SONGS OF THE DEEP

VARIOUS AUTHORS   ALESSIA WINTERS   EMRYS LAINE

NICOLE ZOLTACK   A.L. DAVE   THEA DANE

LEXI OSTROW   A.R. HARLOW   NIKKI PRINCE

JORDAN ELIZABETH   TAMI LUND

MARIE CATHERINE REGALADO   CATHERINE STOVALL

LOUSIA BACIO   MELISSA MACKINNON   D.C. GOMEZ

CASIA PICKERING   TIFFANY STAND   BRY DIG

INTRODUCTION

In 1478 a woman stowed away on a ship searching for gold. She was found and thrown overboard for the common belief that women were viewed as cursed. The ship certainly had a run of bad luck so when they found her, and the crew wasted no time removing her. She was captured by two young men and thrown overboard.

Her legs were tied together to prevent her from swimming and reboarding the ship. As she fell through the dark ocean waters, Poseidon took pity on her, but could not outright save her or risk Zeus' wrath. He allowed her bound legs to form a tail. As she sunk, after 45 seconds her lungs would close and reopen breathing water. She was gifted a voice to destroy men on the sea should any wander close to her.

He told her each woman would receive a gift of magic to aid her as a mermaid as his personal gift for life in his domain.

The woman makes haste against those who destroyed her - murdered her in cold blood. She used her siren song against the very ship that threw her overboard. Though guilt prevented her from using her gift a second time against another ship that sailed across her path.

Poseidon shows himself to her and explains what happened. He offers her a choice to save others like her - she accepts with no concern for the lives of humans who would perish for their crimes against others.

The woman's name: Galene - which meant gentle seas in her native Grecian tongue.

She can only save a life if she SEES the person falling. Meaning not all who find a watery grave had the option to be saved. Over time, she starts to see men drowning and requests to save them. Poseidon agrees.

In a world of magic, Galene is the only mermaid to be immortal as her magic is the gift of saving others and without her, there would be no more mermaids.

A pod formed of the lives Galene saved. Each member received a gift to offer protection, life, health to the pod. Together they lived, traveling the waters of the Atlantic, never to be caught, and saving those they deemed worthy of a life beneath the waves.

A BREAK IN THE TIDES

ALESSA WINTERS

CHAPTER ONE

It all started with the mistaken belief that she could do anything.

Wait, no, it all started when her asshole of an ex-boyfriend told her she couldn't, in fact, sail her uncle's boat by herself. His reasoning was that she's too flighty. Too inattentive. Too easily distracted.

Just like how she was in their relationship.

According to him.

Of course, she had driven the boat by herself before. Taken small little trips, little day journeys to the islands and down the coast to some hidden coves. Left the sleepy little port town and driven the boat into the unknown wild of the Atlantic coast until she could see nobody else and was alone in her thoughts.

Her boyfriend hated those trips, too.

The more she mulled on it, as she leaned against the wheel and let the wind pull wisps of her blond hair out of her braid, the heavier her heart grew.

It's never a fun proposition, to think that one's boyfriend had hated them and everything they did throughout an entire relationship, but lying to herself felt even worse.

But then again, if she had taken the time and looked at herself with anything resembling honesty, she would have seen the gap in her experience of attempting a multi-day trip and not gotten herself into the entire mess.

The entire mess that stared her directly in the face the moment she climbed down the ladder into the compartment with the suspicious engine noises and flicked on the lights.

"Okay," Brooklyn whispered, down in the makeshift engine room/extra bunk space. "Water here. Bad."

Somehow, without her knowing, on the third day of the trip, water seeped through the hull of the boat, leaving an ankle deep brackish sludge soaking the extra mattress and causing the motor to sputter. The sallow lights of the room don't give her any faith, either.

The boat had a bilge pump, but it remained silent.

Brooklyn thumped her hand against the pump, the water sloshing against her rubber boots, a bit cresting over the edge and trickling cold down into her socks.

Nothing.

"Right," she muttered.

She had started muttering to herself halfway through the first day, when the wind picked up and it looked like it might storm.

And she had thought she could last for an entire week alone.

With a sigh, she hooked her hand up on the ladder, pulling herself up to the main deck of the tiny boat, into the darkness one only found on the deep sea at night.

It was a good boat, when it wasn't actively leaking, if a bit rundown and out of fashion. A nice twenty-five footer with space in the front hull for two to crash and two outboard engines. Her uncle had painted the entire deck a pristine white with a garish orange edging at one point, and years of scuffing of boots and splashing of water left it oddly dulled. Illuminated only by the single safety light,

4

it looked even more outdated, more like a haunted house than an active, working vessel.

Now, granted, it's her uncle's worst boat, and he has quite a few with questionable seaworthiness, but still she thought better of it than it'd sink.

Brooklyn grabbed the old, worn down VHF radio from the console, thumbing it on. "Hello, Coast Guard?" She said, into the dull plastic of the receiver. "This is boat *Myth on the Sea* off of the coast of Maine, approximately..." She checked the coordinates. "Eighteen nautical miles from shore, and I'm taking on water."

When she said it aloud, a bit of fear wormed inside of her.

For as much as she was flippant, as much as she was generally a chill person, a ship taking on water eighteen miles away from shore was never a good thing.

The aged plastic cold in her hands, she waited, craning her neck up to look at the sky.

It wasn't too late, just after around 10 PM, but she just saw black instead of any remnants of lit clouds or any stars.

"Again, anyone out there?" She said into the radio, the button rough against her thumb. "This is boat *Myth on the Sea*, taking on water."

Her Uncle had long ago lectured her into memorizing the emergency protocols, but they've always included calling for help and then waiting for help, nothing to do if nobody answers.

"Right," she whispered, then glanced around the small cabin. "Next thing."

She wasn't going to panic, panicking was for flighty helpless people who care what their ex-boyfriends thought about them.

So she gave herself a moment to think. To come up with a plan.

There was the lifeboat, a tiny dinghy with oars and the tiniest of motors. There was the fish gut bucket - thankfully empty - to try to bail out the bottom, so she can find a place to patch.

There were the flares in the emergency bag.

With one last shake of her hands, she carefully placed the radio back in its receiver, the volume cranked all the way up, then she grabbed the bucket from the untouched fishing pile. The faintest sheen of grime adorned the inside of the bucket, but she wasn't going to eat from it, so it'd work.

"Coast Guard, I'm attempting to bail out the boat, please respond," she said into the receiver, her heart in her throat, then straightened.

Right. Onto the bailing.

While she may be inattentive, she may be in over her head, her uncle did not raise someone to give up.

AFTER A GOOD HOUR of bailing out, interspersed with poking her head out to stare at the radio and send out her message again, the water sloshed up to firmly mid-calf.

Which meant it got worse.

Her arms ached, her back ached, and the grimy horror of possibly being stuck out here started to seep into her skin when the lights to the inside cabin abruptly snapped off, plunging her into darkness.

She flinched, she couldn't help herself, the sudden black all but slapping her in the face. The engine in front of her stilled, and, for once, no comforting thrum of the boat still being alive reached her ears.

After a good long second of panicking, she grabbed the flashlight from her pocket and flicked it on, then stuck it in her teeth to climb back up the ladder.

Time for flares, then. Flares and getting down the lifeboat dinghy.

Up on deck, mist swirled around her, kissing her cheeks and puffing around her breath, and the flare she lit up disappeared before it's even twenty feet up, as if it never existed.

Without the onboard lights, without the flare, there's nothing to show where she floated.

"Fuck," Brooklyn whispered, peering off towards the flare, as if the mist will clear and the brightness will flash back into her vision, but nothing came.

Leaving her with only the small flashlight to illuminate the night.

"Fuck."

The boat had a small battery-powered lantern in the emergency bag, but she left it unlit, saving the power for when the flashlight runs out, though her pulse jumped at every little slosh of water beneath her.

The two onboard motors wouldn't move, giving her nothing but a continuing dreading creep, and the boat lulled softly, all but motionless in the fog. She wrestled the teeny lifeboat down and filled it with the spare water jugs and enough food for...

She stared down at the food supply.

Obviously not all of it could fit in the lifeboat, but how much food will she need massively depended on when she thought she could get rescued, and the very idea of needing a rescue filled her with a blank terror. Who knew how long the tiny engine would take to get to shore, supplemented with her meager paddling, and the food was...not all shelf stable.

After a split second of panic, she grabbed as many of the power bars as remained (a Costco pack of fifty), then tossed in anything that didn't need refrigeration or cooking. The pack of pop tarts (eight of them, all brown sugar), the three bags of beef jerky (extra spicy, because of course), the bag of hard candies her uncle always kept hidden underneath the desk drawer (some unholy mix of lemon drops and hard caramels in a hundred pack). The strange energy gel her uncle inhaled when he ran marathons and insisted on keeping a box in the boat. The extra cup, so she's not just drinking from the industrial water jugs.

After a moment of thinking, she tossed in the container of instant coffee. She could drink it cold, and it was better than having no caffeine.

She loaded the battery-powered lantern, the rest of the flares, the thermal blankets and the compass. The satellite phone, the gps tracker, the spare tiny solar panel to recharge them. The emergency medical kit, with the anti bacterial gel and the tourniquets and the meager Advil. The paper map of the waters, carefully marking off the boat's current location with a pen. Her pocket knife and the extra tiny multi tool. Extra socks for herself, an extra shirt and an extra pair of underwear.

The very idea of needing more of that skittered on the edge of her awareness, some looming fear that was far, far too much for her to process, but the boat began to list to the side, and even her rubber boots didn't want to keep grip that strongly.

"Fuck," she whispered again, then threw on her hat and her hoodie and life jacket, and climbed into the dinghy, and off the *Myth of the Sea*.

And as the dinghy started to drift away, Brooklynn put her hand up to her throat.

Her necklace. She had taken it off when getting ready for bed, and carelessly placed it on the side table.

Her ex always told her that was a way to lose precious things, chided her for misplacing things or refused to help her find them, saying it would teach her a lesson.

And the *Myth of the Sea* sunk into the water, and she watched it, a lump in her throat.

CHAPTER TWO

It's a point of pride for Ellis that no boat has sunk in his introvert swimming grounds for quite some time.

Not that most of the Merpeople had introvert swimming grounds. Not that most actually paid attention to things like statistics and boat paths and rates of survival. Most were content to swim always with the pod, going from place to place with everyone they know and love.

Ellis used to be that way.

Used to always stay with the pod, happy to stay with his beloved who saved his life, turned him into a Mer in the first place. Used to always being around others exactly like him, like his beloved.

But death comes for them all, and even the magic in their blood granted by Poisidon and Galena herself couldn't save his beloved from injury.

So here he was, alone in a sea of perfectly happy and mated Mer. Alone, when the only person he had ever loved, the one who campaigned to turn him as well, was gone.

Of course he'd have a place to go swim and be away from all of it.

Sure, he felt the pull back to the pod, everyone did, and he visited just long enough until that itch went away, and headed out to his own swimming grounds.

His swimming grounds were...austere. Austere, but beautiful, with their jagged rocks jutting from the ocean waves and sea birds that clung to everything above the salt. With the waves that tossed more than just the ocean waters, and the wind that chapped the skin of any human who dared to fish in its depths.

Not many did. Most swung up the coast to where the water cleared itself from the rocks and the wind was calmer and the crab just as plentiful.

So when a boat started to take on water in the deep dark of night, Ellis followed.

There was a gash on the outside, the sort of nick that was obvious from below the waves, with water whistling in at a faster pace than most boat owners appreciated. Ellis pressed his hand against the hull, and the splinters dug into the palm of his hand, harsher than they should.

Like the boat was way, way more injured than it should be.

With one push of his tail, he swam enough away from the boat to cautiously dip his head above the roiling waves.

A small figure rushed around the boat, illuminated only by a single flashlight in her hand, casting a glow over the plasticky sheen of a rain slick.

Most boats of this size had two people on them, but nobody else appeared as he watched, nothing more than the top half of his face over the waves. In the dark, he should be safe.

The figure has already brought down the inflatable dinghy all boats like this have bolted to its side, and dumped handful after handful of stuff into it, in quick, clean motions that belie something halfway between fear and adrenaline.

The rain pelted the top of his head, but the figure did nothing to shelter herself from it.

Odd. It was the first thing most humans do.

Ellis had seen boats sinking before, of course he had, but still, the moment the boat started to tilt, his breath caught in his throat in some half remembered trauma.

The human pressed buttons on the radio, speaking, but her words disappeared into the wind, and even from this distance, he could see her eyes squeeze shut in desperation, before she fired off another bright flare.

Another flare that disappeared into the low cloud, with no hope of being seen.

Ellis stilled himself, barely above the waves. He never had to rescue anyone before, and the dread sitting in his heart didn't actually give him much hope that he actually could.

He was, after all, the Mer who lost his beloved to a simple injury.

The human's hair slicked against their cheeks, shining in the pinpoint bright light of the flashlight. She was young, for a solo traveler, with pale hair and pale skin that seemed to reflect the glitter from the dark water back at him.

She shouldn't be out alone.

The thought settled deep inside him, something between despair and frustration. Someone like her, someone so young and so vulnerable, shouldn't be left alone. Shouldn't have had to take out the boat alone, shouldn't have been abandoned.

Shouldn't have been in this place on a boat like that.

The human on the boat lowered the dinghy to the rough water, abandoning the ship far earlier than most people do.

Must not be her boat.

He scoffed, but of course all sound was lost in between the rain and the waves.

Younger than most humans who owned boats in this area, too. Not familiar to him, and he knew most of the boats that go in and out.

He ducked back as the dinghy hit the water, and watched as the boat slowly sank underneath the waves with nary a sound. All the money and chemicals and paint to just sit among his stones.

And then...there was an actual living human alone in a tiny dinghy in the rain without any ability to get help.

"Ugh," he mumbled under water, as the puny engine that would do nothing against the waves dipped below the surface and puttered. There was no way she'd make it to the mainland, not with this mist and rain and wind.

And with the rocks jutting from the waters and the fact that nobody answered her radio hail, it could be days before someone found her.

And she didn't load enough water to survive that, much less clothing and warmth.

"Ugh," he muttered again. The engine sputtered a torrent of bubbles, jerking the dinghy forward, then stalled out.

Even after everything, he didn't want someone to die in his waters.

Avoiding the engine with its valiant attempt at moving the dinghy, he flicked his tail until he's under the nose of the boat, right where the rope rings sit to tie it onto the main vessel, and grabbed one, pulling the dinghy gently to the left.

One of his favorite rock islands was a few miles to the south, with a freshwater pond and a few caves that reach the ocean. It was sheltered enough from the winds that someone could survive there a few days until help could be reached. He would just deposit the human there, keep watch until sunrise, then fuck back off to his introverting.

The human in the boat jerked the engine in the other direction, and he strained to fight against it, but the waves and wind were on his side. There's no way she could see him, not with the darkness, but the back of his neck crawled with being this close to a human after so long.

There were laws why they're not supposed to let humans see them.

The engine jerked again, then, miraculously, turned to follow the direction he tugged the boat in.

It's not like he was inherently a strong Merman, he considered himself rather average, but not having to fight an engine just made things a bit easier.

"Thank you," he muttered, even though there's no way the human could hear him through the dark water flowing through his gills, then, with another push of his tail, he strained with the weight of the dinghy, until momentum relented and it glided through his waters like a knife.

Perfect.

CHAPTER THREE

Brooklynn didn't know why the boat turned sharply to the left, but she stared down at the compass with a lump in her throat, watching as she moved south east. She didn't want to turn off the flashlight, but...

But it may be the only access to light she had for the entire night.

The maps were safely folded up in a waterproof ziplock bag, and with the rain beating against her jacket, she's inclined to leave them there. Leave them until the morning, where she wouldn't need the flashlight and maybe the rain would let up.

Maybe.

"I really shouldn't have come out here," she said aloud to the waves and wind, and a corresponding thump to the bottom of the dinghy seemed to agree.

Maybe she hit a fish. The last time she checked the depth meter, besides the rock islands jutting up from the surface, the water was far too deep for her to have hit ground already.

Though who knew if she already drifted far off course. Who knew where the water was taking her, so strong of current that her engine did nothing against it?

These were the stories that people died from.

The thought rattled around in her brain, underneath the pelting rain and the stinging wind, so she hunkered down in the boat, half laying back, keeping a hand on the engine just in case. With one last prayer to the sky, she clipped the flashlight to her jacket and...turned it off.

The darkness was immediate. Immediate and all enveloping.

No moonlight filtered through the clouds, no stars shone through gaps in the mist. No other boats, no other sources of light. Just black, reaching through the mist and caressing her cheeks.

She ought to stop imagining things, too.

There was no way to know where she's going. She could run aground and not even know it until it's too late. She could unknowingly drive herself beyond all the small rock islands that shelter the coast and into the open ocean.

So, her heart in her throat, she cut the engine, squeezing her eyes shut against the darkness.

She's not someone who grew up on boats, not someone who instinctively knew what to do in the worst-case scenario. Not someone who could just wave her hands and have the solution to her problems on the ocean. Not someone who had the map and radar of the area embedded into her instincts, so they could steer on smell and feel of the waters.

She was just...stuck.

The boat lulled to a stop for a few seconds, buoyed against the waves, then, slower than before, tugged along the same course. With the wind, with the current, and there was nothing she could even do to change it.

"I'm screwed," she said to the mist and the darkness, and just by speaking the words, more fear twisted into her stomach. "I'm screwed and nobody can help me."

Another thump against the bottom of the boat, as the dinghy pulled ever onwards, and she pulled the blanket over her in an attempt to shield herself from the rain.

Without the help of the engine, it took Ellis one and a half hours to pull the dinghy to the island. His biceps ached and his tail felt like he pulled a muscle somewhere along the line. His hand cramped somewhere around mile 1.5, but he didn't let go of the ring, didn't let go of the boat, until he could tug it into the ocean cave, finally free from the unrelenting current and the wind that started to threaten to pull it out of his grip.

The water in the cave was shallow, a narrow cut through of stone, before widening out to a black pebbled shelf of a beach he could lean against and read. Fish lurked in the mouth of the cave, easy to catch cod that can feed him for a few days if he so chooses, and crabs scuttled along the outside of the rocks.

A few months ago, once he established his own pattern of escaping for weeks at a time, he had pulled books from a water-proofed bag in a completely unrelated sunk boat, and he stacked them along the edges of the shelf, along with a found solar charged lamp and a makeshift coffee percolator.

Coffee was probably the biggest thing he missed about being a human. Coffee and computers and unrestricted access to all the reading material he could want.

Propping himself up against the shelf and giving himself a chance to adjust to his top half being above the water, he reached over and flicked the lantern on, bathing the entire cave in a human appropriate amount of light, warm and flickering, then glanced back on the dinghy.

Most humans would instinctively react to the light.

Instead, this one curled underneath a reflective blanket, her hat tugged over her face to shelter from the rain, and, somehow in all the wind and the tension and the rain, she had actually fallen asleep.

Actually asleep.

She could have died in a sunken boat, could have run afoul of the rocks and broken up the dinghy, and she was asleep.

He gaped at her, but she's still breathing, so it's not like the human died on him.

Moving as silently as he can - which was less than easy above the water - he pulled out the length of rope from the nose of the boat, then tied it around the ring he had just spent hours gripping, then looped it around a rock on the shelf.

"Do you have any survival instincts?" He whispered, and she stirred slightly before pulling the blanket tighter around her. "Why did you not stay awake until dawn?"

The dawn that was still a few hours out.

Her hair was slicked back against her neck from the rain, and, still, she shivered. Even in her sleep, she shivered.

And now he had to worry about hypothermia.

"For fuck's sake," he whispered, precariously holding himself above the lip of the dinghy. Though his tail thrashed in the shallow water, he dug through to the other blanket he saw her toss into the dinghy.

It's soaked through, cold and useless, as is the extra pair of socks and extra hoodie she tossed in the boat.

As much as he could, he spread them across the shelf to dry, then ducked back under the water, until he swam to the mouth of the cave.

He could leave her here, go back to his swimming alone in the dark with nobody but the fish and the crabs. She should live through the night, and wake up incredibly confused but safe in the morning.

A SMALL NOISE from the boat, as the human audibly shivered, the sound echoing in the still waters of the cave.

"Fucking humans," he muttered, then swam along the edge of the rock island, where the rocks jut up from the ocean.

Enough driftwood had accumulated around the stones in the

ages of its existence that he's collected enough to store in small pockets of shelter from the rain. He mostly used it for coffee, or the occasional fire when he's moping about being non-human, but it would do. It would warm up the cave to survivable temps, dry out the blanket and clothing, and if he felt frisky, he could even cook a fish over it so she wouldn't starve.

Being responsible was the worst.

CHAPTER FOUR

Brooklynn didn't so much wake up as consciousness slammed into her, cold and clammy, and her eyes flung open beyond her control.

The dinghy was...still. No lull from the wind or the water, no rain hitting her hat or jacket, just the small crackle of a fire and a gentle lapping noise met her ears.

Careful, all of her instincts torn between staying as still as possible and getting the fuck out of there, she pulled the hat away from her face, blinking up from her spot.

There was a roof above her.

No, scratch that, there was a rock ceiling above her, flickering light bouncing against the rough stone and sending shadows skittering across the surface.

She let her eyes drift over, and the ceiling gently sloped downwards.

A cave.

Somehow, her dinghy drifted into a cave, though she wouldn't be able to see more unless she sat up, and her entire body shivered, cramped from the cold and wet.

The fire popped, and a male voice mumbled out a curse.

She wasn't alone.

"Okay, what?" She blurted out, sitting straight up in the dinghy, sending the blanket to crumble around her lap, before she gaped.

In front of her, half propped up in the water, half on a gravel beach shelf, was a dark haired man, whose brown eyes stared at her with the same amount of panic she's felt

He was handsome, in a sort of austere way, though stubble roughed up his jawline and his hair curled wild with dampness.

And he was shirtless. And he held a stick, very clearly poking the small fire. And he was lounging in the frigid water like he belonged in it.

"Who are you?" Brooklynn breathed out, when neither of them moved.

Idly, she noticed that her extra blanket was spread out on the pebbles, damp spots all over, as well as her socks and extra jacket. There was a coffee pot, a rickety looking lantern that hadn't been in fashion for at least a decade, a stack of books, and...

Nothing else.

She shivered again, as if the lack of clothing on him reminded her that she's cold. She was cold, she was clammy, and even out of the wind the cave was still way colder than she likes.

The man in front of her just blinked, looking back to the fire, then to her.

"Did you take me here?" Brooklynn asked, tugging the reflective blanket closer to herself, and a hint of hysteria warped its way into her voice. "Where are we, who are you, where's the boat, where—"

"The boat sank," the man said, and his voice was a bit raspy, like he hadn't spoken to anyone else in a while.

Which, yes, she remembered that, but it did nothing against the panic welling up. "Where are we?"

He glanced back at the fire, and she could see the white of his eyes in the light of the fire, before he looked wildly back at her, like out of all of this she was the strange one.

"Why don't you have a shirt?" She blurted out, when he still won't answer. "What's this cave, how'd you find me, who..."

She sat up further, looking into the water beneath the dinghy, and...

And she couldn't see his legs.

Instead, connected to his torso like a fucking Disney movie, was a black tail. Like the mermaids she would obsess about as a little girl, scaly and glittering and everything.

Her brain shorted out, and she stared, dumbfounded, at the rest of him in the water.

"We're...in my cave?" He said, after the moment stretched on, as her mind tried valiantly to catch up to the reality in front of her and failed. "The storm was just going to get worse."

It was no longer the question at the forefront of her mind, but words disappeared from her use, like they're vanishing away.

She must've hit her head somewhere in the attempt to get to safety. She must've hit her head, she must be hallucinating, she must be dreaming.

But no, the light of the fire flickered across the cave, too real to be a dream, and her skin goosebumped over her arms.

"You were cold, so..." the guy, the fucking merman, gestured towards the small fire. "This seemed okay?"

Her eyes snapped up to his face, searching for something, anything, to show that it might not belong to a full human, but no, it was normal.

He was built stronger than what pre-teen Brooklynn had imagined mermen to be, sturdy and thick, like he's designed to lift weights rather than be slim and sleek. But then again, pre-teen Brooklynn had imagined them more like Legolas than any actual person.

And this one in front of her looked like he's about to bolt away from fear.

"Okay...." She said, tamping down on the panic, tamping down on the hysteria in her voice. "Uh. Thanks?"

He nodded slowly.

"And you are..." She gestured down at his tail, and he shifted, the scales glittering silver in the firelight. "Am I insane?"

"You're the one that went alone on a boat meant for three during a storm," he shot back, though his eyes were wild. "In a poorly mapped place with undersea rocks that are nightmares against hulls."

She supposed that yes, a Merman would probably have strong opinions about marine craft.

And yes, it was foolish.

She lifted her chin. "I had permission."

"Good for you?" He said, then stared back at her, blanching.

She could sympathize. This was top tier insanity, and the fact that he was just as thrown as she felt somehow helped.

"Okay, obviously Mermaid person, who are you?" She asked, shivering involuntarily and pulling the blanket back over her. "If you exist, you must have a name."

His eyes tracked her movement. "You should get out of the boat, sit next to the fire," he said, after swallowing. "All your clothes are wet, it's forty-three degrees out, humans get hypothermia too quickly."

It wasn't bad advice, even if he didn't answer her question, but she still tucked the blanket tighter.

Impulsively, she lifted her hand to her throat to fiddle with her necklace, only once more to be reminded that it's deep beneath the ocean, somewhere on a sunken ship.

Another little loss.

She rested her fingertips against her collarbone all the same, the loss a bit more raw than she would've expected. It's a necklace, those can be replaced, but...

Still.

"I'm...Ellis?" He said, his voice trailing up, as if he had a question about his own name. "I didn't want anyone to die in my waters?"

CHAPTER FIVE

Ellis watched, feeling like a fish stuck in a crab pot, as the human gingerly climbed out of the dinghy, scooting so she's sitting cross legged next to the driftwood fire. Her pants stuck to her legs and her blond hair started to frizz dry in a halo around her heart-shaped face.

Humans were definitely not supposed to see him, and the strange thrill of breaking such a cardinal rule sent a panic down his back, crawling down his tail.

But this human hunkered next to the fire, rubbing her hands together, though her teeth chattered, and sort of glumly appraised the cave.

"So Mermaids are real," she started, then cut herself off, grimacing. "Okay, that's weird. Thanks for saving me? I think?"

He nodded back, unsure of what else to say.

"And you...swam me here? Pulled the boat?"

He nods again, then points at the dinghy, still neatly tied with his rope.

"And you...exist." The fire reflected off of her blue eyes, as she looked anywhere besides him. "Alright. Any other mythical creatures? Anything else?"

He lifted a shoulder into a shrug, because he didn't know how to answer that. He didn't believe in mythical creatures before his beloved, so it was a fair question.

"And you have a normal name like Ellis?" She blinked down into the fire. "Are you sure I didn't hit my head?"

"Not that I saw," he said, extending the piece of information like it's a peace offering. "Please don't panic, I don't think panic is good for hypothermia."

"Right," she said, then, somehow, giggled. "Bad for hypothermia. Logical." She held her fingers out to the flames, and her fingertips were wrinkled, even though they'd been in the cave for well over two hours and they should be normal.

In an ideal world, she should take off her damp clothing to dry, but a flash of inspiration told him she would not respond well to that idea.

"What's your name?" He asked instead. It felt like a normal question to ask. Like something normal people would say.

"Brooklynn, like the city," she said, and it's enough of a practiced answer that it was off the cuff. "Parents thought they were cute."

She shivered again.

Ellis reached over the shelf and grabbed the coffee percolator. The freshwater pond was on the other side of the rock, but it'd take only three minutes to swim there, and anything, anything was better than continuing this awkward conversation. "Stay here," he cautioned, like she was in any sort of state to wander off, then ducked down into the water and swam past the boat, away from the flickering firelight.

The water was cool, a welcome distraction from the awkwardness stealing over his entire body.

Nobody but him had ever been in the cave.

Ever.

The thought itched under his scales as he glided through the dark, cool water. He hadn't tried to share the space with anyone, never tried to bring anyone from his pod.

Not like he was close enough to the pod. Not even Galena.

The fresh water pool, well replenished from all the rain, wasn't far enough away for him to quell the anxious thoughts, although carrying the percolator above water while swimming gave an annoyed edge to them.

The human- Brooklynn - still sat, her knees tucked up to her chest, though her eyes sharpened as he swam into view of the flickering fire. "I tried radioing again, no response," she said, self assured.

She was able to get herself together in that short amount of time, and she finger combed through her blond frizz.

"The receiver should still work, we're still in range," she continued, and it's like she took the little bit of time to address her situation. "Unless you towed me an additional forty miles, which I really don't think you did."

Ellis shook his head, then put the percolator on the flat stone he uses to boil water, then propped it up over the fire. It was a soothing motion, something he could actually control. Something he had done dozens of times.

"So, Ellis," she started, and it's just weird to hear his name above the water, "what's going on?"

"Do I look like an electronic engineer expert to you?" he shot out, his mouth moving faster than his mind, then his common sense caught up. "Probably the storm, there's a relay island not too far away that gets windy."

She blinked her blue eyes owlishly at him.

"That's...that's probably it," he finished lamely. "The coast guard will come out and fix it in a week, probably, and then the radio will work."

"A week?" She said, and her voice pitched up again. "I have to be here for a week?"

He blanched at the same time. "No!" He said, as quick as he possibly can, and shook out his hands, like that could stop the awkwardness. "It should be safe after the storm, and then...then you can paddle. Or try the engine."

The engine wouldn't last a day, and even the best human would have trouble paddling twenty miles with limited food and limited experience. She wouldn't have much of a chance.

She hugged her knees tighter, breathing deeply, and with a shock, he realized that she was scared. She was scared and she didn't want him to know. All the bravado he thought he saw was fake, something she had drudged up as a facade.

It was already difficult enough for him to talk to someone, and now he might have to calm her down.

"I don't know," he said desperately. "I don't keep track of the coast guard, except to avoid them, they might come faster. I can leave tomorrow, I'll leave you alone, you'll be able to just stay here and be safe."

Wrong thing to say, and she flinched, leaving him floundering.

"Or I can stay, I can get you fish and freshwater, and you'll be fine," he said, "Whatever it is, this cave has no predators and is safe from the wind."

"Okay, safe from the wind," she repeated, a bit numbly.

"It's perfectly safe, nothing will bother you, and and and..." he trailed off, because how do you even calm a panicking human, a human who was completely and obviously out of her element and experience level?

He remembered panicking when he was a human and would have drowned, if it wasn't for his beloved.

He took a deep breath of the dry, warm air, then settled himself so he leaned his arms against the shelf, most of his body perfectly submerged and comfortable in the cool water.

"I don't have any coffee right now," he said, gesturing to the percolator. "But hot water will still help. I think. With the hypothermia."

She nods, though her lips curl up just a bit, sending a jolt through him as she looked towards the dinghy. "You drink coffee?"

"When I get it," he said, tapping the heat safe handle of the percolator. "Not easy to get, though, out here."

"Makes sense," she murmured.

"You could try to sleep, it's still a few hours until dawn," he said, hoping his voice was more reassuring than he felt. "The cave is nice with the sunlight."

She raised an eyebrow at him before her face twisted.

"Well, I guess if you were gonna kill me in my sleep, you wouldn't have towed me here," she said with a hint of irony.

He weighed being offended, before absolutely conceding her point. Waking up with a stranger who wasn't even human would have weirded him out before his beloved, and adding in any trauma of the boat sinking and the storm would've just made it worse.

He'd be wary, too.

"I think I'm too wired," she continued, and it had been a few years since he was human, but he's fairly certain the slang hasn't changed too much. "Waking up in a strange cave does that to ya."

"Fair," he conceded, though he really, really had no clue what to do with her if she wasn't resting. "Just..." he trailed off, staring at her.

She stared right back.

"It's been...a few weeks since I talked to anyone." As soon as the words were out of his mouth, he wished he could take them back. Far too vulnerable. "I know most people stay in the pod, but I'm...not that person."

She said nothing, and he didn't know when human facial expressions got so foreign.

"Hell, most wouldn't be out this far. The entire pod thinks I'm crazy for always being alone," he said, and as try as he might, the words kept coming. "So it's either crazy or they pity me and I...I don't make good company or conversation."

He hadn't for far too long, now.

The firelight flickered in her eyes. "I take it from the word pod that there's more of you?"

"Many," he said, slouching against the shelf, as much of him in the water as possible. "So, so many."

"Can you tell me about them?" She asked, and her voice was smaller, somehow. Softer. "Or...I dunno. About your social structure? Society?"

It's way more than he wanted to talk, but she's still hugging her knees, still curled up against herself, like she was one wrong thought away from utterly losing it once more.

So he talked.

CHAPTER SIX

She drank three cups of the hot water, as he talked about the other Merpeople. About the curse-slash-blessing from Poseidon, about the nebulous government they have, with an immortal Mermaid at the center.

About how he used to be human, just like her, and his apparently dead wife got him turned to be with her. About how when he was human, he was a normal elementary school teacher, with normal problems and normal friends and normal, you know, legs.

He briefly touched on his ex-wife, about how she died in an accident, about how he just couldn't put up with things afterwards.

She understood that, at least.

He talked about the ocean, about how he hunted and ate and slept. About how he could swim for miles without tiring, and the act of towing her dinghy wasn't the most difficult thing he'd done, though he didn't enjoy it. He even rhapsodized about the beauty of the dark, of the very deep, of when the light didn't even filter down, and all he could see is the vague shapes of the fish around him, moving past him like ghosts on the wind.

She believed none of it, of course, but the conversation was nice.

29

He was clearly insane - or she is - and clearly full into a delusion so deep that she wasn't fully certain if it came from her or from him.

But still, when his words ran dry along with the hot water, she was a little bit calmer, stretching her legs out and leaning against the wall of the narrow cave.

Being a merman sounded exhausting, by all metrics. So much swimming and politics and being around people that she would absolutely run away as soon as she could as well.

He looked exhausted, too, pillowing his head on his arms on the shelf, tilting so she remained in his view, his long lashes casting shadows over his cheeks in the dying fire.

If she had to guess, it was roughly four AM.

Six hours after the boat had sunk and six hours of complete silence from the radio.

Even though she wanted to stay awake, even though she wanted to stay as alert as possible, the hours tugged at her eyelids and fogged up her mind, until even yawning was almost too much effort.

And Ellis had done nothing but talk to her and refill her mug with hot water.

The adrenaline from earlier had completely worn off, leaving her aching.

She stretched her legs out on the shelf, and even the blanket was now dry.

"So, do Mermaids sleep outside the water or under?" She asked, and a flicker of relief filtered into his gaze.

"Under," he replied easily, stretching his arms. "I mean, I can sleep with my head above water, but my throat hurts when I do that."

She nodded, swallowing. "And nobody will come in here if you sleep?"

His eyes crinkled up, but he didn't quite smile. "I don't think anyone has ever come here but me." His voice was soft, almost wistful. "I leave my things here, nobody ever disrupts them. No birds fly in, and the fish stay at the mouth of the cave."

Apparently, that mattered to Mermen.

"So it's...safe," she said, repeating his words from earlier. "Nobody will do anything if I sleep."

Still, the small not-smile. "I'll sleep at the mouth of the cave, so not even the crabs will come in."

She wasn't terribly worried about crabs, but still, she made a show of stretching again, then tugging the blanket over the pebbles. It wouldn't be the most comfortable sleep, but even she would admit that she felt better now that she wasn't wet and freezing.

And not, you know, dead on the bottom of the ocean.

With only an uncertain nod towards the now smoldering fire, he waited for her to pull the blanket away from it, then pushed back and disappeared under the water with barely a ripple.

Her breath hitched, but without the sun and without any stronger light, she couldn't see through the black water to catch any hint of him.

Like he never even existed.

"Okay," she whispered, to the dead still air of the cave. "Sleep. Then see if I hallucinated."

She bunched the jacket underneath her head in some sort of makeshift pillow, curling up on her side, and stared out at the dim view of the mouth of the cave. It was barely more than a slightly darker section of rock, and the dim light of the fire barely made its way to it.

And somewhere underneath the water, a merman that she probably made up in some sort of head trauma infused mania, slept and kept watch.

She shuffled a little, until the pebbles underneath her hip were a hint kinder, then let her eyes close. Let the worry and the hysteria and the adrenaline wait until the next day.

She could decide if she's sane tomorrow.

IN A SHARP CONTRAST to the night, the morning light shone directly onto her face, and pulling the blanket up did absolutely nothing to impede it.

"Ow," Brooklynn muttered, scrunching her face down, as if that would help. Everything ached, her shoulders and neck and legs, everything she wouldn't think about being used in a shipwreck.

Shipwreck.

For the second time in way too few hours, she jolted upright, clutching the blanket to her.

Grey skies peek in from the mouth of the cave, and the pebbles shone in the morning light. The water lapped gently against the rock shelf, throwing off glistens that reflected up the cave wall.

And, unfortunately, it was bright enough that she could see the impact of rain against the water outside.

"Fuck," she breathed, then made herself unclench her hands.

Not a dream. Not a nightmare.

The dinghy floated innocently, still beautifully tied up against the rocks. A far better knot than she could ever hope to tie, crushing the idea that she could have done this alone.

Wind howled past the opening of the mouth, and even though she was tucked deeply inside, she shuddered. The cold didn't reach this far into the cave, but even the memory of the harsh wind from the night before brought a lump to her throat.

If she got jumpy each time there's a bit of a breeze, she was gonna need a lot of therapy to still live in Maine.

She stretched out, then pushed herself to stand. The cave ceiling was high enough that she could extend her arms on her tiptoes, but it still gave the overall impression of being low and a bit claustrophobic.

The ashes of a fire and percolator propped up against the rocks were other small bits of evidence that she didn't come here alone.

She gave herself thirty seconds to despair, thirty seconds of mind crushing angst that she still might be insane, before she shook herself out of it and dug into the boat for one of the pop tarts she threw in there.

Might as well contemplate the impending doom of her own brain while hyped on sugar.

It was less than ideal, it was less than what she pictured for herself for the entire trip, but at least she was relatively uninjured and completely dry.

With nary a ripple in the water, Ellis poked his head above the surface, his wild curls slick against his head.

He blinked wildly at her, a stark mirror of her exact emotions at the exact time.

"So I didn't dream you," he said, leaning his arms against the rock shelf. "I convinced myself that I hallucinated."

"Same," she replied, toasting with the pop tart.

The wind howled again, and he threw a look over his shoulder, then back at her. "There's no way they've repaired any broken relay yet, and in my professional opinion you absolutely should not try to paddle back yet."

"Professional, eh?" She said, bouncing on her toes a bit. "Lots of economic structure among the mer people?"

He gave her a nervy look, like he wasn't sure he wanted to talk as much as the night before.

"I have instant coffee," she said, before she stops herself. "You said you liked coffee."

His eyes lit up immediately, and without even another word he grabbed the percolator and disappeared under the surface once more.

"Okay I can bribe him with coffee," Brooklynn said to the now empty cave. "Useful."

His head broke through once more, right at the mouth of the

cave, and fuck, he must move fast if he got there already. "I'm not being bribed," he said, indignant, and she briefly wondered about the physics of him hearing her from under the water, before she dismissed it because mermen exist. "You offered."

"It was sarcasm," she called out to him, and he rolled his eyes, before disappearing once more.

CHAPTER SEVEN

It took him little time to get the water and restart the fire from the night before, but he still found himself waiting for it to percolate.

The human puttered around on her actual legs on the rock shelf, like she couldn't help herself but move, and he caught himself watching her from underneath his lashes. She was smaller than the firelight of the night made her out to be, less intrusive. Less taking up all the space and air of the cave and more dwarfed by it.

And she probably couldn't leave today, and unless something changed with the storm, he doubted tomorrow was likely either.

Meaning she was stuck here, and by her blank look as she ate a pop tart - of all things - she was trying to not think about it.

"Good news, there's a collection of crabs on the far side of the rock if you need more food," he volunteered, after a few excruciating minutes of no conversation and no coffee.

Her brain visibly skipped along his words. "Crab for breakfast is a bit intense." Her chin turned towards the mouth of the cave, the meager light illuminating her profile into something strangely beautiful.

"It's after noon," he supplied, but it probably didn't help. "But yeah, I would've thought so when I was human."

"That's still very weird," she said pointedly, as the percolator finally began to steam, and she busied herself with measuring out the instant coffee for them. "How long since you've had coffee?"

"A few months," he answered, "it's not the most commonly thrown overboard item, and thieving it gets a bit complicated. Not supposed to show myself to many humans."

She poured him coffee into one of his chipped mugs, and he restrained himself from making grabby hands for it.

"Well, if I make it out of this whole thing alive, I'll figure out a way to do some coffee drop off in the area," she said matter-of-factly, as if her words didn't utterly rock him. "Seems like the least I can do to assist in not spending the night in the rain with hypothermia."

He sipped from the mug to stop himself from replying before he thought of an answer, and the beautiful taste of coffee, actual coffee, not watered down and not waterlogged by salt broke his brain. Actually fresh coffee, with just a hint of a roasted flavor, and the sharp bite of caffeine.

"And with enough warning, I can make it better coffee than this shit," she muttered, before plastering on a smile. "I'll write down the coordinates and drop it off when there's...not a huge storm."

"Yes," he babbled.

"Who knows, maybe bring out some sugar and shelf stable creamer, get you the best coffee setup known to mermenkind," she rambled, like she's trying to bargain with him and it wasn't already the best thing he's ever heard, "maybe a French press."

She finally plopped down to sit, still staring out the mouth of the cave, like all the words had left her and they were the only thing keeping her upright.

"Do you have access to another boat?" He asked, after probably a rude amount of time enjoying actual coffee. "Yours sank."

She waved a hand at him. "Uncle has many, all in various states of disrepair," which wasn't a good thing in his opinion. "He'll be mad, but I'll be his secretary for a few months for free and he'll forgive me."

"Convenient," he said, pouring himself another mug and eyeing her little container of instant coffee. There was more than enough for quite a while, even with two people drinking. "So you intentionally went out in a bad boat on the night of a storm."

The corner of her lips quirked up, despite the insult. "I'll make sure there are no hull breaks in the next one."

She trailed off, staring back out at the mouth of the cave, like she contemplated ever going back out on a boat again. Which with what he remembered of human trauma, it'd be pretty amazing for her to do.

"I can also get closer to shore, if needed," he said, in case she's getting discouraged about the idea. "No absolute need to come out this far."

"Thanks," she said, and her blue eyes flickered to him for a second. "What do you do for fun around here?"

"Swim," he replied flatly.

"Should've seen that one coming," she mumbled over her coffee.

CHAPTER EIGHT

After a day spent in the company of a human for the first time since he was turned, Ellis wasn't actually sure if he was unhappy or not.

Sure, they lapsed into quiet more than he thought most people do, and the moment Brooklynn wasn't actively engaged she stared out the mouth of the cave with something between horror and longing, but the tension relaxed its way from her shoulders and the worry from the lines between her brow.

She ate from her cache of bland looking energy bars despite his offer to catch fish or crab for her, and he only swam off a few times for more water.

It might be the most words he's spoken since his beloved died, and he couldn't even say it was distressing him.

It should.

She paced around the rock shelf, stretching and making the small idle motions that somehow he had forgotten were so common with humans, moving her hands while talking and even when she's not. Her hair was a frizzy pale halo around her face, and sometime around midday she took off the rain slick and there were tiny freckles all up and down her arms.

He wasn't sure if it was the depth of the water or his lack of paying attention, but he couldn't recall if any Merpeople have freckles.

But as the light dimmed under the wrath of the storm and the night, she reached into the boat and pulled out a completely normal hoodie instead of the rain jacket.

"I'm not...interrupting you for anything you need to do, right?" She asked, after a day of chatter and stories and even some joking, as he rekindled the fire into something more suited to light than for making coffee. "You're not playing hooky from a job or anything?"

Any job or function he had in the pod faded away when his beloved died, so he shook his head.

"My entire plans were to swim around the area until I wanted to return to the pod for a bit," he said, "I'm not exactly the most useful person around."

She nodded, the slightly pinched expression returning for a hint of a second, before vanishing again. "Same," she confessed, like it's some sort of secret shame. "I just live with my aunt and uncle, do work when they ask, and...nothing else."

From what he's observed of her from the day, it seemed unusual.

"I mean, I have a degree, I have all this possible promise and potential and I...do nothing with it," she said, staring towards the now dark hole of the mouth of the cave, her fingertips resting against her collarbone, like she missed something. Like she normally wore something around her neck, and the lack of it distressed her.

"There's not much use for a kindergarten art teacher in a society where there are no kids," Ellis said, and his voice was less bitter than he thought it would be. "So that degree is pretty useless."

She gave him that, nodding, though her lips twisted in the same way they did when he first told her that Mer don't have babies like humans do. "Not many kids get thrown overboard, huh?"

"Not while I've been around," he said, because he's heard enough stories from Galena about how bad the seas used to be.

"Do you miss it?" She asked with unerring focus, staring him down. "All the things you've spoken of, all the small things you can't get, all the skating around mentions of your ex wife, do you actually miss having legs and walking on the ground?"

Her words landed between them, settling into the pebbles on the rock shelf like a stain that no amount of salt water would be able to remove.

"No," he let out, before he let himself think about it too hard. "I...I can't imagine going back. Picking up like this never happened. Like she never happened."

"That's not the answer to the question," Brooklynn whispered, her voice softer than the words have any right to be.

"Do I miss things? Sure," Ellis said, almost desperately, opening his arms wide and causing ripples on the surface of the still water of the cave. "I miss cafes. I miss restaurants with things like bread and pasta. I miss books, I miss people who will leave me alone, and I miss stores like Target and Home Depot where everything is convenient." He paused, and even the water against his tail was almost too much sensation. "Do I miss being above ground and dealing with people? No. Do I miss politics and air pollution and sunburns? No."

She nodded, neutral, like she wasn't the one who sparked this rant.

"Do I think, even for a second, that no matter how much I miss that I would go back? No." He shifted, and her eyes caught along the glittering scales of his tail, because of course they did. "It would be another little death, to be without the ocean."

"Another little death," she repeated, before ducking her head away, looking back to the fire. "Grim."

As if his own words were the only things keeping him upright, he slumped over against the rock shelf, and she sat down, instead of pacing, so she was a little bit closer to him, and he was very, very aware of every little air current moving through the place. Of every little whisper of motion in the sea, of the wind teasing prickles on his arms as some of it breezed in through the cave.

She remained quiet, just watching him for a long moment, and it was different from all their other small silences that they've had that day.

He had never talked about anything he's missed, not to anyone in the pod. He and his beloved briefly discussed it, once when he was first turned, and then never again, as she had some things she missed as well. Always small things, like roses or pastries or headphones, but never anything that actually impacts their world.

"You really don't talk to many people, do you?" Brooklynn said, after his brain had run out of the little regrets to think of, of things he should have said instead.

He shook his head, and his curls had been above water for so long that his hair was actually dry, a sensation that he hasn't had in ages.

Telegraphing her motions, she reached around him to the dinghy, and pulled out...a loaf of bread. A loaf of bread, carefully inside a ziplock bag, pre-sliced and everything.

"You didn't bring waterproof blankets, but you grabbed a loaf of bread?" He asked, and she offered him a smile, something unguarded, before opening the bag and handing him a slice.

"I also grabbed peanut butter," she informed him, and the knot in his chest that he wished he could say came on with just the rant but knew that it was older than that, loosened up. Just a bit.

"A lot of people throw peanut butter jars overboard, and they rarely finish them completely," he said, taking the slice of bread and holding it gingerly in his fingertips. "People are sometimes the worst."

"You're telling me," she said, grabbing a piece of bread for herself. "I can't help with all those things, but I can offer bread."

It was a kindness he's not sure he would extend to someone else, not in his normal prickly state, but here, in his cave and talking to this strange woman who now knew more about him than he's told anyone in a year, it was almost painful in its simplicity.

"When the storm is over, I'll tow you back to the harbor if you bring me more," he said, and meant it. "It'll take a day, but it'll be easier than waiting for the coast guard."

"Deal," she said, "I'm not good at keeping to a schedule but I'll figure something out. Some way to communicate when I can do it."

"Something," he said, and he hadn't kept an actual trackable schedule since his beloved died. "Either way, it'll be more than I get right now. I'll be responsible for getting you home, you'll be responsible for the bread and the coffee."

Her smile faded, just a bit, and he raised an eyebrow at her. If he gave up those details about himself, if he said all those things, then a strange maw inside of him wanted to know what would make her look like that.

"My ex said I was too irresponsible." She said, grimacing a bit. "Why I came out here alone, to prove to myself I can."

Without being able to fully help himself, he glanced at the dinghy, at the ramshackle collection of items she grabbed for herself, and she coughed out a laugh.

"Yeah, I haven't exactly done anything to redeem that, have I?" She said, carefully zipping up the bread again and tucking it against the wall of the cave. "It's what I always do. I think I'm breaking out of being flaky, I think I'm getting my life together, and then something happens to completely ruin it all again."

Once again, he didn't know what to say, so he stared down at the delicate bread that would surely disintegrate if he brought it under the surface of the water.

"That's why he's an ex?" He asked, finally, after receiving no guidance from the slice of bread. It shouldn't be a meaningful thing for him, not with all the heartbreak he's had in his past, but here, holding the piece of bread and still propped halfway up against the bank, it was somehow very important.

"Pretty much," she replied dryly. "Said he couldn't stand me.

Dated him for three years. He ended it because I couldn't keep dates straight in my head and plowed right through our anniversary and forgot his interview day." She shrugged, some sort of faux casualness that didn't even begin to appear real.

Somehow, someway, this was something that bothered her.

"You're being kind," he said, and she blinked at him in surprise. "You're being kind to a stranger, that has to be more important than being flaky."

Her lips quivered and she ducked her head. "The rest of the world doesn't see it that way."

"The rest of the world is out there," Ellis said with something almost close to bravery in his gut, nodding towards the mouth of the cave. "Right now, you're being kind, and that's way more important."

She didn't look up at him, but the firelight played off of the smile all the same.

CHAPTER NINE

The next morning dawned with something resembling hope.

After setting up the beginnings of a fire and the water to boil, Ellis glanced towards the mouth of the cave, then back at the sleeping human.

With the fire this low, with how crystalline cold the freshwater was in the morning air, it'd take it far longer than usual to percolate, giving him time.

Sunlight flickered through the water, beguiling and beautiful, and with one last glance to Brooklynn, he ducked back down underneath the water.

There was still more cloud than sky visible, but he let himself glide through the water, in the first few feet of the surface where sand dances and tiny fish flick up to eat the bugs landing on the sea.

It was gorgeous, and his heart felt lighter than it's been in ages. As if something inside of him, from hunkering in from the storm, had changed on some fundamental level.

It was a little like peace.

With barely a thought, he swam back toward the sunken ship

Brooklynn came in on, and without the lashing rain and the laden dinghy, it was a far easier trek, and the dappled sunshine played along the surface.

The wind still pushed the clouds at an alarming pace.

The wreck was easy to find, of course, not many newly sunken boats in this area, and it rested against a rock outcropping, the cabin tilted at a ninety-degree angle. The gash in the side of the hulk grew over the course of the sinking, and a crab even poked around it, before scuttling away when Ellis passed overhead.

There was the familiar taint of spilled oil, bitter against the back of Ellis's throat, but he ducked closer into the boat anyway, into the flooded control room.

All the electronics were dark, no blinking lights to show its once life, and when he rested his hand against the console, nothing happened. No small spark of electricity, no indication of signals being sent, nothing.

Piece of crap boat indeed.

He scoffed, and another fish darted away, like it took him speaking for it to realize he's there.

"I'm going to make sure the next boat is better," he said aloud to the silvery fish, like it could understand him. "I'll wait outside the harbor and everything."

He would, too, he realized with a jolt, and the possibility of it actually sent eagerness down his arms and over his tail. Like making these tentative plans was...right.

He swam into the cabin, where ruined bedding floated, half on the mattress and half off, his eyes catching a hint of neon orange fabric, shining and reflective even this deep in the ocean.

"I bet she'll want that," he murmured, pushing away the curtain of blankets to pull it out.

A dry bag, fully functioning and sealed, and even if she didn't know it existed, he still admired the seal job on it. Most boaters get lazy.

He tossed it onto his shoulder. If it's something important

45

enough to be fully sealed, then Brooklynn - or her irresponsible uncle - will want it.

A few more small silver fish flickered around the small kitchenette, but there was no real salvageable food anyways, not after two days underwater.

The boat creaked in the current, and if he was a more superstitious man, he would call it haunted.

A glimmer of gold caught his eye, pulling him deeper into the cabin, until he found the small bit of light.

A necklace, delicate on a chain, pinned down by a book. Obviously casually taken off and then not grabbed in her mad rush to get off the boat, and when he pulled it free, there's a small glimmer of precious stones on the pendant.

She would definitely want this.

BROOKLYNN SWIPED the grit out of her eyes, and her back ached from sleeping on pebbles for two nights in a row, but the sunlight peeked through the mouth of the cave, watery and weak, but there.

If she thought the water glistened under the light from the clouds, it was nothing like the sparkles of the actual sun. Prisms shone through the entirety of the cave, lighting the ceiling and the walls in some sort of strange glitter.

It was beautiful.

It was beautiful, and she would have never been able to see it if she hadn't sunk the boat.

She would have never gotten to see this cave, to share coffee with a mythical creature, to make tentative plans for food drop offs and meet ups. She would have never been able to talk so frankly about her flaws, and have them be so completely seen and yet dismissed.

She wasn't quite sure she'd ever had someone not care so

quickly. Everyone seemed to always give pause if she told them before they found out, and it never works out when she waits for them to discover on their own.

For someone who was so completely hell bent on being alone, Ellis was certainly not bad at people.

She pushed herself up, and a small fire already burned, the percolator on the rock to heat up, slightly steaming. She couldn't see Ellis, but he must've been around to set it up already, and he hadn't woken her up.

Another little kindness.

She finger combed through her hair - it was a disaster - before twisting it into a braid the best she could. She wasn't her most glamorous, but all things considered she thinks she's doing well.

Not how she thought the trip would go.

Almost methodically, she started to measure out some of the instant coffee into the two mugs, almost like it was a routine. A routine started with just one day, somehow settling deep within her bones as something correct.

It's not even that cold out anymore, though the wind still whistled over the stones.

Carefully reaching into the dinghy, she plucked the radio from the haphazard pile of stuff she brought, thumbing it on.

Still nothing, not even a crackle.

With a glimmer of movement at the head of the cave, a dark form slid quickly through the water, and her breath hitched. With the sunshine, she could actually see him, see the power in his motions and the speed of which he swam. See each thrust of his tail, the motion of his shoulders as he pushes through the water.

It was a lot more kinetic than she had thought.

There was a bag slung over his shoulder, easily identified as one of the ubiquitous neon orange dry bags that came with every boat.

With barely any time at all, he swam up to the shelf, popping his head above water and giving her a wide, slightly sheepish grin. "I went for a quick swim," he explained, pulling the dry bag off his back and plopping it on the pebble shelf. "Turns out I'm a bit faster when I'm not pulling a boat, got to your wreck much easier."

She eyed him, and he's breathing a bit hard, but nothing extreme. "You said it was 2 miles away?" Even if someone above water sprinted, it's still an insane speed.

He shrugged. "Water's nice right now." With a practiced tug, he opened the bag, pulling out the plastic protectors to the boat's paperwork and insurance information. "Figured you'd want these, at the very least. Help get everything all sorted away."

"I'm surprised he had insurance," Brooklynn murmured, turning the pages over. "He's not really the type to be that careful."

"Also, found this," Ellis said, then held up his hand out of the water.

Twisted in between his fingers was a delicate chain and a small gold pendant.

Her necklace.

She jolted upright, sitting straight. "How'd you find that?"

He shrugged again, one gloriously bare shoulder, as if it was nothing. "It was floating in the cabin, half pinned down by some books," he said, holding it out to her. "Didn't know if it was yours or your aunts, but thought it good to grab just in case."

The chain was wet, and little droplets dripped down the back of her neck as she clasped it into place.

"I took it off to go to sleep," Brooklynn said, resting her fingertips against the tiny pendant, a lump growing back in her throat. "I thought it was...gone."

He watched her from underneath his eyelashes.

"My ex always told me that I'd lose it if I did that, but I..." she swallowed, the small gesture of grabbing the necklace for her growing, much bigger than it should be. "Thank you."

He took the chipped coffee mug and poured the steaming water over the instant coffee. "Didn't weigh me down," he said, a half-smile playing along his lips. "Glad it's something good."

"Yeah," she said, not able to take her touch away from it nor her eyes away from him. "It's good."

The moment was weighty, somehow, something twisting into something else. That the action went far beyond just grabbing a necklace from the bottom of the rocky seabed, changing the very air that they breathed.

His gaze flickered back up to her and caught.

Most people don't bother doing something so nice for her. Most people wouldn't be bothered. Even her ex would've called it too small, too insignificant. That she was immature for putting such emotions behind an item.

And Ellis just did it casually. Like it was as easy as existing, as easy as being. Where he saw something that could be done and just did it.

"Hey," he said, setting aside the coffee cup, eyebrows raised. "You okay?"

She wasn't sure if she's been okay for a while, not if this was how she reacts to something like this.

The thought hit her like wind in a sail. That beyond all her flaws, beyond her immaturity and her irresponsibility, she never had someone do such a meaningful small gesture for her, without mocking or expectations or...or something.

"It just..." she swallowed again, and the lump in her throat didn't disappear. "It means a lot, all your help, saving my life and all that, and then you grabbed this."

In some fit of emotion she couldn't quite define, she settled herself on her stomach, propping her head up, and it felt right. She can't very much get in the water and stay there with him, but this little bit of closeness soothed something in her.

His brows drew together, like he was having trouble figuring out why it's such a big deal, before he extended his hand to her.

And so she took his hand, sitting there on the pebbles on a rock shelf, her hair still frizzy from seawater and the rain, and tried not to let the strange tide of emotions break over her.

His thumb swiped along her palm, sending some sort of sensation she can't define up her arm, and she shivers.

"Why is it that someone who's a mythical creature is the nicest guy I've ever met?" She spouted, after just long enough of silence.

He huffed out a laugh with a crooked smile, and there were lines around his eyes at the motion. "I'm not anything special, I didn't do anything outstanding, I'm just...someone who was here." Still, his fingers tightened around hers, ever so slightly.

The water gently lapped against the rock shelf and the light filtered muted through the mouth of the cave, just the two of them, and his face turned thoughtful, before his eyes flickered to her lips.

And her attention was caught, just like that.

"Why do I get the feeling that people aren't generally kind to you?" He murmured, voice so low. "You spend so much kindness everywhere, and then don't get any in return."

"Not really," she said, and it's a horrible revelation to have.

"And the guy you call your ex, he certainly didn't help," Ellis continued, tapping a finger against her palm.

"Not really, no," Brooklynn replied, and to horror of horrors, she was on the brink of actual tears. That such a little kindness would do that to her.

"Well," he started, and his jaw was sticking out strangely, like this vexed him, but his grip on her hand was still gentle, still soothing, "I don't think you should have to put up with that."

Not even the dull lull of the water could disrupt the moment, and she was close to him, so close. Even with him in the water and her on the pebbles, their faces were close.

He exhaled, his eyes on her lips, and she spared a quick thought for what a merman's actual respiratory system might be, before he leaned forward, ever so slight.

Waiting for her.

Before she could talk herself out of it, she tilted in as well, and, somehow, miracle of miracle, their lips met.

He tasted of salt, which shouldn't surprise her, but the moment she opened her lips to him his hand reached into her hair, tangling into her frizz and pulling her closer.

It's perfect. It's perfect and it didn't reek of obligation and annoyance. Didn't feel like he's only doing this because he was supposed to, didn't feel like he only did it to get something. Didn't feel like an annoyance.

It's beautiful, and she shivered, once, and he broke the contact.

"Are you okay?" He whispered, reaching a hand out and tapping where the pendant rests against her collar bone.

Instead of answering, she pulled him back in and kissed him again.

CHAPTER TEN

Mid afternoon, after a few more stolen kisses, sunlight streamed in, brilliant and cold, through the mouth of the cave.

They both turned to look.

"One moment." Ellis murmured, then disappeared under the surface of the water.

With the sunshine, she could see him swim, all long lines and smooth motions. He was beautiful, unreal and mythological and somehow intimately powerful.

His head bobbed up right outside the opening, just his eyes and his curls sticking out, the droplets sparkling in the light, before he turned and glanced back at her.

If the weather has cleared, then he could help her back.

Back to her normal life, back to her bed and her shower and her boring job with her aunt and uncle and the ex-boyfriend who never loved her and the world that treated her like an inconvenience.

Keeping his eyes on her, he swam back, and it took him far less time than it should.

"I could get you back," he said, and his voice dips lower. "It would take a few hours, but you could get back home."

"Yeah," she said, though her stomach dropped. "Home."

They stared at each other, how they stared at each other the first night, when she awoke in the dinghy and first found out about mythical creatures and fucking mermaids.

Slowly, she piled the blankets back in the dinghy, almost numb, before she stopped herself. "One week," she declared, without knowing if she could make it happen. "One week, I'll meet you on the edge of the rock islands."

A little spark of something, almost hope, entered his gaze. "You'll see me again?"

After the time they've had, after the kisses they shared, anything else was unreal.

"Hey," she said, and his smile was as watery as she felt. "I owe you coffee."

EPILOGUE

Ellis wasn't one to give into hope, but he found himself at the edge of the rocks one week later, twitching his tail restlessly near a particularly rough patch of rockweed that collected at this point of the Maine waters.

She didn't specify what time of day, she didn't specify exactly where, but still, he watched every boat as it motored by, to see that familiar frizz of pale hair. He watched as boat after boat passed by, all without her, and his heart sank, moment by moment.

It's too much to think about directly, so he pretended he's just watching to count the boats. To make sure nobody is in trouble, despite the brilliant sun and the non-existent wind and the completely mild current. To check the hulls that go by, to see if any have the telltale sign of damage that only he could see.

Not like he could do anything, but still.

The afternoon sun dipped low on the horizon before he settled himself on an underwater ledge, a smidgen of hurt winding up against his spine. Still, he stared up at the boats, all cleanly sliding by the spot she had pointed out.

Until.

The sun was almost set before a catamaran, small and more beat up than really advisable, chugged up to the point of the rocks and killed the engine.

He stirred, squinting up at it, but it idled in the gentle waters, the paint of the hull cracked and peeling.

"No way," he muttered, staring up at it, before he pushed up towards the surface of the water, a cautious distance away.

The boat was even worse above the water, but Brooklynn leaned against the railing, her face fresh and her cheeks pink, staring out at the water, her eyes searching.

Searching for him.

"Hey!" He called out, before he could stop himself, and she spun to look at him, a smile brightening up her entire contenance. "You came."

She grinned at him, and she was beautiful in the sunlight. "Of course," she said, ducking beneath the awning of the boat for a split second, before lowering the ramp to the catamaran.

It was entirely the wrong weather and the wrong ocean for this type of boat, but she laid against the ramp, as if she would dangle her hands into the water , and he swam right up to it, propping up against it.

His face hurt from his grin, despite all of it. "This is a horrible boat for these waters."

"Yeah, well, Uncle didn't want me to get on one of the nicer ones," she said, but her tone was teasing, her eyes brilliant and blue in the setting sun. "Here."

She set a coffee mug on the edge of the ramp, the sort of cup you get in chains all up and down the coast, the sort he hadn't even realized he missed.

He coughed out a laugh, and she reached into her bag, pulling out a croissant and another pastry and a can of whipped cream, setting it all up for him.

"Took me a bit to convince him that I was safe to," she continued, and he wasn't sure he had been so happy for so long, in years. "And

55

then everyone was weirded out by the coffee run, but..." she shrugged, laying against the ramp, and just...

Smiled at him.

"It's good to see you," he let slip.

"Yeah," she said, "you too."

Then, with only a barest of breath of hesitation, she leaned towards him, and he captured her lips into a kiss.

THE END

A Mer's Hunger

EMRYS LAINE

CHAPTER ONE

Music thrummed through the hot, summer-night air, almost as if it pulsed along the mass of bodies that danced to the rhythm in the center of the room. The strobe lights in the corners flashed and switched color, a dance of their own in the music, and encouraged the patrons to dance even more with them. Any voices heard were just blurred to the drum of the club, lost to the voices singing along to the words of the songs.

Groups of men and women swayed back and forth with one another, they danced between partners and among friends, drawn like moths to a flame, drawn to the center by an unseen force.

Sweat glistened off of Lucia's deep-tanned skin, her long, brunette hair stuck to her neck and her arms as she pressed her body between a short-haired, blonde woman and a dirty-blond-haired man. He pressed his hands against the flesh of her exposed stomach, they danced up her body to caress between her breasts and teased along her neck.

Her eyes were shut, one hand reaching back to grab the base of the man's neck to pull his head closer to hers, while the other danced along the hip of the smaller woman before her. Painted nails trailed

59

up the side of the blonde's stomach, her hand stopped at the hem of the blonde's crop top, and she moved to keep their dance in tandem.

She barely knew either of them, but their bodies moved as if they had danced together their whole lives. Their hips rolled slowly like a wave to the sensual music. Blind touches of hands that roamed new territory, Lucia moved her hand to grab the nape of the woman to press the blonde to her chest. She felt gentle kisses get placed on her exposed sternum just above her top. Lucia dropped her hand from the blonde locks of the other woman and allowed it to rest on the waistband of the woman's jean shorts.

Lucia's silver-scaled top reflected the light and dragged more eyes to watch the rhythmic dance. Eventually, the blonde woman turned to mold herself to a new participant, a raven-haired man that had come up behind her and pressed against her as she danced. Her arms quickly wrapped around his neck as she continued with the rhythm that the couple behind her danced, ensuring no contact was broken with the other two dancers of their little pile. The hypnotic movement of her body swayed almost in a serpentine pattern, her torso and hips moving parallel in their dance.

The two couples danced and ground their hips in tandem, and more bodies joined and departed their bubble of movement, as the group appeared to breathe as one. Several women made their way to the center of the bubble, hands reached to casually touch and kiss one another as they joined the group. A lot of the group had started their own dance, the massive in-sync wave of bodies had become individual droplets that collided but did not conflict.

Some hands reached in just to give a tight squeeze and to depart moments later, the eyes from members of the knowing group would briefly open to watch where the ones that left departed to, then would return closed, enjoying their dance. Lucia never did though, she only focused on the strong touch of the man behind her and the gentle press of the body of the woman in front of her.

Lucia's hand trailed down from the neck of her partner, down his broad shoulder, until she grabbed at the belt loops of his pants, and her second hand moved from the hip of the blonde before her and darted up to the dirty-blond, gelled hair and roughly clutched a fist full with inhumane strength. She jerked his head back from the crevice of her neck where her shoulder met her neck. A strand of saliva glittering in the light was the only thing that connected his mouth to the part of her body that he had licked and kissed. The straps of her silver, strappy top which had been pushed to the side, slid down into its place. She could feel the carnal gaze he was giving her. Her strength in the grasp of his hair never faltered and she only clutched tighter to dig her nails in momentarily then released to claw down his neck.

The music changed, the pace faster, and kohl-lined eyes opened to reveal pale-gray, almost white, eyes—a ghostly and eerie color that lit up with the strobed lights. Her eyes were the only thing that indicated something otherworldly about her, but her nature drew others in despite the intensity of her gaze.

She pulled the man to her side and reached forward with her freed hand to give a tight squeeze on the hip of the blonde before she detached and guided herself with her partner away from the center of the mass of bodies. She felt the beat of the new song in her blood. It sang with the desire and hunger in her bones, and the hands that caressed her body answered the call that her body sang.

SHE LET the man take the lead to take her toward the bathrooms of the unfamiliar club, her eyes hooded and hungry, and her intense and predatory gaze went unnoticed by her partner. The man turned his brown eyes to her and walked backward once he found the door to the restroom. A boyish smile graced his lips as he pulled her in, unaware of the fierce hunger that he had drawn out of her. He pulled her onto his body, and the weight of her forced his body into the door, her hands scrambled to reach back and lock the door to the restroom. Their teeth clashed and clicked as they all but devoured each other in the kiss, strangers to one another's bodies.

Lucia used her teeth to bite down on his lip, she pulled away slightly and his lip dragged out with her, and forced him to gasp out in slight pain. She was fast to take advantage of this, their mouths collided again as she delved her tongue into his mouth and encouraged him to explore her mouth as well. They barely pulled away to breathe until he pulled back fully to suck in a breath of air, his eyes heavy-lidded. Her eyes dilated as she watched this display, she ground their hips together against the door where he was pinned, they both gasped out at the friction when their jeans rubbed together, and a new spark ignited in their bodies.

He lost his large hands in the tresses of dark-brown hair, her lips crashed to meet his own as they both let go. Hunger fully took over the two when they collided again, the buildup of the dance they had done around one another for a good portion of the night boiled over. He let out a hungry noise as he grabbed her thighs to pick her up to hold her tightly against him. She let him carry her further from the door, placing her onto the sink counter of the room.

In the dim light of the bathroom, he could see just how intensely her eyes stared at him with an almost predatory, indescribable hunger. She chewed on her bottom lip, her ghostly eyes dragged down his form, and they followed his v-cut t-shirt down to land— and stare—at his tented, dark jeans. His dark-blond hair glowed gold in the lights of the bathroom, and the sweat-soaked fringe hung in his eyes, giving the brown of his eyes a deep smolder.

The man moved to get on his knees before her, his large hand reached to undo the buttons of her black, tight jeans that clung to her body. She slid down from the counter and captured his jaw in her hands, her pupils were blown wide with want for the man below her, and the light stubble rubbed against her fingers as she guided him back to fully stand.

"No," she panted out. She let her ethereal gaze rake up and down his body. "Right now I want to taste you."

The words took a moment to process in his borderline-drugged mind, the desire clouded his ability to translate her words. His eyes dilated and his breath quickened when his brain caught up with the accented English that demanded only to be obeyed. He nodded fast and moved so that he was leaning against the counter instead, his legs spread out some for her to fit between them.

She hungrily kissed him again, she let her hands slide along the trunk of his body, she felt all the parts of his torso, the wider waist that promised a sturdy and full body below the shirt, his softer pecs that firmed up as her hands danced along his flesh, and the bits of belly she felt that sat softly against his fitted jeans. Chub, her favorite. She kissed down his neck, trailing along the new parts she had just mapped out on her way down to sit on her knees before him. It took so much power to hold herself back from going in to bite on the flesh beneath her lips.

She groaned and thanked Poseidon for the power she felt from how desperate the man before her was, he hurriedly reached down to undo the top button of his pants for her. She let her long fingers reach up to drag down the zipper. She applied pressure on the bulge below when she encouraged him to push his jeans down further for her. His hips pushed off the counter of the sink long enough for the thick material to get below his ass. She made fast work to get his boxers to slide down and reveal his length, it gave a slight bob as it bounced back up at full attention before her face. It had width but not much length, the heavier weight of it sat in her hands as she pressed back the skin to reveal the tip.

"Lucia..." he breathed out when she pressed the tip to her lips, carnal eyes looked up to him from between his legs, her name in his mouth made her even more hungry, as messy and unfamiliar as it sounded from him.

She mentally thanked Poseidon that she'd found the man earlier in the night. She hummed her response, she didn't move forward but she didn't back away from her goal, her tongue darted out to lick her lips and the edge of it grazed the tip just an exhale away. He let out a gasping noise, she paused where he had stopped her, and her hot breath danced on his member. Intense, white-gray eyes looked up at the man above her.

"I do not think... Ah, Dios," he moaned. She moved her gaze to the member in her hand then back up to greet him with a hungry stare as he tried to think of what to say. "I do not think I will be long," he confessed.

She gave a satisfied grin, excited further by what he admitted. "That's okay, Matías." The way his name rolled on her tongue was nice, she had decided. She kissed his tip as she gave him a pump with her hand.

He groaned out as she swallowed him down, she was done with words and the want to taste him in her mouth had become too much. She felt the stretch of her jaw quickly due to his girth, not going too far down to test the waters first as she licked and pumped the length of his cock. With each bob of her head, the pullback was emphasized by the drag of her teeth along the flesh in her mouth. One of his hands reached to hold onto the bathroom counter, the other clutched to her dark-brown hair that he pulled out of her face into a sloppy ponytail, this bettered his view of her as she devoured him.

She let her eyes flutter closed with the taste of sweat and the heady flavor of his length along the flat of her tongue. The strain on her jaw as she swirled her tongue on him grew to a comfortable ache, she was able to relax and let her mouth open wider to lick up the base of his cock, she took a moment to look up and see how destroyed the man above her was.

She released the length with a loud pop, nuzzled her nose, and kissed down him slowly, white eyes never looking away from him. His eyes barely opened to watch her press his length against her face as she licked base to tip. His jaw clenched and unclenched, it matched the tight grip on her hair and the white-knuckled grasp he had on the counter. Lucia wanted him to fully let go, to let the desire ride through him.

She let her lips dance around his length, they moved to kiss and suck his skin down to his thighs, her fingers continued to pump his length, keeping his attention on her hands as she sank her teeth in and bit down slightly on the flesh where the thigh joined the hip.

"FUCK!" he shouted. He jerked her head away from his hip, the pleasure twisted in his face to full-on pain. It didn't stay long as the shock of the shallow bite passed, "Sorry," he hurriedly released her hair and reached back to clutch the counter of the sink again, "you can't just surprise me with that."

Lucia was not fazed, she seemed to be even more excited with his reaction, the roughness of his hands in her hair, and the satisfaction from the bite hot in her head. She stuck her tongue out to him, and her teeth appeared brighter against the pink of her tongue, "Sorry, I'm a bit of a biter." She scrunched her nose and gave a toothy smile to emphasize her point as she looked up at him then drew her gaze back down to the softened erection, she wanted to continue what she was doing.

Matías caught his breath, the predatory look that crossed Lucia's playful face made him panic for a moment. He saw something dark swim in her intoxicating and ethereal gaze, for just a moment, and then it was gone. He dismissed the fear as a trick of the light or just from the intensity of her stare, it quickly became replaced with the heady arousal that this woman dragged out of him.

She purred as she gave apologetic kisses up his thigh, she never broke her otherworldly stare from him as she made progress back to her goal. Gentle bites that she teased up his leg, were much more to his satisfaction. He nodded his head to her, licked his lips, and bit the bottom of his lip as he relaxed back into her touch, he leaned against the sink, and his right hand slid back to where it held her hair before. His head dropped back, his brown eyes closed, and gentle words of encouragement fell from his lips.

Content with him back to how she wanted him, she laved her tongue along his cock. She worked until she was satisfied that she got his shaft to return to its full glory. She slid it fully into her mouth, both her hands placed on his hip bones to hold him in place. Matías let out a loud, appreciative noise to this, he moved both of his hands into her hair and pushed her further down on him, her nose brushed his much darker and curly pubic hair at the base of his cock. She let him guide her down and held herself there, regulating her breathing through her nose to adjust to how far he went down her throat. Lucia was very done with the way she teased him and wanted to get him to completion so they could continue with their night, and she didn't plan on that being done here.

Lucia practiced swallowing around him, she made sure to breathe in slowly and took her time to ensure she wouldn't gag around him. She would test the water again with biting later, something she very much wanted to do. Hypnotic eyes looked up at Matías, his darkened eyes stared through thick eyelashes to watch what she did. She did a slow press downward, to push his length as far back as she could down her throat before she pulled back up quickly, her mouth caused a suction around his length, pulled up to the tip then quickly slid back down to the base.

She breathed only through her nose, she used her hands to push herself away and let his hands be the force that pulled her back down. He seemed to hesitate when he realized she had put him in charge of the force and speed of which she came back down on his length, only going slow and shallow for a few thrusts.

He twitched in her mouth, his hands gripped harder with the hope of quick completion, his confidence in the power she gave him turned him on further. He pushed her face down quickly, a slurp filled the room as she swallowed him down, and her head moved as she was guided.

His breath had hitched as he moved quickly, Matías could feel the edge of release, and the soft and warm mouth that obediently swallowed him down promised to be what undid him. Lucia scooted herself closer to him, painted nails dug into his thighs where she had grabbed onto him, the flesh under her nails turned pink with irritation, and her knuckles slowly turned white from where she clutched him tightly, the action encouraged him to go deeper down.

He twitched in her throat, she felt his body tighten up above her and she knew that his release was there. She swallowed deeply as he shuddered, his deep gasps and groans which were once desperate for release, had become higher and relieved as warm fluid gushed into Lucia's mouth. A stream of swears and curses in many languages spilled from his lips. Lucia took back control and continued to bob her head, she encouraged more of his release to fill her throat and gave another swallow. She looked up at Matías's face, his head hung backward again, no longer able to see her hungry stare up at him, the predatory assessment of if she would get what she needed to satisfy her desire.

She dragged the flat of her tongue along his shaft and gave slow, lazy pumps along his length to push out any last drops of his release. He mused out soft words of praise in what she could only assume was Spanish. Matías's hand patted and gave gentle strokes through her long, brown hair that was released from the ponytail that he had made. Lucia let her eyes flutter closed, she pressed her head into the gentle touch, and she reveled in the praise she felt in his tender caress.

THE THRUM of the music gradually reminded them of where they were. Lucia stood first, her joints cracked quietly as she dusted off her knees from the dirty floor. She checked herself in the mirror, straightened her top, and quickly schooled her face back to the sensual gaze she had perfected. Matías was slow to open his earthen-brown orbs to let his sedated gaze roam over her figure. He rolled out a blur of words, Lucia was sure it was not even an attempt at English.

"Do you want to go back and get some more drinks?" she offered, she watched him with a singular eyebrow raised, to get a read of what he wanted.

He swallowed and nodded, shrugging his boxers and jeans back up over his length, it was tucked securely back in before he zipped and straightened himself out. She smiled and gave him a kiss before she moved toward the door to unlock it and enter the club again. The dirty-blond was not far behind her, he held the door open and followed her out.

He let his hand drop down to rest behind the small of Lucia's back to walk her out back into the club. Once out of the bathroom, her eyes darted around to look through the crowd, no longer sensing or seeing the massive pulse of breath in the center. She let her ghostly eyes roam through the center of the dancef floor in search of a familiar face, she couldn't see the one she looked for in the crowd, although she doubted the one she sought would be in there.

Lucia let her gaze drift over the rest of the room toward the walls where the tables lined the dark sections, the occasional lights drifted over to illuminate the tables. She knew that the one she searched for shouldn't be far, but she watched as the lights lit up the dark-red hair of someone familiar, which meant the one she searched for was nearby.

CHAPTER TWO

L ucia took the lead and walked ahead of Matías to serpent her way through the throng of the crowd toward the redhead; once closer, she could see the ones further in the shadows by the table. The long, scarlet-red-haired woman chatted with two others. One with short-cut, black hair and random snow-white streaks, the hair was buzzed along the sides and longer on top, and another young woman with sandy blonde hair that was pulled back into a romantic braid. Lucia's eyes settled on the one she had searched for, she slowed her pace, she moved so Matías's hand dropped from her back, and her urgency dissipated when she watched the one with the spiked black-and-white-speckled hair survey the room.

Deep, chocolate-brown eyes paused in their scan of the room on Lucia as she approached, they darted to Matías behind her, then back in a knowing manner. Lucia gave a large smile as the redhead turned to look at who had joined them, a near empty glass clutched in her hand. Her arms spread wide, offering a hug of greeting to Lucia. Lucia accepted and kissed the cheek of the redhead.

"Lucia," sang out a slur-tinged voice, the redhead released her and took a sip of the deep-red drink with fruit slices in her cup, "we were wondering if you were gonna come back!" Plump, pink lips, stained a darker red in the center, tilted up in a teasing smile followed by a wink.

"Don't worry, Val. I always do." Lucia smiled back at the redhead, bright amber-brown eyes met her stare. Lucia watched the colored contacts slide as the smaller's gaze moved from one eye to the next, her own pale eyes confident and tender. Val broke eye contact first, seemingly overwhelmed and flustered by Lucia's stare. She gulped down the last of her drink and placed the glass on the table. Val's deep-brown skin flushed pink as she dared a glance at the taller brunette again.

"She knows I would hunt her down if she didn't come back," spoke up the one with black-and-white-speckled hair. Lucia let her eyes slide down to meet the deep-brown gaze of the shorter that did not cease in their stare at her. Val giggled and nodded at the commentary, Lucia surmised that the redhead had probably drunk multiple glasses of alcohol since she had gone to the dance floor earlier. Lucia let her eyes gaze back over to the short-haired speaker.

"Of course. If you didn't, I would assume you didn't love me anymore, Em," Lucia teased. She reached over and rubbed the shorter's arm with a smug grin before she leaned down to give them a kiss on the cheek. "You wouldn't let your elder wander around a strange country by themself, would you?"

Brown eyes narrowed before they were rolled away to look over at Val who excitedly moved her hands to speak with the sandy blonde. Val bounced her body with the music as she signed to the blonde, her lips mouthed along with the song that played overhead, so they could only guess that Val was translating the song to her friend across from her.

She glided her hand over the sandy blonde's arms to gain her attention, passing a few Euros to her, and mouthed slowly to ensure the younger could understand her, "Hannah, can you grab me some drinks from the bar? This should be enough." Hazel-green eyes flicked to Matías who bounced his head and swayed to the music's beat. She nodded with a big smile before she drifted to the bar.

"You should have told her what kind," Em laughed, "otherwise she'll get the most expensive thing the bartender tells her to get."

"Nah, I'll make sure she gets something good!" Val practically yelled as the music changed to a more upbeat song. She shuffled around the tight crowd near the table to catch up with the blonde.

Em scooted closer to the side of the table where Lucia and Matías stood, the deep stare of eyes raked over the man behind Lucia that was chatting with another man standing at a table nearby. Lucia watched their eyes, her pale eyes followed the outline of the shape of the younger's brown eyes that reflected the light of the club, down the wider strong jaw, and along the neck to their pronounced collarbone. The tilt of their head drew her attention back to the younger's eyes, they were unimpressed with Matías, and she wasn't upset with the opinion, Lucia knew that it took a lot to impress the other.

Matías's hand grazed up the waist of Lucia's jeans, he let his fingers slide into the belt loop at the top that rested on her hip bones. He gave a gentle squeeze to her side, still in deep conversation with the man at the table next to their own. She could tell he wanted to return to their dance on the floor, she wanted to do much more, but she knew she needed to check in and calm herself or she wouldn't hold back like she needed to. She leaned back to put some of her body weight onto Matías, his body pressed back, and held her weight against him.

She directed her attention toward the bar that Val and Hannah had disappeared to. Hannah didn't speak much Spanish, but Val went with her and it wouldn't take the two much time to retrieve their drinks. She looked around at the packed club, noting the summer energy, that night, swam through not just the club but most of the city, and figured it might take a lot longer than she thought.

Em had also directed their heavy gaze to the bar, they had spotted Val who spoke to the bartender, but Hannah was not in sight. They nudged Lucia to see if she had noticed what the younger had. Lucia stood taller than Em and was able to spot Hannah at a further end of the bar, two drinks in hand but a large hand sat on her shoulder, holding her in place as a person tried to talk with her.

Lucia's jaw quickly set, and ethereal eyes shifted to Em, they had a look on their face that she could only assume mirrored her own. Her white-gray eyes swam with a darkness that screamed to be freed, her jaw clenched tightly, and her nostrils flared out a shaky breath. She turned to move, but realized the hand at her hip had disappeared. Matías was suddenly at the bar by Hannah, he pushed the hand off of her shoulder, and carefully put himself between her and the stranger that held her in place. Hannah scurried over to where Val was at the bar. She quickly took one of the drinks from Hannah's hands and guided them both back over to the table that the others were at. The wave of relief washed over the two once the blonde was back at the table.

Em pressed their hand against Hannah as they pulled her closer, Lucia moved herself to place Hannah between both herself and Em, and the other's eyes shifted to focus solely on the guy being berated by Matías and some of his friends who had moved over to join him. The men argued with the stranger in fast-paced Spanish. Val placed the drink she had procured on the table before them, she took the other drink from the shaken blonde and placed it down as well.

"Are you okay?" Lucia pressed, she spoke slowly once she was able to get the young woman to look at her face while she talked. She knew better than to try and yell for the other to hear her, for she couldn't over the noise of the club.

"Yes." Wide, hazel-green eyes looked back and forth to the ghostly-white eyes and back to the pink lips that spoke to her. Lucia waited for any more info to come from Hannah, "He would not let me go, even though I told him I didn't understand." Her speech was slow and slightly monotone, with misplaced inflection on some words. Lucia nodded and rubbed her hand along the blonde's back, comforting without the use of words. Hannah's eyes drifted to Em, the younger didn't speak but brushed a thumb across Hannah's forearm.

Lucia dragged her eyes over to where the man once stood, Matías and his friends stood alone at the bar now, any upset that might have been in their body language was gone, and a relaxed expression matched their calm shoulders. The Spaniard headed back to the table with one friend in tow, they slid up to the table but made sure to maintain distance from Hannah and the visibly angered Em.

"Do not worry about him," Matías smiled confidently. "We apologize for the misunderstanding that happened." Lucia dared a glance at Em who continued to look in the direction where the stranger once stood. Em refused to look away, Lucia understood the rage hiding in her friend's stare.

"Misunderstanding." Em echoed back the word to the Spaniard, not a question but it asked for clarification. The shorter's white-and-black-speckled eyebrows furrowed and showed the displeasure that they held for the term.

His lighter-brown eyes darted from Lucia to the shorter one next to her, his smile faltered as he thought of a way to answer. Em's glare only moved momentarily from the direction that the stranger disappeared in, to meet Matías's uncertain gaze. They lifted their chin, narrowed their eyes in speculation, and then let the intense stare return to where they previously looked.

"Sí..." Matías let his hands come together in an apologetic manner, "Our friend mistook your friend for someone he knew."

"Some friend," they stated, Lucia let out an uncomfortable sigh at Em's words but she didn't disagree with them.

"Ah." uncomfortable eyes shifted from Em back to Lucia.

In an attempt to break up the visible tension in the group, Hannah nudged at the drinks that she had gotten for Lucia, she pushed them toward the brunette. Lucia tapped on Matías's hand and gestured to the two drinks, his hand grazed over the beer toward the red drink that looked similar to what Val had drunk earlier.

"Gracias," he said loudly to Hannah, she stared and nodded her head to what she assumed was a comment to her, a tight smile and eyes looked to confirm that she understood him correctly. The young man held up the drink in a 'cheers' fashion and waited for Lucia to grab her drink as well. Val shifted herself to be closer to the side of the table that Matías and his friend were at, their group fully encompassing the small, round table.

Lucia quickly grabbed the beer and clinked it into his raised glass and took a long sip from the bottle. She dropped her hand that was pressed against Hannah and tucked a stray strand of hair behind the girl's ear, the petite blonde jumped at the touch and turned to face her again. Lucia flattened her hand, touching the pad of her fingers to her lips, then moved the hand in the direction of Hannah with a gentle smile. She mouthed the words 'thank you' to the blonde and pointed to the drink in her hand.

Hannah broke out in a warm smile and nodded, she understood what Lucia was trying to convey. Lucia mirrored the smile on Hannah's face, glad that she was able to express her gratitude to the slender blonde. She wished that she had studied sign language in her old life to make the blonde more comfortable in their talks. She softened her face, drank from her beer and let an arm rest around the blonde's waist to hold her close, and drew her line of sight to the bar again.

There were many things that Lucia wished she had done when she was younger and still in school, things that she had taken for granted, and language was one of the things she had greatly overlooked back then. After being saved by Galene a few years prior, that had become even more apparent. When she met new members of the pod, she was sometimes reminded of this shortcoming. She knew she wasn't alone in this, most people didn't think about different ways of communication until they were faced with a person who didn't speak the same language.

Her eyes watched the movement of Em out of the corner of her eye, their hand grabbed her arm and squeezed before she felt their presence move around them to disappear toward the crowd.

She wanted to go with them but turned her vision to look at Val, she was in a deep conversation with the friend that had followed Matías to their table. The brunette couldn't understand the little bits that she heard, the Spanish too fast to keep up with, so her eyes wandered to Matías.

"I think I will return to the dance floor, yes?" he questioned. She observed his empty glass on the table and his antsy stance, then gave a nod. He smiled and pressed a kiss to her cheek, "Have a lovely night." He quickly disappeared, the dirty-blond hair no longer visible in the glow from the overhead light.

Lucia clenched her jaw and let out an irritated click of her tongue, no matter where she went people had the attention span of a jellyfish. She tried to calm herself with another swig of her beer.

She felt the aggression as it settled in her bones, she kept her eyes trained back on the bar, ghostly eyes scanning in search of where Em had disappeared to. Hannah leaned against Lucia, content with the protective hold that she had around smaller's waist, the deep tan contrasted against the exposed pale skin on her belly. Lucia glanced down at the blonde that rested on her, Hannah had a smile, and hazel-green eyes watched Val's lips while she talked with her. The mindless buzz of arousal was long gone and a new tune sang in her bones. The incident from before had triggered a new craving in her body, and not much could scratch the itch. She stroked the side of the bottle as she focused on the drone of the music overhead to ignore the song in her blood that screamed for violence.

Val drifted back over to where Hannah and Lucia stood, "Do you want another drink?" She moved her hands to ensure that Hannah was able to understand her question as well. The redhead noticed that Lucia had zoned out and repeated louder to snap Lucia out of it.

Lucia nodded her head slowly in reply, she broke her gaze away from the bar, and she blinked quickly out of whatever trance she was in when she looked at the curvy redhead who smiled expectantly. Ghostly eyes drifted to acknowledge the now empty beer in her grasp.

"I'll take another one of these," the beer was raised then discarded on the table. Ghostly eyes looked to the redhead, "if you don't mind."

Another wide smile and nose scrunched up to a button that Lucia decided were adorable, "Of course! Is just whatever brand okay?" Lucia just nodded, and that appeared to be enough for Val, her eyes drifted to Hannah.

Hannah nodded and raised her hands to sign and speak at the same time, "There was this drink that the bartender was making earlier that I saw that looked good," she said with slow words but excited eyes. "I think he called it the *Tinto de Verano?*" She spelled the name of the drink with the same hesitance that she spoke it out with, the inflection of the Spanish-named drink placed in the wrong areas. Val just bounced her head in confirmation, she knew the drink that the other asked for.

"I gotcha! I'm gonna get some drinks, too, so I might be a bit." Lucia nodded and zoned back into the music of the club, she swayed herself and Hannah to the beat.

She moved her gaze over to the floor of the club, the lights illuminated the center showing a familiar head of dirty-blond hair bouncing around that danced between two women. She didn't dwell on Matías for long, her eyes returned to searching for her counterpart. Em usually wasn't one to up and disappear without her, after years of knowing the younger, she knew that they could be up to something, but she trusted them.

She remembered the first time she had met Em, unconscious and hurt. She had found them as they drowned underwater, she kissed them to get them enough breath so she could get them to Galene. She had begged her creator to turn the smaller to save their life, not experienced enough in healing to treat the wounds. Since then, the two had been attached to one another. A shared hunger and desire was between them and they were closer to each other than any others of their pod.

Lucia thought that Poseidon had blessed her when he had

brought them together, a kinship in their pasts that they slowly healed with one another. She felt that she would never have healed as much if not for Em, and she knew that they felt the same way.

She mindlessly swayed with Hannah to the music, her hand protectively squeezed the other as she thought of the past. She refused to fail to save another person again. After all, Galene couldn't turn them all.

CHAPTER THREE

E m drifted into Lucia's peripheral from the dark shadows of the club, a baggie with what appeared to be rock candy was held in the younger's hands. Lucia didn't bother to ask where the other got it from, she could spot the signs that advertised the flavored candy that the bar sold. Lucia slowed her dance with Hannah to greet Em and watched as their head swiveled around.

"Where is Val?" Em, ever the vigilant watcher, asked.

"She ran to the bar to get some more drinks, it might be a bit." Lucia glanced down at them from the corner of her eyes, their head turned in the direction of the bar to find the energetic redhead. Said redhead was pressed up against the bar laughing with the bartender and a few other patrons.

Em nodded their head once they spotted the woman and turned back to Lucia. The bag of candy was placed on the table before them. Painted nails reached out expectantly toward Em, a single, speckled eyebrow raised, and deep-brown eyes looked to the hand and back up to the brunette.

They opened the bag of the crystal candies and popped one into their mouth, their eyes trained on Lucia to watch her as they crunched down on the crystalized sugar. Brown eyes lazily blinked at the older, a slow smile spread on their face as they crunched down on more pink and purple candy, never breaking eye contact with the bright-white eyes.

She let out a huff and pouted out her bottom lip at the other, they just let out a snicker and popped another candy in their mouth. "Such a bully." Lucia huffed again and grabbed a candy for herself, having given up on the hope the other would pass one to her.

Lucia relished in the sensation of the crunch, the irritation in the back of her head slowly dissipated as she crunched on the candy. She knew why Em disappeared to get the candy, she knew the younger had the same itch in their skin after what happened. They needed to let out some of their aggression.

Lucia grabbed a small bunch of the rock candy and squeezed Hannah's hip, the blonde snapped her head over to them, eyes bright in the question of what was needed of her attention. "Do you want some?" She spoke slowly and close to the device that looped around Hannah's right ear to ensure the other could hear.

Hannah nodded and accepted the sweet, and smiled as she realized that Em had returned to the table. "Thank you!" she chirped before she crunched down on the candy.

Em just nodded their head slowly, the younger gradually relaxed and continued to snack, not breaking their stare from the bar. Neither brought up the lack of Matías or his friend that had hung around to talk with Val, but Lucia knew better than to think that the smaller didn't see that the men were gone, for they saw all. The deep-brown eyes were aware of others and their intentions, that's what made their stare so intense. Lucia never inquired about how it worked and they never explained, she just trusted her friend's call on a person. After all, Poseidon blessed them for a reason.

Lucia let her hand rest on the table next to the candies that Em mindlessly ate, their hand eventually paused and ran short nails along her arm back and forth, a subconscious caress for comfort. Lucia angled so that she leaned against Em's smaller form while Hannah stayed in the crook of her arm. She kept her eyes on the bar to watch Val, who laughed and joked with some of the others waiting their turn.

VAL ENJOYED her time while she waited for the mixed drink that she ordered for Hannah, there were many people also pressed against the bar to get their drinks so she knew it would be a wait. There was a buzz of different languages around her, mainly English and Spanish and she wasn't surprised. There were several cruise liners that were at the Spanish port, that included the one that she and Hannah were from as well.

She bounced on the balls of her feet as she turned back to see if she could spot the blonde toward the wall, the dark club didn't aid her endeavors, but she knew that her best friend was in good hands with Em and Lucia. The redhead was so grateful for the duo, who didn't judge Hannah. Val watched a couple of the girls that she recognized from the cruise come over to the bar, the cluster chatted about shots as they approached the open area beside her.

Once in the light of the bar, she recognized a short-haired brunette as the girl from the cabin next to her on the boat. Val joined in on the energy, added a shot for herself to her tab, and she raised the tequila shot to knock back with the group of girls who cheered in the joy that someone joined in.

"Will you do some more shots with us?" the brunette neighbor with big hazel-green eyes begged. Val looked at the drink that the bartender slid over to her and the beer for Lucia, but no sight of the cocktail for Hannah.

She grinned and nodded, the girls cheered and ordered another round, and the redhead followed suit. Val made sure to ask the bartender to get a small side of limes for her shot.

"Another round for them, on my tab," an accented voice spoke up behind her, a shot glass raised up to grab the bartender's attention. The bartender nodded and quickly poured duplicates of the women's drinks

"Thank you!" cheered the brunette, similar thanks came from the rest of the group. The girls moved to make room for the newcomer, most excited that someone had bought them shots.

"Oh! Thank you, but you didn't have to do that." Val quickly turned to see a young man with sandy-blond hair that stood behind her.

He gave the group a big smile, "It's okay, it's my last day in port on my cruise and I wanted to make sure I had fun!" his deep voice was filled with his Irish accent, and pale skin displayed several freckles along his cheekbones.

The bartender set the new shot for Val on the counter along with the drink that she had ordered for Hannah. She grabbed one of the limes that she was given earlier and put the citrus in her mouth. Corralling the drink with Lucia's beer, she eyed the new shot the man bought her.

"I appreciate the shot but I gotta get these drinks to my friends!" She smiled. She was tempted to take the shot but she knew she had been gone for a while and didn't want her friends to worry. Some of the girls booed at the announcement of the loss of their drinking buddy.

The man placed his hand on the drink, "I'm sorry, lass. I didn't mean to inconvenience you, I'm sure your friends are thirsty."

"It's just a shot! Just one more with us?" the brunette begged Val and grabbed onto her arm. Val knew that she had drunk a lot already, but her tolerance was high, so one more shot wouldn't hurt. Especially since the whole point of her and Hannah going to the club was to party and drink.

"It'll be super fast!" one of the girls gulped down a shot to emphasize their point. Val chewed on the rind of the lime to get all the juice out as she thought. Her eyes glanced at the drinks in front of her, then over to the shot that the blond man offered her.

"It's taking longer for you to think about it than to drink it," a raven-haired woman chimed in.

"Another! Another!" the brunette pressed against her chanted. Val discarded the lime and pressed her lips into a line, she really wanted to take the shot and they all had good points.

Val sighed deeply as she looked back over to the guy that still held the drink, he held it up to offer it to her. The girls cheered when the redhead took the drink and smiled as she knocked it back quickly. The group was quick to ask for another shot for her, the brunette doubled the order and pressed close to Val in hopes that she would stay longer.

Val smiled and gulped down shot after shot and chased them with limes. The flush of her previous drinks slowly started to crawl on her cheeks, a deep red appeared on her dark skin, and her smile got wider.

She knew how slippery the slope was when she agreed to stay for another shot, but she wanted to drink more as well. It also helped that she greatly enjoyed the attention of the brunette pressed against her. Val blushed and let the brunette press against her, each touch of the short-haired woman lingered longer.

The blond man talked with the whole group, he knocked back his own shots with the girls, and he even drew in other guys to join in on the party that slowly grew at the bar.

Val bounced along to the music, the blur from the alcohol made her feel flushed and heated, her eyes closed as she enjoyed the music and the press of the woman that moved with her as she danced. She didn't pay mind to the shots offered and just danced with the brunette.

"I think your friends' drinks are getting warm." The Irish accent drew her out of her daze. He held out another shot. "One more for the road?" He had his own shot in his other hand and quickly drank it down. He lifted her shot up again then placed it on the counter near her.

"Will you come back to join us once you drop off their drinks?" The brunette gave her big, puppy-dog eyes in hope that Val would return.

"I will have to see if my friends want to stay longer." Her hand drifted to the drink, she definitely felt the effects of the tequila and this would be her last one for the night, she decided.

"Maybe you can invite them over to join us," Irish-painted words suggested.

"Maybe." Not a definite answer, but the girls of the group cheered anyway and the man nodded.

Val quickly drank her last shot and rushed to get a lime, her face screwed up at the strong taste, and the tart citrus quickly covered the strong alcohol. She reached over and grabbed the drinks for Hannah and Lucia, the beer was covered in condensation from being out, and the cocktail was in a similar state. She detached from the group to navigate to the table where the others sat.

LUCIA FELT her blood run cold, she focused only on the beat of her blood that rushed in her ears, the noise blurred everything much like how her eyes had begun to glaze over. Everything went cold, Lucia was lost and her body vibrated to a drum that called to her.

Violence. Hunger. Lucia was familiar with it.

White eyes were laced with anger and glazed over a predatory hunger, her jaw clenched tightly, and with an aggressive and strained breath exhaled, she stood stock still.

Her eyes only followed the drink that was outstretched to the redhead in the distance, she saw the liquid become disturbed with a substance that was dropped in. Her jaw locked and unlocked. Her hands had begun to shake with the energy that suddenly flooded her body.

Horror filled her body as she watched her friend gulp down the laced liquid and turn toward the blond man beside her. She felt her blood rush and scream for vengeance. She moved to rush toward the other, to get her to safety, but an olive-skinned hand held her in place.

CHAPTER FOUR

White eyes whipped around to glare at the one that stopped her movements, violence redirected toward the one that got in her way. Intense eyes were met with deep-brown eyes, eyes that reflected the same violence in her own. She inhaled sharply, a shaky breath released as they had a silent exchange in their eyes. Em held a strong grip on her arm, their knuckles were white from the hold.

Their eyes didn't remain on Lucia for long, the younger turned to watch Val move toward them with drinks in hand. Their eyes darted to the man at the bar who watched the redhead, said redhead walked with the drinks in hand, a slight sway in her steps.

Lucia jerked her head around to glare in the direction of the man that lounged at the bar, the group around him had continued to take shots and loudly party at the bar. He joined in the festivities of the group but Lucia watched him look over in their direction, toward Val. Lucia listened to her pulse thunder in her ears, she needed to get her friend out of the club and she needed to do it fast.

A soft hand touched her left arm, Lucia looked over to Hannah, and her soft, hazel eyes gave a questioning look of concern. Lucia realized that she had suddenly moved and let go of the younger girl, which probably startled the other. "Ah, I just felt woozy for a sec," Lucia lied. Her eyes looked over to Em, their eyes focused on the bar, on the blond.

Val finally returned to the table they all stood at, she swayed significantly more now that she was stationary. Two drinks were placed carefully on the table, a big smile on her face.

"I'm so sorry I took so long! Some people from the cruise were buying me some shots!" Her words ran together as she rushed to speak, her face was flushed a deeper red.

"We noticed," Em said flatly. They refused to look over at the drunken redhead, they just stared blankly at the bar. Lucia knew better than to believe that they weren't focused on something though, they had been together long enough for her to know that those eyes tracked every move that their target made.

Lucia's gaze moved up and down Val who swayed to the music. Hannah had moved over to her friend to get the cocktail, Lucia's eyes glanced over to the beer placed down for her.

"Honestly, I think we should probably head out soon," Lucia said slowly, Em nodded their head, still with a heavy gaze in the distance. Hannah turned to look at Lucia, she took a long sip from her drink and smiled at the taste of her drink.

Val furrowed her brows in confusion. "But you just got your drink."

Lucia's eyes went back to the beer just out of reach of her hand. She licked her lips nervously, she tried to think quickly of something to get the two women to agree to leave the club. Em was no use, their glare and focus were solely on the bar.

"What's up?" Hannah asked, her eyes going from Val to Lucia.

"Lucia wants to leave soon." Val pouted, she made sure to sign her words to Hannah. The blonde nodded as she looked over to Em and Lucia. The brunette shoved some more rock candy into her mouth as she stared from Em to Val. Em seemed disinterested in the conversation, their eyes just stared into the distance, seemingly elsewhere in their thoughts.

"That sounds good to me," Hannah agreed.

"We can finish our drinks, though, you went through all the effort of getting them for us." Lucia offered, she noticed that Val's face relaxed into a smile.

"Okie dokie!"

Lucia eyed the drink as she pulled it close to her lips, she raised her eyebrows and inhaled as she took a drink. She didn't detect a strange taste in the drink, she gave a side eye to watch Hannah who enjoyed her drink, and offered a taste to Val. Val took a sip and proceeded to dance to the Spanish song that played overhead, her moves becoming more sluggish and lethargic.

Lucia trusted in herself and swallowed down the beer as quickly as she could. She thanked Poseidon for his gifts to her and looked at Em, they watched the bar like a hawk, the prey would be unable to escape their hunter's eyes. They spared a glance over to Lucia, then back over to their target.

Lucia put a practiced smile on her face and forced a laugh, "I think your shots are catching up with you, Val!" Val forced her eyes open, the sluggish dance had stopped and her energy seemed to slowly disappear from her body. "Are you okay? You don't look good." She furrowed her brow as she watched Val become affected by whatever was laced in her drink.

"It.. all hit at once I think..." her voice slurred and slowed. She grabbed her head, she blinked with as much effort as she could muster. Hannah furrowed her brow and grabbed at Val's shoulder, she leaned to get a look at the redhead's face.

"Maybe it is time to leave," Hannah looked up at Lucia.

"Yeah.. we need to go." She nudged Em.

They snapped out of the trance they were in, moved toward Val, gently grabbed her under her elbow, and slowly made their way to leave the club. Lucia walked with Hannah in tow, the smaller blonde held her hand as they weaved through the darkness. Lucia never lost sight of Em or Val, she didn't let the two get much further than a few people away. She kept an eye over her shoulder, not to watch Hannah though, she squeezed her hand, but to keep an eye out for the blond man from the bar.

She knew better than to think he wouldn't notice them when they moved to leave. Predatory white eyes gazed around the club, she kept the bar within her peripherals as they moved to the exit. As expected he had his eyes trained on the redhead in front of her.

He didn't move to follow the group as they left, Lucia internally hoped that he would follow, it would make it easier to deal with him if he did. She spied the displeased look that crossed his face as he watched them leave, he turned his body back to the bar and returned his attention to the group of girls that still took shots at the bar.

"Fuck," Lucia muttered under her breath, her jaw clenched and her hand tightened around Hannah's as they got closer to the door.

THEY MANAGED to get out of the crowd where they met up with Em who held up a very lethargic Val in their arms. Lucia reached her free arm to intertwine Val's other arm with hers. She shared a look with the younger, she jerked her chin up, and they nodded their head in acknowledgment. They started to walk to the door, Hannah walked ahead of them to get the door open.

The warm, summer air rushed into the club, the darkness of the club became brighter with the outside lights. Hannah stepped out to keep the door open for the others, the two assisted the redhead through the threshold into the fresh air. Val took in a deep breath, her head tilted back to relish the night breeze. It was a struggle for Val to take a step, her weight fell into Em and Lucia's arms.

"Is she okay?" Hannah worried, the two looked at each other before they looked at the blonde that wouldn't take her eyes off her friend.

"I think she just had too much to drink," a nonchalant reply to calm the other. "However... I don't think we will be able to get her back to your cruise ship."

"We would have to carry her all the way to her room. I doubt they will let us on the ship," Em said flatly.

Large, hazel eyes looked up at them, concern covered her face. She chewed her lip in worry, she looked to the redhead who was all but deadweight in the two's arms.

"We could go to our hotel," Lucia offered, "You guys can crash there until morning." Hannah gave a long stare at the redhead. "I know I would feel better knowing she's okay."

"You know her best, if you wanna go back to the cruise ship, we will do our best to get her there," Em reassured. "But you're more than welcome to stay with us for the night." They readjusted their hold on the redhead, ensuring they had a better grip on her, but also made sure she wasn't uncomfortable.

"I used to be a nurse so if anything goes wrong I can help her," Lucia added in, "I have some meds that can help."

Hannah nodded her head and looked into Lucia's eyes, "Which way?"

Lucia and Em gently set Val down on the only bed in the hotel room. It was one of the only places where the pair could get an extended stay with cash. It was close to the port where the cruise liners were docked, but far enough away that it wasn't excessively expensive since they didn't have much cash. The tiny room was made up of one large, queen bed that appeared to actually be two single beds pushed together, a bathroom, and a dresser with a small television.

Hannah turned on the lights, the dim lights of the old lamps flicked on, they gave off barely enough light to fill the room, but Lucia reached over and tapped a button on the side of the wall next to the nightstand, the side-table lamp kicked on to give some more light to the room.

"What can we do for her?"

Hannah sat on the side of the bed next to the unconscious Val. Em had crouched down to tug off the redhead's heels and they moved to set the shoes at the foot of the bed. The speckled hair disappeared into the bathroom without a word.

"We can get her some water and have some meds ready for when she wakes up, but the best thing for her is to sleep it off and keep an eye on her." Lucia sat next to Hannah, she reached over to gently fix Val's hair. Em appeared from the bathroom and moved over to place the mentioned water and meds on the side table.

"I don't know how she got so drunk, she hasn't been this drunk since college," Hannah pondered with a sign.

"She mentioned that the group at the bar was buying her a lot of shots, it's likely she drank more than she realized," Em suggested. Their eyes met with Lucia's, the unspoken agreement that passed between the two went unnoticed by Hannah who leaned down to work off her own shoes.

The quiet of the room was filled with Val's soft breathing, her chest rose and fell, and Hannah gave a wistful stare to the redhead. "Thank you, guys, I don't think I would have been able to do this by myself." Lucia rested a hand on Hannah's, she gave her a soft smile. Em gave an equally as soft smile to the blonde, the pair were also thankful they were there for the other two.

"Let's get some rest, it's been an eventful night." Lucia patted the bed next to her. She slid off the side of the bed so that Hannah could lie down and moved to the side of the bed that Em stood at, kicking off her shoes to climb into the bed. "Sorry it's only one bed, Em and I are used to cuddling." She laughed.

Hannah smiled, "Doesn't bug me, we share a bed when we visit each other." She reached up to her right ear and hesitated. "Are you okay if I take out my hearing aid? It's not super comfortable to sleep in. I can still kinda hear without it, though! It'll just be harder if I'm not paying attention or awake," she rushed out in a blur of words, her hands came together in an anxious movement, and her fingers intertwined and worried at one another.

"Don't worry about it! It doesn't bother us if you need to take it out to be comfortable." Hannah looked up to meet Lucia's white eyes, the nerves slowly melted away from her. She dared a glance over to Em, their head nodded in agreement with the brunette.

"Thank you," she said with a soft smile.

THEY WAITED until Hannah's breath slowed and evened out; soft, little puffs that danced along Val's neck. It didn't take long for her to fall deep into sleep given the night they had. She was snuggled close to the redhead, her arms tangled around the other. Lucia moved from the other side where she cuddled Em and walked over to the edge of the bed where Val laid unconscious. They had positioned her that way in case she woke up and needed to throw up, but Lucia wasn't going to let Val suffer from the drugs in her system for much longer.

She spared a glance at Hannah, her hearing aid sat on the nightstand to the side of the bed. Em had suggested to charm the sandy blonde to ensure she slept through the night but Lucia rejected the idea. Lucia sat down on the ground, she heard the younger shuffle in the dark of the room, but she paid no mind to her friend.

"I need to heal her first," she whispered to the unspoken question from the other. She couldn't see the deep-brown eyes, but she knew the other wouldn't disagree with her.

Lucia gently brushed the hair from Val's dark skin, she softened her face and muttered under her breath. White eyes closed and melodic words of an Italian lullaby were sung quietly as Lucia let her hands drift over the redhead.

A gentle, white glow began to warm her fingertips. She ghosted them over Val's skin, she barely made contact with the skin as her fingers drifted over the supple body. Lucia continued to sing her lullaby, she pressed her warm hand to Val's forehead, the soft, white glow grew stronger.

Lucia prayed to Poseidon and Galene as she sang, she felt a tear roll down her cheek. Her body was cold compared to the warmth that radiated from her fingers, all of the warmth moved from her body to the hands that worked over the other. She fought off the images of a cruise ship balcony, rough choppy water that moved below, and gray clouds warped from under the water. Her words choked for a moment, caught in the memories.

Val didn't move, her body just a loose ragdoll on the bed. Lucia pressed a firmer touch into Val, she didn't know what drug was given but she prayed with everything to rid it from the redhead.

The lullaby stopped and the glow dissipated but Lucia remained on the ground, quiet tears sliding down her cheeks. She pressed her forehead against the side of the bed, she held Val's hands in her own. A careful hand pressed on her shoulder, she looked up to Em, the white parts of their hair the only thing that was visible, she couldn't see their face but she felt the strength in their touch.

"Let's get that fucker."

CHAPTER FIVE

They stalked in the streets, the dark of the night allowed them to go by unnoticed by the drunk patrons of the night.

Em had changed into a black t-shirt, loose, dark jeans, and some tennis shoes. Lucia, however, had changed into a black sports bra and a black hoodie, she remained in the jeans and shoes that she had on earlier. Her long hair was pulled back into a thick braid, the dark-brown hair pulled out of the way for their hunt.

They made their way back to the bar where they had last seen the man. Lucia prayed to Poseidon that their prey hadn't left the bar or worse, found a new victim. She clenched her jaw at the thought.

The pair usually hunted together, this was nothing new to them. Usually, they had the advantage of being in the water, they had struggled with their recent hunts on land, but they made it work. Their expressions matched when they shared a glance, anger and hunger. Not many in their pod kept to the old way of hunting, but they did. The thrill of the hunt and the taste of the blood in the water drove them on.

Their instincts were strong under the moonlight, and it fueled their desire for their hunt. The end of their phase approached soon and they would return to their home, the stiffness of their bones let them know this.

Em moved from the shadows of their spot, the shorter started toward the still-active club. Lucia knew to stay in the shadows, she was less noticeable in the darkness and she didn't hold the power that Em did. Their eyes would find their target with quick ease, and they wouldn't let him get far if he was still in the club. She waited in the dark shadows, Em had left her sight, but from years of them being together, she knew the younger was able to manage themself. She just kept her eyes on the exits in sight while she awaited her partner to find their target.

EM SNAKED THROUGH THE CROWDS, they kept to the shadows and slipped by the entrance of the club with a group. The first place to check was the bar where the man was at last. Although it had been over an hour since they left, they were sure he would still be there, he had made this his hunting ground, after all. Dark eyes darted around the club, they didn't get to see the man up close, but they knew what he looked like.

Em melted into the crowd of the club, they let their more primal side slip out and take the reins. They slid between people, the push of the club no different than the pull of currents. Their eyes roamed past faces in the center of the club, quick scans of the dancers that rolled against each other like waves.

With no luck in the center they moved to the shadows of the wall. The tables had barely any light for the quick search, but they found the group of girls that was at the bar earlier with Val. The party girls crowded a table, empty shot glasses filled the glass table. Em took a chance and approached the table.

"Hey, do you guys know where the guy that was here earlier went?" They shouted loudly over the music. Some of the group turned to them, drunken smiles and glazed eyes.

"Which guy?" a brunette who giggled and hung on to one of the other women at the table asked.

"Tall guy, blond hair?"

"Ohhhhh! The Irish guy?!" a blonde with buns yelled. "He was taking shots with us at the bar."

Em nodded. "Yeah that's the guy, where is he?"

"We moved over here cause the bartender got mad at us." The blond pouted. "I don't know what his problem was, we were taking shots and drinking."

"But where did the guy go?" Em asked, they tried to hide their frustration that laced their voice. "I found his phone and want to get it back to him." They hoped the girls wouldn't see through the lie.

"Right! Oh my gosh, he just left to smoke outside." the giggling brunette finally said. "He said he would get us more drinks on his way back." The other women nodded in agreement.

"You can hang out with us until he comes back," the blonde offered. The group chorused about it, one chanted about shots.

"To smoke? Okay, thanks." Em ignored the comment and abruptly left the girls. They weren't sure where the smoking zones were but they would find them rather quickly.

Instincts urged them to follow their nose, they kept to the walls and moved toward some doors that smelled of smoke and tobacco. They prayed to Poseidon that it led to an open outside.

They scrunched up their nose at the strength of the smell when they swung the door open. The sick smell of tobacco lingered in the air and they scanned the gated patio. Tables littered the area and two couples smoked near the gates, they talked amongst themselves, not even acknowledging Em's entrance to the area. The man wasn't there.

They sucked in a sharp breath, biting down on their inner cheek with sharp teeth. They rushed back into the club, the smell of cigarettes followed them. Em wove through the crowd of people toward the bar again, another spot he could be, given what the girls said. A quick scan of the bar showed the blond man wasn't there.

The only other place that could be a smoke zone was out near the front. They huffed and moved toward the side door by the entrance, the subtle smell of cigarettes came from beyond the door. They slipped past the door into the second open-air patio. This patio was just beside the entrance, large concrete archways that decorated the area, a small gate, and the waterfront walkway beyond the walls.

Leaned against one of the concrete walls with eyes directed toward the entrance stood a figure. A lit cigarette balanced between fingers as they took a drag from it. Em knew the person saw them enter the area, the tall figure shifted from the shadows and exposed short, sandy-blond hair.

Em sucked in an exhilarated breath, they had found their target, and they were alone. They tried to steady their breathing, they couldn't take him alone in their current position.They needed to get to where Lucia could see them, they took a step forward past one of the concrete columns. They glanced to see if they could spot Lucia, no sight of the brunette in the shadows.

They resolved that they were going to have to charm him to come with them when they watched him take another drag from his cigarette.

"Need a cig?" an Irish voice offered, he had pushed himself fully off the wall toward where Em stood.

"Yeah, I could really use one." They pursed their lips as the guy approached them, he was a foot taller than them and broad, but they just needed him closer. He reached into his pocket to pull out a white box.

Em stepped closer to him, they felt their hunger grow, their movement became more fluid. They let their body sway in a way to entice the man before them. He watched cautiously as the shorter approached, he slid the cigarette out of the box and offered it between his fingers to them.

"Rough night?" he inquired, he didn't remove his eyes from Em as they let slender fingers brush against his when they took the cigarette from his hands.

"Yeah, you could say that," they started slowly, as they let their eyes flutter up to meet his. "I just really need a *stress reliever*."

They let their intense eyes stare into his blue-green eyes. They prayed to Poseidon to have all their siren charm draw the man in. They stared deeply into his eyes, their white-and-black-speckled eyelashes fluttered when they stared at him.

"A stress reliever?" he echoed back, unable to look away from Em's stare.

"*Yeah*," they let out in a sultry tone, "*something to get rid of that itch. Ya' know?*" Em slowed their words, the blond nodded his head slowly.

"Ya need a light?" he offered sluggishly, even without a reply, he had pulled out the lighter, unable to break away from Em's entrancing stare. They gave a seductive smile and nodded, lifted the cigarette to their mouth, and leaned forward to the lighter. Their eyes never left one another.

Em drew in a breath from the cigarette after he flicked the lighter on. His own cigarette dropped to the ground, forgotten in the hypnotic stare. They blew out the smoke through the side of their mouth. There was another presence that stood in the shadows that Em sensed, they were comforted by the familiar energy from the bystander. A hand reached out and squeezed their arm before it melted back into the shadows. Em discarded the cigarette to the concrete, their running shoes stomped down on it, not bothering to look at it.

"*What's your name?*" They drawled out, a tongue pressed to the top lip. They looked down at his lips for a second to release him for a moment before they pulled him back in.

"Eli," he took a moment to process the question, a single breath before he drowned in the deep-brown eyes.

"*Eli...*" They drawled out slowly again, holding his eyes that glazed over. The presence behind them fully stepped out to reveal Lucia, "*Let's take a walk.*"

· · ·

Lucia took the lead with the direction they headed while Em continued to keep Eli under their charm. She walked ahead of them on the sidewalk of the waterfront, the paths were desolate for the late hour. Once the older was sure that they were alone, she led them toward the sandy shore at the water below. Both Em and Lucia felt a surge of confidence, their bodies thrummed with the beat of the waves at their feet. Em kept contact with their prey, their hand pressed against his elbow to urge him forward. The younger walked beside him in the water, unaffected by the sogginess of their shoes.

Lucia noted how far they were from their goal, the hill of rocks which was right beyond a large structure that blocked vision from anyone who would walk by. After a couple more minutes of their walk, she guided them behind the wall and determined they were out of sight enough. She stopped in her tracks and turned around to look at Em. Her face had an odd sense of calmness that had come over it, long gone was the aggressive and hostile hunger, she seemed almost serene.

She felt the call of the ocean, the energy of Poseidon, fill her body. They had maybe a day or two before they turned, Lucia knew that Em felt it as well. She grabbed at Eli's free arm, the calm look on her face hardened with the hostility that filled her body when she looked at him. The brunette had taken the charmed Eli from Em's grasp.

"Come join me for a swim, Eli." His head swiveled over to her, the glazed blue-green eyes followed her as she moved deeper into the water. Her voice was a siren song and he was the sailor.

Her knees were submerged in the water when he finally followed after, a tether pulled tight with her own charm that enchanted him. She urged him deeper into the water, the quiet of the night was filled only with the gentle splash of water against the rocks and their bodies. Em entered after them to swim to the deeper water, they treaded around and relaxed as the energy of the water filled them.

Lucia's braided hair became saturated the deeper she got Eli into the water. She got down to chest deep before she let her feet out from under her and used them to push her deeper into the water. Eli was taller than the two and in his trance, he managed to get deeper into the water before he had to tread water. The air shifted once the ground was no longer under his feet, the pair closed in on Eli as they forced him deeper into the waves.

"We know what you did to our friend, Eli," Lucia said coldly, she grabbed on to one of his shoulders. *"You slipped a drug into her drink, in hopes that she would be vulnerable so you could take advantage of her."*

Em circled around them in the water, a predatory gaze filled their eyes as they watched Eli in the water. Eli swam there unresponsive to the commentary, the trance they had put him under held him in place.

"We can tell this isn't your first time doing this, you were too calm and smooth with it," Em chimed in and grabbed his other shoulder. Their legs were much stronger and the muscles were far more used to swimming in water. *"Were you planning to go for one of the other girls next?"*

Lucia pulled his arm down and began to force more of his body under the water. She had a coldness in her icy, white stare that watched Eli, Em's eyes mirrored the same coldness.

"So, we're going to give you the same fate," Lucia started as she swam further into the water and deeper under.

"Unable to control your body," Em followed with a tug on his other arm, forcing him deeper.

"Unable to fight back."

"And unable to hurt anyone ever again," Em finished.

Their faces became predatory as they both plunged the man under the water. He didn't thrash in their arms, he didn't even take a breath before he was dragged under. They pushed him down to the sandy underwater until his shoulders connected with a solid rock, the bubbles escaping his mouth in a flurry. The two stayed under with ease, the bubbles were a storm that flooded around them, but they weren't affected.

Lucia dug her nails into his shoulder, the frenzy of anger flooded her brain and she wanted him to fight, she wanted the hunt. She released her trance on Eli. Her white eyes began to glow in the dark waters, inhuman and predatory. The taste of revenge wasn't enough, the anger of her past welled up in her. She kicked her legs in the water to force Eli further into the ground, rocks under the sandy seabed provided a solid surface to pin the large man to. The bubbles from their victim began to slow, the once-panicked stream became small and sporadic, he was almost out of air. Em slowly reduced the hold of their trance on the man, it was already too late for him to escape.

The realization in his face that registered the lack of air thrilled them both, his shoulders struggled in their grasps, a new flurry of bubbles surged from him in his panic. His arms attempted to flail in the water, but Em was fast to pin them to his side. Lucia smiled in satisfaction, her free hand roughly grabbed his hair and slammed his head into the rock below him, a large bubble of air escaped at the contact. The effort of this was much harder underwater but the pair were used to this, their arms moved like the current, strong and sure.

Lucia continued the assault, she used all her strength to smash his head back into the rock. The water began to stain red with each contact she made with his head. The blond's body went slack in their hands, stray bubbles of air drifted from his lips. Lucia wasn't done though, caught in the frenzy of the kill. She dug her nails deep into the muscle of his shoulder until it broke the skin, the blood further tainting the water.

Em slowly breathed out bubbles and released their prey, the body floated in the water. Lucia's grip was the only thing that kept his body to the sea floor, her own body hovered at the bottom, she had latched her legs around a protruding rock to keep herself below as she thrashed his head into the rocks. The dark ocean swallowed up the blood, it dragged the stained waters to the sea.

Lucia slowed her actions, bubbles had stopped coming from her prey, his eyes stuck open with fear and mouth agape. She detached from the rock that kept her down in the water and moved to the surface. Em followed suit, they didn't need to, the air wasn't a problem for either of them, but once at the surface, Lucia breathed erratically.

Her chest heaved as she gasped out and sucked in the air. She released a sob and dragged the body up to a flat rock. She unlatched her hand from the bloody shoulder, ripping the flesh open to expose the muscle below, and grabbed the head with both hands. She aimed it at the sharp edge of the rocks and returned to slamming it onto the surface. The squelching crunch of the contact overpowered the sound of the waves. Aggressive growls and snarls filled the air with each of the wet clashes.

Lucia stopped her assault on the rock, dropping the caved-in head, and lunging forward, she sank her teeth into the throat of the body. She bit down hard on the jugular and jerked her head back, the skin shredding from the prey. She crunched down on the flesh in her mouth, chewing it briefly and then spitting it out to grab more of the gory flesh. The second bite was less clean, she held the body down to the surface to devour the body and growled as she let her sharp teeth rip more meat from the throat.

Blood flowed from the mauled throat, coating her face and spilling down the rocks. Chunks of flesh were scattered around her, floating in the water and in the crevices of the rocks. Bits of flesh stuck between her teeth as she bit down further into the flesh, she kept going until her teeth collided with the bones of his spine.

She moved on to the slashed shoulder, sinking into the muscles and detaching the fibrous tendons. The meat was flung from the arm, Lucia barely chewed before latching back down to keep going. Her nails dug into the flesh she didn't bite down on, holding the unmoving body in place. She dragged the body back up to herself when it slid down from her attack.

Em swam over, their head swiveled around to ensure that no one had wandered over to investigate the sounds. They moved over to the older as she pulled away from the flesh, her tears streaking down her bloody face. A soft hand reached over to grab blood-soaked fingers, holding her in place. They sat like that, for a while until

Lucia's sobs quieted. Every time they had frenzied, Lucia was there to bring them back. This time, they would be there to bring her back.

"Sunrise is soon," Em observed.

Lucia moved her hand to clutch Em's, her bloody hand shook. Her white eyes glazed over with memories. The fog slowly melted away from her eyes, the frenzy gradually leaving her. She turned to Em and then to the sky, the darkness was all that greeted them. Lucia's heavy breathing and the waves were the only sound for several minutes.

"We-" she croaked out, "we should get back soon."

Em pressed their lips together, dark eyes looked down at the body in front of them, watching the water lap at the cooling flesh. A heavy sigh escaped their lips as they slid back into the water, a hand grabbed at a foot of the body. Lucia followed suit, she grabbed the arm that was not mauled and tugged the corpse into the water, and the blood on her washed away with the current.

CHAPTER SIX

They used the cover of night and the dark waters to swim with the body to their destination. Water rushed around them. Lucia floated on her back while she propelled herself with her legs. Em swam on their side, the younger's eyes trained on the coast and docks that they swam toward, a fleet of massive cruise ships loomed over them.

Comfortable silence followed them as they swam under the piers, they kept to the shadows of the pillars, moving the corpse as quietly as possible. Lights from the pier spilled down to the water, the dark water illuminated around the sides. Occasional footsteps and conversations drifted down to the pair in the water, their ears tuned in to every subtle sound. Em directed them toward the closest ship, the massive cruise liner dwarfed them in the water. Water splashed loudly against the sides of the metal behemoth, they used the sound to cover their own splashes as they neared. The pair moved to the side of the ship that was furthest from the dock once they reached the nose, the side they moved toward facing the open ocean.

They swam faster once they were on the side of the boat, they didn't have to hide their noises as much. Lucia huffed, she was the faster swimmer of the two but that was when they were underwater, the surface added more weight to their cargo.

"This would be much faster with our fins," Lucia grumbled, her words were swallowed by the waves. Em rolled their eyes, they both knew that they couldn't speed up the moon phases.

The silence returned as Eli's body was heaved to the end of the ship, the pair examined the end of the boat to find their goal, the propeller of the ship. Lucia released her hold on the foot, submerging herself into the deep water. Em remained with the body and floated pressed against the side of the boat while they waited for the older. She shortly returned, hair that had escaped her braid pressed against her face. She nodded to confirm that she had found the propeller and moved to take his body below. Em held the body and stopped her, though.

"His wallet," they whispered.

Lucia sucked in a breath as realization crossed her face, they didn't get it earlier when he was tranced. She quickly moved her hands over the pockets closest to her, feeling for the wallet. The older shook her head when she didn't discover it on her side. Em looked in the pockets on their side and discovered it in the back pocket of the jeans. It took a second for them to get it out of the pocket, the jeans were soaked under the water and clung to the wallet. It proved more difficult for the shorter one to slide it into their own pocket after they retrieved it.

A nod of the younger's head signaled to Lucia that the wallet was secured and then they submerged. She guided them down deep under the water to the propeller of the ship, the dark waters moved with them. Their eyes adapted quickly to the water, the darkness not a problem for their siren eyes. They kicked hard through the current to get the body to the large fan-like propeller of the ship. Em pushed the body into the crevice of the propeller between two of the blades. Lucia made sure that they got the body wedged in enough that it wouldn't pre-emptively become dislodged by any sea creatures or currents.

Satisfied by their work, they returned to the surface. They swam in silence back to the shore, they avoided the shoreline where they had killed Eli at and favored a shore that was closer to their hotel. Their clothes clung tightly against their bodies as they walked out of the surf. Lucia wrung out her hair while they walked through the small patch of sand, she flicked the braid back over her shoulder when she deemed it fine. She reached her hand out to Em's hand, the shorter accepted the touch and glanced over to her.

"You okay?" Their dark eyes watched her.

Lucia let a long pause hang between them, her white eyes focused on the path ahead of them. The question was valid. She hadn't frenzied on their prey before like that with Em, not in the two years that they had been together in the pod. She knew she had done it before when she had just turned and she was healing mentally. She continued her hunts for the thrill after the rage and desire for revenge died down. When Em turned and joined the pod, they joined her on her hunts, but Lucia had never frenzied. None of their victims had given her the flashbacks she had, until then. She got lost in the memories of their past, Em gave a gentle squeeze to draw her attention back.

She let out a slow breath, "Yeah. I'm okay."

DAWN HAD STARTED to break when they reached the hotel, the sky had begun to change colors with the warmth of the sun. Lucia and Em had managed to stop dripping water before they slipped into the hotel and back to their room. Em started the shower in the bathroom while Lucia checked on the girls asleep on the bed. Val had rolled over in her sleep into Hannah's arms, the blonde held the other against her chest. They breathed softly in deep sleep. Lucia was careful to caress a hand against Val's forehead to check for a fever.

When she found none she returned to the bathroom and locked the door behind her.

Em stood in just boxers, their shirt, and jeans were discarded across the toilet to dry. They had pulled out the wallet and were going through the contents, wet bills were placed on the counter, and a passport was next to the money. They pulled out a baggy between their fingers, the still-dry contents of a powdery substance and pills were visible in the clear packaging. Lucia scrunched up her nose in disgust.

"Leave it. When they find his wallet, they will know what he was." She pulled the hoodie over her head and it landed with a wet slap. Her shoes found a place by the sink before she worked off her jeans and kicked them to the shower.

"They aren't gonna dry properly if you don't hang them," Em scolded as they separated the Euros that they had laid out on the counter.

"We are going back to the pod soon, why should I care?" Lucia scoffed.

"You're such a brat."

She gave the younger a playful smile and picked up her clothes and hung them on the towel rack. Lucia released her braid and worked her fingers through it to get it unraveled. Once done, she walked up behind Em and circled her arms around their waist, her chin nestled into the crook of their shoulder to look at the money on the counter.

"Ignoring his credit cards we got about two hundred Euros," the older bounced her head in a nod to Em's words, her damp hair tickled at their back from the movement.

"So, enough for some food and such."

"With some left over," Em confirmed.

Lucia pressed a gentle kiss to Em's throat, "We could bring some souvenirs for the others." Lucia suggested. Em made a noncommittal noise in their throat, they leaned back into Lucia's taller body.

"Not much will survive down there."

"We survive down there."

"You know as well as I do that the reason we can is 'cause of Galene." Em scrunched up their face at Lucia's suggestion, but she just laughed lightly.

"Who knows, maybe Poseidon wants an offering," the older teased. Em whirled around in her arms to glare at the brunette. "I'm kidding!" she defended. They glared at her for a moment before they gave an angry huff and set their head on her chest. Lucia rested her head on the top of their hair.

The two stayed in the moment for a while, Em held closely in Lucia's arms, both their eyes closed. Lucia loosened her arms and removed her chin from Em's head.

"We should probably actually shower," she gestured when they detached.

"I guess," they still moved to take off their boxers despite their reluctant words, and they placed them on the toilet seat with their clothes. Lucia pulled her sports bra overhead and flung it in the direction of the towel rack, her panties followed after, and both articles missed and slapped to the floor behind the toilet. Em grumbled and picked them up for her, who apologetically smiled.

Dark-brown eyes watched her in the mirror. They couldn't pull their eyes away from the brunette, her long hair reached below her hips. Her tanned skin showed all the marks along her body, love marks on her thighs, and scratch marks down her back. They gave a smug smirk at the marks on her body, they knew that there were more along the front of her body, they had put them there days prior. They knew that they had similar marks from her littered along their body, mostly bite marks.

Lucia stepped into the warm spray of water, she relished in the warm water. They wouldn't get to enjoy it for much longer. She already felt the itch of change in her bones. White eyes stared over to her counterpart that stepped in front of her in the shower, she was sure the younger felt it as well. All of the joints in her legs hurt, cracking and aching with each move, and it was barely soothed by the warm water. She internally wished that her healing powers helped remove the pain of the change.

She ghosted her hands over Em's small waist, cupped water against their belly, then released it so it fell all at once. They laughed in unison and pressed the side of their heads together. Em's wet, short, black-and-white hair pressed against their face. Lucia guided them out of the water so she could have her back in the water, the shorter gave a noise of complaint at Lucia's actions.

"Everything hurts," Em mumbled and dropped their head back onto Lucia's shoulder. She kissed the top of their hair in sympathy.

"I know, I know." Lucia reached her hand up to push Em's hair from their forehead.

"Is it tomorrow or the day after?" She knew what they meant, the moon phase to turn.

"Tomorrow, I think." She hummed thoughtfully.

She kissed their head again, ran her hands down their soft chest, and rubbed their sides. That was where she ached the most, so she figured it would help their pains, too. Their groan confirmed her assumption, so she continued to massage the side of the younger's hips. A soft laugh slipped from her lips and she rotated them so they were half in the water and half out. She rolled her head so it rested on their shoulder to look at the younger's face. Water splattered on their faces while she spied a small patch of hair on the side of their head that was white at the root under the jet-black hair. She reached up a hand to stroke the spot.

"You have another speckle," she mumbled with a smile, her fingers carded through the shorter's hair.

Em made a noise in their throat, and dark eyes opened and blinked through the water. "Yeah," they shifted some in her arms, "I have another one appearing on my undercut as well."

"Do you think it'll be entirely white one day?" She looked around the undercut to find the mentioned spot. Lucia detached to turn them so she could kiss the new spot.

"I don't know, probably." They shrugged, their hands rubbed

against their body to wash off the saltwater. "Some people just have a streak or two."

Lucia pondered it and smiled, "I love it. They're like freckles." She kissed the side of their head again then ran her hands down the other's back.

"Yeah, yeah. Let's finish up in the shower, the other two will wake up soon." They reached for a bar of soap to emphasize their point. The brunette laughed and wrapped her arms around them in protest.

"No! I wanna keep holding you," her bottom lip pouted out.

"You get to hold me all the time." The younger turned in her arms, and they shot her a strong look with a raised, speckled eyebrow. She was unfazed by the look and just laughed more, swaying their bodies together.

"Fine. Fine. It's not like we live in the ocean or anything," Lucia grumbled and separated from Em's body. The younger laughed at her statement and passed her the soap.

CHAPTER SEVEN

The pair quickly dried off with towels. A towel hung over Lucia's head, her hair dripping water on the floor under the towel. Em had a towel wrapped around their chest and used a smaller towel to dry off their hair properly. Lucia propped her leg up on the toilet to dry it before switching to get the next one, eventually she deemed them dry enough and wrapped the towel around her own body. She moved on to her hair, rubbing her dark-brown locks with the towel and watched Em put together the different items to hide.

They stashed away the wallet and passport in the bathroom behind the toilet tank to discard later, the wet cash was wrapped in a hand towel and hidden under the sink. Neither of them had grabbed a change of clothes so they would have to go back into the room to get dressed. Lucia peeked her head outside to see if either of the women had woken up.

The light from the bathroom spilled into the room, allowing her to check on the two. Hannah had rolled over so her face was toward the door and Val had her back pressed against the blonde. Lucia checked the water and saw that it had been drunk and the pain meds were gone. The brunette nodded and went over to the small dresser to pull out a change of clothes for each of them. She quietly stepped back into the bathroom for them to get dressed.

Em grabbed their clothes from her, slipping on a forest-green V-neck shirt and black boxers with some dark-wash jeans. Lucia shimmied on a black sports bra and boy shorts, a light-gray shirt with white, faded lettering that said 'Spain' on it, and black sports shorts with a white stripe along the seams. Her loose hair left wet marks where they sat on the shirt, the damp strands hung over her shoulder and down her back. Em leaned against her, watching their reflections, and gave a tired sigh.

"Come on, let's go lie down." Lucia bumped her shoulder against them. Em nodded and followed the brunette, clicking off the light as they left the bathroom.

They managed to scoot Hannah over on the bed to make some room for the both of them. Lucia checked on Val before she let herself lie down next to Em. They got situated on their sides so that Em was pressed against Lucia's back. She was further down so her head was pressed against Em's chest but still on the pillow, careful to keep her hair out of Em's face. They protectively wrapped their arms around the older woman, they held her tightly to their chest. She relaxed into their arms and gradually went lax as she dozed off.

They checked on the brunette asleep in their arms, they felt the slow rise and fall of her chest as she slept. They softly hummed and pressed a kiss to the top of her head, leaving their face pressed into her damp hair. The younger one inhaled deeply, pressing another kiss to the crown of her head then rested their chin on her head closing their eyes. They dreamed of the ocean and brown hair that moved with the waves.

LUCIA WOKE UP FIRST, her face was tucked into Em's chest, her long legs tangled with the other's, and her arm wrapped around their middle. This was how they usually slept when they were with the pod, their tails usually twined together. She nuzzled her face back into their chest and closed her eyes, willing herself to fall back asleep. She heard movement on the other side of the bed, it dipped and someone got off of the bed. The person shuffled in the dark to the bathroom and the door clicked closed.

The other body on the opposite side of the bed sat up, the mattress moved as the person looked over to the cuddling pair. Lucia turned her head, letting a white eye peek open to see Val rubbing her face.

"Mornin'," her half-asleep voice was gravelly. Val turned back toward her on the bed, surprised to see that the brunette was awake.

"Good morning," the redhead sounded much more awake than she looked.

"How long have you been up?"

"A little while," she paused. "I only got up 'cause Hannah went to the bathroom."

"Ah."

"You?"

Lucia slowly untangled herself from Em's hold, "I only just woke up." She swiped her hands over her face and yawned. "How are you feeling?"

"A little hungover, but overall okay." Lucia sat up on the bed, her arms stretched upwards then reached to click on the lights. Calculating eyes examined the redhead to gauge her health.

"I can get you some painkillers if you want."

"Nah, I'm just a bit queasy." Val looked around the room, "What time is it?"

"Uh..." Lucia looked over her shoulder at the clock on the nightstand, "It's a bit after one." She received a groan from the redhead.

Hannah emerged from the bathroom, the two looked over to the bathroom, neither had registered the flush of the toilet until the door opened. The blonde had undone her braid and pulled it up into a ponytail. Hazel-green eyes blinked widely at the two women awake on the bed conversing.

"Oh," she walked over to the bed and grabbed her hearing aid from the nightstand. "Good mornin'," she chirped once the device was attached.

The two echoed the response to the blonde, she sat cross-legged on the bed next to Val and looked between the women. Lucia adjusted Em to avoid waking them, she leaned against the headboard and put their head in her lap, their arms wrapped around her leg. She stroked their hair mindlessly in the conversation, the soft locks slid through her fingers.

"We have to get back to the ship," Val sighed and leaned back onto the bed. Hannah scrunched up her face but nodded.

"The ship leaves port tomorrow?" White eyes didn't look up from the speckled hair.

"Super early tomorrow, last boarding is at ten tonight..." Hannah informed.

Lucia nodded her head in understanding, she remembered from her experience on cruises. She gently moved a stray hair that attempted to go into the younger's eyes and ghosted her fingers over their eyebrows which were splotched black and white.

"So, you need to head back soon?"

Hannah nodded her head, "Yeah. I still want to get some souvenirs for my little brothers and my uncle."

"And I wanted to find a cute outfit. So, we'd have to head back and change, eat, then try to go through all the different shops." Val continued. "Man, it sucks that you can't join us on the cruise! Then we could chill more."

Lucia rubbed at Em's shoulder to rouse them awake so they could say their goodbyes to the girls. They nuzzled their face into her leg, attempting to return to sleep. She laughed and rubbed their arm more firmly.

"Wakey, wakey, sleepy head." The younger groaned, "Aw come on, Hannah and Val are about to leave." A dark-brown eye cracked open to peer at the brunette. Lucia tucked a hair behind her ear as she looked down at them, "Their ship leaves tomorrow, so we might not see them before then."

THE GOODBYES WERE quick when Em finally mustered enough energy to get up. Hannah had insisted on giving Lucia their numbers for the states, demanding that the duo should text them to meet up when they got back. Lucia smiled and accepted a scrap of paper with the phone numbers scribbled out on it. She made sure to keep up the appearance of their cover story while she saw them down to the lobby in their parting.

Em was stiff in the hug from Val but smiled anyway. They offered a side hug to Hannah, which she gladly accepted. Lucia was more than happy with a full hug from both women, her white eyes were the only thing that gave away her sadness at the parting with the pair. Lucia and Em went back up to their room when the girls finally left.

Em went over to the closed curtains and pulled the corner all the way over to prevent any light spilling from the small window. Lucia clicked off the lights that had been clicked on and slid into the bed, stretching out as much as she could. Em climbed in after her, pushing her limbs aside so they could stretch out as well. Lucia listened to Em's breathing even out as they fell asleep first, she just looked up at the dark ceiling and let out an excited breath, they got to return to the pod soon. Eventually, she managed to doze off.

EM WOKE UP BEFORE LUCIA, they glanced over to the clock and saw that it was an hour until midnight. Every single joint in their legs and body hurt, so it was impossible to move from the snare of Lucia's limbs. She had snuggled up next to them in her sleep, her arms tightened around the younger's chest. Em tried to roll over to face her, their legs complained with the effort. The brunette grumbled in her sleep, she pulled the other closer in her arms. The smaller smiled and pressed into the hollow of her neck, kissing along her neck, sleepy moans slipped from the brunette's mouth.

"Mmmm," her hands slid so one was in the speckled hair and the other pulled their hips closer to her.

"We need to get up. It's almost midnight." Em mumbled against her throat, still pressing kisses up her throat toward her jaw.

"You should wake me up like this more often," a deep, groggy voice mused, massaging the younger's hips, they laughed into her skin.

"I'll try to remember," they nudged her to lie on her back, trailing their kisses to her collarbone. They rolled to lie on top of her and just pressed soft kisses against her.

Lucia groaned in pain, she held the smaller one to her chest, adjusting her arms to accommodate the new position. She stopped rubbing circles on Em's hips, opting to move her arms up their back and their sides. Em closed their eyes and just rested their head on the older's chest, they basked in the soothing pressure to their pained body.

"We should head to the water soon, it'll help with the pain in our legs." Em gave a hum in acknowledgment, listening to the beat of Lucia's heart below their head. "Come on," she urged, lifting her torso to sit up. Em groaned and rolled off her chest, flopping onto the bed. Lucia reached over and clicked on the table lamp, looking over at the younger, they had rolled onto their back and just stared at the ceiling.

"This is torture."

A moment of vulnerability. They didn't look at the brunette, afraid to see her face while they were confessing this. White eyes turned to the younger, and sorrow bubbled in her chest. Lucia could see the wetness of their dark eyes, they attempted to blink away the tears but some still escaped down their cheeks. She didn't comment on it, she knew exactly what they meant. The fact that they could return to land for a limited time, but had to go back. They were believed to be dead, they technically did die, so even though they were able to go on land, they could never go back to their old lives. Poseidon saw it as a blessing, but to some, it felt like a curse. They were grateful for Galene saving them, everyone from the pod would really be dead, if not for her. They were still allowed to grieve.

Lucia rubbed Em's arm in comfort and reached her other hand to cup their olive-toned face. She pressed a firm kiss to their face, letting her soft lips slot into their chapped ones. They pressed back deepening the kiss, their hand reached to hold her closer to them. Tears spilled down both of their cheeks and the brunette pulled Em on top of her. She used her free arm to stroke their back, slowing down the kiss, and gradually pulled away. They panted and took the moment to wipe their face free of tears, the corners of their angled eyes tinged pink. Lucia scrubbed her cheeks with her shoulders, not breaking the comforting rubs on their back.

"You okay?" Lucia comforted.

They rubbed their hand through their hair, "Yeah, I'm okay." Em dared a glance at the clock on the other side of the room.

"Not enough time for one last celebration of having legs?" she joked with a wiggle of her eyebrows, looking at Em's face. They scoffed.

"Unfortunately not." They smiled and pressed a kiss to Lucia's lips before they rolled off the bed. Lucia let out a sigh and joined them in getting out of bed.

"Do you wanna just trash all the stuff or...?" Lucia gestured to the dresser with all the clothes that they had bought while on land. Em spared a glance and just shook their head.

"Not worth the energy, but we do need to ditch the wallet and cash somewhere."

"They will be looking for it when he is found," Lucia agreed.

They didn't bother getting changed from the clothes they had slept in, Em disappeared into the bathroom to get the things from behind the toilet and under the sink. Lucia rifled through the drawers and grabbed the rest of the cash that they had stowed away.

She didn't have pockets to slide the money into so she followed after Em who was tucking the wallet into their back pocket.

They put all the money together then put it in the front pocket of their jeans and let out a final sigh, looking to the door of the room. White eyes stared at them then the door, she pursed her lips and let out a similar sigh.

"Ready?"

"Ready."

CHAPTER EIGHT

The pair discarded the wallet at the club that they had been at the night before. They snaked their way through the crowd of tourists attempting to get into the busy nightclub. Lucia casually dropped it behind a group of men who were distracted by each other. The pair disappeared into the night quickly after, making their way to the beach.

Em suggested that they split up the cash and give it to some of the homeless people that slept on the beach. Lucia nodded in agreement and they began their search for a small group of people. Lucia tried to split the money as evenly as she could, enough for a couple of meals individually at least. White eyes spotted the small group that was camped out at a sitting area near a restaurant. The benches nearby the restaurant housed three people curled up on the seats. The busy restaurant ignored the people in rags on the benches, but Lucia and Em walked right up to them.

Em nudged one of them gently, urging forward their siren charm to calm them if they startled. Lucia rested her hand on one of the people's shoulders on another bench, soothing words laced with charm garnered their attention.

"Excuse me."

The two that they woke, rose up, a man and a woman stared into the sirens' eyes, the owners of those eyes were crouched down beside them. The third person roused at Lucia's voice, jolting their head quickly in her direction, and froze under the icy gaze.

"We wanted to give this to you," she soothed, holding up the cash.

The trio just nodded thankfully while she reorganized her pile to fit the smaller group. She released the weak trance on the group and passed them each a handful of cash. She struggled to stand back up due to the pain in her legs, the joints cracked and ached as she stood.

Em was already over at the sand leading to the beach, their shoes in hand, and stood stock still just staring at the waves in the distance. Lucia ignored the voices of the people on the benches and walked up behind the younger. She bent down despite her complaining bones to work her shoes off and picked them up in her left hand. The pair stood there, staring at the dark horizon and what it promised beyond.

The brunette was the first of the two to walk on the sand and move toward the water, the sound of the waves pulled her in with each ebb and flow. Em hesitated. Dark eyes closed and brows furrowed, they pressed their lips together in frustration as they tried to ignore the call of the water. The crack of their bones is what pushed them to move forward, after the tall brunette.

They scooped up Lucia's free hand when they managed to reach her, she had kept her pace slow to allow them to catch up. She squeezed their hand gently, her white eyes gazing over at the other as they walked along the beach.

Their feet splashed into the water when they reached the shoreline, the dark waters lapped at their feet. Lucia kept walking, guiding them to a more secluded area of the beach. With the late hour, it wasn't too hard for them to do, most people that were out were at the different restaurants that dotted the shore.

Em chucked their shoes to the sand, their bones cracked as they shimmied to kick off their jeans. Lucia lovingly admired her friend as they undressed, the deep olive of their skin, the cant of the hips, the cowlick of hair that flopped in the opposite direction of their hair, and their deep-brown eyes that stared back at her. She could see each bite mark on their body that she had left on them, one peeked above the line of their boxers, some were less prominent on their chest, and scratch marks down their hips. Lucia smiled, she thanked Poseidon once again for bringing them into her life. Em looked around the beach again before they discarded their shirt, they left all the clothes in a pile by the shoes and jeans.

Lucia plopped her shoes next to where Em had put their clothes. She slipped off her sports shorts, toeing them to the side, and reluctantly took off the soft, gray shirt. It was Em's turn to gaze at her, their dark eyes soft and filled with an emotion they dared not to admit. They traced the curves of her hips, the healing hickeys on her inner thighs, and the outline of teeth marks that peeked out of her sports bra. She shimmied her body, having noticed their stare. They smiled at one another, relishing the last moment they had with their legs. They moved toward the surf, the crashing waves greeting their return.

The deep waters beckoned them in, it drew them deeper. Em slipped off their boxers and Lucia took off her boyshorts, the articles of clothing floated away in the waves. The pair swam through the water, getting further from the beach.

Lucia changed first, her long tail was covered in white scales and a frill of fins. She plunged down and spun in circles, the ache and pains of the change melted away with the exercise. Em plunged down after her, their tail was dark as night, white scales speckled throughout randomly. They swam around her, pushing deeper into the water. She admired their body, the soft curve of their hips where their scales traveled up. She saw that her bite mark at their waist was on full display.

She lingered keeping parallel with the coast. Em flipped around to look at her questioningly. Lucia gestured to the coast.

"We didn't eat earlier." She flicked her tail out.

Em grinned, sharp teeth on display. "I guess we should get some takeout then."

A RISING TIDE

Nicole Zoltack

CHAPTER ONE

The storm was terrible, vicious, wicked. The sky had never been darker, and the tide? It rose higher than Varina had ever seen it before. Even so, she stayed near the surface, watching, wary.

Chances were, this storm would devastate any and all who dared to sail about.

And chances were, there was at least one fool who had not been able to read the skies to realize such a terrible storm was coming.

Despite the whipping wind and the slashing rain, Varina could make out a ship. A longship to be more precise. With a sigh, she swam over. In a storm like this, she didn't need to be quite so careful to hide the fact that she was a mermaid.

Before Varina could reach the longship, it tilted over to the side. The massive waves kept beating against the longship until it finally tipped over, capsizing.

Varina flew as quickly as she could over to them. She had only seen two on the longship, but it was possible she missed someone in the darkness of the mighty storm.

"Frea, are you all right?" a man asked. He sputtered out some water as he lifted a redheaded woman from the water.

"Of course I'm all right," Frea grumbled. "A little water isn't going to kill me."

"No? Are you sure about that? The way the other—"

"Water is necessary for all life," Frea said. "Ubba!"

She yanked him out of the way before a large piece of wood, perhaps a piece of another ship, almost slammed into the back of his head.

Ubba groaned, and Varina's heart squeezed. Had he been struck after all?

"What now?" Frea asked as the two bobbed up and down in the water.

"Well, it seems only fitting that I would save you and then you would have to save me."

"Ah, so I don't owe you, hmm?"

"Of course not!"

"You could own me for this," Frea said.

She lifted a hand, and somehow, the longship rocked until eventually, it was floating atop the rocky waves once more. A might bit soggier than before, but still.

Varina gasped. These two weren't humans. Whoever Frea and Ubba were, they weren't human.

As Ubba helped Frea onto the longship, even though Varina assumed Frea did not need the help, the storm began to slowly die. By the time the rain stopped and the waves turned gentle, Varina found a spot near a boulder to hide behind so she could continue to observe the couple.

"Now that was an adventure," Ubba was saying.

Frea groaned. "Hardly."

"Oh, you would think an elf would want to have fun."

"Fun? I can show you a fun time, but almost drowning? That isn't it."

"You can control the wind," Ubba said dryly. "You can just push the water away. You weren't in any real danger."

"All the more reason why I didn't need you to pull me up above the surface of the water. I was fine."

Ubba huffed. "That's some fine gratitude you're showing your husband."

"How's this for gratitude?"

Even though Varina turned aside to let the couple kiss in peace, she also shut her eyes. Their easy banter, their playfulness... the two of them clearly loved one another dearly.

When the kissing noises start, Varina thought about making her way back to the pod. Instead, she lingered. Did Ubba have some magic of his own? Was he also an elf? No, she deiced. He didn't have the same ear shape as Frea did. Her hair was long and red, such a beautiful shade.

Unlike Varina. Hers was as black as the night. Her eyes, though, were as bright blue as the sky on a sunny summer day.

"You should be grateful for me and all I did for you," Frea finally said.

"Why's that?" Ubba asked.

"Maybe because I saved our longship."

"She's still mine."

"We're married. What's yours is mine," Frea said dryly.

"Can I have some of your red locks then?"

"Why do you want that?" she asked.

"Do you have to know everything, woman?"

"Do you have to be so difficult, berserker?"

Ubba laughed and laughed. "Yes, I do believe berserkers tend to be difficult. You married one. That's your own fault."

"I suppose so," Frea said with a laugh. "I do sometimes wonder what I was thinking."

"You weren't thinking. You were in love. Foolish of you, wasn't it?"

"Not nearly," Frea said. "You should be counting your lucky stars that I've been willing to be away from land for so long."

"As if the land doesn't have life within it," Ubba protested.

Varina's eyed opened. Was he referring to mermaids? Or to the fish?

"I care most of all about trees," Frea said.

"Are you certain you aren't part dryad?" Ubba countered.

A dryad. Varina had never met one of those magical beings. They were said to be tethered to trees, to the land. A dryad and a mermaid wouldn't have much in common at all.

But who would have thought that a berserker would be with an elf? This berserker, from the looks and sounds of him, was from Norway or thereabout. Her voice, though, suggested her to be one of the Celtic elves. Ireland maybe. How in the world had the two of them met? And for them to fall so deeply in love...

Berserkers were not said to live long, yet he was so much older than Varina would have expected. Not that she had met one of his kind before. She had seen a few other elves before, though, from afar only, not up close

The two of them set off once more, ready for their next adventure. Now, Varina hesitated a long moment before she decided to follow them a bit longer. Their love... That was the kind of love one could only hope for.

Varina wished to find a love like that for herself.

Maybe one day...

CHAPTER TWO

Eventually, Varina veered off. She should probably be returning to the pod soon, but she couldn't help wondering if all elves were as accommodating as Frea was. If Frea could bring herself to love a berserker, maybe another elf could fall in love with a mermaid.

"Not that I need love from anyone aside from my pod," Varina murmured to herself as she swam along.

Still, she wanted to grow and explore and see what there was to the world. She had been a mermaid for decades and decades now. She could hardly remember what it had been like to be on the surface, to walk, to not have a fin. There were times when she could easily believe that she had been born a mermaid, although that had not been the case.

If she thought hard and long enough, she could recall what had happened to her. Her father had perished, how she couldn't quite recall. Her mother had remarried, and that man...

Varina had tried to tell her mother about what the man had done to her, but her mother had threatened Varina, believing her new husband over her. When the husband had come after Varina, she had run away, trying to find a place to hide.

Which had ended up being a ship.

The ship had encountered a storm the likes of the one that had attacked Frea and Ubba. The constant rolling and rocking had caused the sailors to toss overboard anything that wasn't necessary

That had been when they discovered Varina.

And being the suspicious lot that they were, they cast Varina overboard.

To drown.

Only a mermaid had seen everything and saved Varina, bringing her to the first mermaid so that she could be turned into one such as them.

The pod meant much and more to Varina. They were her new family, yet there were ties, especially of late, when she felt the need to go out and explore, to try to find someone for her.

Some of the other mermaids had found lovers. There were even some mermen who swam among them.

But all mermaids were granted a single magical ability. They could not choose what it was. Some could heal. Others could control water. At least one could walk on land.

But Varina? For all of these years, she still hadn't been able to discover what precisely her magical ability was.

She swam and swam and swam. Eventually, she was able to reach the northernmost coast of Ireland. There was a human settlement there, but Varina could see a few pointed ears. She also saw signs that the city had once been destroyed by fire and then rebuilt.

It was the elves rather than the humans who caught Varina's eye, and she kept far enough off the shoreline that no one should be able to see her. Maybe the elves could. They should have superior eyesight compared to a human, right?

Whereas the humans would often go into the water to swim or splash each other with water, the elves hardly ever ventured into the waves. All in all, the elves seemed rather settled in their ways, which disgruntled Varina. Still, she lingered. She hadn't swum all of this way to give up now.

Once the sun set and the moon started to rise, Varina dared to swim a little closer to shore.

A young elf, who had perhaps only seen about twenty summers, stood on the beach. Varina nodded and smiled at him, staying low enough in the water that he couldn't be able to see her true identity.

"The water is refreshing," she called to him.

"I don't swim."

"Can you? I can teach you."

"Of course I can," he said smugly.

"Why not then join me for a swim?" she asked.

"I don't want to. That's why."

She wrinkled her nose. "What's so better about being on the land?"

He tilted his head to the side. "Why do you act like you only are in the water?"

"I'm a water rat," she said with a laugh. "What does that make you?"

"I don't know. I don't care for rats of any kind, water or otherwise."

Varina pursed her lips. "Not very friendly, are you?"

"I don't know who you are, and frankly, I don't care what you think about me."

"You're an elf," she blurted.

He stiffened. "I don't know what you're talking about."

"You don't have to be afraid," she said. "I'm—"

"I don't care who you are."

"Fine. Be like that. You aren't an elf. You're a human with pointed ears. Happy?" She crossed her arms as the waves bobbled her up and down in the water. "You and your kind... the other humans with pointed ears... you don't leave the land much at all, do you? Not even to bathe."

"We bathe," he says hotly.

"You do?" she asked, wrinkling her nose.

He narrowed his eyes at her. "You could be nicer," he said.

"Perhaps, but..." Varina sighed. "You're comfortable on land."

"Yes, we are. You can stick to the water."

"And be alone."

Only now did the elf seem a little curious. "You're all alone? In the water?"

"I'm not alone... and yet I am."

He grunted. "I know that feeling."

"What's going on?" she asked, daring to swim a little closer.

The elf wandered a little closer to the water but not nearly close enough for the lapping waves up the beach to touch him. "Nothing that really concerns you."

"No, it doesn't, but sometimes, it helps to talk, and since we'll never see each other again..."

He sighed. "My father died years ago. My mother is going to remarry."

Varina winced.

The elf didn't seem to notice. "He seems nice enough, I guess, but I just... I miss my father so much, and I can't... I find myself picking fights and staying away because I'm afraid... I'm worried that I'll..."

"You're afraid that you'll be friends with him."

"Well, I don't know about that but... accepting him seems wrong."

"Does he make your mother happy?"

"Yes," he said without hesitation.

"Does she make him happy?"

The elf nodded slowly. "Yes."

"Is he good for her?"

"I... I do think they're good for each other, yes," he admitted.

Varina nodded. "Good. That's good. My... A similar situation happened to me, actually. The man my mother married... he was not a good man. That is not the case here. You can accept him and still honor your father."

"That is easier to say than..."

"I know," Varina said.

She had stopped swimming, and the tide was bringing her closer and closer to him. He might be able to see her tail, but she did not care. All she did was hold out her hand.

But he did not take it. He merely nodded to her and walked off, leaving Varina alone and wishing she could have helped him more than she had.

If she had helped him at all.

CHAPTER THREE

Perhaps it wasn't the smartest of ideas, but Varina still did not return to her pod. She would. Soon. Just not yet.

First, she wished to seek out the berserkers.

It took her much longer, so much longer, to find any of the berserkers. They did not have any noticeable features that set them apart from humans like the elves did with their pointed ears. Yes, berserkers tended to be tall and muscular, but there were tall, muscular humans as well.

The man her mother had married had been short but so very muscular. That had been a part of the problem.

Varina shook her head and tried to stop dwelling on the past. For now, she was debating how she might find a berserker to talk to. All mermaids could walk on land once for a single lunar phase, and she was not about to use that anytime soon, not when she had no true way to know if she would have any feelings for a berserker.

She did not know much at all about the race, although she thought they might be the kind that could enter into a strange state where they could fight and not be injured. Once upon a time, they had been able to shapeshift into a bear, could they not? Perhaps it

was just as well that she did not know. To change into an animal...
that seemed so very strange to her.

After a few days of searching and not finding any sign of berserkers, Varina decided to try something different. She swam out past the
shallows toward the deep sea, but she had only just made it past the
reefs when she saw a ship. It was sailing through the waters, cutting
through them like a sharp blade. She had seen ships before, usually
trading vessels that cast their nets for fish or military ships patrolling
the sea, but this one seemed different. Curious, she followed it until
they reached a small island. There on the shore, she saw a number of
men unload from the ship.

"Come on, lads Let's get to drinkin'!" one of them called out, and
the others all cheered.

Was this what berserkers sounded like? She had always imagined
their voices would be gruff and deep with an otherworldly quality to
them but these were light and melodious, almost lyrical.

Varina stayed in the shadows of the waves, watching and
listening quietly without ever having been noticed. There were eight
men in total.

The more they drank, the louder they became. They were telling
stories of grand adventures, but honestly, Varina thought most of the
tales were of the tall variety.

But then they started to talk about raiding and pillaging coastal
towns.

At the very least, they were vikings, but that did not mean that
they were berserkers.

"Karsten, I can hardly believe ya want to be marryin' an English
lass," one of them said. "An English woman. A human!"

Varina's ears perked up to hear this. They weren't human themselves, but again, that did not necessarily mean that they were
berserkers.

"There aren't enough berserker women to go around," another
protested. Varina wondered if that one was Karsten. His beard was
braided with some beads dangling on the end.

"That may be true, but I'm not sure any of 'em could ever make me as happy as this one," another said, the shortest of the group. "I can feel it in me bones. She's the one."

Ah, he was Karsten then, not the one with the braided beard.

Suddenly, Varina noticed the men seemed to become aware of her presence. They had stopped talking and were staring out into the sea, eyes wide with shock and recognition.

One of them pointed at her and shouted something in a language she had never heard before. His voice was thunderous and commanding, though she didn't understand what he was saying.

Before she could react or flee, the berserkers surged forward toward her like an unstoppable tidal wave, swords drawn ready for battle!

"No, please," she called, waving her arms. "I mean you no harm!"

They ignored her, the berserkers springing into action, drawing even more weapons and wading into the water, swarming around her like hungry wolves.

"I only came to talk... I know of a berserker! His name is—"

"Did you drown him?" a berserker asked.

"Did you sing and lead him into a watery grave?"

"Did you sink his ship as your kind likes to do with our brethren?" the braided, bearded one questioned with a snarl.

They gave her no chance to answer their questions, not that they would have believed her, leaving Varina no choice but to fight back though she was outnumbered. She used her skills as a mermaid to dodge their attacks and retaliate with her own punches and tail slaps and blows.

But their swords? They were harder to avoid, and the same could be said about their guns. Those frightening, terrible weapons. Varina had never seen one up close before, and the sound of them! So loud she feared she might never hear again!

If she could not flee from them... Varina feared for her life.

After all, mermaids were not immortal.

CHAPTER FOUR

Varina fought with all her might, but it was not enough. The berserkers were too strong and too many.

She gasped in pain as she tried to dodge their attacks. The mermaid narrowly missed a bullet that whizzed right past her tail and grazed off the side of a nearby rock.

Still, the berserkers continued their onslaught, pressing forward with a renewed vigor, determined to take Varina down. They hacked at her with their swords and shot at her. Thankfully, they missed her repeatedly, perhaps because they were crowding her too closely and they feared shooting one another, but that didn't stop the salty sea water from mixing with her blood, staining the waves around her red.

"How very human of you," she hissed as she managed to slap a fin hard enough against an arm that the attached hand opened, dropping the sword into the water. "Using weapons to fight your battles for you. Are you berserkers? Or are you cowards?"

That only served to anger them, which, she had to admit, was pure folly. Only seconds later did one of them manage to land a blow directly on Varina's shoulder with his sword, sending waves of pain radiating through her body. She screamed in agony as she felt the metal slicing into her flesh. As if sensing victory was within reach, the berserkers pressed forward even more fiercely now.

Varina knew it was only a matter of time before they overwhelmed her, and that was precisely what happened next. She screamed into the night as their swords clanged against her scales and their blows struck her body like thunderbolts. Varina had never felt such pain before, such an unrelenting onslaught of violence that left her exhausted and defeated.

The berserkers finally left her lying in the shallow waves of the ocean, barely breathing and unable to move. In addition to all the cuts on her body from their blades, there was a searing pain in her shoulder where one of them had shot her with a pistol. She could feel the bullet lodged deep within muscle and bone.

As Varina lay there clinging to life, she cursed herself for ever troubling these men.

Karsten, for his part, had been the one to convince the others to leave. Another, she could not say which one, had been ready to strike her down dead until he had intervened.

Not that he had refrained from attacking her as all the others had.

he had taken down not one or two of them. Three. Half. Impressive perhaps, but not enough. She was far too injured to swim now. Unless one from her pod were to find her... but she hadn't told any of them where she had gone.

Foolish. She had been so very foolish. It seemed that Ubba was not like most berserkers.

She dragged herself onto the shore, exhausted and overwhelmed by the pain that radiated through her body. Her tail felt like it had been torn up by claws and her skin ached from being pummeled with fists and stones in addition to the swords.

Varina could barely move as she lay there on the sand, feeling helpless as she watched the berserkers jump back onto their boat and sail off into the night sky.

Honestly, she didn't even want to go after them. Other mermaids might have felt differently. Many of them had gone after and sirened the sailors or pirates who had cast them overboard to drown.

Varina never had. She had been so grateful that she had been reborn as a mermaid that she hadn't had time to bother with rage or anger or anything like that.

Stupid. She had been stupid and reckless.

Naive.

Even after being alive for so long, she had been too naive and unworldly to handle dealing with land dwellers.

Berserkers. How could she have thought she could see them, talk to them, try to fall in love with one?

She sighed, too weak to move. Moments later, exhaustion began to take over, and she faded in and out of consciousness.

Sleep. Sleep might well be the death of her, and she forced herself to slip into the waves. If she went underwater, perhaps she could manage to near the pod and one of the others could help her.

Suddenly, Varina heard a commotion coming from the sea. She felt a strange chill run up her spine. Had the berserkers come back for her? No, that didn't seem right, but if not them, then who? Her thoughts were interrupted as she saw a tall ship with black sails looming in the distance. It was captained by men wearing eye patches and long coats, waving swords, and shouting orders to each other. Pirates!

Varina tried to move away, but it was too late. The pirates had seen her and were quickly moving in. She dove, but her injuries slowed her to the point that she knew getting away was a near impossibility. Still, she tried to force her arms to propeller through the water when there was a loud splash. She was grabbed from behind and forced up toward the surface. Varina struggled, but the pirate's grasp was too tight. She could not break free.

She was a captive of the pirates.

What plans did they have for her?

CHAPTER FIVE

Despite her best efforts, Varina fought against losing consciousness. The sound of sails flapping against the wind and a strange rocking sensation beneath her drew the mermaid back to the here and now. The sky was still dark, but there were more stars than she recalled seeing before. Time had passed at least a little bit.

The salty air greeted her as she opens her eyes to find herself lying on the deck of an unfamiliar ship being manned by a group of armed men.

Everything came rushing back to her, and she tried to push herself up, but the pin in her shoulder from the gunshot wound caused her to cry out.

"A real mermaid. We should sell her to the highest bidder!" one of the men cried.

"We should keep her. Travel all over the world. Make people pay us to see her."

"I'll die before I'll let you use e for money," Varina said.

But they ignored her, laughing and talking, formulating plans but solidifying none of them. Varina eyed the side of the ship. If she could just drag herself over to the edge, she could tumble down to the waters. Down, down, down... She could get away from them if she reached the waters. She was sure of it.

But before she could scoot over even an inch, already two pirates seized her arms. The cry of pain that burst out of her sounded so very weak, and they laughed and jeered at her.

The two pirates threw her into the cargo hold and slammed it shut. Literally threw her. She fell down hard, and she moaned as a fresh wave of pain shot through her.

With her good arm, she pushed herself up somewhat. It was dark down here.

And then she heard movement. Not the scratching of tiny claws from rats or other small animals.

"Who... Who goes there?" she asked.

From the shadows, a much larger shadowy form rose.

"That there be Ellington," a pirate called down. "Another prisoner. Our slave. He don't talk none, but he does what he's told. You, girl fish, better do what you be told too. You don't want ta see us when we're angry."

The pirates laughed and moved off.

Varina eyed Ellington. He seemed tall, very tall, but he was thin, almost too thin. Were the pirates feeding him at all?

"When were you picked up?" she asked.

Ellington shifted forward a little, into the small sliver of light that came down from the holes in the grated door of the cargo hold. She could see him better now. Brown hair. Light eyes. Maybe green. She couldn't quite be sure. He wore no shirt, and the pants he wore had holes in them. He was barefoot.

"Where are you from?" she asked, trying again to see if he might talk to her. It made perfect sense that someone wouldn't want to talk around their captors.

But still, the young man remained silent.

Varina couldn't begin to guess his age, but he wasn't a young boy. Old enough to be wed if he liked, she supposed.

"Have you any family?" she inquired.

At that, Ellington turned his back to her, slinking back into the shadows.

Fine. If he wished to remain silent, so be it.

But then a terrible thought occurred to her. What if the pirates had cut out his tongue?

She reached toward him. "I won't hurt you," she said. "You don't have to be afraid."

Blood trickled down her arm from the gunshot wound, and she lowered her hand to her tail. Tears trickled down her face.

The bullet. It was still inside her. She had to get it out.

The wound wasn't terribly deep, and Varina dig inside it until she could feel the bullet. It hurt terribly for her to move it.

"Hey, what's be goin' on down there?" one of the pirates called.

"If Ellington wants to have a bit of fun with the mermaid, who cares?"

"If he hurts her worse... She be in bad shape. We need her alive for..."

"She won't die."

"How can ya be so sure?"

The pirates walked off, and Varina finally yanked out the bullet. It dropped to the ground.

So did she.

The floor hardly vibrated, yet she knew Ellington approached. She could scarcely keep her eyes open.

He bent down and looked at her curiously.

Her face.

Not her tail.

The others saw her as a freak, but Ellington seemed to see her.

She sucked in a breath and reached out toward him once more. He didn't flinch or turn around this time, and she touched his face.

At once, she felt pain, so much pain, but pain of a much different sort than what the berserkers had inflicted upon her.

As quickly as she felt that mental anguish, it all dissipated and fled away as if it had never been there in the first place.

Ellington gaped at her, his expression altering from curiosity to relief.

There was no other word for it. He seemed so utterly relieved, and she wasn't at all shocked when he sat beside her.

"What did you do to me?" he whispered.

She blinked a few times. "You can talk!"

He nodded. "I... Yes. My... I haven't spoken in years. Years and years. It must be... maybe twenty years. My parents died when I was five. Killed in front of me. My village, it was attacked, and... I ran away. Like a coward. It's the only reason why I survived."

"Who did that?"

Ellington shrugged. "I don't know. I just stopped talking afterward. I didn't want anyone to know about my past, but... I feel so light now. I feel so free. How did you... What did you do to me?"

Varina laughed. "I did nothing. I..."

"When you touched me... all of the pain I've been carrying... It's gone now. I don't feel guilty. I don't feel grief. All I feel... is me."

Her mouth hung open.

Could it be that she had discovered her gift after all?

Perhaps she could heal. Not physical wounds. Wounds of the heart. Mental wounds. Deep trauma.

Ellington smiled at her. "What can I do to help you?"

CHAPTER SIX

Varina held still as Ellington found some water and cleaned her wounds. Then, he found some rum.

"Not the best thing," he muttered. "It'll sting most likely. Don't cry out if you can. We don't want them to know that I'm helping you, but..."

"What are you going to do with that?" she asked.

"We don't want your wounds to become infected," he explained. "Just hold still."

It had burned some when he cleansed her, but the alcohol on her wounds? Yes, he had warned her, but nothing could have prepared her for the stinging sensation. It brought tears to her eyes, and she bit down hard on her tongue to prevent her from crying out. Somehow, she didn't taste blood in her mouth.

"You didn't scream," he murmured. "Some of the pirates, they would do this to each other... They'll cry or scream like little girls. Ah... no offense."

"None taken," she murmured, a bit dazed.

"Some didn't flinch at all, though. Some are tough, and it's not always the ones who look the toughest that actually are. The silent ones, they're the ones to look out for."

"Like you?"

He snorted. "Not hardly."

"If you say so," she whispered. "Are you going to..."

But the young man was already looking around. "There used to be... aha! Here it is." He held up a stray shirt. "A pirate threw it down here. I think he didn't like it. He drank a bit too much, ate a bit too much, and now his belly's too big, but it'll work."

Immediately, Ellington ripped it into strips that he then used to cover her wounds.

"Not the best, but... There. That's as much as I can do for you. I... ah..." He cleared his throat, looking at her tail and then away.

"If you have any questions," she asked.

"No. Ah, no. Not a one." He shook his head emphatically.

"Thank you," she murmured. "You didn't have to do this."

"I did," he insisted. "You helped me. I help you."

She smiled at him, but already, she could feel the water leech from her body the longer she was away from the sea. She needed to go home, to return to her pod.

"Have you ever thought about escaping?" she murmured.

"Escaping? No. I have nowhere to go to, and they at least have food for me. I don't know... I've been with them for... months, maybe. Could be a year. Two years. I don't really keep track. It's been better... Let's just say that my life has been worse off previously."

"You really want to stay here?" She could hardly believe it.

He shrugged.

"But you and I, we could escape together."

He snorted. "I'm not trying that."

"You won't even try? Why not?"

"Where would I go? I can't breathe underwater. We aren't near shore anymore, and I don't know if I could swim far. They feed me, yes, but not enough for me to keep up my strength."

"Are you sure I can't convince you? I can maybe help you to sure."

"How?" he asked bluntly. "I don't mean to offend you, but you're hurt. Are you even going to be able to get away to safety yourself? Maybe you should stick around. Heal up some. Recover your strength and then try to escape."

"If I do that, will you come with me?"

He hesitated and then shook his head. "No."

"Why not?"

"Why do you care what I do? Don't get me wrong. I can't thank you enough for what you did for me. I don't think I ever would've talked again if not for you, but... this is my life. Maybe one day, they won't view me as a slave. If I can make them happy, maybe they'll let me be a pirate."

"And you'll be a party to kidnapping others? To enslaving others?" Hot anger filled her.

"No. I don't... I have to survive. You wouldn't understand."

"You're right. I don't understand."

He grunted. "You don't know me. I have to do what's best for me."

"No matter who gets hurt, right? So long as you're all right."

Ellington wrinkled his nose and turned his back to her. "I'm going to sleep," he announced. "They're liable to put me to work in a few hours."

"Sweet dreams," she mocked.

He grunted again and laid his head down. on the floor of the cargo hold.

What a terrible life he had to look forward to. Yes, she had helped him, but he was still choosing that to be his future? It bothered her terribly, perhaps more than it should, but what could she do? She wasn't about to force him to come with her. That would be another form of slavery, wouldn't it? It wouldn't matter that her intentions were to save him. He didn't wish to be saved.

She used her arms to drag herself over to beneath the door of the cargo hold. It pained her shoulder and arm wickedly to do so, but she managed. Once in position, she listened for a long time. Two pirates were blabbering back and forth, but eventually, they fell silent, and then she could hear snoring, not just from Ellington but from above.

The pirates on watch overnight had fallen asleep.

If ever there was a chance for her to make an escape, now was the time.

CHAPTER SEVEN

Varina gripped the door to the cargo hold. To her shock, it wasn't locked. In fact, despite the pain it caused her, it was all too easy to lift up. She only allowed it to open enough for her to peer about.

The two pirates were off to the left. One was sitting. The other was leaning against the railing. Neither was moving.

She lowered the door to rest on her head to give her arms a break as she waited and watched them long enough to be certain the one standing was also slumbering. Then, she slipped onto the floor of the deck of the ship and lowered the door to the cargo hold behind her.

It pained her emotionally far more than the physical pain to leave Ellington behind, but he had made his choice.

Just as she had made hers.

With her good arm, she dragged herself over to the edge of the ship. She looped that arm around the railing and stood on her fin and—

"Halt!"

"The mermaid!"

"She's trying to escape!"

Varina dove, but she wasn't quick enough. Arms wrapped around the top of her fin, and she was thrown back down violently. Her elbow slammed against the deck, and tears sprang to her eyes.

Her heart hammered in her chest. Her voice. She could control the men, could get them to let her go free.

She could even convince them to let Ellington go too.

Why hadn't she thought of that before?

Her lips parted, but before she could utter even a single sound, tight fingers wrapped around her throat.

"We're going to have to bound and gag her, won't we, lads?" one of the pirates said with a wicked tone to his voice and an even more wicked glint shining in his eyes under the silvery moonlight that glistened on the calm dark waters all about them.

"Don't," cried out a loud voice, audible over the sound of raucous laughter from the other pirates.

"Who said that?" a pirate asked. His eyes were a bit glassy.

"I think that..." Another glanced toward the cargo hold.

The door burst open, and Ellington climbed out. His longish dark hair was more than a little crazy, sticking up every which way. His eyes—green she realized now for certain—were wide, and he stared at Varina. She couldn't reach the expression in his eyes, but his stance... standing as tall as he could, shoulders back, chin lifted... He was trying to project strength despite his thin frame.

Strength when he was a slave. This was not going to go down well.

She tried to speak, but the pirate holding her throat tightened her grip. She gasped and choked, hitting his arm, which only made him squeeze even harder to the point that her vision grew spotty.

"Did you say something?" the glassy-eyed pirate asked, his tone accusing, his gaze fixed on Ellington.

"Let her go," Ellington said clearly.

"Look at 'im," another pirate said. "He can talk."

"Could all along," another said. He was missing a tooth, and he walked with a limp as he crossed over to Ellington and seized his arm.

"I asked her to fetch—" Ellington couldn't continue with his lie as the pirate holding him punched him hard enough in the stomach to release air through his mouth.

The other pirates aside from the one who still gripped her throat all circled around Ellington. She couldn't see what was happening, but the thuds and the stomping, the punching and the kicking... She could imagine all too easily how the punishment was going for Ellington. She choked on her sobs, gasping for air as she cried, weeping for him and for herself.

In the end, she and Ellington were both tossed back into the cargo hold. Ellington was bruised and bleeding all over, and she was bound and gagged.

"You remove that gag from her, and we'll cut off an eye and a few fingers and toes. Can't have a slave without a hand or foot. You'd be even more worthless if you're less a hand, but if you don't do as told, we won't be needin' ya at all, understood?"

The pirate laughed as he clamored back out of the cargo hold.

Varina just sagged against the cold floor. Tears still leaked from her eyes. She hadn't meant to have Ellington get hurt. If he had come with her...

They might still have gotten caught.

There was no hope for them now.

Briefly, she wondered how it was that the pirates had known Ellington's name when he couldn't talk to tell it to them. Maybe the pirates had named him. If so, that might have been the only kindness they had ever shown, giving him a name so he wouldn't have to be called slave all day long.

Ellington grunted and groaned, but she didn't look his way, too ashamed that she had caused him so much agony.

Abruptly, she felt hands on her, and then the gag was removed.

She gaped at him as he went on to remove the rope around her wrists. "You..."

"You aren't just a mermaid, are you?" he whispered. "You're a siren too."

She nodded.

"You could have saved yourself immediately. Sang to them and gotten them to let you go or to help you first and then let you go."

"But then I wouldn't have helped you," she whispered. "It's... Everything happened as it should."

He eyed her but said nothing.

"Flee with me," she begged.

His nostrils flared, and she wondered if he was thinking what she was.

That she could force him to let her save him.

But she wouldn't. She had never sirened anyone before, and she wasn't going to now.

"No. I won't go with you," he finally said. "Not unless you make me, but... I will cover for you."

"I don't want to leave you here," she said desperately, still whispering. "I won't let you—"

"It is my choice," he said, his eyes wide. "Don't take that from me."

She hung her head and nodded. "Don't cover for me, though. Don't say anything. Don't..."

Varina inched a little closer to him and hesitated. She wanted to cup his face, but she didn't.

"Do you want me to help you with your wounds?" she asked.

"No."

"Should I wait until tomorrow night? They might—"

"They won't have more guards. Once they're asleep, the ones watching the deck, you can slip away, so long as you don't wake them."

"They won't post more guards?"

"They're not the brightest lot, and... There had been one other slave. He did escape. Took him three tries. All the same night. I don't know if he made it to shore, though. The second time, they cut off two fingers. He... I think he was afraid that they cut out my tongue because I... I couldn't talk then. I physically couldn't. I wanted to assure him that I didn't talk not because of them, but... I don't know. I was afraid, I think. I wouldn't have had to talk about anything I didn't want to, but I didn't... I was afraid I would blurt out every-thing about my parents, my village... how scared I was... I didn't want to experience that all over again, but telling you... I was foolish to be so afraid."

"Fear is not something to berate yourself over," she murmured. "I'm afraid."

"You'll be fine."

She lowered her head. Varina wasn't just afraid for herself.

She was afraid for him too.

CHAPTER EIGHT

Varina waited until the pirates watching over the deck fell asleep. Once she made it onto the deck, she scarcely moved, inching forward ever so slightly and then pausing, not wanting to run the risk of being overheard. Nothing was going to disturb them this time.

And then she reached the edge. As quickly as she could, she slipped over and dove into the water, hardly making a splash.

When she was far enough away that the ship was barely visible, she still didn't feel safe. If anything, her heart felt ready to burst.

Leaving Ellington felt wrong.

Was this love? No, but the possibility existed that in time she could grow to love him.

Uncertain of what to do, she swam a little closer to the ship. Being in the water helped to soothe some of her aches. Even so, swimming caused her pain. Until she healed entirely, she would always have pain.

But what was pain when Ellington faced a lifetime of servitude?

The closer she neared the ship as the moon nearly sank into the sea so that the sun might rise, the more raucous noises she heard. The pirates had realized she was gone.

And Ellington was paying the price.

But instead of cutting him, she could just see that they were binding his hands and legs.

And then they tied a cannonball to his legs.

They meant to drown him!

Varina bobbled in the water. She could feel anger and rage as never before. Her lips parted, and she wanted to sing about a rising tide that would sweep over the ship. She longed to curse the men with her silver tongue and force them all to drown so that Ellington might be saved.

They should beware the rising tide, the rising anger within her that would doom them all.

But she held back. Instead of using that fierce anger to doom the sailors, she poured that anger into energy, and she dove under the water and swam despite the agony it caused her. The mermaid reached Ellington as he started to sink, and she struggled to untie the cannonball. Varina couldn't completely undo the knot, but she managed to loosen it enough that she shoved it off him.

His face was turning blue, and unthinkingly, Varina kissed him. Air flooded his lungs, and his eyes widened. He struggled a bit before relaxing in her arms as he realized he could breathe underwater now. It wouldn't last forever.

Quickly, she wrapped her good arm around him even though she had to use her wounded shoulder to help them cut through the water. Once they were far enough away, she had them pop their heads over the surface of the water.

"Please," she begged. "Let me take you to—"

"Where? The shore?"

"You can be a merman—"

"What?"

"We can be together!" she cried. "I won't have you die!"

"I..." He chuckled. "I'm not going to die. Look. They're sailing off."

She followed his gaze. The ship was almost out of sight once more.

"Do not worry," he said softly. "We can rise together even if I remain a human."

"What... What do you mean?"

"Help me to a village. A coastal one. I'll learn how to make boats, and then I'll be able to sail and find work wherever you are."

"Ellington..."

"You have done so much for me," he said, "and I don't know if I can ever repay you. You healed me. I was broken, and I don't think I even knew how broken I was, but you..."

"Why won't you be a merman?" she whispered.

"I just... I'm fixed. I'm not broken. You saved me, and... maybe... if I do follow where you go, together we can save other humans. If I learn how to make boats, I can maybe learn how to build houses. The humans who might need your help might be like me. They might have nothing at all. Just the clothes on their back. If you can heal them inside, I can help them on the outside. You... Can you have two legs at all?"

"I... Only once ever for one lunar cycle."

"So for thirty days of your entire life. That's all?"

She nodded.

"Well, then, it's settled. I wouldn't be able to build boats or houses if I'm in the sea, and we can make a difference together, you and me. Maybe... I don't know how mermaids age, but maybe one day when I'm old and gray, maybe then..."

"To be turned into a merman, you would have to be at risk of dying. You would have to be drowning," she mumbled.

"In that case... I could drown myself, and..."

"Ellington!"

"We could wed first," he continued, reaching out with his still-bound hands to grasp hers as they bobbed in the calm water. "Then, I could go out to the water—"

"It is a painful process," she murmured. "You... you will die first and then be reborn. Mermaids... we aren't immortal. I'll die one day. You will too."

"We can help people, and then we can be together. I... I ran away. I had been frightened. Too scared to fight back. I would have died most likely, but maybe I could have saved at least one other person, but I didn't. I want... No, I need to help others now. It's the only way I feel that my life will be worth it. You saved me for a reason. Not just for us to be together."

Her lips curled into a smile. "I don't need more time," she murmured.

He furrowed his brows.

She untied his hands and hugged him tightly despite the pain in her shoulder. "I already love you," she whispered. "Your heart..."

His lips claimed hers.

"I love you too," he said once they parted.

She ducked her head, certain she was blushing.

"My heart is yours, but I must do this."

"I know, and I will help you as I can."

"You've already given me a second life," he said. "I will be a merman one day..."

"But for now, we'll be a rising tide to all those in need."

"Indeed."

Together, they swam to shore, and Varina watched from a distance as he spoke to some of the natives there. As the natives walked ahead, presumably to help Ellington, he turned back toward the shore and waved to her.

She waved back, her heart full.

And then she swam back to her pod. She will be returning to Ellington shortly, but she could not deny her pod much longer.

A rising tide... Her heart had never felt so light.

Varina belonged to her pod, of course, but she had found another home in Ellington too.

If you enjoyed this story, consider checking out Nicole's Magical Hunters Academy trilogy about a school for paranormal teens to train to fight evil creatures.
You can also join Nicole's newsletter here.

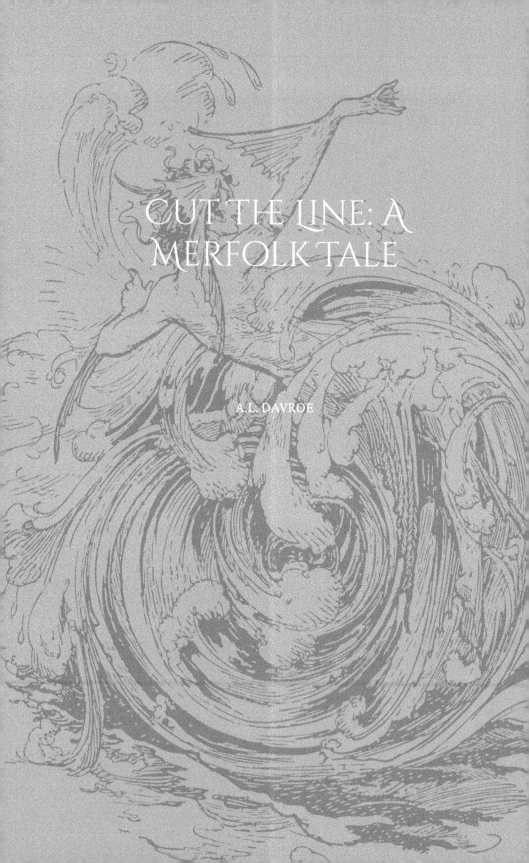

CUT THE LINE: A MERFOLK TALE

A.L. DAVROE

CHAPTER ONE

Nissa was missing. She'd been missing since yesterday. He'd brought her to Portland to watch the fireworks on the 4th of July. Nissa had whined and complained about wanting to come back to shore. She missed many aspects of being human and Sinter didn't blame her. It happened to all the newer merfolk. There was a period of adjustment and she was still young. So, he'd offered to take her back to land for a few days.

Galene had grudgingly allowed it.

As a rule, Galene never allowed the merfolk to go off on their own. There was safety in numbers, of course. And she believed that, once turned, a mer should focus on their new life, not their old one. But she made special compensation to two types of folk: Those of the folk, like Sinter, who could call up legs at will, and those of the folk who were newer and were having difficulty adjusting to life in the ocean.

Sinter often volunteered to either run land-errands for Galene or take the new folk back to shore. He wasn't fond of life in the pod and he needed as many excuses to get back on solid land as he could get.

It wasn't as though life in the pod was bad. Everyone had a role.

They all had a home. They were secret and safe and life underwater was as modeled after life above as it could be. But it wasn't life above. Above there was pizza and muscle cars and bonfires with friends. Above there were more people than Sinter could ever hope to know. One could get lost and stay lost. One wasn't controlled by strange magical constraints.

Sinter counted himself lucky that his magical gift was being one of the merfolk who could go on land at will. He didn't know how he would handle the constraints of this life without it. Even still, he only got to go up on land very rarely. Galene had flat-out started refusing to let him go off on his own until he cut the line connecting him to his humanity and truly accepted his merpersonhood. She kept saying it was high time he leaned into being a mer and utilized his gifts appropriately. She encouraged him to seek vengeance on those who had attempted to kill him, that it would be cathartic, and he'd finally understand what it meant to be merfolk.

He thought she was a homicidal maniac. So, he was strictly limited to visiting land with new merfolk, but it wasn't as if there were new mers all that often. Nissa was the newest and it had been almost a year since she'd joined the pod. Still, she wasn't adjusting all that well.

And when Anita, a mermaid whose magical skill allowed her to read the true nature of a thing, had determined that Nissa would, with time and training, be a land-walker like Sinter, Sinter had suggested that he might take Nissa back to land to train.

Nissa, who had become like a little sister to him at this point, readily joined in the pleading and they'd finally convinced Galene to allow him to bring her on land with him.

Sinter had made lots of plans.

He was going to make Nissa feel like she was a normal little girl again. He'd been so excited to share everything with her, to help her have some good experiences that would make her forget her current miseries. He wanted to be a good big brother.

But he hadn't been.

He hadn't accounted for how sensitive little girls could be. First, he hadn't expected how afraid she'd be to try and turn back. The transformation hurt. Turning from human to mer was excruciating. Turning from mer to human was just as excruciating. Some mers never survived the transformation. It sucked, whether you were a new mer or changing into one for the 800th time.

He'd gotten her all the way to the docks in Portland by cover of night. He'd transformed and, panting, clung onto an algae-slick length of rope hanging off of the pier and encouraged Nissa to make an attempt. She'd stared at him, wide-eyed and terrified, and then shook her head.

He couldn't blame her. It was scary to willingly inflict that much pain on oneself, even for adults.

"Don't you want to try?"

She wrinkled her nose. "What happened to your tail?"

Sinter wasn't sure. He had been turned as a young adult and in the time since he'd been a mer person he'd watched himself mature as one. When he was younger his scales had been an opaque white with violet tinges along the edges—like the inside of a quahog clam shell. As he'd aged, he became darker and darker, the purple overcoming more and more of the white like a spreading bruise and, as he came into what would equate as mermanhood, he'd developed dark striping like a tiger fish.

The other mermen, few as they were, made fun of his purple coloring and it made the females of the pod wary of him. He couldn't understand why, he was a fine male specimen, mer or otherwise. Perhaps that was why he enjoyed his legs so often. He never questioned where those scales went when he turned. All he knew was, when he took human form, the purple scales were gone and the women on land seemed to be inexplicably drawn to him.

He knew that draw still had a lot to do with his being mer. There was something about the mer that drew humans in. He was fairly certain it was the mer voice. Even when he wasn't singing, the cadence of his voice tugged at a human's attention. He had no money or clothes when he took to land, but he could usually find both quite easily. All he had to do was ask.

"It's magic," he eventually settled on. Sinter tried to encourage her. "Don't you want to do something fun, Nis? Mini golfing? The amusement park? The zoo? Anything you wanna do."

She bit her lip. "What about clothes?" she'd asked.

"Don't worry about that. I'll get us some. Any kind you want."

For a long moment, she stared at him. Her eyes dark, inky pools floating about the glittering obsidian water. "I want to see my parents."

Everything in Sinter froze up. There was one rule Galene had told him never to break with the newbies. Never take them to see their families. Something in his face must have showed that rule to Nissa because it had gone downhill pretty fast from there. They'd gotten in an argument and she'd sped off. He'd still been in his human form and in the time it took to transform back into his merfolk form, he'd lost her.

He'd *lost* her—which was the one thing he wasn't supposed to do.

And it had been over a day now and he couldn't find her.

The idea of something having happened to her made his chest tight and his stomach sour. He quickened his pace, thrashing the water with his powerful tail. Galene was going to kill him when she found out. *If* she found out. Hopefully he could find Nissa before she did.

As he swam, he felt the press of the pod on his mind. It was always calling, dragging the folk back together. It tugged at him, always reminding him that he could never be free of this life. He wanted to swim so far that the cord snapped. He'd tried it a number of times. Even went so far as to take legs and just walk away. He'd made it as far as the Mississippi before the drag of the call had him shucking his stolen clothes and throwing himself back to the mercy of the water.

The transformation back to a mer hurt more the longer one was out of the water. No one had ever taught him that. He'd learned that all on his own the hard way, thrashing and screaming in the deep muddy water of the river. He'd nearly drowned that day. That was when he knew he was trapped in this life.

Nissa would have to accept that as well. One day.

The summer water was warm close to the surface and whooshed against his body, but the water was getting colder as he drew farther from shore. He was going back and forth across the bay, calling for Nissa. She had to be somewhere.

And once he found her? He was going to find some chains in a sunken ship and fasten them to her fins. He grumbled to himself, sending a stream of bubbles across his cheekbones, and rolled his eyes. Why were children so unreasonable anyway? This wasn't how he'd wanted to spend his weekend.

His stomach chose that moment to growl at him loudly. It occurred to him he hadn't eaten since yesterday and he hadn't stopped swimming either. He was no good to anyone if he made himself sick. He needed to stop for a bit. Rest and eat. Maybe then he'd be able to think of where she might be hiding.

Sighing, he arched and dove deep, wriggling down to the ocean floor. This part of the coast of Maine was flat and sandy bottomed with only rocks and trash to decorate the floor, not like farther south where lovely coral reefs decorated the seas. But, desolate as it seemed, food was plentiful when one knew how to look and he knew it was flounder season.

CHAPTER TWO

Herron sat huddled against the superstructure which was the only shade she could find on the *Bertie May* without being in the way. She'd already been thoroughly yelled at by Mike and Jasper and she didn't relish either fussing to Clapton about him bringing her aboard. He'd already raised a hot stink about it when he'd found her hiding below deck.

"Boats ain't a place for women," he'd insisted for what felt like the millionth time in her life. A woman on a boat was bad luck. He believed it as strongly as their late father had. He was in such a mood he'd threatened to haul her overboard right then and there.

She'd told him she'd just swim after them and climb back in.

Herron was curious and stubborn and she had a reason for wanting to be on the boat. She wanted to try out her new Nikon F3. She'd saved up months' worth of wages and had taken the ferry to the mainland just to buy it. She had a future in photojournalism and she wanted to see what the camera could do.

Frank paused on the starboard and put his fists to his hips. The light was perfect—framing his stout body and really bringing the yellow of his waders and his bush of a beard to life. Crouching, she lifted the camera and brought it to her face. Point, focus. *Click*. She slid her finger under the lever and advanced the film.

Frank glanced over his shoulder. "You get a good one?"

She grinned at him. Frank was older than dirt and sweated pure whiskey, but he seemed like the only one excited to have her on board. Probably because he liked women as much as he liked his Jack Daniels. "You bet I did! You're made for the camera."

It was that moment that Clapton came brushing past her, bumping her so that the camera slipped out of her hands. The weight of it snapped around her neck. Thank god she'd been smart enough to put the strap on. "What the heck, Clap!" she growled at him as she lovingly scooped up the camera. "You almost made me drop this."

Reaching up, he pulled his headphones off and sneered at her. "Woulda deserved it."

She flashed him the bird. "This thing was expensive."

He rolled his eyes. "Don't even."

She sighed. He was pissed at her as it was for spending so much on it. They weren't exactly swimming in money. Their tiny little island fishing village was going down the tubes and newer fishing restrictions weren't making it any easier for their livelihood.

She knew she should have used the money to help the family. It had been hard since their father died. Their mom had died when they were kids and after their father passed, Clapton was constantly out at sea and struggling to make ends meet.

But Herron wanted off the island. She didn't have skill with much, but with pictures she seemed to be good. She was good enough that, with a little practice, it could take her places.

Clapton was putting his headphones back on now. He practically lived with his Walkman attached to his hip. "Stay out of the way, we're about to bring in the nets."

Herron did as she was told, backing up and pressing her body against the cabin. Half a dozen men started gathering around the aft of the trawler. Clapton pulled a lever and the winch started dragging in the dual chains. They rattled and clinked as they spooled up and out of the water, dripping all over the deck, dragging salty seaweed with them and summoning a mass of squawking seagulls to hover like vultures over the water.

Reveling in how much of a photojournalist she felt like, Herron raised her camera and took candid shots as the men bent to their various tasks and yelled to each other. And then the net came up, gushing with water, silver and white bodies sparking and wiggling in the sunlight. And there, another body, dark and huge against the others.

At first her mind told her it was a dolphin, but then she saw the arms and his head.

Point. *Click.*

"What the fuck?" someone said.

She glanced toward the voice. Mike was staring up. They were all staring up. She looked back and realized it was only a man. A man. Naked and caught in a net ten miles from shore. He stared down at the men collected around him.

"I could have sworn," Frank breathed beside her.

Pulling his headphones off, Clapton squinted at the man in the net. "Who the hell are you?"

The man in the net, perhaps not much older than Clapton, frowned down at him. "That's my business. Let me out, I've got things I need to do."

Herron blinked at him. There was something about his voice. Something...propelling. Her fingers itched to reach out and release the net.

"Like hell," Clapton barked, leaving the headphones slung around his sunburned, sweaty neck like some new-age torc. "I know what I saw."

The man remained quiet, his expression petulant.

Clapton turned away from him and addressed the others, a huge grin on his face. "Looks like we caught another one."

Wait, what? Another one? Confused, Herron looked back at the man in the net. How often were people caught in fishing nets in the middle of Casco Bay? How was this dude even alive after being dragged for miles along the bottom of the ocean?

Clapton and Jasper high-fived.

"What are you talking about?" Herron demanded.

Her brother glanced at her, like he'd forgotten she was even there. "Nothing."

"What? But—" He wasn't listening to her anymore. He headed below deck as the others started to maneuver the net over the deck.

She shifted foot to foot, caught between wanting to watch the men unload the net and interrogating her brother. She decided to stay and then get answers from Clapton once they released the stranger from the net.

The men pulled the net over the side and let it sag into the deck, the man inside struggling to stay atop the rest of the catch. Paulie released the bottom of the net and fish bodies slithered across the weathered wood like they'd been birthed, crabs skittering in all directions. The man was a jumble of limbs, struggling to free himself from the net and the momentum of slimy fish bodies, but then Clapton's men were on him. He began to struggle but someone knocked him unconscious with the flat of one of the shovels they used to sort the fish.

Herron stared, frozen and horrified as the man hit the deck with a thump and the men struggled to roll him back into the net and winch him back up. He hung there, seagulls squealing and pecking at his unconscious, naked form as the men went about their task like this was nothing new or strange. For a long moment, she simply clutched her camera and stared as the remaining men sorted through the fish, ushering their slick bodies down chutes that led to holding tanks below.

After a long moment, she gravitated toward Frank.

"What is all this?" she asked, horrified and confused.

"Eh?" He mopped sweat off his brow with a rubber clad arm. "Oh, that?" He gestured toward the man in the net.

She nodded.

Frank shrugged. "Donno, exactly. But he had a tail like the last one."

"Last one?" she urged.

Crossing his arms, Frank looked up at the net and squinted against the light glaring off the water. "Caught a fish with a human top just yesterday. Er...a human with a fish bottom? She didn't grow legs again like this one, though. She stayed all fishy."

Frowning, Herron adjusted the strap around her neck. The camera suddenly felt far too heavy. "Clapton didn't say anything."

A chuffing scoff rattled Frank's body. "Of course not. Who is he gonna tell? Who's gonna even believe him?"

Herron opened her mouth to tell him she would, but she wasn't sure. Mer people were only myths after all. There had been folktales about the merpeople around Maine for a long time, but nothing concrete. The real world didn't actually believe in them—no more than unicorns or faeries, anyway. She wasn't even sure she'd seen what she'd seen. Where did this guy's fin go? How'd he suddenly get legs? So quickly, too!

She fiddled with the camera in her hand. Perhaps she could prove it to herself? Still... "What happened to the other one?" There was no place back home to hide something like that.

"Clap handed her off before we even came home yesterday. Likely he's arranging the same thing right now."

Was it this one's mate? Perhaps he'd come looking for her. "Handed her off?"

Frank side-eyed her for a long moment as if weighing whether to tell her more. "There's a special kinda place for off market things. Sometimes we find a little something and we can make some extra cash on the side."

Extra cash? "You mean like when you sometimes sell the stuff that accidentally gets caught in your net?"

He nodded.

"But this isn't a stray dolphin," she reasoned. Her chest suddenly felt tight. "And, isn't that illegal?"

Frowning, Frank released his arms and rubbed the back of his neck.

She pressed him. "Black-market shark fins are bad enough, but this is human trafficking."

"Don't know nothing about that," he dismissed. "All's I know is, most of the time, what we find? It ain't human and it brings good money. Kinda money we don't see all too often and most of us can't make ends meet as it is. Ocean ain't gonna miss a few souls. Lord knows she takes as many as she gives."

Desperate, she gestured at the net above her. "He clearly is human, though. How can you say he isn't? Frank, we need to let him go right now!"

For a long moment, Frank just stared up at the man creaking above them. He was beginning to make soft moaning noises. He was coming to. "I can't account for what the creatures of the deep can or can't do. All I know is this ain't my boat or my catch. I'm just a hired man and I can't lose this job. Your brother's the only one who'll keep me hired with this...affliction of mine. He's a good man who does right by us. What we could make on yesterday's catch alone will feed our families and pay off mortgages. You really wanna challenge all that?"

No. Yes. She glanced around at the remaining men on deck. It was only Alphie and Tad and they weren't looking at her and Frank, but she sensed they were listening closely. She held her breath for a long moment. These were people she'd known all her life. They'd either worked with her father before he died or she'd grown up with them. Hell, she'd even dated Tad in her less intelligent days. She didn't wish harm on them or their families and certainly didn't want to steal the food from their mouths, but... She looked back up at the man in the net.

He was awake now, blinking down and around as if trying to clear his vision.

This was wrong and she knew it down to her core. Sighing, she turned away and stomped off toward the cabin where she assumed Clapton was.

"Herron," Frank called after her, but she didn't respond.

As she drew around the side of the cabin, she heard someone speaking low and quick. Jasper. She slid close to the door and stood just out of eyeshot.

"—isn't like the last one. This one has legs. How can we be sure?"

"Look," Clapton's voice chimed in. "I know what I saw and we couldn't all have imagined the same thing."

"How's it possible then?" another voice—Mike, maybe—reasoned. "What if he's just some dude we dredged up? A competitive swimmer or some kind of immigrant or someone who fell overboard."

Clapton made a growling sound. "He's not. Trust me."

"Still, how are you going to prove it to Musgrave? I mean, you ran off and called in to him so quick, but if you show up with someone who just looks like some dude you stripped and knocked out he ain't gonna be happy. He's doing us a favor handling the last catch, you know? He said he'd get it in front of big buyers. This could mean something for us. If he thinks we're screwing with him? We can't fuck it up."

"I know that, Jasper." Then, Clapton was so quiet that she could hear his headphones blaring Kenny Rogers over the sound of the boat and the sea. "The auction isn't for another few days, right? We'll just wait for him to turn back."

Mike said, "And if he doesn't?"

Another drag of silence. "We make him."

Swallowing hard, Herron glanced down at the camera dangling from her neck. She had a picture of this merperson. She could prove he was something other than human. That may at least save him from whatever convincing was on Clapton's mind.

She shook her head. What was she even thinking?

Her stomach felt sour.

She'd always known her brother was mean. He'd always had a temper and plenty of nasty things to say to her. Sometimes he even raised a hand to her. She could swear her ear wasn't quite right since he'd gone after her for buying the camera. Still, after he'd calmed down, he'd let her keep it in the end and she'd always assumed she sort of deserved his wrath. She was willful after all. But she'd never really thought of him as someone who would stoop to poaching for the black market or human trafficking, and certainly not torture.

But then, money did things to people. So did desperation and she knew they were in dire straits when it came to the mortgage. Their father had refinanced the house when their mother got cancer to pay for the hospital bills and now Clapton was drowning in the debt.

Herron tried where she could, but her seasonal jobs left holes in a concrete stream of income.

She closed her eyes and pressed her back against the warm metal of the cabin wall. *Bertie May* felt familiar and warm, her body oozing ruddy rust where her bright white paint had chipped away. She'd been her father's boat and now she was Clapton's. She wondered what secrets the old girl held. How many poor creatures had met their end on her creaking deck. Sighing, she slumped to the floor. Sure, she might prevent this merman from enduring torture at Clapton's hand, but to what end? He was going to some sort of auction and what would happen then?

She couldn't let it happen.

The rest of the men were filing past her, their boots squeaking on the deck as they all piled into the cabin. Frank was last and he was already hollering about a celebratory drink because they were all going to be rich.

Herron hugged her legs and listened to the still screeching seagulls, letting *Bertie May* rock her like her mother. It took her a long few minutes of sitting like that before she realized that she was alone on deck and then she was scrambling to her feet and creeping back toward the aft.

The merman watched her with piercing eyes that were more gold than brown as she stared up at him and then stared at the control panel for the winch. It occurred to her that she had no idea how to operate the winch and even if she did, most likely, Clapton's men would hear it.

She glanced back over her shoulder. She could hear them talking loudly. Congratulating themselves. They weren't very far away. Slowly, she gravitated toward the starboard side of the boat where someone had left a fileting knife sitting on a sideboard. It was dull and a bit rusty, but it might work. She snuck back over to the mermaid and held the knife up for him. She wasn't tall enough to cut through the net herself, but she assumed he'd know what to do.

For a long moment he just stared at her. "Take it," she hissed. "Before they see."

He did.

And then she backed up and turned away, heading back toward the cabin. She made a big show of climbing up along the bow and taking a lot of pictures. The windows to the cabin pointed in every direction but behind. The men inside could see her clearly. And she could see over the cabin freely. Could see the merman slowly sawing away at the nylon netting around him.

She watched as he cut himself free, dropped to the deck, holding her eyes for a long moment, and then turned and dove off the aft of the ship.

CHAPTER THREE

Sinter surfaced just next to a small rowboat that tugged at its line, the weathered rope creaking above his head. He wasn't entirely sure where he was. They were farther north now, a small fishing village. He had no idea if he was closer or farther from Nissa, but all he had was the promise of a few choice words overheard while hanging from the net on that ship the day before...the promise of the girl who'd freed him.

She was at the end of the pier, her camera in her hand. Her attention was fully on the gulls that were squawking at each other from among the mess of lobster traps heaped around a shed. There was nothing especially pretty about her. She was plain, the sort of girl who his mother might have approved of since she never liked anyone outshining her. Sinter didn't go for those types. He'd brought home girls who made his mother feel as old and ugly as possible. He'd never really had a desire to please his mother.

He sank beneath the water and dove down under the dock. Murky light blasted down through the wooden slats above, illuminating the water to a green hue. He grasped the pier supports, barnacles pricking into his hand, and pulled himself forward. Above, he could hear the gentle thumping of the boats, the *tsss*ing of bubbles popping. The pressure of the water was like a weighty blanket. He wove support to support, the stalking of his prey observed only by sea stars and urchins.

Finally, he slithered up the last support and noiselessly broke water. He leaned against the green algae ring around the support, his head just a few inches above the lapping water and tipped his head. He couldn't see her, she was just above him, but she was speaking.

"There we are, you pretty thing, I won't hurt you. Just...stay... still..." *Click.* "Perfect. You're so photogenic."

He smirked despite himself. What had that man on the boat called her? Herron? Like the bird? Licking the salt water from his lips, he rose just a fraction more and let his senses absorb the world around them. It wasn't busy on this dock. It wasn't busy in this place at all. It seemed like a sleepy, unhurried sort of place with few people. Plain as she was, she didn't seem like she belonged here. Not with her grungy fashion sense and that frizzy brown hair.

He took a deep breath and grasped the ladder beside him.

Shifting for Sinter was painful. Of course it would be, turning from a fish to a man involved all kinds of changes in bone and skin. It felt like an eternity of torturous pain when in reality it was only a few seconds. It never got easier, but Sinter had learned to keep himself silent and still as he did it. When it was done, he clung panting to the rungs of the ladder. He held his breath, willing his thundering heart and shaking limbs to still. He focused on her voice.

"It's all right, I'm not going to hurt you. Just a little closer. Shhh..." He closed his eyes and rested his forehead to the slimy plastic. She had a soothing cadence to her voice.

When he was sure he had enough strength to do so, he checked their surroundings one last time before slowly climbing the ladder.

CHAPTER FOUR

Herron straightened and wound her film. "You did well!" she told the seagull perched on the top of the pier support. He cocked his head, examining her with a golden eye. She grinned at him then turned to find another victim. Then froze.

There, standing maybe only five feet away in the relative shadows of the transit shed, was a man. A naked man. One with a face she knew.

She gasped and didn't realize the camera had slipped between her fingers until the weight of it snapped against her neck, knocking her off balance so that she had to take a step forward to catch herself.

His hand came up, as if to catch her, but she caught her weight and stumbled backward and away from him instead. Some unholy noise erupted from her throat—something between a cry and a squawk—and she backed into the line of traps behind her, knocking them over. The resulting clatter and crash sent the gulls screaming into the air and a number of the traps tumbling into the water. She clamored over the mess, but there was nowhere to go so she clawed

177

at the massive iron ring bolted to the wooden pile and clung there, half hanging out over the water.

The man. No, the *mer*man, glanced back toward the wharf, his amber eyes narrowing beneath a wet mop of charcoal hair. After a long few minutes of stillness on shore, he fixed his gaze back on her. "I'm sorry, I didn't mean to startle you."

Herron blinked at him. His voice was just as calming and magical as it was the day before. Velvety smoke, inky brushstrokes, the lull of dreamland wrapped into a gentle accent that she could not place. Despite herself, she relaxed a little. "Wh—" she tried, but found her throat was too tight.

"You're shaking," he said, his eyes flicking toward her hands. "You could fall."

She was. She couldn't help it. She was shaken enough by what she'd seen yesterday. She half thought she'd imagined it. And yet... "Your...your tail—"

Those golden eyes flicked down, examining the lines of his obvious nakedness. "Would you prefer a tail? I figured legs would be better." He glanced up. "Though, I guess not."

She bit her trembling lip. It was less the legs and more the nakedness.

"Come down." His voice was some sort of command that her body ached to obey. "You'll fall."

She shook her head against the dark pull of it.

"Please," his voice tugged again. "I don't want you to get hurt. I'm not gonna hurt you."

His words were truth and promise and comfort. She found herself obeying and before she even knew what she was doing she was stepping back onto the pier and pressing her back to the pilon.

"That's better."

It wasn't, she was sure of it. But he did stay standing where he was. For a long moment, they just stared at each other. Herron began to question her sanity. And yet...and yet, the whole of the crew of the *Bertie May* had seen this man with a fish tail. Clapton had even voiced that there was another. And pictures didn't lie. She'd developed the film, she had a picture of him like that. He didn't have a fin now, though, so it had to have been a trick.

Anxious for something to fill the silence, to fill the voice of uncertain dread in her, she spoke. "Do you often make a habit of swimming with a fake fish tail in the middle of the ocean?" The logistics of such an accusation were all off. There had been no boat nearby to the *Bertie May*, nowhere for him to have come from. He couldn't have swam that far from shore on his own...wearing a fake tail.

His expression told her as much. "You think I was pulling a prank?"

A scoff escaped her. "I believe you're some kind of deviant." She gestured at him.

Another glance down and he pursed his lips. "Ah, you don't like how I look." It was a statement, not a question, and the tone of it sounded almost offended.

It wasn't that. Not at all. Hadn't she dreamed about this? After seeing this creature caught in a net, after having given him the knife, and endured Clapton's rage...she hadn't had nightmares.

She hugged her arms around herself, comforting herself against her own profuse blush at remembering how her subconscious mind had conjured him just like this. Beautiful and bare and accessible, his dark voice purring against her skin. She changed the subject. "What are you doing here? Are you even real?"

His chin tucked. "You want to touch me and find out?"

She pressed herself harder against the pilon. "No. S-stay there."

Cupid's bow mouth quirking up slightly, he shot her a dimple. "As you wish."

Unnerved, she looked away, staring instead at the scuffed graying toes of her Converse sneakers. How was this creature so lovely? It wasn't fair.

"Thank you," he said after a long moment. "You helped me yesterday, I owe you one."

She closed her eyes. So that's what this was about. She took a deep breath. "You're welcome."

"I..." he trailed off.

His silence made her peek back up at him. He was looking off toward the mainland, his teeth gnawing his lip. His expression was vulnerable, like when he'd been caught in the net. She couldn't stand it. "What is it?"

He closed his eyes and kept his face turned away from her. "You got in trouble."

"Ah," she closed her eyes and forced a smile, "so you heard Clapton lay into me, huh?" Lay into wasn't quite the right phrase for it. Despite no one being able to prove she'd helped the merman escape, Clapton knew otherwise. He'd screamed and backhanded her so hard that she'd gone flying. He might have beaten her bloody if Frank hadn't stepped in. She was lucky to have gotten away with as little as she did.

When she opened her eyes again he was right in front of her. She shied back but she was already pasted against a pilon with only the water behind her.

He reached out and she flinched, but his touch was very gentle as he touched the throbbing bruise on her cheek. She had a black eye and a pulsing headache, but that wasn't the worst Clapton had done to her in his rages. "He hurt you." The merman's voice was a mere whisper, something filled with dark anger and shadowy tenderness. His touch was cool and a little wet, as expected from someone who'd crawled out of the ocean, but it felt good on her hot skin. "It's my fault."

Herron's innards squirmed and she let out a breath she hadn't realized she'd been holding. "It's not so bad." It was a line she'd told herself many times.

The merman's hand slid away. "A man should never hit a woman."

She cocked her head and stared up at him. This close, she could see he was quite tall. Tall, lean, dark featured...beautiful...promising... She wanted to shove him away, put distance between them. And yet, she could never bring herself to do such a thing. "There are mermaids as well then?"

His chin tucked. "That's why I am here, actually. I'm looking for one. Nissa. I came to...ask for your help."

"Oh." She couldn't help her disappointment. Foolish of her to think he'd come back because of her. Of course he had someone.

He took a step back. "I know it is a lot to ask and I already owe you...but Nissa...she's missing and I heard the other men on your ship speaking of another mermaid that had been caught. I thought maybe..."

"I don't know anything about it," she admitted. "That was the first I'd heard of it. Until yesterday, you were nothing but a fairy tale." She sniffed. "I'm still not entirely convinced you're not."

The merman nodded, his mouth set in disappointment.

For some stupid reason, it made her chest ache and she found herself reaching out toward him, taking his hand. "I can try to find out what's happening, though."

His fingers twitched around hers and he grinned, teeth flashing pearly and slightly fanged in the orange glow of oncoming dusk.

She forced herself to let go, to sidestep. She was being stupid, letting her childhood fantasies take over. Honestly, she should be running away screaming. Any normal person would. But Herron had lived with her head in the clouds all her life, had always wished for something exciting and otherworldly to happen to her sleepy little life. She didn't have it in herself to act like an adult and tie herself to reason and doubt. The best she could do for herself now was not to let her foolish crush on this...thing get the better of her.

His charcoal timbre pulled her back to him. "How can I see you again?"

Her heart leapt into her chest. She balled her fists. "I'll come back here again. If I find anything."

"I'll wait for you."

She did not acknowledge those words. Knew the lie her mind

was interpreting in those words. His voice was a sin. A thing that cast awful spells without promise. Still... She eyed his naked form. "Maybe not here. There are too many people who could see us. Er, you."

His chin dipped in agreement. "Where then?"

CHAPTER FIVE

Sinter was a few hundred yards from the shore hunting for breakfast when he surfaced and was surprised to see Herron coming down the lupine speckled hillside late the following morning. Anxious to hear the news, he dove under the dark waves and raced back to shore.

As agreed, he was lying in wait in a small alcove she'd described to him. It was hidden under an overhang of ancient spruce trees that clung to the rocks at an angle. The great cone-laden bows knit together like fingers and dipped low, hiding the entrance to the alcove in shadow. One wouldn't be able to find it unless they were daring enough to brave the jumbled rocks and pricker bushes on the landside. He marveled that she'd been able to find it at all, but as he watched her weave her way toward him, he could tell she knew this place well.

When she eventually pushed through and stopped short on the rock ledge above him, she stared down at him. He felt more naked and vulnerable now than he did the day before. Part of him wanted to shy back, but there was nowhere to escape her piercing brown eyes.

The cove wasn't large, perhaps ten feet wide and it didn't exist as more than a pool when the tide was out. Still, it was quiet and hidden and anyone trying to make their way through to it made enough noise to warn of their approach. The tide was mostly out now, barely a foot of water attached the pool to the Atlantic and the pool itself was barely three feet deep. His tail was obvious and she was staring at it.

Resisting the urge to shift back to having legs, he said, "Did you find something?"

Her lips twisted down and she shook her head in the negative, but her eyes remained fixedly on his lower half.

He looked away, half annoyed by no news and half annoyed by how she was staring at him.

When he finally looked back, she was moving—crouching slightly, her attention on her hands and feet as she half-slid, half-climbed her way between the jumble of boulders. She was wearing the same scuffed pair of Converse sneakers from yesterday. Her socks, a mismatched florescent pink and blue, were pulled over the cuffs of her acid-washed jeans and the shirt tucked into her high-rise waist was a fluorescent yellow. None of the ensemble lent to covert operations and he wondered whose attention she'd garnered on her way across the island.

When she got to the edge of the cove she tucked the faded purple windbreaker she had tied around her waist under her rump and sat on a wet hillock of stinking seaweed. He mentally gave her some credit for doing that. At least she wasn't prissy. In fact, he assumed she must be the adventurous type. "Have you eaten?" she asked, not looking at him.

He felt annoyed she wouldn't look him in the eye, but supposed he didn't blame her. "I was going to."

She unslung a small jean backpack patched with a parade of Grateful Dead bears and tugged at the drawstrings. He gave her another point for similar taste in music and was about to ask what her favorite album was—because he felt that one could glean a lot about a girl on whether she preferred *Terrapin Station* over *Anthem of the Sun*—when she pulled out a tinfoil-wrapped parcel. "Can you eat people food?"

Startled, he blinked at her. "People food?"

"Bagels?" She held the round parcel out.

He held back a moment. "What flavor is it?"

"Cinnamon raisin," she offered. "Toasted with plain cream cheese."

He reached for the bagel. "I prefer everything."

For a long moment she watched him as he tore back the foil and took a bite. He closed his eyes and groaned to himself as the tart flavor of the cream cheese bloomed at the back edges of his tongue. "Fuck, I miss bagels."

Her quiet scoff had him opening his eyes. "What?"

"I guess I never expected a mermaid to swear," she said with a shrug.

He took another bite and spoke with his mouth full. "Man. Merman."

"Uh, right." She glanced away with a blush. A long moment passed as he ate, then she said, "You said you *miss* bagels."

"Yeah," he swallowed and glanced at the half-finished bagel. "The mouthfeel mostly."

Her shoulders crimped up again and she tucked her fingers between her knees. "How do you know what a bagel even tastes like?"

Crimping a brow, he frowned at her. "What kind of shitty New Yorker doesn't know what a bagel tastes like? I didn't grow up under a rock."

Looking sheepish, she said, "No, just under the sea. Where bagels definitely don't keep their texture, but..." she paused. "New York? Are there mermaids in New York Harbor?"

He couldn't help smirking at her and decided not to correct her again. "Only when we want to be."

She shook her head, obviously confused.

Sinter threw her a bone. "I was born on Long Island. I ate a lot of bagels before I became one of the merfolk."

"Oh," she breathed. "So, you weren't always one?"

Bagel half-clamped between his teeth, he shook his head.

Thoughtful, her eyes ventured back toward his tail and stayed fixed there as he finished eating. When he was done he balled up the foil and tossed it at her head. It hit her in the forehead with a solid "thwack."

"Hey!" she yelped, rubbing her forehead.

"Oh come on, that didn't hurt." He hadn't thrown it hard enough.

"So? What's the big idea?"

"You were staring. Don't you know that's rude?"

Grumbling to herself, she looked at her shoes. "Well, it's kind of hard not to look."

"You didn't stare so bad yesterday," he reasoned.

She met his eyes again. "You didn't have a tail yesterday."

He looked away and down at his tail. "Is it really that ugly?"

"What?" she squeaked. "No! It's...it's actually really pretty."

He didn't look up at her. He didn't want to see any evidence of a lie in her expression. He slid his hand over his scales. No one had ever called his tail pretty before. "It's not a normal color," he reflected. "Not for a male, anyway."

"I like purple," she said. "See?"

He glanced up to see her grasping at the windbreaker under her butt.

"And stripes are in," she added matter-of-factly.

He scoffed and looked away again.

"It's a lot easier to talk to you with your tail on. The other way is...distracting."

He wanted to argue that she seemed more distracted by the tail than his bare male bits, but didn't.

"So, you *became* a merperson then?"

He nodded.

"Is that like a coming-of-age thing? Puberty?"

He fought a smirk, despite the painful memory. "We're...made. By other merfolk. Usually as a necessity. A," he fought for the right word, "mercy. That's how they see it anyway."

She was quiet for a long moment and he knew she was mulling over his tone and wanted to ask more questions. She didn't, though. Instead, she changed to an adjacent subject, "Why aren't you trying to hide your tail from me?"

"You already saw and you already know."

She took a deep breath. "I wasn't 100% sure, you know? Part of me thought I was seeing things. Even when I developed my film and I saw for sure..." She closed her eyes and shook her head. "I kept telling myself it must be the angle of the camera, a trick of the light."

"I'm merfolk. Whether I like it or not."

Her fingers grasped around her ankles. "You have legs sometimes, though."

He dipped his chin. "That's my special power."

"Special power?"

"We all get one special power when we turn. Talk to fish, control the water, create light with our hands. Mine's to take on human form at will."

"So why not choose to stay human?" she wondered.

A bitter scoff escaped him and he stared up at the canopy of needles above him. "It isn't as if I haven't tried. I can't stay in my human form. It gets too painful after a while."

"Oh."

More silence and her staring at her feet. Sinter felt antsy, like he'd said something that put a wall between them, shut her down. It bothered him. He wasn't sure why, but he wanted to try to pull her back over that wall. "I've never talked to another human about any of this before. I'm supposed to keep it a secret."

Her fingers suddenly white-knuckled her shoelaces. "I won't tell. I promise. I already destroyed the picture I took. The negatives, too."

"That's...not what I meant. I trust you." And he meant it. Something about this girl made him feel like he could talk about anything. He hadn't felt that way with anyone, human or mer. The realization was mildly unsettling and he found himself retreating back to his side of the wall with a clearing of the throat. "So, you're here. Did you find something out about Nissa?"

Herron's shoulders seemed to crimp in even farther and she pressed her face to her knees. "No."

"Oh." He couldn't hide the disappointment in his voice. "So...why are you here then?"

He couldn't see her whole face at that angle, but he could see her eyes shut. The bruise around her eye was more evident without the distraction of her big brown irises. Angry at the sight of it, he balled his fists.

Her hand detached from her ankle and wandered to where the foil ball fell after he tossed it at her. She rolled it around in the small puddle it fell in, creating concentric ripples. "I thought maybe you'd be hungry and maybe a little lonely."

Her distant voice pulled at something in his chest. She was right, of course. He was hungry. Hungry and lonely. Was. He didn't feel either of those things now. Thanks to her. "Thank you." He shifted in the water, antsy for no reason. "Though I'd give up the bagel for some good news."

"Sorry."

The disappointment in her voice made him go still. "It's not your fault. I'm just worried about Nissa. I mean, she's just a little kid. She must be terrified."

Herron's head came up then, her eyes wide and startled. "Little kid?"

"Yeah, I mean, she's only like...ten?" He wasn't sure, exactly. He'd never asked—which seemed sort of dickish now that he thought about it. He didn't even know when Nissa's birthday was, let alone how old she was. He really was a shitty older brother.

"Oh." The word came out in a shudder. "I...thought Nissa was your girlfriend or something." Sinter grimaced and it made Herron chuckle. "So, she's your daughter?"

He rolled his eyes. "Do I look that old?"

"Sister?" she ventured.

He shrugged. "She's my...charge, I guess? I'm her babysitter for the time being. Or, I was. And then I lost her and now she's been captured. I can't go home without her." He shook his head. "I could never do that."

Crossing her arms, Herron took a deep breath and let it out. "I'll do everything I can. I think it's shit what they're doing. And to a kid no less. Until then? Well," she grinned at him, "the least I can do is bring you bagels to keep your spirits up."

He grinned back. "I'd like that."

"And in return," she said, "I'd like to know your name."

He smirked. "I'll tell you mine if you tell me yours." He knew she was called Herron already, but he wanted her to give him that name.

CHAPTER SIX

Days passed. Herron spent them visiting Sinter and keeping her head down at home. Clapton was still in a mood and would bluster about whenever she was in the room. He was angrier with her than he'd ever been and she was genuinely afraid he'd hurt her again. The only time the tension seemed to break was when she went to see Sinter and she found herself spending more and more time with him as the days passed.

She brought him food, even brought him some of Clapton's old clothes to wear, though he'd turned his nose up at the tee shirt and worn Carhartts and said he'd rather go naked than wear the clothes of a guy who hit women.

They talked about music and his life at sea. She told him about her dreams and he listened intently when she talked about photography or her friends on the mainland. He even asked questions and no one did that, ever. Not even those supposed friends on the mainland who were too engrossed in their own lives to much care for her sleepy island life.

Despite the discomfort of it, she still kept her mind on the task at hand. She knew Sinter was only sticking around because he needed her to find out about Nissa. All the time he spent enduring her was probably just him feeling like he had to pay a price for what Herron could do for him. So, she made sure to always leave in time to get home before Clapton and she always stayed close to him while he was home.

It was hard at first, given how angry Clapton was, but he cooled enough to eat dinner in the same room with her by the end of the week.

The silence spreading the distance of the long table between them was punctuated by the higher notes of Whitney Houston on his headphones. Feeling awkward, Herron cleared her throat and reached for another helping of peas. She wasn't hungry anymore but needed an excuse to stay at the table. She attempted small talk. "Weather's been good."

Clapton grunted around a mouth full of bread. She couldn't tell if it was a response or a request to get her to repeat herself. He often couldn't hear her when he wore the headphones.

She frowned, she was terrible at this. She mulled over asking him a stupid ice breaker question but the phone suddenly rang, making her jump.

He was up and out of his seat in an instant, chair clattering to the floor as he tore off his headphones. She blinked at him as he yanked the receiver off the wall and held it to his ear. She hadn't seen him this anxious to get to a call since he was dating Sarah Walton. "Hello?"

A man's voice sounded on the other end but she couldn't hear what he was saying.

Clapton glanced at her, then turned toward the wall as if that would fix anything. "Yeah. I told you not to call this number, Musgrave."

Musgrave? The dude Jasper had mentioned?

The man on the other side gave a few short words.

"Uh," Clapton breathed, dragging his fingers through his hair. "No. No, I'm sorry. My bad." His hand released his hair and white-knuckle-gripped the phone wire which, after so many years of phone calls spent wandering the kitchen and hallway, was now less polite, organized coil and more lazy, tangled wave.

Herron narrowed her eyes at Clapton's back. He was actually apologizing to someone? Just who was this person on the other end?

More speaking from the other side. Clapton hunched and reached for the stub of a pencil that had rolled halfway down the counter and wedged itself under the empty fruit bowl. "Yeah, go ahead." He began to write something on the pad under the phone. "Okay. Okay. Three o'clock. No, just me and Jasper, in one car like we agreed. I'm meeting him at Tony's beforehand and we'll take my car. All black. Mask..."

Mask? More illegal activities, no doubt. She rolled her eyes at the phone and studied the fading artwork on her Welch's character glass. Tweety was missing half his face due to too many harsh scrubbings.

"Just drive up and they'll let us in? A guest list? Wow, that's pretty fancy. Okay. I'll be there." Clapton hung up the phone with a clack.

"What was that all about?" she wondered.

He scowled at her over his shoulder then ripped the note free of the pad. "None of your fucking business."

"Geez, I was only asking. Take a chill pill."

He shoved the note into his pocket and stalked away from her. "I'm going out."

"Where?" she demanded, getting up and following after him.

He turned and rounded on her. "Why are you in my business today?"

She stopped short, out of arm's reach, and shrugged. "Well, if you're trying to pick up a chick you're not gonna do it in that grody get-up."

Easing his headphones into place with one hand, he flashed her the bird with the other and then shoved out the door.

She waited long enough for him to walk down the driveway before turning on her heel and practically running back to the phone. She grabbed the pencil and lightly shaded over the pad. Clapton wrote with such a heavy hand that she really didn't need to but the graphite shading made the transferred imprint below stand out more clearly.

Belvedere Auction

Friday @3

black & mask

POP Terminal 4 Berth 5

She frowned at the indented chicken scratch, trying to puzzle it out. She assumed POP meant the Port of Portland which was the nearest port that was large enough for terminals and berths. But she wasn't sure whether the auction started at three or he was to be onboard at three. Either way, she was sure this must be the auction they'd been anticipating. Jasper was going, too, after all, and Clapton had called the guy on the phone Musgrave.

"Friday," she breathed. That was tomorrow. That didn't leave much time. Gnawing her lip, Herron tentatively reached up and grabbed the phone. She held it cradled between her chin and her shoulder as she chewed chipped fingernails on one hand and plugged her fingers into the rotary with the other.

Christie picked up on the fifth ring. "Donner residence."

"Chris, it's me."

"Hey, stranger." Christie's tone changed from bored to light in an instant.

Herron grinned, pleased to hear the voice of her best friend since kindergarten. "It's been like two weeks since my last visit."

"That's forever. When are you coming back to me?"

Christie was right, of course. That was sort of forever for the both of them. But, since Herron was between her seasonal jobs, she hadn't had a reason to go to the mainland in a while. Plus, she'd been a bit occupied with Sinter lately. "That's what I was calling about, actually," she said, feeling guilty.

"Oh?"

"I need a teenie favor..."

CHAPTER SEVEN

Crashing through the underbrush woke Sinter. Worried about being found, he slid off the rock ledge he'd been sleeping on and into the cove which was now full with the high tide. He submerged most of his body and pressed close to the rock, counting on the overhanging ledge to hide him. His heart hammered as whoever it was drew closer. And then a shaft of weak yellow light slid over the water.

"Sinter?"

He relaxed at the whispered voice. Herron. She sounded winded and panicked, though. Clearly something was wrong. She'd been making a habit of visiting him, but didn't usually come in the middle of the night to see him. He pulled away from the ledge. "I'm here."

The light lanced down toward him and he held up a hand to keep it from blinding him. He could see nothing of her. "Oh good." She kept the light on him as she moved toward the tumble of boulders.

"Don't come down, you might fall." He turned his face away and blinked away spots. "I'll climb up. Just kill the light, you're blinding me."

"Sorry." The flashlight snapped off.

Sinter grasped hold of the ledge and held his breath through his shift. He was still shaking slightly as he puzzled his way between the rocks. When he made it to the top he squinted into the darkness and found her just-barely-there shape—black against the deepest of sapphire blue night. "Are you okay?" he demanded, stepping toward her and grasping at her elbows.

She felt the heat of her palm against his chest. "I'm all right."

He slid his hands from her shoulders to her jaw. "You're shaking." Had Clapton hit her again? Sinter was going to kill him.

"It's cold," she reasoned, her other hand also coming to his chest. "Aren't you cold, too?"

His skin felt tight with goosebumps but it wasn't from the cold. "No," he answered honestly. In fact, he felt a little hot. With adrenaline, maybe, from the fright she'd given him. Or...maybe something else.

He felt himself drifting a little closer to her, canceling out the distance between them. Sinter was at a tipping point with this girl. She hadn't much appealed to him at first. And yet...there was something about her. Something that, over the past week of getting to know her, had gotten under his skin. Now that he was touching her in the dead of night, it seemed obvious to his body what was going on. He liked this girl. He wanted to touch her more.

It seemed like she welcomed the idea. Her arms weren't pushing against him and her jaw tilted slightly, nuzzling into his palm. But then she spoke. "Get dressed."

He went still and blinked at her. "What?" That seemed like the total opposite of where his mind wanted to go right now. He wanted less clothes, preferably on her, not more clothes on him.

Her fists balled against his chest. "We don't have much time, come on."

Feeling like a cold bucket of water had been dumped over his head, Sinter stepped away from her and searched the ground for the plastic Filene's bag she'd brought him Clapton's clothes in. He spoke as he pulled out the clothes and dressed. "What's going on?"

"I think I found out about Nissa."

He paused, one leg pulled into the khaki-colored pants. Right. Nissa. This was no time for girls or sex. "What?"

"The auction," she explained. "It's happening today. We have to catch the morning ferry and get to the mainland ASAP."

He unstuck himself and continued getting dressed. "Tell me everything."

CHAPTER EIGHT

"**A**re you about done? It's almost time and we still need to get to Tony's," Herron whined as she squirmed under Christie's crimping iron.

"Sit still," Christie hissed.

"How much longer?" Herron whimpered, glancing sideways at the clock. Her scalp already felt itchy from all the bobby pins and her head felt a number of pounds heavier. She tugged at the edge of her dress.

Christie popped her gum and chewed it like cud as she spoke. "You wanted a classy updo. Rome wasn't built in a day."

Herron grimaced, she wasn't sure if she should take offense to the comment or not. She glanced at Sinter who sat on Christie's bed looking bored and delicious in a charcoal polyester suit Christie had stolen from her parents' closet. It was a little dated—still sporting the large lapels and matching vest of the late 70s where nowadays things were trending looser and suits were mostly two-pieces, but he still looked delicious.

Blushing slightly, she looked away and fussed with the edge of her sleeve. Herron's outfit was an evening gown that Christie had worn to the last Navy ball with her long-time boyfriend, Chad, who worked at the Portsmouth Naval Shipyard in Kittery. It was a black sequined thing with a high slit along the thigh and long sleeves that puffed at the shoulder so that Herron felt bigger than she actually was.

"Chin up, honey."

Herron looked back at the mirror. She started at her blushed cheeks and the dark lines around her eyes and darkening her brows. The golden shadow Christie had chosen really made Herron's eye color stand out. She looked like she belonged on a magazine cover. "Thank you for doing this."

"Eh," Christie breathed, setting the crimping iron on the vanity with one hand while holding the strip of hair between the bright pink nails of her other. "What's the point of dropping out of beauty school if you can't help a friend out sometimes?" She grabbed a can of Aquanet and aimed it at Herron. "Close your eyes."

Herron did as she was told while Christie held the hair in place and plastered it. Herron coughed slightly and waved her hand over her head when she was done, examining her friend's masterpiece. "You've outdone yourself."

Grinning, Christie stepped back and chewed her gum. "Your hair likes this style."

Herron rolled her eyes. Her frizzy hair was her worst feature, but she couldn't argue that it added something to the bouffant, tousled look Christie had given to her. She turned to Sinter who was thumbing through an old issue of *McCall's* from Christie's night-stand. "What do you think?"

It took him a moment to realize she was talking to him. When he did his golden eyes slid up, widened, and then he grinned. "You look good."

Her stomach turned over and began to flip around like a fish tossed on the beach. Blushing harder, she looked away and tried to focus her mind.

"You have the masks?"

Christie disappeared from the room for a moment.

Herron slid out of the chair and smoothed her hands down the dress. She felt weirdly exposed and awkward in Christie's black pumps. "This dress is too tight. So are the shoes." She sucked her stomach in and turned sideways. "I feel fat."

"I think you look amazing."

She touched her cheek. "Least you can't see what's left of the bruise anyway."

She heard Sinter set down the magazine and his borrowed shoes creaked as he stood. He came up behind her. He was tall and broad and lean as an athlete. The differences in their appearances were painfully obvious to her in that moment. He was dark, beautiful, and comfortable. She was unpolished, awkward, and clearly a fraud. As she stared at him in the mirror she felt his hand splay across the small of her back.

"Here we are," Christie's voice made them both jump as she rushed back into the room with a blue duffel bag. She stopped short when she saw the two of them and grinned.

She'd been asking all kinds of questions about Sinter since they'd arrived and Herron had fended them off valiantly, explaining that there was nothing between them—because there wasn't—except a common goal to free a young mergirl from traffickers, but that was hard to explain. "Am I interrupting something?"

"No." Herron took a step away from Sinter.

"Oh," Christie sounded depressed and she probably was. She was constantly trying to hook Herron up with one of Chad's Navy buddies. "Well, my brother has plenty from his theater days so take your pick." Christie dumped them out on her pastel floral comforter.

CHAPTER NINE

Sinter held tight to Herron's hand as she crouch-walked behind a row of parked cars in the back lot of Tony's Bar and Billiards. The clutch purse and the strips of sequins down her dress kept catching the light and sending lighthouse flashes of their location as she led him toward their target. Finally, she stopped behind a boxy brown Cadillac and tugged him close.

"It's that truck, right there," she said, pointing at a rusted out red Ford.

Sinter frowned. "How are we supposed to hide in that thing?"

"There's a tarp in the back. Clapton uses it to cover the groceries."

Sinter didn't like this, not one bit. He'd thought, well, he wasn't entirely sure what he'd thought, but this wasn't it. Herron had explained her plan to him while they took the early morning ferry to the mainland but that felt like a lifetime ago—something lost to the gray haze of dawn and the pounding of adrenaline in his veins.

Herron shoved up her sleeve and checked the cheap plastic watch strapped to her wrist. "We better do this."

Nodding, Sinter followed her across the parking lot and watched the back door of Tony's as Herron opened the tailgate and awkwardly struggled to climb in. She lost a shoe in the process.

He scooped it up and hastily tossed it in after her.

"Ouch!" she hissed.

"Sorry." He took another glance around and followed after her.

He shut the tailgate as softly as he could while she made more noise than necessary struggling to get under the weathered blue tarp. He took a minute to reposition the cinderblocks Clapton had weighing it down before climbing under after her.

"This is such a bad idea," he muttered as he squirmed in beside her.

He was already sweating. Already miserable. The suit he was wearing was stifling and his body already wanted to shift back. He'd turned too much in the past few weeks and his tolerance for his own legs was lower than normal. Plus, he hadn't noticed until he'd been sitting in the calm of Christie's bedroom, but he was beginning to feel the strained pull of the pod lessen slightly. That could only mean one thing—the pod was coming toward them—and that couldn't be good.

He'd been fretting ever since he realized it. Wondering how long they'd been coming toward him. He'd been distracted all morning.

Herron wriggled around next to him, trying to straighten her dress and pressing her backside into him in the process.

He grasped her hip to still her. "Would you quit moving?" Her teasing him was the last thing he needed at the moment.

"Sorry, my pantyhose are twisted."

He held his breath and endured her for another few seconds, his face pressed into his upper arm. He wanted to hike the dress over her hips and rip right through the pantyhose, but it wasn't the time. He tried to focus on something else. "It smells like fish under here."

"Well, duh. He's a fisherman." She kicked at a pair of old waders crusted with scales and dried fish guts for emphasis.

Sinter wrinkled his nose and was about to demand how she expected to pass at a fancy ball if they both smelled like fishmongers, but the sound of voices and gravel crunching made him swallow the words and pull her tight against him to keep her still. He pressed his face close to her ear and shushed her.

A shiver shimmied down her body and she took a breath, but then she must have heard it, too, because she went still against him.

He felt her heart thumping out the back of her rib cage and against his chest as the voices approached. Two men, deep in jovial conversation, their spirits clearly lifted by alcohol but they didn't sound drunk. Still talking, they split apart—one to either side of the truck—and then they stopped. Sinter heard keys jingling as Clapton said, "This is going to be a turning point for us."

"Buy my own boat."

"Pay off the mortgage." The door opened with a creak, then slammed. The truck rocked slightly as, Sinter assumed, Clapton leaned across the bench seat to unlock Jasper's door. The other door opened, and Jasper started saying, "I've seen some real beauties down in Portsmo—" but the door slammed again and Sinter could only hear muffled tones from within.

Herron let out a shuttering breath and relaxed against him. The truck came to life with an unhealthy rumble and the smell of tarp and fish was quickly overshadowed by the smell of diesel. Sinter pressed his face into Herron's neck, inhaling the smell of Dove soap and Aquanet off her skin. She shivered again, but didn't try to escape him. In fact, despite the heat, she snuggled deeper against him.

CHAPTER TEN

Heron had fallen asleep in the rocking comfort of Sinter's embrace when the sudden jarring of the truck going over a bump and then a strange rumble strip woke her. She heard men's voices all around her. Confused, she moved to sit up, but Sinter held her down.

"Hush," he whispered.

She did as she was told and a second later the truck came to a stop with a soft squeak of brakes. A moment later the slow whining crank of her brother's window and someone's voice from outside of the car said, "State your names."

"Clapton Jones and Jasper Hernandez."

There was a shifting of paper. "Okay, I see you. Special guests of Mr. Musgrave. Masks are required from this point on. Drive up to section A there on the left then take the stairs to level B. You're in seats A-6 and A-7, auction starts at eight. The viewing rooms will open once we're past the twelve-mile limit. There are cocktails and hors d'oeuvres in the main ballroom until then. Take everything with you when you go."

"Thanks."

Clapton didn't bother rolling the window up as he slowly accelerated forward. They were definitely inside of something from the sound of it.

"You see the way that dick looked at us?" she could hear Jasper demanding.

"Just suck it up. We only have to deal with it for a few hours and then we're done."

"Why'd we have to come to this anyway? Couldn't we just get the cash when Musgrave is done like always?"

"Cuz I want to see and hear the final bid myself," Clapton explained. "I've got my suspicions with him lately and he can't stiff us our cut if we know what the real bid is, now can he?"

Herron had to give her brother some credit for thinking that deeply, she didn't think he had that kind of brain.

The car jarred to a stop a moment later and they got out, the noise of the doors closing sounding cloistered as if they were in a garage.

"Whoa, are you seeing this, man?" Jasper squealed. "A Lamborghini Jalpa!"

"Don't touch it," Clapton hissed.

"The money in this ship alone... We're gonna make so much money!"

Clapton said, "Would you shut up and look a little bit like you belong here? People are staring."

And then they were too far away to hear anymore, their voices swallowed by the echoing of cars and voices and slamming doors and high heels shuffling. Herron lay with Sinter for what felt like forever. She needed to pee, she was sure her hair had collapsed from sweat, and her hip was all tingly. Eventually the noise died down entirely. There was a massive *whump*ing noise and suddenly a deep thrumming.

"We're in a ship," she whispered, recognizing the noise.

"You think it's safe?" Sinter asked.

Herron slowly leaned forward and grasped at the edge of the

tarp. The crinkling noise it made was far too loud in the quiet, but she figured it was better to just pull the band-aid off and ripped it away. For a long moment, she lay there breathing hard and listening as the blessed cool air touched her skin. No one seemed to be moving or speaking.

She peeked her head up and squinted in the orange glow of the low overhead lighting. It looked like they were in some kind of metal parking garage. She realized then they were on some kind of RORO. She sat up entirely.

"We're in a ship?" Sinter wondered, glancing around. "What kind of ship is this? A ferry?"

"Possibly." She struggled to her hands and knees. "Or a RORO or a CONRO. Maybe someone's personal hybrid?"

He grasped her hand as she attempted to dismount the truck on jelly legs. "A what?"

"Never mind," she grunted as she stretched. "Ugh, I stink."

"Yeah, I was afraid of that."

"Here, gimme my purse."

Sinter rummaged around in the canvas they'd been lying in and joined her on the knobby floor. He stretched and straightened himself as she dug out a travel-size bottle of Baby Soft and proceeded to douse herself in it. Then she turned it on him.

"Ugh," he breathed. "I don't want to smell like that."

She puffed one last spritz at him and then tucked it back. "Powder and floral is better than fish."

He wrinkled his nose, but said nothing else.

"Come here." She gestured for him to lean closer.

He gave her a suspicious brow lowering, but did as she requested. She straightened his tie and then combed her fingers through his sweaty hair, tacking it back into place. He looked like he'd had a sweaty row. Probably she did, too.

She pulled her hand back. "Do I still look okay?"

His eyes flit around her. "Your cheeks are pink and your hair is a bit messy. And you look like you're...what's that word...glistening?"

Scoffing, she looked away. At least he was trying to be polite. "Well," she breathed, pulling her mask from her bag, "maybe we can just pretend we decided to take our time coming out of the car. People won't ask too many questions. Too awkward." She pulled the mask across her face and began to tie it. "You see a stairwell anywhere? I can't see over these cars."

"Yeah." Sinter's hands slithered over hers and he took up tying her mask for her. When he finished, he turned her and clasped her chin, examining her. And then, suddenly and without warning, he leaned in and kissed her.

He kissed her long and hard and she kissed him back, aggressively. She had so many questions in her head but she silenced them and took joy in the feeling of his teeth biting and sucking at her lower lip. She was ready to explode for want of more when he finally pulled away and hovered less than an inch from her mouth.

"Wha—" she panted.

"We have to look believable, right?" he whispered, his own breathing heavy. She could feel his body hard and demanding against hers. She hated her clothes, hated that there was anything more important than this. "You weren't breathless enough," he added. Coming back in, his tongue snaked out and lapped gently at the crease of her mouth again. "Your lips weren't swollen enough."

Shuddering at the gesture, she forced her eyes closed. Of course, there was a reason. A good one. He wouldn't want to kiss her just to kiss her, how foolish. Taking a deep breath, she pulled away from him and forced a grin. "Well, how about now?"

His eyes seemed to burn along her skin as he took her in. "You look like you need more."

She turned away. "Well good. Then, it worked. Let's go."

CHAPTER ELEVEN

Sinter felt like he was going to explode. Out of his clothes, his body, his manhood, his mind. Everything was unspooling. He was going mad. Still, he forced his mask on and led Herron through the cars and toward the steps. They climbed up and up, their shoes ringing on metal as they went. They met no one as they moved.

And then they came to Level B and there were two men in solid black fatigues. Guns gleamed heavily in their hands. Herron's fingers tensed around Sinter's as they came onto the landing.

Sinter forced a smile and tried to remember everything he could from Bond and Gatsby. "Evening, gentlemen." He dragged Herron close to his side and kissed her forehead and she was smart enough to throw her arms around his waist and giggle like a drunk idiot. "This way to the ballroom?"

The men glanced him over, glanced her over, then looked at each other. One of them smirked slightly, then reached out and depressed the bar on the door, opening it for them. "This way, sir."

"Thank you, my good fellow."

Herron held onto him like a clinging burr until they were through the door and the door closed. They were in a narrow white hallway, alone again.

She released him but kept close to him. "Guns. Big ones."

He narrowed his eyes. He hadn't been sure what they'd be facing once they got onto the ship, but he hadn't really thought about any kind of security. As they rounded the corner and went through a set of double doors, he realized he hadn't been expecting anything like what they'd just walked into.

The ballroom was larger than any event space he'd ever been in. Massive crystal chandeliers hung low over intricate wood flooring. There were half a dozen banquet tables piled with dozens of kinds of cheeses, crackers, breads, fruits and vegetables. The bars were massive and carved in deep wood. There were black-tie waiters floating through the crowd balancing trays of fluted champagne, mixed drinks, and hors d'oeuvres. It smelled amazing.

And the people...there were hundreds of them, and even though Sinter had grown up in a well-to-do Long Island family, there was something about the milling black-clad mass that spoke of a sophistication that was beyond him. Even the conversations he caught snippets of seemed beyond him.

He didn't belong here. Neither did Herron.

Still...

"Champaign, sir?"

He glanced at the server to his right. Nodding, he took a crystal flute and tried to hold it like he'd been taught. Herron took one, too, and a second later she was swigging it like a shot of tequila.

He leaned close to her. "Take it easy."

"I need something to steady my nerves," she whimpered.

He squeezed her hand, telling her she wasn't alone. "Stay close."

"No worries here." She placed her glass on a passing tray and her eyes flashed across the crowd. "So, how do we find Nissa?"

It was a good question, one he didn't really know the answer to. She'd gotten them to the auction, but neither had really known what they'd be walking into so that made rescue a bit difficult. "I'll take ideas."

"Well, in some ways this is easier for you."

"How so?" He hadn't told her anything about his youth, being dragged to dinner parties and charity auctions.

"We're on a boat," she reasoned. "All we have to do is get you two outside and you can jump ship and escape."

She had a point. Being on a boat made things infinitely easier. Once they were in the water there was no hope of pursuit. They just had to break Nissa free and get her in the water. But... "Nissa and I can go, but what about you?"

She waved a hand dismissively. "I'll just climb right back into the truck and go home with Clapton. Go back to my boring life."

He frowned. The way she was talking annoyed him. Like they weren't going to see each other again. And maybe they wouldn't. He hadn't really thought that far. Hadn't thought about the fact that once he'd gotten Nissa he'd have to return to the pod. The press of them was just under his skin, tugging at him. The pod was closing in.

Once Galene found out what happened, she'd never let him go to shore again. He'd be lucky if she let him live. She always seemed to be looking for a reason to be rid of him. It was as if she regretted turning him in the first place. He didn't blame her. He didn't deserve to be one of the merfolk. He'd been told by the older merfolk that she'd needed a lot of convincing to turn him in the first place.

Merfolk weren't born, they were turned. Usually one really had to prove themselves an ally to the merfolk to be turned. Sinter hadn't done that. His father, Ezra Caldwell, had. Sinter only knew what he'd been told and according to those accounts, the merfolk had owed a debt of gratitude to his father. Anita, with her ability to read the true nature of a thing, was able to determine if a soul was worth saving.

His father had been a politician who had lobbied heavily for environmental protections and had helped to block a number of waterway harmful bills from passing. In the eyes of the merfolk, this made Ezra Caldwell worthy of saving.

But, when his father took him on a father-son fishing trip up to Cape Cod and some terrorist blew up their boat, it wasn't his father who was turned. It was Sinter. Galene claimed that it was because it had been his father's wish to save Sinter and the merfolk, for good or evil, always paid back in kind.

Sinter wondered how often Galene regretted paying that favor to Ezra Caldwell.

He regretted it often. His father had deserved to be saved so much more than Sinter had.

Herron was tugging on his sleeve. He blinked down at her, bringing his attention back to the present. She was holding some sort of puff pastry up.

"Try this, it's amazing."

He leaned down slightly and she placed it in his mouth.

"Mmmph," he groaned, closing his eyes as the crust burst and oozed the flavors of cheese, spinach, and chicken into his mouth.

She grinned. "I know, right?"

Mouth still full, he smiled back. Who cared whether he deserved being a mer or not? It had brought him to her and that was enough.

A moment later, there was a crackling over a PA system. "Ladies and gentlemen, this is your captain speaking." A sudden hush fell over the room. "I'd like to personally welcome you to the *Lady Belvedere*. At this time, we've just passed the twelve-mile limit and we will be taking anchor. The preview period for the auction will begin shortly. Please proceed through the main corridor and onto the main deck. Bidder registration will be conducted in Gallery A just outside of the auction theater. The auction will begin promptly at eight PM at which time the assets will be secured. Once the auction is complete, we will begin our journey to our second port of call. Please feel free to settle up your accounts and return to the ballroom where a second round of refreshments will be served for the duration of the journey."

Sinter and Herron exchanged a furtive glance. He set his glass down on the edge of a table. "That's our cue."

CHAPTER TWELVE

They were definitely on some kind of private CONRO. It was far smaller than any cargo ship Herron had ever seen in the port and way more glamorous, but there was no denying it once she was on deck and saw the neatly arranged lines of shipping containers. All of them were black and labeled with a white block letter that read *Belvedere*, and none of them were stacked.

As she and Sinter shuffled across the deck to make room for all the people filing out behind them, some fifty some-odd armed security men—each stationed outside of one of the containers—turned and began to unlock their respective containers.

Herron glanced around her. The only thing that separated the crowd from the containers was a line of theater-style stanchions. Everyone respected this barrier, the black-clad bodies giving a respectable distance to the burgundy velvet cords strung between the golden stands. There was an eerie sort of hush and stillness to the crowd. Anticipation.

She spotted her brother, obvious with his headphones slung around his neck. There were two men standing beside him. One, she assumed was Jasper, was whispering to a middle-aged, graying man with a mustache. She assumed maybe that was Musgrave. She turned her attention forward so as not to garner their attention. She didn't think her brother would recognize her or Sinter but one could never be too sure.

Sinter leaned close to her. "There are a lot of containers here."

She nodded. If one of them held a mermaid, she didn't want to see what might be in the other ones. Even so, they'd have to look in each in order to find Nissa. She dreaded the idea. They were here for Nissa and Nissa alone. They'd not thought up a way to save more than one of the poor souls that must be held in these containers. She knew there wasn't a way they could and it killed her.

A dark-haired man in a tailored suit and two guards on either side of him was making his way through the containers, his sharp, nearly black eyes glaring over the contents of each as if checking to make sure all was well before he accepted the key from the attending guard and locked it into a small, coded lockbox mounted on the door of the container. When he was finished, he shuffled toward the stanchions and, without a word or directive, unhooked one of the cords and opened a path.

Everyone went still like a held breath as the man turned back and retreated with two of his guards in tow. The other two remained. Only after he was out of sight did the two guards step away from the stanchions and let the people through.

Everything went at an unhurried, dignified pace. No running, no yelling. People didn't follow a queue. Instead, they fanned out, slipping in and around containers like smoke. Sinter led Herron to the container at the end of the farthest row and they made their way back and forth, aisle to aisle, eyes skimming over the contents of each.

Herron felt sick and dizzy.

A strange war of wonder at what she was seeing and disgust that it was here being sold off for some rich asshole's whims was occurring within her. Some of the items up for auction were recognizable things she'd expect at an auction. Art stolen by Nazis. Artifacts obtained from national historic sites. Jewels fabled to kill their wearers. Rare plants that only grew in the Himalayan Mountains. The only breeding pair of some strange monkey she'd never even heard of. Black-market biproducts like tusks and fossils.

Some items were vague and required her to stop and read the placards set on elegant stands within. They were favors. Guaranteed without question. Services of certain individuals and agencies. A hit on anyone. Something erased from a record. A politician's vote.

Some were information. The bank accounts of 200,000 individuals. The identity and whereabouts of a political spy.

Other things made her question her sanity. A unicorn haltered at the far end of its container. A pixie banging about in a metal birdcage. Items from these strange creatures: A kraken's tentacle in a massive tank. A dragon's egg. She wouldn't believe they were possible if she wasn't leaning so hard against a merman in an effort to keep from fainting.

Worse were those who were human, or close to. A woman purported to be a witch. A glass coffin containing a sleeping man who was supposedly a vampire. A massive wolf pacing in an enormous silver cage that was a werewolf. And then there was Nissa.

Sinter stopped short when they got to the entrance of her container and Herron bumped into his back. Confused, she glanced around his shoulder. There were three people in front of them, their bodies leaning over the stanchions placed across the entrance of the container and the armed guard leaning menacingly close with his gun white-knuckled in his hands. Herron could just make out the glowing blue of a massive glass tank and inside of it the dark waving locks and the silvery tail fin.

She stepped sideways, trying to see Nissa more clearly. The girl was slumped in a corner, her face turned away from the crowd and her arms and tail pulled in close.

Herron felt Sinter's fingers tighten around hers, almost to the point of pain. He was staring intently into the container. Herron nudged him slightly, trying to push him into action without causing a scene. He didn't want to move. She pushed her hand to the small of his back. "Let's move along, dear, other people want to see."

Sinter's feet reluctantly unstuck and he slowly plodded a few steps. She ushered him to the end of the aisle and around the corner of the last container where he sagged against the metal. Nervous, she glanced around but there was no one except a deck-hand at the far end of the ship who didn't seem to be paying attention.

She crouched in front of him. "You all right?"

He took a deep, shuddering breath. "I...I don't know. How are we going to do this?"

That was an excellent question. She was certain that, once the preview period was over, the containers would be locked up again and she doubted that the guard assigned to each was going anywhere anytime soon. She glanced at the crane system looming above her but, even if she knew how to operate the crane, what was she going to do with the locked container? There was nowhere to put it except to drop it into the sea. Which was all well and good except it was locked and leaving Nissa locked in a container at the bottom of the ocean didn't seem any kinder.

She nibbled her fingernail for a long moment in thought. "Okay, well, I'm sure we can agree the best time to try getting her out is either during the auction when everyone is back below deck and we only have security to contend with, or maybe wait until after the auction and try to follow her to her buyer's house and spring her then?"

His chin lifted and his eyes drifted back down the aisle. "What about the others?"

Yes, what about them? Clearly he wasn't just focused on Nissa anymore. She liked him more for that. She gave him a sad smile. Practicality called for a pincer move, something small scale and quick, but neither of them had it in them to sacrifice anyone for the price of another.

"Okay," she huffed. "There's got to be something we can do. If only we were on land and we could, like, pull a fire alarm or something to get everyone to leave the boat for a little bit."

Sinter straightened suddenly. "Alarm, no. But we do have a siren."

Herron knit her brows. "Huh?"

He shoved to his feet, hauling her up with him. "Come on, we need to find the bridge."

CHAPTER THIRTEEN

S inter leaned against the wall and peaked through the small glass window. There was only one person on the bridge that he could see. Most likely the captain was off somewhere else since the ship was anchored and he was not needed for the time being. The remaining person was dressed like one of the security men. His gun was propped against one of the consoles and he was sitting, feet propped up, his head bobbing to some rhythm and his eyes wandering across the screens in front of him. They were clearly hooked up to security cameras stationed all over the boat.

Sinter could see waitstaff bustling around the ballroom cleaning and setting up for the second round of refreshments after the auction. A few mask-clad passengers wandered the corridors along with various members of the crew. Security stood at most doors, but the bulk of them were on deck, stationed at their containers. A few passengers were already sitting in the theater with their paddles but most were split between making rounds of the containers and the registration table in the atrium.

Slowly and as quietly as he could, Sinter grasped the handle and turned it. It felt like eternity creeping into the room without being noticed. He doubted the guard could hear much of anything over the blaring boombox propped on the console. As the guard started singing along to Prince, Sinter reached out, eased a pair of noise canceling headphones off the radio console, and passed them back to Herron.

She gave him a questioning expression and he mimed to put them on. She did as she was told and gave him a thumbs up. He pointed at his ear and then the boombox, asking if she still heard anything. She shook her head no.

He took a deep breath, steeling himself. And then he reached for the gun.

CHAPTER FOURTEEN

S inter cracked the guard in the back of the head with the butt of the gun. Herron squeaked in surprise as the man crumpled to the floor. For a long moment, she stared at the blood welling from the man's bald head and pooling on the floor. She'd known Sinter planned to incapacitate the guard, but she hadn't expected something so violent.

Mouth too dry, she swallowed. What had she expected? It's not like a merman would know some secret *Karate Kid* moves.

Shaking, she looked away from the man and back to Sinter who was examining the switches, dials, and buttons on one of the consoles. Her heart was racing. She glanced back toward the door, anxious that someone would come. But no one did.

A moment later, Sinter waved a hand at her to get her attention and then gave her a questioning thumbs up. He was holding the microphone for the PA system in the other hand. Biting trembling lips, she nodded.

He flipped a switch. A light went from red to green on the console. He lifted the microphone and his lips started to move. He was singing, she could see that, but she couldn't hear him. She wanted to hear him. Her fingers twitched and she felt an itch to pull the headphones off. He was watching her and seemed to understand her urge. Still singing, his eyes turned to a warning and he nodded his head back toward the mounted screens.

Eager for something else to look at, she turned her attention to the milling bodies on the black and white screen. Like little ants, passengers, crew, and guards alike were all in perfect step slowly swaying and bumping their way away from what they'd been doing moments before and toward the bridge.

It was working. It was actually working! Heart lifting, she grinned at Sinter who smiled while he sang and waved a hand toward the door.

Herron went.

When she rounded the corner and ran smack into the chest of who she could only assume was the captain, she thought she was done for. But he didn't even look at her. He just shuffled past her and trundled down the hall. She watched him go, worried for Sinter, but when the captain got to the open door to the bridge he just stood there and stared into the room. Stared at Sinter, she assumed.

Satisfied that he was probably safe as long as he kept singing, she turned and made her way down the stairs and toward the deck where the containers were. She passed what felt like the entirety of the ship on her descent, but no one stopped her. It was the opposite, in fact, she stopped each member of the crew until she came to the person she was looking for. One finely dressed, dark-haired gentleman with a briefcase cuffed to his wrist. He shuffled forward like a zombie as she rooted through his pockets for the key to the cuffs. She relieved him of the briefcase and ran down the hall with it.

Halfway to the deck she came across an emergency ax stored in a glass case. She clawed the case open, took up the ax, and began to hack at the case.

While she and Sinter had been in the ballroom, Herron had caught an interesting conversation going on between an old man and his much younger date. It must have been her first time at the event because she said something about wearing her emerald out of the auction house and he'd made a point to correct her.

The man explained that upon payment directly after the auction, they'd be given a container key and a code. Upon reaching their second port of call, the attendees would disembark in their personal vehicles and were expected to head home. Each container would be unloaded and sent separately via secure transport to the agreed upon location where the attendee would use the key and the code to retrieve their asset for further transfer.

His little date was not pleased with the delay in her expected present, but Herron had found it quite interesting. As expected, this black-market auction required some special measures. The boat made a point to move at least twelve miles from shore. It wasn't entirely lawless in these waters, but it certainly was easier than conducting shady business in a clear jurisdiction. They'd left from Portland and clearly wouldn't return there because it would look suspicious after only a few hours away from port and none of the cargo having been unloaded. Having the auction attendees drive into the boat allowed for the carrier to go to any chosen port of call without actually telling them where they'd be let off. And the containers made so much sense. Letting the customers just off-board with their asset was too risky. Using shipping containers offered a cover as well as a method to move the assets, no questions asked.

Herron marveled at the genius of it and wondered how long it had been going on. Once they moved on deck for the preview, she'd made a note to pay attention. She'd watched the dark-haired man take the container keys and secure them in coded lockboxes mounted inside each of the containers. Watched the guards take up position right in front of those coded boxes.

As she and Sinter walked aisle to aisle, she saw that in each container, the asset was contained in a secondary way within the container, an added level of security, no doubt. Locked cages, doors, and display cases.

She'd guess that the codes the auction attendees would be given would open those boxes, but there was no point in getting codes to the boxes if they were also handed the container key...unless there was something else in each of the coded lockboxes. And she was almost 100% sure the coded boxes contained a way to open the second level of containment.

Finally, the edge of the case splintered apart. Herron bent and dumped out the contents. A stack of manilla folders slid out across the floor. She grabbed one and skimmed its contents. When she found what she wanted, she scrambled to gather them together and hugged them to her chest as she continued to make her way to the deck.

She wondered how long Sinter could sing before getting tired. At least a half hour? 45 minutes? Concerts were usually at least an hour long, right? But she assumed he wasn't a trained vocal artist and even vocal artists stopped singing between songs. He'd have to keep singing, right? One song's final lyrics stringing into the beginning of another one. And what happened during the natural pauses? What happened when one took a breath?

She shoved her worries out of the way as she made it to the deck. Every single one of the containers was left open and abandoned as expected. Her heart, the only thing she could hear in this place, seemed to know exactly where the correct containers were.

The first one she came to was the unicorn. She shoved the stanchion over, set the files down on the metal floor, and shuffled through them until she found one with a number that matched the unicorn's container number. The unicorn was nothing but a number to these monsters. Annoyed, she stood and punched in the code she found on the bottom of the page into the lockbox. A light blinked and it snapped open. A shuddering breath escaped her as she found not one, but two keys hanging inside. She'd guessed right. One had a tag matching the container number, so she assumed the other, smaller one was for the lock on the unicorn's stall door.

She grabbed the key and advanced on the stall door. The key fit the lock and the door swung open. The unicorn pranced on cloven hooves and swung away from her, tugging at its lead rope.

Breathing hard, Herron stepped inside. She didn't have the time to worry about her own safety. She only hoped the creature understood she was trying to free it. She tiptoed through the hay, her hands held up. The unicorn lifted its head and eyed her. She went still, staring at it a long moment. Herron tried her hardest to think friendly, *I'm here to help* thoughts. Its nostrils vibrated in a snort and it lowered its head, allowing her to reach forward and unfasten the buckles to the halter.

When the leather halter fell away, the unicorn demi-bucked and charged out of the carrier. Herron knew it had nowhere to go, but she assumed that now it at least had a fighting chance.

She moved on.

The pixie who dive-bombed her as soon as it flew from the cage. The monkeys who wouldn't leave their enclosure.

It was slow going so she changed her tactic and went to Nissa next so at least she'd be able to free the little girl if shit went to pot at any moment.

When Herron got to Nissa's container, the mermaid was upright in her tank, palms pressed against the glass and face turned toward the bridge as if listening. She clearly recognized Sinter on the loud-speakers.

Herron opened the lockbox, removed the key, charged forward, and climbed the short set of steps to the top of the tank. Nissa swam to the bottom of the tank and curled into a ball, clearly afraid. Herron focused on the metal grate locked over the top of the tank, but her fingers were so shaky and sweaty that the key slipped from her fingers and landed in the water.

"Shit," Herron breathed. Herron banged on the grate to get the mermaid to look at her. "Nissa, I'm here to help!"

Nissa looked up but remained at the bottom of her tank. Maybe Nissa couldn't understand what she was saying through the water?

"I'm here with Sinter," Herron explained, growing more panicked by the second. What if Nissa wouldn't leave with her? It was bad enough the monkeys had just stayed sitting in their cage staring stupidly at her. She dug her fingers into the grating. "That's him singing, can't you hear him? We're trying to free you."

Nissa backed up to the far side of the tank and surfaced. There was just enough clearance from the top of the water to the grate for her head. She said something.

Herron shook her head and pointed at the headphones. "I can't hear you." She pointed downward. "I need you to get the key."

Frowning, Nissa looked down but stayed in place.

"Nissa, honey, I swear I'm not gonna hurt you. I'm going to take you back to the ocean as soon as you get that key for me."

Nissa slid back under the water. Even though it was only a few feet it felt like eternity waiting for her to come back up. When she did, she shoved the key back through the grate for Herron. Herron went back to the lock and then hauled the grate up.

"Okay, come on," she offered Nissa her hand.

The little girl stared at it and then back at her, but eventually her cold, skinny fingers slid into Herron's. Herron hauled with all her might and managed to get Nissa up and over the side of the tank and tumbled backward with her. They both went over the rail and landed hard between the tank and the wall of the container.

For a long moment, Herron felt nothing but pain and cold wetness. Nissa was squirming around on top of her.

"Okay, okay," she breathed, trying to shove the mermaid off of her and sit up. "We need to go. You gotta put your legs on."

Nissa gave her a baleful expression and shook her head.

"No? What do you mean no?" Herron grunted, shoving the little girl backward. "It will be faster." She finally managed to sit up.

Shrugging, Nissa gestured to her flopping silver tail.

Crimping a brow, Herron studied her. "You can't?"

The girl nodded.

She couldn't make legs? Was she limited in a way Sinter wasn't? She shook her head and got to her feet. She didn't have time for guessing games. "Okay, I'll just have to take you like this." Nissa was young, but she weighed more than any ten-year-old had any right to. Herron couldn't carry her so she hooked her hands under Nissa's arms and dragged her out of the container.

"Look, kid," she grunted, her shoes slipping on the deck. "Once you get overboard I'm gonna need you to go to the bow and sing your little heart out. You gotta lead them away from Sinter so he can get out."

Nissa glanced up at her and nodded.

She was just turning the corner at the end of one aisle when something came out of nowhere and slammed into her.

She felt Nissa's body wrench out of her grip with the force of it. She skidded on sequins a few feet before hitting a shipping container. For a long moment, she was stunned to stillness, couldn't see.

Someone was going at Nissa, their hands grasping at her. Nissa thrashed in the man's grip, striking him with her tail.

"S-Stop!" Herron managed to yell. She took the only thing she could reach—her headphones—and pelted him in the head with it. It distracted him enough to loosen his grip on Nissa, who wriggled away. The man stumbled after her, but out of nowhere the unicorn charged at him, rearing and making him fall backward. The unicorn lowered its head, menacing him with its horn as it stood guard between Nissa and the man.

Herron was just starting to regain her feet and then suddenly the man was turning and coming at her. He slammed into her again, his shadow looming over her, his hands on her neck.

As he lifted her in a painful squeeze, her eyes came clear again and she realized the man choking the life out of her was Clapton. Her own brother. His mask was gone, his face red with hate. His headphones were perched on his head blaring something with a heavy country beat. He couldn't hear Sinter.

Wait, *she* couldn't hear Sinter.

He'd stopped. Stopped singing.

No. No, no, no. Herron kicked, grabbed hold of Clapton's wrists and tried to wrench herself free. She tried to wriggle in his grasp, tried to plead with him.

"Cla—" she whimpered. Didn't he know it was her? Couldn't he tell? Did it even matter? So many times she'd been certain he was going to kill her. He never did, though. Something always stopped him.

He slammed her backward, smashing her head into the container. Grey was closing around the edges of her vision. "You stupid bitch, you thought you could steal from me?"

He was gone. Insane.

She clawed at him, at his face, at his headphones. She got tangled in wire.

"It's my money. Mine!" He slammed her again.

Black. Black and spots. Pain around her neck burning in her lungs. She choked and whimpered. He was going to kill her this time. She knew it. She just knew it.

CHAPTER FIFTEEN

Sinter had been watching it all on the screens in the bridge. He'd sung louder and higher with each of Herron's little defeats. Getting the briefcase and the codes—he'd not even noticed such a thing! And her success at freeing the unicorn, the pixie, the monkeys, and Nissa! He was so proud to see her dragging the little mermaid out of that container he practically crowed.

But he didn't. He just sang, jubilant and with a stupid grin on his face. He didn't notice other movement on other screens. Didn't see Clapton charging into Herron until it was too late. He faltered then, his breath whooshing out of him. The world felt still and silent as her body flew one way and Nissa went the other.

He'd held his breath for the next few seconds. The man going for Nissa, Herron and the unicorn stopping him. And then Clapton advancing on Herron. And nothing intervened for her.

"No," he whispered.

He didn't understand. What was happening? Why hadn't Clapton come to the bridge like everyone else?

Someone grabbed him from behind, pulling him away. "No!" he screamed, whipping around and trying to run. Trying to get to her.

227

To stop Clapton. They wrestled him down to the floor, knees and hands pressing into his back.

"Herron!" he screamed.

He was crying. Hysterical. He trashed and wailed.

"Stop him, he's gonna kill her!"

"Take it easy. Take it easy," someone said.

And then the hands were gone. The crushing knees were gone. Sinter whipped around, but the bodies that had been holding him were nothing but retreating shadows on the hallway wall. He clamored to his feet, threw himself at the console, his eyes raking the screens. Where? Where was she? He couldn't see her. Not her or Clapton.

"Fuck," he breathed and turned back toward the door. He was shoving past shambling bodies in the hall when he realized that he could hear shrieking.

He recognized the sound of Nissa wailing as if her hair was on fire. He'd heard his little sister's cries so many times in the past year. Sinter's breath wobbled out of him. At least she's still alive, but that screaming? Was Clapton going after her now?

He darted around bodies, finding the ax Herron left abandoned in the hallway with the broken briefcase and held it high as he waded through the people bottlenecked at the exit to the deck. Sinter practically climbed over them, not caring who he hurt in his effort. When he finally got through, finally found the spot he'd seen in the camera, Herron was slumped a few feet away on the deck. Unmoving.

He skidded to a stop and fell to his knees beside her. He shook her. Called her name. There was nothing left, her eyes were open and lifeless. He couldn't find a pulse and her crushed neck warned him no amount of mouth-to-mouth was going to work. Herron was gone.

Red lanced through Sinter's vision. His hands found the ax and he was on his feet again. The shuffling mass that had followed his song all the way to the bridge was now making its way toward the bow. It occurred to him that Nissa was still shrieking and the shrieking wasn't so much mindless wailing but a keening sort of song. And everyone was now following it.

After all, it wasn't about the song or whether the singer had a good voice. It was about the lure within that voice. The magic and intent.

At the forefront of that magic was Clapton. Shambling and mindless, his still blaring headphones dangling from the cassette player clipped at his belt. The sight of that stupid little crescent somehow managed to anger Sinter more. Roaring, Sinter bolted forward and buried the ax in the back of Clapton's head. Clapton's body buckled and hit the deck.

Breathing hard, Sinter hefted the ax over his shoulder and glanced over the side of the ship. When Nissa saw him she stopped her keening song and grinned at him, relief clear on her face. He didn't grin back.

He could hear the people on deck again. Someone screamed. He knew what he looked like and he was ready for justice.

A head popped up in the water beside Nissa. Galene. More heads quickly followed.

The pod had finally found them.

A tightness released inside of Sinter, but the pain went nowhere.

Galene began speaking to Nissa. They were too far away and the chaos on board was growing too loud for him to hear what Galene was saying, but he thought he already knew. There was only one true law for the merfolk and it was vengeance.

Yes, he thought, turning back toward the people scrambling on deck. There were security people pointing guns at him now. *This is what being merfolk is all about.*

"Hands above your head!" one of them shouted.

In response, Sinter said, "Sing." And then he screamed it. "Sing!"

And they did. All the merfolk down below began to sing. One voice joining another in an overlapping chorus—that haunting siren song that had made them infamous and nightmarish in the folktales of humans.

But they weren't folktales. The merfolk were real, and he was one of them. So was Nissa. And vengeance was the one sweet consolation they were granted.

One by one, the zombie-like passengers and crew stumbled past Sinter and threw themselves into the sea. There, they would drown.

Maybe.

Perhaps there was a worthy one among them. Perhaps Anita would see the virtue within someone and Galene would turn them into a mer as she had with everyone else in the pod.

Sinter doubted it, though. The only worthy person on this ship was lying still and lifeless, beyond the shambling hoard clogging the bow. She was not destined to be a siren like Sinter. Instead, she would become a muse...a reason for him to sing. It was because of her he was now ready to cut the line.

DEEP SEA DREAM

Thea Dane

CHAPTER ONE

G*alway Bay, 1720*

EVERY TIME NYANZA came ashore to work her merchant stall at the marketplace, she was reminded of just how loud and crude humans were.

"Fresh fish for sale," a fishmonger bellowed. She heard him clear down the other end of the beach. "Get half a barrel at a quarter of the price."

She wrinkled her nose as the stench of rotting fish assailed her with the change in wind direction. Clearly, the fish was not fresh but who was she to keep another seller from making a profit? She yawned while observing people from the town move in the direction of the fishmonger's voice and his smelly wares.

Ah, such was life. Fish didn't fare so well on land. Even those who were only half-fish. Seated on a bench behind her table of shell and sea glass baubles, Nyanza wiggled her temporary feet beneath her voluminous skirts.

It was the last day of the phase of the new moon. The sea would soon be calling for her to return home. She looked at the blue-green beads strung on her brown wrist. She sold twelve such bracelets this morning. With luck, she'd be able to sell the rest of her jewelry before she left land again for another month to join the rest of her pod.

Her eyelids drifted down. Nyanza always got sleepy before it was time to return to the waves. Galene, the first siren, as timeless as the ocean itself, once told her it had to do with her gift. Rest was important for Nyanza's gift to flourish.

In addition to crafting pretty jewelry, she could interpret dreams.

"You, girl."

She glanced up as a man and woman came to her stall. The man who spoke to her was dressed in the drab garb of the town's street sweep. His dirty brown hair was fixed in a shoulder-length braid that kept unraveling in the wind. His companion was dressed in similar fashion, although her hair was cut short at the chin, likely due to a case of head lice. She scratched at her scalp as she perused the items on the table.

"Good afternoon." Nyanza addressed them with politeness even though she'd just been referred to as a girl. Admittedly, the nutrient-rich waters of the sea kept the skin soft and supple, but there was nothing about her twenty-eight-year-old bosom and hips to indicate girlishness. "What can I interest you in today?"

"How much do these fetch?" The woman lifted one of the necklaces and dangled it between her stained fingers like a minnow she snatched from a creek.

Nyanza restrained herslef from taking it away from her. She worked hard on those necklaces and didn't wish to have the beads spilling across the table and into the sand. "The one you're holding is one pound, two shillings. The ones with smaller beads fetch for eight to ten shillings."

The woman scoffed. "How to you expect to sell these trinkets for such a price?"

Simply say you can't afford them and move on. Nyanza kept the thought to herself. "They are popular and sell well in other ports, my lady."

"Hm." She set the necklace down. "I don't think you'll have much luck here in Galway, but good day to you."

Nyanza straightened the necklace as the woman and her companion walked away. Nyanza never had much luck in Galway.

To be honest, that was an understatement.

It would've been better had her family never set foot in town to do business all those years ago. They were part of the *daoine goirme*, the Black African Irish. Her father was a carpenter. Her mother was a cook and midwife.

How different things were today than they were almost ten years ago. She closed her eyes, succumbing to the desire to sleep. Although, she didn't want to dream. A decade had passed, and she could still hear the sound of chains hitting the water to this day. The cruel laughter carried on above her from the pirates who were paid to throw her overboard.

Nyanza's limbs even now recalled the heavy helplessness as she once sank beneath the roiling waves. But nothing was heavier than the sinking feeling of her dashed hopes of being rescued.

"Pardon me, Miss."

Another man's voice cut through the roar of the ocean. She opened my eyelids and shut them again at once as bright sunlight brought pain to them. The roar of the ocean in her head was replaced with the noise of the busy marketplace.

She must have been dreaming again. Always, the same dream.

She put her hand above her eyes to shield them. When she opened them again, the man who addressed her stood directly in her field of vision. He shifted, and his tall, broad-shouldered form blocked the sun.

"Sir, I didn't see you standing there."

The sun tried to peek above his wheat-colored short hair. "Most people don't say that to me. I'm hard to miss." He presented a playful smile.

Nyanza didn't return it. Instead, she searched his face for hidden vanity or a proposition behind the blue eyes. Out here by the sea, away from their warm homes and rules imposed by the church and the nobility, men tended to loosen the ties on their civilized masks. They showed their greed at the promise of riches at sea or the warm, supple body of a washerwoman plying her wares both in and out of the stall.

Nyanza was not in the business of selling promises or pleasure. So what brought this man to her stall? She took note of his garb. The fabric of his white shirt and grey pants were weathered as though he'd been out to sea, yet the fine seams indicated wealth. Despite the cool day and brisk wind, he wore no coat like a nobleman or rich merchant. Instead, his shirtsleeves were rolled high above his elbows. He had the tanned, muscled arms of a sailor. "Sir, I work with both the jewels of the sea and of the mind. Which of those two can I interest you in today?"

The fabric of his shirt stretched taut as he folded his arms across his chest. Despite the cool day, heat wound through her body. She shifted her gaze from his arms and saw that he glanced at the jewelry. "Ah, a gift for a lovely young maiden, perhaps?" She swept her hand over the selection of sea glass jewelry. "Would the lady enjoy a bracelet to adorn her graceful hand?"

"The jewelry is pleasant to look at." He frowned as he granted her the compliment. "I don't wish to buy any."

Nyanza ceased my flowery language to address him plainly. "Then I'm afraid I'm of no use to you. This is what I have available at this stall. Now if you're looking for something else—"

He dropped a brown drawstring bag on the table. She heard the distinct clink of coins. "Tell me about my dream."

His eyes held a wild, near desperate gleam to them. How could she not have noticed the first time? Too distracted by a pair of strong arms. She chastised herself while folding her hands on the table. She would not reach for the bag of coin right away, though she could tell it was heavy with currency from the way it fell on the table. "Your dream, sir?"

His shoulders tensed. "You are a seer, are you not?"

"Not quite. For you see, a seer is someone who can see what the future holds. I can tell you what I see, but the meaning may have more than one interpretation."

"I don't need all that flowery language." He waved his hand. "If you can interpret dreams, then you are the woman I'm looking for."

Patience was not his strong suit. Then again, it wasn't with most men who were in desperate search of something. Nyanza peered at the one who stood before her. Perhaps he was still in his twenties. The sun may have weathered his clothes and bronzed his skin, but the lack of lines on his face told her this man was still young. "Are the dreams troubling?"

"Very much so." He looked around. Most of the people in the marketplace were gathered near the fishmonger. "I wish to do this in private."

"I can't leave my stall."

"One of my hired guards is standing nearby. He will keep watch on your stall while we speak."

Nyanza glanced about and saw no one in particular who stood out from among the crowd. It could be a good thing for a guard to pass unnoticed. But who was this man who had the arms of a sailor, the clothes of a noble, and the face of a painting? Why did she get the strangest sensation that she'd seen him once before?

She reached for the bag. The coins jingled as she slid it into her lap. It was indeed heavy. Whatever dreams this man had, they must have been quite disturbing for him to offer this price for their meaning.

"Shall we go?" He held out his hand to help her to her feet. This was different, a man of the merchant or noble class offering a hand to a nameless stall vendor. He didn't want people to know he sought an interpreter of dreams. He needed to be careful for other people not to see this, either.

Heat laced through her body again, increasing as their hands touched. Did he notice, too? "That is quite chivalrous of you to aid me to my feet. Careful, though, you never know if there are noblemen and women who might protest to you touching the hand of a foreigner."

He observed their joined hands. His long fingers covered hers. "My mother, before she died, taught me to always be kind to women."

"Your mother is wise." When she once lived in Galway, Nyanza remembered a woman with the same sea-blue eyes as his. She would visit Nyanza's mother's house to buy cooking and medicinal herbs. She spoke often of having to brew mint tea to soothe her sensitive stomach. Was this man her son?

The question never reached Nyanza's lips. She struggled to keep up as the man practically pulled her along in the rocky sand until they were yards away from the marketplace in a different location on the shore. She noted he was very tall. Her head came towards the middle of his back.

"If you're going to tow me along like a fresh catch, I'd at least like to know your name."

He slowed his pace and walked alongside her. Their hands were still entwined. "Apologies. My name is Caelan."

Now where did she hear that name before? She wanted to search her mind, but the name was not an uncommon one for this land.

They stopped walking once they reached the beginning slope of a cliff face. He stood in front of her, concealing her from view of those in the marketplace. "What do I call you?"

Miss will do. She almost uttered the words she reserved for most people who came to her stall. Another strange sense came over her. She didn't wish to be curt with this man. He looked so desperate for answers. "Nyanza."

He repeated her name in his Irish lilt. "It's a beautiful name."

"Thank you, Caelan. I don't think you brought me here to compliment my name. Tell me about this dream of yours."

His face turned glum. "I must warn you, it's scandalous."

"Aren't all the good dreams?"

Her teasing did nothing to lift his mood. He stared out to sea with a torn look in his eyes. This dream must have vexed him for days. "I can't have scandal. I'm betrothed to a merchant's daughter. Her father owns four spice ships and leases half of the properties in town."

"I see." Nyanza knew there had to be a maiden involved. Maybe he should've bought a necklace after all to smooth things over. "Perhaps you simply don't tell her about the dream, yes?"

"No. You don't understand. This wasn't a single dream. I keep having it, and every single time, I fail to learn who the woman in the dream is. I only know it is not Maire."

"Be truthful with me. Is there another woman?"

"No." He turned back to her. "I mean, not in my life. In the dream. I have to know who she is."

"Forgive me for prying, Caelan, but could it be this woman exists only in your dream?"

"I want you to pry. I will pay more for you to pry if I have to. Just tell me who this woman is. I feel as though I've seen her before."

"I'll see what I can do, but I make no promises." Nyanza stretched her arms to take him by the shoulders. There was both strength and tension in them. "Lower your head to mine. You must not be shy."

He inclined his head. Nyanza's feet were sinking in the sand. Her attempt to stand on tiptoe to make contact with him was laughable. *We should have taken the bench with us, either for him to sit or me to stand.*

His brow touched hers. She felt his breath on her face. A new recognition curled in her stomach. This was an interpretation of dreams, not a lover's tryst. Besides, he already said he was betrothed to some maid named Maire. Nyanza needed to see about this pesky

239

dream of his so he could get back to planning his wedding and securing that small fleet of spice ships.

"Just hold still. I'm told it feels like a tickle inside your head."

Nyanza closed her eyes and began the ritual. She attuned herself to the sound of his breathing and the feel of his skin, letting the distant noise of the marketplace and the ever-present ocean drift away. Soon, the bright sun faded. She no longer felt the soft sand shifting beneath her feet.

Now she stood in a darkened area. Was this a room? No, she heard the sound of gentle lapping water. This was a small water cavern or grotto.

More sounds. Breathless whispers, pleasured gasps. She concentrated, searching for the source. Then she saw an image of Caelan, naked in the water, his torso glistening with saltwater and sweat. His eyes were closed as he moved in the throes of lovemaking.

A woman clung to him. Both of their images were faded as though being viewed from clouded glass. The woman's legs were wrapped around his waist. Nyanza could not make out the shade of her hair. The shadows covered it. She focused on her limbs. That's when she saw the woman's legs gleamed, not with water but they had patches of shimmering green scales.

This woman...was her. In human form.

Her heart raced as she tried to escape the sight. This couldn't be right. That couldn't be her clinging to Caelan.

She opened her eyes and pulled away from Caelan. His eyes were wide open. His lips were parted. He gazed at her with an intensity that made her body feel like it was on fire and doused in an ice bath at the same time.

"It was you." His voice was hoarse.

"No." She stepped away from him.

"I saw it this time. The woman in my dreams is you."

She could only keep shaking her head. "I'm sorry. You are mistaken." Her hand trembled as she reached into her pocket for the bag of coins. She tossed them in the sand at his feet and ran away.

CHAPTER TWO

C aelan went over what he'd just witnessed. Nyanza was the woman in his dreams. All this time, the picture was blurry in his mind. He could never see the woman in his arms.

Until now.

And just as soon as he learned her identity, she slipped away. He stared at the bag of coins she tossed in the sand at his feet. She ran across the beach and disappeared behind the foot of a cliff to go around to the other side. It was too late for him to catch up to her.

Small waves rolled up to the escarpment before retreating towards the sea. The tide would arrive soon. Nyanza must have been hiding a pair of webbed feet beneath her dress in order to climb over those rocks so fast.

His humor left him as quickly as it formed when he remembered he still faced a dilemma. He was drawn to Nyanza, almost to the point of feeling that he knew her before. Was such a thing possible?

Now that he knew she was the woman from his dreams, he would not wed Maire. He had to tell her and his father.

He pocketed the bag of coins and returned to the marketplace.

His guard stood near Nyanza's stall. The guard looked to him for instruction.

"Keep watch on the woman's stall until I return. See that no one takes anything from it. If she returns before me, say nothing and move away."

The guard nodded. Caelan took his leave of the marketplace and started back on the path to town. His steps were heavy as he thought what this new revelation meant for him moving forward. He came close to being struck by a falling barrel from an ale cart.

"Apologies, McDonagh." The driver called him by his surname. "I didn't see you behind the cart."

"It's good I saw you. No apologies needed, except for the person who purchased the ale."

Caelan hurried on about his business. As the man was one of his father's merchants, he would normally stay and converse. Today, he had no time to lose.

He marched past several businesses before arriving at the building that housed his father's office. He pulled open the door and found his father at his desk.

Rhodes McDonagh poured over piles of leather-bound ledger books with a magnifying glass and a quill pen. His calloused fingers were stained blue-black from the ink. He heard Caelan enter and peered up at him with a deep-seated scowl on his face. "I figured it might be you barging in. I heard the ship returned from the Capri Isles early this morning."

"Yes, father. I took some time to visit the marketplace first."

His scowl deepened. "That rabble. You have no need to go there. Nothing but strong drink and a soft pair of thighs to purchase."

Caelan was used to his father's insinuations. In his former life, Rhodes studied to be a man of the cloth, but his family ran out of money for his education. He also got caught with Caelan's mother. Caelan was the product of that scandalous discovery and an ever-constant reminder to his father of his thwarted ambition.

What Rhodes McDonagh couldn't accomplish from the pulpit, he made do with his pen, executing orders and keeping track of the men who moved his mercantile across town and over the seas. Anyone who crossed him was reported to the town's authorities and dealt with swiftly. Cruelly, may have been a better term.

"I didn't go to the marketplace to carouse, if that's what you mean."

"Why are you here, then, boy? Can you not see that I'm busy going over this month's sales and exports?"

Caelan steeled himself. Even though he was a fully grown man now at twenty-five, his father's dismissiveness left a bitter taste in his mouth. "I cannot wed Maire."

Rhodes's pen ceased moving. Ink dripped on the white space of his ledger book. He didn't notice as he gave Caelan a coarse glare. "What did you just say?"

"You heard me, father. I'm calling off the betrothal. I've never seen or spoke to Maire in person so it won't be too much trouble for her to forget this whole thing. I'm going to write to her family, offer my sincerest apologies, and send a sum of appeasement."

His father's knuckles were white as he gripped the pen and flattened his other hand on the desk. "Clearly, you thought this through enough to plot your leave of a successful and wealthy match. At least tell your old father what inspired this sudden burst of creativity?"

"If you must know, I met another woman. It would not be honorable or fair to Maire for me to pretend this won't affect our arrangement."

The pen clattered to the desk, sending ink droplets splattering across the wood surface and the front of his father's neatly-pressed shirt. Rhodes did not notice. "You carried on with a whore from a distant port and now you wish to throw away your betrothal to a woman from one of our country's richest mercantile families?"

Caelan's ire rose at yet another false accusation. This one was directed at Nyanza. Even though there was mystery surrounding her, he felt compelled to defend her honor. "She is not a whore and we did not 'carry on'."

"Well, then, who is she? What's her name? Does she come from a prominent family?"

All the questions he threw at once. Caelan couldn't answer them all. The one he could answer, he chose to remain silent, knowing his father's history of making his enemies' lives miserable. "I don't know." He admitted the truth. He knew little about Nyanza, except that something inside told him he had to find her again.

His father gave a humorless laugh. "You don't know? You would throw away everything you and I worked for over an unnamed woman."

"She has a name."

"What is it?"

He saw the look in his father's eyes, that intentional, fixed gaze. He was ready to put his pen to work again, launching an investigation into yet another person. "I cannot say. No, I won't say."

Rhodes launched to his feet and jabbed a crooked finger at him. "Do not dare to clench your fists at me, boy. Now, I don't have time for games. You will keep your betrothal to Maire. I don't want to hear any more about some unnamed buxom port wench, do you understand?"

"I understand you, father. Now you understand me. I will make my own decisions when it comes to whom I wed. The betrothal is off. I'm writing Maire."

Caelan turned to leave. Something sailed past his ear and shattered against the door. He watched as ink splattered and stained the polished wood. The broken well lay on the floor in pieces.

"Get you gone." Rhodes clenched his teeth. "I never in my life expected to have such a worthless brat. Get on a ship and do not return unless you have something or someone worthy of the McDonagh name."

Caelan stepped over the broken inkwell, opened the door, and left his father's office.

Outside, the sun was setting over the horizon. He stayed in his father's office going back and forth with him for too long. He broke into a run, following the path of lanterns through the town and returned to the marketplace. He grew uneasy as he saw most of the merchants had torn down their stalls for the night.

Was he too late? Did Nyanza already leave?

His loyal guard was still at his post when he arrived. So was Nyanza's stall. The guard gave him a shrug. "She never came back."

How strange for a merchant to leave their wares and stall unmanned. Did Caelan frighten her with the dream? Did she know more about it that she didn't have a chance to tell him?

Questions swirled in his brain like a whirlpool created by the tides against a rocky shore. He would've kept it to myself if he'd known this would upset her.

But he had no prior inkling that the two of them would be connected.

"We can't leave her stall out here all night. Someone will pocket the jewelry."

The guard looked helpless for a solution. "A storm's coming in."

Caelan felt the strong wind against his back. At this rate, they'd be finding Nyanza's jewelry half-buried in the sand by morning. "We'll take down the stall, store the jewelry, and put both on my ship. If Nyanza doesn't come back in the morning to claim it, I'll keep it safe for her until I return to port."

"You're leaving?"

"I have business in a neighboring port." He kept the details of his departure to a minimum. It would be best for all parties involved, his own father included, for him to leave as soon as possible. The marketplace traveled. Hopefully, he'd see Nyanza here or at another port soon.

He wished he asked her how she traveled but it would have been prying. He wanted—no, had to—learn all he could about her. A forbidden heat traveled down his body at the thought of her soft dark skin and mass of braided black hair on her shoulders, adorned with gold pieces and shells from the sea.

He vowed to himself to find Nyanza. He wouldn't stop looking until he saw her deep brown eyes again.

Ψ

*VERDANT ISLAND, two miles off the coast of Galway
One month later, new moon lunar phase*

NYANZA DIDN'T RETURN to the marketplace in Galway Bay to collect her jewelry or take down her stall. Instead, she set up a new stall at the market on Verdant Island, an area close by.

She couldn't risk coming back and finding Caelan in Galway. Her behavior felt evasive, childish, even, but she never experienced seeing herself in another person's dream. What did it mean?

Let things stay in the shadows that wish to stay in the shadows. She remembered her mother's words to her when she was a young woman. She used to be a headstrong girl. She failed to live by those words, having wanted to use her meager gift at the time of seeing visions. The gift cost her former life, and yet, gave Nyanza something more, along with a freedom she never thought she'd experience.

She no longer had a family outside of the pod. She lost track of how many new moons had passed since Rhodes McDonagh had his paid mercenaries haul her from Galway and toss her out into the cold water far from her family's home.

That's what happened to women who did not fit within the seams of tightly-bound society. They were called witches and companions of devils for looking different, for being different. Nyanza only wanted to be of help to the distressed women who came to her mother, needing more than medicinal herbs and care for their bodies, but for the dreams that troubled their minds and stirred their souls.

246

Once Rhodes McDonagh heard from a loose-lipped woman that Nyanza could peer into dreams, he cut her trade and life short.

When her new life with the pod commenced, her gift grew stronger. She grew stronger. So why didn't she have enough fortitude to return to Galway Bay and retrieve her sea glass trinkets?

It had nothing to do with those baubles. Every time she thought of Caelan, her body grew tingly like she was a silly girl discovering boys for the first time. She was still a virgin. Sometimes the thought of being with Caelan was enough to make the sea around her boil.

How revolting.

Nyanza was one of the pod members now. She could swim as fast as a sailfish with her mermaid tail. Her retractable fangs were as sharp as a shark's and could penetrate flesh just as easily.

Truly, with these attributes, it did not make sense for her to think of that man.

But her sex did not care that she could only walk on land one week out of the month. Her body was awakened to the desire for a man's touch.

I am being unreasonable. She let that man's dream get into her head. Hopefully, he was able to put the whole thing from his mind. He probably was planning to wed his betrothed. Things were better this way.

"There you are."

Nyanza stilled at the sound of the familiar voice. She only moved her eyes as Caelan strode towards her stall.

"I've been looking all over the nearby ports for you in the past month." He rested his hands on the table and leaned forward, staring in her eyes. "Where have you been?"

CHAPTER THREE

Nyanza stood up from her seat. "You shouldn't be here." She walked around the table of her stall, giving Caelan a wide berth. "You need to leave."

"I mean you no harm. I have your jewelry you left in your stall in Galway. It's on my ship."

She cast her gaze left of the harbor where the larger ships were docked. "You have a ship?"

"I work on one of my father's merchant ships. Well, I should say, I formerly worked."

"You have the leisure of sailing all day and searching for female merchants minding their own business?"

He gave a small laugh. "That is so specific." He lifted his hands from the table. Nyanza noticed his forearms were a deeper bronze than from the last time she'd seen him. "I'm not searching for women. Only one."

"I returned your money."

"I don't care about it."

"Then why follow me?"

"I feel as though I've seen you well before. Did you used to live in Galway?"

Her heart picked up speed. Did Caelan recognize her? How? "I don't recall ever running into you in my life." Her family used to live on the fringes of town, and she and her mother were only visited by women for help with childbearing or interpreting dreams.

She planted her feet in the sand, resisting the instinct to hop back and run as Caelan drew close. He lowered his head and did his studied gaze into her eyes. "Does that mean you lived in Galway?"

Nyanza nodded. "Years ago, but I'm certain our paths never crossed. I would've remembered you since you're so persistent."

He smirked. "There was a girl, a *daoine gorm*. She had brown eyes like yours, shaped like almonds. I liked them."

"How old were you when you saw this girl?"

"Fifteen. She had to be two or three years older. Her parents passed from smallpox years ago after she left."

Nyanza let the ache of grief wash over her. In her own dreams, she knew her mother and father had gone on, but now she learned the cause. Sickness was horrible, though at the very least they didn't suffer the same fate of being murdered as she did. "How sad for this young girl. She would be a woman by now."

Caelan affirmed her statement with a nod. "I never saw her much in town before my father had her sent away, but people called her Nancy."

Nyanza stepped back, but not before letting out a barely audible gasp.

"What is it?" Caelan's concentrated expression turned to worry. Then he looked at her again and his mouth parted. "It's you, isn't it? You're Nancy."

She could hardly catch her breath. This man who laid open his mind to her and showed her his dream, could he be the son of the man who had her killed? "Is your full name Caelan McDonagh?"

He nodded.

Nyanza grabbed the edge of the stall table to keep herself

upright. Caelan rushed in to aid. She held him at arm's length. "Do not come near me. Your father is Rhodes McDonagh."

"He is. Unfortunately, I can't change that fact. Nancy, I'm glad to see you again."

She stepped away when he reached out an arm. "My name is not Nancy. I am Nyanza." A flurry of emotions filled her head. Anger from old memories surfaced. "Your father had me removed from Galway."

"I know. I'm so sorry, Nyanza." Caelan's face turned somber. His mouth flattened. "I resent him for how he's treated people who are different from him. Good people who only want to make their living and raise their families. He delights in making enemies."

Nyanza drew in a ragged breath. She couldn't control the way her voice shook with both pain and fury. "He did more than make me his enemy." Her words came out in a rasp.

Caelan straightened, keeping his eyes on her and appearing startled. Good. Let him be frightened. It would protect him. It would be for his own good.

"Go back to your daddy's boat. Go play with your spoiled, pampered rich girls and forget about your youthful fascination with me."

"We are not youths anymore. You are a woman, a beautiful and mysterious one at that. And I'm a grown man. I will repay the debt of my father banishing you."

"There's nothing you can do. No amount of money in the world can change things." Tears formed behind Nyanza's eyes. What was this? Was she on the verge of weeping? When was the last time this occurred, when the waves swept over her as she gasped in vain for air as a human that one final moment before drowning?

She squared her shoulders and met Caelan with a steady gaze. He would not see her tears. "I was innocent once. I was a young woman. Did I not deserve a chance at life and love on land?"

"I don't quite understand. Do you mean a life in Galway?"

"Forget it." She shook her head and turned away as a single tear rolled down her left cheek. "You don't need to understand."

"I want to. Help me, Nyanza. What is it I can do to help make the rest of your years right?"

She felt a touch on her arm and a slight tug as Caelan turned her to face him. He saw the tear on her face and reached out to wipe it away.

"I hate that my clumsy way of speaking brought up these memories and made these tears."

Should she have told him he was wrong? It had little to do with his speech. It was a sudden desire that cut through her. He tore through her strong and reliable resilience. "I want to tell you that this is your fault. This could've all been forgotten had you just walked away after I saw your dream. Now you've stirred up old memories that should stay buried."

"Is it just memories that trouble you? Is it also your own unmet dreams?"

She stared at him. "I have no more dreams."

"You must have had them once. Surely, you and your family had dreams and plans. My father took them away from you when he sent you away."

Why did Caelan keep referring to her being drowned as being sent away? Unless...he didn't know his father had her drowned. "I may look like an ordinary woman to you, Caelan, but trust me, there's so much you don't know about me."

He put his warm hands on her cold shoulders. His blue eyes were clear and earnest. "I want to know more about you."

Nyanza had never been with a man before, though the heat behind his stare was unmistakable. Images of his dream revolved in her head, of their bodies writhing, limbs entangled. She experienced an unfamiliar throbbing between her thighs. It ached and yet felt strangely good at the same time.

What was happening to her?

"I have to leave." She shook free of Caelan's grasp. Before he could step forward, she pointed a finger at him. "Do not try to follow me."

Nyanza kicked off her shoes, gathered the hem of her long skirt, and trodded across the sand. Caelan trailed after her. "You cannot keep running away from your problems."

"I can and I will. Watch." She yanked the skirt away from her waist.

"Nyanza." He closed in on the gap between them. "You and I must speak about the dream."

She kept walking in her chemise and pantaloons. "I told you already to forget about me and go to your betrothed."

"I ended the betrothal. I want you."

Her bare feet touched the cool water along the shore. She looked over her shoulder. Caelan still followed her. He was stubborn as an ox. With the stature and face of a Grecian statue. "Do you not understand me? Go away."

"I won't let you drown in the ocean."

She turned a rueful smile up at him. "You're too late." With that, she raced into the shallows and used her legs to spring into a dive towards the deep.

The water called out to her, cool and welcoming in its salt embrace. She stretched out her arms and invited the transformation. She heard the fabric of her clothes tear away as her feet sealed into a long, strong green tail fin. Her two legs became a fish tail, ending at her waist. The torso retained the appearance of a human female.

Water rushed past her ears, pushed through her beaded braids. She rejoiced in the sensation. This was her home. Her freedom and true sanctuary.

Then she heard him. The kicking and the splashing. That stubborn man actually went in the water after all. With a weary sigh, Nyanza whirled around and swam back to Caelan.

He treaded water much better than she thought he would. He still was a sitting duck in an ocean full of predators.

"You should've listened to me and stayed back on shore where it was safe."

"I can swim. Maybe not quite as well as you but I can keep up." He gave her a playful splash.

She sloshed the water back at him. "You have no idea where I'm going. I don't want to be responsible for what could happen to you."

As she arced her hand to send water in his face again, he caught it and pulled her towards him. His chest was solid as he held her against him. His lips were hot as they slid across hers.

Nyanza felt her feet beginning to form again. The more Caelan kissed her and her body responded, her tail fin started to disappear.

Caelan spoke against her lips. "If anything happens, I know I'll be rescued by a beautiful sea maiden."

She pushed at his chest, separating herself from his embrace. Her fins formed where her feet were previously. "Are you sure you want to cling to that fairy tale? Out here in the deep, there are no fair maidens and magical spells." She lifted her tail fin out of the water and flashed him a broad smile, showcasing her fangs. "Only the strong live out here in the open sea."

CHAPTER FOUR

Nyanza showed her fangs and fins to Caelan. This was the moment she expected him to shirk back in horror and flee for the shore. Instead, her fanged smile shrank in surprise when she saw his mouth broaden into a grin.

"What are you laughing about?"

"The men who sail with me have tales of sirens at sea. I thought they only talked to pass the time while they drank rum. I never thought sirens existed."

"You do realize you grin at me knowing that I have the power to lure men to their deaths?"

"I don't intend to be drowned. And I don't think you intend to be the one to do it."

"What do you think you're doing, Caelan?"

"I intend to follow you."

She folded her arms and used only her tail to remain afloat. "I doubt you can keep up."

He did a funny wiggle of his eyebrows. "Is that a challenge?"

Nyanza dove beneath the waves. Caelan never ceased to surprise her with his stubbornness. Well, if he wanted to bob out here in the currents by himself, that was his choice. She stretched her arms and propelled her fins to take her even further below the surface.

She knew these waters, the crags and rocks on the ocean floor. Ships could run aground here on the sharp rocks and meet their end. Humans who dared to swim among them could easily get their clothing caught on the sharp edges and never reach the surface.

She wove expertly through the rocks, circumventing the crags. The path led to an underwater tunnel. She swam through, the narrow walls were inches from her shoulders. With a flick of her tail, she reached the other side, finally swimming upward to breach the surface of the hidden grotto.

The water bubbled in front of her before a wheat-colored head broke the surface.

She groaned in disbelief. "How did you get here?"

Caelan pushed back his wet hair. "Following you of course." He looked around. "Who would've thought this place existed below the surface?"

"There's much you humans don't know about the sea."

"I want to know where your fin came from and where your legs went."

"Repulsed that you put your lips on a fish, are you?"

"Not by far. I'd happily do it again." He found her waist under the water and drew her towards him. His eyes sparked with desire as he looked at the tops of her bare breasts. "It appears a mermaid and the ocean have no use for modesty."

Nyanza readied her hand. "If that was a chastisement, I'll splash you again."

"It wasn't a criticism."

His kiss was soft and deep. Nyanza settled into him, wrapping her arms around his shoulders. The low pleasurable ache returned to her center. Was this what desire for a man felt like?

As the feeling built within, she felt her feet emerge and her tail fin go away. She opened her eyes to find she and Caelan drifted close to the grotto floor. She felt his hand drift from her waist to the curve of her lower back. His hand delved deeper before he paused.

"I suppose you answered my question about how your legs form." He stroked her thigh.

"Underwater, it's a response to you kissing and touching me." Nyanza took in the sensation of desire as it knitted its way through her body. She found herself getting a bit bashful as she explained the phenomenon. "My tail goes away underwater because...I enjoy what you're doing to me."

As he pulled her even closer, she felt his hardened, enlarged cock graze her abdomen. "I want to pleasure you." His fingers ventured to the front and pressed between her legs. He found the small bud there and stroked it tenderly.

Nyanza squeezed his arms as the desire he wrought in her body intensified. Between his touch and the water lapping between them, she thought the pleasure might make her burst into tiny different pieces that scattered across the seven seas. And that would be alright. "These sensations. They feel so good it's nearly wicked."

"There's nothing wicked about pleasing you." He covered her mouth with his before moving to lift her out of the water. Nyanza's legs sealed and her tailfin formed.

The scaled barrier left her with unfulfilled longing. "I am unable to leave the water on human legs," she explained.

Caelan settled back into the water with her. "But you were just walking on land minutes ago."

"I can only go on land during the new moon. It ended today."

"No wonder I didn't see you for thirty days after you left Galway." He stroked the back of her neck while placing kisses on her ear.

Nyanza's moan was a soft echo in the grotto. She found her legs again and rubbed them suggestively against his with a womanly instinct she didn't know she possessed. "That's not the only reason why I avoided Galway. You were there and I had to protect you from me, from your dream being fulfilled."

"If my dream means that you and I are to be joined, I accept. Do you want this dream to be real, Nyanza?"

It was already real. She and Caelan together alone in the protective shroud that was the grotto. The desire that wove itself between them. She couldn't deny this or the exact feeling she experienced when he showed her his dream. She nodded once before taking his face in her hands and bringing her mouth to his in a crushing kiss.

The more he touched her body, the more her womanly form came into being. The length of his cock pressed against her leg. She dipped her hand beneath the water to undo the ties of his pants. Between breathless kisses and moments of shared laughter, she helped him tug the pants down and off. He flung them on the grotto floor. Before they had a chance to land, he lifted Nyanza's legs on either side of his waist. Still in the water, Nyanza let out a gasp as the tip of his hot, engorged cock slid between her folds.

Caelan's eyes were heated, blue like the heart of a flame. Nyanza locked her gaze with his as he plunged into her with one stroke.

The bit of pain she experienced having been penetrated for the first time quickly gave way to a sense of pleasure and fullness. Caelan gripped her hips as he moved inside her. She noticed everything, the way her walls tightened around him. The pleasure she had before only deepened with this iteration of physical pleasure.

She clutched his shoulders while he showed her this sensuous dance. Her head tilted back, her eyes squeezed shut as their rhythm changed and became more fervent. Water sloshed against their bodies as they rocked and grinded against each other, chasing the pinnacle of their pleasure. An instinct Nyanza had no words for told her there was more.

The pleasure climbed higher. Their bodies were joined in the water, buoyed by its gentle swaying rhythm. Nyanza clenched her thighs hard around Caelan's hips. The sensation pushed at her until it sent her careening into the depths of her climax. Her cry echoed along the walls.

Caelan held her tight while her body convulsed around his cock.

His fingers dug into her flesh. He buried his face in the side of her neck. Nyanza felt his lips move against her skin but couldn't hear his inaudible words. His whole body went stiff before his cock pulsed hard inside her.

Water continued its gentle assault on their backs while they remained in the grotto, bodies still entwined. Some amount of time passed before Caelan withdrew and let Nyanza's feet touch the shallow side of the grotto pool. She stepped out of the pool onto the grotto floor and sank into a crouch as her legs became her mermaid tail once more.

Caelan dropped beside her. They rested on the grotto floor while water lapped at them. Nyanza stared up at the dark ceiling. Tiny pinpricks in the rock allowed light from the nearby harbor to penetrate. It colored the water indigo blue and tinged their forms in grey. Was this grotto the very same place in Caelan's dream? She looked around and saw that it was so.

A light tickling sensation traveled along the side of her tail. She discovered Caelan lightly running his fingers against the scales. "I had no idea a siren lived in town all those years ago."

She leaned on one elbow and gazed at him. "I wasn't a siren then."

He drew his brows together. "But my father had you sent away. He said it was because you were different."

"He discovered I was reading the dreams of women who visited my mother for medicine and midwifery. He thought I was a witch."

"He didn't know of this?"

Nyanza lifted her fins and dragged them through the water. "I will tell you something. If you flee from me, then I'll understand."

Caelan gathered her in his arms and pulled her on top of him. "When will you stop trying to convince me to run away from you? It will never work, especially now."

Nyanza watched the tiny gold beads hanging from the ends of her long braids as they brushed against Caelan's shoulders. Her hands trembled as she recounted the truth buried for all these years.

"Your father did more than send me away. He hired pirates to take me on their ship, *The Steadfast*. It still goes into nearby ports to this day." She turned her gaze away from him for a moment.

"Nyanza." Caelan brought her face back to his. "You don't have to hide from me."

Her heart beat against her chest as she lay on top of him. Could he feel it, too? "They bound my wrists and ankles in chains before throwing me overboard. I did not make it to shore. That was when I was given a choice by the first siren Galene: become a mermaid or die by drowning. I made the choice to bear the terrible pain to become what I am today."

She watched as Caelan's expression shifted. He rolled onto his side, taking her with him, still holding her. "My father hired men to drown you?"

"Yes, but becoming a mermaid is what saved me. I am freer now than I would've been living in Galway. I'm freer than any man, even the rich privateers."

Caelan pressed his mouth flat. He voice took on a grim tone. "All this time my father has been lying to me, to everyone."

"Do you see why I didn't want to say anything? You're angry."

"I'm furious." The light in his eyes, once languorous from sex, turned into a harsh, brittle glimmer. "My father plotted and paid to have you killed when you were barely a young woman."

"The past can't be undone."

"No, but there can still be consequences." Caelan rose and donned his discarded clothes.

Nyanza raised herself to a seated position on the grotto floor. "Where are you going?"

"To find my father. He will answer for this."

"Caelan, you must stop." Nyanza called after him as he got back in the water and treaded towards the opening leading back through the tunnel. He dove beneath the surface.

CHAPTER FIVE

Caelan knifed his hands through the water once he breached the surface on the other side of the tunnel. He never swam so fast and sure in his life. He didn't want to leave Nyanza back in the grotto, but this matter had to be settled between father and son.

I should have guessed my father was a murderer. The single thought went around in his head as he stepped ashore. People gawked at him as he strode into town, shirtless and without his boots. He strode past them all, heading for the building with a single lantern light shining from the window.

He all but kicked the door down to get in. "I figured you would be burning the midnight oil better than any devil."

Rhodes McDonagh—it was hard to call this man father now—jolted upright from his chair. "What in the hell do you think you're doing here, boy? Did you come back to put your mistakes to right?"

"Indeed, I have."

The man who sired him stopped and studied him. "It seems you couldn't wait until morning to tell me. Did you leap from a ship and swim all the way here?"

"It's extraordinary how fast the body can swim without hands and feet being bound."

Rhodes gave him a wary eye. "Have you been in the rum with the sailors? What talk is this?"

Caelan returned his father's hard stare while his hands formed tight fists. "I know what you did to Nancy. To Nyanza."

"Why is that little witch's name on your lips? She hasn't been in town for years."

"Because you had her dragged out to sea by mercenary pirates."

Rhodes's narrow eyes widened for a moment. Then as the light flickered from the oil lantern, he put his face back in its continual cold, stoic expression. "I don't know how you came by this information, but it matters not. The witch is gone, as are other trouble-makers whom I've disposed of previously."

"People have gone missing from the town. Now I know why. You had them all killed."

Rhodes lifted a deceptively thin, wiry shoulder in response. "Galway is better for my actions. A civilized port has no need of witches, dream readers, and other rabble."

Caelan stared down the man. "Call her a witch again."

"Or what? You'll dare to raise a hand to your father?" Rhodes peeled back his coat to reveal both a dagger and a flintlock pistol holstered at his belt. "Leave my office. Leave my town for good before I shoot you down like a dog in the street."

Caelan saw the lantern flicker on the windowsill again. He seized it and stormed out.

"Where are you going with my property?" Rhodes shouted like a banshee behind him.

Caelan kept on walking, out the door and the town. The man he once called father followed him all the way to the docks where the ships were anchored. Rhodes kept braying and shouting for him to return the lantern. "You'll inherit nothing of mine. That is my lantern."

Caelan stopped before an old brigantine. Faded red letters that marked *The Steadfast* still clung stubbornly to its side. "You won't need your lantern. I'll light up the whole port for you." He drew back his arm and launched the oil lantern high into the air.

The lantern sailed over the rails of the brigantine and crashed onto its freshly swabbed and oiled deck. Caelan felt a primal thrill of satisfaction as the deck erupted into flames.

"You ungrateful, disloyal bastard." Rhodes's screech carried across the port. He dashed at Caelan and struck him across the mouth. "I wish you died years ago instead of your mother."

Caelan tasted blood in his mouth. He spat on the ground while the flames grew behind him. "God rest her soul, at least she did not have to see you at war with the world."

"You insult me and then set fire to my ship." Rhodes sneered as he whipped the dagger from his belt. "I will show you war."

Nyanza swam as fast as her fins could carry her to Galway's shore. Her mind was filled with fire and blood, all connected to thoughts of Caelan. Where was he?

She moved below in the dark depths, but she saw the light from flames on the water's surface. When she reached the top, she gazed in shock as a ship burned in the port. The flames rose high on the deck while fire and smoke billowed from the disintegrating sails. Wood splintered and crackled as the ship was preparing to meet its fiery end.

Movement caught her eye. Next to the brigantine, two figures were on the docks, trading blows. Nyanza swam closer to see Caelan engaged in fisticuffs with an older man.

Her blood turned to ice when she discovered the man's identity.

Rhodes shouted and hurled curses at his son. He moved like a wild animal, fresh from being caged. In his right hand he swung a dagger inches from Caelan's face. Caelan dodged, sidestepping in time, but his bare feet were at a disadvantage on the splintered docks. Rhodes had better footing in his boots. He missed getting his son in the face, but he let the knife come down, tearing into Caelan's leg.

"Stop."

Both men halted their violent advances. Caelan grasped his wounded leg and turned to Nyanza. She realized it was her powerful siren's shout that reverberated across the peer.

"Nyanza," Caelan called out to her. "Get away. You're not safe here."

Rhodes slowly turned his whole form to face her. The blood drained from his face in a sickly pallor as though he'd seen a ghost. "Nancy?"

At the mention of her old Anglican name on his lips, she felt the fangs lower in her mouth. Using the full strength of her mermaid tail, she leapt out of the water and landed on him. With the unnatural strength gifted to her from the transformation to a siren, she pinned down Rhodes. Her gleaming white fangs were reflected in Rhodes's large, frightened eyes. "My name is Nyanza."

She lowered her head and bit down hard on his neck. Warm blood splattered her face as she severed flesh and tendon. Rhodes howled in pain before he shoved her off.

Caelan rushed forward, right leg buckling. Nyanza felt his strength waning as he lifted her and carried her to the edge of the dock. He released her to fall to the safety of the water.

Nyanza heard a sharp crack of gunfire above. Her stomach sank to the bottom of the ocean while she kicked her fins to swim back towards the surface.

Caelan was on his knees, blood streaming from both his leg and now right above his heart. Rhodes staggered to stand over him, a smoking pistol in his hand. A crimson stain covered half of his white shirt. "Whatever this devilry is between you and that witch, it ends tonight."

Helpless to do anything but watch as Rhodes raised the pistol again, Nyanza panicked. She saw a flash of a blade as Caelan pulled the dagger from his leg and threw it at his father.

The blade landed in Rhodes's chest. Caelan's father dropped the pistol. It fired harmlessly on the dock as he staggered backwards towards the burning ship. He lost his footing and fell, plunging into the flames that swallowed the deck.

Caelan grunted and fell forward into the water. Nyanza shot forward to his side. She held his head above water while his blood stained the port waters red.

His blue eyes were glazed over with agony. "I'm dying, Nyanza."

"You are." Tears fell from her eyes to land on his pale, blood-drained face. "But I can help save you. It will be painful and there's no going back."

He lifted a hand to wipe the tears from her cheek. "The pain of death is worth the risk to be with you."

"You are a stubborn one, Caelan McDonagh. No wonder we can't stay away from each other." Nyanza planted a kiss on his lips, along with a secret wish, and dove with him beneath the waves.

EPILOGUE

G*alway Bay, 5 years later*

NYANZA'S HEAD appeared above the water's calm surface. The seas were peaceful today. The pod was moving on to warmer waters in the Mediterranean but had paused in a nearby port for other members to sell and trade crafted goods.

Nyanza watched as people walked about on Galway beach. On the port side, new ships were anchored. It seemed the town carried on with its business as usual. At least, she hoped business was more equitable for all involved since one of the former leaders had been removed.

"What are you doing up here?"

She turned around and spotted Caelan. Water dripped from his hair and fell on his bare chest. That familiar rush of heat filled her body. Her feet took the place of her fins.

"What am I doing up here? You're one to talk."

He splashed her with his large grey tailfin. "It's a good day. The sun is shining. The warmth of new waters call us."

Nyanza worked hard to tread water with her arms and legs. "I'm going to keep losing my tail if you don't stop smiling at me. And then how will we reach those warm waters?"

"I'll happily carry you." He reached for her hand.

Nyanza took his hand and together they swam away from the port. "Are you...alright, Caelan?"

He didn't so much as spare a glance at the world on land behind him. "In the years we've been together, I've not once regretted my decision. You are who I want to be with, whether you walk the land or swim in the sea."

She'd come to enjoy his poetic way of speaking. "It is the phase of the new moon. I can walk on land."

"I can think of better things to do on land besides walking." His mouth broadened into a mischievous, lusty grin.

She laughed. "Then let's see what the Mediterranean has to offer."

They held hands as they flipped their fins and swam on to join the pod, eager to carry their love onto more pleasant shores.

Enjoyed this story? Be sure to leave a review! Follow me on social media and sign up for my newsletter so you can be the first to know when new stories are released. If you want more hot alien romances (or vampires, shifters, fantasy romance, reverse harem, etc.), check out my list of titles.

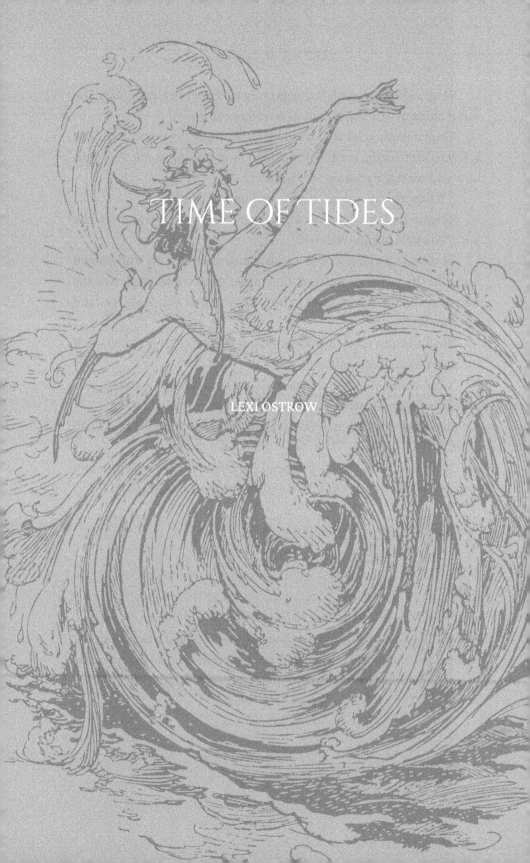

TIME OF TIDES

LEXI OSTROW

CHAPTER ONE

Jaws snapped mere inches from Ariana's face. She rolled to the side, her tail fin flipping her over effortlessly as the angry Tiger Shark circled back for another go.

"Throw the damn javelin!" Tanessa, one of the oldest in the pod, screamed at Ariana.

She'd forgotten the stick was in her hands. She was not a hunter. This was not her role in the pod. She taught, not tortured.

"Damn it, Ariana, now!" Tanessa snarled again, bursting through the water with her gift of speed and snatching the weapon from Ariana's fingers when she hesitated only a second.

Red exploded into the water as the point speared through the shark's eye and likely brain. Its back was arched, the creature forming a c in the middle of the water as it began to sink beneath them.

The smallest ripple of the vast ocean pushed toward Ariana as the now-dead shark's body began its descent. The very same descent she would have made had she drowned.

Had she not been saved.

She watched helplessly as the finned beast spiraled until it

269

landed in the net several mermaids held open below it. The four who held the net buckled and bent just slightly under the weight of the massive shark. Their grip was steady, ensuring the success of the hunt despite her failure to react and kill the tiger shark.

"We have to eat, damn it." Tanessa's tail fin knocked against Ariana's arm as she moved by. "Not all of us live on kelp."

Ariana ignored the taunt. She wasn't the only one in her pod to eat meat as infrequently as possible. It had been the same before she'd found her life beneath the waves. Before Poseidon had found her. No, it was not the Greek God but Galene, the mermaid who began it all. The siren she owed her life to.

Then why do you feel so miserable now? Why can you be so closed off to the men and women who've been your life for nearly a century?

Mermaids didn't die of old age - not that she'd ever heard. That's because they were, in essence, already dead.

And they weren't mermaids - not really. Not the creatures she'd been told of bedtime stories.

Ariana may find fault in killing, but it didn't mean she didn't partake when necessary. Not one second after she took her first breath underwater did she feel the need to kill pulsing within her veins. It was the gift and the curse the sea god gave to people thrown into the seas.

His seas.

Everyone knew the tale of Galene's transformation and what followed. The race of sirens who spent countless decades luring men to their deaths, the same way they'd discarded women to drown centuries ago.

Centuries ago, when Ariana had not been alive but held no disbelief in the tales the eldest sirens told. Tales that spurred their kind on, watching plenty inhale the deepest, saltiest water into their lungs until their eyes bulged and their breaths ceased.

Even Galena didn't know what the mighty god saw in her, only that she had been given the greatest gift and curse. In exchange for her life, Galene and the sea god worked to churn the waters of the boat she'd been cast from. All had perished, many looking Galena in the eye and dying believing she was the cursed witch they thought her to be when they thew her over.

Only the lucky ones were given the gift of life underneath the waves. *Then why do you not feel so fortunate as of late?*

Ariana loved her life and what the second chance had brought her, but it didn't stop the little things from prickling under her skin. She wasn't a hunter. They all had their place, just like in the world above. Hers was with the newly turned, guiding them through their transition as a siren. Aiding them in destroying those who threw them over. With the belief in curses and tides a thing of the long distant past, many deaths were now accidental.

Every transition came with more than the promise that the siren would bring Poseidon the gift of more citizens of the deep and a gift to help them along their way. Ariana's gift was precious, it allowed the siren a chance to change their mind.

The gift of life wasn't accepted. It was thrust upon a dying soul, and before Ariana's transition to siren herself, it was permanent. She could weave the moon and spin the tides, turning back the hands of time. Once a siren took their debt, Ariana could offer them the chance to return to the life they had left.

It hadn't been her idea, but Galene's. And it wasn't offered in all cases. It could only be done when the newly turned were young or held something in them that created a gift that could not help the pod.

What about my gift to help myself?

Ariana shook off the thought and set her eyes back on the kill. She'd been useless. She could turn back time and kill the fucking thing, erase the hate and annoyance Tanessa threw her way.

But she wouldn't. Ariana didn't play with her gift - except to steal more orgasms from her husband. She would never tire of them, and Poseidon didn't care how they used their gifts so long as they murdered and took souls into the deep for him occasionally.

"Back to the pod!" Brinna, a siren from before Ariana had even been born, blew into a disfigured conch that somehow blared through the ocean's dense waters. Sound should not have carried, but it did, and it always would when Brinna commanded it. Her gift of communication made hunts possible in groups to bring in more food at once.

Below her, the four with the net flicked their fins and began to rise. She loved the feel of the rush of water over her body. Always had, even before her untimely death and transition. Ariana hadn't belonged on land even when she'd been alive, and the waters had always called to her.

Maybe she could hear the sirens singing from everywhere she went. She never met the god and couldn't ask him if some people were fated for this life or if it was all chance and circumstance because a siren couldn't be born without Galena watching them die.

Only she no longer cared for her life in the pod. Only her husband and the waves they swam in.

Hundreds of her kind had tried to regain their humanity. And nearly every siren created was questioned to determine their power, with plenty hoping they'd have a gift better than Ariana's.

Sirens, mermaids, whatever they were called, didn't get to return to the living. They had died. The cold hand of the ocean had wrapped around their throat and pried open their mouths before reaching in and drowning them. The life bled from their bodies even as the gift filled their souls. They would sink, the frigid ocean floor trying to claim there before Poseiden and his gifted prize could do what needed to be done.

No, a siren couldn't return to their life as human without Ariana's gift and Galena's blessing.

They were dead. And dead was dead was dead.

Only they weren't dead. They were indebted to one another in a way that kept them alive in the only way that mattered.

Orion won't like these thoughts. Ariana tried to force the ugliness away. As she did each and every day.

· · ·

IT PAINED him to watch Ariana suffer. The simple look of agony in her gaze couldn't be ignored when -she cast her glance at him. The usual life that shone from her bluish-green eyes was murky, almost brown, when she looked at him as the hunting party returned.

To him, his wife was the most important person in the entire world, and yet, she looked away the moment his gaze turned concerned. He'd get to the bottom of her discomfort soon enough. Ariana did not like hunting, but it was not enough to set off the unease he saw. She was guarded. If she showed any emotion, there was a reason.

"You did it," he swished his tail through the water and crossed the space to her.

Her stunning smile did not grace her lips. Ariana did not even look up at his gaze. Orion didn't hesitate to wrap his arms around her, tugging her against his body. Even with her upset, the tension left her shoulders as she settled against him.

They were two of a kind – both quieted by the other's soul and perhaps one of the only mercouple pairs truly destined for one another. Poseidon told him as much the day Ariana was tossed – albeit accidentally – into the sea. The Greek god himself demanded Galena grant Ariana the gift of second life, claiming her power would be one to save countless lives.

It wasn't until that moment that Orion realized each person's gift was not a gift but merely something in their being unlocking when the magic flowed through their veins.

He placed a gentle kiss on the top of her head, squeezing her against him to offer her comfort. "This is not just about the hunt." He didn't ask and so, she didn't answer, not really.

"It's about everything. What if I'm just tired of this lifestyle?"

Orion frowned. This was not the first time she'd brought up discontent with the pod, but he swore the last time was just that … the last time.

"Then you are tired of me so easily?" His voice did not hold the teasing tone he usually found naturally with his wife because there was nothing humorous about her statement.

There was no way to leave the pod except death, and her death was not something he would ever allow to come to pass. He hadn't thirty years ago, and he wouldn't now. Even had Poseidon not demanded Galena save the drowning woman who became Orion's whole world, he would have beseeched the siren leader to do so.

Orion was as transfixed with his wife today as he'd been the moment her bright eyes fell on his and she no doubt believed lack of oxygen led her to hallucinate a man with flowing dark locks and a fucking tail approached her.

"I will never tire of you." Her lips found his, and though this kiss was chaste, it set his body on fire the way it always did.

"Then tell me what's upsetting you. The death of a shark is not terrible when it feeds the pod. You've never been upset by it before."

Her sigh weighed on his heart, but the weight increased as her palms lay flat on his chest, and she pushed away from him just slightly. It showed Orion the darkness in her eyes was more so up close. A turbulent swirl of color met his gaze. A turbulence he'd never seen before.

Ariana was the gentlest woman he'd ever met – on land or under the waves. She regarded all life as precious and went to great lengths to ensure none were harmed if she could control it. The woman staring back at him did not shine with that light. She appeared tired – as she indicated.

"We will take a leave. I will clear it with Galena and the pair of us with spend some time on the outskirts of the city, away from the pod. I will not have your well-being tarnished by whatever you encountered today."

"It wasn't just today," her voice grew hard, and she pressed against his chest.

Orion allowed his grip to loosen, allowing Ariana to swim backward if she genuinely wished. When she did, his heart fractured just a bit. She never shied away from him, not from the moment she'd re-awoken from her first death.

"Come," he gestured for her to follow but didn't dare take her hand. He respected her boundaries and she'd already pulled away from him once.

Orion half expected her to stay put, not willing to speak to even him about what troubled him, but the gentle flow of water passing over his arms from behind let him know she did.

They swam in silence, the first uncomfortable silence of their time together. It ate him – the quiet did – made him worry for all the things that she'd experienced without him there to help her. She was the strongest woman he knew and seeing her so defeated cut him deeply.

Only when the pod was miles behind them did he turn and offer her his hand. They could remain upright in a stasis if they choose. Flipping their fins was only to move through the water. They stood still much the same way as a person did on land.

"I'm sorry," she whispered so quietly the sound did not reach his ears. Only the moving of her lips gave her words away.

"You will never have anything to be sorry. Tell me what happened, help me understand so I can chase the gray from your gaze." He cupped her cheek in his hand and she leaned into it. "I would give you the world if I could."

Her smile was sad. "You already have. Time and time again. You saved me, and in doing so, I found you. I just," she sighed, her shoulders sagging in defeat. "The pod grows large. Some day, wouldn't it be nice to slip away?"

He frowned and watched as the joyous light in her eyes seemed to fade even darker than when she approached.

A shift in pressure sent water brushing over him, drawing his eyes up.

"Fucking hell," Orion snarled as he stared at the small form in the water above.

Bubbles obscured the overall form, but Orion knew a child when he saw one. He watched as hair whipped the water, tangling in fingers that flailed to propel the young body to the surface.

Seconds ticked by and his skin began to itch with the need to do something. He couldn't touch the small human fighting for their life, his gift was near a curse and would send the child to death.

Ariana's tail flicked past his face - a dark rush of green in the empty vast blue around them.

She pushed up, propelling herself as quickly as she could.

He knew his wife. She would save that young person even if it exposed her. *And then the pod will destory her.*

Without a thought, Orion pulled at the small shell around his wrist, jerking it free rather than just lifting it to his lips. It was impossible to feel temperature underwater with the ocean all around him, but he knew the shell would be warm, heated from it's place against his skin. Orion's lips wrapped around it as he pushed as much breath as he could into the small charm.

No sound blasted through the water, but the small shell they all received connected them back to Galene.

Orion held no clue how the original siren transported herself to and from drownings in action but she always did. This time was no execption.

Galene's pale blonde hair swished and floated behind her. Seagreen eyes pierced into his soul with knowing. There was only one reason that she was beckoned.

"The child!" Orion watched as Ariana reached the young child so far above their place near the bottom of the ocean.

Galene's gaze turned upward as if urgency was not of any importance to her.

"That young girl is not for our kind. Her soul does not speak out and there are none who know her to bargain." She'd returned her gaze back to him as she spoke. Pain shone in her eyes, but her decision would be final.

No one understood why Galene made the choices she made, but Orion couldn't keep his gaze on the scene above. Not when Ariana's scream pierced through the depths, even though the sorrow tugged at his heart in ways that made him wish he could save her from what hurt her.

He couldn't. Death could hurt them all and they just needed to accept that. Evey being thrown over would not live to take a breath under the waves.

CHAPTER TWO

White hot pain sliced through Ariana. The same pain she'd felt as she'd gasped for the last breath of air before Galene shook her world to its core. Every molecule in her body heated to a boil as she clutched the small girl in her arms.

She cradled the lost one like she did so many of the young in their pod. Only this girl would never smile up at her and reach her arms around her neck. The girl was not saved.

Tears blurred her vision - the strangest thing she'd known as a mermaid - and it was only as she released the young girl, trying to return her body to those who may have lost her if there were any - that she saw Galene's distinct blonde hair below her.

"You were here?" Ariana hissed, the snarled question no doubt reaching the other woman even though only her husband looked up at her.

Fury replaced the pain and spurred her to swim faster. Everywhere the burn of loss had been was replaced by the ice of fury that wrapped around her like a fortress protecting her from what could come of her next move.

"Galene!" Ariana screamed the name, daring the other woman to show a sign of recognition. "Look at me!" Ariana nearly choked on the water, something that only occurred during intense emotions that drew the water into the lungs.

Galene spun and even the sorrow darkening her pale green eyes was not enough to calm Ariana's path.

"You were here, she could have been saved." her tail swished rapidly in the water, churning it underneath her. Preparing her. "I'm going back and you'll fix what you were too late to handle."

"Ariana, no." Galene's voice was calm but loud. "That young child is not for our world."

"No one came for her!" Ariana's nose burned as the threat of tears began to build larger.

Galene only nodded. "We are too far out to see. If she had been wanted," the other woman cast her gaze down.

"Is that not what we are for?" Ariana's heart slammed aggressively against her ribcage, the hammering jacking up her intensity as if they were connected. "Then we sink the boat that dared to destroy a young life! We lure them to their deaths with our song until their eyes bulge with recognition as the last of their air supply is stolen from their lungs."

Her anger mounted as the other mermaid continued to look at her with zero intention in her eyes.

"Avenge her!" Ariana snarled, her jaw jutting out in her anger.

"You know our laws. We avenge those who wronged us. While the death of one so young should never be celebrated, we are not to _"

Galene's words were knocked away as Ariana's fist connected with the exalted leader's nose. She smirked as the words stopped and the woman's head snapped backward from the surprise of the force.

"Ariana!" Orion called, horror in his dark brown eyes.

"You could have saved her!" Ariana lunged forward, her fingers intwining in Galene's hair as she whipped the woman side to side.

"Her death was not needed!" Tears rolled down her face as she thrashed the pair of them about.

Ariana's fragile hold on pod rules set her on fire as the ice over the senseless death removed her fear at what she'd done.

Galene's arms flailed against Ariana, but she couldn't make the connection. Galene was not a fighter - not that Ariana was - but also small for her younger counterparts.

Ariana lost sight of everything as the two sirens tumbled through the water, tails flicking in erratic patterns as one fought to be free and the other sought to cull her rage. Something slammed into her gut, but she didn't let go.

Galene couldn't be killed, certianly not by drowning at the very least, but Ariana didn't care. She didn't feel as she pushed downward, trying to take Galene down to the dark, rocky, seafloor.

She knew the arms that wrapped around her better than she knew her own.

Orion tucked her close as his hands clasped around hers.

"Let her go, Ari. Let her go before he comes."

Ariana knew the danger in attacking Galene. Death. By Poseidon's hand.

She continued her assault and Orion's grip was firm. The same grip she flourished under during their lovemaking now tried to stop her from her attempts.

"I love you, and I will not allow you to do this, Ari." He pressed a little firmer on the pressure points in her wrists, and they both released as if by magic.

"Orion!" She snarled, whirling on him.

"Do not think I did not understand your goal." he pulled her close, pressing her against him as he kissed her brow. "We never got to have that conversation of ours, but I refuse to allow you to convince Poseidon to take you away from me."

She sagged against him, the tears wracking through her as Orion cradled her, loved her, held her in place, and allowed her to unleash all the events from the past days in a single moment of weakness.

"I will forgive this attack because I know you've struggled for some time," Galene swam somewhere behind them. "But if you go against me again, you go against the pod."

Ariana couldn't bring herself to care. She was so tired of not saving everyone. She'd long ago lost her streak for revenge and cold heartedness. If more people lived beneath the waves than above them, who would care. The ocean's were vast and covered far more miles than the land.

"What were you thinking?" Orion's voice was calm as he whispered against her ear. "I could have lost you forever."

"I want to use my gift." She ignored the slight tremble as the clarity took hold of her and pulled the remaining emotions away.

"She's already told you it will do no good. The death of a child is a horrific event, but do not tax yourself to have the same result."

"No," Ariana shook her head, watching as her dark black curls floated around them, framing his face as if to caress him. "You misunderstand me."

His fingers traced the line of her jaw even as his eyes searched hers for the words she was afraid to say. When Orion set his forehead against hers, her resolve nearly crumbled.

"You cannot mean what I think." he refused to look at her, leaving them connected in the gentle touch of their heads.

"I do," she whispered, all of her fire and ice from the fight with Galene a thing of the past. It had been such a very long day and it was a day she could reset and erase - along with hundreds and nearly thousands of others that had come before.

"Then you are mad at me too?"

"No!" she pulled back, surprised that he would ever think she loved him any less than with her whole heart. "I would find you."

"Would you?" He scoffed and pulled away, his eyes storming over as hers had moments before.

"If I turn back time before you are turned, I would lose my fins as well. We could be together."

"I waited thirty years for you to fall into the ocean. You go back before my time and you won't even be born."

"I am in control of my gift. Time will work for me as I need it. I cannot write myself out of existence. Think how foolish of a gift that would be." She reached for him, his hand slinking around his wrist. She used her weight to pull her closer to him.

"Aren't you the one who always says how our gifts are curses we cannot see that way?" He narrowed his eyes as he stared her, the waves of anger rolling off him.

"Orion, I love you and I am not trying to end our time. I am merely sick of living for the pod. I want to live for us. For me and you and the family we could create together."

At the mention of family, his eyes softened, and the dark chocolate brown shifted lighter as if changing with his shifted emotions. He'd always fought for the children who fell into the water, but he never dared suggest they take one in. His response was all Ariana needed to know.

Her gift could undo everything.

Ariana knew what she needed to do.

One last thing.

Just a few specific lives to save with her gift.

CHAPTER THREE

Orion's entire body was numb with worry as he stared at the most important person in his world.

She'd entranced him from the moment he lay eyes on her. His quest to save her had been foolish and driven by his desire to feel her lips against his, but Ariana was his world. She was everything he'd ever dreamed of, and now she spoke as if she could simply take all that away and hope their connection was strong enough.

"Ariana, promise me."

"We don't make promises, you know that." Her hand weaved in the thick hair on the back of his head and pulled him close.

Numbness gave way to desire as she pressed her lips to his and sought to deepen their kiss as her tongue dared to tease his lips.

Orion's hands wrapped around her with a low growl of approval, but he found he held nothing.

"Ariana!" Orion spun, knowing full well she'd used her power over his rationale thought to slip away.

He knew his wife. She wasn't changing their timelines, not yet.

She was going after the little girl.

Unlike some gifts, his included, Ariana's held no boundaries except that she couldn't return to the same place twice. Well, and that she could only go back, never forward.

He kept his stare at the body floating lifelessly on the ocean's surface.

His gut churned that he'd forgotten about the young child in his need to protect Ariana from herself.

"Any second now." Orion would never remember what Ariana did, wouldn't remember the conversation or the brief scuffle that took place before it.

The minute Ariana adjusted the timeline, she was the only one who would bear the memories of what had passed in an alternate timeline. Technically, she could continue with her plan to undo their lives under the sea and he'd be none the wiser.

The last thoughts he could have of his wife would be these. Dark thoughts wondering why her loyalty to the pod was so pushed over the edge this day when she rarely seemed at odds with anyone every day that came before.

A single shark was not enough once she saved this small child, but he would never know. All of this would be gone, little more than a fever dream the second Ariana succeeded in the timeline she created.

Orion studied the body on the top of the surface. Watching it, waiting for the slightest shine that Ariana's gift was at play. The body would appear to blur and then shimmer for mere seconds before it vanished and took his memories with it.

As he watched, a pit formed in Orion's gut that he couldn't shake. A weight that tried to drag him lower and force his gaze from the surface.

Had Ariana changed their paths before?

Never in their sixty-one years together had he worried for such, but it was a thought boring into his brain like an eel diving for the safety of the holes in the coral.

A splash somewhere overhead revealed a man sinking too rapidly.

"Already did then," Orion ignored the deceased man, knowing full well the ocean would make a meal out of him when it was time.

"Orion!" Ariana's voice pulled his attention from his thoughts.

What were you even thinking about? Orion shook his head and pulled his gaze from teh water's surface to see Ariana swimming towards him. The smile on her lips spoke of mischievous events, but he couldn't understand.

Moments ago he'd been swimming with her, trying to find a space for them to discuss what haunted her so he could chase the ghosts from her soul. She'd rushed off and he'd been keen to keep up, but she'd ascended too quickly so he'd stayed behind assuming she missed a glimpse at the world she'd given up.

"And now she's grinning at me like she stole an extra helping of dessert kelp."

He scratched the back of his head, trying to figure out what she'd seen and how'd she'd gotten to the surface, versus just behind him.

"You did something." It wasn't a question. He knew his wife.

She nodded. "This is the part where you tell me you haven't seen me smile in months." She stopped swimming before him, just out of his reach.

"Nu-uh my love," he reached for her, her hand happily grabbing on to his. "I've seen an entirely different on your face when I bring you to release." Pulling her close he allowed himself to drop a kiss to her neck.

When her hand ran down his bare chest and smoothed a path over his cock Orion stilled in the water as all rationale thought and means to tease her vanished. His tail, like hers, provided modesty, not an inability to pleasure one another.

Grabbing her wrists playfully, Orion jerked her close and slanted his mouth over hers.

She tasted like ripe strawberries and wine. Flavors he would always taste on her tongue as he tangled up with hers because it was the final thing she ate before her demise. A blessing he would always be fortunate for.

Their tails twined together, keeping them connected as Orion allowed his hands to trail over the somewhat cliche shell top that Ariana wore. His hand splayed over her back as

Relations out in the open ocean were dangerous, but if his wife weren't careful, he would run the risk.

"What did you do, wife?" he whispered against her lips.

Her chuckled response would get them both killed.

"I used my gift the way I wanted to for a life. Not that way I'm instructed to." She pulled back, knowing full well an onslaught of questions were about to spill out from him.

"Are you mad?" Orion's voice still held the deep husk of his arousal. Though he still held her close, Ariana knew this was not the time now.

She hadn't realized how light she would feel after saving the young girl's life. Part of her life as a siren meant strength to destory those who wronged her.

She'd seen a single man on a small fishing boat before she'd gone after Galene. He'd seemed relatively unaware of the young girl's death, but when he hadn't jumped in to save her, Ariana knew the truth.

Twisting time to race ahead of Orion as they swum hadn't been an issue. He'd followed her for a split second, trying to understand why she'd rushed.

It took him longer to catch up because he'd been unprepared for her rushed speed and lingered back. She'd strangled the man in seconds. He'd clawed at her wrists but must have been drunk because she could smell the booze on the air.

Tossing him over, she knew Poseidon would thank her for the gift another time. Even though he would also always know she'd attacked his precious Galene. A quick word of warning to the young girl and she'd dove back under.

Everything from the day vanished. Her gift had allowed her to save a life. To give back what had been stolen from her. And though they all believed their gifts were only to be of service to the pod, Ariana knew they all held small joy with their talents.

Melanie lived for the thrill of camouflaging like an octopus to spy.

D'Angelo thrilled in his ability to construct homes for them from a mere squid ink sketch.

Brittany secretly enjoyed shifting the temperature of the waves to piss them off when it suited her.

Even Orion relished in his ability to instantly take the life of a human with a single touch.

Once upon a time, her husband had been bloodthirsty. Or so he tells her. In all their years, the one thing Orion begged her not to do was see his past. To see the man who fought in wars.

So she hadn't.

And now you must.

"Ariana," Orion growled, this time his annoyance showing in the way the sound grew louder toward the end.

"I am not mad. I had a life to save, and you were too slow."

He glanced at the body sinking ever lower, getting closer to them as it went.

"That was you then?"

She nodded. "A young girl's life hung in the balance."

"Jesus, I hate when an entire life span happens, and you can undo it to give people their life back."

She glanced away, unable to lie to him properly and unsure if he would accept that she'd changed fate without approval.

"Ari," he held out the end of her name in annoyance. "What did you do, my love?"

Sighing, she allowed herself to drift gently on the current.

"What if we could go back and make our choices again?"

The Orion from eight minutes ago had not been impressed. This version may be different.

"You'd ask me not to save you?" his eyes darkened, and he crossed the small space in a blink, his hand cupping her cheek.

She could undo her gift, but she'd never live without him. He was her rock, and there was no life without him. She would undo his acceptance and erase her choice. She wouldn't drown because she'd have her current self to save her past self.

The plan was a jumble in her head, formed only as they'd swum in silence. Ariana couldn't do it - not without his approval and not yet. There were too many details to work out, but staring into his dark eyes, she knew it would be for the best.

They would live together in his country - away from the hellish internal wars and damnation in hers. Normal jobs paled compared to what she did now, but she'd always intended to be a doctor and save people that way.

If Ariana could prevent Orion from drowning, her present self would remain human because she could get caught by the timestream. It was the only warning she'd been given when Poseidon spoke to her shortly after she'd been reborn.

The pain of her transformation had barely worn off. Still, the sea king came to her, and she'd listened with rapt attention even as the need to murder those who caused her undoing ate at her.

Her gift would allow her to walk amongst the waves and the pull of tides the moon created each month. She could go as far back as she wished, but should she create turmoil within the time-line that sprouted to her life, she would be stuck, unable to ever return.

It's the real reason she'd never dared to learn the secrets of Orion's life that he undoubtedly didn't share. She couldn't risk being trapped alone should she alter somthing in his life.

This was different. If she could save him, her timeline would be altered, and she would be forever stuck.

Which is why you must have legs when you do this, or all is lost.

288

Ariana swallowed. One wrong move and everything vanished permanently. But she could do this.

Would do this.

Life as a human was undoubtedly not as wonderful as her life as a mermaid, but it was the pod she was tired of. Not her Orion.

"Take me to the surface."

"That's how you intend to end this conversation?"

She nodded. "I did what I did to save a young girl. I've had a terrible day, and sinking my toes into the sand is still my favorite sensation."

"Oh?" A dark brow quirked upward. "I should hope there is a sensation you enjoy much, much more."

Laughing, she ignored the growing desire. Her dismay from earlier lifted. Her gifts had come in handy, for now, they'd chased away the sorrow from the hunt.

"That is precisely why I want to use our cycle. I want to make love to you on the beach."

His eyes darkened for the fifth time in as many minutes.

"You make my head spin, love, but yes, if you wish for time on the surface to erase what ails your soul, then I will give it to you."

"Not because I planted a very wonderful image in your head?"

He snorted. "I can take you on the sand in the black of night without the fear of humans."

She grinned, thinking of all the times the pod had been near shore and they'd slipped away. "Then you'd better make this one extra special." she winked and darted forward, the internal compass they all shared pointing her to the nearest land mass - America this time.

She blew out a breath. *Legs, check.*

Ariana had no doubt she could do this correctly, but still, the slightest fear that she'd save him and fail to get stuck and merely propel herself into the future and drown began to creep from the corner of her mind to the forefront.

She would get this right. She had to.

CHAPTER FOUR

Ariana's heart should have beat erratically in her chest as they swam for shore. Hours had passed, and hours more would. They would be spent when they reached the shore and would spend most of their first day sleeping. She should have been under a crippling weight to speak to her husband about her plan, to ask his permission.

But she wasn't.

Since saving the little girl, her entire being was calm. The tension in her muscles from her discomfort with her role in the hunt vanished. The agonizing fury from the unnecessary death of the young child depleted and merely lingered like a minor headache from a time only Ariana could remember. All that remained was a sort of certainty she hadn't experienced in months.

Changing her husband's fate should have been his choice. He'd never expressed any concerns with their life as merpeople, but, then again, neither had she until earlier. Orion also only seemed concerned with how they would find one another again.

And we will.

He wouldn't remember loving her, but she would remember and

290

could start the process over again for them both. It didn't matter if it took time. He'd spent a few years chasing her before she'd given in to the sexual tension between them.

Not because Ariana hadn't loved Orion from the moment she saw him, but in spite of it. There were so few of their kind - far fewer men than women - that she didn't want him to regret choosing time with her if it didn't work out.

So much has changed. The thought pulled a smile over her lips. In the sixty-one years that followed, they'd spent nearly every day exploring one another, learning the secrets of the past and the joys of the present. Ariana never expected to be with a man longer than her human life. Still, every day with Orion made her love him more.

They would get back what she was about to steal from them.

The darkness from a new moon made the journey harder, but only in the sense that the extreme blackness around them kept trying to lull her to sleep.

"You're quiet. What's on your mind?" He took her pinky in his and tugged her closer as they continued to swim.

"You. Us." she grinned at him. "We've had a long time together, and going to the land always excites me more than ever with you by my side."

His grin sent her heart flip-flopping in her chest.

Orion had that effect on her since the moment she took her first breath as a siren. She preferred that term to mermaid - mermaids from her childhood were filled with goodness and light, but a siren was born in darkness from death.

"Keep looking at me like that, and we won't make it to land," Orion teased, his gaze heating up as he looked at her and swam backward.

Ariana hadn't realized her own lusty expression had risen, but it wasn't a wonder.

"Much as I would like that, I want this on land." *I want this to matter so much more than every other time.*

She swallowed back the small wave of unease brewing in the pit of her stomach. She would save them both and have a normal, human life.

ORION EXTENDED his hand to her, the moonlight serving only to highlight the lust in his gaze as she rose from the waves to stand beside him.

"The moonlight suits you," he gently pulled her close, "almost as much as legs do," he dipped his head and captured her lips against his.

Ariana shuddered into their kiss, her mouth parting to invite his seeking tongue inside.

Every kiss with Orion sent her body on fire. Even the gentle, soft kisses had a way of making her desire him.

His hands trailed down the curve of her breasts as they kissed, and hers cupped his ass, dragging him closer. His erection brushed against her thigh, and his growl of warning sent a spark through her. Ariana encircled his length and stroked him twice before leaning back onto her heels.

Lovemaking under the water came with one very intense drawback for them, and she intended to make that a thing of the past. Spreading her knees, she sunk lower into the sand and ducked her head, swiping her tongue across the head of his cock.

"Ari," he hissed his appreciation as his hands sunk into her hair.

Smiling, she slipped her mouth over just the thick head of him, swirled her tongue across the slit, and tasted the salt of his cum. His hands fisted in her hair, and she took him to the hilt, his impressive length grazing the back of her throat as she began to suck.

Ariana was lost as his hips began to thrust in time to the bob of her head. The sounds of the ocean gave her peace as her body cried out for a shift in the location of his dick. When one hand left her hair and pushed between them, circling her clit she nearly stopped fucking him with her mouth, taken back by the jolt of pleasure as they teased one another.

"Ari," Orion growled, his hips steadying. "Enough," the single word was strained; a request, not a command.

Smiling, she slid her mouth down once more before releasing. Beg as he had, his finger continued to rub against her clit, drawing stars to her vision before she could even consider resuming her torture. Ariana's body quaked from the startling release.

They didn't speak, and could barely see each other in the bare light from the new moon, but when Orion laid her back into the sand and sheathed himself in a single thrust, she moaned.

Ariana let her hands slide over Orion's back as he held himself up with hands on either side of his head. Her legs wrapped around him and took him deeper.

Over and over he thrust, and Ariana's body moved in perfect tempo with her husband's. The waves crested behind them as every fiber of her being began to light up with a second release. She nipped his lower lip and pushed upright, forcing Orion onto his back so she could ride him.

"Gods, Ari," his hands wasted no time finding her breasts and massaging them.

Her hips bucked forward as his thrust up to meet hers. She gave into everything and let her head fall back as their bodies bumped and ground together and frantic speeds. She couldn't keep her eyes open as colors burst behind her eyelids as the second orgasm took over.

Though Ariana couldn't keep up the pace as her body exploded with pleasure, Ari's hands landed on her hips and controlled them, his forceful thrusts drawing out her waves of pleasure until he came, grunting her name as he did.

"I love you more than should be possible," she whispered, leaning forward so her lips could brush against the taut muscles of his chest.

"And I love you just the same," his arms wrapped around her, and his squeeze was almost enough to keep her pressed against him.

Almost.

She closed her eyes, picturing his gaze as he'd looked down at her with a fury of passion just minutes before. She'd give anything to stay connected to him like this, but she had a job to do.

Lifting off his dick, Ariana lay against him on the sand, her ear laying over his heart. There was comfort in the rapid, post-release thump of his heart, and comfort knowing she'd created such a release in him the same way he had for her.

"I love you, Orion." She whispered the words and merely thought the year and was gone.

CHAPTER FIVE

H is heart cracked beneath his rib cage as Orion's palms crashed against his chest.

Ariana's words of love, her passion, and insistence on coming to land made sense to him now.

She hadn't heeded his warning or listened to a word he'd said. She was determined to find her freedom from her mermaid form, and she'd left him to do it.

Orion ignored the burn of tears in the corners of his eyes. He had to pray and hold onto the belief that she would find him and remain stuck in time with him. He had to hope against hope, Poseidon didn't track her down in his fury and smite her where she stood.

Laying his hands flat on the sand beside him, Orion tried not to give into the grief swirling through him. If she never found, if she couldn't stick herself in time, they'd never remember one another.

"Worse, if she succeeds in saving me but not cementing her place by my side, she'll be gone."

No other mermaid or merman had been present when he found Ariana. Only the necklace had saved his wife.

And if I'm not turned, she'll be dead.

Orion pushed back the thought. He had to believe Ariana made it to nineteen seventy as safely as possible.

There was nothing he could do now but wait. Wait and wonder until everything becomes a blur as a new reality replaces the old reality - his current reality.

Once, he'd tried to explain to Ariana what it was like for those she left behind when she slipped through the Tides of Time. It was an empty existence and went on for as long as it took her to complete her task.

She could be gone days sometimes, minutes others.

There was never any way to know the outcome. It left a cold sort of deadness in his chest.

His entire world was somewhere in time, potentially fighting for his life, and Orion could do nothing.

Truth be told, his wife was a force of nature with her gift. She could travel at will, and while she had never tampered with anyone's life without their consent before, she could at any time. The people in their pod respected her - and a few others - for the intensity of their gifts. They didn't hold her at arm's length, though. They welcomed her and treasured what she could give their people.

And it still wasn't enough. Orion sighed and ignored the way the squish of wet sand went to a place in his body where any kind of sand had no business being.

He couldn't lay on this beach forever. If this reality changed, if she didn't come back with a change of heart, he would vanish, but potentially not soon enough to stop someone from seeing a whole bunch of man they might not have been invested in seeing.

Pushing upright, Orion glanced at the pants they'd grabbed from their home before their travels. He slipped his jeans on forgoing boxers, ignoring how constricting they were around his thighs.

Being a merman was freeing in a way he could never imagine. May never imagine if Ariana succeeded.

What if what she saw was not something she wished to see?

Would she make haste and return to their time only to hate him for the human he'd been.

Orion dragged his hand through his short hair with a disgruntled sound. He'd been no one special when he'd died. The fear of death never left him. Orion believed Posiedon left them with those vivid memories to ensure they never forgot what was done to them.

Sitting back on the sand, but further from the shoreline to keep his trousers dry, Orion looked out over the calm ocean. The barely visible waves were made stunning by the glint and glimmer of moonlight off the dark water. He could watch them for hours and would do so to ensure if Ariana somehow appeared in the water, he would be the first to see her.

Gazing out and the silent night, Orion couldn't help but stop the flashes of memory of his life as a human. Of the senseless violence he'd been forced to carry out in the name of his people as those of other religions attacked his homeland. He'd never told Ariana, but he'd taken close to a hundred lives before he lost his own.

Looked into countless sets of eyes before pulling the trigger and cowardly killed many others by not looking them in the eyes as he brought them to their death.

The man he'd been before was the reason he did not aim to hurt any in his new life. He would if necessary, and had on many occasions, but he wasn't the pacifist his wife was led to believe.

Once upon a time, I deserved the drowning death I'd found. Maybe if she succeeds, Ariana will make me a better person the same way she'd help take the coldness from my soul as a merman.

His stare stayed on the waves.

Whether he had minutes or hours, he would never know. The waiting was a death in and of itself, but for his wife, he would always wait.

CHAPTER SIX

Ariana's legs nearly failed her a third time as she stumbled across the broken cobblestone street.

Israel was nothing like the photos she'd seen in her time, but it was not the vast and barren desert Orion led her to believe it was either.

The streets were a bustle of activity before her - with cars and people moving and weaving together as if there wasn't a care or concern in the world for how much traffic was out on the street.

Her skin ached as the sun bore down on her.

She'd never been to the desert, even as a human. The strength of the sun was enough to torch her skin instantly. She had no sunscreen and no money. All she could do was hope the small dress she'd grabbed off a clothing line would keep the bulk of her skin safe.

Ariana could - and would - apologize to her shoulders later with a soothing kelp wrap.

Despite her legs, her genetics were still that of a creature who belonged beneath the waves. Being in direct sunlight zapped her strength in a way she'd never thought possible.

Stumbling, her arms flail to the side of their own accord as she crashed against someone's back.

"Whoa!" a deep voice chuckled as arms wrapped around her.

Arms that did not belong to Orion.

She glanced up into the dark, almost black, eyes of a very attractive man, but that man was not her husband. Large muscular arms felt more like a trap than comfort, and the hard planes of his face gave him a dangerous - almost malevolent - air.

Pulling back, Ariana tried to calm her nerves before she spoke up. She didn't have much time before her husband would be called to battle. She needed to find her before then, ensure he never went to the shores. Coming across like a blathering idiot would do her no favors.

"‫אתה בסדר?‬"

Ariana spoke very little Hebrew, only the words of endearment Orion had taught her.

If she spoke Spanish, it was unlikely he would understand. Instead, she used English in hopes it helped. "I do not speak your language. Apologies for visiting your country without learning it."

"Not a worry. My English is rough, but my parents taught me." His voice was deep and gruff.

"Yes, I'm sorry." she gestured at the ground around them. "A tourist," she hoped she could find her long-forgotten Spanish accent to help guide her cause. "I am unused to roads like this," she flashed him a smile she hoped spoke enough to leave her alone.

A dark brow raised. "You sound Spanish. I know there are cobblestone roads there." his gaze traveled over her body and rankled her. Her eyes landed on the silver band on his hand, and she realized she had a way out.

She prayed she could remember how to heat her cheeks to a flush. "Perhaps I was looking for a way to introduce myself."

He smiled. "While you are stunning, and am I happy to have saved you, I fear my wife would not be pleased."

"Drats," Ariana tried to force as much upset into the single word as she could.

"Do not tell her I looked," he gave a wink, and her stomach rolled.

"Could you help me find someone? I'm here searching for family."

For the most important family. My husband.

Though they'd never visited Orion's home, she'd heard many stories and would never forget the address because it was an important piece of his past. She didn't know the exact date of his death because he hadn't remembered it himself.

Just that Orion Levi died sometime in the early fall of the very year she'd transported to. It was summer, and she hoped that meant she'd get to him before he was called to fight for Isreal. Not because she needed time to make him love her in this time, but because she needed to ensure she could save him when his drowning began.

Save him as a human, not as a mermaid.

"Yes, I would be honored. We're not such a large city that I cannot assist."

Ariana started to give him Orion's address and froze.

Her husband walked out of the store just half a block up, and he was as perfect as the man she'd left naked and pleasured on the beach.

His hair was a little shorter, buzzed like many military men did from her time. Still, the thick black hair begged her to slip her hands inside the strands and kiss him until he fell in love with her. Otherwise, he looked exactly like the man she left some ninety years later on the beach somewhere in the United States.

"Nevermind," she moved away from the stranger and toward her husband.

Three steps closer and she stopped.

How the hell can I introduce myself to him and not seem like a desperate lunatic?

. . .

ORION TURNED and found himself unable to move. Unable to do anything except at the exceptionally beautiful woman a few shops back.

Truthfully, she didn't look very different than all the women he'd met locally, but there was something about her, some sort of magic that reached out from her like a beckoning finger and called him close.

Her dark black hair was short and curled just slightly at the ends, as if intentional and not natural. It framed a tan face with striking features. Her brows were thick but not unshapen and framed the most stunningly aquamarine eyes he'd ever stared into. A pale orange dress covered her shoulders and draped to her knees, but it did nothing to hide her shapely form. Round breasts stretched the fabric too tight at the top, and the curve of her hips was unmistakable through the cotton of the simple dress.

This woman was not from here, of that he had no doubt. She was far too stunning to have gone unnoticed in this city.

When she looked at him, it was as if time stopped. Orion could not hear a single sound around him. The cars paused in street. All the laughing and shouting vanished. There was nothing but the woman staring at him head-on.

She's searching for me.

The thought was the most illogical he'd ever had, but he still couldn't shake the feeling that she was here for him.

You're fantasizing before the war claims you.

The war with the Palestinians would never end. They were furious their land was divided up, and if Orion were honest, he didn't blame them.

But he would do whatever it took to keep the families of Isreal safe from them and the bombs they dropped with reckless abandon.

What's one for the road before I throw myself to the enemy lines?

Orion didn't know when he would leave, but he knew he would. The Army came calling time and time again because the threat didn't stop. That was no reason he couldn't have a little bit of fun with a stunning visitor before his time was up.

His mother's voice sounded off in his brain, telling him not to think like that, but Orion couldn't help it. He'd been on edge since the last time the Army called for him. He'd come home when many hadn't. It was the same story every war, every battle, every insurrection, but there was this sensation deep in his bones telling him the next time they came for it, it would be the last.

"Miss?" he spoke in English, assuming she would not speak his native Hebrew as so few did who weren't born and raised in Isreal did. Even the Jews in other countries who spoke Hebrew dwindled as they all moved to this part of the world.

"Hello," her cheeks turned damn near strawberry red with her flush, and she stepped toward Orion as he walked toward her.

"I couldn't help but hope your eyes lingered on me." He wasn't a flirt, but he would be for this woman.

"I'm afraid they were," she extended her hand. "Ariana de Gasol."

Orion's fingers slipped over hers, and static shot through him.

"Sorry, must have been our connection," he teased and couldn't figure out where this brazen man came from. He was attractive, but he'd never been so aggressive in pursuing someone. "Orion Levi, a pleasure to meet you."

Again, she flushed, but this time her eyes held the heat of desire he usually only saw in a woman's eyes after pressing against her or drinking far too many drinks.

"Do I know you?"

She swallowed visibly, but her eyes did not give away if she were embarrassed. "I would like you to."

His grin was unstoppable. "Are you certain you mean to speak me out? Not to distract you from your attraction, but this is not the norm where I am from."

She tucked a strand of hair behind her eyes. He had the unmistakable urge to do the same - to trace his finger along her cheek and over the curve of her ear until the stray hair was well and truly tucked.

"I'm certain. I've come a very long way for someone just like you."

"Well, then, please, allow me to buy you a drink." he gestured for her to walk beside him before he began to move. "What brings you to Isreal? We aren't the standard tourist spot."

"As I said, I came looking for someone just like you."

The lust dancing in her words made his throat dry and his mouth parched. He had never met a woman so upfront, never mind one as stunningly beautiful as Ariana. Orion would bet men chased her around her homeland - which he presumed to be Spain from the sound of her accent.

"Keep talking to me like that and we won't make it for the drink." he offered her a playful wink and swore she stumbled on her feet as if he flustered her the way she was beginning to do to him.

"Promises you've always made." She spoke so low under her breath he almost missed it.

"Come again?"

She flushed. "Nothing, please that drink would be wonderful now that I've made a fool of myself."

"No," he stopped and couldn't ignore the urge to take her hand, this time intertwining his fingers in hers. The moment he touched her, a spark of pain began near his temple.

He wasn't one for headaches, but he also didn't pick up beautiful women for drinks in the middle of the day. He tried again, focusing on the swirling blue in her eyes.

"Never apologize for yourself. Be focused on what you want, and direct in how you'll get it."

Something that looked like hurt flashed in her eyes but was gone a second later.

This woman was strange and beautiful, but he chose to simply believe she was strangely beautiful.

"All right, I won't." she didn't move to pull her hand from his, and they stood on the sidewalk, staring at one another. "That drink?" She prompted after a moment.

"Yes, the drink," Orion shook his head and tried to refocus himself. Never had a beautiful woman done more than turn him on. This one seemed to stir emotions he swore he'd never had, determined not to widow a woman as a stray bullet had done to his mother.

He walked again, gently guiding her down the street until they stood before the small restaurant. "I may have stretched the truth when I said drink, but water should be good all the same."

Her laughter set his soul alive. He'd never heard a more musical sound. It called to him, made him want to thread his fingers in her hair and kiss her until the world fell away.

Perhaps she's a siren come calling to distract me from my work. He chuckled at the thought, and she tilted her head to the side.

"I'm not certain what amuses you, but water would be wonderful. I'm not used to such heat."

Orion guided her in. "And what weather are you used to?"

"Humid. Rainy. Wet." She shrugged as if he should understand. "So the opposite of here, but it was important I come."

"To meet someone like me," he grinned as he guided them to a table.

"Precisely."

"You must entertain me while we quench our thirst." he let go of her hand as she slipped onto the booth seat before joining her on the other bench. "Why come looking for someone like me?"

"To fall in love," she held the most serious expression for a few moments before it twisted with laughter. "I should not have played such a trick, but it is not so far off."

He exhaled a breath he hadn't realized he'd held.

"'I'm here because I made a promise to someone that I love that I wouldn't go and change history alone."

"So you're planning to make some waves?"

She laughed again. The sound of whistling and magical bells filled his ears.

"One might say that. Tell me, Orion Levi, what is it about you that makes me unable to look anywhere else?"

"I could have asked you the same question, Ariana de Gasol." The sound of her name on his lips had an unexpected response. Blood rushed south as if he spoke her name in the peak of passion.

He let his hand shift over hers, wondering if he moved far too fast with a woman he'd met on a street corner. A strange calm washed over him when she didn't tug hers out from under his.

They sat like that, talking about everything and nothing for so long the sun began to set in the sky. They'd drunk, shared food, and everything in between that two people could do while trapped in a meal hall.

"It would appear I've drastically altered your day," her lips wrapped around the lip of the glass, and Orion swore he'd cum in his pants at the simple action despite not having been hard a moment prior.

"Let me take up more of your time. Dinner. Tomorrow night. I know this is crazy, but I can't shake the feeling I'm supposed to have met you. I promise I'm a fantastic cook, and you'll have nothing to fear joining me at my home."

"Yes," she responded so fast he thought he'd asked an entirely different, easy-to-answer question.

"You will?"

She nodded, a curtain of hair falling in front of her face.

"I don't have anywhere to be for a few days, I came looking for adventure."

"I thought you came looking for someone like me?"

"And couldn't you be one and the same?"

Blood pounded through him as if she'd somehow torn down every wall and desire he'd ever had and saw right through to his soul. He'd wanted that - to be someone's safe space and adventurous partner.

"I'll get you my address. Tomorrow at six?"

"Tomorrow at six," she nodded, her eyes fixed on his as if there were nothing else in the world more important for her to look at than boring old Orion Levi.

CHAPTER SEVEN

"You're perfect," Ariana mocked what Orion said to her anytime he found her standing before a mirror in their home. She hadn't cared how she looked to anyone but him, and his words never failed to make her feel like the most special woman alive.

"Then why don't you feel perfect?"

She dropped onto the bed of the hostel she'd wormed her way in to. She shouldn't have taken off without the bag she'd packed, but Ariana knew she needed to leave or never be able to. Laying in his arms had always been her favorite part of their relationship. A single delay could have jeopardized her willingness to hope this worked.

"But it is working," she looked at the woman in the mirror and tried not to care that the dark black dress she'd stolen was slightly larger than required.

The man she ate with yesterday had been truly perfect. He was her husband in every way even if he didn't have so many years as a merman under his belt.

Orion Levi was as perfect as a human as he was a siren.

All that was left to do was get a job so she could stay near him.

She knew where he would go - where he would lose his life - but it wasn't somewhere Ariana could hang around and wait.

She'd never survive. Perhaps if she'd been gifted with invisibility, all would be well, but that was not the case. Time travel didn't work inside of itself. She couldn't hop around and hope she found him. Ariana's gift worked once per cycle. She always needed to return herself to her most recent present moment when she was done.

It could be weeks before the fateful day, but she couldn't think of a single useable skill in her arsenal. Before her death, Ariana had been a general practitioner - something utterly impossible not only in the seventies but in the Middle East. She needed to find something, maybe waitressing, if she wanted to be around and fall more in love with Orion every day.

Glancing at the circles under her eyes in her reflection, Ariana exhaled and walked to the door.

Seventeen minutes later, she stood outside the address she'd already known by heart but had written on a piece of paper. She made a good show of gripping the paper as she walked to knock on the door.

It flung open, revealing a sinfully sexy Orion in nothing but a pair of jeans resting low on his hips, showing off his muscular, tanned body. She swallowed back a wave of desire and couldn't help but wonder if this outfit was intentional. Her husband was not a tease, but he did know what she liked. Perhaps he knew because women before her liked it.

The thought drew her lips down in a frown.

"Shayna, that is not what a man likes to see when he greets a woman at his door."

She didn't need to ask what Shayna meant, he used it all the time to call her beautiful in his language.

"Perhaps I'm not used to seeing men casually naked."

He scoffed. "You are from Spain, which is practically the French-Riviera. You have seen many naked men."

She wanted to correct his geography but decided against it.

Instead, she found herself smiling at the same way this version of her husband could put her at ease.

"Who said my frown wasn't because my mind was very sad I would not get to eat whatever delish meal you cook?"

"And why would that be?" Orion extended a hand and, when she took it, tugged her inside.

"Because your state of undress has me believing there is something else on your mind."

His eyes went dark with lust. "It is not polite."

"Fuck polite," Ariana hadn't meant to sound so crass, but seeing him before her only served to remind her what she fought for. Her lips were against his in a split second.

He tasted of spices and butter - obviously tasting his cooking as he did at their home in the future as well. His kiss was hungry from the start, proving he still wanted her despite not even knowing her - and it wasn't as if she was the definition of beautiful.

"You taste like strawberries and wine," he spoke against their kiss and then swiped his tongue over the seam of her mouth.

She would always taste that way to him, but she'd never known him to taste of anything save for bread - his last meal hours before his death. Perhaps she could find a way to bring him a different last meal.

His hand brushed across her back and pulled Ariana from her thoughts. His fingers nimbly traced circles over the bar portion of her back where the dress did not cover near her shoulder blades.

Every stroke sent a flick of desire through her. There was something illicit in believing she was about to bed another man. He was her husband, but he wasn't, and something in that set her body on fire.

"Please tell me to stop now if I must," he trailed kisses along the nape of her neck until he reached her collarbone. "I will not take advantage of you when I asked you here for dinner."

She let her hand trail between them, brushing over his growing hardness before cupping and rubbing more intently. "Never stop."

She let her fingers glide over the metal button, grasping the stupid metal between her and him until it pushed through the hole. Ariana's hand slipped under the waistband and found him hard as ever inside his briefs.

A small snicker was spared as she acknowledged he lied, telling her he was a boxer man before there was no need for underwear.

He was all hot steel in her grasp, and Ariana suddenly couldn't remember anything save for how he pumped into her on the beach just nights ago.

"Will you respect me if I tell you how badly I want to be intimate with you?" She tried to force the words to sound time appropriate even as his hands had moved to her breasts and rolled her braless nipples between his fingers.

"Never," he took his statement to heart, and his hands trailed away from her breasts down her body. They lingered momentarily alongside her thighs and then grasped the bottom of the stolen dress before tugging up and over her head.

She was forced to release his dick from her stroking for a moment and found herself pinned against the wall a second later, his fingers splaying tantalizingly over her wetness, stroking over but not entering her.

"I assure you, my invitation had been innocent, but I cannot help myself."

Ariana could have pointed out that she was a siren, that as a human, he was helpless around her if she wanted his affections, but she wasn't certain that's what this was, and she sure as fuck didn't want him to stop.

"Orion!" She gasped when his fingers pushed inside her pussy, bare from underwear because she'd not wanted to steal more than she needed to.

"You came ready," he whispered against her ear and added another finger, they moved in tandem, thrusting and scissoring inside her dripping center as her hips began to thrust.

"I came for you," she cried out as the orgasm crashed over her so quickly.

Their mouths found one another's again, harder this time, demanding and hot.

"That was," Orion held himself above her, sweat clinging to the hair on his forehead. "That was fucking incredible." He rotated his hips, punctuating each word as if they hadn't both just come together.

"I'm going to have to agree," she swirled her fingers over the planes of his back. "Do you think you can go again before you feed me?" She nipped at his earlobe, knowing full well he would not rise to the occasion after the frantic way they'd just fucked.

"The food!" his face twisted into regret. "It'll be burned."

She laughed softly and used her hands to cup his face and bring him down for another kiss. "I promise, this was so much better."

CHAPTER EIGHT

Orion gasped for air as he rolled off of Ariana. There was something about this woman that he couldn't seem to get enough of. It wasn't just the way he craved sinking deep into her body either.

She was brilliant, far more so than most women he'd met. She had a way of focusing on a situation and delving into it, probing the conversation for all it was worth and challenging him to do the same.

Never in his life had a woman gotten under his skin in the way she had. Everywhere he turned, he wondered how Ariana would fit into the moment or what she would have to say about something. Her intelligence was just one piece of the puzzle that fascinated him.

Two weeks.

"What about them?"

He hadn't realized he'd spoken out loud until she responded.

"I was just thinking that it's only been two weeks, and I cannot imagine a day that you have not been part of my life." His eyes widened when he realized the strange confession was likely as terrifying as the way they'd fucked the second she'd come in the door for their first official date.

"I feel the same," she moved to lay her head on his chest, her dark hair fanning out over his body like a curtain.

"I know this will sound crazy, but would you wait for me if I were called to war?"

She went absolutely rigid against him.

"That was the wrong thing to ask -"

"I would wait, but I would rather you not go." she cut him off before he could continue to blunder things up. She sat upright, not bothering to cover herself with the sheet.

He'd never told a woman he loved her before, but he couldn't shake the feeling he loved this woman already. Or that perhaps he'd been destined to love her. The thought was foolish but one he couldn't shake.

"Orion?" Ariana gazed at him.

"I love you."

"What?" her jaw dropped open.

Orion winced, his error evident. "I'm sorry if that was too fast."

"No! I love you, too." She grinned at him and bent forward to kiss him quickly. "I just wasn't expecting you to say that."

"Trust me," he kissed her again, longer this time, "I hadn't expected to say it so soon, but I cannot deny the truth. I have fallen in love with the pretty Spaniard who's invaded my thoughts."

"Then do not go to war. If the Army calls, stay home." Terror laced her words, and he understood why. War was not for marriages.

"It is my job. They will arrest me if I ignore a summons." he let his hand cup the right side of her face, and she leaned into his touch. "I promise that if I know I have you to come home to, I will never find harm in battle."

Her face paled so much he worried she may pass out. She didn't though, but when she closed her eyes, he could not ignore the dusting of tears clinging to her lashes so quickly. "I love that about you, you know that? Your unwavering loyalty once you commit your-self to anything."

She spoke as if it were something she'd told him a dozen times. He couldn't recall ever showing her this side of him in the last two weeks, except his promises to make her scream his name every time he saw her.

A smile spread over his lips just thinking about all the ways he'd fucked Ariana in the last two weeks. They'd been unstoppable, barely able to come up for air once they began their heated explorations of each other.

A knock interrupted any further thoughts. The action banged through the house as if the person knocking had life or death conse-quences should they not get him to come to the door.

"Ignore it," she whispered, letting her hand trail down his stom-ach, teasing the skin and sending blood surging to his cock already.

He didn't need to be told twice.

Until the knock came again.

"Orion Levi, this is the Israeli Army. Open up."

"Fuck," he snarled just as Ariana had slunk down his body and pressed her lips against the head of his dick.

"Leave them be," she whispered.

His stomach tightened as he did the unthinkable. Despite his desire to stay between the wetness of her lips, he gently pulled her head back. "Save that thought." Rolling away with painful quickness, Orion grabbed his pants off the floor where they'd been thrown last night and damn near jumped into them. The fabric was rough against his straining erection, and he knew if this wasn't a fast conversation, he may finish from the way his pants caressed him.

Jerking open the door, he was unsurprised to see two men standing in full attire.

"Gentlemen," he stepped out and closed the door behind him. He would not allow these men to see Ariana.

"It is no secret that our enemies grow braver by the day. You have served your time well, but the call to action comes again. You'll receive your orders and stationing within the day."

The world seemed to flip upside down on him as the officer spoke. There was no possible way this came to be the second he and Ariana confessed their love and spoke of it.

"Dismissed." The second officer spoke with a nod of his head, and they left.

Numb everywhere, Orion turned and set his hand on the doorknob. He struggled to twist it, his mind a haze of pain and confusion that destroyed the lust coursing through him fucking seconds before.

"Orion?" Ariana stood in the hallway, dressed, with a frown on her lips.

"How could you have known?"

She winced, and the tears began rolling down her cheeks. "I didn't, but I've feared it since you told me what you did."

He crossed the space and tucked her against him, setting his chin on the top of her head as he ran a hand over her back.

"I swear to you, I will return. When I do, I'll speak to them about my discharge. I've surpassed my service expectations."

She nodded, the action oddly slow under his chin.

"I'll come back to you. What we have may be new, but it's wonderful, and I'll not let anything get in the way of that."

Her sniffle was louder than she likely intended it to be.

"Come, let's get dressed. I want to show you a special place you can go whenever you miss me while I'm gone."

"When will you go?" the question was little more than a whisper.

"I won't know for a little bit. But if they've come to me versus ringing, our enemies have gotten braver, and if I can help save even a single life, I cannot ignore this."

Ariana nodded again but said nothing.

Orion couldn't stand the way his heart contracted as if squeezed from the inside. He'd fallen in love with this woman on a whim, and her happiness meant the world to him.

CHAPTER NINE

O rion cast a glance down at the paper under the pen. The words blurred together moments before he dragged the pen across the page, scribbling everything. Nothing was coming out the way he'd intended it to.

He'd been gone less than a week, and all he wanted was to send Ariana a letter that told her how important she was.

The look in her eyes as he'd gotten on the plane haunted his every waking moment. His dreams were plagued with memories of their bodies intertwined and even a few fantasies of what they would be in the future. She encompassed his every thought in a way that shouldn't be possible so soon, but he wouldn't dare let it go.

"Then write what you need to write, damn it." Orion sneered and ran a hand through his hair, still clutching the pen in the other.

Everything had been so uneventful he didn't believe there'd been real reason to send his unit. Not for the reasons everyone thought.

The Americans weren't the only ones who stuck their neck out to help others. It seemed his country followed in its path, maybe due to the help America gave them almost thirty years ago. Instead of protecting Isreal, he sat in a tent on the fucking beach of Normandy, as if another war would come to these shores.

Dropping the pen, Orion tore the page free from the pad, relishing in the satisfying rip of page from page as if it signified ripping something of himself that he hated away. The clean page taunted him as much as the poorly written love letter had.

An explosion of bullets thundered through his ears and paused any attempt at writing to Ariana.

"Let's go!" A voice he couldn't recognize of a soldier he didn't know well enough spurred him on.

Orion jumped up, the shitty folding chair collapsing underneath the quick spring of weight. All around him, he watched lips move but he couldn't hear anything over the sound of the bullets - sounds he prayed remained just bullets.

Leaning, he grabbed his gun from where it was propped on the side of the bed and took off. Around him, men darted toward the danger with great speed. His eyes blurred everything around him except the bullets flying toward his people.

Every single dark pewter object nearly stopped him in his tracks. Orion dodged two as his feet struck the sand. Running was damn near impossible, and he lunged to grab a fallen soldier as they gave into the difficult terrain and slipped.

"Thanks," he swore he heard as he jerked the other man up.

Orion's heart slammed in his chest as he continued to run. Closer and closer, he pushed until water splashed against his pant legs. He wasn't the best shot in the bunch, he needed to be close to take the enemy down.

He looked at them, stared at the men stomping closer to them with no identifiable uniform. His mouth was dry as he loaded the chamber on the shotgun, and he pulled back, his finger snapping away to release his own bullet.

It made contact with a man's shoulder, but it didn't slow him down. Around him, Orion heard the sounds of war, sounds that would shake a grown man to their knees, but he couldn't seem to duck and protect himself.

Firing off another round, he took a step closer, aimed, and fired again. Pain seared through his arm and stopped his pursuit of the advancing army. Orion didn't need to look to know he'd been shot. Thankfully, it slammed into his left bicep, an arm he didn't need to shoot them all down. Whoever they were, they came to destroy this unit. Orion refused to go down without a fight.

An image of Ariana formed in his mind as he fired off another bullet. Her eyes were bright, her smile brighter. She had her arms open, beckoning him to run to her.

The distraction cost Orion as pain so blistering hot he believed himself on fire raced through his chest. He fell, the water both cushioning his fall and covering up over his mouth as salt streamed into his mouth.

Stop screaming. He couldn't hear himself, but he knew the sounds of pain - at least some - came from him.

Pushing his feet into the ocean bottom beneath him, Orion tried to bend his knees and push up, tried to roll to the side at the same time, but the motions canceled each other out. Out of the corner of his eye, he saw another fall and a rush of water explode upward.

Then everything went blurry, and finally, he let his eyes close. He may die here, the pain in his chest was too intense to push past.

I'm sorry, Ariana.

Something squeezing his arms woke him. He blinked, trying to clear the fog, and the pain came back, searing through him like a bolt of electricity.

He was dying.

Ariana tugged him backward, toward the shore.

The sounds of war were gone, and when he turned his head, Orion saw far too many bodies lying in the water around him.

"I'm not letting them take you. Not this time."

Ariana's words didn't make much sense, but he was happy to see his final moments of lucidity conjured something as wonderful as the woman who'd stolen his heart in less than a month.

"I love you," he choked on salt water and sputtered, but he knew the words were audible.

"And I love you, which is why I'm doing this. Those morons left you for dead." She continued to rant, but his ears were failing him.

He closed his eyes. Imagining her was the perfect way to go if he had to die. She would pull him to safety, and he would sleep.

When his ass smacked into a rock, he realized this wasn't some pain-filled on-the-brink-of-death dream.

"Ow, fuck."

"Sorry, my love." she glanced down at him and grimaced. "This is as far as I can take you. I can feel the time shift coming." Her voice broke into sobs. "It wasn't supposed to be like this. I was supposed to stay!"

Her anguished cry tore at his heart far stronger than any bullet ever could.

"You're leaving?"

She began to blur, and Orion swore he could almost see through Ariana.

Maybe this is a death dream after all. It was only a few more seconds before he could no longer feel her grip on his arms.

"Over here!"

"You got a live one?"

Orion wasn't certain what the fuck was going on anymore, but he just needed to sleep.

CHAPTER TEN

The frigid water rushed into her mouth, exploding past her tongue and poured down her throat.

Ariana clutched at her throat, even as her legs flailed to push her to the surface.

No!

She screamed, her eyes adjusting to the burn of the salt water far quicker than should have been possible. Her lungs screamed out for air because she wasn't a mermaid, not now, not yet.

She remembered this moment, remembered the crushing fear and the intoxicating pain as her chest seemed to explode without air.

Ariana stopped trying to force the water from her throat and began to tug herself toward the surface. She could push herself up if she didn't panic this time. She didn't need to die at the hands of those fucking drug lords a second time.

Kicking, she almost broke the surface until a hand shoved her under.

Ariana kicked and tried to slam her hands against the arm attached to the hand that drownd her, but she was too weak.

Almost sixty seconds had passed, and her body would begin to shut down any moment.

Something went wrong. The whisper-light thought passed through her mind. She'd saved Orion. She was supposed to stay stuck in time.

But you aren't. You're drowning again because some drug lord used your boat as a getaway vehicle.

Ariana tried to channel the peace she knew could come from being under the waves, but as her lungs began to cry out, the peace slipped away. Her thoughts grew slow as the oxygen vanished and couldn't be replenished.

Ariana wasn't a mermaid.

She was a human.

And Orion wasn't a merman to save her.

Everything grew cold the longer the hand shoved her beneath the waves. Her head smacked on the boat, and her vision started to fade.

"You're going to owe for this," Galene swam before her. With a touch, everything went black as Ariana foolishly opened her mouth to scream for underwater air.

She sputtered, and everything went black.

Her mind was free, drifting somewhere, and then it wasn't.

Ariana's eyes flew open, and she screamed.

This scream did not suck air into her lungs.

Galene's obnoxious pale green eyes stared at her, fury etched in the line of her brow and the straight line of her lips.

Ariana took a deep breath and then another.

"Why wasn't I a mermaid just now?"

"Because you somehow fucked a timeline up beyond repair." Galene growled.

"Be kind. How would you feel if it were me?" Liam's familiar baritone came from Ariana's right.

"If you're so pissed, why did you save me? How did you know where I'd be without Orion to bring you here?"

"That would be my doing." A very disgruntled voice came from the depths before a man - not a merman - seemed to rise from beneath them.

Ariana knew Posideon's voice. It was sensual but commanding and somehow gentle but terrifying, all in a single note.

Long blond hair, a shade more golden than Galene's, was perfectly flat against his head despite the current underwater. His bare chest tempted her in ways it shouldn't because of her love for her husband, but a god's beauty was impossible to ignore. His trident glowed a faint yellow in his hand, and his brilliant eyes narrowed on her in anger.

The handsome god flashed them away, dropping them in his castle.

Ariana allowed herself to float into a chair before trying to understand anymore.

"What were you thinking, child?" Poseidon bellowed, damn near shaking the shell walls of his palace. "What I gave you was a gift!"

"What you gave me was a never-ending life in service to someone else. I was tired." She slumped in the chair, knowing how selfish all of this was. "Is Orion alive?"

All three nodded at her. "He's alive and human." Liam spoke, ever the peace bringer.

"Which is a problem for me." Poseidon crossed his arms over his chest, the action causing every fucking muscle on display to flex. "My dear, when Orion called to Galene it was I who commanded her to save you. I knew your love of time travel would suit our needs - needs to save the pod which is always my first priority. It was I who did so again, but it seems we have a small problem."

"And now you'll kill me?"

His bark of laughter was more sensual than it had any right to be.

"Not in this lifetime. Now I will work to undo what you fucked up. The pod needs Orion's gift the same way it needs yours. His ability to suffocate with a single touch saved many mermen and

322

mermaids who would not have survived their trip for revenge. A second life that lasts only a few hours is no gift at all."

"Why was I human?"

"Because your plan failed, as it would have all along." Poseidon almost seemed saddened she'd tried anything that would harm her.

"Getting stuck in time is a punishment, not a gift. Also, it is not for you to control. Chronos - bastard that he is - is supreme in that. He found your attempts amusing, and so when you saved your husband, you catapulted back through time to the moment of your death."

Ariana had no memory of that, just of saving Orion and then drowning. She always kept memories of multiple timelines when she created them, so this wasn't shocking, but it fucked with her ability to tell up from down right now.

"Galene and I saved you because we need your gift. A gift is once in a pod's lifetime. We are not done using yours as of yet. However, because you are clearly wound up in Orion's life, we bartered with Chronos in his pit for a boon only he could give."

She didn't like the harrowed sound in the god's voice. Ariana knew the Greek mythos and knew what Chronos was to his family. And to the world.

"You're not going to ask what this boon is?" Galene lifted off the chair and swam to linger before Ariana.

"Apparently, it was my life."

The leader gave a small scoff. "Not so much. He's given us the ability to allow you to travel back into Orion's timeline - the erased one - and fix what you stole."

"I won't condemn him to this life."

"Did he hate this life?" Galene's voice boomed around them. "Or did he love you so much he allowed your recent hatred to seem like his?"

Ariana paused before she spoke. She knew the answer. Orion was terrified of losing her to her plan. He'd never mentioned wishing to be away from the pod, only that he couldn't lose her.

Tears burned the bridge of her nose before forming in her eyes. She did her best not to acknowledge them and appear weak in front of the important trio.

"So here is the task at hand. It is not a deal, so I will not call it such." The god's trident glowed before spitting out an image of Orion on the beach. "You will go with Galene and murder this poor soul. He must take his rightful place beneath the waves."

"I will never harm my husband!"

"Which is a problem because if he doesn't die, you'll snap back to the moment before your death, and no one will know you're there this time. We only knew this time because Chronos spoke in my head, gloating about the dangers your gift would cause the pod." Dark blue eyes stared into her, damn near seeing her soul while he played out the scene like a projection.

Ariana couldn't watch, couldn't stand to see the figures of herself and Galene.

"The choice is yours, my daughter of the sea. Destroy him and save yourself, or destroy yourself and many within this pod."

As quickly as everything appeared, Ariana was alone with Galene, her tail brushing against a shallow ocean bottom.

"What will you do, sister?"

Galene's words echoed in her mind and pulled Ariana into a cyclone.

If she never saved Orion, would someone else in the pod? *Of course, they would.* He would survive in one way or another to save her one day.

But what if he doesn't die beneath the waves? What if it happens on land, and then we're both free?

The thought slammed into her, causing Ariana to stop the gentle tail swish that kept her upright. She didn't want to escape life, she just wanted to escape life as a mermaid.

"I'm saving my husband." She spoke through a clenched jaw, not because it wasn't the choice she wanted, but because it was accepting that everything would start again. She would live as a mermaid and eventually tire of the constant need to be with the pod.

"What you're feeling is common, sister." Galene set a hand on her arm. "It can be quite a lot living life in service to another."

For the first time, Ariana realized that perhaps Galene carried a weight on her shoulders that no one else could bear. Without her, there was only death if one could not escape the watery hands that grabbed the feet of those unfortunate enough to fall in unprepared.

"Are you prepared to see this?"

Again, the other woman was kind and compassionate. Ariana knew that once, but she'd forgotten with her anger over the years. Galene watched countless men and women take their final breaths, only to decide if they would ever take another.

"I'm sorry for your burden." Ariana set her hand on Galene's shoulder.

"I'm so sorry for what you must bear. Chronos was definitive in his torment. You must drag him to his death to save his life and countless others."

Ariana took a deep breath, thankful that the water did not rush into her lungs as it had just half an hour before.

"You must take us there." Seafoam green eyes filled with sympathy. "When you are ready," Galene held out a delicate hand.

Ariana nodded. *When I am ready.* She blew out a slow breath. *When you are ready to kill your husband so you may one day be together again.* Another deep lungful of air over her gills, and Ariana set her hand on Galene's.

"Will I recover from this?"

The older woman shrugged solemnly. "I cannot answer that. I live with the choice of death for many. It is nowhere near the same, but I should think a part of you will always live with this."

Nodding, Ariana focused on the frigid waters just off the coast of France, pinpointing the exact date that Orion had told her time and time again was his new birthday.

The bubbles swirled around them, the only sign that she made any effort to travel through the tides of time.

A bullet whizzed past her arm, some of the danger undone by the force of the water the bullet crashed in to.

"It's a war," Galene reminded her, nudging her forward. "Orion, he's shot in the shallows, isn't he?"

Ariana nodded, trying to figure out a way to get him into the depths without her tail being seen.

I remember the life fading from my body and then being tossed, throne further out to sea, likely so they didn't have to bury a body. Orion's pained voice sounded in her mind.

"How could I have forgotten?" Ariana shook her head. "We don't move. We stay here. Someone will do their worst to him." Her stomach grew heavy. "This is not a punishment, correct? I will not drown my beloved for you to watch and taunt me?"

Galene's features twisted as if Ariana struck her. "I will not give that a response."

They waited there in silence, thanks to Ariana's thoughtless question, as bullets and men fell into the water. Ariana wished they could save more, but Galene did not much no matter how many took their final breath beneath the sea. They were here for Orion, and though her soul broke with each death, Ariana knew they would only save her husband.

Every splash drew her eyes to the source. Every ripple twisted her insides with what would come.

Orion had never told her a siren drowned him to save him, and she couldn't help but wonder if it had always been here. Was this merely one step of a loop they always saw out?

"There!" Galene's hand landed on Ariana's arm, and her other hand pointed to where Orion floated mere feet from them, a trail of blood leaking behind him. "You know what you must do."

Ariana's tears tracked down her face as she swam closer. Orion's eyes were closed, but she could see the faint rise and fall.

"I'm sorry," the words were lost to her sobs as she grabbed his hand and began to swim down.

Down and down she went, stopping only when the darkness familiar to their home surrounded them. He flailed at one point, likely coming awake as his body noticed the deprivation.

"I love you," she cried. "I'm so sorry." Her hand tightened around his wrist as her heart thumped so wildly in her chest that she almost let Orion go to float to the waves.

"That is enough, my child." Poseidon's deep timbre filled her mind, and a blinding white light forced her eyes closed.

CHAPTER ELEVEN

"Don't you ever do that again," Orion snarled at his wife the second her head returned to his chest. "Don't you ever fucking do that again." His hand trailed over her hair, his heart trying to escape his chest with worry as the fear of a life never lived slammed into him.

"What do you mean?" Ariana's voice cracked as she sat upright.

"Don't play stupid with me, wife." He snarled the word like he regretted the truth behind it.

"You remember?" She tucked a hair behind her ear and tried to look away.

"I don't think so," Orion caught her chin with two fingers and jerked it upright. "You're not running from this conversation. I didn't give you my fucking consent."

"I'm sorry," she whispered, her glittering eyes filling with tears.

"I didn't give you consent to steal decades from us by damning us to a mortal life." His lips captured hers, and he didn't care that he was aggressive. He was pissed. "I didn't consent to the loss of a single fucking second with you," he spat when he pulled back from his bruising kiss. "And I never will."

"I'm sorry, I needed out."

"You would trade decades with me for a chance to live like a normal human?"

"When you say it like that, it sounds so foolish to give up what we have."

He snorted. "You're damn right it's foolish, and I'm going to remind you why." His hand slipped between her legs, wiggling to spread them apart as a finger brushed over her clit. "Every single second of our lives together is important to me." He pressed a finger inside her body, and her legs fell open on a gasp.

Orion still held her chin in his other hand. "Look into my eyes, Ariana. Stay with me as I make you remember."

Her body responded to the pressure of his finger thrusting in and out of her pussy. Her hips bucked slightly, and he almost lost her stare as her eyes fluttered.

"This, he growled and added a second finger into her heat. You're wet for me already." Releasing her face, Orion captured Ariana's lips with his and thrust his tongue against hers the instant the kiss began. This wasn't about gentle and tender.

A lifetime of memories slammed into him - memories that shouldn't exist but did.

Memories of her in his home. Memories of them saying I love you at a time when she'd not even been born yet. Memories of dying in her arms and being saved by them as well.

He'd had time to be furious because the memories came before she did. Time to think about if he would walk away from her for her selfishness or fuck her into she couldn't think straight. When she'd left, he'd not been overly worried, but knowing that life, the one she almost gave him and then stole by walking away on the beach,

His erection grew with every thrust of his finger into Ariana. They'd never had hate-sex before, but damn it if he didn't understand the appeal.

"Orion," she gasped as she began to ride his finger, her body pressing against the heel of his hand to give her the relief she craved from his touch.

"Ariana, this is about more than lust, but god damn it if I can't think of another way to prove to you how furious I am right now is to deny you what you crave." Ignoring the thrum of blood in his cock, Orion slipped his finger free from her body only to use his body to crowd her backward into the sand. "This is what you want," he used his hand to grasp his hard length and trace it over her opening. She was slick and so close to the edge a single thrust would send them both over.

"Orion," she reached between them and took his shaft in her hand, stroking him with so much force he nearly came in her hand. "Show me."

She nipped at the muscles in his neck, and he lost control. He slammed into her heat, knocking her hand off his dick as he did. Orion's thrusts were merciless as he slammed hard and pulled out to the tip, only to strike against her again.

His breathing caught in his throat, but he didn't slow down. She would come first. It didn't matter that in this timeline they'd just made love. He knew the way her body tightened around his that she was about to crest.

"Come for me," he flicked a finger across her swollen clit and screamed his name into the night. Her body clenched around him, pulling his orgasm before he could pace himself to draw hers out.

Panting, Orion allowed himself to rest on top of her even as he rolled his hips for small, slow thrusts.

Nothing was said, and nothing could be heard except their heavy breathing and the surf rushing onto the shore.

"If you crack a joke about doing that again for the sex, I swear I'll tie you up in our house and never let you leave."

Her laugh was as shaky as his words. "I'm sorry, Orion. I thought it was for the best."

"Promise me that whenever you feel overwhelmed or used or burnt out, you'll come to me." he kissed her gently this time, and pulled free from her body. He rolled onto his back when he was done.

Orion started up and the sky and tried to imagine the life they could have had as humans, but it never happened. In the alternate timeline, they never met. He died alone, never having found a reason to marry.

"How long were you away in the strange timeline after my death?"

She sighed. "Long enough to hate the world without you and me together in it."

"Good."

"Good?" She huffed.

"Yes, because if you hated it that much, then I know you'll never try this again."

"Never, I love you too much to run the risk of never getting to know you. Never getting to feel you fuck me like you just did - which by the way, please get angry with me more often."

He chuckled and tugged her close. "I think we can make arrangements."

"I love you, Orion."

"And I love you, every single version of you I've ever and may ever meet."

ARIANA'S HEART thudded in her chest even as the orgasm's intensity died down. She loved the man beside her, and even though she had found flaws with the pod, she understood the pain and suffering Galene dealt with.

The first mermaid was a broken woman, and she relied on the pod to keep her together. To keep her from hating what Posiedon made her, what the great god created for them all.

"Come on, we still have a lunar cycle to enjoy," he stood, and Ariana couldn't help but enjoy the view.

"You look as perfect as you did as a human."

"Good," he winked and offered her a hand to stand up.

"Did you ever intend to tell me how many revenge kills you made for the pod?"

He froze, the smile slipping slightly from his lips. "I'd hope to keep the darkness I had to bear a secret."

"Never again. Let me unburden you when those days come. We may be built for revenge, but it's not all we are."

"No, my perfect Shayna, it is not all we are." He tugged her to her feet. "But I am tired after somehow living two lifetimes in a single day. Are you coming?"

She smiled, "There's nowhere else on land I'd rather be."

EXILE

A.R. HARLOW

PROLOGUE

"Come on, take another shot!"

Castiela shook her head. "Bart, you know I've already reached my limit." She gestured to the six empty shot glasses on the bar top of their boat, The *Exile*. "I would much rather take you back to bed and have some fun." She purred seductively, putting her lipstick-stained lips against his ear. She gripped his arm, her fingers twisting in the blue material.

He shuddered in her grasp and backed away, straightening his button-down shirt. "Fine, fine. But first, let's go see the moon over the water. I hear that sometimes in weather like this, you might even spy a mermaid coming on land to escape the violent throes of the sea." He shot her that million-dollar smile that had won him and his mother many of the elections in town. It made her knees weak and her core wet and she couldn't think straight when he sent her looks like that.

"Alright, but I better see a mermaid if it's taking the time away from getting laid." Her unfiltered state was something to marvel at because she certainly wasn't a drinker, and it didn't take much.

"Lead on, Captain." She fake saluted him and he led her out onto the deck of the boat.

The moonlight sparkled down across the water with a beauty that took her breath away. It was worth the delay to seducing her fiancé back in their cabin. "Wow." She stared up at the sky and could make out so many stars and constellations and she backed up toward the railing of the boat, her fingers tracing the sky with wonder. "Look at how beautiful." She chuckled then and pointed to the water. "But I don't see any mermaids." She fake-pouted and he approached her.

At first, he took her hands in his and they slow danced by the side of the boat. Vaguely, Castiela thought of it being silly to be that close to the railing when the waters beneath were churning with a untamed violence, but the thought faded as Bartley pulled her in closer. "I'm sorry." He murmured against her ear. "One day, maybe you'll look down on me and be proud of the man I became after this."

"What—" she couldn't finish her thought. She tumbled into the raging waters that were violently thrashing the boat. She fought to keep above the surface, his expression of nonchalance burning into her memory as she struggled to swim through the waves that threatened to repeatedly push her below.

The boat moved, slowly at first, and then it was off at as quick a clip as it mustered, and she choked on water and the salt of her own tears. Sobs threatening to drown her as much as the water was. She was fighting a losing battle; she couldn't tread the vicious waves forever. Castiela slipped under the surface for longer bouts each time and found it harder to swim up against the crashing waves. She knew she couldn't make it to the far rocks nor to the shore that lay a mile away. Truth be told, she wasn't even sure she wanted to. Her fiancé threw her overboard. As the image of his face came to the forefront of her mind, she lost her battle to keep her head above water and began to be pushed down.

Down.

Down.

Down.

Her vision darkened as she struggled to hold her breath. She didn't even know why because she couldn't make it out of this one. There was no way except for an angel swooping from the skies or a mythical beast from below catching her and saving her. But Castiela never was much for fairytales and as she breathed water, she knew why she never believed in them.

Agony.

Her veins burned. The sensations that spidered throughout her body were worse than that first breathe of water. Her lungs filling with liquid and beginning to ache to the point of bursting was easier and less painful than her current reality—whatever the hell that was. One moment, she had been breathing water with her vision fading to nothingness and the next she was awash with feelings and...life?

Castiela experienced moments of her life playing in her head like a movie. Each memory a mixture of emotions that were wholly over-whelming. If it was Hell, she hated to think that this would be her eternity—and that's what it felt like was eternity swirling around her. A mixtape of pain, agony, grief snaking throughout her entire being. It was hard to be in her body and part of her, a naïve and childish part of her hoped that it was all a nightmare, and she would wake up with a hangover in the cabin of The Exile and kiss her sleeping fiancé.

She knew it wasn't a nightmare. She didn't know what exactly it was. All she knew was she wanted it to end. She felt disconnected from herself yet present in a strange and disjointed way. It was hard to focus, hard to think, hard to breathe. The pain ensnared her senses and overrode most of the primary ones, hide away her questions. But slowly, ever so slowly, that pain became to morph into a singular train of thought.

Revenge.

He will pay for what he has done.

Before everything faded for Castiela once more and she remembered no more.

CHAPTER ONE

Castiela shot out of the water, the moonlight illuminating her only briefly before she disappeared back below the surface. She swam through the depths, spinning around and around as she went further into the darkness below. In the brief glimpse of above, she knew that the boat she was waiting for wasn't out there. It hadn't been for several months. She knew. She was watching as often as she could.

Of course, that wasn't as often as she would like because she did have a life after all. She was now an owner of a successful *Curiosities from Above* shop, with the oddball items that found their way to where the pod was. There were a good number of precious gems, metals, and even technologies that fell into the seas and Castiela was one of several that appreciated collecting those things. Oftentimes, the things that she collected were obsolete beneath the waves—and even useless when any of the mermaids or mermen could go on land. Cell phones and other electronic technologies didn't care too much for water and by the time Castiela could get them to the surface... well... they were too waterlogged to do much with for any of the merpeople.

She wistfully remembered the joys of owning a smartphone and the pleasure of showing off diamond earrings in the sunlight. While she could walk on land once during the lunar phase, it wasn't quite the same as having a life up there. The shop did little to abate the sorrow she felt at the loss of the *human* aspects of the life she once lived.

Castiela had thought many times about the life that had been stolen from her and the existence she had now. It wasn't a bad existence. It just wasn't what she wanted for herself. While it was possible to walk the shores and spend time on the surface for an entire lunar phase, she couldn't pop in and out of their lives. They had lives that would certainly be ruined if she just resurfaced now, so long after she had vanished. She often wondered what they were doing, how they took her disappearance, and just what lies he spun.

"Castiela!" Her head swiveled around to meet the dark-skinned mermaid, Enita. "Searching for that boat again? None of the pod have seen it, well, at least the ones that are looking." Her dark brown eyes bore into Castiela's vibrant blues, and she shook her head, her red hair fanning out around her.

"It will return. He won't stay away from the water forever. Especially not the waters of Peyton Harbor." She stated this fact with such simplicity even though nothing about her situation was simple. "Was there a reason you came looking for me, Enita?"

Enita shook her head, black dreadlocks bobbing everywhere. "Nope, just figured you could use a friend. I know how much this bothers you."

You have no idea what this does to me. Her thoughts often turned dark. There were days she cursed Galene for saving her and transforming her into a mermaid, though she supposed if she were to voice such an opinion she might be outcast from the pod. Galene had given her a second chance, to use how she saw fit, and Castiela was going to serve justice to the man who had stolen her heart and then cast her away, leaving her to die in a tempest many months ago.

Her story wasn't the only unhappy one, of course most everyone knew their origin story, though she guessed some may not remember it to the fullness that she recalled her own. Her underwater friend, Enita had been younger, just barely a teenager, who had followed through on a stupid dare to swim as far out into stormy waves as she could and circle back around a buoy near her hometown. The waves overpowered her, and she disappeared beneath the surface to never be seen again. Enita expressed uncertainty over who decided that she should be saved by Galene, but she was one of the ones that was happy with her new life, it beat the old one she had back on the surface.

Castiela could feel the swell of the waters as someone sidled up alongside her. She *knew* his presence the moment he came within a certain proximity to her. "Argose." She tried to keep him at a distance. Because his very being bore into hers in ways that made her uncomfortable. He was her friend and occasionally her lover but that didn't mean that she wanted these feelings and *that* connection. Trusting someone so deeply was what landed her in the merpeople pod to begin with.

"Enita, Castiela," his rough timbre made her weak in the tail and she just floated there, her eyes stealing glances at the olive-skinned merman. He was sculpted and she would have sworn he was taken after one of the gods for how chiseled and perfect he looked. "What brings you out here?" He gestured to the water around them. They were some distance from the pod's settlement.

Enita swam close and poked her finger into his chest, jabbing hard into his breastbone. "That, mister, is none of your business." Castiela stifled a chuckle. Enita and Argose had never been friendly with one another which made any social activities that she had both on her side for awkward from the tension. It would remind her of how her friends on the surface felt and acted when around her fiancé, Bartley. But Argose was not Bartley and Enita would never be Nicki or Alison. And Castiela wasn't sure she would ever feel at home.

"Not out looking to get revenge, are you?" Argose gazed into her eyes knowingly with the slightest smirk. "You've got a successful business here, a home in some of the finest purple coral this side of the sea, and us for friends." He winked suggestively and she felt her cheeks redden. While Argose would have no problem discussing their relationship or situationship or whatever it was, Castiela liked to keep it quiet.

"So what if I am?" She retorted, facing away from him. "It makes little difference at the moment, because the *Exile* hasn't been out in this part of the water for some time, I guess since he cast me over- board." She couldn't keep the bitterness from her tone.

"As much as I think Argose needs to piss off... We both want the best for you and maybe revenge isn't the best thing to focus on. You know?" Castiela didn't acknowledge that, she couldn't. She didn't accept that as an option for her.

Argose reached over and tucked loose strand of hair behind Castiela's ear. "Enita is right." She knew they were both right, but she wasn't letting it go. They didn't understand.

CHAPTER TWO

"I swear to god, he killed her."

"Alison, don't you think you are taking your dislike of the man a little too extreme?" A curly-headed brunette questioned. "I mean, he was like over the moon in love with Castiela, why would he do that?" She shook her head and looked at her chipped green nail polish.

The other woman shook her head. "Nicki, I'm serious. She has been missing for a year! He was the last person to see her." Alison ran a hand over her short hair, feeling the spiky contours of it with her manicured fingertips. "It's not like Castiela to just leave. Her parents haven't heard from her and even more, we haven't heard from her. The whole story that she just left and left him a note and nothing for anyone else? It doesn't make any sense."

Nicki met the other woman's gaze finally. "Alison, we have no proof. That is the most vital thing to remember! He is someone, if we go stirring up trouble now, we can forget all about the wonders of living in a beach town, because we will be sitting in a prison cell with matching jumpsuits. Him and his mommy run this place and anything to the contrary will sink this ship——"

"That's how he did it! I'll bet my savings on it. He took her out on the water in his boat. He used old love letters or one of her short stories to make it seem like she wrote him a goodbye letter to cover up pushing her off the boat. We never thought to look because he covered it up so good, and now, now they would never find her body. But he made it look so damn good. Nicki, I'm telling you, he did it." Alison's voice rose until Nicki clapped a hand over her mouth. They were someplace far too public to continue that conversation and Alison realized that after Nicki gestured around them to the people that were across the street from where they sat at the *Muffingford Speakeasy.*

"We will continue this conversation later on." Nicki mouthed. "God did you see the way Johnny killed that wave? I swear he could smoke everybody with his skills. He looks damn good, I'm telling you." Nicki could easily transition from topic to topic and any busy-bodies would be convinced that there had never been a discussion of the Mayor's son killing his fiancée because of how smoothly she could play conversations.

Alison shrugged and went along with it until she finally pulled Nicki away to their shared apartment. Once inside, she met Nicki's uncertain gaze. "We have to look into this. She's our best friend. I refuse to just accept this any longer. It seemed weird at first, but I was too heartbroken, now... though." Alison grasped Nicki's shoulders in her hands. "Now, we have a chance to at least somehow, find the truth of what happened."

"I..." Nicki cleared her throat and backed up. "Jeez, Alison, I don't know. Like I said, if we do this, we've got to be smart about it. Because any missteps and we will be sunk. Our careers, our apartment, everything here that we know and love... if he really made Castiela vanish...killed her, well he could easily make people like us disappear too, don't you think?"

Alison sensed Nicki's anxiety rising and took a few steps back to give some space. "Let's do a meditation?" She hated leading in meditations despite her ability for sensing emotions and knowing how to stabilize them in the moment.

When Nicki nodded, she went on, "Okay, we are going to visualize the sea. First, noticing the blues and greens lapping against the white sand. As the water bathes the sand, we are going to slowly inhale to the count of five. So, water is coming in, inhale, one. Two. Three. Four. Five. We are going to hold that there, like the water often pauses on the beach, we will pause, holding our breath for three. One. Two. Three." Alison kept her tone level and took slow breathes. "Now, we are going to visualize the rocks that surround the shore. The water is going to break over the rocks. As the waves increase, we will exhale with them. To the count of five. We are exhaling all the tension and stress. All the worries."

Alison allowed herself to sneak a glance at Nicki, seeing the other woman's expression relaxing. "We aren't going to judge it; we will let it flow through us and notice it. Exhale to five. One. Two. Three. Four. Five. As we begin to come back into ourselves, we will picture the water slowly receding as the sun sets. That is our emotions coming into balance. We will not judge them or try to change them. We will accept them. As we acknowledge and accept where we are, slowly come back into yourself and let yourself reconnect with your surroundings." Alison always felt she was rushing through meditations when she led them, but she guessed it worked because when Nicki finished the exhale and opened her eyes, she seemed more at peace then she had moments before.

"You're getting better at those." Nicki said softly. "Thanks for giving me the space. It's a lot to process and a lot to think about."

Alison nodded. "I know, and you were closer with Bartley." Alison's tone lacked malice. "So, to imagine that someone you once knew to be a friend in grade-school could be," she stopped herself from saying *a murderer* and met Nicki's glassy eyes, "well to imagine he could be someone else must be hard to think about."

Nicki nodded and collapsed back into her sofa seat. "Yeah. He was always kind to me in school, it was only after he got to high school that he acted like a dick. But then that all stopped again when I introduced him to Castiela right at graduation." Nicki shook her head. "Listen, I don't think you are wrong, but I don't know if you are right either. Let's sit with this and think through some different ideas, because we want to make the best decision we can in how to go about this."

Alison wanted to argue about all the different reasons why waiting was a bad idea, but she bit her tongue, knowing that maybe Nicki was right about going about this the best way possible. She didn't want to risk screwing everything up for them or their families. If there was one thing Alison knew for certain, it was that those in power often stayed in power because of the way people feared what they could do, and Nicki and Alison both had a lot they could stand to lose if they dove into this too hard and too deep without a proper plan.

CHAPTER THREE

Enita swam around the alabaster coral that she called her home in a frenzy.

Each day, like clockwork, Castiela could be found out in the more treacherous waters, where the boat that dumped her off sailed. While Enita and other merpeople had the ability to lure sailors to their deaths, it wasn't exactly a common practice anymore, at least not in this portion of the pod. Now, with other portions and people groups of the pod, yeah, it totally happened. But with theirs... not so much.

Enita had never revealed her gift from Galene and Poseidon because it would probably cost her the delicate friendship she had with Castiela, but Enita could read thoughts and perceive intentions within them with almost 100% accuracy every time. So, she knew the depths of Castiela's heart and the plans she concocted daily in her head. Enita worried for her friend and just how much the lust for revenge was driving her away from more positive experiences and true healing. Enita began patting on eyeshadow from her palette onto her eyes in thick gobs. She followed that by an intense spray of goo onto her dreadlocks. Finally finishing by brushing her scales from waist to tail until they shone the deep dusk red that she so adored on herself.

Enita regarded herself briefly in the mirror that she had hanging in her room and decided she was good enough to go out again in search of her friend. "Enita!" She froze where she was and turned half-way around, a snarl rising to her lips. *Well, fuck.* It was Argose, of course, the merman she couldn't stand that had somehow made his way into Castiela's life despite what Castiela had been through before.

"What!?" It was impatient and rude, and she didn't care. She hardly ever even wasted her time skimming his thoughts because they seldom were focused on anything of importance, barely managing to string thoughts together it always seemed. *Maybe that's why I hate him, he either can block out my presence or he just is that air-headed.* She wasn't sure which to be the truth, but she didn't care really either. She tolerated his presence simply because there were days, he seemed to make Castiela not hate being a mermaid.

Argose didn't flinch, only quirked an eyebrow. "She's not out there today. I couldn't find her. I thought we could look together, as it is not normal for her to be...absent." His eyes twinkled with worry and Enita cursed under her breath before nodding.

"Yeah, we best look together. So, you said she's not in her coral and she's not out in those badass waters?" His head bobbed. "Maybe we should try her shop. Sometimes on days like this, she is there." She led the way, knowing that he was following behind her.

When she stopped in front of the shop, she took in the empty looking building and sighed. She refused to allow herself to worry yet, she didn't believe it would do any good until they had checked out all the options and assured themselves that something bigger might be going on. She didn't think that was the case, it was probably just that Castiela needed away or...

"Maybe she is collecting from the dumping spot that the surface-dwellers have. Her shop did seem lacking the last time I visited."

Enita pulled a face knowing that his visit was rarely ever a normal social calling, it was a booty-call plain and simple.

"Lead on," she gestured, and mock bowed at him. Swimming behind him, she noticed the scars along his tail, and she wondered, not for the first time what some of his story was. He was older then both she and Castiela and he had been there longer, he was there when she was first saved. Just, he wasn't part of her everyday life. Not until Castiela came along and he took a shine to the woman. Enita couldn't really blame him for that either, because Castiela was stunning.

She was redheaded, pale skin, and scales in beautiful shades of blue. She was a vision if ever there was one. From day one, Castiela had attracted the attention of many of the mermen and mermaids in the pod if nothing else but for a wistful *wow* about her. Enita shook herself firmly to remind herself what they were doing.

Argose led them through the pod's dwelling and town, out into shallower waters that sat near some of the more scenic and populated beaches. The sun bore down into the waters and that always made Enita leerier. It wasn't that people didn't know mermaids existed, but often, their existence was either highly sought after by people wanting to use their scales or hair in experiments or wanting to capture them and study them or they were believed to be mythical or long extinct. Either way, Enita wasn't fond of the more daylight excursions closer to where the boats and ships were and all the people that were on-board them.

"There she is." Argose gestured to Castiela's wave of red hair billowing out as she used a net to catch items that were either being thrown from above or had fallen. Enita gasped, knowing how risky it could be considering how close to the surface that Castiela was bobbing. Under the brilliant sunlight, her red hair could easily be noticed if someone were really looking. "Enita, steady yourself. Castiela has a handle on what she is doing. Outside of that, most of the boats that make it to this point are party boats with drunkards who can barely notice their own feet before them much less anything else." Enita wanted to chastise him for his arrogance, to prove some sort of point about how he could be wrong. She didn't get that chance as the surface above them exploded with a whoosh and someone sank down.

Enita swam toward the person. In these waters, people barely made it back to the surface even with help. Her eyes widened when she realized it was a child. A boy that was barely old enough to walk, let alone swim or be in the waters. Panic filled her. All the thoughts of her friend left her, and she focused solely on the child that was still sinking. His eyes wide and terrified and her heart broke.

It seemed to take forever to get him, to stop his rocket-like descent into the deeper waters where the currents grew swifter and the danger greater. "Galene! Poseidon!" Her screams rang loudly, she wasn't sure how it worked or how the ocean-god and goddess would know when a situation like this occurred, but she knew what she was about to ask of them. Enita kissed the boy, granting him one hour to breathe underwater.

Enita held the boy in her arms and began to swim in the direction she believed that Galene might be. But her own worries and the thoughts of the boy that she was perceiving made it hard to keep swimming and she stopped. Resting until Galene appeared, though Enita couldn't be bothered to know from where as she stroked the boy's hair. "Please, grant him life. Please spare him." She knew he must have had a family above and her mind raced with the beauties of that family, concocting an entire story about what his life must have been like. It felt like ages passed between her request and Galene's answer, but the soft nod and the boy being swept from Enita's arms told her that the goddess of the sea was going to try to save him. It didn't always work, but Enita hoped that he would be saved by the seas and given a second chance.

‡

"CASTIELA! WAIT!"

Argose swam toward Castiela, watching as her red curls fluttered at the waters boundary before her head broke the surface. "Damn." His tail flicked in the water with haste and the muscles in his arms rippled as he raced to break the surface. He exhaled as his head popped out, just above the water. He tried to get his eye to focus.

The sunlight was blinding, even as it started to set off the beach. "Cas—"

"Shush! Look!" She pointed her finger at the boat the boy had come from. A man with a sneer stood there with a bead of drool rolling off his chin, a bottle of beer clasped tightly in his porcine hands. The man seemed entirely unaware of their presence on the surface, casting his empty beer bottle down into the water carelessly once he drained the last drop.

"Got the little bastard. Let the seas have him. Won't be missed." Deep-bellied laughter followed the statement and Argose felt sick. He knew that it happened, there had been many cases where the merpeople had requested Galene's gift to save someone who had been cast into the waters. He didn't know the specifics of that ability, just that there were times the person was saved and transformed into a merperson and others where they weren't so lucky and would perish anyway.

Argose heard all he needed and dove back under the water. He tried to quell the sickness, but turned away from where Castiela would be and retched. *Such cruelty.* The thought circled him like a noose. His own origin story as a merman wasn't a very pleasant one. Maybe it was why he related so well with Castiela—their stories at the core, weren't much different.

Argose eyed Castiela, laying on his bed. He had asked her several questions and now, it seemed like the tables had turned as she began her own interrogation of his origins. "Do you know how you came to be here? Since you seem so keen on knowing how I became a mermaid." Her tone was biting but oh-so-tired. Argose leveled his honey-brown eyes on her.

"It's not really something that is... pleasant to share when I had hoped we would be making love." He was sincere. That wasn't a story that put him in the mood to be around anyone, much less the other activities he had in mind when they first came back to the shell he called home.

Castiela propped herself on her elbows and quirked her eyebrow at him. "Well, you could tell me and then we could still fuck or... I'll just ask again later." She undid her top and let it float to the floor.

Argose swallowed hard. She was like a dog with a bone when she got onto a topic—a trait he was learning he liked and disliked in her. "Cas..." The look she gave him made him shake his head. "I was a human on the surface from a town called Prescoit Fall's. Fairly large town along the beachfront. One night when going to lay out and look at the stars, I discovered a mermaid sitting on the beach by the cove I like. I couldn't believe what I was seeing, a real mermaid? I thought they only existed in myth and legend, not in the flesh."

His eyes glimmered with the wonder he felt, but sorrow soon filled them. "She and I talked. She was feeling sad about losing a friend and so I put aside the whole lives-under-the-water thing and offered her comfort. After I went home that night, I didn't think I would see her again. But she was there again on a starry night a few weeks later. It continued and eventually I fell in love." His eyes darkened and he looked away from Castiela, not able to take her in whilst reliving the memories.

"That doesn't sound so bad." Castiela offered with her usual level of snark. "But I'm guessing there is more to this story then that or you wouldn't look so...broken about it." She seldom minced words and he chuckled mirthlessly.

"Something like that." He exhaled and forced himself to look in her eyes. "She convinced me that to be together like we wanted, I would have to trust her. Now you and I both know, Galene doesn't just change someone because she deems it fit, no... there has to be danger involved or a reason beyond love. Well, being the surface-dweller I was with experience of one *mermaid in my life... I just believed it was a matter of her requesting that I be changed. So, while she handled what I thought was that topic with Galene, I put everything in order on the surface, said goodbyes to friends because I wasn't sure if I would be allowed to see them again, quit my job, gave the house to my sister."* He felt the pain flare in his chest, the anguish that he still hadn't dealt with.

"She put you in danger." It wasn't a question. Castiela swam over to him and put her arm around his shoulder, rubbing small circles where her hand rested.

He laughed. *"She didn't just put me in danger. She had me so convinced everything would be simple and smooth. She had me swim out into the water and I was attacked by some sort of deep-sea animal that dragged me beneath the waters. See, her gift was communicating with animals, it's incredibly common because well, it would seem like some hokey or campy child's film down here if everyone could speak to the sea creatures."* Argose turned and embraced Castiela, holding her and stroking her hair. *"Galene saw what she had done and spared me. Meanwhile... Nethya, that was her name, her plan backfired and the beasts she thought she had trained turned on her and devoured her. Perhaps a twist of fate, karma unfolding for her devious plan. Either way, the life I thought I was coming here for was gone in the blink of an eye and the transformation near killed me."* Castiela stiffened in his arms and pressed a kiss to his adam's apple.

"I'm sorry." He could tell she was. Castiela wasn't soft around the edges and her coming to comfort him signaled that she knew something about the sting of betrayal.

"You've nothing to be sorry for. You've been my bright spot since you arrived." He pulled back and kissed the crown of her forehead with tenderness. To Castiela, it might just be fucking, but to him his time with her was precious and the feelings of love deepened with each coupling.

"My fiancé threw me overboard our boat, the Exile." She whispered it against his skin and he felt his heart ache for her. *"So... now that we have our sob stories out of the way... want to just... lay here?"* It was unlike her to offer cuddling or other affection, but Argose wasn't going to deny her it.

He doubted he would deny her anything.

Argose shook away the memory from not so long ago. His focus returned and he waited for Castiela to come back and breathed with relief when she descended, her blue eyes filled with concern. "Are you okay?" She reached for him, and he took her hand in his.

"Yes and no."

Castiela nodded. "Me too."

Argose glanced around and noticed that Enita was nowhere to be seen. "I think that Enita requested Galene save the boy. I hope that she chooses to try."

Castiela swallowed and met his gaze. "I hope he survives it." She shuddered and he nodded along. "It was... well I couldn't imagine it when my fiancé threw me overboard, but a child? Why would someone do that?" He wanted to ask that same question, but he knew there were no good answers to be found for it.

"Let's see if we can find Enita. This is her first request." As it was explained to him and to all others, a mermaid was only given three requests in their lifetime or else something dark would happen to them and they would die. The first request for some mermaids was a big deal and often overwhelming. Argose knew that his presence would be unwelcome, but Castiela's would bring Enita comfort.

CHAPTER FOUR

Nicki had tossed and turned all night with what Alison said.

She knew Bartley pretty well. They had gone to school together. She was the main reason why he and Castiela ended up dating after all. It was a hard pill to swallow that Alison suspected that he killed Castiela. "Dammit Alison." She squeezed her green throw pillow tightly before chucking it against the wall.

They had to be discreet in the searching. Even more secretive in what they uncovered if anything. Nicki couldn't quite believe that Bartley had done it all his own accord. Nicki decided she needed to be the one to head the investigation she and Alison would be launching. There were so many things they needed to investigate before just deciding that Bartley had killed Castiela.

"Alison, I'm going out for my run." Nicki opened the bottom drawer of her nightstand and grabbed out a camera that was tucked beneath some papers from lack of use. She pushed it into her running pack and waved at Alison when she went out the front door and began her run toward the far beach's cliffs. It was one of several routes she ran around the town. One of her favorites, because she could stare out from the clifftop and see everything. It was that on top of the world feeling that she loved.

She waved at passersby and ran past many of the slower walkers and joggers that were out at this time of morning. When she reached the peak, she looked around and slowed to a jog and then to a walk. After double-checking her surroundings, she unzipped her pack and pulled her arm back, launching the camera as far out into the water as she could. She glanced around to make sure no one had seen her do that, people didn't like littering and she didn't want to go through all the trouble of deleting old nudes from the camera, so it was just easier that way.

She sighed with relief at having at least gotten rid of one problem item that had been taking up space in her life for far too long. Now she had to help Alison solve what really happened to Castiela.

Alison rang up her final customer of the day with a smile and, "Have a wonderful evening!", handing the man his latte. Her shift was over. She could grab her iced mocha and head out for a night on the town. Well, more like a night of researching all articles around the time that Castiela disappeared.

She took off her apron and walked toward the door, stopping short when she heard someone talking in a whisper on the far side of the nearly empty coffeehouse. "I still think it's odd that that Bartley fellow's fiancée just vanished into thin air. And with all that stinkin' money you'd have thought he could have expended more to find out what happened. I mean c'mon, get real, what girl would leave a guy like him with all that money just out of the blue?"

She recognized his voice, and she decided then that she needed to hear the rest of this unfold. She knew there had been rumors and talk but she almost never caught anything worth staying for. Alison ordered a cake pop and took a seat, turning away to make it seem she was people-watching instead of eavesdropping.

An older woman that was sitting across from the man nodded along. "Ah yes, little Cassie. It really isn't like her to ghost people. Never known her to be that sort. Just seems fishy. He's got a lot of connections, maybe their relationship wasn't what everyone thought it was. They made a beautiful power couple, but there's often more to it than meets the eye." The woman broke into a cough and covered it with an embroidered handkerchief.

The man reached over and put his hand on hers. "Easy there, Lav. I think we'll find out what happened eventually. But best not continue this right now... I see the Mayor; she might come in here."

Shit. Alison knew she couldn't get out of the café without making a scene now. *Please don't come in, go to the next shop.* She begged whatever deity might be listening, if there was one out there, she needed their grace. She hadn't spoken to Mayor Hale since the day Bartley contacted them to say that Castiela was gone.

"As I live and breathe! Castiela's bestie!" And that was why Alison seldom prayed or believed in higher powers because they always seemed to fail her. "My dear. How are you doing? I feel we never see each other anymore." The woman pouted while kissing Alison on both cheeks.

"Mayor Hale, it's been a while." Alison stood awkwardly and shuffled her feet. "How is the campaign going?" That was a safe topic, one everyone would ask the mayor about.

Mayor Hale smiled. "Seems like everything is going according to plan. I have it in the bag." She whistled happily. "I must get my matcha and then off to another press conference! We must get together soon, dearie." She blew some air kisses before approaching the counter and Alison was left staring where the woman had been standing wondering what the hell just happened.

CHAPTER FIVE

Enita swam back and forth, knotting her fingers in her thick hair.

"Let him be okay, let him be okay." Became her solemn chant with each pass by where Galene had taken him to watch over him for signs that the transformation would succeed or fail. Enita knew she could join the watch over him but she worried that the intensity of her distress would interfere with the transformation somehow.

"The first one is always the worst." It was Kilina, a mermaid that provided support to new mermaids. "It is not much easier with the second or third. But the first sets the tone. That's what I'm here for, to ensure you have all the resources you need." Enita nodded, though she wasn't absorbing it. "You really should rest. The boy will need you, should he make it through. You will be the most familiar face he has." Kilina touched Enita's arm, running slender fingers along ridges of it.

Enita shrugged away from the unexpected contact. "While your concern is appreciated... I want to stay nearby for whenever the transformation is complete. Like you said, he will need me when he wakes from this." Enita met Kilina's eyes with a fierce glare. "I'll update you should I need your assistance." Enita swam closer to the door that led to where the boy was.

Kilina left without saying anything, perhaps she was used to indifferent responses. Enita could have used her gift to find out what Kilina was experiencing at her rejection, but that required energy and effort that she didn't have for that.

Enita tried to steady her breathing before entering but found that it was too hard to concentrate on it when all she could think of was the boy inside that's life was changing. A slight pang of regret sank in, but she shook it off knowing that there was no way she could have gotten him back on the boat that he had come from.

CASTIELA FOUND where the boy was and in turn, where Enita was. "How's it going?" She floated close to Enita, stretching out her hand for comfort.

Enita nodded toward the room. "He's having a really hard time with the transition. Galene has been by his side. I was in there for a little while, but my emotions are running too high to be much good in there." Enita took Castiela's hand and clasped it. "Tell me, was it an accident?"

Castiela hesitated but shook her head. "No... it wasn't. A drunkard threw him overboard." Castiela wasn't the best at conveying messages in a sensitive and thoughtful way. Oft she had been compared to a bull in a China closet. That was to say, she had no skill for presentation of any information, but particularly anything that required the truth. She was brutal or she lied, there was no middle.

Enita nodded. "Something told me the circumstances were... unsavory. Had hoped to be wrong though. I can't imagine wanting to throw a little boy overboard like that." She wiped at her eyes and Castiela saw the sparkle of a tear before it was brushed away. "I just hope he makes it."

"Me too."

Castiela stayed with Enita for several hours, until darkness fell and there was still no change. As Castiela was getting ready to leave, Galene came out. "The boy shall live. Enita, please, tend him." Galene swam away and Enita's eyes widened with relief.

"I will leave you to it, I'll catch you later." Castiela bid Enita, relieved at the outcome. She knew from other mermaids that there was no guarantee that a person could be transformed.

"How is the child and Enita?" Argose didn't waste time with pleasantries, he had to know how things were.

"The boy will live, his transformation was successful and Galene turned him over to Enita's care." Castiela closed the distance to where Argose was reclining.

Argose nodded. "Good, good." Argose gestured for Castiela to join him. With the stress beyond them, it shifted Argose's focus to the more immediate, pressing things on his mind. "What would you like to do?" His eyes twinkled suggestively.

Castiela was receptive and her scales parted. Argose kissed her hard and fast, deepening it as she moaned into his mouth. His scales parted to reveal his pulsing manhood. He didn't hurry to drive himself home, he took his time kissing down her neck, leaving trails of little love bites. He reached behind her and unclasped her silky blue top, revealing her breasts. He kneaded them in his hands until her nipples became hard, and she let out soft moans, increasing into a whine as she bucked upward against him.

"Stop teasing me. I need relief." She grasped him, aligning their cores.

He hissed but didn't argue. He drove into her until they were both crying out each other's names. When they finished, Castiela didn't rush to dress and leave as she often would. She curled into his side, pressing her lips against his neck.

CHAPTER SIX

Nicki gasped and the paper fell soundlessly from her hand to the floor.

"Alison!" The other woman came running into the room. "Look! That letter... it... well it is different than what Bartley told us." She pointed to the page that lay face up.

Alison bent and picked it up, reading through it. Her eyes widened and her hand covered her mouth. "Castiela thought that Bartley was cheating? Where did you even find this?"

Nicki struggled to meet her eyes. "Well... I still had that key Castiela gave me for watching the cats that time. So.. "

Alison gasped. "You went through Bartley's house? Without his permission?"

Nicki frowned. "What was I supposed to do? Show up and say, 'Hey, we think you killed Castiela, can I look in your house for proof?'" Nicki put her hands on her hips. "I thought you would be happy that I had something. I mean, think, if he was cheating and he knew that she knew... all the reason to get rid of her, right? I mean his mother is the Mayor, it could hurt her re-election, among other things." Nicki turned away from Alison, her frown deepening at her friend's reaction.

"It's not that I'm not glad that we have something. But what do we do now? Confront him?" Alison folded her arms and returned the frown.

Nicki pursed her lips. "Perhaps we should confront him. Ask him about Castiela and if he knows more about why she left. Since he attests she left."

Alison nodded. "Alright, want to see if he will meet us someplace?"

Nicki pulled out her phone and shot a text to him. Within minutes, it chimed with a new message, and he agreed to meet them at the dockside bar, *Sink n Swim Bar and Grill.* It used to be the place all of them would get together after work a few nights a week.

ALISON COULDN'T PLACE her finger on the strange feeling she got when she saw the letter Castiela had written, but she couldn't ignore the feeling either. She didn't express that she felt some unease to Nicki. Her friend usually took it personal when people didn't just go along with what she was thinking or saying or didn't agree with how she came about something. Alison was just glad that there was some sort of lead, or something that pointed to why something had happened to her best friend.

Alison sat in their usual spot and before long Bartley joined her, Nicki following close behind. "Have you heard anything from Cassie?" Alison wasn't mincing words, despite the glare Nicki shot her.

Bartley, for his part, acted like he was still heartbroken that Castiela was gone. "No... of course not. Not since that fateful letter."

He sniffled and Alison struggled not to roll her eyes. The bartender brought their drinks and Alison took care of the tip.

"Well... could you walk us through what happened again... the day that Cas disappeared?" Nicki had a way to her that she could sell anyone on anything. "We miss our bestie."

Alison noticed something then, a small look that passed between them. It was so brief that she wondered after it if she was seeing something or not. She took a long swig of her beer and settled her gaze on Bartley.

He undid the buttons on his shirt sleeves and rolled them up to his elbows. He threw back a shot and followed it with his rum and coke. "Everything seemed normal. Just a regular day. We went to our jobs, saw some friends, and I decided to take the *Exile* out in the weather. It turned a little nasty and I didn't get back until the wee hours of morning and didn't see Cas. But I figured she was with one of you or her parents, I was so tired that I didn't even look. But then morning came, and I noticed the letter. Saying she was going out and would return at some point, but not to wait up. I was so distraught." He wiped fake tears from his eyes and Alison sighed.

"Why would she just leave though?" Alison wondered that question so often since Castiela had vanished. "I mean, her cell phone was never found... but she never answered any calls or texts. No one has seen her in any of the nearby towns and her parents never heard anything from her. I mean, they even moved because of this." Alison shook her head and frowned.

Bartley shrugged. "I wish I knew, really. I do not though. She was just gone. We weren't having any problems... the sex was great. Your guess is as good as mine as to where she went and why." He finished his rum and coke, but the server wasn't nearby so none of them could get a refill without having to get up.

Alison went to stand, but Nicki waved her off. "I've got this round." Nicki set her phone down and Alison glanced over, noticing that it was open to her messages because she must have been texting right before she went to get them more to drink. Alison was about to write it off when a new message popped across the screen before it went dark.

Bartie : I know babe, but really no one knows anything. We will get through this. Trust me. Xo

Nicki came back at that moment with the drinks. Alison's stomach churned and anxiety knotted up in her throat, making it impossible for her to form her thoughts into words. She mutely accepted the drink with a nod. She had to check into something, like now. She stood abruptly. "I've just thought of something I need to check. It's really urgent. Catch up with you later. Thanks for meeting us."

Nicki pouted. "Come on, don't be a party pooper."

Alison put her purse over her shoulder. "No, it's something big. I gotta go take care of it because otherwise it'll be a big mess in the apartment." She knew Nicki wouldn't want to help her clean up a huge mess, hell Nicki, when she was there at their apartment seldom lifted a finger for the basics.

"Hope you can get it resolved." Bartley smiled at her and threw back his rum and coke. *Drink while you can when I figure out how to stick it to you... I'm gonna make sure you pay.* Alison wasn't normally that sort of person, but with the information she was thinking she just found... that changed a lot of things.

Including her friendship.

CHAPTER SEVEN

Enita tossed Heliro off the back of a sea turtle.

The boy floated for a moment and began to laugh a deep belly laugh that shook his entire body. He didn't seem to know many words. Or he was shy. Enita couldn't discern which was the more likely of the two options, she just knew that she enjoyed teaching the child and spending time with him.

She couldn't believe how much time had passed since she had saved him. Over a month. In that time, he had learned to swim and learned to dive down to get shells from the sandy bottom. Castiela and Argose had worked together and set up a new room in the corral that Enita lived in and Heliro had his own little space to play and learn in.

The best thing that came from Heliro's rescue was that he was taking up both hers and Castiela's free time, meaning Castiela wasn't out on the hunt for revenge. Enita would never fault her friend for it, but it brought her deeper peace to know her friend wasn't luring anyone to their demise in the depths.

She found that she liked the extra time she was spending with Castiela. Begrudgingly she would admit she enjoyed some of the time that Argose was around too. Enita found the merman trying to wrangle another sea turtle for them to catch a ride on.

"I want to tell you why I don't like you." His head shot up. "It's because one of the boys who dared me to swim so far out to the buoy... he looked, sounded, and acted a lot like you do at times and it... bothers me. I thought I was less of a person because it was bothering me, but... it seems like that is the only way to work through it and to heal from it and come to an agreement on certain aspects of life." Enita met his burning eyes finally.

"I..." He wasn't sure how to act now. "I guess... thanks?" He shook his head seeming to realize that was probably not the best answer. "I... well. Thank you for sharing with me, but I am sorry it was someone similar to myself that put you in that position to start with. That must be triggering at times and makes it hard to truly find that healing because inside you feel so empty and just want to feel something."

Enita nodded. She wasn't sure that they would be best friends, but it was a start.

ARGOSE HAD HELPED ENITA for several hours with the sea turtles and Heliro, finding true joy in the simple action of being there with them. His happiness began to wane as his heart yearned to find Castiela and talk to her about something.

Argose went first to her shop and noticed it was closed. At first, it seemed a little odd, until he looked up and saw the way the light was reflecting off the water and realized how late in the day it was. His next stop was her corral apartment, but he found that empty too. *She's probably out looking for the damn boat again.*

He found his mood souring as he entered his shell-home. The sourness evaporated when he saw Castiela lounging in the bed, fidgeting with one of her recent finds—a shiny bracelet engraved with 'Fearlessness'. She stopped throwing it and catching it, her eyes landing on him.

"I was wondering when you would get here. I was getting bored." She yawned for emphasis and his smile widened.

"I had no idea you were here. I thought…" He left the thought unspoken because they both knew where he thought she was. "I'm really glad you're here." He closed the distance, taking her hand in his and bringing it to his mouth. He placed several kisses along the back of it before flipping it over and kissing her palm.

Castiela sighed at his touch. "I wanted to be here."

"I want you here." He saw her expression. "I… well… you staying around after we have sex and now finding you here when we didn't really plan anything… it's nice. Really nice. I could get used to this if you'll let me?" He knew he was making a fool of himself, but judging by her expression he wasn't doing too bad.

Castiela shifted. "I… would like that. For you to get used to this. And… to keep doing it." She blushed and his heart felt like it would burst with the love that filled him.

"I love you, Castiela." He kissed her on the lips, feeling a spark erupt through him.

Castiela smiled against his lips. "I love you too, Argose.'

CHAPTER EIGHT

S ome time had passed as the odd trio settled into a new routine with each other and the addition of Heliro.

THEIR TIME WAS SPENT in several ways, mostly it seemed like they worked and when they weren't working at their jobs, they were all taking turns with Heliro and educating him on all the things about being a merperson. Recently, he had started forming words and expressing ideas and feelings. It was limited to the simple things, but the glow from Enita at the way the boy was progressing brought joy to just about anyone who witnessed it.

CASTIELA AND ARGOSE were settling into their own sort of dance. Castiela had gotten rid of her corral apartment when it became apparent that it was no longer needed with her staying at Argose's place as their relationship evolved into a committed one that was recognized in the eyes of the merpeople.

. . .

She was realizing that there was happiness to be found in her life, as she began to really settle into being a mermaid. It wasn't without challenges but most of them were easily overcame with patience and the right support.

It had even been a while since she went out to watch for the *Exile* to make an appearance. She was certain that one day he would return to that spot and a large part of her still wanted to get revenge for what he had done. One late evening, she went out to her watching spot.

Her waiting paid off. The *Exile* came into view and so did its captain. He stood proudly in front of the ship's fancy white wheel, the waves gently lapping at the exterior of his boat with the eagerness of a lover. Several people on-board the ship milled around, laughing and drinking.

"Once cast aside
   Now given new life
   Join me, the water can be nice

Oh hear *you*
   This song of longing
   Wanton beings are calling

Dive deeply now, *sailors*

Come, chase the mermaid flavors
Delight in our songs

COME LAY *ye down*
   Under the waters
   Slowly drown

SAY GOODBYE NOW
   You should have thought about the crimes
   As your sins are paid for by your last breath of life."

CASTIELA WATCHED as the men that were partying on the boat with Bartley one by one began to dive from various parts of their boat. Her eyes sought out Bartley's face. He was still the same man, broad frame with soft blond curls dangling in his eyes. His hands had left the wheel of the boat as he tried to figure out what was going on. Confusion had his brows knitted together as he walked to the railing of his boat and gazed out, noticing the men and women aboard his vessel were in the water, drowning. His daze started to lift, and she opened her mouth once more,

*"*TO THE DARKEST *depths*
   You will be taken
   No longer shall you awaken

REVENGE, *once beloved*
   Truly is as sweet as it sounds
   While I listen to you inhale the water

. . .

AND SLOWLY DROWN."

HIS EYES GLAZED over as the power of her voice, her commands turning his own body against him took control. He climbed the railing and jumped into the water, his arms flailing because he was a poor swimmer at best.. Each person aboard started swimming to her. Some were struggling in the ebb and flow of the waves. Her power to control the water meant that she could choose how high the waves would rise before they crashed down upon themselves. Her emotions rose, reaching a peak, the waves rising with it and at the crescendo, Castiela thought she would feel relief.

CASTIELA'S EMOTIONS dissolved and she struggled to understand why getting her revenge hadn't felt as good as she imagined it would. Why there was no sense of vindication from what brought her here. She wanted to feel something as deeply as she had the night she went into the water. But as the last body bobbed in the water, his curls disappearing as he was pulled by a current into the blackness, she felt nothing.

CASTIELA WATCHED until Bartley's lifeless corpse disappeared beneath, and she swam, her tail swishing through the water expertly as though she had always been a siren, a mermaid from the deep. Castiela was desperate to feel something and made a split second decision of how she would find that feeling.

THE SHORELINE with its glimmering sands grew closer and soon she could make out the edges to the crags and rocky overlooks that jutted proudly along the spot that was their favorite spot for over two decades. With the lunar phase just begun anew, she had one goal in mind—reconnect with her best friends, something that until this point, she felt she could not do until her heart was at peace. Though she couldn't place any emotion to the emptiness she felt, there was a small comfort to be found that Bartley would never again haunt the water with his presence again. She had gotten her revenge on him and even if she felt nothing, it counted for something.

Turning the page to the new chapter meant taking a step out of the life that had become hers. Reverting to a previous life where mermaids were whispers, and the sirens were tales meant to scare away boaters and placate naughty children.

She swam close to the shore and began to slip and slide between the rocks until there was barely any water covering her torso. Castiela felt strange, unlike herself as a more humanlike form began to come from the waters. She began to pull herself out of the water, the transformation beginning as more and more of her emerged from the water until she traded her scaly tale for two, slightly less scaly legs.

She stood, wobbly and unsure of herself. In her quest for revenge, she hadn't allowed herself the pleasure of being human. *I will embrace both the good and the bad within me and within this situation,* she vowed as she unsteadily walked toward a faint firelight. Castiela knew many people camped out on the water at this time of year, so she only hoped that Nicki and Alison hadn't stopped the tradition in the time that she had been gone. She wasn't sure the consequences, if any, for revealing her merperson status to them when she knew that they would never join her beneath the surface, but she was willing to take chances in letting them know.

· · ·

As Castiela approached the distant firelight, Enita and Argose came out of the water. "Cas! Stop!" She turned around and met the now rather human-looking duo. Enita was holding something.

"What's that you're holding? A camera from my shop?" Castiela shook her head and turned back. "I can look at it later, I need to see Nicki and Alison. I've put it off for too long in fear of what they would think of me."

Argose grabbed her wrist firm but not unkind. "That's why you need to look at this. It came on when Heliro was helping in your shop, and you need to see the picture." Castiela's gaze shifted to the outstretched camera, and she took it. She wasn't sure why it was— her eyes locked onto an image that burned deeper into her mind then Bartley's face when he pushed her overboard.

Nicki.

On the *Exile*, wrapped in Bartley's arms with her holding the camera out to take a selfie as he kissed her cheek. She squinted at the stamp in the corner of the image, that showed the date the photo had been taken and her world stopped spinning.

Nicki was on board the Exile the night she had been pushed off. Nicki was the one who whispered about how sorry she was. Not Bartley. The camera fell from her hands and the screen went black when it hit the sand beneath it. Castiela's hands covered her mouth in horror.

. . .

SHE BEGAN to collapse into the sand and Argose's strong arms were the only thing that prevented it. The sobs that ripped through her weren't unlike the ones that she experienced when she had been tossed into the water and left to die. Yet, somehow, they were different as a new pain erupted that eclipsed the pain of Bartley's betrayal. Her best friend choosing to kill her instead of just... breaking the relationship up? She shook violently and was only vaguely aware of Enita stroking her arms and whispering softly.

WHEN CASTIELA PULLED HERSELF TOGETHER, her eyes burned with the salt of her tears, and she pulled away. "She deserves to join him." Her mutter caused her friends to jerk their heads in her direction.

"IS THAT A GOOD IDEA?" Enita asked first, beating Argose to it.

"I DON'T GIVE a damn what is a good idea or not. She was my best friend. Instead of just telling me she was in love with him, instead of just getting us to break-up, she tried to kill me. She *did* kill me, or at least the version of me that everyone here knew." Her words came through gritted teeth. "I probably would have walked away had I known. How can I let her just go on living? After what she did?" More tears brimmed her eyes, but she wiped them away, refusing to cry more.

"CAS... I understand how you are feeling, I've been betrayed by someone I cared for immensely. That's how I became a merman. Enita experienced betrayal of her own. Heliro too. He's just a little boy that was thrown overboard because they didn't want him anymore. We all have a story, some happier than others." Argose tried to reach for her, but she walked out of reach.

. . .

Castiela realized something else and shook her head more frantically. "But it's not just me that I have to worry about. Alison was my other friend, she won't just let this go and if she gets close to uncovering what happened... if Nicki was willing to kill me, why wouldn't she be willing to kill a liability?" Castiela didn't wait for Enita or Argose, she took off running on shaky legs. Drawing closer to the firelight.

She crested the hill and she saw both Nicki and Alison seated. They were talking by the campfire, both barefoot and relaxed. At least at first glance. She went down the hill on the side where she could stay hidden in the dark rocks and other shadows that shrouded the beach. She stubbed her sensitive toes on many small rocks and sticks that were along the sand. "Shit." She murmured trying to be quiet.

"Nicki, I know what happened." Alison stated without looking at Nicki.

"What do you mean? I thought that's what we came here to figure out with that letter and with what Bart said." Nicki sounded confused, maybe a little worried. Not as worried as Castiela began to feel as she tried to get closer without giving herself away.

Alison shook her head and chuckled without humor. "You see, I wondered about some of this for a while. Some pieces didn't line up. You accepting the answer from day one without much thought to Castiela's tendencies. But I wrote it off as grieving in a different way." Alison picked up a stick and poked the fire. "Then you had the letter from a key from watching the cats. Except... you weren't the one who watched the cats because you hate cats. I was the one with the key and I realized it was a lie when I went into my drawer for the key." Castiela saw Nicki shift, not able to see her face, but watching tension creep into the woman's back.

GOOD.

"WHAT GAVE it away in the end though, was when we went to speak to Bartley and you went to get us more drinks from the bar and you left your phone open to your messages. While we were sitting there, Bartley responded to your message. I saw it flash on the screen and what he said... well let's just say it sent up alarms." Alison turned toward Nicki with the flaming stick. "That's when I figured it out. You and Bartley were having an affair. Rather than talk to Castiela, who with her infinite good qualities would have probably turned him loose, you decided to throw her overboard. Into the storm that night. Bartley swore from day one that she stayed home, and he came back, and she was gone. But I knew otherwise, because she told me that day she was looking forward to going out on the waters again because it had been awhile. But I wrote it off." Alison stood and Castiela could see the anger in her face.

"ALISON, do you hear yourself? That's crazy." Nicki put her hands up and shook her head, playing dumb.

ALISON'S EXPRESSION morphed into something almost animalistic. "Don't lie to me!" Her voice echoed in the rocks around them. "You pushed her overboard that night. Didn't you?" When Nicki didn't respond at all, Alison thrust the fiery stick close to her face. "Didn't you!?" This time Nicki nodded slowly.

"I DIDN'T ACCOUNT for anyone asking questions. It seemed fool proof. And maybe your right, but if I couldn't have her friendship and the relationship, then one of them had to go." Nicki was nonchalant in her explanation and Castiela bit back the bile.

ALISON SWUNG the stick at Nicki. "How could you!? She was my best friend!"

"TOOK YOU LONG ENOUGH TO LOOK." That was all it took for Alison to lunge for Nicki this time. But Castiela wasn't letting it go further. She already had some blood on her hands from the boat and the guys that Bartley had on it with him.

"ALISON! STOP!"

BOTH NICKI and Alison's heads swiveled, and shock etched across their faces. With Nicki, it was surprise and fear. With Alison, it was relief and joy at seeing her again. But her expression did show curiosity and Castiela could guess why. Even in the faint light the fire cast on her, she still had some scales that were visible.

"WHAT THE FU—" Nicki didn't get a chance to finish her question before water came up out of a pool that was formed on the beach. The splash knocked her to the ground.

. . .

"Castiela...?" Alison was tentative. Castiela put her hands out to show Alison she meant her no harm, approaching slowly.

"Yes?"

"You have scales." Alison seemed like she was trying to hold back tears. "But you aren't dead."

Castiela nodded. "I'm not dead. I was... saved by a mermaid. Sometimes when someone is drowning, they can be saved by a special mermaid in the sea. I was one who was saved. I can't walk on land all the time. It's too much to explain right now. But I don't want her blood on your hands." Castiela gestured to where Nicki was trying to get her bearings.

Alison looked to Nicki and back to Castiela. "But..."

Castiela shook her head. "Believe me. I've already got blood on my hands. I got revenge against Bartley."

That statement got a rise out of Nicki and she was on her feet and charging. "What did you do to him?"

Castiela laughed as she side-stepped her. "What did I do to him? Well, I guess you will get to see for yourself." Castiela met Alison's eyes. "Go, come back another night and we will talk. But now, now I have one more score to settle." Alison looked at Castiela for a long moment and nodded.

"SEE YOU AGAIN SOON, MY FRIEND." Alison left without asking what Castiela meant, and she was grateful. Her friend could claim ignorance later.

CASTIELA BEGAN to walk back to the closest access point of the water. Nicki was hot on her heels, and Castiela used her command of water to sling the occasional ball of water in her face. As soon as she could, she got to a rock and dove into the water, her legs reverting to a tail.

NICKI STOOD on the edge of the water and glared at her, out of breath and soaked. "So, you'll just swim away? I'll reveal you as a mermaid to everyone. Get the hunters and make a bunch of money. Have them kill you for those scales." She was spewing all the hatred she could at Castiela, and Castiela just smiled.

"No, that's not what's going to happen at all."

"ENLIGHTEN ME, what the hell can you do from there?" Nicki took a step back, seeming to remember that Castiela had been throwing water at her.

"BETRAYAL IS the sweetest sound
  Watching me as I drown

Kissing he who was mine
Claiming all that was as thine.

YET DEATH DIDN'T LAY *its claim*
    A mermaid came to my aid
    A plan so perfectly laid
    But in the end it didn't pay.

FIRST THE EXILE *with its traitors sank*
    His last breathes the restoring grace
    There was one more card to be played
    A best friend once owed a debt that mercy couldn't stay."

NICKI'S FEET began to drag her to the water against her will. As the realization sank in that her body was moving on its own accord and she couldn't stop... the expression of terror was something Castiela would relish in her memories. "Forgive me!" Nicki cried out before the trance took hold of her and she went beneath the water. Castiela used the control of the water to push Nicki farther away, deeper and deeper into the trench where she would either drown or be devoured.

ENITA AND ARGOSE came to her side, both in their merprson forms again. "It is done then?" Argose inquired. He reached for her, and she took his hand, needing to find some sort of comfort in the moment.

CASTIELA MET HIS EYES, her body starting to shake.

• • •

"Revenge has been served. Now I am free from the hold its had over me."

The END

IN TOO DEEP

NIKKI PRINCE

OCEANU'S GROOVE

Crucified - Army of Lovers
Kiss or Kill - Stela Cole
Psycho Killer - Talking Heads
Barracuda - Heart
Paper - Kinzie
FU In My Head - Cloudy June
Superstition - Stevie Wonder
Control - Halsey
Gangsta – Kehlani
Bones - Imagine Dragons
Keeping Me Alive - Jonathan Roy
Blood // Water - grandson
Wicked Game - Ursine Vulpine
Chains -Nick Jonas
Trouble - Annella
The Otherside - Jake Daniels
Blind Spot - Saint Chaos
Hide and Seek - Lizz Robinett
Fuck Apologies - (feat. Wiz Khalifa) JoJo

Bad Bitch – (feat. Ty Dolla $ign) Bebe Rexha
I See Red – Everybody Loves an Outlaw
Who Is She? – I Monster
Villain – Bella Poarch

Find the playlist here on Spotify!

CHAPTER ONE: BECOMING OCEANU

"My soul is full of longing for the secret of the sea." – Henry Wadsworth Longfellow.

Looking out at the sea as the small boat rocked back and forth, Olivia Tate wondered once again why fate had her tied up like an animal in a boat with mad men. The choppiness of the water became even more apparent once the boat was propelled forward by the motor. In fact, sea water splashed in and hit her fully in the face, drenching her from head to toe. The saltiness of the air and the water filled her with dread. She was going to die.

What was it like to drown?

This was a question she'd never thought she'd be asking herself. It was also something she'd learn in full when her captors decided it was time. She shivered as a chill ran up her spine. God help her, this wasn't going to be pleasant. Her clothing had been ripped from her body and lay in shreds at the bottom of the small boat. A chill ran over her, giving her goosebumps.

She didn't consider herself to be someone who always stayed on the straight and narrow, she'd never been a troublemaker either. Tears formed in her eyes even though she knew it was useless to cry. These men didn't know what mercy was and because of the evil deeds her father had done she would pay with her life.

"Daddy can't save you now little girl," one of the men said.

Both of her captors started laughing as if they'd made the greatest joke ever. They knew what she was thinking, which meant they'd done this kind of thing a lot.

The laugh was on them. She felt sure her father didn't even know she'd been taken. She'd moved out of the familial home a month ago. Busy with her own thing and trying to distance herself from the dirty dealings of her father. She'd only wished she'd been able to bring her sister with her when she'd moved.

In hindsight, however, having left her sister at home had been the best thing for her. She would now be facing the same fate had she been with her. She didn't know where her father was at this point. They'd tried everything to get Olivia to stay, but it had been futile and now here she sat. He'd always been way too busy making kids and coming up with a new scheme to get rich rather than worrying about said kids. Papa was indeed a rolling stone.

"This is the price he pays for stealing from Mr. X."

The gravelly voice of the older man in the boat shook her from her musings. *Is that what this was all about? Her father stole from Mr. X.* She let out a half laugh, half sob as the full scope of why this was happening hit her. In one of her father's schemes, he'd tried to make money by stealing from one of the biggest loan sharks in the country. The man whose real name was Lofton Exeter but he preferred to be called Mr. X. She suddenly felt like she was in her own laughable 'B' movie, but she knew this was very real. Nothing to laugh at. She'd always thought she'd live to the ripe old age of at least eighty.

Her life wasn't one for tempting fate. Hell, she hadn't even had more than one boyfriend or done anything crazy. She'd always made sure to live her life to make her mother proud. At least she'd hoped she'd been doing that all along. This morning, she'd woken up, got dressed, and headed to the university to teach a class in the healing of the mind and body. Now she was trussed up like a damn chicken in a boat headed for the deep.

The water lapped against the hull and even though the motion seemed to be soothing, it was terrifying at the same time because she couldn't see far within the dark depths. Her fear of dark water was about to be realized. Olivia heard chuckling behind her and she stiffened. Sure, the tears still fell but at this point, she just wanted them to get it fucking over with. Death couldn't come too soon.

Another sob escaped her. *Who am I kidding?* She didn't want to die. She hadn't lived her life fully. Her bucket list was still... just a list. She'd never been on a cruise. A small giggle escaped her as the thought that this was her cruise filled her.

"I'm surprised the bitch ain't pleadin' for her life still," one of the men said gruffly,

"Naw, little princess would never plead for her life," the other one replied. "She's too fucking stuck up to do that. She'd rather just cry."

"Ha! Jed, she doesn't want us to touch her little sister."

"Yeah, that shut her up really quick, didn't it, Tim?"

"Well, she already knows that we plan to kill her," Tim replied.

"It's sorta a shame. I wish the boss would have let us play with her longer," Jed grumbled.

"Yeh, me too...such a beauty. What a fucking waste, but we have to do what the boss says and when he says it." He sighed.

Olivia didn't even turn around to see who had made the sound.

"Yep, or it will be us floating at the bottom of the sea."

The words from her captors were said so straightforward that she knew crying and pleading wouldn't help her. When she'd tried to beg for release hours before, each of them had taken turns beating her and raping her. Her body hurt like it never had before. She'd also been told if she didn't shut up that they'd go for her younger sister next.

Olivia had gone cold at that point and silent. The only thing showing that she was still present were the silent tears drifting down her cheeks. It was apparent her voice would no longer help her. What did words matter? She wouldn't allow them to harm her sister Kaila. So at this point, what did her tears matter?

Squaring her shoulders as best as she could, she willed the tears to stop. Men with hearts of stone wouldn't feel empathy for her. Men who could kill innocents wouldn't even bat an eyelash at tears. In her mind, she sang the words to a song her mother had sung to her when she was a little girl. When she'd lost her mother to the god-awful disease called diabetes, her father had turned to illegal ways to support the family to pay off his wife's medical and funeral expenses. The path he had taken had finally led to this—her execution.

Death lay beneath the waves....a cold death where no one would ever find her. She would be just as alone in death as she had been in life. Closing her eyes, she prayed to God for mercy and to any divinity that could get her out of this. Olivia prayed like she'd never prayed before to survive. Then she would get revenge of another kind on her captors and Mr. X. She prayed to be able to rise again and bring these very men to their knees. An eerie calm came over her and she felt like her prayers would be answered. She didn't know by whom but the feeling that revenge would be sweet made her smile.

"That bitch is smiling, Tim!"

"She won't be smiling for long. This shit must have scared her enough that she's lost it."

"Well, gotta hand it to her, least she bucked the fuck up and ain't crying like a baby anymore. I have to give her props for that. We've had men piss their pants and cry like little fucking babies."

Olivia not only felt but heard the motor turn off. A shiver moved through her. She felt so cold. The night air plus the spray of the waves hitting her naked body was almost more than she could bear. However, being cold was the least of her worries.

"Time to go and meet your maker, girl." Jed jeered.

Olivia knew she'd finally lost it when she started to laugh at the asshole's choice of words. *Meet her maker? Who said that anymore?* Apparently, it had been the fucker who now grabbed her and brought her to the front of the pitching dinghy. Maybe if she held her breath, she'd be okay and she could break free somehow.

Rough hands pushed her from behind and then she was falling into the cold, dark sea. Olivia closed her eyes and held her breath though she knew it would be futile. How long could she hold her breath? What was the point when death was imminent? How long would it take her to die? Did time even matter? It was going to happen and she was sure it would be painful.

Her chest started to burn as she struggled against the ropes that expertly tied her. Finally, she gave it all up to the sea, letting go to its magnificent splendor.

Olivia heard the most beautiful singing and a resplendent feeling hit her. This was what it must feel like to be in heaven. Opening her eyes, she watched as bubbles rose towards the surface while she drifted down at what seemed like a snail's pace. This must be what blessed peace felt like and she knew no more.

Wake up child of the sea...

Child of the sea? I'm Olivia. Olivia Tate. Besides, she didn't want to wake up. She felt so warm and cozy. She'd been dreaming of her mother. Nothing could harm her where she was. Why would she want to wake up?

In another life, small one. You are now of the sea.

I'm Olivia!

In another time and place...now pick a name. You and the ocean are one.

The voice sounded ethereal, and she couldn't quite place where it was coming from. *One with the ocean? That doesn't make any sense.* She squeezed her eyes tightly and opened them again—yes, she was still underwater and apparently alive.

Blinking, she groaned and then it all came flooding back to her. Abruptly, she sat up with a gasp, eyes wide while looking around to see who spoke and why she was alive. Or at least she thought she was alive. She reached up to frantically touch her chest and then it hit her that she was in water. She had to be dead. *Very dead.* She was breathing in the water and that was impossible. Her hand went to her chest. She felt the vibration of her heart beating against her hand. Even though she remembered drowning.

"How?" she asked this question aloud as she continued to stare at her hands in the water. From what she could tell, she was intact. She reached up to touch her head and felt her long black braids wrapped around her fingers. She was all there.

"Don't worry about the how. Worry about the when of revenge."

Revenge.

She finally looked towards the voice who had been speaking. Really looked and then found herself staring. "You're a mermaid?"

"Indeed I am. My name is Galene and I still don't know the name you've chosen."

"Did I hit my head and die and now this is heaven?" Olivia questioned.

"You tell me...look at yourself," Galene suggested.

Olivia glanced down and a smile spread across her face as she noted the very gilded fishlike tail she had of her own. She was alive, but not the same. The mermaid was right, Olivia didn't fit her anymore. The scared girl she'd once been needed a new name to fit the gilded tail she had now instead of two legs. Despite how wild it seemed, she was now *of the ocean* as Galene had stated. So why not choose a name for her new life. "I'm Oceanu," she said softly.

"Who?" Galene wore a fierce expression on her face, as she crossed her arms over her chest and stared at her with the most intense sea green eyes.

"I am Oceanu," she replied with a conviction she finally felt.

"What a pretty name for a very pretty mermaid. I knew there was a reason I saved you."

"You—you saved me?"

"Yes, don't you remember? I saw those nasty men throw you into the water. At first, I wasn't going to help...but then something about you compelled me to. Maybe it was the songs I felt in you."

Oceanu didn't question what this meant. She frowned as she stared at Galene unsure what she should even say to that. "I don't remember much after drowning," she said softly.

"Well, I don't just save anyone. The world would be overrun with mermaids and mermen."

"There are mermen too?"

Galene laughed. "Yes, there are mermen too. Now you really should rest a bit."

"How long have I been here?" Oceanu touched her tail and gasped softly. Oh, this was very real. The tail was real. She stroked fingers along it once more, amazed at what it felt like. She'd heard of mermaids but like any sane person, she'd thought they were only made-up tales. Then now, here she was a living mermaid, breathing in the water with an actual freaking tail!

Galene cocked her head at her. "Do you mean how long did it take for me to save you and for you to awaken?"

"Yes, that part."

"It's been a month since your transformation. It wasn't pleasant...it is never pleasant."

Oceanu stared at her in shock. "It has been a month?" How could it possibly have been that long since she'd drowned? It felt like it had only happened yesterday. In fact, it felt like only moments ago when she was struggling to breathe.

"Transformation isn't always easy. Some adjust quickly and for some, it takes a while. There is no set timing for this, Oceanu and it will take you time to adjust."

"But I died."

"You were reborn," Galene stated the fact firmly.

"Reborn for?"

"A siren song...what else? Mermaids sing and bring the world of men crashing down."

She nodded her head at this even though she didn't understand it. Moving a bit, she wanted to see if she could get up and if it would be easy to adjust from legs to a tail. "A siren's song..." Oceanu repeated and instantly, she was filled with all the memories of what it meant to be a mermaid. She realized that she was now a Siren...A dark mermaid. "Now what do I do?" she asked while holding her hands out to touch the wall of the room they were in. Because it was indeed a room, not like she was used to back on land, but a room just the same. Magical looking, sparkling, lit with coral, anemones, and other sea creatures.

Surprised by her immediate agility, Oceanu swished her tail back and forth and smiled as she was propelled forward.

"What is it you wish to do?" Galene asked.

Oceanu glanced over at the blonde-haired, green-eyed mermaid and knew exactly what she wanted to do. She wanted revenge in the worst way. She remembered who had done this to her and why. She wanted to the end of Mr. X. A smile spread across her lips. "I want to be the ending of men."

"All men...?" A small smile showed on Galene's face.

"No, just a few." Oceanu knew exactly who she'd marked for death, and they wouldn't even see her coming.

"Do what you need to do, Oceanu, but do it safely. None can know we exist."

"I'll be very careful."

CHAPTER TWO: BROKEN

Scott

"The broken will always be able to love harder than most because once you've been in the dark, you learn to appreciate everything that shines." –
Anonymous

Scott Roby stared out at the deep blue sea and wondered for the hundredth time what it would feel like to just jump in from the pier he sat on and drop into the deepest part of the dark water. He could even tie weights to his legs, so it would be quicker. He'd been thinking about it a lot. He remembered his life before leaving home for the first time to join the military. Suicide and death had been on his radar in his purview for years now.

The salty breeze tickled his nose and sadly reminded him of the last time he'd talked to his mother before she'd passed. He'd been pushing her in a wheelchair along the dock and they'd been chatting about life. She'd been his only family. The military had allowed him to go home early on leave to bid her goodbye as she'd been wasting away from cancer. She hadn't told him about her illness, as her many letters had always sounded so cheerful. If he shut his eyes, he could still see her lying in her hospice bed weathering away.

Scottie, it's so good to see you.

Mama, I'm so sorry.

Why? You didn't give me cancer.

But I wasn't here.

You were in spirit. Besides, you were doing something important. Serving our country.

They would have let me come home, mom.

You had more important things to do and as I said, your spirit was with me.

Scott remembered thinking that his mother was a saint in those moments. Dealing with what she'd dealt with all alone and not angry with him for not being there. He'd tried to not be with himself because common sense told him his mother wasn't. Yet the rage never left. Anger and guilt was a part of him. Guilt struck him again as he'd thought about how he hadn't always written back. He wondered if there was something on the other side, as they liked to say.

What if there was nothing on that other side? Did this mean his fellow soldiers all died in vain? A lot of them had died calling out to their deity to help them. It would mean his mother's death had been meaningless as well. She'd lingered in pain for there to be nothing on the other side.

Oblivion.

Nothingness.

The water looked so peaceful in a world that wasn't peaceful at all. Well, other than the crashing sound, it made as it hit against the rocks where he was settled, gazing out as if something magical would lift him to the sea and sweep him away. His green eyed gaze searched the surf for some magical form of release. Sighing, Scott shut his eyes and tried to center himself like his therapist had requested for him to do when he was feeling off balance.

Who am I kidding?

Meditation had never worked for him. It would never work for him and yet, he kept trying. When he meditated and tried to clear his mind, he would see and feel the helicopter going down. He'd remember floating on debris after waking up in the icy depths and finding that everyone else aboard that helicopter on a practice flight was dead but him.

Bodies floating everywhere.

He could still hear the cries of the others as the copter went down. The scent of death still lingered in his nostrils. He'd been sent home on leave then medically discharged with post-traumatic stress disorder, PTSD.

He ran his tongue over his dry lips. The medication he was forced to take through orders from the military doctors made his mouth so damned dry. Well, the word *forced* was a strong word but that's what it felt like to him. His doctor said *take the meds, meditate, journal what was happening—rinse, wash, and repeat.* How the fuck was that shit supposed to get the demons out of his head?

A watery death would be good for him. It would be what his men and women had experienced.

Retribution.

Men and women he'd fought with overseas and bonded with. Why the hell was he still alive? He had nothing left. His mother was dead now. The military had let him go, citing that he was not fit for duty anymore. He wasn't fucking fit for duty, as he couldn't get over what had happened in that crash.

Come to think of it, he really didn't have to take the meds or do anything they asked at this point. He had always been such a creature of habit, a man who liked order and rule. A fat lot of good that had done him. He'd been discharged anyway. Yeah, he had been honorably discharged but then he was jobless while living off the very money he'd been sending home for his mom. After she passed, he had found out she'd just put it all in the bank for him, having never touched any of it.

He'd had to use it to pay the rest of her medical bills and then found himself looking for a job. No one had wanted to hire a vet with issues, so he'd had to go to the underground. That had been where he'd found Mr. Lofton Exeter—a man who you didn't question and didn't ask questions. A hired gun was what he needed; a hired gun was what he'd get. He'd do all the dirty jobs and do them with relish.

Lately though, the water had been calling to him. One would think he would be scared since the accident over the Atlantic but here he sat staring at its depths, wanting the water to welcome him as it had the others. Why had the ocean spared him? Why did it seem inviting?

"Scottie..." A gruff voice said from behind him,

It broke him out of his reverie. *Fuck.* Scott sighed and opened his eyes. "What is it, Blanchard?"

"The boss has a job for us."

"What kind of job?"

"Does it matter?" Jedidiah Blanchard growled out. "When the boss has a job, the boss has a fucking job, now come on, sailor boy. And how many times do I have to tell you to call me fucking Jed?"

Ever since Blanchard had found out that Scott had been in the navy, he'd been calling him 'sailor boy.' Scott thought it was some kind of slur, though he didn't even care. He rolled his eyes and ignored the question from Jed. "Where's Tim? That's who you usually take." He stood and began to move off the pier with the other man.

"Not sure, can't find him." Jed grunted and walked swiftly down the dock.

Scott paused at this news. Tim and Jed were inseparable, so it seemed a little weird that he couldn't be found. He turned to Jed as they headed towards the Pier One bar run by Mr. X as a legitimate business to cover up the illegitimate things he did. "Let me guess, he wants us to round up some women for his trafficking."

"Scottie, how about you yell it even louder, so the cops can hear?" Jed snapped.

"What fucking cops? Just tell me what the fuck we're doing," Scott retorted.

Jed turned quickly with his gun pointed at him.

Scott was faster and had the muzzle of his gun pressed into Jed's side. "Want to try that again?"

"Whoa...Scottie...whoa." Jed let out a nervous laugh. "Come on now..."

"Put the gun away, Jed. You know I was hired because I'm an expert gun handler, don't make me handle you."

"I was just playin'," Jed said, his pale face turning red as he put his gun away.

Other patrons on the boardwalk made a wide berth around the two.

"No. Playing is what you do every night in the booth as you fucking jerk off to the dancers. Pulling your gun out is serious. Next time you do it, you'd better be prepared to use it." Scott put his gun back under his jacket and nodded to Jed to keep moving. He already knew to watch out for Jed as he was as shifty as they come and if he pulled a gun once, he'd do it again. Stupidity knew no bounds.

The bar itself was a huge multi-level building that marred the beach front. Jed opened the door to the seaside bar as they were both blasted with jazz and voices of patrons. The same music always played here, as Lofton Exeter claimed he was a jazz connoisseur. They headed up to the second-floor deck, this way had always been a lot quieter and easier to be in then out.

As they reached the top platform, Scott noted the man in question Mr. X was settled in his private space with several young women in different states of undress straddling him or sitting close enough for him to be able to touch them. Exeter didn't have a certain type so there were Caucasian women, Asian women, and women of color all around him. He also didn't care about age. The youngest one looked to be about 16.

Scott drew the line for himself as underage girls were not his thing. He had to once again stop himself from rolling his eyes at the overt display of money, power, and just plain lust. Not that lust was a bad thing, as he liked fucking just like the next man. However, he felt sure Lofton Exeter's excess and love of very young girls would be his eventual downfall. Until that day came, Scott would take the fucker's money and do whatever he was required.

"Scottie, just the man I wanted to see," Lofton Exeter said as Scott stopped next to his chair.

"Yeah, boss I found him just like I said I would," Jed cut in.

"Jed, go fucking make sure things are running smooth at the bar."

"Sure, boss, right away boss." Jedidiah backed up as Exeter frowned at him. He scurried away towards the bar.

Scott kept his attention on Exeter.

"He is fucking driving me insane." Exeter watched Jed run off. "Why the fuck do I keep him around?" As he spoke, he worked on preparing a Cuban cigar.

Scott didn't answer him because knowing Exeter, this wasn't a question he wanted answered it was rhetorical. He placed his hands behind his back and waited patiently for the boss to talk.

Finally, the older man turned gray eyes in his direction. "Scottie, how long have you been with me?"

"About six months, sir," Scott stated, giving the man respect with the use of 'sir.' He had to wonder where Exeter was going with the question if anywhere at all. This man sold illegal drugs and used his own product so sometimes he wasn't lucid.

"Six months..." Exeter trailed off.

Scott determined it was one of his in between lucid periods. So, he'd probably only used a bit of the coke. "Yes, sir."

"Right...so in those six months, what have you learned about Lofton Exeter?"

Scott ground his teeth together to hold back a retort. *Christ, why the hell did he talk about himself in third person?* What he wanted to say was that he used his own shit and talked in circles a lot, but he knew better than to share his opinion. He paused for a moment and then spoke, "I've learned that you are a man who takes what he wants, when he wants it."

"Bingo. This city is mine; these bitches are mine...and you're mine."

The girls around Lofton just giggled at being called *bitches*.

Scott stiffened but didn't say anything. Fuck, this is what happened when a man ran out of options. He winds up working for a dipshit. He still felt amazed at the things he had to do to pay the bills.

"I need you to aid Jed in a clean up job. I don't know where the fuck Tim went."

"How long has he been missing, sir?" Scott interjected.

"According to that fuckwad Jed, about two weeks. Just up and disappeared. I think he just walked. No one just walks on Lofton Exeter!"

"So let me make sure I know exactly what you want. You want me to find Tim?"

"Amongst other things, Scottie. You do me right and I'll make you my right hand."

Shit.

Jedidiah would not like hearing that bit of news. He already thought he was Lofton's right hand. All he needed was to have to look for Tim as well as making sure he didn't get a knife in his back from Jed. As far as he was concerned, Jed could have the damn job, but Exeter was the boss on that. "Whatever you need, boss," Scott said.

"Don't tell Jed, I put you in charge. He thinks he's in charge, I know."

"Whatever you say, sir." The man loved his games and right now, Scott knew he had to be careful, or he'd get caught up in a very dangerous one. Tim, if he'd indeed left and hadn't gotten himself killed, had more than likely ran off to hide.

"I also want you and Jed to gather some girls. I need a new

singer. Someone who will bring in the men and the money. She needs to be fucking sexy. You got that, Scottie?"

"Yes sir, she needs to be sexy, someone who will bring in the patrons."

"Not just patrons, but the patrons with fucking cash."

"Got it." *What the fuck is he doing?* Scott was better at shooting people. He knew the moment Lofton was done with him when he began to kiss and play with the women on his lap. Dismissed, Scott left quickly to find Jed to let him know what they would have to do today.

CHAPTER THREE: FIRST KILL

Oceanu

"Everybody wants to go to heaven, but nobody wants to die." – Unknown

Oceanu stood in the shadows of the *Triple X* staring up at the well-guarded bar owned by Lofton Exeter. She knew she would never be able to walk into this place and just kill him. Although, the thought of doing that filled her with a huge amount of pleasure. She noted how the women were dressed along with who the bouncers let in. So, to get in and to get close she needed to be sexy enough to appeal to the blatant lust apparent in the eyes of these men.

She'd get to that later. Right now, she had to get back to the place where she'd tied up one of Lofton's men. He'd been easy to lure from his post and she'd had enjoyed scaring him. He'd been one of the men who had tried to kill her. Or should she say one of the men who killed Olivia Tate. This capturing and stalking men wasn't the kind of thing she would've ever done before, but this was now the course of her life. This Tim character wouldn't like how she intended to finish him off. Though to be truthful, Oceanu knew she'd make him suffer.

Why not?

Drowning wasn't as quick as some thought. Perhaps she'd have a little fun with that. Drag him out to sea and then let him take that long dip without any air. It would be appropriate to watch him struggle and sink. Swim around him and let him realize that no help would be coming for him. Let him feel the terror she'd felt when the water had begun to fill her lungs, making them heavy. A numbness sliding through the body as organs began to shut down. Plus, even though the water was warm this time of year, she knew a cold like no other would creep into his body where he'd never feel warm again.

Hell, why not just kill all the men who worked for Lofton Exeter? If she just cut off the tentacles of one, wouldn't another grow in its place? So, killing the lot of them would be the best bet. After all, Galene was fine with revenge. Yet, she could not draw attention to what she was. Which meant she couldn't just rush in and kill the men here without the possibility of drawing attention to who and what she was. Olivia Meredith Tate coming back from the dead in the form of a mermaid would be a tasty headline she knew she couldn't afford.

Hmm. So this did pose a few issues for her. How to kill about thirty or so men without drawing attention? It would have to be something she thought about and took her time in doing. Right now, she only had one of those men and though she felt sure Lofton knew he was gone, he was none the wiser as to why.

What fueled her to continue the path she was carving out for herself was knowing she'd never be able to see her sister again. Having gone to see her, she'd found that her father and sister had left the area. Her dad most likely left because Exeter wouldn't have just wanted her dead. He would want him dead too. He would have wanted his money. Period.

Oceanu was about to turn away when she saw a tall male with dark red hair taping some signs on the windows of the bar. Both arms were covered in tattoos and his arms showed his strength without him even flexing. From where she stood, she could tell he was handsome and unfortunately, one of the men who worked for Exeter. No, he wasn't the one who'd been with Tim when they dumped her into the ocean.

She had to wonder what was on the sign.

The handsome guy finished putting up the signs. He paused and looked around as if he knew she was watching him. After a minute, he shook his head and went back into the building.

She ran her tongue slowly over her lips. He looked nice enough to dirty up. What possibilities could arise? In that moment, she made it up in her mind to meet this man and if he didn't piss her off, she'd just fuck him and not kill him. She was suddenly hungry for blood and sex. The only thing she could figure out was that her transformation and rage at what had happened to her had made her feel everything more keenly. The odd thing was, she didn't mind it one bit.

Two women walked up to the sign and snickered.

"They want a singer. You can sing, Deb!"

"The auditions are tomorrow morning at ten," Deb replied. "Girl, I won't even be up at that point."

They chuckled then went into the bar after flashing their IDs at the bouncer.

Ah, a singer? What about a siren? She grinned at the thought. They were going to get more than they bargained for she'd make sure of that. Singing was something she knew she could do and it would get her close to Mr. Sexy and Mr. X. She slipped away silently and headed back into the water, heading for the cove where she had been spending most of her time with Tim.

EYES ON THE PRIZE. This thought kept running through her mind as she entered the small inlet. It seemed eerily silent but she expected that, seeing as she had Tim tied up with a gag shoved into his mouth and a blindfold over his eyes.

Of course, he was currently on the sand squirming and trying to get loose.

She padded barefoot over to him, straddled his clothed body and laughed softly. Her laugh was humorless though as his body stiffened.

Ripping the blind fold off his head first, she watched his dark eyes widen as he saw who was above him.

The fear she noted in his eyes was sort of like a high for her. "Hello...Timmy." She cocked her head to the side and smiled wickedly. Water still clung to her skin from her swim over to the cove.

It dripped down onto his face and he blinked.

"Oh Timmy, a little water won't hurt you. But I promise you, I will." Oceanu laughed.

Mumbling frantically against the cloth in his mouth, he looked terrified.

She jerked it down off his mouth so hard his lip bled. Leaning in nice and close to him, she spoke quietly, "Any last words?"

"Please, please d-don't kill m-me!" Tim sputtered out, spit dribbling down his stubbled chin.

"And why should I give you grace?"

"Because...because I can get you money! You like money. don't ya?"

Naked and not caring one whit, she cocked her head to the side as she played with one of her braids. "Why on earth would I need your dirty money?"

"Because every beautiful woman wants money," Tim said quickly.

"Do you remember about a month ago, the young woman you killed? What did you tell her when she begged for her life?" Oceanu still played with her braids as if she was asking about the time of day.

"I-I-I...don't remember."

Oceanu growled and slapped him hard across the face. So hard that her handprint shone brightly on his pasty skin. "Try again!"

"I've killed a lot of women!" he screamed out, his voice echoing in the cave.

"And that's supposed to make me want to let you live?"

"No, I just don't remember you," Tim whined.

"Not that it matters in the long run, because you will still be dead. But you don't remember the young girl you threw into the ocean not so long ago?"

Tim stared at her blankly.

Oceanu grinned and then mimicked his voice and the words he'd said not long ago, *"She won't be smiling for long. This shit must have scared her enough that she's lost it."*

A wild recognition crossed over Tim's face and he gasped, as he looked panicked. He jerked his body around and looked horrified as he lost his bowels. The dark yellow and brown color stained his jeans.

The putrid smell rose and hit her nostrils and she grimaced. "Remember me now?"

"How is this fucking possible?" Tim's face was beat red with spittle on his lips and chin. He looked like a dog frothing at the mouth.

"In the long scheme of things, does it really matter, Timmy boy?"

"Puhlease...mercy! I promise I won't tell anyone. I'll leave and no one will ever know that Olivia Tate came back from the dead!"

Oceanu growled as her teeth sharpened. "Olivia Tate is no more. You made sure of that. Mercy doesn't live here anymore."

"I'll do anything!" Tim screeched.

Oceanu could taste the actual fear in the air and felt a thrill wash over her. This dying and being reborn thing was fucking cool. "There is nothing to do, but die, Tim and that is what you will do." Standing, she grabbed him by his bound feet, dragging him towards the ocean.

Tim's wails filled the air, as he was met with an echo of his own voice and a crash of white caps hitting against the shore.

Oceanu turned to look back at Tim flailing in the dark, the night lit by the perfect moon. Luna as some called her. She loved to think of her as sister moon. She remembered reading as a kid in school that the earth, moon, and sun helped the tides with their gravitational pull. An amazing thing really.

Finally, she reached the water, knowing she had to drag him in quickly as her legs would soon form her gilded feet. She ran into the water and let go to grab the rope that tied his upper torso so she could keep him afloat.

Oceanu swam far from the cliffs and land so there wouldn't be any witnesses to what she was about to do. Just like porpoises loved to play with their prey, she'd be doing the same thing, and relish every moment of it. She intended to make sure his eyes were uncovered as well as his mouth. He would drink the sea and it would be the last thing he ever did before he got sent to hell.

No mermaid would save him as Galene had to be present, and she would not be. Death was his only escape.

Tim had stopped begging as the only noises he made sounded like a grown man crying. Heavy sobs could be heard as she turned to him to face her in the water. Oceanu gazed into his eyes to see if there was an ounce of remorse within them or if they only held fear and a need to save his own skin.

Smiling wickedly, she thought of a better way to torture him. She swiftly untied the rope and moved away a bit. Just as she suspected he would, he tried to swim towards the distant shore. She figured his limbs had to be aching. Waiting, she let him get about a yard away and then began to sing her siren's song.

He stopped swimming and turned in the water back to her. His eyes were filled with the terror of knowing he couldn't do anything against her song.

"I want you to feel what I felt," she said softly as she moved forward.

Tim kept treading water looking desperate and horrified.

When she came within inches of him, she began to sing more soulfully. It didn't matter what words she sang, as the melody and lilt in her voice had him enraptured and caught in her siren's spell.

He was panting hard and tiring out.

"You at least aren't bound like I was," she stated sadly.

Tim stared at her and heard her words. Before too long, his rotund body weakened and he began to sink, even though he struggled to stay buoyant.

Oceanu sang him into his doom, "Just give up."

Tim stopped, outwardly giving up and sank down into the deep blue.

She followed him.

He tried to hold his breath. Smallish bubbles escaping his nostrils, spiraling up towards the top of the water. Tim began fighting again when it became apparent that he could no longer hold his breath. He took a deep gasping breath which filled his mouth with water. Next, his legs went stiff and his eyes widened at the taste of the sea water slowly filling his body.

Oceanu didn't have to guess about the next stage.

Now he was starting to feel the heaviness of his lungs as they filled with the water he was drinking.

Oceanu swam around him, circling his body like a shark did with its dying prey. She thought of giving him air, as the human in her still had some feeling. But why do that? He deserved this painful death. He'd even said he killed many women. Well, he would kill no more.

His body twisted and turned as a gurgling came out in the form of large bubbles. His eyes stared into the distance at nothing but a strange smile broke out on his lips—like he felt happy.

Ahh, the blessed hallucinations. This was the point when she remembered thinking of her mother, her sister, and how short her life had been. It had a sort of a calming effect on her and she'd just floated down to unconsciousness.

Galene had witnessed her drowning and had saved her then welcomed her into the pod. Oceanu intended to make sure she honored that gift of life.

She felt the moment his spirit was leaving his body and she moved in close, capturing him as he continued to sink. She sank her teeth into his neck to drink his life's blood as it was still tinged with fear and adrenaline. Once more, the orgasmic feeling flooded her body, close to shattering in a million pieces of pleasure. Having conquered one of her demons in an easy game of cat and mouse or in this instance—human versus shark, she felt victorious.

Tonight, she would feast on the flesh of her enemy. "One by one, you will all succumb..."

CHAPTER FOUR: THREE WEEKS LATER

Scott

"No notice is taken of a little evil, but when it increases it strikes the eye."

—Aristotle

Finally done with things at the club for the night, Scott headed to his car in the parking lot. He checked his phone... 3 a.m. which meant he'd only had a little bit of time for sleep before he had to get back up and do it all over again. He'd found that he never slept when he worked for Mr. X. At this rate, he should probably sleep in his car. He had his duffle bag in the trunk with clothing so it wouldn't be a problem. They had a locker room with a shower at the bar, so he could potentially shower there and be back on the job.

He really hadn't slept much since seeing combat while in the military. As something about carrying dead friends out of a warzone certainly seemed to change a man. The meds usually kept him up as well. So, his life was filled with an hour or two of sleep, then back to work so he wouldn't overthink things. The jobs he did for Exeter were no different from seeing combat, other than it had been legal to kill for the military.

He paused in the middle of the parking lot and looked toward a few of the outlying buildings. He couldn't shake the feeling of being watched, but he didn't see anyone. It came with the territory he knew, being wary of one's space. The possibility that someone wanted to end him had always shadowed him. He worked for Exeter, who had lots of enemies though Scott had even made some of his own. He gazed around once more as he made it to his vehicle. Getting in, he started the car to warm it up as it had been parked since earlier this morning.

He was never without his gun. He slept with it under his pillow and had it near the shower when he was showering. His gun had become an extension of him so if someone out there meant him harm, he or she would be taken care of. If someone were coming for him, they'd catch more than a couple of bullets.

He still needed to find Tim Wyatt. That fucker had disappeared without a trace. His place hadn't been slept in recently and his car still sat parked at the small house where he stayed. He wasn't a family man so Scott had no family to contact to see if he'd left with them or if they knew where he was. It had become such a fucking mystery when it shouldn't have been. Tim had been an asshole, but he hadn't been one to shirk his duties. At least from what he'd seen.

He also had the task of finding a singer that Lofton Exeter would be pleased with. As it stood now, he'd denied over twenty singers. Granted, the women hadn't been even close to comparable to Billie Holiday but they hadn't been bad. He ran a bar on the beach, why on earth would someone who even sounded close to Billie sing there? Fuck, if he knew.

He pulled his gun out, checked it and then set it within reaching distance. He needed sleep, in a few hours it would be the start of a new day, a new chance to find this miracle singer. He adjusted his seat so he was laying back. He'd slept in worse places.

Bunkers, caves, Humvee's, to name just a few of those places. There were other tight spots, so sleeping in his old sedan was cake. Opening the glove compartment, he took out a bottle of pills and a small bottle of water he kept in there. Scott tossed the pill into his mouth and took a swig of water, then screwed the top back on. Putting the bottle into the cup holder, he sighed. Placing his hand on his gun, he then closed his eyes. Nothing that a little shut eye wouldn't cure. If it didn't cure it, fuck it, he was still a man who did his job.

Sergeant Roby! What do we do? We're taking on water!

Scott sat frozen inside the fallen copter as he heard the panic rising in his men and women, filling him with dread. He stared blankly in the distance. What could they do? It was hopeless out there in the middle of the ocean. The helicopter shifted. Just what was needed to wake Scott up. He quickly undid his seatbelt and tried to save his squad from drowning. However, in the next moment he was thrown out of the sinking bulk of metal and thrust into the water. No saving his people now but he still tried, swimming as fast as he could back to the wreckage.

Scott kept swimming, trying to reach them as the water and the expanse just seemed to widen. He called out for his men to answer him so he could help them, tears mixing with the salty water. No matter how fast he swam, the distance seemed to get further from those he wanted to save. Those who deserved to be saved rather than him.

Scott woke up with a cry and realized he'd been dreaming. Tears were streaming down his cheeks as he ran hands over his face to fiercely swipe them away. "Fuck." He hissed. The nightmare had always been the same, him wishing to save the others from the wreck. The guilt he felt for being the lone survivor was never ending. The other soldiers, Mick, Parisa, Statler, Washington, and Hailey all deserved to go home to their families.

He kept his head back on the seat then realized his hand was on his gun, he could end everything right now. What or who would stop him? His hand tightened on the gun and he brought it up slowly, just as a knock sounded on the door of his car.

Quickly, he aimed his gun at the window. "What the fuck!" Once the initial adrenaline wore off, he realized one of Lofton's men, Gallagher stood there. He put his weapon down in his lap and then rolled the window down.

Fred Gallagher held his hands up in the air while wearing his properly pressed gray suit complete with a red tie. His brown bald head shone brightly in the early morning sun.

"Fucking, idiot," Scott swore. "I could have shot you!"

"Sorry, Scottie. I just got in and noticed your car here. You sleep the night here?"

"Yeah." He rubbed a hand over his face. "What did you need?"

"Nada, bruh, was just checking on you. I'm going to head in. See you in a bit?"

"Yeah, yeah. I need to shower and then I'll be ready for work. We're going to spend today trying to find Tim. Then later, I need to finish those auditions. We have four more."

"Mr. X is kinda picky."

"Kinda doesn't even cover it, bro."

Gallagher chuckled as if Scott had said the funniest thing in the world as he nodded. "See you in there in a bit then." He gave a salute and headed towards the bar.

It wasn't open for the public this early in the morning, but it served as the base of Lofton's business, all his businesses. Scott wasn't sure how the man had gotten away with it so long, other than a lot of the cop's hands were greased with Exeter money.

Scott watched as Gallagher walked away and took a deep breath. He was losing it. This time, he'd been so close to ending it when

Gallagher showed up, stopping him. He felt sure if the other man hadn't been here, he'd have done it. The sadness he felt went so deep that he knew he might never get rid of it. Who wanted to live a life while not living at all? He spent his sleeping hours with the dead, where he felt he should be.

Tucking his gun away, he got out of the car, moving to the trunk to grab his bag. *Baby steps,* they called it. He needed to get through the day and then he would again try to get through the night. Locking his car, Scott leisurely made his way to take his shower, get dressed, and fuck shit up. Most often, that was the kind of state he lived in.

Fuck shit up. Rinse, wash, and repeat.

THE DAY HAD HELD SO much promise after his shower as the comforting hot water brought him out of his funk. Then it had been thrust back into the mire when he'd found out from Exeter that there were two other missing men missing. How was it possible that all these men had just vanished?

First, it had been Tim Wyatt. Then now Pedro Villareal and Gregory Dempsey were gone. If Tim had been a dumbass, those two had known what they were doing and had perfect street smarts. So, who was picking them off and leaving no trace? None of it made sense and he had no time now to look further into it, as he had to do these stupid songstress interviews.

He hoped to fucking god that the jazz singer his boss wanted would be in this last handful of singers. He'd grown tired of hearing *Sentimental Journey.* A favorite of Lofton's and what the women had to sing to get the part, but Scott was starting to feel like...*if you heard it once, you've heard it a million fucking times.*

He entered the area of the bar where the stage was and saw Mike the sound man making sure everything was set up again for the live singers. Looking to the right, he saw Exeter sitting up on his 'throne' kissing one of the underage girls again. Scott had to suppress his disgust. Which had been getting harder and harder to do. He stared down at the list in his hand, noting there were four girls who were supposed to be coming to sing for the chance at the job.

"Scottie."

Scott turned to the sound of his name to see Gallagher standing there. "What's up?"

"There's only one girl out there to sing. She's a real looker. So hopefully, she'll be what the boss wants, because I don't see anyone else here."

Scott took a deep breath and nodded. "Mmm, well let's hope so because I sure as fuck am tired of looking. We have better fucking things to do than find someone to sing him into hardon heaven."

Gallagher agreed with him, "He's looking for someone who can sing jazz which seems kind of stupid to me. When he wants to attract a younger crowd."

"The boss told me the other day it's not just about jazz," Scott replied. "Like if she can sing that, she has range. Whoever gets this job will need to be able to sing anything and everything." He shrugged his shoulders and moved to the area where the girl was said to be waiting. He stopped just inside the small waiting area next to the building's office, his hand on the door frame and paused.

Fucking hell.

Blinking his eyes, he stared at the dark-skinned beauty. Her long braids flowed down her back as she sat in a tight black dress with legs crossed as she wore red heels. Instant lust. He felt his cock harden and his grip on the doorframe tightened. The dress she wore should be illegal on her curves. *Shit.* Change that...her curves should be illegal all on their own, no matter what she wore. What the actual fuck was a woman of this caliber doing on Lofton Exeter's turf? He cleared his throat.

Her dark eyes gazed at him beneath a fringe of thick lashes, her full red tinged lips curving into a smile over her pearly white teeth. She looked at him with sultry eyes.

He continued to stare, as he wanted to fuck her right then and there, in this very office. He could envision her pressed against the office wall, her dress up around her waist, her legs tight around his body as he thrust into her repeatedly. Lustful dirty thoughts, salacious and delicious filled his brain.

The vision then spoke, "Going to just stand there and stare at me?"

Scott grinned. "Definitely wish I could."

She released a husky chuckle.

Scott was hooked. How it was possible to want to fuck someone senseless after just seeing them for a few seconds? He didn't know, but that was exactly what he planned on doing, fucking her till they both couldn't think. Gallagher's words rang into his mind. *She's a real looker.* Those four words were a fucking understatement. He found himself looking her up and down, as he wondered what treasures were hidden under that sexy dress.

The woman in the sexy dress cleared her throat.

He swung his gaze back up to her face. "What's your name?"

"I go by Oceanu."

"Oceanu...Just Oceanu?" Scott found himself repeating the name.

Her mouth curved into a luscious smile. "Mhmm...Oceanu," she repeated slowly.

Scott blew out the air he'd been holding and spoke again to gain control of himself and the conversation, "And you're here for the audition?" He had a job to do and he could think about doing her after said job was done. He knew he sounded stupid but damn if he didn't want to just keep her right here in front of him. He didn't even want to take her to Lofton Exeter. The old bastard didn't deserve to look at such beauty.

Oceanu stood from the chair. "Yes. Did the job already get taken?"

Scott was just mesmerized by her. The heels, though they made her taller still had her right under his chin. The perfect height. Compact size for pleasure. He stared into her dark eyes and blinked again like an idiot. His thoughts about fucking her and her words didn't register.

"Um, maybe I should go," Oceanu said, softly. She moved towards the door.

Scott managed to block her path. "No." His brain had finally disconnected from his cock enough for him to realize he was fucking shit up.

She flicked her long braids back over her shoulder and stared up at him, an ebony brow raised. "What do you mean...no?"

"No, the job isn't taken," he muttered.

"Ok, going to take me to where I can sing?"

"Yes, this way." He moved to the side so she could move out of the room.

She walked away and out the door.

Scott couldn't help but watch her ass as it jiggled in that dress. Fuck, he was going to have so much fun with that ass.

CHAPTER FIVE: OCEANU

"He was the very breath of my need." – Nikki Prince

Oceanu stared over the top of the mic directly at the male who'd told her to sing. Swaying her full-figured body in the borrowed dress. The fabric felt smooth on her skin and wrapped around her body snuggly, showing off every curve. The darkness of the fabric was offset by a soft sparkle that mimicked the clear night sky.

She'd managed to get the outfit by singing it off a woman the night before. She'd been on the boardwalk outside one of the fancy restaurants, headed to her car. In no time, the woman had taken her to her home and handed off several items she'd need to play the part of singer to grab the attention of Lofton Exeter and company. She also had the woman give her a suitcase to pack the things in, so she could hide them at the cove. The one thing she remembered from her life before was to never get anything that would wrinkle terribly, so she made this request to the woman as well. No harm came to her, as she wasn't the one she was after.

In the dimly lit room, she could see Lofton Exeter in his spot with his *women* all around him. He sat in a large black, padded leather chair as if he were a king. She felt so ready to dethrone him it was unreal.

She could also see how many of his men were around. Perfect for her and much easier to pick them off one by one. Something she'd already started as Oceanu had been paying attention to make sure she didn't draw attention to herself nor attention to the fact that men were disappearing. Slow and steady wins the race.

"Okay Oceanu, we want you to sing, *Sentimental Journey,*" Mr. Hot Man with the dreamy green eyes stated.

A siren was a siren for a reason. And she was a siren so she could sing any song they threw at her. Oceanu nodded at *Mister Yummy* and began to sing as the track started to play. She intended to fuck him tonight. It was written plainly on his face. She swayed to the beat, singing the notes of the old song like a pro. She knew it and the men out in the club knew it too.

Even waitresses stopped what they were doing to set up for work to listen to her sing. Several men came from the back area of the club to listen.

Mr. X sat up straighter in his chair, not paying attention to his little playthings any longer.

It angered her. The girls were so young, like junior high young. She made sure to keep her face neutral. She couldn't allow her true feelings or intentions bleed out into the song. In the end, she would enjoy dicing up Mr. X and feeding him to the fishes.

Oceanu finished the song as every person in the bar stood and clapped. She bowed slightly still holding on to the mic like a long-lost lover's cock. Pointedly, she looked at Mr. X, and then at her soon to be *fucktoy.* She smiled slyly at him when he stood there clapping like the rest of them.

She had them all in the palm of her hand.

"Well?" Oceanu asked.

"Well, what?" Mr. Gorgeous just stared at her like a fish out of water.

"Do I need to sing more, or do I have the job?" Oceanu questioned.

"She has the fucking job!" Mr. X yelled. "Everyone back to fucking work!"

The small crowd scattered, heading back to work.

Oceanu looked over at him and winked. She had her prey right where she wanted him.

"You heard the boss; you have the job," Mr. Hot stated.

"Now isn't that just awesome," she purred.

The man's eyes darkened to an emerald color as he stared at her.

To stop herself from laughing she bit her inner cheek. Oceanu loved the look in his eyes. His intense gaze spoke of things to come.

"Head with me back to the office, we...um..." He cleared his throat as his eyes roamed over her. "...have some paperwork to fill out and some things to discuss."

Oceanu ran her tongue over her bottom lip as she returned the favor by looking him up and down. He looked well-muscled in all the right places. She could see this fact even with him in a pair of black dress pants and a white button-down shirt. The sleeves of the white fabric on his arms bulged with power.

She knew just what they'd be discussing, and it wasn't how much she'd be getting paid. Nodding her head, she followed him off the small stage towards the back, where she assumed there was an office. He headed into an office after opening the door and stood there looking at her, so she followed him in. Once she was inside, there were no words said as she heard the lock click.

Turning towards him, she advanced and pressed him back hard against the wall near the small office door.

Immediately, he leaned in and kissed her deeply. Both groaned as their lips touched. Oceanu bit his bottom lip roughly and then sucked on it hard as she heard him hiss. His hands were all over her body. Then just as she'd thought of earlier, he was inching the dress up above her waist. She wasn't wearing panties. As he pulled her dress up, she worked at the button of his pants and then zipped them down as quickly as she could. Staring up at him, she slipped her hand into the hole of his boxer briefs and gripped his cock. Eyeing him, she licked her lips, as he was the perfect size. He would make her feel full. He still wore his shirt, but she could see his impressive, chiseled abs just above his boxers.

He hissed softly as he brushed her fingers away and kicked her legs apart to thrust into her without ceremony.

She gasped softly as he turned her to the wall and began to fuck her. His hands tightened on her waist as he impaled her again and again. This was not a slow taking and she didn't care. She ached and needed to come hard all over his cock. This felt like pure bliss and lust...damn, did she revel in it.

"Is one expected to be a gentleman when one is stiff?" — Marquis de Sade

SCOTT COULDN'T HELP the grin on his face as he heard that delightful little sound of a whimper as it escaped her full lips. He could literally not get enough of her. Her hands gripped his shoulders tightly as did her legs around his waist. She felt like tight, wet, silk. Fuck, if he wasn't careful, she'd have him blowing his load fast. He slowed his pace a bit while slowly sliding every inch of his throbbing cock into her wet pussy. Gripping her hips, he made sure he could control their speed. Every thrust made her moan and tightened her pussy on his cock. He felt like he'd ascended to heaven.

Her long nails dug into his shoulders and then one of her hands slid up to grip the back of his head. The pain was delectable. He arched into her nails and bent his knees a bit, so his cock hit deeper into her.

"Ahh..." she whimpered.

"Take every damn inch, baby," Scott growled out.

"Mmm fuck, yes. Harder," she whispered as she nipped his earlobe.

He almost exploded right then. He sped up. No more playing around he needed her to shatter on his cock as he flooded her with his cum. Scott pressed his face to where her neck met her shoulder and breathed her in. Her scent filled his mind...Lavender and the sea. A strange but very sexy, potent fragrance.

"Fuck, kiss me," Oceanu said.

Even her voice was entrancing. Scott raised his head and kissed her, mating his mouth to hers, as he slid his tongue inside. He lapped at the inside of her mouth in time to his furious thrusts and felt his balls drawing close. Man, he was about to come hard in this entrancing, hot woman who smelled like the sea.

Oceanu rolled her hips and matched his rhythm perfectly. Her timing as she rocked into him was everything. Her pussy swallowed his cock and then released it, almost unseating him, then tightening so thoroughly, he groaned out her name, "Fuck, Oceanu, I'm going to bust."

"Then bust, cause' I want every bit of your cream."

Her words sent him over the edge. Before he knew it, he was shooting ropes of seed into her tight recesses just as she began a whole-body shiver and came as well. Her inner muscles contracted around his dick in spasms milking him completely.

Scott stopped thrusting and rested against her. While still inside of her, they both panted heavily. This had to be the best sex he'd ever had in his life. He couldn't believe it and he still wanted her. The carnality of it all floored him. He'd known her for all of a half hour and she had him ready to lay himself bare for her. To do anything and everything she wanted. Hell, he only knew her by her first name, how fucked up was that?

"So, when do I start?" Ocean asked softly.

"This evening. Is that too soon?" If she wanted to talk while still seated on his cock, he'd let her. He just didn't want her to get off his dick. *Keep talking baby, keep on talking.*

"This evening is fine." Oceanu rolled her hips.

He groaned. "Damn girl, you want more?" He felt her squeeze his cock as he took in a deep breath.

"Isn't it apparent?" She began riding him.

Scott found himself caught up in her all over again as he moved to her beat. If she wanted more, he'd fucking give her more and then take more of what he wanted as well. She was secured against him with her legs wrapped around his waist and her arms around his neck. Raising his hand, he tugged one side of her dress open and pulled a breast free. She had perfect dusk-colored areolas, and he immediately sucked her nipple into his mouth. He played with it, licking around it and drawing on it with loud smacks of his mouth as she held on.

Scott rammed his cock into her tightness, her juices causing the sound of sex to fill the small office once more. Damnit, he couldn't think of anything else but her. How she tasted, how she smelled, how she felt around his cock. It was all her. He pulled back to watch her face as they fucked. The breast he'd freed from her dress bounced wickedly with his saliva shining on it.

It felt as if he had marked her with his claim and he liked that feeling of power. In this moment, she was his and his alone. He shivered as pleasure rolled through him. Then all thought just slipped away as he growled out her name and felt his climax take over. The feeling was indescribable.

"Fill me," Oceanu sang the words in his ear.

Scott was done for as he came hard within her yet again. It was so intense that stars exploded behind his eyes. He was spent, having no more in him, the temptress had drawn it all out of him and this time, his legs were weak. He had to stagger to the office chair with her still on him. He sank down panting wildly as he felt her body give way to another climax. Her juices gushed all over his lap and he held on to her as her body shook.

"God damn," he muttered, his body still trembling with ecstasy.

"Mmm..." she moaned.

Scott chuckled softly. "That all you have to say about it?"

"What's your name...?" she asked.

"Scott. Scott Roby."

Oceanu leaned in to kiss him hard and then she slipped off him while pulling her dress down.

Scott knew his cum had to be sliding down along her legs as she stood and that only made him want her more. She had a picture-perfect body as far as he was concerned. Round ass, full breasts and meat on her bones that he loved on a woman.

He could see the intelligence in her eyes, so she wasn't just some piece of ass. She was the whole package, and she knew it, he could tell. He wanted to ask her to stay, yet that was foolish, wasn't it? Besides, he'd see her later in the evening. With her and his appetite combined, he was sure they'd have fun again.

"See you tonight...Scott Roby," she said, winking at him.

Then before he could say anything, she walked out.

He stared after her even as the door shut closed with a soft *Shick* sound. A few seconds went by and he blinked. He shuddered, as his body seemed to remember the ecstasy he had felt from being with her. Lord help him, he was hooked and he knew it. She was even better than the meds from the doctor. She was a fucking aphrodisiac.

"Fuck me..." he muttered, as he chuckled.

Literally, she had fucked him and exceptionally well. He smiled at the closed door and fixed his clothing. Tonight couldn't arrive soon enough when he could see her again. The next time he had her, he hoped it would be in a bed.

LATER THAT EVENING after Oceanu's set, Scott was tasked with clearing out the club and making sure everyone left, the money counted and the place closed up. He missed Oceanu leaving but not the note she left him.

YOU WERE BUSY. So, we'll have to take a rain check. Don't worry, we'll fuck again.
Oceanu

DAMMIT. The woman was a firecracker and he loved every minute of it. The anticipation was astounding to him. The promise to have sex with her again made his cock throb. Now he'd have to suffer blue balls the whole night or need to stroke it out. This hadn't been an issue for him in a long time. It sounded a bit better to him than carrying around blue balls, but it wouldn't be as satisfying as being between Oceanu's thighs. What had happened to him? He felt different about everything. He felt...*alive.*

CHAPTER SIX: POWER STRUGGLE

Scott

"The greater the power, the more dangerous the abuse." --Edmund Burke

Scott stood in front of Lofton Exeter's desk with his hands behind his back as the man rattled on and on about how he was the king of this castle and they needed to find out why his men were missing.

Jed stood next to him. "But boss——"

Scott winced, knowing what was coming.

"Mother fucker, did I ask you to speak?" Exeter Lofton's fist hit the desk and his eyes became wild. Spittle came out of his mouth and he didn't care as was evident when he didn't wipe it away."

Jedidiah was shaking his head. "No...no... nooo...boss," he stuttered.

"Then don't fucking speak unless I ask you a mother fucking question!" Exeter roared. "Fuck, this is why you aren't in charge.

Fucking Scott is in charge. He knows when to speak and not to speak!"

Scott bit the inside of his mouth to stop himself from retorting. He hadn't wanted it to be known that Jed wasn't in charge. It would make it harder to work with him.

Jed turned and glared at Scott.

"What are you looking at Scottie for, Jed? I'm the one talking and your attention belongs to me right now."

Jed turned his attention back to Lofton, his hands tightening into fists being the only sign of his anger.

Scott knew he wouldn't hear the end of it from Jed after the meeting was over.

Exeter went on, "Just this afternoon, we have had four more men just up and disappear. Now this tells me it isn't random."

Hell, the last three should have fucking told you that. I work for an idiot. Scott stared at the angry man who kept ranting.

"Four more of my damn men. This can't be a coincidence." Lofton spun around in his chair and stared out through the office window towards the beach and the boardwalk. It fell silent in the office for a few moments and then Lofton spoke again, "What are we going to do about this?"

Scott knew the 'we' meant him and Jed. Lofton wouldn't do shit. He never did shit, but then he was the one with all the money. Which gave him absolute authority. "Boss, we're going to leave here and go look for them," Scott suggested.

"Mhm, isn't that what you've been doing?"

"Yes, sir." Scott said. "We—"

"Are you going to tell me that I've given the job to the guy who didn't deserve it?" Lofton interrupted as he remained in his chair with his back to them.

"No boss, I deserved this job." Scott knew the disappearances couldn't be reported to law enforcement. Lofton Exeter was never on the right side of the law. His men, him included, had done some gnarly things so the police were a no go. He had no fucking idea what had happened to the men. The only thing he could think of was that Lofton had a new enemy or enemies who wanted his turf and his money.

"Someone knows something," Lofton offered. "And when we find that someone, dodging my bullets won't be easy."

Scott knew this meant they needed to head out and talk to the locals to see if they'd spill. Perhaps this was why he'd been feeling like he was being watched lately. The enemy was at their door and invisible.

"Boss, what about that guy Jeff Brannigan?" Jedidiah offered up. "He's been talking about wanting to take you out. Remember?"

Fuck me. That idiot didn't know shit from a hole in the wall. He couldn't have done this. The man was all talk. Drunk and drugged up most days if not every day. He opened his mouth to say exactly this.

Lofton spun back around to pinpoint them with his gaze. "Find this Jeff Brannigan and bring him to me."

Good lord, he took Jed seriously. This would be a fucking wild goose chase that I have neither the time nor patience for but it's his dime. The one thing Scott knew for sure was no matter what he did for Lofton he would get paid the same amount. If he wanted Jeff Brannigan tracked down, he'd track him down. He nodded his head and said, "We'll have him for you by this evening." He already knew where the man in question liked to haunt. Brannigan wasn't guilty of this, as the man was sloppy as hell. However, he might know something even in his drunken stupor. A rat was always great at telling others.

"Sounds good, now get out of here and send in my favorite girl, Jorja." Lofton turned back around to the beach.

Jed glanced over at Scott as they both turned and left the room.

"Do you really think that old drunk has anything to do with this?" Scott asked as they walked down the darkened hallway to the back door leading out into the parking lot behind the bar.

"Nah, just wanted the boss to let us go," Jed admitted.

Scott glanced over at him. "You do realize you're playing with fire?"

"I've been around too long and know too much the boss ain't gonna do nothin.' Besides, I'm married to his fuckin' sister," Jed said with a laugh.

"What?" *Fuck me.*

"Didn't know that?" Jed raised a brow at him as they headed to the area where their cars were parked.

"No, I didn't know that. I stay out of other people's business here unless the boss asks me to get into their business. You can be in charge, but in front of the boss, shut the fuck up." He reached into his pocket and took out his keys. "We're going to take my car." Now he understood why Jedidiah was tolerated and had been put in charge. He'd hate to be at that family dinner. He could only imagine the bickering involved along with the threats.

"I got no problem with that. Gas is high anyways." Jedidiah chuckled.

Scott didn't trust Jed or his seeming laughter. The man was a snake. He was still going to watch him. "That is the truth." Scott pushed the key fob and unlocked his car.

Jedidiah slid into the passenger seat.

He got in the car himself and buckled up, then started the car. "We're gonna head to Tim's place first. Maybe there's some clue there that we've missed."

"What about getting Jeff?" Jedidiah wore a scowl creasing his brow as he stared at Scott. The older man was all about his Jeff idea. Which made no sense since they both knew that Jeff more than likely had nothing to do with the missing employees.

Scott pulled out heading towards the freeway before he said something, "Maybe he knows something as he's always on the boardwalk watching. But we need to make sure we didn't miss anything with the first man, and then the others. Then we will grab Jeff."

"Alright." Jed went silent.

Scott just concentrated on driving. Tim's place was about thirty minutes from the beach and at this time of the morning, it was rather busy. So it might take about forty minutes to get there if they were lucky. He turned on the radio, playing a light rock station just to fill the silence within the car.

He could feel Jedidiah brooding on his side of the car and he didn't want to have to talk to him at all. He really wished he could have chosen to work alone on this. He wasn't quite sure if Jed would fuck shit up on purpose just to get back into his brother-in-law's good graces.

"You know we're gonna have to square up about you taking my position," Jedidiah grumbled.

Scott sighed and glanced over at the other man. "I wasn't trying to take your supposed position, Jed."

"But ya did," Jed argued back.

"You're making beef where there shouldn't be any. I don't fucking want your position. I just want to get paid for the shit I do... like anyone else. Fuck, dude, calm down." Scott shook his head and concentrated on getting through the thick morning traffic.

Thankfully, Jedidiah didn't say anything else.

Scott hummed the song playing on the radio to center himself once more. Days like this made him want to just blow a mother fucker's head off and keep on trucking. He was never sure when Jed would calm down or just go off the handle.

"Do you think there will be anything at Tim's?" Jed asked.

"I'm hoping. There must be some clues. Too many men have just up and vanished. No money has been taken from Mr. X." Scott turned off the freeway towards the street where Tim lived.

"And no one has reported them gone," Jed stated.

"Yes, because we can't. The police would be all over this and all over Mr. X. Which means they'd be all over us."

"I know we can't report it. Was just stating the fact that no one else has reported it. Fuck, this is just crazy. Tim was flaky. I get him, but the others? Greg, Zach, and Marlon?"

"You're right, it doesn't make sense." Scott drove down the quiet street while making sure to check in his rearview to see if they were being followed.

Tim's place was next to an alley so that is where he parked. He and Jed got out of the car and headed to the back fence of Tim's property. Scott knew Jed had a key and waited for him to unlock the gate. Once that was done, they both went in through the back door, using another key and they entered the washroom. It looked fine, if a bit unorganized, but Tim was disorganized. So, it fit. Scott expected the whole house would be like that.

He walked in behind Jed. "You check down here and I'll go upstairs and check around. Maybe there's something out of place." Scott had been to Tim's house a time or two when he'd had to come pick the other man up, but he wasn't as close to him as Jed was. He only knew Tim briefly in fact.

"Gotcha." Jed headed into the living room.

Scott headed through the kitchen up the stairs to the second floor of the two-story home. On a brief glance, nothing looked out of place. When he stepped through the place, a familiar scent drifted in the air and he halted.

He entered Tim's bedroom then flipped on the light switch as the curtains were closed in the room and it was dark. The bed hadn't been made, but to him that wasn't something out of the ordinary. Tim hadn't been the neatest person. He moved to the bed while glancing down at the floor to see a bit of sand. At least it looked like sand.

He bent down, touched the granules, and rubbed them between his fingers. Sand. Just like he thought. He stood up while looking around. Was the sand a clue? Or was it him overthinking again? Not everything had to be a clue. He knew that. However, everything was important until he could discount it. The scent he smelled through the whole house was one that he'd smelled before.

Lavender and the sea. The scent reminded him of something—of someone.

Oceanu.

Oceanu smelled like that. He didn't even think she'd known Tim. She'd just come to the club for the audition. Therefore, the scent perhaps was a new perfume a lot of the women were wearing nowadays. Otherwise, he would never believe Oceanu had been in Tim's house of all places.

He moved to look out the bedroom window facing the back of the house where one could see the beach. He wasn't far from the beach at all. He sighed. Shit. Now he'd gotten off of his task because he was distracted by remembering her. His cock hardened in his pants and he shifted to ease the discomfort. He wanted her. Sighing, he stroked a hand over his military styled haircut. The woman was a distraction he didn't need. He wasn't ready for an entanglement with anyone. He wasn't fit for it either. He knew he and his life was fucked up.

He left the master bedroom after checking the bathroom and entered the second bedroom. Nothing looked out of place here either. In fact, the room was neat by Tim Wyatt standards. This room was where he'd let his buddies stay in such as Jed, and some of the others. They at times would come to Tim's to play Rummy or some other card game and have bets going on. He'd come once to Tim's for such a party. The second bathroom upstairs was just as spotless and left no hints of any wrongdoing.

"Mmm fuck, yes. Harder."

Oceanu's words whispered through his mind just as if she were standing here begging as prettily as she did the first time. Scott turned away from the window and headed out of the room. He took a deep breath to see if he detected the essence of Oceanu. He swiftly figured out that the smell had been the strongest in the main bedroom.

Heading back down, he hollered to Jed that he was done and had found nothing. What did he expect? If this were a hit from another boss, trying to take territory there seemed to be nothing left to tie him or her to the disappearance. If Tim had a woman here maybe she wore that scent and Tim had been with her. It didn't mean his death or disappearance came from that. "Let's head out," Scott said to Jed.

"I didn't find shit in here. The place is just like Tim always left it." Jed's face showed his disbelief that there wasn't anything to glean from. "It's just fucking weird."

"Yes, it is fucking weird," Scott agreed.

"The last thing Tim and I did together was to kill Dante Tate's daughter."

Scott turned to look at him. "Tate?"

"Yeah, he stole money from Mr. X. That's a big no-no."

Scott paused, he felt glad he hadn't been in on that. He refused to kill a woman. No fucking way. Unless it was to defend himself, even then he would try not to kill her. "Think Tate has something to do with this?"

"Nope, cause not long after we killed her...he left town with his other daughter."

"Well, something happened and I'm not sure what it is, but Tim and the others have vanished and it looks like they've left no trail."

Jed nodded his head and went through the doorway.

Walking back outside, they left the way they came with Jed locking up.

CHAPTER SEVEN: "DODGING MY BULLETS WON'T BE EASY." –LOFTON EXETER

Lofton stared at the door after Jedidiah and Scott left. It was hard to find good men to trust these days. Men who wouldn't try to take what was rightfully his. Jedidiah was getting old and slow...Scott?

Well now, he wasn't quite sure if he'd made the right choice of placing Scott in charge. In fact, he was playing the two against each other as he was getting bored. It was time to spice things up. Neither man would do anything to him, so he was safe in that regard. Jed wanted to stay in his good graces and well, Scott was loyal to a fault because of his military background.

However.

They would be fun to play against each other. The only reason Lofton had hired the incompetent Jed was because his older sister had insisted that Lofton bring him into the family business. So, Lofton hired him. In the beginning, everything had been cool, but the older they got the more incompetent Jed got. How in the hell could all of his men just be disappearing, and no one knew what the hell was happening?

Perhaps putting Scottie in charge would help with finding out what was happening and put an end to it. Scott was a much better choice than Jed. Lofton rubbed his hands together. He'd been running things too long in this city to lose it all now. So, he'd watch Scott Roby and see if he'd picked the right man. If he found that there was an issue, he'd just kill him.

Yes.

That was the plan, watch Scott, and see if there were changes.

Good changes. His changes. What he wanted. If he found he didn't like Scott's way of handling things, then he'd take care of him and find someone else who could enforce his rules better. In the meantime, things could continue as they were now. Of course, he'd want them to get to the bottom of the issue of his men being gone. He wasn't a boss without employees.

Now that was his only worry. None of his businesses had been touched. It had just been his men running off. He'd give Scott some time to find out what was going on. If anything else happened, he would make sure that heads rolled, and hearts stopped.

Lofton chuckled and settled back in his chair, grabbing a cigar to smoke. What did a man do when he had everything? He played God and manipulated circumstances into the way he wanted.

Death was his playground and the people around him were all the unsuspecting pawns.

Scott

"Learn as if you will live forever, live like you will die tomorrow." — Mahatma Gandhi

. . .

SCOTT STOOD in the back of the club watching as Oceanu sang her last set. The bar since her hiring was filled to the brim with patrons. Exeter seemed to be happy and hadn't hounded him or Jed for any more information on what had been happening with his men.

Scott was stumped in a few ways. Mostly, Exeter's silence but the other two factors still bugged him. Exeter was up to something. Whatever it was, it wouldn't be good, even if he was just playing games with him and Jed.

Men vanishing as if magic played a part in their disappearances, as there hadn't even been a small trail left by the men. One or two men leaving he could understand but now, they were getting close to the double digits.

Oceanu hit a note that made Scott look up and his cock hardened immediately. He had to wonder if she was some sort of enchantress to be able to grab so many people's attention at once. Damn. He wanted her as much as he needed to breathe air. It was almost sickening how much he needed her.

Their eyes met.

She smiled at him and winked.

At least he thought it was for him. Though he saw men and even women responding to her charms. Her words entangled him in a spell. There had been times when he could have sworn he heard her whispering his name over and over again. This woman could seriously end up being the death of him. He'd become wrapped so tightly around her little finger that he'd do anything for her.

He was crazy. It was crazy right? How could he fall so fast for her? Why would she even want him? She had her pick of men or could have. *But she picked you.* He refused to ask the how and the why of it. She'd brought sunshine into his dark life in such a short span of time and he intended to enjoy every bit of it.

He winked back at her as she continued to sing the soulful melody which sounded as if she was putting her very soul into the song. An aria that made him want to be on his knees in front of her, worshiping every inch of her as he touched that glorious body of hers. He watched as she swayed to the beat, opening her arms as if inviting the crowd in. From the claps and whistles, he knew everyone in the room felt as enthralled as he did.

Scott felt the beginnings of a possessiveness he'd never allowed in his life over a woman. He had no doubt that if someone came between him and Oceanu that it would be their end. She'd managed to break through the walls he'd built up, ones that had become more prevalent after his stint in the military. He'd fucked women but he'd never even let lust guide the way he was feeling. He had to admit that it couldn't be just lust.

Whatever it was he was going to ride the wave and take from her what she was willing to give him. She was better than any drug he'd been prescribed. He'd in fact stopped taking them, as he didn't like the way they made him feel. For the first time in a long while, he was feeling clear about everything and that was a beautiful miracle. The phenomenon was Oceanu. If only he could bottle her, so he had her forever.

Lucidity was beautiful.

Lucid.

He just wished he knew what Oceanu was all about. Why would a woman of her quality even be here? He had already thought about the obvious. Was there any connection to her sudden appearance and the missing men? Scott couldn't get past the little niggling of doubt that she was in some way responsible. Her innocence couldn't be based on the fact that she was a woman either. Women could be vicious and deadly just like men.

Scott wasn't a foolish man. He'd always been on top of things. It would be silly of him to just dismiss his suspicions just because she was a gorgeous female. Through the centuries, women had shown they had the tenacity, the viciousness, and the intelligence to bring men to their knees. Oceanu would be no different from others in that regard.

Scott moved away from his spot in the shadows to his job, making sure everything in the bar was on the up and up for his boss.

Even if he detested the man, he respected the business part of it at least. He circled the bar checking on the other men who were left as well as the bartender and bouncers at the door. Everything seemed to be going as smoothly as he'd hoped. Tonight, he wanted to head home to get some sleep in bed for once.

What would she look like in his bed?

He allowed himself to dream about what it would be like with her on a more intimate basis. He already loved how she melted into him when they were connected in lust. How would she connect to him in passion? Scott thought briefly of inviting Oceanu over, but the moment the thought hit him, he brushed it away.

He already felt like he couldn't do without her. So he didn't want her knowing the need for her ran so deep. Scott needed to get her out of his system. There was no room for him to fall in love. Lust he could deal with. Loving someone seemed to be a curse for him. She was becoming a big-time distraction.

He ran a hand through his hair and leaned against a far wall watching the show right along with the patrons.

"She's gorgeous."

Scott turned his head towards the voice.

It had been Larry, the newest bartender.

"She is," Scott admitted.

"Man, there is something about her songs that make me feel some kinda way."

Scott just nodded. He'd long suspected that Oceanu had some kind of magical voice. It pulled a person in and made him or her feel giddy and needy all at once. In a way, it had been exciting to feel the way he did for her. On the other hand, it was a bit disconcerting. He always thought himself to be strong, a man who didn't rely on anyone. Now, all he wanted to do was to rely on Oceanu. To be there for her, for whatever reason.

"I'd fucking do her in a minute," Larry said.

Scott growled. "I think you'd better get back to fucking work, man."

439

"Alright, alright, no disrespect meant." Larry hurried away.

Fuck. Scott now knew he was well on his way to being sprung and he didn't like the feeling one bit. He pinched the bridge of his nose to fight back the headache brewing along with the dark thoughts of what he wanted to do to the new bartender for even daring to think he could touch Oceanu. She was his. Even if it was for only a little while.

His.

He needed to get her out of his system. The only thing that could happen with them continuing any kind of relationship would be his downfall as he fell irrevocably in love with her...something he had to nip in the bud. No love. No long-term entanglements because he was staring down the barrel of death on a daily basis. Once again, he moved from his spot and made his rounds around the bar. It was almost time to lock up.

Scott headed over to Lofton Exeter. He waited for the man to get up and head towards the side door where his vehicle was parked. It was Scott's job to make sure that Exeter made it to his car safely and was headed out before the bar closed. Exeter always said he wanted to have a grand entrance and exit. Two new bodyguards along with Jed would be driving Exeter to his beachfront property. Scott had tried to argue it would be better if he took him seeing as men were disappearing, but Lofton of course dismissed what he'd said.

"Scottie, make sure to lock up and get some sleep," Exeter said to him as he opened up the car door for his boss.

"Yes, sir. That's the plan. Some rest in a nice warm bed."

Jed came out of the club and patted Scott on the shoulder then slid into the back passenger side on the right next to Exeter.

Once all the men were settled in, Scott waved them off and headed back in to get things shut down.

CHAPTER EIGHT: MORE MISSING A WEEK LATER

Oceanu

"Karma has no problem getting back in touch with you when need be."

−Unknown

For her, the most exciting part was the hunt over the actual killing. Trailing after her prey and making sure they felt like they were being stalked. Then catching the person – allowing the fact that they were going to die – to sink in.

It had all been so gratifying. Galene had mentioned that she needed to remember she was reborn...not immortal. This thought alone sobered her enough so she wouldn't get cocky. She could die for real this time if she wasn't careful.

Oceanu swam through the waters at a leisurely pace headed for the shore that held her game. Sure, the taste of ocean wildlife was appealing at times but there was nothing quite like the taste of human flesh tinged with fear. However, not just any human flesh. The human populace didn't have to worry about her going on some monster rampage. They didn't have to worry about her at all. In fact, she was doing a favor for the public, ridding them of an evil menace. She'd made sure no one knew who or what she was.

She just wanted to end Exeter and his people. Well, except for Scott Roby. He was too delicious in other ways to kill and eat. She found herself wondering about him often. Which at times made it difficult to do what she had set out to do. It wasn't a smart thing to do, thinking of him more than she should. However, her brain seemed to be doing what it wanted.

Exeter had his men out looking for his missing. What a shame that they were on a wild goose chase. She smirked to herself. She'd made sure they'd never find the bodies as she fed them to the sharks and the other carnivores of the ocean. Waste not...want not. Or in her case, if she didn't want it, she didn't waste it.

It had been two weeks since she last saw Scott. Yes, he was a good fuck, but that was all he could be right? He was very much human and she was a mermaid now. A thing of fantasy in most humans' minds.

Then why are you swimming to him now? Because I want him and I'm going to have him. Fuck. Now she was talking to herself and even answering. He thrilled her, gave her his all, pleased her like no other man ever had. She hadn't had much to do with men before her death, but he was as addicting as one could get. She wanted another taste of what they'd done after her audition. He was wrapped up in the spell of her singing, but she had also been wrapped up in just him.

Mermaids sing and bring the world of men crashing down.

That was supposed to be the objective...To bring the world of men crashing down. She was moments away from that happening. The closer she got to shore the closer she got to being truly free from the anger that simmered just on the surface. She'd avenge her death and she'd be appeased. One more fuck. Then she could swim away and forget him. It wasn't love she was feeling but lust, right?

She couldn't help but to wonder about the very human, Scott.

Could she just leave him? Did she even want to leave him? What kind of future would there be with him? None really when you looked at it. She was tied to the sea in more ways than one. Sure, she could walk on land, but it was limited. She could not reproduce either.

The only way to make a mermaid was for Galene to save that woman, child, or man from drowning. As Galene had done for her. Most men wanted children, didn't they? So why would he want a forever with her? She wouldn't be able to give him children.

Ever.

Oceanu came up in the shallows, her legs beginning to form as she rose out of the water. Soon she was padding naked towards the protection of her cove. Time was running out. She would only be able to walk on land for a few more days, the lunar cycle for her kind being twenty-eight days. Time to kill and get this done finally. Time to eat the evil man responsible for this mess then fuck Scott Roby and bid farewell to him.

She had a plan, now she needed to make sure she followed it. She'd be able to head back to the pod as soon as she was done with her payback.

Eating the evil.

She chuckled to herself. She didn't used to be so sarcastic with her thoughts but dying by the hands of ruthless men had a way of doing that to a person.

She'd found out where Scott or Scottie, as they called him lived and she planned to be waiting for him to come home. He had a nice warm bed, she was sure, so why not try it out. See if he was just as good in a bed as he was out of it. She made her way quickly to where his home was. Oceanu had it on good authority that he'd be coming home tonight. Of course, she had ear-hustled and found out where he was going after work.

Earlier that evening after her set at the bar she'd heard him mention to one of the other men that they'd be able to contact him at his house. She'd followed him home once before to see where he'd gone in the evenings when done at the club. His place was surprisingly cute. A small little bungalow not far from the beach strip.

It had also been easy to get to, enabling her to stick to the shadows as much as she needed to. She was quite pleased with how close he lived to the ocean. She could hear the waves hitting the shore. Tonight, she was dressed in a small red number that had a slit up the side and shimmered lightly in the moonlit sky. It fit so well and almost looked like her skin.

Reading the numbers on the tightly clustered homes, she finally found his number and went to stand in the alcove of the bungalow. She settled on a chair on the porch to wait for him. It wasn't hard to imagine him sitting outside on the porch late at night, listening to the sound of the ocean, the night ocean birds, and smelling the wonderful salty air.

Just as she relaxed into the chair, she heard Scott's car pulling into the driveway. She stood waiting for him to notice her.

Scott came up to the door and paused, looking into the darkened porch. He raised his head and breathed in deeply. "Oceanu...how did you find me?"

"Does it matter? I found you. I wanted to try out your bed for a change." She grinned coming out into the open where the porch was lit by the lights in front of the car port.

A smile spread across his face. He no longer wore a look of 'how the hell did she find him.' Just a look of pure hunger. "You're not cold?" he asked, as he looked her over.

"I figured you could warm me up." Oceanu held her hand out to him and smiled as he placed his hand in hers and moved closer to her. She moved in for a kiss and moaned softly when their lips touched. She groaned when he parted the kiss.

"Come on, let's go inside." Scott unlocked his door while still holding her hand and led her inside, closing the door with his foot. Nothing else was said as he took her from the front door towards the back.

Oceanu didn't even have time to check out the home and she

didn't mind that one bit. She wanted him just as fiercely as he wanted her.

They entered the bedroom, where they quickly tore at each other's clothing, dropping every article to the floor.

She purred softly as he pressed his naked body to hers and covered her lips in a hard kiss. His mouth taking hers over as he thrust his tongue in while walking her backwards to the bed. Oceanu slid her arms around his neck as they both fell onto the mattress sideways. Wrapping her legs up high around his waist, she groaned again as she felt his cock in between her legs, her moist heat ready to accept him. Rubbing her mound against his hardness hungrily, she felt that thrill only this man could give to her. He always felt amazing.

Scott growled low in his throat continuing to rub against her without slipping inside of her. "Fuck, I need you." He buried his face into her neck for a moment, then nipped her flesh.

Oceanu squealed with pleasure.

He pulled back up to gaze into her eyes.

"I'm right here," she whispered.

Scott cupped her breasts and squeezed them.

Oceanu found herself pushing them even more into his large, callused hands. The roughness of his hands had always turned her on. Nothing was more attractive than a hardworking man. She licked her lips in anticipation of having him fill her with his cock.

Scott pushed forward and they groaned in unison as he slid fully into her. He stopped moving and she held onto him, panting softly. He stretched her so full. There was nothing small about him.

Leaning in, Scott took one of her nipples into her mouth and sucked hard. Raising his head, he stared down into her eyes.

Oceanu stared right back at his brilliant green eyes that reminded her of the finest coral in the sea. The man was just so damned hot and strong. Scott ground his hips into her and she hissed softly as his cock hit deep. The passion she felt for him was indescribable. She was so close to exploding just from what he was doing.

Scott must have realized this because he stopped altogether, when she started to pant harder. "What the hell is it about you that I can't get enough?"

Oceanu didn't say anything. She didn't want it to be because of her Siren song. She honestly wanted him to want her just because he wanted her. But she feared it was the song. She covered his mouth with hers and kissed him hungrily to stop him from asking questions that were painful. She just wanted to feel this high they went on every time they were together.

She could deal with this Scott. The Scott who just wanted her madly. The other Scott asked too many questions she could not answer. Ones she didn't want to answer. "Move," she groaned out.

"So bossy," Scott mused as he reached between them and played with her clit. He pressed his thumb against her clitoris and rubbed it.

Oceanu couldn't help but try to move against that insistent thumb. "I still need you to move." She shuddered, closing her eyes. Being connected to him was wonderful but what she needed was a fast release that only he could give her.

Scott pressed back into her slowly and then pulled almost all the way out.

"No!" She cried out at his teasing as he gave her less and less of his cock. Oceanu clutched at him trying to pull him in deeper with a tightening of her legs about his waist. Scott chuckled as she leaned up and bit his shoulder hard.

Growling, he snatched his head back. "You want it rough, Oceanu?"

She licked her lips with a strong sense of anticipation for what he could give her. "I want you so hard that all I feel and taste is you."

"You're going to come way too soon," he reasoned.

"Yes, that's the fucking point! Please!" She wailed.

Scott began to pound into her like she craved and soon she was exploding into a concerto of orgasmic sensations. This man owned every part of her at this point as she sobbed and shuddered.

Finally, he roared with his own climax as the warmth of his cum filling her body added to her own ecstasy. This man gave her pleasure she could not even begin to describe. Never in her short-lived life had she ever considered such a desire for anyone. The one guy she'd been with had been safe. Oceanu realized this now as she held Scott close. He made her feel things she'd never experienced before. Having lived in fear because of her father she'd played it safe with the guy she'd chosen. Choosing Scott had given her so much more – a myriad of feelings, a wild sort of fire that lit her up from the inside out – she wished she could keep him.

CHAPTER NINE: ONE SHOT, ONE KILL

Scott

"All that we see or seem is but a dream within a dream." — Edgar Allan Poe"

It is only by way of pain one arrives at pleasure." – Marquis de Sade

Scott was bone weary. They'd been to all the missing men's homes and every one of the houses smelled like lavender and the sea. They hadn't of course been able to find Jeff Brannigan either. Scott had checked around and was told the old man had finally been picked up by his family and taken to a rehabilitation center. So that door was closed. They had no hope in finding out if and what he knew about anything. Then to top everything off with a big fat juicy fucking cherry, Jed was missing.

Common sense told Scott that it couldn't be a coincidence. Smelling the lavender and sea in places where Exeter's men had been. Everything pointed to Oceanu, but why would she want to kill

Exeter's men? Hell, on that train of thought why hadn't she killed him?

He didn't want to be sensible though. Sensible would mean the men being gone was somehow Oceanu's fault. Unable to shake the odd feeling, he'd waited in his car at the end of the evening for Oceanu. He intended to follow her tonight to see where she went and who she was with.

What if I'm wrong?

Hell, he fucking hoped he was. Because this shit didn't make any sense. The woman he wanted beyond reason was a serial killer if she was the reason the men vanished. Or at the very least a kidnapper? Scott sighed, raking his fingers through his hair. He could still smell her. Her scent was the most tantalizing thing he'd ever smelled. He wanted to fucking bathe in her essence.

How would she be able to do what she was doing without being caught? This part confused him to no end, making him think he was barking up the wrong tree. Oceanu didn't seem the type to kill indiscriminately. What type did she seem like? A seductress to be sure, but he had never seen her go sexually for anyone else except him. So, if she was killing Exeter's men. What made him different?

So, he finally decided to trail her and what he found astonished him to no end.

Scott now stood in a dimly lit cave. Luckily, the moon shone brightly enough that he could see her as he trained his gun on her. The part that hurt the most was thinking that she would kill him given the chance. Just like the poor man who laid on the ground between them both.

Jedidiah Blanchard. His eyes vacant and staring up in horror at the cave ceiling.

The last of Lofton's men to go missing. Well, if Scott didn't include himself.

"How did you find me?" Oceanu asked.

"So, we're going to make this about you?" Scott murmured.

"You tell me. You followed me. I'd guess it is about me."

She sounded so nonchalant to Scott that he tensed. "Did you do it, Oceanu? Did you kill those men? This man?" Of course, she did. He knew he sounded like an idiot asking her something so ludicrous and yet, true. How else would she be right here with the evidence? Jedidiah Blanchard's twisted and dead body. The other men that had left with no trace, were nowhere in sight which was still puzzling to him.

"There is no simple answer."

Scott stared at the woman he'd come to adore and need as surely as he needed breath. It dawned on him that she had killed all of Exeter's men. No way was Jed the only target seeing as the disappearances had been going on for the better part of a month. He had his gun drawn on her and it was painful for him to know they'd come to this. He did agree though...the answer to his question wasn't simple. But a killer recognized a killer. The fact that she'd been able to kill all of these men and he knew she intended to finish Lofton Exeter off as well... was frankly, fascinating.

Dark eyes stared back at him unapologetically.

He couldn't say he blamed her at all. Lofton was pond scum emblematically. "No simple answer. In my line of work that is understood. But you?"

Jed was Exeter's kin even if he had despised him. How would Scott even begin to protect Oceanu from the wrath of Exeter?

"But me what? Just because you fell for a singer, you think that makes me innocent? I once had a time of innocence, but that has been gone for a while." She smirked. "Besides, you'd never have touched me if you thought me innocent." She stared at him waiting for him to answer.

"True. And the way we danced that first night, I knew there was much more to you."

"Is that what you call it? Dancing?"

Scott nodded. "Because we had perfect timing together."

Oceanu's lips stayed in that tantalizing smirk which made Scott just want to kiss her again. The temptress was back. The darkness in her soul matched what was in his. He wasn't afraid of her; he was as enthralled as ever. He just needed to hear the truth. "It's called many things...the little death by some," Scott answered her.

"We fucked, Scott." Oceanu said simply.

"You and I both know it was and is more than that." Scott growled.

"What are you going to do?"

Scott sighed as she brought the conversation back to why he'd followed her to the cove. "There isn't a simple answer as you said." He kept his gun trained on her. His hand steady not showing the turmoil roiling in his belly at the thought that he'd even had to raise it at her. This whole experience was leaving a nasty taste in his mouth.

Oceanu

"No simple answer then, so just drop this and let me go." Oceanu wanted to get the discussion back on course. She didn't feel comfortable with talking about their sex being more of a connection than just lust. She glared at him, unwilling to let in the fact that his words affected her. Immensely. It wasn't just his words. He affected *her*. He made her feel some kind of way that she didn't want to wonder about and she almost hated it. Almost.

If only things were different.

"Sco–,"

"Ocea–,'

They both stared at one another as they both tried to speak at the same time.

Oceanu crossed her arms over her ample breasts and raised a brow.

"You go ahead and go first," Scott suggested.

"What else is there to really say? They had to die."

"I had a feeling you were involved." Scott sighed.

"How? I covered my tracks quite well." Oceanu sauntered over to a part of the cave that jutted out and settled back against it, staring at him with much more than just the defiance she felt. She refused to allow him to stop her from getting back into the water. Even with his gun schooled on her.

"Your scent. It is the one of the things I love about you. How you smell."

Scott sounded wistful, but the determination she heard in his voice grounded her, it trapped her. She knew she could sing and have him just walk away or point the gun at himself. But those were the two things she didn't want.

She didn't want him dead, nor did she want him to walk away from her either. No. She wanted him just as she had the first time she'd laid eyes on him. However, to keep him she knew he'd have to be dead or near death to be turned by Galene.

Why would he give up anything for her? Time with him had always been such a sweet distraction. She'd gotten well over her head in this when it came to her feelings.

In Too Deep.

Oceanu took a deep breath and closed her eyes. "There is so much you don't know about me, Scott."

"Well, I'd say." He raked his fingers roughly through his hair. He had a penchant to do that when he was upset about something. "Fuck. You're a killer."

Oceanu gave a chuckle. "Isn't that a bit hypocritical of you? What makes me different from you? You kill and almost on a daily basis if Exeter asks."

"Yes, but..." Scott hesitated.

"But what? No difference between me or you with the exception that money passes between a coward's hand and yours."

Scott raised a brow though his hand did not waver from pointing the gun at her. A gun she could easily make him turn on himself. "I just didn't picture such a sweet voice and sexy face to be..."

"Ruthless?" she asked.

"Yeah, that." Scott released a heavy sigh.

"I am what I was made to be."

"And what exactly what were you made to be?"

"Do you really think you can handle it?"

Scott's expression showed how troubled he felt, despite his calm demeanor. "I can take anything that you tell me as long as it is the truth, Oceanu. Who are you? Who are you really?"

"Is it necessary to know who I am? You're asking the wrong question."

"It's necessary to me. There have been times where I feel that I know you. Then something else happens and I understand that I don't know you like I should."

They stared at each other.

Oceanu didn't say anything else. How did one tell the man that they'd been intimate with that they were not human anymore? That she was a mermaid. *Um sorry, handsome but I was killed by your late coworkers and turned into a mermaid?*

Scott cocked his head to the side as his emerald eyes bespoke his confusion.

"It's not easy to tell you more than it would be to show you what I've become. The story starts with a young Black woman being taken by Jed and Tim. Sent to her doom and drowned," Oceanu explained emotionlessly.

The look on his face was one of *show me or I won't believe you.* Scott dropped his hand with the gun. "If you're the girl Jed talked about, you wouldn't be standing here."

"Oh, but I am. They took me out to sea and dropped me into the water."

Scott grabbed her by the arm and turned her towards him.

Staring at his hand, she waited until he let her go. His grip, though not painful, was strong.

"Tell me the truth."

"I'm a mermaid."

Scott took in a huge breath, then exhaled it with laughter.

Oceanu just watched him. She crossed her arms waiting until he'd stopped laughing.

No mirth showed in his eyes as his laughter faded away. "If you can't tell me the truth, show me. Because all this shit that you're saying can't be true. There are no fucking mermaids!" Challenge glinted in his eyes.

"Are you sure?" Oceanu asked softly. What was the worst that could happen? He'd hate her. He'd try to shoot her, and she'd have to kill him. *Shit. This was either going to turn out okay or be messy.*

"Show me," Scott growled out. "Quit stalling."

Ocean nodded and turned to head out of the small cave. "You must follow me."

"Into the water?"

Oceanu heard the uncertainty in his words. "Yes, the water is where Oceanu begins."

"You're talking in fucking riddles."

"I'm trying to make sure you understand when you see what happens."

"What the hell does the water have to do with this?" he demanded.

"It has everything to do with this. It is the reason I breathe."

"Are you sure you haven't taken any drugs?" Scott queried.

Oceanu released a small chuckle as she finally stepped backwards into the water. There wasn't a lot of water, so the process of her changing was slow. However, soon shiny gilded scales began to appear, the moon's reflection making them sparkle.

"What the—" Scott's otherwise handsome face wore a huge scowl. He stared at her feet, eyes wide and mouth open.

"Why is she still breathing, Scottie?" A voice came from behind Scott along with the sound of a gun cocking.

Oceanu tensed. Her last target was now present and holding a gun as well.

Exeter Lofton.

Fuck.

Scott turned to look at Exeter. "I..."

"I what? So fucking wrapped up in pussy that you can't do your fucking job properly? She's the bitch who's been killing my men. How she did it, I don't know, and I don't even care why. She did it and she needs to fucking pay with her life."

CHAPTER 10: FIN

Scott

"*When things change inside you, things change around you.*"
—Unknown

In one moment, he was staring at the transformation happening to Oceanu and in the next, he was spinning around to see Lofton Exeter with a gun pointed at them both. Scott also noted that Exeter had that wild look of a user on his face. This wasn't going to end pretty. Someone would be dying today. He couldn't let it be Oceanu.

"Well, what is it, Scott? Why is she still alive? You and I both know she's the reason that the others went missing. Jed is over there fucking dead. What am I going to tell my sister?"

"Boss—"

"Don't boss me! You don't respect me, or you would have done what you were hired for!" Spittle flew from Exeter's mouth.

"She's innocent boss, why would you have me kill her? She brought money to the club for you," Scott tried to reason with the other man though in his heart he knew it would be futile. Exeter was right...she had killed the others. That alone would be enough for Exeter to want her dead.

"No one in this life is fucking innocent," Exeter said with a smirk on his lips. "Now unless you want to die...you will finish the job I assigned you and kill her."

He knew the deranged drugged up Exeter was serious. Scott didn't care if he died. He just didn't want her to die. He stared squarely at him. "I'm not going to let you kill her."

"Then you'll die along with her." Exeter pulled the trigger.

On instinct, Scott moved into the path of the bullet as he heard Oceanu cry out and felt a burning in his chest then he hit the ground. He heard a wailing melodic sound. Before his eyes closed, he could hear Oceanu singing. Oddly, it was comforting to him. Turning his head to the side, he heard another gunshot.

Exeter had turned the gun on himself. He fell on the beach with his brains splattered around him.

Scott closed his eyes, as he had relished this release for a long fucking time. Oceanu was miraculously alive and knowing this one fact, he could die in peace.

Oceanu
"No siren did ever so charm the ear of the listener as the listening ear has charmed the soul of the siren." – Henry Taylor

"GALENE!" Oceanu cried out frantically as she swam as quickly as she could to find the other mermaid. The only mermaid that could save Scott. She refused to let him die. She had one hour to find Galene or Scott would die and it would be her fault. That fucker, Exeter had done his last evil deed. One that made her wish she had died as well. Scott was fading as she could feel the struggle within his body to give up.

Finally, she knew why from the moment she saw him, she couldn't kill him.

The immediate rush of need, a pure animal magnetism that she'd never had in her human life hadn't just crept up on her but slapped her in the face so hard she couldn't think when she was around him. He obviously was dealing with the same issue. Why else would he have jumped in front of her when Exeter had fired off his gun? *Oh, Poseidon, why had he moved in front of the bullet?*

The only thing she could think of doing was to give him air and then get him as quickly to Galene as she could. She could only hope he didn't hate her. She'd seen the look on his face and the absolute horror in his eyes when he saw she was for all intents and purposes a fish. He might hate her but she'd rather live with that fate than for him to be dead. The best thing to do was to get him turned and deal with his hate later.

She screamed Galene's name through the water once more so loudly that a school of fish swimming nearby immediately went into a bait ball. Oceanu ignored the fish and continued to swim at top speed. She looked down at Scott's face to see there was no fear there, but his eyes were closed. She could feel him breathing though it was shallow. The breath that she gave him helped to ease his lungs from the pressure of being in the ocean.

All she wanted was for him to live. To be able to see him again even if it was with him shunning her. His death would be her real issue.

In record time, she made it to where the pod lived and headed to Galene, still screaming her name.

The other mermaids moved out of her way quickly and stared at her as she passed.

Finally, she saw Galene's blonde tresses as she swam up to her. "Please, I beg of you to help him." Oceanu knew he didn't have much time left.

Galene looked from Oceanu to the male whose breathing had become shallow. "There is no time to waste, child of the ocean." Galene closed her eyes and spoke some words.

Scott was surrounded by the most beautiful song Oceanu had ever heard. The same one she'd heard at her birth. The bullet within his chest moved free of his flesh, the only proof of the shot being the blood that dispersed into the sea and the sinking bullet that Oceanu caught in her hand.

Then Galene opened her eyes and pinpointed Oceanu with her gaze. "He will awaken soon. Take him to your chambers to rest. You should be the one he sees first."

"Thank you, Galene. For healing him and for letting me be the one he sees." Still holding on to Scott, she swiftly swam to her chambers to get him settled there. As she was laying him down, she saw his tail beginning to form. The change could be painful or it could be pure bliss as it had been for her. The process was dependent on the one who was changing. She could only pray to Poseidon that his death and rebirth wouldn't be painful.

Scott
"Peace begins with a smile." —Mother Teresa

AWAKEN CHILD OF THE OCEAN.

Scott heard the words, but he felt so comfortable. Comfortable for the first time in his own skin. He didn't want to wake up, so he just kept his eyes closed, but the voice became so insistent. Groaning, he opened his eyes and saw Oceanu peering down at him. Seeing her brought it all flooding back and he clutched his chest for the bullet wound.

It wasn't there.

Right then, he noted he was in water. He wanted to ask how but the memory of how he got here flooded his mind. Instantly, he sat up to press his back against the wall and just stared.

Oceanu stared back at him. "I know you probably hate me. I'm sorry but I didn't want you to take a bullet for me."

Scott shook his head. "I didn't want you to die either."

A look of relief appeared on her face.

"Now I have no choice but to believe you were telling me the truth. I take it I was changed too or how else would I be in this water?" He looked around noting the coral here and there, the sparkling of the ocean floor along with the passing by of fish outside the chambers.

"So, you don't hate me?" Oceanu asked.

"No." Scott shook his head as he looked down at what used to be his feet. His chest was bare and there were emerald-colored scales that covered the area where his legs used to be. They were now one large fin.

"This is a lot to adjust to. You're okay with this, just like that?" Oceanu asked.

"For the longest time, I just existed." He scoffed as he admitted, "I'd become lost. You don't know this, but most of the time, I wanted to check out. I hated my life and myself. I lived with nightmares on a constant basis." He gazed up at her. "Until I met you. When I'm with you, that all fades away. I felt alive for once."

Oceanu stared at him as the worry on her face disappeared. Gracefully, she swam across the room and leaned in to hug him.

Scott released a long sigh, feeling as if he'd truly and finally had come home. Wrapping his arms around her, he smiled as he heard her begin to sing softly.

Oceanu

"At first, all I felt was rage for having been killed the way I was and all I saw was revenge," Oceanu whispered as they laid on her bed together, their arms still wrapped tightly around each other as if they'd never let go. "But I couldn't bring myself to kill you. Something about you pulled me in. Like I could feel your sadness and despair. Somehow, it mirrored mine."

"Jed had mentioned that he'd killed an Olivia Tate, but I didn't put two and two together."

"You only caught on because of my scent," Oceanu stated.

"Right..." Scott nodded then chuckled. "It haunted me. I knew it was you, but I just didn't want to admit it to myself."

She snuggled her face to his neck. "You'll need a new name. Like I have. Something more fitting for your new life here."

Scott nodded and looked like he was in deep thought.

Oceanu let him think it over. Choosing a name was a serious step forward into this world and she wanted him to pick something he was comfortable with.

"Since this is my new life...I'd like to be called Bourne."

Oceanu grinned. "Bourne as in born again, or reborn?"

"I guess you could say that. It just feels powerful."

"We are powerful but most especially, we will be...together." Oceanu waited for confirmation from him that they'd be together, but he didn't say anything. Dread began to fill her. Sorrow too, as she tried to pull away from him.

"Where are you going?" he asked.

"You didn't say yes to us being together," she whispered.

"I'm sorry Oceanu. I'm adjusting to the fact that mermaids are real and I'm a merman."

"Forgive me for rushing you. I know you've been through a lot and I shouldn't expect that you would want things to continue just because I saved you."

"It's not that," he replied with a shake of his head. "I don't feel beholden to you because you saved me after Exeter shot me."

"But?" Oceanu queried.

"There is no but." He looked into her eyes. "We saved each other. I want to spend whatever time we have left as mermaid and merman with you. I am just adjusting to the fact that what I thought was fantasy is real."

Oceanu cupped his face with both hands. "I want you to know that I think I have loved you from the very beginning. Almost like instant love. You gave me peace and comfort where I had none. You made me feel more than rage."

"And you have made me feel more than hopelessness and sorrow."

"Yeah?" She searched his eyes for the truth and found that those emerald eyes were even a deeper green now. More importantly, his eyes held the same heat and passion as they had before.

"Yes. I love you Oceanu," he said simply. "Truth be told, the ocean has always been a place of peace for me. I'd contemplated ending it within these depths. Even now, you have saved me. This is home, you are home."

Joy filled her.

Home.

"You are my home too, Bourne," she practiced saying his name. She felt so excited to have witnessed his turning and him choosing his new name. She'd never be able to thank Galene for all that she'd

462

done for her. She leaned in and kissed him with all the love she felt. Her rage was gone, she felt lighter and new all over again. Her heart was hammering in her chest as he pulled her tightly to him and kissed her back. His kiss took her by storm even more than it ever had before. She'd come full circle as she'd found her place, resolved her pain, and had the love of her reborn life wanting her as much as she did him.

Finally, he broke the kiss and asked, "So can I sing too? I mean like you?"

"Well, not exactly like me...but mermen have their own songs, so yes."

He grinned. "That will be a change from my singing then. I never could carry a key."

"Yeah, I heard you once." Oceanu laughed at the memory.

His eyelids drooped a bit. "I'm tired," he said softly.

She knew it would take a while for his body to adjust to this new form. "Then rest, we have nothing to fear anymore and we're together."

"If this is a dream," Bourne whispered to her ear. "I never want to wake up. Keep me with you, Oceanu. Don't ever let go." He snuggled closer to her.

"Never," Oceanu whispered back as she held him close.

IVORY COVE

JORDAN ELIZABETH

CHAPTER ONE

The house phone rang. Hawker froze, his laundry bag in hand, and it took him a minute to remember landlines existed. His mother's voice drifted through the open bedroom door. "Hello. Oh, hi, Jenny."

Hawker groaned as he tossed the laundry bag onto his bed. Clothes spilled out across his monster truck comforter, the one he had since he was twelve.

"Not much new here," his mother said from downstairs. "Hawker came home. No, he's here to stay. Yes, it just didn't work out at the school."

He reached for an undershirt but ended up sitting on his bed instead. Memories from the school flashed by.

The boy who'd punched Hawker in the face, leaving a bruise that lasted for weeks. The other boy who'd elbowed him in the eyes and broken his glasses. The girl who'd bit him in the arm, through his shirt, and left marks.

His principal had told him to "get it together." Planned ignoring didn't help. Instead of hurting him, they hurt the other children, and

467

when the parents complained, the principal threw Hawker under the bus.

"I always told Hawker he was too soft to be an elementary school teacher," his mom continued to Cousin Jenny. "You have to be tough to handle kids these days. He should have been a librarian. I always told him he should be a librarian."

Hawker wiped his hand across his face. It would take too much energy to walk across the room and close the bedroom door. A calendar from the humane society watched him from the wall. It still read June. He'd moved out in June when he was twenty-three and excited about his brand-new teaching gig.

He'd lasted three years. That should count for something.

He should have gotten a new comforter. The one from his apartment fit a queen, his old bed, all of that now dumped into a storage unit that he had to pay rent on.

"You're exaggerating," the principal had said the week before Hawker quit. "The class can't be that bad."

"Hey." His little sister leaned against the doorframe. "Did a parent really threaten to kill you?"

Hawker looked up through heavy-lidded eyes. "Yup."

"Why isn't said parent arrested?"

"Because she says she never said it." Even though a second irate parent heard the conversation. "Some kids said it too, but they always say it."

She tipped her head to the side, her dark hair pulled back in a ponytail. "You only wanted to be a teacher because that was Grandma's dream."

Hawker flopped backward and smacked his head on the wall. "Yeah, well, I like it when kids learn something. I like seeing that lightbulb go off."

"Bullshit," she whispered.

He flipped her off and stood up, rubbing the back of his head.

"You wanted to be a marine biologist and you wanted to be an artist, and Grandma wanted to be all that too."

"She didn't want to be a librarian."

"Mom wanted you to be a librarian."

He jerked open the dresser drawers to stuff in his clean clothes. They were half full of the old stuff he wore to college and high school.

"Now you work at the mall," she said.

"I'm a manager."

"Of a store that sells body jewelry. You have a ring in your nose now and you wear nail polish."

"Whatever." He lifted out an old pair of plaid boxer shorts to throw at her.

"Ew, gross." She kicked them away.

"Wait until next year when you get to go to college and Mom picks all your electives for you."

"Hawker?" Mom called. "Emma?" Her slippers hit the stairs, then flopped along the hallway.

"Just helping Hawk get settled back at home." His sister grinned.

His mother didn't bother with the doorway – she walked right in to sit on the desk chair. "Jenny called. Do you remember your grandmother's cousin Eleanor?"

"Of course, Mom." Hawker pulled out more boxers that looked too small and dropped them on the floor.

"Eleanor passed away." Mom let out a loud sigh.

Hawker paused.

"Wasn't she like a hundred?" Emma asked.

"Ninety-eight." Mom sighed again. "Jenny is so distraught. Her mother's last wish was to keep the summer camp in the family, but it's so far for Jenny to travel now that she lives in Texas."

"What summer camp?" Emma asked. "Like with marshmallows and friendship bracelets?"

"It's in Maine," Mom said.

"It's just a house," Hawker added. "We used to go for the family reunions. You had sports, Emma."

"Oh yeah. Dad and I had pizza every night."

Mom huffed.

"I'm sorry she's dead." Hawker shoved his clean clothes into the drawer and pushed at the edges to make sure they all fit.

"Hawker." Something about Mom's tone made him look over his shoulder at her. "Hawker, I told Jenny about your predicament."

A muscle twitched in his jaw.

"She asked if you want to stay at the summer camp for a while. Jenny's keeping it, at least for the rest of the summer. She thought you might like to get away for a while."

"But he's a *manager*." Emma wrinkled her nose at him.

"Oh." Hawker tightened his grip on the drawer. "Really? That big house in Maine?"

"Maybe you could look it over for her, see if anything needs to be fixed up if she decides to sell? It's been a few years since the family's visited, not since Eleanor broke her hip."

The house on the seaside where his grandmother had spent every summer as a child. Her stories had been of glistening waves and playing with her cousin in the forest, and of seafaring legends, and evenings at the village ice cream shoppe.

"I'll go." Hawker closed the drawer.

Hawker maneuvered his car around a branch in the road. Wind shook the trees that lined Center Avenue. A few green leaves danced over the windshield. The rain had stopped, but the gray storm clouds threatened more.

He turned up his music so he wouldn't have to listen to the wind.

Center Avenue opened out from the woods into the village. Parking spaces provided spots for cars in front of a coffee shop, post office, library, and dollar store. He slowed as a red-brick restaurant came into view. If the downpour came back, he'd be stuck carrying his suitcases in while soaked through. Hawker kept driving. A woman with a yellow lab hurried along the sidewalk, her head bowed against the weather. The dog barked at a leaf.

Hawker slowed at the intersections, checking for the next road. A cemetery loomed to the left. The limestone and marble stones watched him behind a wrought-iron fence.

When he'd been a child and they'd come to the family reunion, he and his grandmother had walked along the gravel paths until they found her father's grave. It was under a maple, alone, Hawker's great-grandfather's name on it.

She'd been buried back home, where Hawker's parents still lived, and so his great-grandfather waited for a companionship that never came. His grandmother had buried her mother at a cemetery closer to home.

Hawker and his grandmother had placed pebbles on top of the marble, and they'd promised to return – and then came the last year. They didn't return after that. He'd been a teenager, fifteen maybe.

Hawker shook off the memories. Next to a huge Victorian with manicured bushes, he spotted the sign for MacTurk Road. The *dead end* sign rested next to it as if warning visitors off. He drove by more Victorians, and imposing federals, and some small brick buildings. One boasted a sign for antiques. The houses became fewer, more spread out, with patches of woodland, and MacTurk Road angled upward.

Thunder rumbled far off as the road ended at the bungalow perched on the cliff.

His mother had laughed when he'd called it a cliff. *"It's just the ocean, Hawker. There's always rocks at the shoreline."*

Hawker parked next to the front porch instead of at the far-off detached garage. With his hands on the steering wheel, he studied the bungalow through the windshield. Earlier rain had dampened the roof and lack of sunlight kept the windows dark. Someone had mowed the lawn, but the flowers Cousin Eleanor used to love had died. No more tulips or rose bushes or black-eyed Susan's. Industrial, plain-green grass offered the only bit of vegetation.

He opened the door. Gravel from the driveway crunched under his sneakers. Out near the garage, the branches of a weeping willow shivered.

"I wish I could take it home with me," his grandmother used to say. *"I used to sit under there, and I would read..."*

He bent his head against the wind as he ran up the porch steps. They creaked and moaned, as did the porch, but the old wood held his weight. He pulled the key that Cousin Jenny had sent, and he had to jiggle it in the lock before it would open.

A weird odor slapped him – must and old air freshener. Dust hung thick in the air. He flipped the front light switch. The overhead lamp in the ceiling blinked on, along with an old-fashioned lamp on a table. He'd always loved the fixture, refurbished from a Victorian oil lamp. Hawker ran his finger over the surface, leaving a thin line. The caretaker hadn't done a great job.

"Hello?" Hawker's voice echoed through the downstairs. "Anyone here?"

Not that a home invader would answer. He listened for footsteps, but none came. Pulling his leather jacket tighter around his shoulders, he headed back out for his suitcases.

After two trips, the downpour came. With no one in sight, he left the car unlocked, but he bolted the front door. A clock nearby ticked.

The house moaned in the wind.

"You're crazy," he said to the foyer mirror. "There's nobody here, just you. You want to be alone."

Rain slashed against the house. The windows rattled with each gust of wind.

Hawker walked through each room switching on the lights. Only one bulb seemed to be out. With the electrical glows and old furniture, it could have been ten years ago. He closed his eyes, imagining his grandmother entering the parlor with a cup of tea. They would watch the waves crash against the rocks – that didn't count as a cliff – and savor the wafting scent of chamomile.

He checked the pantry. Nothing. Not even a box of stale crackers.

"Should have stopped at the restaurant." He opened the fridge. "Also empty. Nice." The dishes were still there, so he ran the kitchen sink for a few minutes before filling a cup.

Hawker took it to the parlor window and raised the drink to the sea. "This is for you, Grandma. It's not flavored leaf water, but it's close. It's water." Shadows seemed to shift around the room as if she joined him. He smiled and sighed. "I wish you were here."

The waves reflected the darkness of the storm clouds. Mixed in with the crests, he could have sworn he saw something silver flash in the ocean.

CHAPTER TWO

"Here you go." The waitress set his plate of pasta primavera on the table. "Let me know if you need anything else."

"Thanks." Hawker's mouth watered. He shouldn't have waited until the storm passed – now his stomach wanted to devour the entire plate and the silverware too. "I feel like I haven't eaten in a week."

The older woman laughed. "That's what traveling will do to you."

"Yeah, but from now on, it'll have to be the grocery store." His wallet couldn't handle restaurant prices for every meal.

She might think that comment was rude since she made her living serving food to customers. "I mean, since I'm going to be here a while, I'll have to eat at home too." Hawker shoveled a spoonful of warm biscuit into his mouth to keep from rambling.

"Are you staying here in Ivory Cove?" She smiled down at him, wrinkles forming around her mouth.

He swallowed. "The bungalow." His grandmother had always called it that. "The Drake house."

Her eyes widened. "Are you a relation of Eleanor's?"

"A cousin." A very distant cousin.

"Getting it ready to sell, then?" She glanced at the bar, and he looked over his shoulder. Two men drinking coffee had turned around on their stools to face Hawker.

"I don't know about that. I'm staying here for a month." Or two, or three. He could stay until his savings ran out until he figured out his next career move.

Now, he wanted her to walk away so he could devour the steaming food.

"Good luck there." She headed to another table, and he stabbed his fork into a hunk of chicken.

"I don't remember you being one of Eleanor's kids," one of the men at the bar said.

Hawker almost groaned, but he smiled at them, the food still on his utensil. "Her daughter Jenny said I could come."

"But you're a relation of Eleanor's." He didn't smile, but he didn't frown either, his bearded face more stoic.

"Her cousin was Clara Drake. She was my grandmother."

The man next to the talker coughed. It was a pointed cough, and he narrowed his eyes at his companion.

"Did you know my grandmother?" Hawker asked. They were older men, but if his grandmother still lived, she'd be ninety. They weren't that old. Seventies, maybe.

"Everyone knows the Drake house," the coughing man said.

The talker turned back to the bar and took a sip from his coffee mug. "It will be interesting to see it leave the Drake family."

Hawker could have sworn the other man said, "About time they left."

Hawker had to have misheard. His grandmother had never acted like the family wasn't liked in Ivory Cove. Eleanor had kept the house until the end, and the family reunions had lasted until she couldn't go anymore.

It probably meant nothing. He bit the chicken off his fork and savored the warmth of food in his mouth.

WIND BLEW OFF THE OCEAN, carrying with the scent of saltwater. Hawker stood on the edge of the rocks. Boulders fell away into the ocean. Waves beat against the smooth rocks and the land underneath. With a clear sky above, the surface seemed dark and blue. Past a few inches, he couldn't see below the surface.

What world dwelled under there? Fish and plant life and shells and...

Monsters. The word came from the past, whispered on the wind. Despite it being August, he shivered. Goosebumps rose along his arms.

"Eleanor and I always looked for sea monsters," his grandmother would say. *"Every summer, we saw how far we could take the boat out. Father never let us go far. We would look down and see if we could find one."*

"What kind of monster?" he would ask.

She would smile, her hazel eyes wide. *"One never knows what could be in the sea."*

The old Drake rowboat was gone. At least he'd never seen it. The Pacific Ocean stretched out until it disappeared at the horizon. Seagulls flew by to land on a large rock a few feet away from the shoreline. A large wave crashed against it, splattering the birds with droplets.

Tucking his hands into the pockets of his jeans, Hawker walked along the land, keeping away from the rocks. The sun should have warmed and dried them, but they appeared slick, shiny. He could fall and hit his head, and no one would find him, no one except a sea monster. Hawker shivered again.

Grass and weeds mingled with dirt and more rocks. A weathered picnic table waited for Eleanor's family. He paused beside it, picking at a sliver of peeling red paint. They'd eaten there once, he and his grandmother, at one of the family reunions. She'd talked about how her father had built two in the same spot all those years ago.

Hawker walked the short distance more to the woods, where the property ended. Wind stirred the trees. Ferns grew along the ground. It wouldn't be far, if he kept walking before he would meet the neighbors.

He couldn't remember the neighbors, but they had a white house bigger than the bungalow.

Hawker turned on the heels of his sneakers to head back to the house. Waves continued to crash against the rocks. A couple miles away, part of the land jutted out to support the Ivory Cove lighthouse. His grandmother had taken him there, too.

The lull of the ocean wrapped him in warmth despite the wind. He found himself humming. He hadn't done that in forever. The memories of the school and the kids and the principal faded away as if beaten to death against the boulders.

"Hello!" Hawker spread his arms out to the ocean. "Here I am! My name is Hawker and I'm free."

Free for however long freedom lasted. He whooped and the wind threw his shouts back at him, at the bungalow.

He imagined the other generations doing the same thing, standing at the shore, calling out with all their might.

Eleanor used to keep photo albums in the little parlor. He headed inside, and although he left the wind behind, he felt colder. He pulled his jacket off the hook in the foyer and shrugged it on. Black and white photographs watched him from the walls.

The photo albums were still in the built-in bookcase between two windows overlooking the Pacific. He stacked the albums on the floor before sinking into a needlepoint chair. Eleanor's mother had made it – she used to rave about it. The springs squeaked now and jabbed into his bottom. Hawker shifted for a better position.

In the first picture, Clara and her mother sat on the front porch playing with kittens. Hawker rubbed his thumb over the image of his grandmother. She couldn't have been much older than five.

He kept flipping through, watching Clara and Eleanor age. They played under the willow tree and on a rope swing in a maple. The entire family at the picnic tables. They slid down a slide and played on a teeter-totter.

His great-grandmother and Eleanor's mother stood by the lighthouse. His great-grandfather and Eleanor's father – brothers – stood by an old-fashioned car near the garage.

In the last album, there were only pictures of Eleanor and her parents. Hawker switched back to the others. Clara seemed to be twelve at the oldest. That had to have been when her father died when she stopped coming until Eleanor, married with grandchildren, started the family reunions.

"Wait," Hawker said aloud. The ticking clock on the mantle answered him. Long before Clara and her mother stopped appearing in the photographs, her father did. Hawker flipped back through, but there was only one of him, the one by the car.

He'd recognize the man, long and lanky with thick, dark hair, thanks to photos back home. There were other men in some of the pictures and other children, probably people from Ivory Cove. Had his great-grandfather been the photographer?

Some of the pictures were curled up. He rubbed his finger along one edge, peering underneath. There appeared to be a glue mark where another picture had been torn out.

CHAPTER THREE

Hawker yanked on the cord that hung from the attic trapdoor. It didn't budge. He yanked harder, grunting, and the trapdoor swung open, dust settling around him. He stepped back as he coughed, waving his hand in front of his face.

He'd been in every room of the bungalow before, or at least glimpsed the insides, but never the attic. His grandmother had never mentioned it either.

A ladder descended from the square in the ceiling. Once his lungs and eyes stopped burning from the dust, he climbed up. Grit on the rungs bore into his palms. Dim light filled the space. Windows at either end tucked away in the eaves, provided it, but he didn't see any lightbulbs.

"Should have looked for a flashlight," he said to no one.

Roughhewn boards were laid across the center of the space and off to the sides, it looked like fiberglass insulation.

"Mental note. Stay in the middle." The boards creaked as he walked along the narrow space. On either side were stacked cardboard boxes with faded writing and bushel baskets tucked with canvas tarps. Antique paintings leaned against a weathered steamer trunk. A wardrobe with a broken door stood tall over the jumble of items. He stopped his trek there to peer inside at the clothing. Metal hangers supported a fur coat, a tuxedo, and a wedding dress.

He ran the back of his hand over the white silk. "Who wore you?" An old pillbox hat rested on the bottom. When he picked it up, the material making up the center cracked and crumbled.

Hawker lifted the tarp on a couple baskets. Most contained porcelain figurines or hand-painted dishes, all wrapped in rotten newspaper. He noticed a couple dates from the fifties, sixties, and seventies. His grandmother had already stopped coming when they were packed away.

When he reached the steamer trunk, he moved the paintings aside to open it, and he paused. The seascapes were signed – Bradford Drake. No one had ever told him his great-grandfather painted. At the back of the pile were two framed, black-and-white pictures. In one, five men wore old-fashioned gym uniforms and held basketballs. He recognized Bradford on the far right. Next to him stood his brother, but Hawker didn't know the others.

In the other picture, Bradford and nineteen other men wore suits. They stood outside of a brick building with huge windows framed in ornate woodwork. They all smiled at the camera. Bradford's imposing height left him towering over the others. He'd have to ask Jenny if he could take them back home when he went.

Why hadn't his grandmother brought Bradford's artwork?

Hawker opened the steamer trunk to handsewn quilts and crocheted afghans. Someone had made them with time and love. At the bottom, he found a pewter trinket box. The lid wouldn't budge. Turning it over, he spotted a space for a key. Hawker set it aside to search through for the key.

Inside of a cloth bag, he found cameos pinned to unraveling cloth, and under that, he came upon a jar of buttons. At the bottom of the trunk, his hand thumped against a large tin box. He pulled it out and sat cross-legged with it in his lap. A faded picture of a sailing ship was painted across the lid.

He opened it to curling photographs, none of them in color. Hawker worked his cell phone free of his back pocket and flipped on the flashlight feature to see better.

The photographs were all of Bradford. Bradford sat on the porch, in a bedroom, in the water wearing what appeared to be an old-fashioned swimsuit. Hawker studied the backs of the pictures. Most of them had scraps of black paper stuck to them, similar to the paper that made up the photo albums.

Someone had torn out the pictures of Bradford. Why hadn't they been given to his grandmother? He couldn't believe she'd never wanted them. Her memories of her father involved playing in the water, going sailing, and listening to the radio. He'd taught her how to play the piano from the parlor downstairs.

He lifted out a yellowed newspaper clipping. "*Local villagers search for sea monster.*" *Hawker skimmed the cramped, faded type. On August 2, 1942, the residents of Ivory Cove would take their vessels into the ocean to search for the sea monster rumored to call victims to their death.*

"An enchanting song can be heard from over the waves," Hawker read aloud. "This song lures young men to their doom. We will eradicate the monsters that call our youth to drown." He snorted. "Probably the wind."

The next newspaper clipping talked about a local man, Bill Abbott, who drowned. His family claimed the sea monster had lured him out during a storm.

"Wind," Hawker muttered.

Another clipping mentioned a Daniel Cromwell, who wanted to hunt down the sea monster. He gave various stories and claimed to have a photograph of the monster. Hawker continued through the box but couldn't find any clipping with the rumored photographs. They were probably hoaxes, like the Loch Ness monster nonsense.

He picked up the last newspaper clipping, and "*Bradford Drake*" jumped out.

"Bradford Drake of Utica, New York, was found slain in the woods near the Ivory Cove Lighthouse early morning of August 1, 1942."

Slain. A chill crept over Hawker. His great-grandfather hadn't been murdered. He'd...died. No one had ever told him how the man died.

Hawker continued reading as goosebumps formed over his bare arms. Bradford had been found by his brother, who went searching for him after he didn't come home after meeting friends. The friends would be questioned by local police, the article explained. Bradford had been found with multiple stab wounds and a blow to the head. Daniel Cromwell of Ivory Cove claimed it to be the work of the sea monster.

His great-grandfather had been murdered. No wonder his grandmother and great-grandmother stopped going to Ivory Cove. Why hadn't his grandmother ever talked about it?

Hawker's hands shook as he set down the box. Why had they been torn out of the albums? Had Bradford's killer attempted to erase evidence? Hawker pulled up the internet browser and searched for Bradford Drake. Cemetery death records came up, but he already knew where the stone was.

Why had they chosen to bury him in Ivory Cove when he'd been murdered?

Hawker glanced over his shoulder, but no villain crept up the attic ladder to kill him.

He called his mom's number.

She answered on the third ring. "What is it, Hawk? How's the weather today?"

"Did you know that grandmother's dad was murdered here?" He tried to stay neutral, keep out the shock and rage.

A pause. "What do you mean?"

"Didn't grandmother ever tell you?"

"He died in Ivory Cove. Is that what you mean? A heart attack."

"He was murdered. Here, I'll send you a picture." Hawker found the clipping and sent her a picture of it.

When she didn't reply immediately, he called Jenny. She answered on the first ring.

"Is everything okay at the house?"

"Was Bradford Drake murdered?"

A pause. "Hawker, you didn't know that?"

He squeezed his eyes shut. "No. None of us knew that."

"Clara would have known. She was there when it happened."

"She saw his body?" Hawker ground his teeth.

Another pause. "My mom always said that Clara was so distressed, she shut right down. Her mother took her right home to Utica."

His grandmother might have blocked it out, or just couldn't remember the bad, only the good about Ivory Cove and the bungalow.

"Is that why they didn't come back?" Hawker asked.

"Yes, I imagine so. It's why Mom was always surprised you came to her family reunions."

No one had ever mentioned to them about the murder. Maybe they kept it quiet to as not to distress Clara.

"Who killed him?" Hawker whispered.

"No one knows," Jenny said. "They assumed it might have been a drifter. Ivory Cove has always been close-knit. Everyone loved the Drakes. Did you know that your...hmm...great-great-great-grandfather built the bungalow?"

Bradford had been murdered so close to the bungalow, and Ivory Cove didn't know a thing about it. A sea monster wouldn't have done that.

Hawker lifted a picture of Bradford standing beside Clara, holding her porcelain doll. "Don't worry. I'll figure it out."

CHAPTER FOUR

Hawker walked along the shore, waves striking the rocks to his right, wind blowing through the trees on the left. As it whistled through the branches, he sensed a voice whispering to him. "Find me. Find me. Find me."

He curled his hands into fists, his pace increasing, but he forced himself to slow down. It had been well over fifty years. There might be nothing left to solve the mystery.

There had to be something, some clue the police had overlooked, or some tidbit that had been left by the villain later. Someone would have told someone else, and the answer might still circulate through town. He clenched his jaw.

His great-grandfather's life hadn't been worthless. He'd been an electrician with a daughter, a wife, a brother. In his pictures, he laughed and smiled, his eyes crinkling. He didn't appear to be a man with dark secrets who might harbor enemies.

A large wave hit, spewing droplets into the air. Hawker walked closer to the edge so he could stand over the rocks. The ocean spread out, gray with white foam, nothing visible beneath the surface.

"Bradford Drake," Hawker yelled at the waves. "If you can hear me, know that I will find out who killed you. I won't let the answer get lost forever." It had already been lost for too long.

He turned away from the ocean with a new determined step. The murder had taken place somewhere in the woods between the bungalow and the lighthouse. Ferns and bramble bushes grew beneath trees. Some of the trees were thick and ancient – they saw the murder – but others were narrow, young saplings. Hawker rested his fingers against a thick, dark trunk. A split stretched down the middle, and one side seemed to tip, the branches reaching toward the earth instead of at the sky.

"You know what happened." Hawker waited. It was madness, the wait, and even more madness when disappointment struck that nothing here was going to answer.

Scowling, he walked on, and the woods opened to a stretch of dirt, grass, and rocks. The land dropped away again into the ocean, and the lighthouse rose to stand guard over Ivory Coast.

Hawker kicked a rock. It rolled away toward the gravel parking lot for those who wanted to visit the historic building.

No answer to the murder resided in those woods. He didn't have a metal detector. He didn't even know exactly where it had taken place. Any possible DNA evidence would have been gone decades ago.

If the trees wouldn't talk, someone else might.

"Bradford Drake," Hawker repeated to the woman who stood near the bookcase in the Ivory Cove Historic Society. "He was murdered here in 1942."

The middle-aged woman looked at the bookcase. "Here?"

Hawker blinked. She couldn't be serious. "Not *here*. Here as in Ivory Cove, out by the lighthouse. By the Drake bungalow."

She shook her head as she walked past him, heading toward a desk with a computer. "I'm sorry, I don't remember hearing about a murder. That sweet woman died recently. Eleanor Drake. She was married, though..." the volunteer's voice trailed off as she sat at the computer.

"I'm her nephew." Many times removed. "I'm staying at the bungalow."

"Lovely house. Is she selling it? It will bring in a lovely fortune being so close to the water."

"I don't know."

"Ah." The woman pointed a manicured finger at her computer screen. "There are a few articles we have on file about the murder. Funny thing, I've never heard of it. He was a relation?"

"My great-grandfather."

"How sad. I'm sorry. I'll pull the files."

He waited while she left the small reception room. Distant sounds filtered through the floor from the Ivory Cove Post Office below.

Had the murder been quick? Had his great-grandfather been forced to think about everything he lost? Had he pictured his family as his mind faded and blackened?

She returned, her heels clicking the tile floor. "Here are the news articles." She sat a scrapbook on a table. "There are only three, as far as I can tell."

His palms sweated as he hurried to the table. This could be it, a mention of a name, or a found article, like a unique button.

"I already have a copy of this article." Hawker pointed to the first one.

"What about this?" She flipped a page.

The article mentioned Bradford's calling hours, but no details about the murder.

The third article stated that the police gave up on the investigation without more evidence.

"That's it?" Hawker blinked at the yellowed articles stuck behind plastic.

"Well, yes."

"They never found out who did it?"

"I have no idea." She tapped her wedding ring. "You're his family. I would think the police would have given you more information than we received."

"But it happened?"

"Yes. It seems it did."

He could have growled and shouted and punched the table.

"It was 1942," she said. "I doubt they had a lot of forensics. Murderers got away with things all the time."

That didn't mean it had to be that way with Bradford Drake.

"What about families?" Hawker asked. "Is there anyone still around who might remember something?"

"They would have told the police."

"But maybe they forgot, or a family member was told something, and they're ready to come forward now?"

She spread her hands. "Ivory Cove families don't tend to move away. My family has lived here since the Revolutionary War."

"You knew about...?" Hawker trailed off. She hadn't known about the murder. Her family hadn't spoken of it.

Her expression softened. "I'm sure it wasn't brushed aside. Ivory Cove takes care of its people. Everyone would have done all they could for Bradford Drake. It's an awful thing that happened. I'm sorry we can't give you anything else."

He nodded, wanted to say something, but kept nodding. It had been a long time ago. Ivory Cove was small, but a murder would have been big news.

As he opened the door to Main Street, she called after him: "If you're at the bungalow, watch out for the sea monster!"

He couldn't tell if she joked or not.

HAWKER PARKED NEXT to the porch, but instead of going in, he stormed back to the seaside. Afternoon would transform into twilight. Oranges and purples would streak the sky and color the ocean.

"Hey!" Hawker spread his arms. "Sea monster. Are you the one who killed Bradford Drake?" Ivory Cove talked more about that than an actual murderer.

The waves struck the rocks, and not far from them, a head broke the surface. Pale white skin, almost translucent against the dark water, stretched over an oval face. Dark hair plastered against her neck and shoulder, and strands floated along the surface. The young woman didn't appear to have a swimsuit on, for she bobbed in the water enough that he could see the tops of her rounded breasts.

She tipped her head at him, her eyes dark and large. "No. I didn't kill Bradford Drake."

CHAPTER FIVE

"What are you doing?" Hawker looked along the shoreline for a boat or company for her, but only rocks met the oncoming waves. "This isn't a safe area to swim."

Or was it? His grandmother and Eleanor had swum by the bungalow. He'd seen the pictures.

"You should at least have someone nearby in case something happens." He stuck his hands in the pockets of his cargo shorts to keep him from flailing like a maniac.

She cocked her head and offered an unsettling grin. "My friends are nearby."

"Oh. Good. Good."

She bobbed a bit higher, and her nipples peaked over the surface.

She was skinny-dipping. He sharply turned away; her laugh wrapped around him, sweet, musical.

"You look like him," she called.

"Like whom?" He ran his fingers through his hair.

"Bradford Drake." The merriment in her voice faded to dismal misery. It caught around his heart as if to suffocate him. Hawker gasped, and the sensation vanished.

Her words registered. "You knew about his murder?"

She still bobbed, her breasts hidden again, and she nodded. Misery oozed off her. He'd never read anyone's emotions as clearly as he could read hers.

"Did your family talk about it? Do you know anything?" He paced along the shore. "I can't believe they never knew who did it. Someone must have seen something or found something."

"I don't know. He was gone, and I heard the rumors. Bradford Drake was dead. My pod left then. It wasn't safe here." Her misery settled into something darker as that wicked grin returned. "I could have destroyed them all."

What was she on? He tugged at the ends of his hair. "You could have destroyed who?"

"The killer. Ivory Cove. They could have all been mine."

The skinny-dipping girl was psycho. She'd probably seen him pull up to the bungalow and get out. She knew where he lived.

"Is there someone I can get for you?"

She laughed, the sound coiling around him. It held promise and magic and—

His sneaker slid on a wet rock. Hawker yelped, jumping backward onto land. When had he started to walk out to her?

She ceased laughing, but her smile continued. "Bradford Drake was kind to me. He didn't deserve murder."

Her skin was smooth, her cheekbones high, her eyes deep-set – none of it gave her the appearance of being one-hundred years old. "You didn't know him. He died in 1942." Hawker could have slapped himself. People didn't argue with a madwoman.

"I'm quite old. You might even call me immortal."

"I see."

"Actually, my pod does call me immortal." Her laugh returned. "I'm not, though. I live for two hundred years."

Her pod.

"I need to go." He could drive back to town. What if she broke into the bungalow?

Back in town, he could ask where she belonged. Someone might be searching for her.

She sobered. "I heard you speak of him and knew you were safe. Let me help you find his killer."

"I don't have any leads." He shouldn't argue with the crazy swimmer.

"He called me Ivory, like the town." She held up her arm. "My skin is pale as ivory, is it not?"

"It is," Hawker said because he was crazy enough to keep the conversation going.

"I've been here for a long time."

"Because you're immortal."

She spread both arms out and flopped back. "Because I'm a monster!" As the water closed over her, a wide, long fishtail flapped free. Silver scales reflected the summer sunshine. Blue and green streaks flashed along the large fin.

"Watch out!" Hawker jumped onto the first boulder, bracing himself not to fall. "There's a huge fish near you."

She surfaced again, and the tail flapped again, and—

"You're a mermaid." He had gone mad too.

She twirled through the ocean, and he caught a glimpse of where the white skin of her belly gave way to the scales of the fish portion. When her head resurfaced, she spit a stream of water at him. "Yes. A monster." Hair fell over her face, but she didn't brush it away. "If you know who murdered him, tell me. They will die." The ocean swallowed her.

"Wait!" He hurried across the rocks to reach the water. A wave splashed across his Converse sneakers.

Ivory didn't reappear. Had he imagined it all? Mermaids didn't exist. She could have a fake tail that only looked realistic.

Even that close to the water, he couldn't see to the bottom. It had to drop away fast.

Before Bradford Drake's murder, the town was going to have a monster-hunting day.

Ivory the mermaid was the monster. She had to be a siren, the way her laughter had pulled him toward the waves. She didn't appear to have qualms against murdering innocent people based on the articles he read. But given what she had told him, it made sense that she wanted to kill the lost murderer. She seemed to enjoy killing.

If Bradford Drake had known her, he might have tried to stop the monster-hunting event. That could have been the motive for the murder. She might know who wanted her gone the most.

"Come back!" Hawker shouted.

She didn't resurface.

HAWKER WORKED at the garage door until it opened on squealing hinges. The lawnmower rested in a little shed, along with gardening tools. The groundskeeper didn't seem to use the garage much. Old bicycles hung off hooks on the wall. Tarps lay over other items.

The wooden floor dipped as he walked. Judging by the style of the building, once it had been a stable. A broken-down buggy rotted near the back.

He found a long, wide item and pulled the tarp off to find a little rowboat. It could have been the one from the pictures of his grandmother and Eleanor. It rested on a wagon with wheels, but when he pushed on it, the wheels didn't budge.

Hawker found music on his cell phone, then began moving the junk away from the front, locating oil in the shed to loosen the wheels. Darkness descended by the time he got the rowboat through the garage door.

"Tomorrow," Hawker said to the ocean. "Ivory, I'm finding you tomorrow."

CHAPTER SIX

Hawker sagged against the oars, his biceps aching and his lungs wheezing. That was hard. So hard. He never should have assumed he could row out into the ocean. One oar wanted to do one thing while the other wanted to do something different.

He could still see the bungalow on shore, and it felt as if he'd rowed for three hours. He checked his phone. Only forty-five minutes had passed.

Even getting the boat into the water had been an ordeal.

He gritted his teeth and tried again, but the oars still didn't want to work together.

"Hello?" he called. "Mermaid? Mermaid!" His shout carried across the ocean before the waves pummeled it away.

Seagulls swooped along the shore. In the distance, a motorboat roared by. A sailboat skirted along.

Ivory wouldn't come. He had imagined her. She'd been a crazy girl out swimming, or not even there at all, and his desperation had conjured her up.

A head emerged from the water next to the rowboat. "You have

494

found the killer?" Ivory watched him through narrowed eyes. Her upper lip peeled back to reveal sharpened teeth. Fangs.

Hawker gulped. It might not have been a good idea to seek her.

"I...I didn't yet."

"Then why are you here?" She lifted her chin, sunlight glinting off those fangs.

"I wanted to talk to you." It sounded stupid now.

"Humans do not talk to my kind." She laughed, and once again the sound coiled around him to tug at his heart.

He blinked, but darkness thickened around his vision. "I...I wanted to know what you remember of Bradford Drake."

Her dark eyes softened. "He showed kindness to my pod when we were labeled as monsters."

"How did the people of Ivory Cove plan to kill you?"

"They wrapped their faces," she hissed, "so they couldn't hear us! They had spears and guns and nets. They planned to corner us and poison the water."

"They couldn't poison the entire ocean."

"They were going to trap us near the lighthouse." She sank, vanishing.

"Wait!" He leaned over the side.

"Yes, human male?" Ivory spoke from the other side of the rowboat.

He leaned that way, the vessel rocking. "What about Bradford Drake?"

"He said we should not be killed." She leaned back her head for another one of those laughs that seemed to pull out his soul. "We, who lured those to drown beside us. He wanted us safe. Imagine." When she lowered her head, her smile chilled him. "I met him. Bradford Drake."

"You tried to drown him?"

"Never Bradford Drake. His heart was different. He had no darkness inside." Ivory took hold of the rowboat to heave herself out of the ocean. Rivulets of water trickled over her chest to plink back in. Her long hair clung to her breasts, hiding her nipples.

Hawker averted his gaze.

"Humans have darkness inside of their souls." She braced herself. With her hands gripping the wood, her face was even with his. "When I sing, I sing to that darkness. It is the sweetest reward. I pull out that darkness from them, and when they died, it is that darkness that brings up their fear."

Hawker's nose almost touched Ivory's. She smelled of saltwater and something else, something sweet.

"Bradford Drake held no darkness in his heart," Ivory whispered, "and you do not either."

Hawker gulped. "But you still make me feel things."

"That is what I do." Her lips parted on a breath, on a kiss.

He could kiss those cherry-red lips.

He could not kiss a mermaid's lips.

"Do you remember any of the names of the people who wanted to kill you?"

"Everyone but Bradford Drake."

Hawker doubted that. His grandmother wouldn't have. "What about Bill Abbott? He was mentioned in an article."

"They all died," Ivory said.

"Right. It's been a long time—"

"They hunted us," she hissed, "and so I sang them to their dooms! Everyone on the hunt died."

"Oh. The hunt still happened?" He'd assumed it hadn't.

Bradford Drake had wanted to protect the sea monster. But he also might not have wanted the townsfolk to die. He would have known she had the power to lure people to their doom.

"A storm came," she chortled. "All of them drowned. I watched them all drown. I laughed at them."

"You knew Bradford Drake was dead?"

"No." She sighed, stared at him, and dropped back into the water.

When she resurfaced, it was to show only her face, her skin so white beneath the dark. "His daughter told me long after."

And Ivory was gone.

His grandmother had spoken to the mermaid, and she'd never told.

$$\psi$$

"Everyone died?" Hawker asked the volunteer at the historical society.

The same woman as before blinked at him from over the computer. "Excuse me?"

"At the sea monster hunt. Everyone who did it died? It was the day after Bradford Drake was murdered."

"Sea monsters aren't real."

Except they were, and they were sirens.

"See this article?" Hawker held it out to her. "Bill Abbott wanted to lead a sea monster hunt, and Bradford Drake wanted to stop it. He died, and then at the hunt, everyone else died."

"I'm certain there's never been a time when everyone in Ivory Cove died." She typed on her keyboard. "Let's see what we have."

While she went to get scrapbooks, Hawker studied the pictures on the walls. Some were paintings and others were enlarged photographs. Men and women stared at the camera.

The largest painting depicted a sea monster like the Loch Ness monster rising near the lighthouse.

Ivory looked nothing like that.

"Here we go." The woman returned. She flipped through the scrapbook pages at the table. "There have always been rumors of sea monsters, especially the one here. No one's ever seen it. There's pictures, but they're always blurry."

"Of course." His response felt automatic.

"Here you go." She pointed to a yellowed article. "There was a sea monster hunt in 1942, but there were always sea monster hunts. My dad used to say they happened every summer."

Hawker scanned the article. "Fifteen men went out and all of them drowned."

"It wasn't a sea monster." Her lips turned downward. "People like to imagine the unknown as something real. Storms come up fast around here. The boats overturned. They didn't wear life jackets back then, I wouldn't think."

"Since Bradford Drake wanted to stop the hunt, do you think any of them would have murdered him?"

"No! No one in Ivory Cove would have murdered someone. It had to be an outsider."

But the villagers of Ivory Cove had no qualms about murdering a sea monster.

The article mentioned names, and Bill Abbott jumped out from the list. He'd organized the hunt.

"Bill Abbott is mentioned." Hawker tucked his hands into his denim pockets to appear causal. "Do you know if any of his descendants are still around? I'd love to talk to them."

She cocked her head as if trying to read his intentions, but then she smiled. "I believe they are. I'll reach out to them and send them to the bungalow."

CHAPTER SEVEN

"Y ou should not seek me out." Rivulets of water trickled over Ivory's face from her hairline. The tresses didn't hide her nipples this time; they were rosy and bright, peeping out from the surface.

Hawker reminded himself to look at her face.

He forgot what he wanted to say as the rowboat bobbed in the ocean.

"My pod will move on soon," she said, her voice all kinds of wistful. The melody of it wrapped around his heart. It might be all an act for her.

"When?"

"You can't miss me!" Her voice hardened and he felt as though it had slapped him. "Your kind doesn't miss mine. I'm a monster to you. I pull you down that your lungs meet the seawater, and you never rise."

But she didn't strike him like that, even when her eyes narrowed, her face sharpening. The water around her seemed to darken.

"I don't know how to find the murderer," Hawker admitted.

"You feel failure." The sharpness in her shifted into curiosity.

"I failed at my job. Now I'm failing at this."

"This is your job." Not quite a statement, not quite a question.

"Is it?" The wind caught his baseball cap, yanking it away. It spun out before landing in the water. She didn't move to get it for him.

"The murderer will cease life!" she hissed.

"What if you've already killed him? Maybe he drowned that day. Or could have died since then." The wind pushed the cap closer to the boat.

"The murderer deserves death." Ivory disappeared down into the depths of the ocean.

It could have been a woman who killed Bradford Drake.

That train of thought left him with as many questions. Sighing, he grabbed the cap from the water and shook it.

As Hawker walked back to the bungalow from where he left the rowboat, a car drove up over the gravel. A man a little older than Hawker sat behind the driver seat, another man, an older man, sitting in the passenger seat. Hawker leaned against the railing until they got out.

"Are you Hawker Drake?" the young man asked.

Not a Drake, but close. "Yes."

The older man used a cane to make his way toward the bungalow, the younger companion at his side. Something about the older man seemed familiar.

"I saw you in the restaurant the day I got here," Hawker said. "You were drinking coffee."

When the older man didn't answer, the younger one did. "Probably. My grandfather's always there with his friends."

"You were asking questions about Bill Abbott," the man said.

Hope blossomed. "Yes, I was. I saw an article about him starting a monster hunt—"

"I'm not here to talk about sea monsters," the man interrupted.

Unease replaced the hope. "Oh. Um—"

"You were asking questions," the man continued, "but it's good to let that sort of thing die down."

"I'm looking into my great-grandfather. Bradford Drake. He was murdered the day before the hunt."

The man snorted. "That's got nothing to do with my uncle."

The younger man cleared his throat. "I think we'd better all start over. I'm Jim Abbot and this is my grandfather, Paul Abbott. Bill was his uncle."

Hawker drew a deep breath. "I'm sorry if you felt attacked. I came here for a few months, and I wanted some answers about Bradford Drake."

"I don't know anything about a Drake," Paul Abbott said. "All I know is you were asking questions about my uncle. News spreads in Ivory Cove. I don't want anything said again about Bill Abbott. He was a good man who wanted to keep Ivory Cove safe."

Hawker reminded himself it had been almost one hundred years. The younger generation wouldn't have been alive.

"Sea monster hunts are in the past," Paul continued. "Folks died and that's the end of it."

His grandson coughed again. "How did you find out about it?"

"The hunts? It was—"

"About Bradford Drake?" Paul snapped. "How'd you find out about him?"

"There were newspaper articles here in the attic and photographs."

Paul looked at his grandson, who looked out at the ocean.

"Most folks didn't want to think about Bradford Drake," Paul said, "especially not with so many dying the next day. It wasn't a good time. Ivory Cove doesn't talk about any of that."

"The mayor?" Hawker prompted. "Did he go on the hunt?"

501

"Bill Abbott was the mayor," Jim said.

The mayor. How had the volunteer at the historical society not known that? Then again, he didn't know the history of mayors in his hometown.

"Bill Abbott wanted to keep Ivory Cove safe," Paul said. "You go upstairs, Mr. Drake, and bring me whatever you have on Bradford. We'll make sure it's all kept safe."

"The newspaper articles are already in the historic society."

"The pictures. Bring me the pictures." Paul beamed a smile.

The smile twisted Hawker's stomach more than the siren's had. "My family pictures. I can make you copies..." Paul Abbott wouldn't need copies. "I can make copies for the historic society."

"Don't worry about that. I'll take them." The smile spread even wider, so at odds with the man's earlier attitude.

Hawker shifted his stance. "I already sent them home."

The smile vanished into a scowl. "What's that supposed to mean?"

"I sent the pictures to my mom."

"Get them back."

"They're my family's pictures." An edge burned his voice. "I'm not giving them to you. I'll make copies—"

"I want the originals!" Paul shouted.

Jim set his hand on his grandfather's arm. "It's all right. I'm going to take him home. Sorry to have bothered you, Drake."

Hawker took a step to follow them. "Why do you want them?"

"Historic value," Jim said when Paul grunted.

Hawker rubbed his bare arms as a chill crept over him.

CHAPTER EIGHT

Hawker's grandmother called to him. Breakfast...maybe something about breakfast. She'd made pancakes with blueberries and squeezed fresh oranges into juice. He needed to get downstairs to eat.

He rolled over on the bed, the sheets rough. They weren't the soft jersey material that he had on his bed back home. With his eyes still shut, he sighed. Those queen-sized bedsheets were all boxed up and he had to deal with threadbare cartoon ones on his little twin bed.

Something clicked. The sound was loud and foreign, and unease settled over his nerves. Hawker opened his eyes to the wall painted sea-foam green.

"Don't move," a man said. He was far too close and this was far too wrong. No one other than Hawker should be in the bungalow.

Hawker's heart pounded. "Who are you?" The voice sounded familiar.

"Get up," the man said, "and don't do anything funny."

The sudden image of dancing around naked pretending to be a monkey jumped through Hawker's mind. He could make sounds and scratch under his arms.

"I have a gun," the man said.

All mirth shot away. Hawker sat up, pushing the blankets down. "I'm naked."

"Get up. Don't reach for anything."

Hawker shifted on the bed to swing his feet to the floor. Paul Abbott stood next to the dresser with a handgun aimed at Hawker's chest. The man wore jeans and a hoodie, but he hadn't attempted a mask. That couldn't be a good sign.

"What do you want?" Hawker fought to keep his voice level. This wasn't school, where kids and parents threw out threats at him daily.

This was a man with a gun.

"Get up and walk toward the door," Paul said.

Hawker lifted his hands enough that Paul could see he didn't have anything – he was naked, besides – and walked toward the door. The floor creaked as Paul followed.

"What do you want?" Hawker asked again.

"Go down the stairs and out."

Hawker's heart kept racing as he made his way down the staircase. The glow of early morning light shown through the windows. "How did you get in?"

"Karl keeps the key in plain sight." Paul's laugh sounded raspy.

"Karl?"

"The groundskeeper." Paul's laugh faded. "Go outside."

"You took the key from Karl to get me at gunpoint. I don't have anything of value." Hawker stepped out onto the porch. The rays of dawn splashed bright and warm across the sky, reflecting in the ocean. "I have nothing."

"I have to do this." Paul's voice hitched. "I have to do it for Grandpa. He wants this done."

"I swear I've done nothing to your grandfather."

As Hawker stepped off the porch, he stumbled. Jim Abbott had acted weird about the pictures. He'd acted like he wanted to erase Bradford Drake.

Now he wanted Hawker, a stranger, dead. Hawker had been asking about Bradford Drake and this brought up the name of Bill Abbott, the uncle.

"Bill Abbott killed Bradford Drake," Hawker said to the salty wind.

"Shut up!" Paul snapped.

"I don't have any evidence." Hawker fought to sound calm, his tone even.

"Shut up!"

He didn't have any evidence, but now he had Paul threatening him at gunpoint. Hawker ground his teeth. Lockdown drills at school hadn't prepared for a moment like this.

Paul edged him toward where he'd pulled the rowboat onto shore. "Get in." Only the woods watched what happened. No one would be within eyesight. A lone sailboat skirted the water, far too distant to see what went on.

No one had seen Bill Abbott murder Bradford Drake.

"Why did Bill Abbot care so much about Bradford Drake?" Hawker might get Paul to talk more, to figure out that blood didn't need to be spilled. "I know he wanted to end the sea monster hunts, but the Drakes only came in the summer. Bradford Drake wasn't a threat, wasn't a threat to Ivory Cove."

"The sea monster hunts were a big draw," Paul said. "Tourists came to do them, and if they died, that just made it better."

"If the *tourists* died?"

"It doesn't matter!" Paul snapped. "The hunts ended with Bill Abbott."

"So why are you threatening me?" They reached the boat. Nearby, waves struck the land. The sun rose higher. Soon, it would chase away the colors of dawn to make everything clear and blue.

"Bill Abbott died a hero, and he will stay that way."

"But no one will know anything." Hawker didn't have any proof – other than the gunpoint threat.

"Get the boat out," Paul said.

He could row away. Fast. Hawker could suddenly, miraculously row like a champ and get far away from shore, and find someone to help him call for help—

Paul climbed into the boat after him. "Row."

"Where?"

"Just go." Paul scowled. The gun still wavered in his hand, but less so, as if he'd come to terms with what he had to do.

Sweat slickened Hawker's hands. His teeth chattered, a bit from the cold, a bit from fear. He fought with the oars to get the boat away from shore. No one would hear him call for help. No one had heard Bradford Drake.

"Keep going."

Hawker strained to keep going. Would Ivory come?

"Now get out."

"Out? Like, into the water?" Hawker had assumed he'd be shot in the boat.

That would leave bloodstains. Evidence.

"Get out," Paul repeated.

Hawker still shook as he climbed out, half-falling into the water. The cold shock to his naked body left him gasping. His teeth chattered harder.

"Now swim away," Paul said. "Swim out that way."

The sailboat had almost disappeared. No one would see anything. Shore seemed too far away.

Could he dive down and make it back? Could he climb out and run for safety?

He'd never been a good swimmer. He could swim enough not to drown, but that was it. The cold was already numbing his limbs as he struggled to keep his head afloat.

"Swim!" Paul pointed with his gun out at the Pacific.

He would shoot Hawker. Hawker knew it, could read the reality of it on Paul's face, that look of being lost and decided on a given task.

A sound started. A song. Sweet and beautiful. Alluring. A glazed expression spread over Paul's eyes.

Then he shook himself and a gunshot echoed over the waves. Pain exploded in Hawker's thigh. He flinched and screamed, and water closed over his head.

That song started again. It wrapped him in a blanket, a warm and fuzzy blanket, and it cushioned him. Darkness swelled around his eyesight, but he still saw blood winding up to the surface, spreading out in the water. He sank down, down, down, and still the song continued. It heightened and ebbed.

Water flowed through his nose and mouth. His lungs fought for oxygen, but there was only water, so much water. It wasn't even cold anymore. It was just...water.

The song brought an odd sense of peace. He saw his grandmother in front of him, and then the water was gone. She stood on the porch of the bungalow beside a tall, lanky man. Bradford Drake. Hawker stepped away from the rocks, and he was dry. His leg didn't hurt. He wasn't cold. He wasn't warm either, but then his grandmother ran down the steps toward him. She was a child. Twelve, maybe.

He hugged her, and she said all sorts of things that made no sense but meant true love. She took his hand to lead him toward Bradford Drake. Bradford reached out as if to shake with Hawker, and all the while, the song continued.

The water returned, and Paul dropped into the ocean. He sunk fast, his mouth open, his eyes wide, pulled into the ocean by the song. The gun dropped from his fist and sank. Air bubbles escaped through his orifices, and then they too stopped.

The song ended, and Hawker gasped, only he could find nothing to breathe except water.

"It's not your time yet!" his grandmother shouted from far away.

Ivory swam up between Hawker and Paul. Her dark hair floated around her, around him, a curtain against the world. She clasped his face between her hands.

The darkness took hold.

"Galene will turn you," Ivory said. She might have said that. The darkness was thick.

HAWKER'S BONES BROKE. He howled and twisted. His spine snapped. His legs burst apart. He howled again, reaching for something, anything, but the pain refused to go. Everything was hard. The ground was there, then above, then to the side.

When he tried to picture his family, he was met with only pain. His feet were gone, crushed into oblivion. He had nothing, no one, only pain.

"You will be one of us," Ivory said. "You will be one with the pod."

It made no sense. Nothing made sense anymore, only the pain. He was pain, and the pain was him, and nothing else mattered.

EPILOGUE

Jenny locked the front door of the bungalow and stepped back. The stained glass of the door window reflected the sun. A salty breeze blew off the water.

The bungalow had been times of fun and merriment and family. Their summers had been spent in the yard and on the water. Summers without her mother, without the bungalow, hadn't felt right.

Locking it up now felt right. Selling it felt right.

Ivory Cove had claimed Bradford Drake and now Hawker, and that poor man from town, Paul Abbott. Paul's body had washed up on the rocks outside the bungalow, along with the rowboat.

The ocean had claimed Hawker.

"Maybe it was the sea monster." Jenny said to the house, and as the wind blew, the house seemed to sigh in agreement.

She walked down the steps and to the seaside. It felt as if she walked forward, with the wind pushing her back, the house pulling her, as if it didn't want to let go.

The sunlight glinted on something rising from the water. It could have been a man swimming, with only his head visible. Hawker?

Then it was gone, and she turned away. The sea monster could take the bungalow and Ivory Cove. The Drake family was done with it.

MERMAID'S TAIL

TAMI LUND

PROLOGUE

The need for revenge is as deep as the sea

Fifteen years ago, Asia was tossed over the side of a ship and left for dead. Galene, the first mermaid, and Poseidon, the god of the sea, saved her and turned into a mermaid.

For fifteen years, Asia has been biding her time, waiting to seek her revenge.

But now that she finally has her chance, she runs into a roadblock in the form of Conall Nowak, a handsome human man who takes her breath away and gives her all the feels...and makes her wish for a future that cannot be.

513

Because she is a mermaid, and Conall has a secret.

He knows who tossed Asia overboard.

CHAPTER ONE

Generally, Asia enjoyed her job. Thwarting sailors and fishermen who drew too close to that section of the ocean above her home—the pod of mermaids tucked deep beneath the sea—was usually fun.

She had a dark side, naturally—she was a mermaid, after all—and deceiving humans fed her inner bad girl in a way that nothing short of a good drowning could.

And she did it all without ever leaving the water.

The last time she'd been out of the sea was the day she drowned —more accurately, was tossed overboard—and Galene, the original mermaid, had saved her. She'd given Asia the ability to breathe underwater, had turned her legs into a fish's tail. Then Galene's magic had forced shimmering, purple scales to grow over most of Asia's body.

The turning had been a long and miserably painful process, made twofold by the fact that Asia had not understood what was happening until it was over and she was part fish instead of fish food.

"You have a new assignment," Bella, the head of security,

informed her. Sometimes, it irked that Bella had been chosen for the job instead of her, but truthfully, Asia would rather be out there in the open sea, her tail fin flapping, her body undulating furiously as she chased off sailors, than down here dealing with personnel issues and bureaucracy. She'd only been fifteen when she'd been forced to trade her human life for life as a mermaid, but she recalled enough of the human world to acknowledge that neither world was run all that differently.

"I just cleared the waters," Asia replied. "Are you saying there's another ship encroaching already?" They had to have been going at breakneck speed, because when she'd left the surface a few hours ago, there'd been nothing on the horizon.

"Not exactly," Bella hedged, and why was she fidgeting with her blue-green scales like she had something to say and wasn't exactly keen to say it? "But my intel says they should be near enough by tomorrow. I need you to intercept them."

"Okay." This wasn't anything different from what Asia did every single day.

"And I want you to board their ship." Bella glanced up at the dim light that only just filtered down to their depths. "We are exactly at the right time in the lunar cycle. You will be able to shift into human form."

Asia shook her head. Dark tendrils of hair floated through the water. "Nope. Not happening. I do not go on land."

"It's not land, it's a ship. In the middle of the ocean."

"You mean like the one I was tossed from, fifteen years ago?" Was Bella nuts? Why did she think Asia got such a thrill out of waylaying ships, sending them far away from the pod?

She had issues. And they were directly tied to being tossed from a boat in the middle of the ocean and getting turned into a mermaid. And she wasn't the only one. The only way to become a mermaid or merman was to nearly drown, to be on death's door, and be awarded Galene's gift of life. Anyone would have issues after that experience.

Bella sighed, as if she'd expected this argument. "I understand how you feel, Asia."

"Yeah, you do. So why—"

"I've been working on this assignment for months, for years, truth be told. I've exhausted all other options."

"You've..." Why was Asia just now finding this out? She was the best of the best at guarding their piece of the ocean against those asshole sailors. If there had been an ongoing investigation, she should have been part of it, damn it.

"Don't look at me like I just stole your pet seahorse," Bella chided.

Asia jutted her chin and crossed her arms. The action lifted her purple scale-covered breasts.

Back before she'd been tossed overboard, when she hung out near the docks, she'd overheard plenty of sailors as they speculated about the existence of mermaids. Generally, sailors believed they were a myth, a legend used to explain away mysterious occurrences like a competent swimmer or captain falling overboard and presumably drowning even though a body was never discovered.

As with all myths, the tales grew exponentially with time.

Sailors had convinced themselves that mermaids were all naked from the waist up. Half the allure was the desire to see a woman's breasts, even if the bottom half of her body was a fish's tail.

Now that Asia was a mermaid, she knew how wrong they were. Every mermaid was different—not unlike humans, she supposed. Her scales, for example, extended up, from her tail all the way to her breasts. It looked like she was wearing a strapless evening gown.

If a sailor were to ever catch a glimpse of her, he'd be disappointed indeed.

"There is a reason I was chosen as head of security over you," Bella said.

Asia's flippers quivered. She hadn't known Bella was even aware she'd expressed interest in the position.

Bella sighed. "Do you want to know the reason?"

What she wanted was to be done with this conversation. "Just give me the assignment," she snapped.

⚓

CONALL LOVED THE SEA. Out here, on a ship far, far from any shoreline whatsoever, it was so peaceful, despite the memories this trip evoked, the edge of what he supposed was grief—or, more likely, bitterness—simmering just below the surface of his subconscious.

That sensation was a large part of the reason he'd stayed away from the ocean for as long as he had. He'd feared it would be too overwhelming.

He kept bracing...and then nothing happened. And as they were at this point, so far out to sea that he could see nothing but roiling, churning water and endless moonlit sky, he was good. He could quit anticipating and just sit back and enjoy.

"Ahoy, matey!"

He grimaced. "Butch," he said shortly.

Butch Rutgers considered himself a historian. Conall considered him an idiot. Nothing he'd drunkenly spewed since they'd cast off had any basis in fact. And here Conall was, about to endure another onslaught of utter nonsense.

"Keeping an eye out for mermaids?" Butch asked, clapping Conall on the shoulder before stepping up to the rail. He reeked of beer. The one thing Butch was exceptionally good at was drinking everyone under the table.

Conall glanced down at the barrel-aged bourbon in his own glass. He wasn't a big drinker, but on occasion, he did appreciate a nightcap before heading off to bed. Butch, by contrast, liked to start drinking around noon and not stop until he passed out.

Butch had informed Conall that he was guiding them around the mermaid pod sailors whispered about in the taverns of shipping towns.

The man was fascinated with that chunk of the ocean, had studied it more extensively than any other person in the world—or so he boasted. He also claimed that was the reason the captain of this ship had invited him aboard for this journey.

They were traveling from A Coruña, Spain, to Portland, Maine. Conall had a job interview in Portland in two weeks' time; he was finally getting back to trying to carve out a normal existence after his father's unexpected death had thrown his life into upheaval.

There had been no justifiable reason except curiosity to choose this method of travel over booking a flight.

And maybe to prove something.

He wanted to negate the rumors. The whispers that mermaids had killed his father. The insistence that it hadn't been a drowning, a freak accident that could have happened to anyone, even a sailor with decades of experience under his belt.

"Haven't seen one yet," Conall said carefully. He didn't even believe in the legendary creatures, not that Butch listened when he'd told him as much.

No one alive could claim they'd seen one, although plenty had stories of fellow sailors who'd supposedly died as a result of their meddling. The fact that bodies often were not recovered only enhanced the stories.

Conall thought that part the most ridiculous of all. There were plenty of carnivores in the sea that would happily devour a dead body—a perfectly logical explanation for not having recovered someone who had drowned in the middle of the ocean.

"Me neither, but we will," Butch said, his voice pitched low, like he was afraid someone might overhear their conversation. No idea who he was hiding from; Butch normally told his mermaid tales at full volume.

"Our captain thinks I'm taking us around the mermaid pod, but really, I'm taking us right over top."

Conall jolted, sloshing the liquid in his glass. Maybe he didn't believe in mermaids, but he did have a healthy respect for the sea, and when sailors for generations said to stay away from a particular area, it was wise to abide by their warnings.

"Why would you do that?" As curious as he had been when he'd booked this trip, he'd honestly believed they would go around the mysterious section of the sea where his father had died. He'd not truly wanted to sail right over it, for fuck's sake. He'd just wanted...

What? What had he been hoping for?

Hell, he wasn't even sure.

"I know about you," Butch said, leaning on the railing and angling his body toward Conall. "I know about your dad."

Conall lifted his glass and drained the contents. It wasn't nearly enough to help him through this conversation, damn it. He ought to walk away, escape to his cabin. Butch was plenty drunk enough at this point that he'd probably not even remember that they'd talked.

Conall stayed where he was.

"Don't you want to know?" Butch asked.

"Know what?" he said tightly.

"What really happened to him?"

He ground his teeth. "Even if I thought the reports were wrong and something else did happen, how is sending us across the section of the Atlantic Ocean known for its high number of drowning deaths going to prove or disprove anything?"

"If we pass over their pod, I guarantee we'll see a mermaid."

"That's a bold statement."

"Trust me. I know what I'm talking about."

Conall didn't trust anything about the guy, except that he'd pass out at some point—probably soon—and wake up tomorrow and do it all over again. Butch was nothing if not a creature of habit.

"The key, of course," Butch continued, "is to get through without the mermaids luring one of us to our death."

Conall pinched the bridge of his nose. "Okay, let's go with this insanity for a minute. What's going to happen, Butch? Why would a mermaid lure one of us to our death?"

"Anger. Bitterness. Revenge."

"Are you saying someone on this ship has wronged them in some way?" No one on this ship—except Butch—claimed they'd ever had any interaction with mermaids. In fact, this ship was staffed with some of the most logical, don't-care-about-mermaid-myths sailors Conall had ever experienced. Which was exactly why he'd chosen to book passage across the ocean.

Butch had been the odd man out, but Conall supposed everybody needed comic relief once in a while.

Turning a full circle, Butch stretched out his arms like the ring-master at a circus. "Maybe not directly, but somewhere, someone in each of our personal histories has, without a doubt." He pointed at Conall. "And you have the most direct, most recent link."

"My father," Conall said, and son of a bitch, he was not really buying into this nonsense, was he? "His body was recovered," he reminded the drunkard. "Cause of death: drowning."

Butch shook his beer can in Conall's face. "I did my research. He'd been a sailor for twenty-five years. He was a swim instructor in high school. He'd been good enough that he probably could have gone to the Olympics if he'd not decided he'd rather captain boats instead of do laps in a pool."

All true, and all public knowledge. Easily accessible, too. The man had died only three years ago, and the story had been splashed all over the internet. Conall had no idea his father had been so famous in nautical circles until his death.

Infamous was probably a better word.

"And he wasn't a good man," Butch murmured, his bleary gaze locked onto Conall's face.

Shit. He really needed another drink. Or to walk away.

"I know it sucks to hear that about your own old man, but you know it's true."

Goddamn it. "You did your research. Congratulations."

That, too, had been splashed all over the internet. His father's misdeeds. How poorly he treated his crew. How he mistreated women.

Hell, most of the articles Conall read had implied his father deserved what happened.

"That's why they killed him," Butch said. "Revenge. Because he wronged one of them."

"He wronged a lot of people." *Including his own son.* "And yes, he wronged a lot of women. Human women, not mermaids."

"I not only did my research, I was *there*."

Conall fought hard not to react. He probably failed. Because, yeah, he knew what Butch was alluding to.

"What do you mean, you were there?" God, why did he even ask? He didn't want to hear Butch's account of things; he'd read plenty, had discussed it ad nauseum with his therapist.

Butch swayed closer. Conall could see the spiderwebs of veins in his bloodshot eyes, could practically pick out his favorite brand of beer by the stench of his breath. This man was going to drink himself into an early grave if he didn't change his habits soon.

"I was on the boat. On that trip. The one where he threw the girl overboard."

MAN ACCUSED of tossing girl overboard released due to lack of evidence.

THAT HAD BEEN the first headline after his father's arrest and subsequent release. Hell, Conall was surprised they'd even put cuffs on him, considering there was no body, no proof that a girl had even been on the boat in the first place. All they'd had to go on was the account of a single person onboard the vessel. They couldn't even pinpoint a specific missing girl who might have been the supposed victim. Five teenaged girls had gone missing from the coastal towns within a fifty-mile radius of the village from which the ship had set sail. Three had been recovered since—alive—but two were still missing, and last Conall had checked, no one was actively searching for them.

Even though the alleged incident had occurred well over a decade ago, both girls could still be out there, somewhere, very much alive. The accusations were not true. His father had been far from a saint, but killing someone was a stretch.

"Don't tell me you were the single witness," Conall said.

That would also help explain how his father had been released so quickly after the accusation. Butch liked to believe he was well-respected in the nautical community, but he was a laughingstock. A drunkard who often couldn't recount what he'd done the day before. The fact that he'd insisted a woman had been tossed overboard when no one else had said the same would have only reinforced how untrustworthy he was.

Captains invited him onboard their vessels for the comedic value, nothing more.

Conall doubted the captain of this ship had followed Butch's recommendations. They weren't going anywhere near that mysterious and not-real mermaid pod.

"Good night, Butch," Conall said, pushing away from the railing. "I suggest you call it a night too. Wouldn't want you to accidentally fall overboard, out here all alone. Somebody might think the mermaids took you."

CHAPTER TWO

Asia found the boat with ease. It was skirting the perimeter of their pod; close but not close enough to justify scaring them off course. The captain of this ship, she'd wager, had heard the rumors and preferred to err on the side of safety. It wasn't all that far out of their way to travel a few knots southwest and then back north to avoid finding out whether mermaids were real.

Darkness had long fallen, but the moon was nearly full, casting a warm, pale glow across the waves and the lonely ship, cruising through the water at a steady, unhurried speed. The passengers and staff were all tucked away in their cabins, save the single officer who had drawn the short straw and was manning the bridge for the overnight shift.

Memories of her childhood, when she had still been human, assaulted her. She'd so desperately wanted to learn how to captain a ship. The dream had consumed her; she'd hardly been able to concentrate on her studies, because all she wanted to do was either be out to sea or read about being out to sea.

And the first time she'd been afforded the opportunity, she'd been tossed overboard, like stale bread for the seagulls to fight over.

Because she hadn't belonged there.

She swam up to the side, where there were two perfectly aligned rows of orange lifeboats hanging, prepared for an emergency situation. Or a mermaid who needed to get aboard.

She still couldn't believe she was doing this, even as she expertly flung the long rope of seaweed up, catching and wrapping around the rod the highest row of boats hung from.

Was she being punished? Was this because she'd coveted Bella's position within the pod? Because surely, Galene would not have recommended Asia for this particular mission.

Most mer, when first turned, were naturally bitter. Between the comprehension that they were going to die, the near torture of being saved and turned into a mer, and coming to the realization that their life as they'd known it would no longer exist, was it really any surprise the pod was bursting at the seams with negative energy?

Yes, it had been fifteen years for Asia, and yes, she should have gotten her closure.

But she'd not yet claimed her first kill; she'd never lured a sailor to a watery death. All she'd done was scare off those who guided their ships too close to the pod. Mermaids had a bad enough reputation—deserved, at that—Asia didn't need to make it worse.

That was what she told herself. She also told herself that her first kill would be a revenge kill, not a just-because-she-could kill. She was waiting until she came across the one who'd altered her life forever.

Which only made this particular mission even more irksome.

After tugging on the rope to ensure it would hold her, Asia began to climb, using only her upper body since her lower half was currently still in mermaid form. She then hung there, waiting for her scales to dry so they would fade to human-like skin and her tail would morph into legs.

At least this transformation wasn't supposed to hurt. Probably because it was temporary.

Hopefully, remembering to walk was like riding a horse. One

never forgot, right? For fifteen years, she'd only used her fins and arms to swim through water. She'd lived under the sea for as many years as she'd lived on land.

"Focus, Asia," she muttered. A gust of wind whipped at her damp hair and swept away the last droplets of seawater on her body, and the transformation began. Her purple scales shimmered one last time before fading to smooth, dusky brown skin. Maybe this was where sailors developed the idea that mermaids were naked from the waist up, because now she was entirely nude, a rather significant part of the transformation she'd forgotten about until this moment.

Which meant she needed to get aboard and find clothing before anyone spotted her. Crap.

Every mermaid possessed some form of magic; Poseidon bestowed it on them shortly after they were turned. The first time she'd met him, the sea god had been unexpectedly pleasant after Galene's harshness.

He'd given Asia the gift of blending in, allowing people to see what they wanted to see. She'd thought it a strange gift at the time— why did she need to blend in within a pod of mermaids she never intended to leave again?

Yet here she was, climbing aboard a ship, suddenly grateful for Poseidon's apparent foresight. It had never occurred to her to feel modest when she was in mermaid form; her scales covered her breasts and mermaids didn't have anything going on down below. Now, however, shaped like a human, with legs and—she glanced down—lady bits, not to mention bare breasts, all that modesty she'd not thought about in a decade and a half came roaring back like, well, walking, as it turned out.

She climbed over the railing and placed her feet flat on the boards, then stood there for a long moment, staring down at her wiggling toes as if they were foreign objects she wasn't sure what to do with. They *were* foreign objects, but at least she did recall how to use them.

She lifted her gaze and clashed with another.

A human man.

He had beady, bloodshot eyes, a bulbous, red nose, tufts of hair growing from his ears, and he reeked of beer. And he was walking more unsteadily than Asia.

She froze. Shit. She'd thought everyone was asleep, save the first mate, who was captaining the ship and whose attention would be on the dark sea ahead of them, not on some mermaid trying to slip aboard in the middle of the night.

"You're real," the man practically breathed, and she half expected him to keel over, much like that M&M's Santa commercial from her youth, and damn it, now she wanted M&M's. If there was one thing she missed from her human life, it was those delicious little candies. The peanut ones were her favorite, but she had been an all-opportunity M&M's fan.

"I saw you," he said, sounding as if he did not believe the words coming from his own mouth. His gaze darted from her to the rope of seaweed still twisted around the railing. She wouldn't need it when it was time to leave; she could simply dive off the side of the ship, but it was too late to unravel it now.

Quickly, she summoned her magic, wrapped it around herself, and sent out a signal that the man was looking at a human, not a mermaid. This was the first time she'd ever used it, so she had no idea if the magic was strong enough to hide the fact that she was naked, but Poseidon below, she certainly hoped so!

The man blinked rapidly and shook his head, almost like he was trying to shake off the spell. But that couldn't be. Poseidon had assured her humans were susceptible to the spell, more so than any other creature on the planet.

The man's brow furrowed. "Are you naked?"

Clearly, the spell did not extend to her state of dress, although she supposed she should be grateful that he wasn't ogling her. He appeared confused, not aroused.

She cleared her throat. "I...was sleepwalking."

"You've been on this ship the whole time?"

527

Her magic worked! She nodded and tried a small smile on for size. To be honest, she suspected adjusting to walking instead of swimming everywhere would be easier than acting nice and cheery around a bunch of sailors. Especially since Bella had informed her that there was one in their midst who was determined to expose the pod.

He'd been eluding them for nearly two decades, she'd said, which Asia had found curious. Why had she only just heard of this man if that were the case?

Bella hadn't expounded. She'd only told Asia to be careful, to pay attention, to not get caught. To not let anyone know she was not human.

Oops. Although, to be fair, this guy was clearly drunk. Between that and her belated spell, hopefully, he'd forget what he saw before she'd transformed into her human form.

"Of course," she said smoothly.

He shook his head again. Now she'd swear he was trying to shake off her spell, which was concerning. What if everyone she encountered struggled to accept the magic like this? It didn't help that every sailor on the high sea liked the idea that mermaids—the benign version of them, at any rate—were real, which was going to make her mission more challenging than she wanted. She was supposed to weed out the single person with malicious intent and lure him overboard to a watery death, but she had no interest in harming anyone who was completely innocent.

She'd been innocent and had been sent to an untimely death, and she'd vowed to never do that to another. In truth, she wasn't exactly mermaid material. Yes, she was as resentful as the next one, but she didn't sit around the seaweed bed, talking of murder and drownings like so many others.

The man wore a black-and-white track suit with a T-shirt underneath. Shedding the jacket, he held it at arm's length, silently offering it to her. The fact that he wouldn't take a step forward told her he was still not entirely under her spell.

Problematic, but she snatched the article of clothing anyway and draped it over her shoulders before zipping it up, hiding all the girly bits. It hung on her like a sack, but at least she wasn't nude anymore.

She was going to have to figure out how to clothe herself, which might be difficult because there were probably few women on board. Even in today's world, there were plenty of men who held to the belief that having a woman aboard a ship was bad luck. That belief was how Galene had come to be the original mermaid, how the pod had formed in the first place.

Because sailors' superstitions were enough for them to justify tossing a woman overboard, believing that would right their potential bad luck. Luckily, Poseidon had taken pity on Galene and had turned her into a mermaid—the only immortal mermaid—instead of letting her die. Unfortunately, Galene's need for revenge had not been assuaged over the centuries—possibly because the practice of tossing girls overboard still continued—and her hatred for male sailors permeated every secret corner of the pod.

"When's the last time you were on land?" the drunken man asked, his words slurring slightly.

She *almost* answered him truthfully.

"We aren't on land," she said carefully.

He flapped his hand at the boards beneath their feet. "Walking around. On two legs."

Well, hell. She canted her head. "Do you really believe I am a mermaid?"

He nodded. No hesitation.

She massaged her forehead. Was this the guy she was supposed to toss overboard? He didn't seem evil or malicious. He hadn't yet mentioned anything about the pod. In truth, he was acting like probably anyone who wanted to believe would.

Go for honesty. He'll never believe it. "Fifteen years ago." She glanced down at her legs. "I'm a little rusty."

"Is that when you were turned?"

Damn it. Now what? "Um...yeah."

"What was it like?"

She lifted her hand, palm facing out. "Okay, stop. I've cast magic to make you believe I'm human. How is it you can still tell I'm a mermaid?"

He shrugged. "Probably because I believe so deeply. Trust me, lady, people have been making fun of me most of my adult life. You trying to evade doesn't even faze me. What's your name, anyway?"

"Asia," she admitted. Was this guy for real? Yes, he most definitely was. At least she could be certain of one thing: he was not the one she was supposed to lure to a watery grave. "Yours?"

"Butch. Butch Rutgers. I met an Asia once. Long time ago. Pretty name. Means sea nymph. Was that your name when you were human?"

"I'm not supposed to talk about this stuff. It's breaking every rule in the"—she almost said pod—"book. So let's just assume I'm not going to answer any more questions."

His face drooped like a disappointed child who was told no as he and his parents walked past the ice cream shop. Hopefully, the rest of the humans on board this vessel were not so strong in their beliefs. Otherwise, she might just abort the mission.

No, she couldn't do that. She was certain this was a test. Bella had deliberately chosen her to do this task. There had to be a reason. Maybe she was being considered for a promotion after all.

If she didn't succeed, she wouldn't get to move up in the ranks. What was that phrase people used? She'd heard it a few times in her youth, when people were trying to complete a difficult task.

Failure was not an option.

CHAPTER THREE

Conall woke with a start, his eyes popping open to stare at the ceiling of his cabin, barely visible in the dim light provided by the green button on the smoke detector affixed over the door. These cabins were barely large enough to accommodate a single bed and a wardrobe bolted to the wall, and yet every single room had a smoke detector with a little green light that glowed all day and night.

Man, he was really getting edgy if he was this annoyed by smoke detectors.

Shoving the thin blanket aside, he lowered his feet to the cold floorboards, the shock waking him more fully and chasing away ridiculous frustrations about smoke detectors.

He knew that wasn't his *real* frustration anyway.

Damn Butch for putting ideas in his head.

He'd had himself convinced this was a leisure trip, maybe a final goodbye, at most, to all the drama his father's death had brought on. He'd had no intention of thinking about or being curious about or wanting to see a mermaid.

They didn't exist, and they certainly didn't kill his father.

Except Butch had been so damn adamant, and he was the last person Conall had spoken to before heading off the bed, so naturally, his dreams had centered around—yep—mermaids.

Not *The Little Mermaid* kind but vindictive, evil mermaids.

Sexy, vindictive mermaids.

He swiped his hand over his face and glanced down at his dick, which was taking its sweet time deflating after that last, particularly erotic dream.

It creeped him out that Butch's mention of the mythical creatures had this sort of effect on him.

Conall pulled on a pair of sweatpants, slipped his feet into his tennis shoes, and dragged a hoodie over his head before stepping out of his cabin. After a quick trip to the lavatory, he headed up to the deck. Maybe a lap around it, with nothing to keep him company but the cool, salty air and the whir of the ship's engines, would chase away all the ridiculousness Butch had put into his head, and he could go back to sleep.

And when he woke in the morning, he'd do his damndest to stay as far away from Butch as one could when sharing space on a cargo ship.

There were no clouds in the sky when Conall stepped out onto the deck, the nearly full moon casting a pale glow on the wooden boards. He started for the railing but changed his mind and headed toward the stern instead.

He stopped. That was Butch's voice. Son of a bitch, that guy was still awake? And who the hell was he talking to? Usually, by this time of night, the only person awake was whichever officer was staffing the bridge.

"Let's just assume I'm not going to answer any more questions."

Wait a minute—that was a female voice. There weren't many women aboard this ship. Conall didn't hold to the belief that women aboard a ship were bad luck. He would not cling to such ridiculous superstitions.

That was as foolish as believing mermaids existed.

Still, curiosity propelled his feet forward, until he rounded the corner and came to a stuttering halt.

Butch was swaying on his feet—not at all surprising—and talking to a woman who was...wearing a track suit jacket probably ten sizes too big—and nothing else.

She had dusky skin and dark hair with hints of auburn. The thick ringlets appeared to be damp, like she'd just gotten out of the shower, maybe. Her body was angled away from him, so he couldn't see her face, and he selfishly took a moment to appreciate what wasn't hidden by her oversized outfit: shapely legs ending in petite feet.

He cleared his throat, and the woman whipped around to face him—and stole his breath away.

She was utterly gorgeous. Big eyes, a narrow nose, plump lips. It was hard to tell under that oversized jacket she was wearing, but he suspected her breasts were more than generous.

How the hell had he not known she was aboard?

Conall was as red-blooded and lusty as the next guy, and he most certainly would have struck up a conversation, subtly checked to see if she was single, and if the answer was yes, he would have hit on her. And if he'd gotten incredibly lucky, sharing a cabin with this beautiful creature would have definitely chased away the sensation of unease that had been dogging him since he'd stepped foot on this vessel.

Wait a minute, what was stopping him from enacting this exact plan now?

"Ahoy, Conall," Butch called out, waving him forward. "Come meet Asia. You'll never believe—"

The woman narrowed her eyes as she glanced at Butch and shook her head. He clammed up and nodded solemnly. What the hell was going on?

"Uh..."

"Asia," Butch said, "this is Conall. He's a good guy. Despite who raised him."

Conall bit back the groan. First, his dad hadn't raised him—he'd been too busy captaining his ships and stirring up rumors, first of infidelity and then, after Conall's mom divorced him, rumors that he often got a little too rough with whomever was sharing his bed at the time.

Second, what the hell kind of introduction was that?

Conall strode forward as he obligingly offered a handshake, forcing a smile that hopefully didn't look strained. "Nice to meet you, Asia. How come I haven't met you until now? It's not that big of a ship," he teased.

Those overlarge eyes widened for a moment before she lowered her lids and her lips lifted into a charming smile.

"It's a pleasure," she said, and he did not miss the way her gaze raked over him from head to toe. Her hand clasped his, and warmth filled him like she'd poured hot water into his veins.

He liked the sensation. But then he frowned. "Seriously, how have I missed you for the last few days?" There had been a casual reception their first evening at sea for the handful of passengers to meet the crew and each other. Why hadn't she attended?

Her gaze darted to the water for a moment before an amused smile played at her lips. "I was seasick." She sounded like she was trying not to laugh.

Was that why she was out here in nothing but that ridiculously oversized jacket? Because she'd been sleeping—nude, by the looks of it—and had felt ill and hurried out here for fresh air?

Damn it, that was a man's jacket. Which meant there someone waiting in her cabin for her. Bummer.

"You're looking well now," he said. She did. Not a hint of the greenish tinge to her skin that usually accompanied seasickness.

Her smile widened. "I feel so much better, thank you. Like it never even happened at all." Her brief chuckle made him think she was teasing him, although he didn't get the joke.

She smoothed her hand down the front of the coverup, and her mood instantly sobered. "I need to find more appropriate clothing," she murmured, almost as if she were talking to herself.

"There aren't that many women on board," Butch said. "And I'm not sure which cabins any of them are in. But one of the crew has a really small stature for a guy. I bet something of his would fit you reasonably well."

"Oh good," Asia said. "I don't suppose you could show me to his quarters?"

"Certainly," Butch agreed.

"Hang on," Conall said. "You don't have any other clothes?" How was that even possible?

"Yes, I..."

"Seasick," Butch blurted. "All over them. Everything is a mess. In fact, she can't even go back to her own cabin. It's that bad."

Damn. "Maybe there's something to that whole 'women are bad luck on a ship' thing, huh?"

What the hell had possessed him to say something so asinine?

"I didn't mean that," he said when her lips twisted into a frown. "Sorry. Totally inappropriate."

Totally inappropriate was right.

For a minute there, Asia had been dazzled by the outrageously attractive human man. Conall. Short, brown hair streaked with blond, which, along with his golden tan, implied he spent a fair amount of time outdoors. The lack of weathered skin on his face suggested that time was not normally spent on ships.

He had startlingly blue eyes, the kind humans liked to compare to the ocean. And the scruff outlining his incredibly kissable lips made her want to drag her fingernails along his jawline.

All of this was attached to a muscular body under a sweatshirt and form-fitting gray sweatpants, and Poseidon below, where were these thoughts even coming from?

As a human, she'd gone through puberty, had all those lusty hormones raging through her body, had had plenty of crushes on plenty of boys. She'd never done the deed, though, hadn't gone any farther than a handful of stolen kisses with a single boy before that fateful day when she'd been tossed over the side of a ship.

When she'd transformed into a mermaid, those urges went away. In their half-fish form, mermaids didn't have the appropriate plumbing for conjugal relationships. They had to go on land—or a ship—during the correct lunar phase and transform into the shape of a human to be able to do those sorts of things.

This was the first time Asia had taken on her human form since she'd become a mermaid. So her heated reaction to such a beautiful specimen really ought not surprise her.

Except she hated human men. Or at least, she was supposed to.

Good thing that rude comment helped to cool her libido. She jutted her chin and gave Conall a chilled look while he blustered through another apology.

"Why don't we go find you some fresh clothes?" Butch suggested. Oh yeah, that absolutely ridiculous story she'd concocted on the spot. Seasickness! It was so absurd she almost started laughing again, but she managed to tamp it down. Didn't need Conall to get any more suspicious than he obviously was.

Hey, at least her magic worked on him. He hadn't even remotely questioned her humanity, only that he'd not realized she was aboard the ship until now and that she was not wearing clothing acceptable to humans.

"Yes, good idea," she said to Butch. Bonus that going in search of clothes would get her away from Conall and hopefully, allow her to wrestle her libido entirely under control.

Did the idea of appeasing her suddenly raging lust tempt her? Yes, most certainly. If she played this job right, she'd possibly never have to transform into her human form ever again, so this was likely the only chance she'd have to see what sex was all about.

Except...what if Conall was the man she was supposed to lure to a watery death? Did she really want to bed the man she was sent here to kill?

"Tell me about him," she instructed Butch after they'd walked away from Conall, who—she surreptitiously glanced over her shoulder—was still standing on the deck, staring after them.

It was still unnerving that Butch was immune to her magic, but on the other hand, having an accomplice was turning out to be handy.

"Conall?" Butch shrugged. "He's a good kid. Has a history you probably wouldn't appreciate, though." He gave her a wink she suspected was supposed to lighten his words, but it most certainly did not.

If Conall had a history she wouldn't appreciate, he was probably the one she was supposed to dump overboard.

How disappointing.

Butch led her down below, to a section of the ship reserved for the staff. Every door was closed, and she caught the sounds of snoring, music, and from behind one door, noises that sounded suspiciously like—

"Jerry and Nate," Butch said, nodding at that particular door. "They've been a couple for years. Just got married, right before we set sail. Clearly honeymooning," he said with a snort.

Another few feet and he stopped. "This is Rick's cabin. He's stockier than you but about the same height, and, don't take offense, but he's probably about the same waist circumference."

"That's convenient," she said, eyeing the closed door. "Now, how do I get inside?"

Butch knocked on the door.

"What are you—"

The door wrenched open, and a smallish man who really did look to be the same size as Asia stood there, blinking rapidly against the bright light in the hallway.

"Morning," Butch said with a smile.

Rick narrowed his eyes. "What the fuck, Butch? It's three o'clock."

Asia waved, drawing the guy's attention. His mouth fell open as he checked out her state of mostly undress.

"I was wondering if I might borrow some clothes," she asked politely, because what else was she supposed to do?

"You don't have your own clothes? And aren't you a woman?"

Yep, magic definitely worked. Too bad it couldn't convince these people she was a man, too.

"Yes, I am, and I do not have any clean clothes. Very long story."

"Pretty gross too," Butch added.

Rick blinked owlishly.

"May we come in?" Asia didn't wait for a response. She stepped forward, and Rick automatically moved to the side. With a little maneuvering, she managed to shunt him entirely out into the hall, and then she smartly closed the door. And locked it.

Time to find herself a wardrobe.

And then it was time figure out who on this ship needed to die.

CHAPTER FOUR

At the age of thirty, Conall had officially become a stalker.

Not that he'd ever aspired to be a creeper. Not that he ever remotely expected he'd be okay heading down this path.

He wasn't, for the record.

This introspection did not stop him from following Asia and Butch—at a distance—after they left him standing on the deck so she could go in search of clothes.

He trailed after them as they headed down to the crew's quarters, then watched from behind a bolted down cabinet as Butch knocked on someone's door and Asia edged the guy out of what Conall assumed was his own room.

He wasn't sure how much time had passed—it hadn't been much—but eventually, Asia reappeared wearing sweats and a T-shirt and carrying a bundle of clothes in her arms. A conversation ensued—probably the poor guy wondering what she was doing with his wardrobe—and then Asia and Butch wandered away, going up one level to where the passengers bunked.

Butch took her to an empty cabin, held open the door, bid her good night, and then left her there while he presumably returned to his own bunk. Conall couldn't confirm that last bit because he'd stayed where he was, tucked into a nook down the hall.

He watched that closed door until the sun rose and the rest of the ship's occupants began to wake.

Finally, he returned to his own cabin, showered, dressed in jeans and a blue golf shirt, and headed to the dining room for coffee, food, and hopefully, another glimpse of Asia.

Passengers came and went while he sat at a table in a corner, drinking enough coffee to make up for the amount of sleep he'd lost last night. But no Asia. Or Butch, for that matter, although that part didn't surprise him. Butch usually needed to sleep off his hangover from the night before, so he often didn't show up until lunchtime.

As the dining staff began cleaning up and Conall assumed she wasn't coming, her shadow darkened the doorway a scant moment before she stepped into view, drawing his gaze and the attention of every cell in his body.

She was still wearing sweatpants and a T-shirt. Her hair had been pulled into a twist behind her head, secured with what looked like a couple of pencils. Ringlets framed her face, which was either devoid of makeup or was layered with cosmetics that made it look like she was fresh-faced.

She was breathtaking. Yep, the obsession he'd developed almost immediately upon meeting her hadn't dimmed.

She went straight for the buffet, practically pushing the attendant out of the way before she filled a plate with enough food for three meals, at least. Adding a tall glass of orange juice, she sat at the table nearest to the buffet and dove in with gusto. Clearly, she was over the seasickness that had plagued her up to last night.

After a few moments' hesitation, Conall stood and made his way over to her table. She glanced up and immediately began choking on whatever had been in her mouth.

"Oh shit," he said and quickly slapped her back a few times, until she shoved his arm away and waved like she wanted him to give her a minute.

After she managed to get the hacking under control, she swiped at her eyes with her napkin and took a tentative sip of OJ. "Pardon me," she wheezed out.

"My fault," Conall said. "I shouldn't have snuck up on you. May I sit?"

She hesitated. She very likely was on this ship with a partner, so he needed to keep his libido in check. Although if that were the case, why had Butch taken her to an empty cabin, where she'd remained —alone—for the rest of the night?

After a moment, she nodded at the chair perpendicular to hers, and he plopped down, promptly blurting out, "Are you single?"

He smacked himself on the forehead. "Sorry. Totally inappropriate. Sorry. Again."

When he dared to glance at her, her lips were twitching, like she found him amusing. That was something.

"I am," she finally answered. "Are you?"

"That answer seemed obvious by the way I'm acting around you. Christ, you'd think I've never been around a beautiful woman before."

"You find me beautiful?"

"Breathtakingly so."

Apparently, he was also on a starkly truthful roll.

"You'd think I've never hit on a woman before in my life." Which was undoubtedly *not* winning him any favors.

She canted her head and studied him for seconds that stretched into days, until she abruptly said, "How do you feel about mermaids?"

He slumped against the ladder back of his chair. "Oh no. Butch got to you."

"What does that mean?"

541

"Contrary to Butch's very adamant belief, mermaids aren't real. Sorry to disappoint you."

CONALL DIDN'T EVEN BELIEVE in mermaids. Which meant he was not the person she'd been sent here to kill.

That was encouraging.

Because, despite what he probably thought, his awkwardness was utterly adorable. And Asia hadn't been able to stop thinking about him since their encounter early this morning. Even after she finally succumbed to sleep, she dreamed about him. About him helping her discover all that pleasure humans had the privilege of experiencing anytime they darn well pleased. She had ten days, and then she'd be forced to return to the sea, to her mermaid form.

Surely, it wouldn't take that long to find the person she'd been sent here to eliminate. Which meant she had time to get to know Conall.

"He's literally the only person on this boat who believes in them," Conall said. "Well, of all the passengers and crew I've met so far."

Actually, maybe she could do both simultaneously: get to know Conall and pump him for information.

"You haven't met everyone?" she asked.

He shook his head. "I was kind of laying low for the first couple of days. Was in a bad headspace. Not the same as you, although I'm sure you can relate to laying low for a while."

Same as—oh, that's right. She supposedly had seasickness. Honestly, she couldn't wait to get back to the pod and tell her fellow mer that joke. It would surely lighten the mood of the entire colony.

"Could you point out the passengers you haven't met yet?" If he could assist her—unknowingly, of course—she could eliminate suspects one by one, until she found her quarry. Oh, and she would get to spend time with Conall in the meantime.

Bonus.

He shrugged. "I'm sure I could. Why? You want to quiz them on their mermaid beliefs?"

She smiled demurely. "Something like that."

He gave her the side-eye. "You don't really believe in them, do you?"

The way he said it sounded as if she wouldn't have the opportunity to get any closer to him if she said yes. If she had any interest in a long-term relationship, that would be problematic. But all she wanted was a little physical satisfaction, so she said, "Of course not."

He blew out a breath. Imagine his shock if she were to leap into the sea and he got a glimpse of her mermaid's tail.

No. She didn't want to know how he might react to that bit of knowledge.

Pushing her plate away, she asked, "Would you like to walk around above deck with me?"

His eyes widened, clearly surprised by her boldness, or maybe he was surprised she'd still be interested after his less-than-stellar attempts at conversation this morning.

He was such a refreshing change from the merfolk she spent all her time with.

"Absolutely," he said, hopping to his feet and sending his chair skittering away to bump into the nearest table. His cheeks went dark as he glanced over his shoulder and then back again, a sheepish look on his face. "I'll try harder to contain my excitement."

She looped her arm through the crook of his elbow and grinned up at him. "Please don't."

He laughed as he guided her out of the dining hall.

The day was bright, full of sunshine, with only a handful of puffy clouds drifting across the sky. They were still so far out to sea that there was no land to be seen. Although she had ten days before her body would revert to its mer form—whether she was in the sea or not—and the trip would take fewer than that. Depending on weather and boat speed, they'd likely be to America in half that time. Perhaps, if she were still intrigued enough by him, Asia might go on shore with Conall, spend the last of her time in human form with him.

She'd never been to America. When she was human, she'd dreamed of sailing there, although she obviously never imagined it would be quite like this.

"What are your plans when you reach the mainland?" she asked as they wandered arm in arm around the deck. She'd been making mental notes as she asked him about each person they passed. Did he know them? If so, did they believe in mermaids?

Of those he said he knew, he had no idea of their mermaid beliefs, although it was Conall's opinion that Butch was the only person aboard this ship who believed in the idea of women who were half fish, half human.

So Asia focused on those passengers he said he had not yet met. She memorized the face so she could return later and perhaps pinpoint the person she needed to dispose of.

"I have a job interview. In Portland. So I may be moving there. What about you?"

She hadn't thought to concoct a backstory for herself, mostly because it had not occurred to her that she'd meet anyone she would actually want to sit and chat with. "I, um, don't actually have any plans."

"Are you vacationing?"

"No, it's a business trip." She didn't like lying to him, even as she knew her answer was bound to lead to more questions, and eventually, she wouldn't be able to answer them.

"Ah. Well, I hope you are able to carve out some free time while you are there. I'm told it's a beautiful area."

"You've never been?"

"Nope. My father traveled the world, but my mom and I stayed put. I've lived in A Coruña my entire life."

"This is a big change, then."

"You can say that again."

She wanted to ask more, so much more. She wanted to know all about him. His family, his life, his desires, his reasons for possibly moving to another country on the other side of the vast sea. And getting there by ship, instead of flying, which had been the more common mode of transport even fifteen years ago when she'd been human.

But she didn't ask, because she did not want to miss him when she returned to her own life.

"There he is," Conall said, and she glanced up to see who he was talking about.

Butch had just stepped onto the deck, dark sunglasses perched on his nose. Despite the shades, he lifted a hand to keep the sun from hitting his face. There were brackets around his mouth and he looked ... ill, actually.

"I admittedly try to avoid him because I don't want to listen to him blathering on about mermaids, but I couldn't help but notice that he'd been absent since we've been up here," Conall said, his gaze glued to the other man. "He doesn't look so well." He paused. "Good God, I think he's sober. I haven't seen him sober the entire time we've been on this ship."

All of a sudden, Butch's body lurched. He covered his mouth with a hand and ran across the deck, grasping the rails as he leaned over and expelled whatever had been in his stomach.

Asia wrinkled her nose, and Conall steered her in the other direction. "Good on him for finally sobering up," he said, "but I don't want to be downwind."

She glanced over her shoulder. Butch was slumped against the railing, the upper half of his body hanging over, even though he was no longer retching.

Why had the man suddenly decided to stop drinking?

CHAPTER FIVE

Conall would be perfectly fine if he never woke from this little fantasy.

Somehow, some way, despite the utterly embarrassing impression he'd made at breakfast, Asia was enamored with him. Enough that she'd asked him to hang out with her for what turned out to be the entire day. They wandered around the deck, they went down to the exercise room together—she said she'd never been inside an exercise room before—they had lunch together, they played games for the better part of the afternoon.

They talked and talked and talked. About the other passengers, about the ship, about his hometown. She was from a small town not too far from where he'd grown up, and she, too, had done very little traveling in her life. They were the same age. They both loved seafood. Both of Asia's parents were from Spain, whereas his mother had been transplanted from Poland, having met his father while vacationing on the coast.

His father had knocked up his mother, and they'd had a small wedding, then a baby, then the troubles had begun.

Conall didn't tell Asia all of that. Only that his parents were divorced and he hadn't had a relationship with his father, who'd died three years ago. He really liked Asia and didn't want to scare her off by pulling all of his skeletons out of the closet.

Asia spoke of her own family wistfully, like she hadn't seen them in a very long time. Of course, a long time to some people could be a few days. Since she said she'd not traveled much, it would make sense that she might be homesick already.

They talked of their careers; she was in securities, while he was a graphic designer. He asked if she wanted kids and then started stammering like a fool. He was beginning to sound like they'd met on a dating app and this was the interview stage.

"Don't be embarrassed," she said, smiling up at him in a way that made him want to wrap his arms around her and kiss her until they were both gasping for air. "I think it's cute how you have no filter."

"Gee, thanks."

She chuckled. "It's refreshing." But then she frowned. "Unfortunately, it doesn't matter whether I want children, because I cannot have them."

"I'm sorry."

She shrugged. "I've accepted my fate. What about you? Do you intend to have children some day?"

"To be honest, I haven't really thought much about it, which makes it even more embarrassing that I asked you."

They were sitting on lounge chairs in the shade, although it wasn't even necessary. Over the course of the day, clouds had begun to fill the sky, until it was a gloomy, overcast evening with rain most definitely in the forecast.

A drop splashed against his pant leg.

Asia glanced up at the sky, a frown marring her brow. "We should go indoors."

"Afraid you'll melt?" he teased.

"Something like that," she said vaguely as she stood and hurried toward the nearest door, not even checking behind her to see if he followed.

Which he did. Of course he did.

Belowdecks was a lounge area overrun with passengers and crew alike. Some were clustered around a television in the corner; they didn't have access to live TV way out here in the middle of the ocean, but there was a huge selection of movies available to watch. Others played cards and boardgames; still others bellied up to the bar on the other end of the room. He spotted Butch over by the television, which was as far from the bar as one could get and still be in the same room.

He really was making an attempt at going sober, it would appear.

"Let's go to your cabin," Asia suggested. "I'm not in the mood to be around so many people."

He wasn't either. He only wanted to be around one person, and she'd just suggested they hang out alone together.

He was all in.

As they passed the bar, he asked, "Do you drink wine?"

"It's been a very long time," she said, "but I'm happy to join you if you'd like a drink."

He asked the bartender for a bottle of red and two glasses, and then he slid cash across the bar top before snagging his prize and leading her to his cabin.

A FEW RAINDROPS wouldn't affect Asia, but a downpour would generate enough water to cause her body to shift into its mermaid form. The captain had announced that the storm should be brief, as it was fast-moving and heading in the opposite direction. Still, rain was rain, and Asia needed to err on the side of safe versus sorry.

When she woke this morning, she'd decided to shower, and as soon as the stream of water hit her, her body had begun to transform, scales covering her skin, her legs binding together, her tail stretching, adding a fin. She'd slid to the bottom of the shower stall and lamented the fact that there were likely no bathtubs on this ship.

Bathing while lying on the floor of a shower stall was not, for the record, a particularly easy task.

Still, it had been admittedly nice to rinse the salt from her skin, out of her hair, and then, after she'd rolled out of the stall and her body dried, she'd slathered on nearly half a bottle of lotion. Ocean scents were amazing, but the combination of lemon, orange, and grapefruit had officially become her new favorite smell.

Her hair was dry—she'd forgotten how curly it was when it wasn't constantly soaked in saltwater—she felt fantastic, and she'd spent a wonderful day with a wonderful guy.

She'd also gleaned enough information about the various other passengers that she knew who she needed to investigate further to determine who was her list.

Oh, and her libido was in overdrive, courtesy of being in such close proximity to Conall for ten hours straight.

When they'd stepped into the lounge and she'd seen all those humans standing, sitting, laughing, talking, she'd damn near had a panic attack. What if her magic wasn't strong enough to hide her in plain sight from so many people at once? Sure, she looked human and none of these folks had any reason to believe she was anything but. However, Butch had figured it out almost instantly, and she wasn't keen to see if anyone else possessed the same ability.

Suggesting she and Conall retire to his cabin had been perfect, for more than one reason.

Mostly, because she wanted to be alone with him.

Conall held the door, and Asia stepped into his cabin. He followed and then immediately began blustering about how this was a terrible idea because there was no furniture beyond a bed and a dresser.

"Pour the wine, Conall," she said, amusement lacing her words. Poseidon below, he was so adorable. So refreshing.

He obligingly did as she asked, leaving the bottle on the dresser and handing her one of the glasses. She touched the rim to his and took a small sip. It was dry and tangy and yet sweet all that the same time. Reminded her of the wine her mother used to serve with dinner. Asia had been allowed only half a glass; however, the practice had been enough for her to appreciate a decent bottle when a handsome guy offered it to her.

She sat on the bed and patted the rumpled blanket next to her hip. Conall hesitated, then sat, with enough space between them that another person could comfortably join them.

She rested her back against the wall. He did the same, and for a short while, they chatted about this and that as the comfort level ticked up and up and up. Before she even took her last swallow, Conall hopped up, filling both glasses before placing the bottle on the floor next to the bed.

When he sat again, he was noticeably closer. Asia smiled and trailed a finger through the scruff on his cheek.

"What was that for?" he asked.

She shrugged, feigning casual. "Curious as to whether it would be soft or rough."

"What's your conclusion?"

She did it again. "A little of both."

"Is that good or bad?"

"Definitely good." She smiled impishly.

"If I asked you for a kiss..."

"Yes?"

"Would you say yes?"

Giggling, she said, "Yes."

He plucked her glass from her hand, placing both on the floor next to the bottle, and inched closer still. "Are you sure?"

"Conall, just kiss me already."

He chuckled, cupping her cheeks with both hands. And then his lips were descending, and she watched, fascinated, only the slightest bit nervous. She hoped desperately that she still remembered how to do this.

His lips pressed against hers, soft, drier than she expected. They parted slightly, and his tongue darted out, tentatively touching the Cupid's bow of her lips, and Poseidon below, electric heat shot through her body.

She opened, wanting more, wrapping her arms around his neck. He became more bold, his tongue sweeping into her mouth, and she groaned, pressing more eagerly into the kiss.

His hands left her face, his fingers skating over her sides, his thumbs skimming her breasts. She arched into his touch.

He pulled away, blinking bemusedly, a silly little smile slanting his lips.

"We're wearing too many clothes," she said, because she wanted him to touch her breasts without the impediment.

He reached for the zipper on the tracksuit jacket she wore, tugged it down, his eyes widening as her breasts were exposed.

"You aren't wearing a shirt."

The guy she'd *borrowed* clothes from hadn't given her much of a selection. It wasn't a subject she wanted to dwell on at the moment. She glanced down at her heavy, full breasts. The dark nipples were so hard she could poke someone's eye out.

"That isn't a bad thing, is it?" she asked, thrusting her breasts toward him. Hopefully, he'd take the hint.

His gaze dropped. He stared hungrily while her body tightened, her inner muscles reflexively squeezing. She was practically ready to start massaging her breasts herself, so overheated was she at the moment. Instead, she said, "You can touch them. Lick them. Suck them. All of the above."

A laugh tripped over his lips. "You are so damn hot."

His gaze unwavering, he cupped her breasts, adjusting his hold like he was trying to determine which way he liked best. Or maybe he was testing to see what she liked best, because when she moaned, he paused, kept his hands where they were, and began gently massaging.

But then he pulled away.

"Hang on," he said, tugging his shirt over his head and tossing it to the floor before dropping his hands to her hips and lifting her as if she weighed nothing at all. He deposited her on his lap.

He sat with his back against the wall, his legs stretched perpendicular across the single-person bed. She widened her thighs so that her lady bits were pressed against his erection. Another zing of pleasure chased through her body. She'd never gone this far with a boy before, and all she wanted was more. More of his hands on her body. More of his kisses. More—

He leaned forward and kissed her breast, his lips encircled her nipple, his gaze looking up at her. She was pretty sure her mouth fell open.

He sucked, and she let out a noise that didn't even sound human as she let her head fall back on her shoulders.

"You smell delicious," he murmured as he nuzzled the side of her breast. "Like citrus and the ocean."

One of his arms wrapped around her back while his other hand toyed with her left breast and his mouth made love to her right one. She fidgeted in his lap, her hips rolling, gasping because it felt so damn good, and she never wanted this to stop.

He slid his hand down until it was on the small of her back, guiding her movements so she was rocking back and forth, her lady bits pressed against his erection, dragging up and down, over and over. She began panting and shivering as her lower belly grew tighter, the tingling growing in intensity.

All of a sudden, he released her breast and chased kisses up the column of her neck until his lips were pressed against hers and his tongue thrust into her mouth. Both hands cupped her backside, dragging her along the ridge of his erection, until she broke the kiss to cry out as an orgasm crashed into her with the intensity of a Category 5 hurricane.

He kissed her neck, her shoulder, her cheek, his movements slowing until she was a boneless mess sitting in his lap, leaning against his chest like she might melt right into his soul.

He didn't seem to be in a hurry to do anything else, which was nice because she was thoroughly reveling in the moment. Not to mention, it was really quite lovely resting here against his bare, muscular chest. She traced patterns over his pecs, which flexed and quivered under the attention.

His reaction revived her energy, and suddenly she wanted to know what it would feel like to do what they'd just done except without clothes. Her fingers wandered lower and lower, until she was toying with the waistband of his pants and his breath was coming in short pants.

She glanced up, and the hunger in his eyes made her gasp before she swallowed thickly. "Um...there's something I should tell you."

His hands, which had returned to fondling her breasts, stilled. "Uh-oh. It's usually not good when someone says that when they're in this situation."

She scratched her nose and dropped her gaze to his lap. She could see the outline of his erection pressing against the material. Oh, how she desperately wanted to see him, all of him, without a stitch of clothing.

"I, um...I'm a virgin," she blurted.

He pulled his hands away, lifting his arms like he was surrendering. "We can stop."

Laughing, she grabbed his hands and brought them back to her breasts. "Are you crazy? That's not what I want at all. I just don't want you to have high expectations."

"Are *you* crazy?" he retorted, wrapping his arm around her waist and flipping her onto her back, so that she lay across the bed while he hovered above her, his palms pressed against the blankets on either side of her head. "My expectations have already been exceeded."

"Oh," she said, because what else could she possibly say?

He pressed a hard, swift kiss to her lips and said, "If you're going to give me this privilege, I'm going to try my damndest to ensure it's the best experience it could possibly be."

He shifted lower on the bed, chasing kiss after kiss over her breasts, her quivering abdomen, until he was licking and nibbling at the sensitive skin just above the waistband of the jogging pants she wore. Hooking his fingers under the band, he tugged them down, his breath catching as they slid over her hips, exposing her lady parts, before he shoved them down to her ankles without dragging his gaze away from the apex of her thighs.

He wasn't even touching her and her skin was warming, something inside her coiling, twisting, like it was desperate to break free.

"So beautiful," he said, stroking her hip, down her thigh, to the back of her knee. He lifted both of her legs, gently wrapping her ankles around his neck.

He crouched at the foot of the bed, his body between her thighs, his face hovering just above her pelvis. "Ready?" he asked.

She really had no idea what she was supposed to be ready for. She trusted him, though. "Yes."

With a jaunty wink, he lowered his face, and then his hands were on her, his fingers touching her lips—those lips, the ones down *there*—and his tongue scraped across the most sensitive part of her body, and if she died right this moment, she would die a happy mermaid.

She didn't, which was a relief, frankly, because that swipe was just a preview. Her entire body shuddered when he nipped at her bud with his teeth, gently, but with enough pressure to nearly send her over the edge again.

She arched, her hands coming up and clasping his head, her fingers threaded in his silky hair, holding him there lest he decide he was done before she was willing to let him pull away.

He nibbled and sucked and licked and stroked, using his tongue, his lips, his clever fingers, sending her higher and higher until she was soaring, her body bowstring tight as she reached the pinnacle, wave after wave of pleasure crashing over her.

When the intensity finally began to ebb, she released her hold on his hair and let her arms drop to her side. She was breathing heavily, like she'd just swam for miles at top speed without stopping, and there was a sheen of sweat on her chest.

"Mm-mm," he said, snagging his shirt off the floor and using it to wipe his mouth. "You taste as sweet as you smell."

"Like oranges and lemons?" she said with a giggle.

"Better."

"Oh." The mood had gone from light and teasing back to intense in a single heartbeat. "More. I want all of you."

He rolled off the bed and shoved his pants down his legs, exposing his jutting, bobbing erection.

She sat up. "I want to touch you."

He didn't move. "Do whatever you'd like."

She reached out, tentatively, and touched the underside of the bulbous head, featherlight.

Twining his fingers on top of his head, he closed his eyes and groaned, his body tensing.

"Does that hurt?" she asked, jerking her hand away.

Without opening his eyes, he shook his head. "It feels amazing."

Ah, she understood now. She'd felt exactly the same way only moments ago, in those few seconds before her orgasm overtook her. It was a pleasure-pain sensation. Nearly unbearable and yet all she'd wanted was more.

Taking that answer as permission, she let her fingers explore. Stoked down to his balls, dragged her nails gently along the underside while he shuddered and groaned again. She touched the tip of his penis, where a bead of liquid had gathered, and she used it to lubricate her hand as she wrapped it around his shaft and stroked up and down, reveling in how good she was obviously making him feel, until his hand suddenly clamped over hers, stilling it.

"I'm about to explode, Asia. If you stroke one more time, I'm going to lose it all over your hand, and I'd need a recovery period before we get to the final scene."

"Oh." She pulled her hand away. He cupped her cheek for a moment, then reached up and tugged the pencils out of her hair. The curly locks fell around her shoulders. He brushed them off so they draped down her back instead, then climbed onto the bed on his knees.

She lay back, her thighs falling open. He nestled between them and rested his elbows on the blanket so he could keep his upper body from crushing her.

"You said you couldn't have children," he said, looking into her eyes. "Does that mean we do not have to deal with protection?"

She swallowed and nodded. He stroked her hair, bent down and kissed her, achingly gently. "I'll make it good for you, I promise."

Laughter bubbled up. "You've already made it far beyond good."

He pressed his lips against hers again, parting, his tongue teasing its way into her mouth, mimicking the act of sex until her hips were moving of their own accord. Without breaking the kiss, he cupped her thigh, lifting her leg and spreading her wider still, while his other hand moved between them, positioning his erection at her entrance. She would have tensed with anticipation, except his thumb grazed her clit and she forgot to feel anything except pleasure as she arched into him and he pressed into her, slowly filling her.

Her body stretched to accommodate him, the sensation of fullness not exactly unpleasant. Her inner muscles rippled, and he froze, the arm still supporting him shaking, while his other hand squeezed her hip.

She wiggled, impatient for more. With a groan, he pulled away slightly and then pressed into her again, going deeper, eliciting a guttural groan from her throat.

"Good?" he rasped as he began to move, thrusting shallowly.

"Better than," she assured him, reaching up and grabbing his backside. The action must have shocked him—he abruptly thrust hard and deep and oh yes, that was exactly what she wanted.

"More," she said, rolling her hips.

"Fuck me," he said. "You couldn't be more perfect if I'd wished you into being."

Apparently, his words were an aphrodisiac, as her body began to twist and coil, already chasing the next orgasm.

He cupped the back of her thigh, giving himself leverage, and increased the velocity of his movements, pressing in and out with powerful, deep thrusts, until Asia was panting and meowling and clawing at his back like a damned wild animal.

"Come on, baby," he crooned, still pumping. "I need you to get there first. Come for me, Asia."

She flung her head back, crying out as pleasure once again swamped her. Conall didn't let up—rather, his movements became more choppy, more desperate, until suddenly he went still and sharp as a statue, practically growling as warmth filled her before he slowly lowered himself so that he was half laying on her, half next to her.

She could feel his chest heaving. He draped an arm across her middle and dropped a kiss onto her shoulder, and Asia smiled as she let her lids close.

CHAPTER SIX

Asia rolled onto her back and stretched, her fingers and toes spreading while her muscles and tendons flexed and slowly came awake.

Sleeping in a bed was certainly one aspect of being human that she had missed. When merfolk slept, they wedged themselves into an alcove formed by rocks—to keep from drifting away—and simply floated with their eyes closed.

Waking up surrounded by softness was a far better experience. Bonus that there was a deliciously attractive, warm, and oh so attentive man sharing the bed with her. Turning her head, she watched Conall as he slept.

He was on his side, his hand resting on her stomach. Last night, they'd curled up together like spoons, and he'd wrapped his arm around her waist and snuggled in close and closed his eyes, and she'd never felt more human in her life.

Or maybe it was that she'd never wanted to be human more in her life.

Stop, she scolded herself. It was foolish to wish for things she knew damn well were entirely unobtainable. She couldn't become human again any more than Conall could become a mer.

Well, technically, he could become a mer. She'd have to ask Galene's permission, and Galene would have to agree to turn him. Asia would need a justifiable reason; Galene had said no plenty of times to a mer who had fallen in love with a human and simply requested they be turned because they wanted to be together.

And Conall should want to be turned—although Asia knew from personal experience that wasn't a requirement. Still, she wouldn't make that decision for him; it wasn't fair.

Which, of course, meant she would need to come clean and admit to him that she was a mermaid. Problematic, since he didn't believe her kind existed.

And again, as she had no justifiable reason to turn him beyond her deep-seated attraction, this whole line of thought was utterly pointless.

Conall's eyelids fluttered and then opened, and he gave her a sleepy smile while leaning forward and pressing a kiss to her shoulder.

Swoon.

"Morning," he said, his voice rusty.

"Hey."

He snuggled more deeply into the pillow and closed his eyes again.

She needed to get out of here. She needed to breathe, to collect her wayward thoughts and remind herself of her purpose here on this ship. And she needed to do so before she gave in and burrowed back under the blanket with him.

He stirred again when she sat up and placed her feet on the chilly floorboards. "Are you leaving?"

She sucked in a breath, let it out slowly, to make sure her words were steady. "I'm starved." That much was true. "I'm going to grab some breakfast." She wanted to go alone, but proper etiquette dictated: "Do you want to join me?"

He yawned and closed his eyes again. "Nah. I'm going to sleep a little longer. Will you come back when you're done?"

She should say no. She was here for a purpose, and it was not to fall for the handsome human man. Heck, if he knew of her purpose, he'd be kicking himself for even sleeping with her in the first place. She ought to tell him. That would certainly force distance between them.

"Yes," she assured him, then gathered her clothes and quickly dressed, twisting her unruly hair into a braid before slipping out the door.

It was still early; the breakfast buffet had just opened when she stepped into the dining hall. There were a handful of guests scattered at a couple of tables, and another table with six crew members; she presumed they were going on duty once they finished with their meal.

Butch was one of the guests, sitting alone at a table near the porthole, nursing a cup of coffee and a plate of toast. Asia loaded up on breakfast foods and filled a tall glass with orange juice—Poseidon below, she loved the stuff—but hesitated before heading over to sit with him.

He looked worse today than yesterday. His skin was sallow, and there was a tremor in his hand as he lifted his mug to his lips.

"Are you okay?" she asked.

"No," he replied, taking her by surprise. She'd expected him to say he was fine even if he wasn't. That's what humans did.

"I quit drinking because two days ago I swore I saw a mermaid."

She quickly glanced around. He was talking at a normal volume, but luckily, there was no one sitting close enough to hear him.

"And as it turned out, it wasn't the alcohol that caused me to see things that shouldn't be there."

Uh-oh. "What do you mean?"

He flapped his hand at her. "You're still here."

She glanced down at herself, in her borrowed sweats, dry,

braided hair draped over her shoulder, legs where a tail should be. "You can tell, even when I'm in this form?"

"No," he admitted, his gaze dropping to his coffee. "But I took a look at the captain's logs, at the guest list. And there is no guest named Asia booked on this ship. Furthermore, I remember why your name struck a chord with me."

"Y-you do?"

He leaned forward and lowered his voice. "I witnessed your death."

"You..."

Stabbing his finger at his own chest, he said, "I was there. In fact, I'm the one who found you, stowed away illegally, on the *Jolly C*."

Jolly C. She'd forgotten the name of the boat she'd slipped onto as a fifteen-year-old who had only wanted the opportunity to go out to sea, to learn the ropes. To maybe someday captain her own ship.

"The boat was named after the captain's son," Butch said.

She didn't respond. She was still trying to absorb this new knowledge. Butch had been there. He said he'd witnessed...

"You know who did it," she said. "Why didn't you do anything about it?"

"I tried," he said, arms spread wide. "No one believed me. That was before I became a full-blown drunkard; in fact, that event was what started me down this path. But I *was* drunk at the time. As were most of the crew. When I went to the police after we docked, the captain contradicted my story, told them how drunk I was, pointed out that there was no proof you'd even been on that boat."

There had been no proof. She'd snuck on board. And before that, she'd told her mother she was going to stay with a friend at their country home for a week. Her mother likely never connected her being missing to the hullaballoo with that captain who had briefly been accused of tossing a woman overboard. She would have assumed Asia had gone missing somewhere between their house and her friend's house, which wasn't anywhere near the sea.

"Why are you bringing this up now?" she asked.

"Well, for starters, it's pretty odd that we would cross paths again, fifteen years later, don't you think?"

He had a point.

"And on a ship, no less."

Another good point.

"I don't think you are here by accident. You have a purpose. Mermaids don't just climb onto ships in the middle of the night and pretend to be human for the thrill of it."

Actually, that did happen sometimes, although it certainly wasn't anything Asia would ever do, and besides, not the point.

"So what is your purpose?"

To buy herself time to think, she took a hefty swallow of her orange juice. It tasted sour.

"I am on a mission," she said carefully. Did he have something to do with her mission? He was the only one on this ship, as far as she'd been able to discern, who had any connection whatsoever to mermaids.

To her.

But he hadn't been the one who tossed her overboard; he didn't seem malicious at all.

"What happened to that captain?" she asked suddenly. She darted a glance around the dining hall. "He isn't here, is he?" There were quite a lot of people on this ship, and she'd been distracted by a certain passenger with sun-kissed skin and lips and a body that ought to be illegal.

It was possible she'd missed the man she was here to exact revenge upon. Bella hadn't told her explicitly that was her mission, but Asia had learned long ago how to read between the lines when it came to communicating with her own kind.

Butch shook his head. "He's dead. Three years ago."

Asia's hand shook so badly, orange juice sloshed out of the glass and coated her fingers—fat, orange droplets splattering against the tabletop. She put it down more forcefully than necessary and focused on using her paper napkin to wipe up the mess.

She wasn't angry. Or bitter. She wasn't upset that she'd not been the one to lure the man to his death. It would have been a justifiable revenge, after all. Perfectly understandable.

Expected of her kind, to be honest. She'd been holding onto her resentment for fifteen years; she should be disappointed that she wouldn't have the chance to exact revenge.

Instead, she was...relieved.

"The mermaids did it," Butch announced. "And no, before you ask, I wasn't there. But I know I'm right."

"How so?" If another mermaid came across the man who killed Asia and figured out that he had ill intent toward women, they'd not hesitate to take care of him in such a way. Usually, they'd return to the pod bragging about their latest conquest.

Asia couldn't recall her interest being piqued by any stories of killing a wayward captain three years ago.

Butch nodded at the porthole. "He died out here. At sea. Under mysterious circumstances."

"That happens plenty enough without mer involvement," Asia pointed out.

"He drowned."

"Still not—"

"He was both an accomplished swimmer and captain."

She opened her mouth to continue to argue, but memories rolled through her head, cutting her off, ensuring she could focus on nothing else.

A teen Asia, strolling along the docks, playing it cool, trying to act casual as she formulated her plan. It had been so simple. Choose a ship. Sneak on board. Try to stay hidden, although if they caught her, they'd likely be too far out to sea to be willing to turn back and deposit her on shore. And surely all those whispers of men tossing women overboard for fear of bad luck were false. No one believed that sort of thing anymore. It was the twenty-first century, for the love of Pete.

Except they did. It was actually quite easy to maintain one's beliefs when one spent the majority of their time at sea, surrounded by like-minded folk. Sailors clung to their fears and superstitions as fiercely as professional athletes did.

She'd thought she'd gotten past it. Finding out the man who took away her human life was now dead—not by her own hand—was a relief, not a disappointment.

Right?

Why were all these memories flooding her brain? Why was she shaking? Why was Butch looking at her with concern?

"You've figured it out, haven't you?" Butch asked.

"Figured what out?" That her own kind likely did kill the man who had tossed her overboard all those years ago? Was that her problem? Was she upset that no one had told her? That didn't make sense; other than Galene, no other mer had been around when it happened. How would they know that particular captain had done it?

"Maybe you should ask Conall," Butch said, not ungently.

Conall. She suddenly had an all-encompassing need to be with him. He would comfort her, he would help chase away these demons. He didn't even believe in mermaids, and he certainly had no issue with women aboard a ship.

She lurched to her feet.

And she fled.

CHAPTER SEVEN

Conall slipped his feet into his tennis shoes. He'd hoped Asia would have returned by now. He'd wanted nothing more than to eat away the early morning hours in bed together, ignoring the rest of the world and focusing on the intense pleasure they created together.

He'd wanted to lie in bed afterward and talk about seeing each other again even after they docked in Maine. Seeing each other again when her business trip was done.

He didn't have to take that job in Portland; he could go back to A Coruña or wherever she was based. He wasn't tied to any place anymore. His mom was gone; even if his father were still around, he didn't give a rat's ass about the man. Conall was an only child. Any relatives he may have on his mother's side hadn't been in contact since he was a kid, and he knew nothing about his father's side of the family, which was fine by him.

All he wanted was to be with Asia, for however long she'd tolerate him. He hoped her tolerance didn't have an expiration date.

Christ, listen to him. He'd sure fallen fast, hadn't he?

Shaking his head at his own folly, he stood and headed for the door, abandoning his hope of spending the morning in bed. Asia had been gone for so long that now he was starving.

So, he'd head down to the dining hall, eat breakfast with her, then they could return to his cabin, bellies full, regenerated for another bout of exhaustive lovemaking.

Yeah, that sounded like a plan.

As he reached for the knob, the door flung open, and Asia stood on the threshold, eyes wide, pupils dilated. Her dark skin was flushed, and her hair was wind-whipped, strands tugged from her braid, as if she'd been running.

Automatically, he pulled her into the room and into his arms, holding her tightly, reassuring her without words that whatever it was, he'd help her deal.

"What happened?" he asked when her shivering finally began to subside.

Brushing her hair out of her face, she strode to the porthole, staring out for a long moment, before turning to face him. "Bad memories. Really bad. Caught me off guard."

He nodded and hugged her again. "I get it. If you want the truth, the reason I'm even here is because of bad memories."

She leaned back so she could look him in the face. "Really? Do you want to talk about it?"

Chuckling, he kissed her temple. "You're the one in distress right now. Why don't *you* talk about it?"

She shook her head. "I am not in distress. In fact, I'm much better now." She said it shyly, like she wasn't sure how he'd react.

He hugged her more tightly. Because he couldn't get enough, didn't ever want to stop touching her. "I've got you."

He felt her smile against his chest. "Tell me your story," she said.

"You sure you don't want to go first?" He was only half-teasing. He honestly didn't want to taint her image of him by letting her know about his parentage, even as he knew if they were to attempt to start a relationship, he'd have to be honest with her.

That was the basis for lasting relationships, right? That's what his mom told him when he was young, when she cut off ties with his father after learning about his infidelity.

"I'm sure."

He still hesitated, but what the hell. If she ran away now, it was better than waiting and falling in love—hell, he was halfway there already—before it happened.

"It was a dark and stormy night..." He chuckled when a laugh burst from her mouth, but then he sobered. This wasn't a fun story.

"The reason I'm even on this ship is because I'm searching for closure. Three years ago, my father died out here. Well, back there." He waved at the stern of the ship. "Where they say the mermaids lure sailors to their deaths."

She stiffened in his arms, and he hurried to add, "I know that's not how he died, although the circumstances were...odd."

"How so?" She'd not relaxed; it felt like he was hugging a board. He loosened his grip. She didn't move.

"He drowned. Apparently fell off the boat. Strange enough given all the safety measures nowadays, but the fact that he was an experienced sailor makes it even more suspect. He had decades of experience under his belt, plus he was an Olympic-level swimmer."

Asia pulled away from him, stumbled backward until she bumped into the wall. Pressing her palms to the flat surface, she looked up at him, her eyes even more wide and dilated than when she'd arrived on the threshold a few moments ago.

"Are you going into shock?" he asked, reaching for her.

She shifted to the side and he pulled his arm back, confused.

"Three years ago," she rasped out. "Near the mermaid pod."

"It was a freak accident," he hurried to say. Did she worry the same thing might happen to someone on this ship? "Besides, we're long past the area by this point. We're going to be fine."

She started shaking her head, long tendrils of hair tugging from her braid and whipping back and forth. "No, no, no, we aren't. We can't."

"No. Don't say that, Asia." This was exactly what he'd been afraid would happen if he opened up about his past. The irony was, he hadn't even gotten to the really bad parts yet. The bit where he told her what a cruel, awful person his father had been. How he'd abandoned his family, abused his crew, beat up women. There were times Conall felt relieved the man was dead.

"Our pasts don't define us," he added, desperate for her to see. He wasn't his father. He'd never been cruel to anyone in his life. His disdain for Butch was probably the worst he'd ever experienced, and hell, that was tied back to his father.

Clearly, he never should have taken this trip. Except if he hadn't, he wouldn't have met Asia.

But based on the look on her face, the rigid set of her body, he was beginning to suspect whatever he thought might grow between them was about to be very short-lived.

"Our pasts very much define us," she said coolly.

THIS COULDN'T BE HAPPENING. Asia's brain felt like it might explode. It didn't want to accept this information. Didn't want to believe.

"What is your surname?" she demanded. Her voice sounded hoarse, as if she'd been screaming. Well, she certainly was on the inside.

"Nowak." She heard his confusion in that single word.

She shook her head. "That isn't it. That isn't his last name."

"Who?"

"The man you say fell overboard three years ago." She used air quotes for *fell*. It had to be the same person. It was too much of a coincidence that there might have been two around the same time and she'd not heard any gossip within the pod.

"Don't tell me you're buying into all that mermaid crap?"

She snorted. "What is your father's name?"

"Why are you suddenly so interested? And what's with the attitude?" He was getting angry. Good. It was better than that puppy dog look he had when she pulled away.

"What is his name?"

"Enrique," he bit off. "Enrique De León."

It was a good thing she was still leaning against the wall. Her knees had begun to quake so severely, they wouldn't have held her up otherwise. "Oh Poseidon," she whispered. "It is him."

"Oh what?"

"I have to get out of here." She took a step but wobbled so precariously, she inched back to press herself against the wall. *Deep breaths, Asia. Compose yourself. You can do this. Get away from him, get back to the pod, and then you can have a meltdown.*

"Why? What's going on, Asia? Talk to me."

"No. I can't." She shoved away from the wall, forced her legs to work by sheer will. One step, two. Halfway there.

"Asia." He reached for her. She shied away, kicking up her pace until she was at the door, her hand grasping the handle.

"I'm not him," Conall said.

"Yes, you are." She wrenched open the door, flung herself out into the hall. A startled crew member in his sharp, white uniform, touched her elbow.

"Are you okay, miss?" His eyes widened. "What are you? How did you get here?"

Great. Her magic was fading. She needed to get back to the safety of the sea.

Shouldering him out of the way, she ran to the stairs, rushed up them two at a time. It was midmorning, not a cloud in the sky when she threw open the door and stumbled out onto the deck. Lifting her hand to shield her eyes from the bright sunlight, she ran to the railing.

The sea was actually fairly calm, even as the ship sluiced through it at a clipped pace. They were a great many knots away from the pod; it would take her a full day of constant swimming to return.

Which was fine. She needed the exercise to burn off all this stress, all these feelings.

Conall was his son. The man who had tossed her overboard. The man who had ended her human life. He'd had a son who was her age.

Someone who did not appear to be anything like his father.

Except he was still related to the man.

Our pasts don't define us, Conall had said.

But they did. Her past certainly had. If she'd not so desperately wanted to learn how to captain a ship, she never would have snuck onto that boat all those years ago. She would still be human.

She would still be alive.

Bella would argue that she was very much alive, but Asia was no longer sure. Clinging to her anger and bitterness, her need for revenge, letting it consume her—how was that living?

She stared down at the water. She had a choice to make. Dive over the railing and go home, her task incomplete. Deal with Bella's disappointment, Galene's wrath, the scorn of the rest of the pod.

Or return to the cabin and finish what she'd been sent here to do.

Because she now knew.

She was supposed to kill Conall. The son was supposed to atone for his father's sins. And she was the one who had to do it.

Could she?

Water sprayed her, and she stepped away from the railing, brushing it away before her body tried to shift into her mermaid form.

Poseidon below, she didn't think she could do it. Not Conall. He was...special. To her. He meant something.

She cared.

"Asia."

She whipped around. He stood near the door to the stairs leading belowdecks, hesitating, like he was afraid to come too close.

"I didn't know," Conall said, without stepping closer. "I didn't know him. He left when I was a kid, and I had no contact with him. I had no idea who he really was, until he died."

She closed her eyes. "I don't want to know." The more he told her, the harder it would be, whichever route she chose.

"Why did you react the way you did? Did you know him?"

Another spray of water hit her. The calm water from a few moments ago was now churning and dark. Were they about to be hit with a storm? She needed to get away from the water.

Or jump overboard.

"I did know him," she finally said. Whatever decision she ultimately made, Conall deserved to know the truth.

"He killed me."

CHAPTER EIGHT

Conall shook his head. "Sorry, did you say he killed you?"

"Yes."

He forced a laugh and waved at her person. "Um, I hate to point out the obvious, but you're standing right here, very much alive."

She glanced down at her legs. "He ended my human life."

"So what are you, a ghost?" Believing in mermaids wasn't enough?

"No."

He crossed his arms and waited for her to explain. He'd come out here to talk to her, to try to convince her to give them a chance. He wasn't his father, damn it. It wasn't fair that the cloud of the man's transgressions would hang over his head—now, twenty-five years after he walked out of Conall's life. He'd been dead for three years, and still Conall could not shake the cloud. If anything, it had gotten worse.

A wave of water leaped up and soaked Asia's pant legs. She turned and snapped at the ocean, "What, are you on his side?"

Grasping the railing, she hauled herself close to it, using only her upper body, as if her legs had suddenly stopped working.

"Are you okay?" He took a couple of steps and hesitated.

"It's all true, Conall." She glanced down to her legs that seemed to be pressing together as if she'd duct taped them.

"What is?"

She wrapped her arms around the railing and clung to it like she needed it to hold her up. "Butch. Everything he said."

Conall snorted. "Butch is—"

He couldn't finish the sentence. He was too busy staring at Asia, his mouth undoubtedly hanging open. Her sweatpants were tearing at the seams, ripping from her body, revealing...

Purple skin?

No, scales. The lower half of her body was covered in scales. Shimmering, sparkling fish skin.

And she no longer had legs. In their place was a giant fish tail, the fin twisting and flapping against the wooden planks of the deck.

How the hell had she managed—

"Don't refuse to believe it, Conall. Not after what happened between us."

"What am I supposed to refuse to believe? What is going on, Asia? Why—why are you suddenly shaped like a fish?"

She glanced over her shoulder at the ocean. "I have to go. I—I'm sorry it's ending this way. I never meant..."

"What do you mean, go? Where are you—"

As if she did those sort of acrobatics every single day, Asia flipped herself over the railing. Conall rushed to the side of the boat with enough time to catch her twist in midair so that she was head down, her diving form more perfect than any professional on earth.

She disappeared below the surface, barely causing a ripple in the tumultuous water.

"No!" Conall shouted. "No!"

He couldn't let her do this. He didn't understand what had happened to her legs, but he did understand that they were in the middle of the ocean and there was no land as far as the eye could see and he was not about to let her go. Not like this.

He dove overboard.

For the record, far less gracefully than she had.

Asia surfaced and glanced back at the ship—and saw Conall climb up onto the railing, waver for a scant moment, and then jump into the sea.

"Conall!" she screamed, diving under water and swimming faster than she ever had in her entire mermaid life.

He was yards underwater by the time she reached him and hooked her arms under his shoulders and began torpedoing upward. He would have surely drowned if she'd not wanted one last look before leaving, because there was no way he would be able to swim back to the surface without her help.

They crashed through the waves, and she expected Conall to sputter and cough while trying to suck in much needed air.

But he didn't. He lay limply in her arms.

"No, no, no! You can't die like this!"

Balancing his upper body with one arm, she tapped his cheeks. His eyes did not flutter. He wasn't breathing!

"Conall, no!"

She couldn't perform CPR here in the water—even if she knew how to do it. She needed to get him back onto that ship, and she was running out of time.

He wasn't breathing.

Keeping his head above water, she swam toward the side. Her seaweed rope was still hanging, the end drifting along with the ship. She wrapped it around him, securing it under his armpits, but now she had to figure out how to get him up and over the railing without anyone seeing her. Galene would have her hide if she exposed her true self, even in this life-and-death situation.

But she could not figure out a way to get Conall to safety without hoisting him up herself, and damn it, his life was far more important than whatever punishment she'd have to endure.

Twisting the rope around her hand, she prepared to climb.

"I've got him," someone shouted from above. She whipped her head up.

Butch!

He grabbed hold of the rope and pulled, grunting and groaning and swearing. She could see sweat popping on his brow all the way from the water. Would he even be able to hoist Conall up on his own? She might have to help anyway. They were running out of time.

Conall's body jerked and then slowly began to rise. Asia pushed up from beneath him, until he was too high for her to reach, and then she held her breath for the excruciatingly long seconds it took Butch to get him up and over the railing.

"Help!" Butch shouted. "Man overboard! Man overboard! He needs medical attention!"

Asia swam closer to the ship, hiding in the shadows, treading water as she kept pace with the large machine. She could hear the sounds of feet slapping against the deck while several people began barking out orders.

Someone was performing CPR. Someone else asked Butch, "How did you get him out of the water?"

Butch replied, "It's amazing what you can do when you're motivated."

And then she heard it. Sputtering. Coughing.

Breathing!

She sucked in an appreciative breath of her own and swiped away a tear that had escaped from her eye. Conall was going to be okay. That was all that mattered.

She glanced up, wished she could see him one last time. But she couldn't risk exposure.

Heart heavy, and yet relieved that he had survived, Asia dropped under the water. She sucked in seawater, her lungs automatically accommodating for the difference, and pushed it out again.

Touching her hair, she watched the tendrils floating freely around her head. They would never be rinsed of saltwater again. The sweatpants she'd been wearing had been torn to shreds when her body began to shift, but she still wore the top. Reluctantly, she pulled it off, let it drift away on the current.

She was back to her mermaid form. Back to the life she was meant to lead.

She'd not accomplished her task. Bella would be unhappy. Asia probably would be assigned some sort of undesirable duty, like corralling jellyfish for a month.

Hopefully, the only wrath she'd have to deal with was Bella's. Hopefully, this mission was too small for Galene to care about.

Even so, Asia didn't care.

Conall was safe. He was alive.

That was all that mattered.

CHAPTER NINE

Asia swam aimlessly. Maybe it was avoidance; returning to the pod meant she'd have to give Bella an update and then face the music when she confessed that not only had she not completed her mission, but she was not going back to do so.

Maybe it was heartsickness. Her heart did feel like it was broken. Shattered into a million pieces, so many that it could never be put back together again. Who had thought that loving and losing was so much better than never loving at all?

They were wrong.

She wished she'd never met Conall. Yes, her life had been empty and meaningless before he came into it. She'd not been happy.

For the short time they'd spent together, she'd been utterly and completely content.

She'd been ten times a fool to fall for him. Even if it hadn't ended the way it had, she still would have been forced to leave him. She was a mermaid; she could only transform into human form once during each lunar cycle.

He hadn't believed in what she was. Even after seeing her tail, she wasn't sure he believed. Not that it mattered. How could they have possibly made a relationship work? She didn't earn enough vacation time to be able to sneak away to be with him for ten days each month.

And she certainly could not discount the reality of their situations: she was a mermaid whose job was to frighten off sailors, not lure them closer. And he was a human whose father had...

The man had killed her. He'd tossed her overboard without a second thought. Snuffed out her human life.

She knew she shouldn't blame the son for the father's sins, but that only made this situation worse. She'd been sent to kill Conall as revenge for what his father did to her.

Asia had so many questions—how did Bella know Enrique De León had died? How did she know Conall was his son?—but she didn't really want to know the answers. Okay, she did, but they weren't important anymore.

How in the world was she going to fit in with her pod now? Asia's need for revenge had shriveled up and blown away with the wind after that short time with Conall. Revenge wasn't what was important; enjoying life in the minute was.

When her tailfin scraped the rocky bottom, she glanced down, surprised to see the ocean floor so close. She hadn't realized she'd swam so deeply—no, the sun was filtering through the waves, so she couldn't possibly be that deep.

She wasn't. She'd swam right into shallow waters unaware. Popping her head above the waves, she shielded her eyes with her hand and glanced around.

There was a lighthouse to her right, the mainland straight ahead. Boats were all around, some of them casting nets or fishing line. She'd certainly gotten lucky to have made it this close without getting snagged in one of them, considering she'd been paying absolutely no attention to her surroundings.

Of course, being this close to land also meant she was awfully far from the pod. Which wasn't a bad thing, to be honest. She was perfectly okay with taking another day or two before returning to face the music.

Where had she ended up? The area wasn't familiar, although, to be fair, she had precious little experience with the various continents. Ducking underwater, she glanced around. Sunfish, a mako shark, which wasn't very telling considering how migratory they were. Oh, there went a haddock. So she was in the northern Atlantic Ocean. She hadn't wandered too far.

Lifting her head above water again, she noted the rocky shoreline, the commercial fisherman, the American flag flapping in the wind.

Had she wandered to the US coastline?

Guess she had wandered far after all.

"As if you needed any more proof of your true intentions," came a deep voice from behind her.

"What?" Asia whipped her body around. All of a sudden, she was surrounded by dolphins, swimming a tight circle around her and—

"Poseidon?" She gaped at the exceptionally tall and handsome man with thick silver hair and a neatly trimmed beard. The only other time she'd come face-to-face with the god of the sea was shortly after she'd been turned into a mermaid and he had bestowed his gift upon her.

"Er, pardon," she said, finally snapping out of her stupor and bowing so deeply her nose touched the waves.

"Why don't we drop beneath the surface so we don't draw attention?" he suggested, and Asia hurried to comply. The dolphins continued their steady, circular pattern around them.

Why was he here? Wait, were her transgressions so terrible they warranted punishment by the top dog of the sea? She had no idea since she'd never not done her job before.

But he remained floating before her, a benign, almost pleasant look on his bearded face, not, well, doing anything. She finally blurted, "Can I help you?"

"I think it is I who can help you."

Okay... "How?"

He waved his hand through the water, bubbles trailing in its wake. "Have you figured out where we are yet?"

She had an idea, or maybe it was more that she wanted to believe. "Off the coast of America?"

"Which part?"

She glanced over her shoulder again, at the rocky sea bottom, the islands in the distance. Another haddock swam past. Surely, she hadn't subconsciously wandered all the way to where Conall was due to port?

"Not due," Poseidon. "He is already here."

Asia once again gaped at the god. "He is? Wait, you can read my thoughts?"

"Not directly, no. It is quite easy to guess what you are thinking. And I am here to assist."

"Assist? You're here to assist *me*?" In what way? And why?

"Do not think it isn't self-serving," he said.

"What do you mean?" She'd had only that singular experience with the god—any god—but she did recall that he wasn't exactly forthcoming with explanations.

Poseidon shrugged. "It is rare that I make a mistake, so when I do, I feel the need to either hide it or fix it. In this case, I am fixing it."

"What's the mistake?"

"You, Asia."

She was a mistake? Gee, thanks.

"Truth be told, it was Galene's mistake. But that woman is so stubborn she would never consider undoing what she has already done." He shook his head again.

"I'm not following."

He narrowed his eyes. They practically disappeared under his bushy brows. "What is your greatest desire, Asia?"

She opened her mouth to say "revenge." She was a mermaid, after all. That was supposed to be her pat answer.

Except the word wouldn't tumble over her lips.

Poseidon caught her eye, lifted one brow.

She cleared her throat. And spoke the truth. "To be with Conall."

"Ah." He nodded as if he'd expected that answer. But how could he have?

"I decided to meddle," he said. "It is a bad habit all the gods have, I'm afraid."

"Meddle? In what way?"

"Who do you think gave you this last assignment?"

"Bella?"

"Bella is a middle manager, not the top of the food chain. Someone instructed her."

"Galene?"

"Are you being deliberately obtuse?"

"No, but... You aren't seriously telling me you gave me that assignment?"

He arched that brow even higher on his forehead.

"Why?"

"You tell me. What did you learn?"

She learned that she wasn't really cut out to be a mermaid.

"Say it out loud, Asia."

Her shoulders sagged as she lowered her gaze to the ocean's floor. "I'm not mermaid material. I don't want vengeance."

"Is that because the one who took your human life is now dead?"

She shook her head. "No. It's because I...I fell in love."

"Ah." He chuckled. "You do know the gods are suckers for the idea of true love, right?"

"Except he's human, and I'm a mermaid. And he doesn't even believe that I exist."

"Oh, he's fully aware you exist."

"He doesn't believe in mermaids."

Poseidon nodded again. "That part you will have to work out on your own, I'm afraid. All I can do—I should say, all I am willing to do—is modify your gift."

"What do you mean?"

"Do you not understand what it means to modify something? Change? Adjust? Alter?"

Asia shook her head. "No, I get it. I mean, you just said you could modify my gift. I thought it was one and done. No adjustments."

There went that brow arch again.

"You can seriously modify my gift?"

Poseidon thinned his lips and shook his head. "I don't think you understand the concept of the gods." He spread his arms wide. "I can do anything I want. I could turn you into a frog." He wagged his finger at her. "Or an ocelot."

"A what?"

"Ocelot. Member of the big cat family, although they aren't terribly large. Native to the southwestern US and Mexico and South America. Utterly adorable. But not good as pets, I'm afraid."

"I don't think I'd like to be an ocelot," Asia hurried to say, lest he decide to follow through on the mild threat.

Poseidon leaned back and stared down his nose at her. "What would you like?"

"I'd like..." She glanced up at the light filtering down from the ocean's surface. Was she truly getting this chance? "I'd like to see if I can make things work with Conall."

Could Poseidon really make that happen? Her gift was to be able to blend in, to encourage people to see what they wanted to see. What did that have to do with Conall?

Poseidon couldn't be referring to turning Conall; first, that wasn't a gift by any stretch of the imagination, and second, Galene was the one who made that decision, and Asia knew damn well she'd not do it just for the sake of love.

Love. It was an emotion she'd never experienced before, beyond what she felt for her family. It was so complicated, and so wonderful, and...

She had no idea if Conall would even take her back if she had the opportunity to reach out to him. Which she didn't, because she was a mermaid, and she doubted very much that Galene would send her to shore anytime soon. If there was one thing in all of this that she was certain of, it was that Conall would stay far, far away from the sea for the foreseeable future. Maybe for the rest of his life.

She'd never wished she were human more desperately than she did right now. If only to apologize to him. For not having faith in him.

"There you go," Poseidon said gently.

She whipped her gaze to his face. For a moment there, she'd been so lost in her own head, she'd forgotten he was even there. Probably shouldn't mention that to the god who expected everyone to be aware of his presence all the time.

"Wait," she said, realization finally, finally dawning.

He nodded, smiling seemingly innocently.

She glanced through the gently rolling water, out toward the middle of the ocean, where the pod was located, then slowly returned her gaze to the water god.

"Are you saying I can become human again?" Was that truly possible? She didn't care that it would probably be as agonizingly painful as transitioning to a mermaid had been. She didn't care if Conall ultimately rejected her—okay, yes, she did care, but this would be worth it just to apologize to him. To set the record straight.

"All I can do is turn you. That is all. You will walk up that beach right there with not even a stitch of clothing on your back. No identification, no currency, no plan other than whatever you choose to do for yourself."

"I'd be starting over. Again."

"When you became a mermaid, you had help. Guidance. A support network. You will have none of that if you request that I modify your gift and allow you to transition to human form."

"But I'll have the chance to ask forgiveness. And if he accepts my apology, a chance at love."

"Aye." Poseidon nodded. Were his eyes a little misty? Surely not. It must be the sea. "What would you like me to do, Asia?"

Her tail swished back and forth, keeping her afloat, and bubbles poured from her mouth as she turned toward shore. "Please modify my gift, Poseidon."

"Good luck, Asia."

In a blink, the dolphins stopped their circling, rushing to crowd around Poseidon. And then they were gone, charging away through the water.

Had he been teasing her? Because he hadn't done anything. She didn't feel any—

She sucked in water and suddenly couldn't breathe. Coughing and sputtering, she lunged up, breaking the surface, abruptly aware that she had legs where a fish's tail had been for the past fifteen years.

She had legs—and she was still in the water!

Gasping in much needed oxygen, she treaded water—using her arms *and* legs—as her gaze darted from the nearest land mass to the nearest boat and she tried really, really hard not to curse Poseidon for dropping this on her in the most inconvenient way possible.

Because she was human—clearly, since she could no longer breathe under water, plus, legs!—and she was far more grateful for that gift than she was annoyed that he'd not made it easy on her to start her new life as a human.

Hey, at least the transition hadn't been remotely painful this time.

Her legs were getting tired already, though, and that island with the lighthouse was awfully far away.

"Hey, what are you doing out here? Do you need help?"

She twisted around in the water. A small fishing boat had moved close enough that the man hanging over the side could toss his life preserver at her.

"Yes, please," she said gratefully, far, far too aware of her naked state.

This was going to be embarrassing.

But at least she was human. Now, all she had to do was track down Conall and hope he'd give her a second chance.

CHAPTER TEN

After foolishly diving into the sea without a lifejacket, nearly drowning, being rescued by Butch, then facing a grueling interrogation, during which he refused to utter the word *mermaid*, Conall was more than ready to get off this damn ship and walk away from the ocean for good.

Never again. He wasn't going to take the job in Portland even if they offered it to him. He was heading inland, as far from the Atlantic as he could go—without ending up near the Pacific, of course. No more large bodies of water for him.

No more beautiful, dark haired, dusky-skinned women, either. Mermaid or human. Didn't matter. He was done with the lot of them.

Mermaids.

When he'd seen Asia's scales and tail, he'd been dumbfounded. Mermaids didn't exist. The way his father died was a rumor, tied to ridiculous urban legends. Asia claiming she'd been thrown overboard and then morphing into a mermaid—none of it was real.

Except the longer he sat in his cabin alone and replayed the events of the last few days, the harder it became to deny that the beautiful, shimmering, purple tail he'd seen had been very much real. And had been attached to Asia.

Oh, and let's not forget his tumultuous, traitorous feelings toward the woman.

The woman who had dived overboard and then disappeared under the sea, never to surface again. That first day, he'd huddled under a blanket, standing next to the railing, constantly scanning the ocean's surface for any sign of her.

He'd spotted a pod of dolphins, but no mermaid. Or human woman.

No one had a clue what he was talking about. There had not been a woman named Asia aboard this ship. The name Asia wasn't on the passenger list.

Butch was the only person who seemed to have any knowledge of what happened, why Conall dove overboard in the first place. Probably, the fact that Butch had sworn off drinking and yet was still determined that mermaids existed, that Asia had, in fact, been on the ship, and no, Conall wasn't crazy, was the only reason Conall even remotely began to doubt his own insistence that the whole thing hadn't happened.

At least, not the way his mind wanted to believe.

It was after that particular conversation that Conall had retreated to his cabin and stayed there until the ship had docked.

Now, with a duffle swung over his shoulder, his hand wrapped around a rolling bag, Conall stepped onto the dock and made his way to firm, solid land. No chance of running into any mermaids there.

As he made his way toward the parking lot, where he was supposed to meet his Uber, a couple of men in Coast Guard uniforms went running in the opposite direction. Mildly curious, like anyone would be, he glanced over his shoulder.

Then did a double take.

The Coast Guard personnel, along with a handful of sailors, were clustered around a woman, who was wrapped in a blanket and otherwise appeared to not be wearing clothes. They were peppering questions at her, and she kept shaking her head and trying to speak, but then someone would speak over her, asking yet another question.

"Asia?"

He hadn't said it very loud, yet she glanced up anyway, and their gazes collided. Her eyes widened, and she shouldered her way out of the group and speed-walked toward him.

He stayed rooted to the pavement, his gaze tracking her movements, his mind trying really, really hard to process the fact that she was here, right in front of him, and she had legs. Beautiful, shapely legs.

Her hair was damp, the water weighing down the curls. Her eyes were huge, full of trepidation.

She came to a stop, clutching the blanket over her breasts.

He scanned her from head to toe. "It's you."

As far as greetings went, it wasn't particularly impressive.

She offered up a watery smile. "It's me." After a pause, she asked, "Can we talk?"

He glanced at the entourage heading their way. "I assume you want to talk without an audience."

"Preferably."

He nodded at the parking lot. "I have an Uber waiting."

"I don't know what that is, but I'm with you."

He'd find it odd that she didn't know what an Uber was if he hadn't allowed himself to finally accept that the woman had the ability to turn into a mermaid. "Let's go."

The cluster of people caught up to them just as the Uber veered toward the curb. They began shouting questions, namely, how had Asia come to be treading water a dozen yards offshore—naked.

Conall mumbled a few words of gratitude that someone had pulled her out of the drink, then he herded her into the vehicle and instructed the driver to get them the hell out of there.

They didn't speak for the short drive to his hotel, although they certainly shared a whole bunch of not very covert glances. Luckily, he was able to check into his room via an app on his phone so they didn't have to endure the questioning stares of the front desk personnel for any longer than it took to hurry through the lobby to the elevator.

And then they were in his room. Asia wandered around, still clutching that blanket around her person, her gaze curious as it touched on the flat-screen television, the view out the window, the bathroom amenities. Herself in the mirror.

Conall flipped open his luggage, searching for something to offer her to wear. He finally pulled out the button-up, long-sleeved dress shirt he'd planned to wear to his interview.

"Here," he said, holding it out to her. "You can put it on in the bathroom, if you want."

Wordlessly, she took the article of clothing and disappeared behind the door. A few moments later, she reappeared. The shirt hung to her knees, and she'd rolled the sleeves up to her wrists.

She was absolutely breathtaking.

He cleared his throat. "Are you hungry? I can order room service."

She chuckled. "I'm always hungry. What's room service?"

Instead of picking up the phone receiver, he dropped onto the edge of the bed. "It's all real, isn't it?"

The smile fell from her face. "Yes."

He stabbed his fingers into his hair and leaped to his feet, striding to the window to look out over the view of the city and the ocean beyond. "I don't know what to think right now."

"Perhaps it would help if I explained."

"Yeah, maybe."

"When I younger, my only dream was to become a sailor. I wanted to captain my own ship someday. But I was a girl, and in the small community I'm from, that wasn't done. It was a foolish fantasy."

"That whole women are bad luck on a ship belief."

She nodded. "Yes. But I refused to let that deter me. I was fifteen when I lied to my mother and told her I was going to visit a friend in the country and instead snuck onto a ship and hid in a storage closet."

"My father's ship." He said the words flatly.

"Yes. And I was caught, of course. Clearly, at fifteen, I was not wily enough to come up with a fail-safe plan to keep myself hidden."

"Butch discovered you."

Her eyes went wide.

"He told me," Conall admitted. "He said he found you and reported you to the captain. To my father."

"I wasn't aware of that part." She tentatively sat on the bed.

Conall nodded. "Butch said my father was furious. One more black mark against him, and he'd lose his ship." Conall dropped his gaze to stare at the designs on the rug. "He wasn't a good man. Even before he threw you overboard. Apparently, his superiors had finally taken notice. He was on probation. He was convinced that admitting he had a stowaway on board—especially a girl—would get his license taken away."

"I remember him saying something about me not ruining it for him, right before he picked me up and bodily threw me over the railing," Asia said.

Conall winced. He wanted to reach out to her, to touch her, to pull her into his arms and hug away all the pain he could hear in her voice.

"Butch told me he tried to report your father, but no one would believe him."

"He told me that, too," Conall admitted. "It was his word against my father's. And no one else had seen you. Even with my father's reputation, without any proof, they couldn't take a drunken man's word over an established ship captain. Especially since there was no body and no reported missing fifteen-year-old girl in the area."

"My mother wouldn't have realized I was missing for another week."

He stared at her legs, recalled with vivid intensity those shimmering purple scales he'd seen.

"I should have drowned, but Galene saved me, turned me into a mermaid."

"Galene?" Conall lifted his gaze to her face.

"She is the first mermaid. She was tossed overboard as well, hundreds of years ago. Poseidon saved her, turned her into a mermaid, and gave her immortality so she could return the favor, over and over again. Although in truth, I don't know how much of a favor it is."

"Why do you say that?"

"It was excruciatingly painful. I essentially died and then became alive again, as part fish."

"But you can turn back into a human."

She shook her head. "Only during the right time of the lunar cycle. And only temporarily."

He fell silent for a moment. That meant she wasn't here for good. He'd thought—hoped—she'd come to tell him she wanted to be with him forever.

"Although I recently found out that Poseidon can do whatever he wants, and if he wants to change a mermaid back to her human self, he can."

"Poseidon?" She'd mentioned the sea god more than once, as a curse or exclamation, like someone else would say "Oh my God."

"Wait. He's real too?"

Asia nodded.

"This is crazy." Except...

She stood, smoothed her hands down the front of his shirt. "I'm sorry for deceiving you."

He swallowed down the lump in his throat. "It's okay. I'm sorry for not believing you."

She smiled a tiny smile. "It's okay."

Silence fell like a stone between them. She stood across the room, fidgeting, curling her toe against the thick carpet, her gaze landing everywhere except on him.

"Um, about Poseidon..." It was still so surreal that he was having a conversation about mermaids and sea gods, like they were real. Oh, because they were. "What did you mean about him doing whatever he wants?"

She twined her fingers, clutching at them until they turned white. "Apparently, the gods are suckers for true love. At least that's what Poseidon says."

"Okay."

She swiftly glanced up. He caught the ruddiness on her cheeks before she dropped her head again, her hair falling like a curtain around her face.

"He offered me the chance to come here, to apologize to you. He's giving us a chance at"—she flapped her hand—"at a happy ending. If we both want it."

"If we both...are you saying you aren't a mermaid anymore?" Was it true? Had she given up her life to be with him? Conall's heart was beating so fast, he was half afraid it would beat right out of his chest.

"Yes. Poseidon altered my gift. Made me human again. If you don't want anything to do with me—which I totally understand if you don't—I'll still be human, and I'll have to figure out what to do with myself, how to survive anyway. I'll just be alone while I do it."

"You won't be alone."

She swiftly glanced up.

"I love you, Asia."

She gasped. Shaking his head, he strode over to her, wrapped her in his arms, pulled her flush against his body.

"I love you," he repeated. "I don't want to live without you."

She stiffened, then stepped out of his grasp. "I cannot procreate. If that changes things..."

"It doesn't. Nothing can change the way I feel about you, Asia."

She collapsed back into his arms, hugging him tightly. "I love you, Conall," she mumbled, her voice muffled against his shirt.

He pressed a kiss to her temple. Suddenly, her lips met his, and his chest swelled as they lingered over the kiss, her fists clenching his shirt, his hands in her hair, holding her close.

In a moment, his shirts, both of them, would be on the floor, and so would his pants, and they'd make love, probably more than once. He'd whisper words of adoration in her ear.

And then they'd begin their life together. Carving a new path.

Together.

"Hey," she said, breaking the kiss. "Can we track down some peanut M&M's? I've never craved something so strongly—except maybe you—in my life."

Conall laughed. And kissed her again. And again.

And yet again. "Of course," he promised.

And then he tugged the shirt over her head.

EPILOGUE

Five Years Later

Asia watched as the child's chunky toddler legs propelled him across the wet sand much faster than she would have expected, given he'd never had this experience before.

He fell forward, landing on his hands and knees, and she held her breath, waiting for him to cry out. Instead, he half crouched, resting on one foot and one knee, and clapped his wet, sandy hands, glancing over his shoulder at his parents, a gleeful grin spreading across his face.

Asia sniffled.

"Are you crying?" Conall asked, sliding his hand up her spine to squeeze the back of her neck.

She swiped at the wetness under her eyes. "I had no idea what to expect."

"For him? Or for us?"

A half laugh, half sob burst through her lips. "Both."

Conall waved at their son, who was busy inspecting a shiny shell, seemingly oblivious to the sea water lapping at his toes. "He's obviously fine. Even more proof that he is nothing more than a product of our love."

"I didn't think I would ever bear children."

Conall kissed the top of her head. "Like I said, a product of our love. And we'll raise him to respect the sea. To respect women." He glanced out over the vast ocean. "To respect the gods."

"Are you suggesting we tell him? About what happened to your father? What I was?"

The crashing of waves, the screech of seagulls, the far-off bellow of a ship's horn filled the gap while she waited for his answer.

"I don't know," he finally said, his gaze never leaving the water. "We'll figure it out when it's time." He finally turned to smile at her. "Together."

"Always together," she agreed, her heart swelling. With love. With happiness. With pride. They'd both come so far. From burning with desire for revenge and answers to finding peace. Together.

Little Kai abruptly stood and started toddling into the shallow waves, and Asia broke free of Conall's embrace to chase after him. By the time she caught him, he'd drenched himself and she was ankle deep in ocean water.

It hadn't felt as shocking as she'd expected it to, even though this was the first time she'd dared to touch the sea since Poseidon had given her the choice to return to her human form.

She and Conall had moved to Colorado, both entirely content to live their lives locked by land. Discovering she was pregnant with Kai three years ago had taken them both by surprise, but they'd embraced the new twist in their love story.

It was her job that had brought them to the seashore today. She was an artist, her specialty vivid underwater landscapes unlike anything any human had ever seen. A client based here in Maine had offered to fly her and her family out so she could be there when they opened an exhibit of her work.

It was Conall who suggested they bring Kai down to the beach. Everyone should dip their toes into the surf at least once in their life, right?

She swept Kai into her arms and rested him on her hip, laughing as he pressed his sand-covered, wet hand to her dress. Movement caught her eye, and she lifted her gaze and then gasped.

"Kai, look! A pod of dolphins!" She pointed at the cluster mammals but quickly pulled her arm back and pressed her palm to her chest.

There was a man out there, swimming with the dolphins.

She knew, instantly, that he wasn't human.

She felt Conall's warmth a scant moment before his arm slipped around her waist and pulled her into his side.

"Is that...?" he asked.

She nodded, still staring. "I think so."

The dolphins leaped and twisted and twirled all around the man, who treaded water and appeared to be watching them. And then all but one of the dolphins disappeared below the surface.

The man placed one hand on the animal's dorsal fin and lifted the other as if—

"He's waving," Conall noted.

After a moment's hesitation, Asia lifted her arm and waved back. With a nod, the man and dolphin dove beneath the sea.

Asia glanced up at Conall, who was steadily watching her.

"I think Poseidon just stopped by to check on us."

Conall smiled. "And I think he liked what he saw."

"Ahoy, matey!"

A fit man who looked like a very healthy fifty-year-old jogged toward them, one arm raised in greeting.

"Butch?" Conall continued staring at the man even after he came to a halt a few feet away. "Is that really you?"

"Hey, Conall. Asia. You both look great. And who is this little guy?" He waggled his fingers at Kai, who smiled and then buried his face against Asia's chest.

"This is our son, Kai," she said. "And speaking of looking great…"

Butch patted his flat stomach and rocked back on his heels. "Yeah, I had an epiphany after that fateful trip across the Atlantic five years ago. Decided enjoying this life was better than chasing after myths."

Asia arched her brows. Myths? But he'd seen her in her mermaid form. Twice.

"Was that who I think it was, out there with the dolphins?" he asked with a nod toward the ocean.

Asia canted her head. "You just said it was a myth."

Butch chuckled. "Everybody else believes mermaids are a myth is what I meant. But I know. Just like I knew, or at least had a very strong suspicion, that the artist whose work is about to go on display at the gallery next to my museum had some firsthand experience with those underwater scenes she painted. Your work is beautiful, by the way."

Asia's cheeks heated. "Thank you."

"Your museum?" Conall asked.

Butch's chest puffed out. "Yep. Butch's Museum of Maritime Legends and Myths. I started it as a hobby, but it's become quite the lucrative tourist attraction. As many people who don't believe, there are twice as many who want to."

Asia felt her eyes widen. "Are you giving away all our—their —secrets?"

Butch quickly shook his head. "Not at all. It's very much a vaude-ville or circus situation. You know, eating fire, the snake charmer, that sort of thing. Except with mermaids and sea gods."

"Snake," Kai shouted. They all laughed.

"Are you in town for the exhibit opening?" Butch asked.

"I am," Asia said.

"Will you stop by the museum before you leave again?"

"Of course," she and Conall said at the same time.

Butch grinned. "I'd better get back. Talk to you all later. Nice to meet you, Kai."

He made it half a dozen steps before turning back to face them.

"I'm glad Poseidon gave you the chance at your happily ever after," he said with a nod before hurrying off down the beach.

Conall gave Asia's waist a squeeze. "I'm glad he did too."

She kissed his cheek. "Me too."

THE END

SILVER SEAS

LOUSIA BACIO

CHAPTER ONE: THE ENDING FIRST

You ever hear the saying that you're in too deep? Yeah, unfortunately that was her right now. The first punch caught her on the chin, snapping her head to the side. Her teeth ground and the taste of blood tinged against her tongue.

She didn't believe in fairies, or mermaids or a white knight who'd ride up on his horse to save her. She'd married her supposed knight and look where she'd ended up: wrists and ankles tied and on a stinking boat with a busted lip.

The boat chugged across the ocean. Archie asked her to go out for a night tour, and then he knocked her the hell out. When she came to, he'd wrapped rope around her legs and bound her arms behind her back. Her joints screamed in pain.

"Asshole," she spat at him over the churning of the engine. "Let me go."

"I shoulda saved some rope for your mouth," he muttered, piloting the small craft.

The waves swelled and she rocked backward. Unable to brace her body with her hands, she tumbled onto her back, knocking her head against the damp wood.

"Whoops. Sorry about that," Archie laughed. "Didn't mean to hurt you."

"Listen, hon," her words sounded slurred even to herself. The cold and the pain gnawed away at her pride. "It's not too late. You don't have to do this. Whatever you want. I'll do it."

She gazed out in the direction where she thought land lay, and the shoreline wasn't even a glimmer in the horizon. Clouds shrouded the moon and the further out they went, the more hope slipped away.

"See, that's where you're wrong—again. I do need to do this. I'm tired of listening to you whine. Even the sound of your voice puts me on edge."

He wasn't always like this, her Archie. But how he wasn't didn't matter for shit right now. It's how he treated her, and about now it seemed like the relationship was over. Dead. As dead as she'd be as soon as they stopped.

He killed the engine. "Well looks like this is it." He stood and set the boat to rocking.

"Looks like what?" Somehow, she righted herself, and braced her elbows against the splintered wood.

"Your final resting place." He tsked, a sound that always put her nerves on edge. As if she'd done something wrong. It meant she'd displeased him and what came next, she always regretted. Regretted every believing his lying promises, regretted hooking up with his cheating ass and regretted living. It wasn't a way to live and hell if it wasn't a way to die.

"Wait." She made eye contact as he grabbed hold of the ropes wrapped around her arms. "I thought you loved me. I thought we were going to spend forever together."

"Yeah," he shrugged. "That's what I thought, too, but hell ... I was wrong."

With those words of wisdom, he hefted her up, the muscles in his biceps straining, the scent of sausage and onions wafted over her nose, threating to suffocate her in his stink. She'd seen enough movies to know some self-defense, and she rammed her head forward, slamming her forehead into his nose.

"Fuckin' bitch!" Blood spurted, and he defensively covered his face. A moment of achievement flared. There was a possibility of hope, of potential for escape, of survival. She'd fought back, and then he pushed her overboard.

The cold shocked her into complete consciousness. Mouth open to scream, the water closed over her fast, filling her throat, blinding her eyes. She gasped, only to draw in more salty liquid. It invaded her lungs. She twisted her body, convulsing, trying to free herself, but somehow now was his time to succeed in something—tying knots.

Her lungs ached and her body spasmed from lack of oxygen. She tried to fight, but nature fought harder. On a regular day, she swam enough to stay afloat but with the weight of waves crashing over her, there wasn't much left to do. Legs bound, she jackknifed upward, swimming like she imagined a mermaid would and propelled her body upward. Every time she made her way to the surface and gulped some air, he waited, pushing her back down.

She went under again and somehow returned to the surface. In her last glimpse, the boat retreated to shore, stranding her in the middle of the Atlantic, or close enough where she had no possibility of rescue.

A deep sense of hopelessness caved in her resolve, and she gave into the watery death. In her last moments of consciousness, a sweet song filled her mind. It was a lullaby filled with loss and hope and love. Soft hands cradled her body and she sank down-down-down. She didn't know if she was imagining it or a mysterious spirit guided her physical corpse, but it offered a reassuring presence.

The world went dark. There was no moment of seeing the light or afterlife. She didn't get a vision any of the friends or family who'd passed before. Simply she was there one moment, and then next gone.

· · ·

UNTIL SHE RETURNED. If dying was agony, coming back to life was even more so. The sky darkened and lightning cut across the nightmare water landscape. She now understood the saying of a "wet grave." The last memory she had was sinking to the bottom of the sea. How now did she end up aware and alive?

He rose from the depths, fury and wind whipping his beard and shoulder-length hair. His shoulders and chest had been chiseled over the years of immortality. She didn't know how she knew so much about him, but her DNA cringed. He was a God, not meant for this world. His eyes glowed a liquid sunshine, and he raised his golden specter and gestured toward her. A flash of light cut from its most top point toward her, and she shielded her face in the crook of her arm. Like when Archie railed against her, it was instinctive but not effective.

Pain radiated from where the surge struck her and spiraled through her body. Her chest seized and she gulped for air. A ragged wheeze squeezed through her air passages and the cascading tremors flexed, leaving cramps in its wake. If she wasn't already dead – because certainly she was in hell right now – she wished for it. Non-existence would be better than living like this shell of pain.

"It's all right," a woman stroked her arm. "It'll pass soon enough, and then you'll be born again, refreshed."

Eyes blinded, she couldn't see who touched her—only hear the soft murmurs. Born through the fires of hell or in this case the depths of the ocean, she didn't care where she ended up, as long as she soon came through other side. Just when she thought it was over, the fire localized in her legs. She twisted, convulsing and her legs bound together tighter than the ropes her evil ex wrapped her. Her ankles turned out and webbing sewed between each toe and her fingers. Sight returned, and she held her hands out before her, unbelieving in what she was seeing. How was she turning into a creature more made for the sea than the land?

She flailed in the water. Her lungs expanded, and she found relief. Oxygen flowed through her body. The ties that bound loosened, and she wiggled for freedom of movement. First, her arms were free and she reached downward, struggling with the ropes around her legs. Her fingertips brushed over a scaly surface, and she repelled. Her mind was unable to comprehend. What was down in the deep with her?

Finally, she fully untwisted the material and attempted to kick her feet, only to be meet with a different resistance. It was as if her legs had been permanently seamed together into one muscular limb ending in a fin.

What had he done to her? She lost consciousness again.

"Is she going to be all right?" A voice tugged at her psyche.

"The change is different for every being," a gentle voice guided her into consciousness. "It'll do no good to push too fast."

"But what if she doesn't wake up."

"They always do," a deep voice reassured. "And when she does, we'll be ready for her."

CHAPTER TWO: A NEW BEGINNING

Not everyone got saved. Some were as evil as those who dumped them overboard. Their bodies sunk as surely as their souls. There was something about this one that fueled the sirens' song — her body harbored a beacon of light that called to Jewel and the others.

Chitter from the sea flowed through the dark waters, and she swam toward the point where the raucous boat anchored. If there was a way to stop the violence from happening, Jewel would. But at this moment, fate had been determined and everything that came before for this young woman led to now. The events about to happen changed the course of her future.

A murmur cascaded through the sea folk as Poseidon flowed through. He only surfaced at special occasions. And while he had abilities many only guessed at, he was selective in his choices.

A splash sent shockwaves through the waters, and she foundered, limbs scrambling for safety. Within her binds, though, she didn't have much freedom of movement. Her blonde hair streamed through the water, creating a halo-like effect circling her body. A spread of pink pulsed in a circle around her. Blood. Even though the Pod ruled this area, other predators would be drawn to her essence.

Above her, a dark figure leaned over the side of the boat. Him. Her murderer. Jewel memorized his features. Now wasn't the time. They never wanted to draw so much attention to the underground lairs. But one day, someday. They would meet again.

As he gazed over the waters, watching her body sink, he met her sight and stumbled backward. *Marked.*

"I will sponsor her." The words came forth from her mouth before she'd fully thought it through. What was she doing? In all her years in the sea, she'd never taken in a fledgling.

Jewel tended to stick to herself. Others had a way of disappointing her. If she didn't get too involved, then she wouldn't feel betrayed. The way this new member had been discarded called to her for some reason, like she possessed a beacon of hope despite what the world had dished her. Jewel had given up her hope for humanity and in particular men long ago.

Poseidon's keen eyes turned toward her, evaluating her features and motives, taking in every nuance. He titled his head. "It shall be. You will be responsible for her care, and for teaching her our ways and rules."

He wrapped the woman with his embrace, and her body convulsed. Even after all these years, Jewel remembered that pain of humanity leaving her physical being and transforming into the underwater creature.

She ran her tongue over her lower lip, wincing at the quick shock of pain. If she hurt, it at least meant she was still alive, right? Slowly, she became more aware of her surroundings – her very wet ones. She blinked her eyes, trying to reconcile what she previously knew of the world compared to what lay before her. She took in the exchange between the man and woman before her, except those descriptions were not correct.

His massive chest drew her attention. Broad shoulders stretched beyond any she'd seen before, more than rivaling a romance hero on the cover of a quality paperback. Silver fox hair swirled in curls around his head, and he clasped a golden specter in one hand. Honestly, he looked like a god, which made her question her continued existence even more. Did what she imagined earlier really transpire? It seemed more like a hallucination.

A tall woman with long, blue-black hair swam forward. The top half of her body was that of a curvaceous female, and the bottom half was a mermaid. "I volunteer to sponsor her."

More discussion passed between them, but it was impossible to catch every word. She blinked in and out of consciousness and spasms radiated through her body.

"Are you sure of this?" the underwater leader asked. "It's not a small undertaking and you haven't done so in the past."

"Times change, and this one needs protection."

His scrutiny of the female made her reevaluate her. The striking mermaid swam toward her. The woman's smile combined a mixture of excitement with trepidation.

"Thank you." She knew she must have looked wide-eyed at their surroundings. The entire situation may be a hallucination brought on by the beating and near-drowning incident. Near?

"I don't know what to think of all this..." She held out her hands. Small webs grew between her fingers. "I don't even know how I ended up here. I mean I remember falling into the water and then waking up here. But what happened in the between. Am I dead?"

"Perfectly normal questions. We all have them. Let's get you settled first and then we can worry about everything else. I am Jewel. What is your name?"

She opened her mouth to respond, and nothing came out. The place in her mind where the recall of something as simple as her name should reside remained empty, out of her reach. "I don't know."

Jewel didn't seem as surprised at this knowledge. She squeezed her hand. "That's all right. Not everyone remembers the before after the transition. For now, why don't we call you 'Lumina.'"

"Lumina." The word felt magical on her tongue, like it was meant to be. Easily, she tread water, her muscular tail undulating back and forth. "My name is Lumina. How the hell did I get a fish tail, and who is he?"

"Poseidon, God of the Sea, Creator of the Pod, Savior. He's the one who granted you this new life as a mermaid. I can't wait to see what type of power you possess."

"I have powers? I don't feel any different, well except for these additions." She twisted her body, bringing her bottom portion of tail and fins upward. The sensation felt similar to sack races as a child, when their feet were tied together and they had to move in unison.

"All mermaids have some power," a merman with shaggy brown hair and mesmerizing blue eyes approached. Like Poseidon and most of the mermaids, his top half was nude. "I'm Liam."

"There are male merfolk," Lumina stumbled on her words. "I thought all Sirens were female." Something about seeing Liam unnerved her. She didn't have to dig deep into her psyche to connect that she hadn't the most positive experiences with men her entire life.

"It's all right," a slender female with wavy blonde hair placed her hand on Liam's muscular arm. "We come in all genders. The Sirens are female and known for their alluring singing. I'm Galene. Welcome to the Pod. We mean you no harm."

"I'm sorry. It's all a bit much." Lumina processed all the new information and sensory details. "When will I discover this power, and what is yours?"

From all the merfolk surrounding her, Lumina was most drawn to Jewel. Perhaps there was a reason they were tethered.

A slight current picked up strands of Lumina's hair. It swirled around her head in a playful dance. With one hand, she slapped it down.

"Have you heard of the nor'easter sailors complain about?" Jewel asked. "That's me. My powers control some of the winds of the ocean. I'm the Northeastern influencer."

"You're kidding me? You're such a badass!" She knocked her fist against Jewel's shoulder. "And to think, you're my mentor."

The woman glanced at her shoulder and then at her like she didn't understand the connection. "Despite what you may think, it doesn't always come in handy."

Lumina retreated, second-guessing what she knew. Not everyone came from the same background and may not react in the manner expected. She looked toward the others surrounding them. Galene placed her hand in the crook of Liam's elbow. Body language completely understood. The others did not seem interested in engaging.

"While we appreciate the welcoming committee," Jewel interjected, moving closer to her side. "It might be a good idea to give my girl here a bit of space. It's been a day and a night and she's newly transitioned."

For the briefest moment, Lumina swore that Galene's green eyes flashed a warning. Just as quick, they returned to normal. "Understood," she bowed slightly. "When you are ready, we can 'catch up,' as they say."

"As long as I'm not the 'catch of the day,'" Lumina said.

The others looked at her for a few beats, and then laughed. She just might fit in this new realm after all.

CHAPTER THREE: UNDER THE SEA

From above, the spires of the dwellings resembled a natural underwater landscape. As they drew nearer, Lumina made out what appeared to be an entire aquatic metropolis and individual entranceways. A sense of wonder filled her.

"It's like a complete under-the-sea city. I don't understand. How do these stay hidden?" Wouldn't any deep diver be able to discover the realm? She might not have the resources but surely others did.

"The Pod is guarded to keep outsiders, well out. Think of it like a giant forcefield that keeps our world hidden. Only those with the abilities can truly see," Jewel explained, squeezing her hand. "Part of your transformation gives you the ability to do more than swim and breathe underwater. It lets you live here."

She'd seen fictional accounts of what underwater kingdoms looked like. The aquatic life. As a child, she liked to daydream about running away, escaping from everyday life and becoming somebody else. As an adult, she learned it wasn't possible. She'd made her bed and had to lay in it. Or die in it.

This wet wonderland exceeded every fantasy. "Like magic." Her voice came out in hushed tones, as if she was a child telling the ultimate secret.

The sky–for lack of a better description it's how she thought of the open waters above them–sparkled with a web of colors like they inhabited a rainbow, but only the portion of blues and greens.

"You can say that." Jewel hesitated outside the door of one home. "Some may say we're blessed. Others that we're cursed. The truth lies somewhere between."

With her palm pressed against an outside censor, Jewel opened the entry. It didn't swing inward or outward like a traditional on-land building but disappeared into a shimmering illusion like it never existed.

She guided Lumina inside the dwelling and the door reappeared. Lumina reached out to touch the surface. Was it real? Would it keep others out? As her fingers neared the entrance, a buzzing similar to electricity crackled. She couldn't push through, though. It felt like real material: solid.

"Some things worked differently here," Jewel laughed. "Most of us take it for granted. If you ever have questions, people will know you're new. Remind me to program to entranceway to allow you in."

"When? Should we do that now? I mean, I wouldn't want to forget…" Panic set in and she flashed to moments when she'd been locked out of her residence, either by accident or on purpose.

"We're in for the night," she brushed it off. "It's complicated and not. The first time you're locked out, you'll remember. I'm teasing. Come here."

The walls were painted a deep purple in contrast to the aquatic themes. It resembled the streaks in Jewel's hair, which were only noticeable in the perfect lighting. She pressed some sort of code into a side panel, and another compartment opened. "Place your hand on that."

Lumina did as asked and the same buzzing feature happened, sending vibrations up her arm and into her body. "Does it read my fingerprints, like a palm reader?"

"More than that. It's biometrics. Don't ask me how it works. I just know it does." A beep resonated and the pulse of light stopped. "There. It's done."

That sense of anxiety evaporated. Nothing of this situation resembled ones of the past. She should have been freaking out from being turned into a mermaid but that didn't happen. Instead, it felt like a new chance at life.

"Since I basically sponsored you, I'm now responsible for you," Jewel explained solemnly. "I'll be here to help you get through the process."

"Thank you. Thank you for saving my life."

A blush spread across the other mermaid's cheeks. "You're welcome. Ultimately, you have Poseidon to thank. Unless it's something big, though, we don't see him much."

"Oh, I wouldn't expect. I mean, I'm just thankful."

"Let's hope you keep that feeling. Time to get you settled. As you might have noticed, most of the merfolk choose not to clothe the upper half of their bodies, unless it's for a special occasion or event. I have some coverings in the drawer over there if you prefer."

Lumina glanced at her chest. She never was overly stacked and didn't need extra support. It felt good to be comfortable in her own skin. "I think I'll go au naturel."

"I OVERHEARD a bit of what you were talking about back there with Poseidon," Lumina said. "How you've never taken in anyone before. Why me?"

"Sometimes you don't know, but you just know," Jewel replied, busying herself by putting odd things away and gathering bedding from a cupboard. Despite having a conversation, she kept her back turned and didn't make eye contact. She didn't want to explain how she'd been drawn to the woman like she was an intended mate.

"What you're saying is that with me, you knew?"

The teasing tone drew her attention, and she turned around. "Don't make me regret it."

Already, it was hard to imagine the mermaid in front of her being the victim of the heinous crime only hours ago. The helplessness of the woman's cries piercing the night and through the depths of the water would have haunted Jewel if she hadn't stepped in. It's not like if she hadn't, no one else would have. Poseidon already marked Lumina for saving. He made those decisions, unless brought a special circumstance and the merfolk pleaded their case for an exception.

Normally that only happened to members of the Pod with a perspective mate when they knew they wanted to be together but inter-species challenges kept them apart. That meant, it sucked to be in a romantic relationship if one was human and the other a merfolk.

Lumina rested on the edge of the chair, fascinatingly flexing the tips of her fins. First one flicked downward and the other turned up. Jewel considered turning on some music for accompaniment.

"It'll become more natural over time," she tried to make her ward feel better. *Goddess. What had she done? Ward.* She was responsible for the well-being of the young mermaid. What if she corrupted her in some way, polluted her like those who dumped trash in the ocean? Maybe she made the wrong choice, and another household would better suit her.

"Hey, slow down there." Lumina placed her hand on Jewel shoulder. "It's like I can read the emotions streaming off you like a pot of crawfish boiling over. Set the lid askew, let off a little steam and let it simmer."

The gentlest touch on her shoulder imparted a sense of peace. That everything might be all right and that the world won't end if she didn't do something right at this moment.

Jewel drew oxygen in, taking a mindful approach to the tasks at hand: Make the bed. Obviously, it wasn't a life-and-death situation.

They could do that simple objective. She finished tucking in the bottom sheet, grabbed the top sheet—a creamy turquoise—and billowed out the silky material. Over the top, Lumina watched her, her eyes taking everything in. A mere glance felt like she was looking directly into Jewel's soul, and they connected. She'd done right bringing her home.

"Why don't I help you with that." Lumina moved to the opposite side of the bed, pulling the sheet tight and tucking the material under the corner of the mattress. As she smoothed out a few wrinkles with her delicate hands, her small breasts with their pale pink tips swayed.

Jewel averted her gaze. It wasn't right to sexualize the newcomer so soon after her arrival. She needed to adjust to the new surroundings. On that note, she hadn't planned the cohabitating aspect of having a roommate.

"Hopefully you don't mind I only have the one bed," she admitted. "I didn't think through that part when I offered to take you in. But there should be room enough for both of us."

"It'll be fine. I trust you."

If Jewel really thought about it, so much had happened without Lumina's consent. First, she'd been attacked, and then turned into another creature, reborn but cursed to the underwater life. She even lost her name. What if she didn't want to become a mermaid? She wasn't given a choice. The temporary moment of peace fled as her mind returned to the attack.

What if that asshole who hurt Lumina returned? She didn't deserve that shit. No one did. Odds were, just because he'd dumped her body over the side of the boat didn't mean his behavior was going to stop. He'd find another victim. Men like him needed to be taught a lesson.

"You know, if we ever capture him, we can chain him up and hold him hostage — unless any of the Pod may want to eat him."

"Eat him?" Lumina stilled.

Obviously, she'd opened her mouth too fast and said too much.

Here she was worrying about the woman's choice being taken away and acclimating to a new environment and then she had to jump straight to devouring that nasty piece of work.

"Archie would leave a bad taste in people's mouths. A guaranteed case of indigestion, I promise you." Evidentially, Lumina followed the jump in conversation. The smile that spread across her mouth reflected in her eyes. "You should see the junk he ate. He'd pass up anything healthy I cooked at home and sneak all this greasy, gloopy takeout. It's a wonder it didn't kill him."

"I have to admit, some inhabitants like to partake in the flesh of the evil." Jewel grinned in a way that she knew showed off her sharp teeth. She ran the tip of her tongue over one. "Think of them like sea vampires who deal justice of another sort out to those who don't deserve to live."

CHAPTER FOUR: SIREN TALES

Lumina woke very much aware of the presence in the bed next to her. When she slept next to Archie, she always felt like she had to not take up space and be smaller, afraid of drawing unwanted attention or making him angry. Even with all the things said last night, she still felt more comfortable with Jewel. She had to be teasing, right? The inhabitants of the Pod wouldn't eat her ex-boyfriend? And seriously, why would she care if he disappeared after how he treated her. He might not have killed her outright, but he left her for dead.

Jewel murmured in her sleep. She shifted her body, curling toward Lumina. Her arm wrapped over her shoulder and her fingers splayed over the back of her neck. The sensation of the scales of her lower half brushing against Lumina's tail elicited a new sensation—one she hadn't experienced before. They moved together, rubbing, interlocking. It was sensually intimate and yet not.

She drifted in a semi-awake state, enjoying the sense of belonging and safety. The warmth and luxuriousness of the bedsheets combined with the waves of acceptance of the water sprite embracing her. She could easily get used to this feeling.

The moment Jewel came awake, Lumina sensed it. The other woman froze as if too aware of the delicate situation.

"Morning," Lumina said, breaking the ice and hopefully dispelling any awkwardness between them.

"I'm sorry. I didn't mean to..." Jewel pushed away. "I must have unconsciously ..."

She didn't complete either comment, but the meaning was obvious. "It's fine. I seem to be saying that a lot. But really, I was enjoying your closeness."

"Same. Maybe a little too much."

Lumina trailed her fingers across the woman's cheek. Jewel closed her eyes and tilted into her touch. "You know my story. Tell me about you. How did you get here? Or should I also ask, when did you get here?"

A shadow passed over Jewel's features, etching her expression into one of unconcern. "Not much to say there. You know the obvious. Some jerk bound me up and tossed me over the side. It's how we all got here."

"If you're not ready to tell me now, that's all right. I can wait, and I'll be here when you're ready. How about the when, though? How long have you lived with the Pod?"

"I'll give you one hint, back then things were much more *groovy*. We had free love that didn't always come free. It came with a price."

Her meaning was all too clear. "You've been here since the Sixties?"

She held up her index finger. "One question, and I answered. You interpret that as you will."

When it became clear Jewel didn't plan on offering any other information, they got ready for the day. Sunlight did bizarre things when you lived deep under the sea. If you were closer to the surface, rays streamed through the water. The Pod possessed its own system that replicated the world above to a certain extent. A huge sun didn't hang above, but as the morning progressed, it grew lighter. It reminded Lumina of visiting Las Vegas and the enclosed shopping areas, except those stayed daylight more often than regular hours and pumped in oxygen in order to keep visitors alert. The Pod more than likely did it to make who lived in the enclosure more comfortable.

Jewel offered a tour along a pathway marked by gems of all sizes and colors. They swam, side by side. Turning into a mermaid should be harder than it was, like a learning curve of skills. Maybe it was the whole being reborn aspect. The new environment invigorated Lumina. She stopped to look closer at some of the stones.

"Where did all these gems come from? They're not natural to the area, are they?" She picked up a few, not much bigger than a dime.

Jewel gave the stones in her hand a passing glance. "Adventures. When members of the Pod go on land or explore somewhere new, they bring them back, add them to our collection. Sometimes they act as a reminder of where we came from."

Some people collected rocks as memories, and some used them to channel energy. Before this moment, Lumina hadn't been drawn to the pastime but something about these gems called to her. A purple one pulsed with power that somehow connected with Jewel. In her mind, she saw it as a symbol of something the other mermaid needed.

She transferred the other stones to her left hand and closed her fist over the hard surface. A pulse of fusion streamed through her body and into the stone.

"What the?" It was as if energy from the universe channeled through her into the material she held. When Lumina opened her eyes, Jewel stared at her. "Why are you looking at me like that?"

"You glowed!" She swept her hands up and down through the water. "This sparkling light emanated from your entire body like some sort of beacon. It was beautiful. What happened?"

"I don't know. One moment I was drawn to this rock and thinking about you and the next. Pow!"

She opened her hand, and the amethyst glowed like it possessed an internal light source. Purple sonic waves pulsed toward Jewel. "I think it's meant for you."

Tentatively, Jewel reached out and her flingers slipped over the rock. Light funneled from the tips of her fingers up her arm and then dissipated into her body.

"How did you know?" Jewel gasped.

"I didn't. Not consciously. It called to me and I thought of you." Lumina studied her friend more closely. "What is it? What do you feel?"

"A sense of connectedness, of knowing. Of having every question I've ever wondered about answered. Peace, happiness, quiet. That's your gift, being able to give someone else what they need the most."

"Quiet?" She was granted one special gift in this life of a mermaid, and she gave someone 'peace and quiet.' She scoffed at the randomness. "As if quiet will do me well in a battle. As if quiet will slay our enemies or protect my love. Why do others get to control the tides and encourage growth among the sea plants and me? Hey, here's a pretty rock for you."

"Oh, stop it. Don't denounce yourself. You never know when your gift will be needed. In that moment it will be the most perfect thing ever."

CHAPTER FIVE: IT TAKES AN UNDERWATER VILLAGE

Around the bend, the pathway opened into a courtyard where several inhabitants gathered. As they passed by, each acknowledged Jewel and averted eye contact with Lumina.

"Did I say or do something wrong?" she asked.

"It's not you, it's them," Jewel explained. "Most are wary when someone new joins the Pod. There's always a question of if it will affect the rankings or status, or how it'll change the group dynamic. Admittedly, she'd done the same thing in the past.

Two mermaids snickered as they approached. Marilyn with her platinum blond hair slicked back in a tight bun raised her voice. "I fully suggested splitting up the Pod into a new group if we got any more newcomers." She angled her body away from them and leaned in to finish her catty comment.

"As if anyone would choose to go with you." Jewel flicked sediment with her fin, sending it shooting their way.

"Ewww. You deserve to be with the new mer-girl!"

Beside her, Lumina stiffened and the corners of her eyes crinkled. "They're not worth it," she said, continuing to swim ahead.

"But you are." For someone who prided herself in not caring, suddenly Jewel did more than ever before. "You want to know what's different about her? She cares."

Anger fueled Jewel's rant. She gazed at the odd group of merpeople in a circle. She'd lived in this community for a long time. Some had come before her and some after.

"Girl, you know we care," Marquez, a mermaid with a thick scar zigzagging across their cheek, snapped a piece of seaweed between their sharp teeth. When they smiled, green glops clung in clusters. "If anyone comes at you, we got your back. She's a little new."

"And I'd have yours, Marky. But Lumina asked me about my life before, and she really listened to me. Most of you never ask."

She let her statement float in the flotsam, mixing with the debris. "By the way, you got seaweed stuck right here." She indicated the spot between her front teeth.

"That's because no one wants to think of the before," said Lacy, a petite redhead mermaid with haunting hazel eyes. "Our lives start new here."

Jewel nodded. "I get that. But sometimes talking about the before truly helps let it go. We don't have to completely erase who we once were. We must take back our lives, and that's what Lumina's taught me in such a short amount of time. Think about it."

On that note, she left the others and returned to Lumina's side, taking her hand. "I'm sorry they were such jerks. It's not always like that. It'll get better once they get to know you."

"I understand. I wouldn't be so open with a stranger, especially considering the background most of them have. I won't take it personally."

The way she brushed off the negative comments and actions was a total defensive mechanism. Sometimes it worked in a positive manner and other times as a disadvantage. It depended upon if she was shutting off reality in the process.

"You shouldn't," Jewel said. "I've got one more spot to show you before we head back home."

"I'm up for it."

On the far borders of the Pod's territory, the two mermaids surfaced. Jewel timed it to hit right when it got dark, figuring Lumina could take in the full effect of living in her new realm.

"The last time you saw this view was probably not under the best circumstances." Jewel wrapped her arms around the other woman from behind, guiding her vision toward the shoreline. One by one like dots on a gameboard lighting up, the city's glow popped up. "I know it's so vastly different where we live. But really, we're not that far away from where you came from."

"Oh, it's magnificent," Lumina said. "You don't know how often I walked along the pathways, gazing out at the sea and wondering what lay beyond the breaking waves."

She rested her head against Jewel's chest and the warmth from the night sky bleed into them both. The waters in the Atlantic were warmer this time of year than in the Pacific, and their body temperatures ran colder anyway. The atmosphere around the Pod's area regulated their heat. Out here, they were open to the natural elements.

Jewel pressed her lips against the seam of Lumina's neck. She tasted salty like the ocean but a stronger, headier scent all her own teased her. The other woman moaned in her arms, tilting her head and claiming Jewel's mouth. Her lips were soft and welcoming. It had been so many years since she'd kissed another that she quickly got lost in the sensation.

As one, they rotated their bodies to face each other. "You have the most delicate features," Jewel twined the fingers of her right hand through Lumina's hair and ground her body against the other mermaid's tail. The scales crackled in friction as they moved side to side.

"Why does that feel so good?" Lumina asked.

"The more sensitive parts of our sexual organs may be covered, but they still exist beneath the surface," she explained. "We only need to delve a little deeper and increase the friction to make it feel even better."

"Tell me this feeling has something to do with who I'm with and it's not just physical," Lumina asked, "because it's never been like this for me before. Granted, I've always been with men until now, and it's been more about what I can give rather than what I get. With you, though, it's more than that."

"I'm not the best measurement," Jewel said. "I don't have a vast amount of experience either. What I feel with you is special, and we're meant to be together. I've known it since the moment I saw you."

FOR SOMEONE who'd been in multiple destructive relationships, Jewel's words might have sent warning signs—red flags—about the deterministic nature of their connection. But in this case, she didn't. Lumina considered the source. Jewel had only been supportive during their short time together.

Softly, she kissed her, being in the moment. The current swayed their bodies, and they moved in unison. "Forget what I said about the view. You are magnificent," Lumina said. "A true gift."

What came next was going to be hard to say, but for her own sake, she needed to be honest. "I'd like to wait a little bit until we take this any further. I rush into things too quickly, and this time I want to do it right."

"Wise actions from a wise woman." Jewel caressed Lumina's arm. "We have all the time in the sea. One more thing: our ability to shift is based upon the lunar cycles. If we wait until then, we'll have our full human bodies."

A more even physical playing ground for Lumina. "It's a date."

CHAPTER SIX: SENSUAL CRAVINGS

A silver hue slicked over the surface of the sea. She watched the dancing waves, undulating and drawing the viewer into their mysteries. A unison of humming began, weaving together a tapestry of song. As the weeks together passed, the more her desire to be with Jewel flared.

Lumina flicked her tail fins, sending streams of color through the water. The moon shined high in the sky, casting a warm kiss over the ocean. On the dock, Jewel stretched her legs out, wiggling her toes.

"Come join me. It's only this time of the month that we change back into our human forms," she explained. "If there's anything you want to do on ground or anyone you want to see."

She shook her head. Really, she had no one who'd really miss her. No one she cared to see. At one time, she had a handful of friends but after a few years with Archie, they gave up on her. Not that she blamed them. They tried but she had honestly given up on herself, too.

He'd isolated her, but she let him.

"I don't think there's anything I want from the city. Too many bad memories right now."

A darkness passed over Jewel's eyes like clouds had suddenly blocked the moon. But it still hung full in the sky. Breathing the fresh air didn't really feel any different now than being beneath the surface.

Jewel slipped back into the water, staying in her human form. "I'm sorry you went through that. You didn't deserve it, and when you're ready, I can help you take care of him, too."

Her meaning sent a chill through her body, and it wasn't all bad. "You've alluded to that before. You'd do that?"

Her question came out hushed, barely a whisper—although who was she afraid of hearing them? It's not like any of the merpeople cast blame.

"No question."

She swam the few arm lengths between us. Her full breasts rose in the water, and Lumina longed to touch her, to feel the softness of her skin. The growing attraction for the mermaid roared. Something about the closeness of Jewel—after dying, being reborn and simply the amazing being she was combined to create this craving.

"Why are you staring at me like that?" She asked in a tone hinting at words and meaning unspoken between them.

A flush burned across her cheeks and over her ears. Thankfully, it wasn't light enough for her to tell. "You're beautiful." Lumina dropped her gaze down to the other woman's breasts again and quickly back to her eyes.

"Do you like these?" Jewel cupped the undersides of her chest and lifted them— rivulets of water trailed across her skin and her dark nipples pebbled.

"Yes." Anything more than the admission stuck in her throat.

"You can touch me if you like. I mean, I'd like that."

"I haven't... aside from before with you, I haven't been with a woman before. Until now, I've only dated and slept with men."

"And how'd that work out for you?" She cocked one eyebrow and a giggle escaped from her mouth, and then another until they were both laughing hysterically.

"Pretty shitty." Lumina admitted. There was no reason not to accept the offering before her. She'd spent the past few weeks evaluating her feelings. It wasn't an impetuous act.

"Maybe you need to try something new."

"The opportunity never came up—some for more obvious reasons than others."

"Have you ever heard the saying 'engraved invitation?'" Jewel pressed her body against Lumina's so they were breast to breast, pelvis to pelvis. "I've been patient, but you're never going to get an invitation more forward than this, right now."

Lumina sensed if she passed over this opportunity, she'd forever regret it–more than anything in her life. She started with the focus of her attention for the better part of the last month—the tempting pert nipples before her. She cupped her hand under Jewel's breast and lowered her mouth, rolling her tongue over the dark center. The most elicit moan came from Jewel and she curved into Lumina's touch.

She lavished loving on her lover's breasts, nipping and sucking, feeling the pebbles on the areola harden further. The more she concentrated on bringing her pleasure, the more heat built in her own core.

Jewel curled her calf around Lumina's leg, locking her in place. She slipped a hand between their bodies, her fingers finding the soft entrance of Lumina's core. She was so gentle, opening her slowly and pressing her thumb against her clit.

"Show me your glow," Jewel murmured against Lumina's ear. "I want to feel you come against me. Ride my hand."

The freedom of taking what she offered, of pleasuring herself on the woman's digits turned Lumina on. She raised her body, her mouth seeking Jewel's, her tongue plunging into her lover's mouth as Jewel's fingers thrust into her pussy. The added friction of the water pulsed into her, in and out and her core tightened. Their kissing grew more frenzied: Two nude women in the moonlight finger fucking and loving and not giving a care if anyone saw them.

The orgasm seized her senses, and the muscles along her thighs tensed. She leaned back, floating on the warm waters and letting the tension flow away. Jewel held her, slowing the caress, understanding the tremors passing through her mate's body.

"That was, oh my goddess, give me a moment." Lumina gushed. She wanted to make Jewel feel as good, if not better.

"You think I'm done with you yet?" Jewel propped her palms under Lumina's ass, raising her pelvis out of the water. "Do you want to know another benefit to being a mermaid?" Oral sex is extra exciting because we don't have to come up for air."

She dipped under the surface, bringing her mouth to Lumina's pussy. With her fingers splayed out, Jewel's thumb caressed the rosebud of her anus, pressing in and adding another physical sensation. At the same time, she thrust her tongue deep inside and over the top, sucking, back and forth, sending her to new heights over and over.

"I can't. No more. You'll wreck me." She loved every moment of it.

When her body totally worn out, Jewel cradled her in the waves, holding her close. "Shhhh. That's the point. Wreck you for everyone but me. I love you my guiding light."

"But what about you? I need to reciprocate, to please you." The thought of leaving her lover unsatisfied caused anxiety.

Jewel teased Lumina's nipple between her fingers. "There are still things you need to learn. Between us, it's not about tit for tat. We're equals. You can let me love you, and you can love me. We'll have plenty of time for that in our lifetimes, and later I can introduce you to some of my toys in the privacy of our home."

CHAPTER SEVEN: THE CLIMAX

L umina grew used to her new life, her love, the fresh air, her siren sisters and brothers, and the freedom of living without fear. She didn't miss anything about her time walking on earth. One concern lingered, though—that she hadn't been the first Archie had tossed overboard and odds were she wouldn't be the last.

About a year past her turn, she sat on a rock looking out at the coastline. The full moon illuminated the dark waters, and she sang the Siren's song of loss, of death and rebirth, understanding its full meaning.

The sound of a boat's engine cut through the stillness and the scales along the back of her neck stood up. There was a familiar chug. It couldn't be.

The soundtrack to her death sounded like *chugga-chugga-chugg —gurgle-chugga*. She tried to block away the sounds, fooled herself that she'd never recognize the clatter of his engine. But the moment it reverberated through the air, instinctively, deep down to the core of her being, she knew. Knew what the lung-clenching exhaust smelled like, knew the way water pooled at her feet along the rotting boards, and knew the way he piloted the small craft with just the

629

right amount of pitch to make her toddle side to side, whacking her elbow, her knee, the back of her shoulder on a rough piece of wood and marking her. Every discomfort he could get in, he did.

"It's him." Jewel surfaced to the right of her. The silver seas shone on her bare upper body and glimmered across her dark hair. She was the siren that gave sailors nightmares. She also was the stuff of Lumina's fantasies.

"Hello lover." Not only had Jewel taken her into her home, she'd given her the greatest gift of all—love—and the belief in herself.

"You know you don't have to do this, right? I can take care of him for you." With a strong thrust of her tail, Jewel propelled her body onto the rock next to Lumina.

With the full moon above, her mermaid form transformed into her human one. Seeing her like this tugged at Lumina's heart. Would they ever have had a chance together if they'd met when they walked on land full time? She liked to hope so, that love found a way no matter what, but probably not. Jewel came from another time, and although many touted "free love," usually that meant between a man and a woman. As for herself, well, she was so indoctrinated not to even think about anyone else that the idea of taking a woman as a lover never factored as an option.

After what she knew now, she'd never make that mistake again. Her heart recognized her soul mate. Did sirens even still have a soul?

"And ruin all the fun? I've been waiting for this, for payback, for too long," Lumina played the situation lightly. If Jewel guessed the truth, she'd never let her go alone.

"I've told you what attracted you to me to begin with, right?" The concern on the other woman's face tugged at her consciousness, and the slickness of Jewel's hip pressed against Lumina, making her wish they had more time together. "Your light. You are not about payback or revenge. You see the better side of people. You give them that gift."

Despite getting a second chance at life, members of the Pod weren't immortal. If killed, they died. They didn't live eternally. Given the chance, she'd love Jewel forever. Life was so precious and

630

fragile. Someone also had taken that from her chosen mate. She gripped the hard granite beneath her fingertips to steady her emotions.

"I couldn't risk something happening to you," Lumina whispered over the echoes of the waves. "You are all I have. It would break me."

"You are stronger than you think," Jewel said. "Shhh. They're coming closer."

As the boat drew nearer, it became more discernable that there were two figures on board. Archie sat at the back, steering and a body lay limp with long dark hair and an arm streaming over the side.

They rested facing the opposite side, hidden from the approaching vessel. Jewel leaned in, pressing her lips against Lumina's, her hand gently cradling the side of her rib cage, curling over her breast. Their breaths mixed together and heat and warmth tunneled through Lumina's body, pushing out the simmering anger. Love replaced the hollowed spaces.

A tear slipped from Lumina's eyes, interplaying with the ocean's mist upon her cheek. "We can't let him hurt her. He cannot be allowed to keep killing."

"I know," Jewel said. With a final kiss, she dived into the swirling waters, a song bursting from her lips.

The engine stuttered and the boat slowed its pace. Archie stood at the stern, looking out over the ocean. "Is someone there?"

In the bow, the woman struggled. She sat up straight, as if she waited for this moment, a distraction, to try to free herself. Lumina flashed to her encounter and the terror coursing through her limbs.

The song of the siren streamed over the waves, weaving a tale of love unrequited, of hopes dashed against the rocks, of men who for generation upon generation bound their women in physical and mental ties and toss them into the depths.

Others from the Pod surfaced, one by one, male and female, and joined the chorus. Archie placed his hands over his ears, trying to block out the madness of the chaotic beauty. Blood seeped from his eyes and his mouth dropped open, without releasing a sound.

An idea formed inside Lumina. In a way, he was instrumental in turning her into what she'd become. The night he killed her, he didn't simply take away her humanity. He offered her a new one in a twisted way. She dug into the rock, fusing the pieces of precious stone together and held it up to the moon.

If she was able to grant Archie one gift, what would it be? Heat flashed in her palm, and she slipped into the waters, swimming toward the rocking boat. If the woman fell overboard, she'd offer one of her turns to save her. Fate required that sacrifice, even if it meant potentially shortening her life.

The other members of the Pod angled behind Lumina and she approached the boat. None worried about him seeing them, because no one expected him to return to land and tell anyone what he'd witnessed.

As if sensing the approaching creatures, the woman leaned over the side of the boat and met the gaze of Lumina. Recognition sparked. It was the waitress from the café they occasionally visited. Archie liked to flirt with her, and one time grabbed her wrist when she went to pick up the payment.

"Chloe." The name imprinted on her mind. She was a single mom with a young son who sometimes sat in the last booth waiting for her to finish a shift. She couldn't be sacrificed. He needed someone to return home.

Lumina broke eye contact and finished the trip to the back of the boat. Archie stood on a bench, peering into the depths. She leapt from the water, strength propelling her upward. The breeze swirled and her hair flew in a funnel around her head. The sirens grew silent, giving her the moment. He stumbled, falling onto his back.

"It can't be. You're dead."

She gripped the side of the boat, slivers of wood burrowing into her skin. Fortunately, over the last year, it had grown thicker and anger made her lose the sense of pain. She flexed her muscles, pulling her body onto the boat.

"You thought you did, but you set me free," Lumina said. "I'm here to return the favor."

The small stone glowed in the light and she forced it into his palm. For the briefest moment, his features smoothed out and she recognized the man she once loved, the man who filled her days with hope until he crushed her dreams. Then the magic kicked in. She granted him the power to see, to feel all the terror and hurt he'd caused over the years.

A scream erupted, shriller than shorebirds fighting over prey. "I'm sorry," he said, before stumbling to the side and tumbling over into the waiting arms and mouths of the hungry Pod.

Alone with his intended victim, Lumina turned to Chloe. "Do you know how to drive this piece of shit?"

"Thank you." She nodded before shivers from the cold and what may have been took over.

From underneath the back seat, Lumina opened the storage compartment and wrapped the woman in a wool blanket. "We'll guide you in until you can find your way." With her sharp nails, she flayed the rope around Chloe's ankles.

"I promise. I won't tell anyone what I saw, what happened," she spoke so fast.

If she was someone who fell for Archie, who knew if she'd hold up to that promise. "I know you won't. Marquez, it's time."

As sure as waves wash away the imprint of footsteps on sand, Marky's gift was washing away memories. From the side of the stern, they placed a palm on Chloe's arm and shut their eyes. Chloe slumped as if asleep. The Pod pushed the boat in the right direction, and when she woke, she'd be able to finish the journey.

The wind picked up from the Northeast and Jewel joined Lumina in the journey toward shore. Her strong aura wrapped itself around Lumina and their energies merged. "You did good," she said. "You saved her."

"And you saved me."

With a final thrust, the Pod turned from Lumina's past and scattered into the swirling seas. The journey from there to here may have been strewn with pain and treacherous seas, but they'd all ended up together as a family.

The End

POSEIDON'S VOICE

CATHERINE STOVALL

CHAPTER ONE: DANTE

The seas off the coast of the new world raged. Waves crested and fell like giant thundering fists, pounding the wooden ship. Men called out in fear and anger, insisting they abandon their mission and return to port before the vessel ended up nothing but splinters on the rocks.

Prince Dante Montoya stood at the railing watching it all as if it were a bad dream. He'd only set out on this damned mission to escape the burdens hounding him in the kingdom of Catari. Now, he longed for home. Being forced to step up as king instead of living the grand life of a second son seemed much less daunting than dealing with the insane man he'd hired to captain his ship. All Dante had wanted was to set out on a voyage to chase myths and legends handed down from his great grandfather. Instead, he was staring down death and madness in the middle of the ocean.

Captain Manford (Dead Eye) Roberts demanded, "Shut up, you lily livered fools. We're almost there. This storm is bound to draw the sea bitches out in throngs. We must capture one tonight." In his right hand, he clutched the sacred conch shell Dante's grandfather had once held in his wrinkled old hands while telling the story of the mer-people.

"They can't resist the call of the horn. They will come," Dead Eye roared.

"Blow the damn thing then," Dante called out. "Do it now before it's too late." The winds whipped his words into nothingness even as they echoed in his head. Six months before, he hadn't believed in the mer-people at all. He'd only wanted to escape his mother's constant nagging about how his brother lay on his deathbed and how Dante must prepare. But now, he believed.

How could he not?

They'd found proof of the pod's movements up and down the coast. They'd nearly come close enough once to call them using the horn, but the mighty sea had fought against the ship until they had been forced to turn back. But tonight, they would finally capture one of the beasts.

The next strike of lightning danced across the open sea, and Dante's piercing gray eyes moved rapidly over the waters. He searched for a glimmer of a fin, a streak of color in the waves, or a beautiful face under the surface of the churning water. At last, he saw a silhouette in the glare of light streaking across the horizon.

Dante clung to the railing of the ship and urged the captain, "Blow the horn, Dead Eye. We're going to be torn apart."

Manford brought the shell to his lips and blew. The haunting wail washed over the raging waters, drowning out all other sounds.

When the sky lit up again, Dante watched the pod swimming toward the ship. Thunder rolled and rumbled overhead, almost drowning out the first notes of the sirens' songs.

"They're here," Dead Eye cried out to his men. "Plug your ears with the candle wax. Do not pity them because they are beautiful, beneath those waters they are monsters. Prepare the nets." With a triumphant shout, he raised the horn and blew once more.

The crew cast out the nets, struggling against the stinging rain and tormenting winds. The ship rocked violently, but the men held fast to their posts. Harpoons stood at the ready in case the wretches managed an attack and live capture failed.

This is it, Dante thought, and he was sure the captain's thoughts were close to his own.

Dead-Eye Roberts had a reputation for being a man driven by his obsession with the myth of the mer-people. Dante had found him drunk in a pub claiming to have lost his eye to one of the sea bitches twenty years before. The wild haired man had claimed the monster had died by his sword that day, but he'd not thought to keep its bones as proof.

Dante of course had thought him crazy when he'd told the tale. But the man's rantings had given him the idea to sail a vessel along the coast in search of proof. The entire endeavor had begun without much ado, in fact. Sailors didn't care if you paid them to sail the world or to jaunt about for weeks at a time near the coast. As long as the king's little brother paid well and fed them well, they were obliged to make the journey.

Dead Eye raised his fist, giving the signal for the men to hold fast as the pod surfaced at the edge of the ship. The mer-people clawed at the wooden vessel and raised their voices higher, blaring their song over the sound of the storm. But the wax plugging the men's ears kept them from falling under the pod's spell.

"Heave," Dante screamed as he raised his arms in unison with Captain Roberts.

The men pulled at the ropes, their backs straining as a torrent of rain pelted against them.

CHAPTER TWO: NAIDA

N aida pressed forward against the raging waters, her mind full of anger, fear, and memories of a past she'd tried to forget. The pod had called her into service, and she had no choice but to fight this battle. But thoughts of what must be done twisted her stomach even as her graceful tale pumped through the choppy sea.

The man captaining the ship was well known to the mer-people and hated more than any other human being. He'd spent years hunting them, trying to reveal their existence to other humans, and he'd even killed poor Luna after she'd ripped his eye out of his head to escape capture. When Perseus, Luna's former mate, had discovered that Dead Eye was on the same waters the pod was crossing, he'd called for help. Of course, the others had come. The captain could not be allowed to live.

Naida raised her face from the water just as the lightning flashed across the sky. The swelling waves crashed against the vessel, rocking it harder. But the men aboard held their places. In a flash of lightning, she saw the captain. Memories of her own past flooded her mind. Rage slammed into her heart, and she dove back down once more to propel forward with new vigor. She didn't see the water churning around her or the other mer-people as they swam alongside. Instead, she saw her life ending ten years before.

Wet, afraid, desperate, and tied to the ducking stool, she'd pleaded her innocence to the witch hunter. But the evil man had refused to believe that she was nothing but a midwife and healer. He'd plunged her down into the cold bay, holding her longer and longer each time. Then, he'd pulled her up again to demand she confess. Even as the water had poured from her ears, she'd heard the crowd chanting—"Drown the witch—" before she'd been submerged again.

In those last moments, her lungs had burned until her body forced her to gasp for air that she could not reach. Water had pressed through her lips. She'd said her silent goodbyes. But then hands had pulled away the bindings, lips had pressed against hers, and oxygen had rushed into her lungs. She'd suddenly been able to breathe beneath the waters of the bay, and her eyes had sprung open.

A beautiful mer-woman with long blonde hair and a tail of gleaming scales had bid Naida to join her. And deep into the sea they had gone. Gaileen had saved her that day. Had gifted her with the dark and painful transformation that had led to Naida's rebirth as a mermaid. Poseidon had then granted her a special gift, one that had both exhilarated and terrified her. Still, she'd used her siren's song and that unique magic to destroy the men who'd murdered her the day they'd set sail to spread their lies and death in another town.

She'd felt the pure release of making them suffer more keenly than any experience she'd had as a human. And for years, she'd lured evil men into the sea to face their death as she feasted on their corpses. But after so long, the killing no longer offered her satisfaction, and she'd chosen to stop. Instead, she'd focused on life in the pod, the happy home she had made for herself, and on healing her soul. That had been four years before, but now she'd return to those ways so that she might avenge poor, sweet Luna's death.

Naida surfaced again, closer to the ship than she'd expected. The memories that had held her within their grasp whipped away as if they had been caught in the powerful winds tearing at the ship's sails. With clawed hands, she dug into the water-soaked wood and prepared to raise her voice alongside the others. The rough seas fought against the pod and pummeled the ship. The ocean was both friend and foe to sailors and the mer-people alike.

Lightning flashed and thunder rolled overhead as if Zeus were cheering them on into battle. Naida's song flowed from her mouth just as her eyes fell on the captain. A large conch shell gleamed in his hand as he pressed it to his lips. A strange sound pierced the storm, and Naida's breath caught in her throat. The noise shattered her mind, her limbs faltered. The sound of the conch shell pulled at her insides as if a chain had been fastened around her heart. Chaos erupted around her as the others struggled against the sound or sank back under the waves.

Harpoons and nets splashed into the sea. The human men screamed to each other in triumph. Red tinged water swirled around her and screams of agony sent cold chills from Naida's fins to her gills. Silence fell as Dead Eye took a breath and prepared to blow into the shell once more. Naida dove, using all her strength to sink beneath the waves and out of reach of the magic in the conch. Realization hit her hard. The captain had planned the attack and had counted on the pod wanting his blood. He'd known they'd seek him out, and he'd waited for them to come near enough to the ship that he'd be able to use the shell.

What he hadn't known or counted on was the gift Poseidon had given just to her.

Naida opened her mouth and called out, "Kraken, come to me. Defend your mistress and her people." Green light poured from her lips and drifted into the deep dark waters below. Time stopped. The strength of her power held her still in the water—dark hair floating around her body, pearlescent fins catching the light of magic and shining like a beacon to the others in the pod. The song she sang was not the siren's song. It was the song of death. The song of the kraken.

The taste of copper filled Naida's mouth as the blood of her friends and pod mates flowed past her, but she held strong. Soon, utter destruction would come in the form of massive tentacles and a beak sharp enough to crush bones and wood into splinters and dust.

CHAPTER THREE: DANTE

"No," Dante screamed as the harpoons fired. "Don't kill them!"

The men were supposed to only fire if live capture wasn't possible. They had the upper hand. The mer-people hadn't suspected the planned attack. The conch had frozen them in place. There was no need for the slaughter happening before him.

"Stop," he shouted as he grabbed one of the deckhands and pulled the heavy-set man away from the harpoon gun.

The man shoved him back and laughed. "Captain's orders, sire," he spat with contempt.

The smell of rotted teeth and whiskey flowed into Dante's face. "You filthy bastard," he screamed back. The feel of his knuckles smashing into the man's meaty face vibrated through his body even as he turned to rush toward Dead Eye.

The rain-slick deck and powerful winds worked against Dante as he half-ran and half-skidded across the schooner. "Dead Eye," he yelled over the storm, "stop this insanity."

The captain never gave him a glance as he pressed the conch to his lips and blew again. The horn drowned out the raging squall just as the ship rocked hard to the right. Dante jolted and slid. His ribs cracked against the ship's rail hard enough to break. His head swam with pain and bile filled his throat. Locked against the side of the vessel, he stared into the now bloody waters.

Bodies floated on the surface and fins disappeared into the chop, but some of the mer-people sat frozen—treading water and hypnotized by the magic in the shell. Like fish in a barrel, they were nothing but targets for the harpoons and nets that splashed into the water.

"Damn you, Dead Eye," Dante whispered, still trying to fill his lungs with the salty, damp air. Just as he gathered enough strength to push away from the railing, his eyes fell on a dark-haired mermaid. For a moment, she'd been caught in the web of magic created by the conch. But, as the trumpeting stopped, she'd grimaced and sank beneath the waves.

Suddenly, the realness of what he'd caused hit him. That beautiful creature and the fifteen or twenty others with her were never going to swim across the seas again. He'd only wanted to own one of them. A sick and childish fascination fueled by his grandfather's stories. But, now, they'd all die. He started to push away again, determined to put an end to the madness even if it meant throwing Dead Eye overboard. But, before he could, a green light caught his eye.

He watched the dark beauty, just below the wicked waves. Arms outstretched and mouth open as if she were still singing the siren's song, she hovered in the water as if the storm could not touch her. Bright tendrils of light, the color of bioluminescent sea glass, flowed from her lips. And beneath her, beyond the gleaming scales of her tail, darkness grew.

The inky blackness spread upward and outward as if the bottom of the ocean were opening up to swallow them all. Dante gasped as the shadow began to take shape. "It can't be," he gasped.

The conch shell blew again, but most of the mer-people had retreated beneath the waves. Their shadows danced under the water as they fled toward the pretty one surrounded by darkness and green light. A few struggled in the nets as the human men heaved them upward. Others bobbed in the bloody water, dead or nearly so. Dante fought to get control of his mind and body. He struggled to find his voice.

The thing in the darkness came higher. And one giant appendage breached the surface.

"Kraken!" Dante yelled, but it was too late. Even if the men could hear him over the wax plugs in their ears, the roaring storm, the sirens' song, and the trumpeting conch, there was nothing to be done.

Seven more tentacles appeared out of the sea, sending torrents of salt water to rain down upon the ship as they wrapped the vessel from bow to stern. The masts cracked under the weight of the beast. Splinters of wood sprayed over them, piercing several of the sailors' flesh. The kraken rolled the ship to its port while Dante clung to the starboard rail, feet dangling. A mighty rush of water sprayed upward as the monster's head breached the surface and its beak sunk into the hull.

All seemed lost. Dante twisted his head from side to side, searching for escape until his gaze fell on Captain Dead Eye. The crazed man stood lodged against the ship's wheel, held upright amongst the topsy-turvy chaos by one of the kraken's tentacles. The magic conch shell remained in his left hand, but he wielded a heavy sword with his right—chopping madly at the appendage trapping him. Pain and hatred poured from the one remaining eye in the captain's face.

Just as it seemed Dead Eye might escape, the snap of wood and bone echoed in the quieting storm, and the terrified screams of dying men pierced the night. The rail beneath Dante's hands gave way as the starboard side collapsed. A weightlessness filled him as his body plummeted, but the water felt as hard as land when he collided into the fierce waves. Pain radiated through his already broken ribs, and for the second time in minutes, the air rushed from his lungs.

Fighting the swells and panic, he struggled to stay afloat until he could swim once more.

This is where I die, he thought. Images of his recently deceased father and his ill brother flowed through his mind, only to be replaced by the sight of his mother weeping over three fresh graves.

CHAPTER FOUR: NAIDA

P ower and magic vibrated through every scale and inch of skin on Naida's body. The strength of the kraken raged through her like a lightning bolt had shot into the sea and filled her with fire. She couldn't see or hear the carnage from where she floated in the water, caught in the whirlpool created by the beast's ascent. But the smell of death and blood flooded her senses. Time stood still as she waited. This feeling of no longer being in control, of surrendering herself to the beast, terrified her. He would not stop once called upon. Not until he'd had his fill of flesh and destruction.

The pod had gathered around Naida. Some clung to her hands, while others formed a circle around her. To protect her meant to protect themselves because, if she should die it would break their link to the monster. Unleashed on the mer-people, it would sate its endless hunger on their bones. For what did a kraken care if it feasted on humans or mer-people?

At last, the sea began to quiet, and chunks of debris drifted by. The dark shadow blocking the light from above moved downward, growing larger as it descended toward Naida and her people. The pod closed in tighter, their fear palpable. But the kraken did not pause. Instead, its gleaming golden eyes locked to where Naida floated, boring into her soul as it swam back down into the abyss.

For a moment, no one moved. Then Perseus cried, "Let us feast upon those who have slain our kind."

The pod rushed to the surface, dragging Naida along with them. Weary from using her power, she could barely swim let alone fight against the hands pulling her forward. As she breached the surface, she gasped in oxygen and searched the water for human and mer-people survivors. Instead, her gaze took in more blood and more carnage.

The mer-people raised their voices and lured the men treading water and clinging to debris into a hypnotic state. The wax plugs they had used to protect themselves had been washed away by the jostling sea. The weak humans stood little to no chance of escape as the sirens' razor sharp teeth bit into flesh.

Unable to force herself to join in the feeding frenzy, Naida turned her back on the gruesome scene. Evil men had murdered her and many of the other pod members. The humans who had discovered their existence were rarely kind and almost always bent on capturing or killing the mer-people. Still, she could not ravage the flesh from their bones or sink their corpses into the sea as fodder for the predators lurking below. She had let the kraken do her killing for her. She couldn't allow her soul to return to that dark place.

"Help me," a rough voice whispered from behind her.

Naida jumped and spun around in the water. Her eyes locked onto the face of a man. A human. Blood dripped down his forehead to completely cover one swollen eye. But the other shined like a blue diamond, reflecting fear and pain.

"Help me, please," he cried again.

Naida bared her teeth and raised her sharp nails. "The only help you'll get from me, human, is being sent to an early grave," she hissed.

"I'm sorry. I'm so sorry. I didn't know this would happen," the man pleaded. "Please don't hurt me. I swear—" His head bobbed under the water, cutting off his words.

Naida waited, watching him struggle and sink. She should hate human men. She should wish death upon them all, but her heart had become too pure. Her wounds had healed too much. With a roll of her eyes, she dipped below the water and gracefully swam until she could reach the sailor. Guilty or not, she would return him to land and hope that his gods sorted the rest out later.

Nabbing the stranger by the shirt, she hauled him up, using her powerful tail to push them to the surface. He was unconscious but still breathing by the time they reached the shore, so she rolled him up onto the sand and swam away.

CHAPTER FIVE: DANTE

It had taken two days before another ship had found him floating atop a large piece of wood in the middle of the sea, and another week for him to recover enough to make his way down to the port. His mother had berated him all throughout the time he'd spent back in the castle, and when he'd left once more, she'd wept. His brother still suffered from the mysterious illness that had taken his father. Dante's only defense for his reckless behavior and need to run from the kingdom full of responsibilities was to remind the queen mother that he was still only a second son as long as Marco still lived and breathed.

Truthfully, rumor had reached him that Captain Dead Eye had escaped the wreckage as well. The boisterous man had been filling the pubs with people every night, still brandishing the conch shell and swearing to return to the sea until he captured the beautiful sea witch that had saved him from the storms, the swells, and the great kraken that had destroyed the prince's ship.

Anger drove Dante forward, but curiosity pushed him as well. He'd seen the mer-people that night. Now, he had proof of what he was chasing beyond a doubt. He was even sure the same dark beauty that had summoned up the sea monster had been the one the captain was claiming had saved him. But even after seeing the mermen and mermaids rip the sailors' flesh from bone, he no longer wanted to hunt them. He was determined to stop Dead Eye from massacring the pod. Especially her. The terrifying magic she'd wielded had shown him just how special the mer-people were.

As he suspected, Dante found Captain Manford in the Boar's Head pub, drunk and slurring out the much embellished tale of how he'd single handedly saved himself, three of his men, and Prince Dante from the mer-people and their sea demon. However, his bellowing laugh stopped short when Dante stepped out from the shadows and glared down at the pompous man.

"That's not quite how I remember things going," Dante said as he picked up Dead Eye's drink and swallowed it in two quick gulps. "In fact, I recall you hacking away at the beast like a child trying to stab an elephant with a toothpick and then leaving me for dead."

The men all jumped to their feet, knocking over chairs and spilling drinks. Except for Captain Manford. He stood with impetuous slowness, his one-eyed glare never leaving Dante's face and contradicting the friendly smile on his lips.

"Your, highness. Surely, you understand that I knew a man of your renown strength and endurance could survive on his own whilst I kept the beasties busy with my sword."

Dante shook his head, disgust written purely on his face. "Tell whatever tales you wish, Captain. I've come to claim what is mine and be on my way. Give me back my grandfather's conch shell. You'll have no more of my ships and no more of my gold to fund your genocide."

Dead Eye blustered, "How dare you? You've seen the evil these things are capable of. You have seen the powers they possess. That shell is my ticket to ridding the sea of them whether it be by death or in a net."

Dante roared, "I saw plenty of evidence of evil on the seas that day, but it wasn't just the mer-people who were the cause of it. And I will not be a part of this insanity any longer."

Dead Eye stood from his chair and reached inside the pouch hanging around his waist to retrieve the shell. His grubby fingers clung to it for a few seconds after he placed it into Dante's hand. "Your highness, I assure you that you are mistaken. If we could only come to some sort of agreement. Perhaps my men were too quick with the harpoons. The storm had them scared and seeing myth brought to life before their eyes overwhelmed them. Sit, drink with us. Allow me to offer my apologies and my assurances before you simply turn away from what could be a truly grand adventure."

Dante knew the man was lying. Every good part of him understood that Captain Manford (Dead Eye) Roberts would do whatever he needed to in order to get what he wanted. Still, a worse fate awaited Dante back at the castle. He couldn't stay and watch his brother die as he had watched his father wither into a gray-skinned, unrecognizable thing.

"What assurances could you possibly give to convince me that you will not do exactly as you did before?" Dante demanded as he placed the conch inside his coat.

"Sit. Sit, my friend," Dead Eye insisted. "I assure you this time will be different."

Dante hesitated for a moment before he took a seat at the head of the table and ordered a pint of ale. *I'll stay for a while. I will listen to his blustering and boasting and his stupid reasoning just so I don't have to go home.*

The night wore on, and ale poured like the rivers into the sea. Manford used his every charm to convince Dante that the next adventure would be a true odyssey. They would shed no blood and cause no more harm to the mer-people. In fact, he had the perfect plan to capture one alive. It could not fail. All he needed was the prince's ship, the conch shell, and a good strong wind in his sails.

Lies, Dante thought. *All lies. But I am to be king, I can control this situation. I can force him to obey my will.*

CHAPTER SIX: NAIDA

Two weeks had passed since the battle on the sea, and still the pod remained near the coast. Many of the mer-people had been injured and traveling had been too much of a risk. Naida had worked day and night to help heal their wounds and to comfort the dying. All in all, the pod had lost five out of the thirty that had gone to war with the humans. But now, the full moon was coming. If they wanted to avoid the spring tides, they had to move on soon.

The humans had learned too much about the mer-people, and their weapons had become too powerful. The man who had killed Luna must have warned the others against the siren's song. But worst of all, the men held the Voice of Poseidon—an enchanted conch shell known to be the only means to summon the mer-people other than by order of Poseidon himself.

The legend of the conch shell had been told to every merman and mermaid who ever lived. It was a sad story of a sorcerer who fell in love with a beautiful young mermaid but was denied his request to join her in the sea. Knowing that loving her from afar but never truly being able to be with her would only destroy her lover, the mermaid vowed never to see the sorcerer again.

Heartbroken, the human magician created an enchanted shell so he could summon his beloved back to him when the loneliness grew too much to withstand. But, when he sailed his boat out to the middle of the sea and used the shell, it called all the mer-people who heard it to him. Enraged by the sorcerer's disrespect and audacity, Poseidon sank the man's vessel, and the mer-people tore him apart as his beloved cried out for mercy. In her misery, the young mermaid made away with the shell and flung herself into the jaws of a great white shark.

The beast swallowed her whole, and there the shell stayed until the great King Phillip caught the shark while on a fishing expedition. When he discovered the mermaid's bones inside the shark's belly, along with the shell, the king became curious. After questioning the locals, he learned the story of the sorcerer. Intrigued by the proof he held that mermaids existed but wise enough to know what men would do if they knew, King Phillip kept the bones and the shell locked in a vault beneath his castle.

The mer-people worried the king might someday expose them out of greed or fear. So, each time one of their people chose to use their gift to walk on land while the pod was near the kingdom, they visited the castle and listened to the human villagers. As the king grew old, he told the story of the conch shell to his children and grandchildren. But because he only showed them the Voice of Poseidon, never the mermaid's skeleton, no one truly believed the story. For the humans, it was a simple fairytale, and the mer-people believed they would never have to fear the evils the shell could bring down upon them.

After the old king had died, the mer-people stopped returning to the castle. Many still believed the story to be true, but others were convinced it was only a myth. Regardless of the tale's legitimacy, it had been over a hundred years since the shell was used. No one had ever expected it to fall into the hands of a madman. But Naida and the others had seen it with their own two eyes and had heard its mesmerizing sound with their own ears. They'd felt the pull of its trumpeting in their very souls. The Voice of Poseidon had returned.

Naida swam toward the moonlit surface, still amazed by the beauty of the sea at night after all this time. She hated coming this close to shore so soon after they'd survived such a horrendous attack and with Poseidon's Voice lost again. It wasn't safe. But, as a healer, she knew the others had to come first. She'd only come here because the thick green foliage would help bind the mer-peoples' wounds as they traveled back home to the deep ocean crevice to hide from the world and recover in peace.

The light danced through the murky waters between the flowing green and brown stalks within the kelp forest. All the world seemed magical in that moment, and fear began to ease from her mind. She wanted to stay there a little longer, to just drift amongst the swaying stems, but she couldn't forget the dangers. With a push of her tail, she torpedoed to the surface and breathed in the cool night air.

Weird how you can miss something so simple as the taste of salt in your lungs when you have gills, she thought. Amused and distracted by little memories of when she'd been a happy human girl walking the beaches at night long before she'd been accused of witchcraft, she almost didn't notice the massive ship leaving the bay in the direction of where the pod was resting.

The same green and blue flag flew from a staff on the stern. The humans had recovered and were hunting once more. Anger boiled in her blood. She hated the humans now more than ever. But she also blamed herself. She should have never let that man live. One act of kindness could have just cost all their lives.

The kelp forest abandoned, Naida sped back down into the sea. She had to warn the others. The winds were not high enough to move the ship rapidly through the calm seas, but she used all her strength and skill to maneuver through the waters. Thoughts beat against her mind like the waves pounding the shores.

Will I reach them in time? Will we be able to escape? Will the wounded be able to survive if the rest of us are injured or killed? Do the humans still have the shell? Naida could see the entrance to the underwater cove where her people were waiting only a single league away. Her muscles ached from swimming so hard and fast, but she knew she must continue. She couldn't stop now. With the push of her powerful tailfin, she shot up to the surface once more to check if the ship was still sailing in their direction.

As soon as she breached the surface, the trumpeting sound blasted into her ears. *It's a trap,* her mind screamed, but her body wouldn't obey her. Instead, she spun around to see a group of human men in a smaller vessel only a few feet away. The conch's song tugged at her and mesmerized her at the same time. She fought against the pull with every ounce of her being once more. This time the song was too loud. The men were too close. She couldn't find her voice to sing the siren's song, she couldn't force herself back into the depths to draw them away from the pod's location, and she couldn't summon the kraken to her aid.

Please let them be too far away to hear the sound, she pleaded as the nets fell around her. Unable to struggle, Naida suffered as the coarse ropes scraped against flesh and scale. Each time the humans tugged the net closer to the boat, she cried out in agonizing pain. Burns formed along her face, arms, and torso. Scales ripped from her fins.

When they finally dragged her to the side of the boat, her head cracked against the wood. The trumpeting paused for a moment, and she pleaded, "Please release me. I won't harm you, I swear."

The human men jeered and roared, celebrating their victory even as she wept. And when Poseidon's Voice remained quiet for just long enough, she tried to sing. Pushing all the hatred, fear, and pain into the first notes, Naida envisioned the men jumping into the sea. She willed them to fall overboard and to be swallowed up by the salty waters. All the old wounds from her human life and her first years as a mermaid opened back up to spill a black bile of abhorrence into her voice.

The first man jumped, his glazed eyes meeting hers a moment

before he hit the water. His promised death gave her strength to continue her song, but the other men's willpower was stronger. Or perhaps the wax was more securely fitted to the ears. Either way, the leader blew the shell once more. Naida fell silent and still as they began to haul her helpless body into the boat. Then she recognized the man who had caused the mer-people so much pain.

The night of the battle, he'd been badly injured. His face had been covered in blood, and the missing eye had been swollen closed. He must have lost his patch during the struggle, because it hadn't been there when she'd rescued him. Naida told herself she would have never been able to tell that he only had one eye. There was no way she could've recognized him. But she still blamed and ridiculed herself.

How could I have been so stupid? A dark cloud of guilt and despair sank down into Naida's soul, twisting and crushing her insides like the kraken's tentacles had crushed the ship. *How could I have spared the life of the man who killed Luna and nearly destroyed the pod? I deserve to die.*

Before she could surrender completely to the desperation and sadness filling her body, the man with one eye picked up an oar and slammed it into the side of Naida's head. Skull splitting pain blurred her vision and she fell into darkness, and her last thoughts were a final prayer that her people had been too far away to fall victim to the sailors' tricks.

CHAPTER SEVEN: DANTE

Capturing the dark-haired beauty had been almost too easy. Sure, she'd caused that nitwit Henson to jump overboard. But other than that, they'd netted her and pulled her into the boat with little effort. As long as she remained unconscious, they'd have no problems getting her back to the ship. Even if she did wake, they only had to continue blowing the shell and keep the wax securely in their ears.

Exhilaration edged through his veins as Dante stared down at the mermaid. They'd done what no other men had ever accomplished. They'd captured a siren.

Dead Eye handed the horn to one of the crew and yelled to Dante, "Don't just stand there, sire. Help me tie the bitch up before she wakes up, escapes the nets, and flops overboard like a fat salmon."

The rope hit him square in the chest, and Dante had to fight the urge to slam his fist into the man's good eye. Even as he bent to tie Naida's hands together, he scolded the captain. "I'll remind you again to watch your tongue, sir. I am a prince on and off these waters, and you are here on *my* ship by both *my* good graces and *my* order."

Dead Eye laughed and took a swig from the bottle of rum in his hand before he secured a dirty rag between Naida's sharp teeth. "I may be here for those reasons, my prince, but I am also the man who just caught you a mermaid. And when we reach Harrisburg in two weeks, I'll be the man that provided the crown with enough gold that the royal family will never again need to borrow from the banks or the kingdom's wealthy families to fund their lavish lifestyle. My contacts are willing to pay the heftiest of prices for such a beautiful specimen."

Dante looked away from the mermaid's unmoving body, but he couldn't meet the leer he knew would be shining on Dead Eye's face. "Yes, you are, you son-of-a-bitch.

The sailors veered the small boat back to where the ship awaited them. Halfway across the distance, the mermaid regained consciousness. The men took turns on the horn, and though he tried, Dante couldn't stop himself from staring into her sad brown eyes. Tears, as blue as the ocean, trickled down her rounded cheeks, and blood leaked from the wounds covering her body.

He had often been told that he had a kind disposition, not unlike his grandfather before him. And Dante wanted nothing more in that moment for that to be untrue. He wanted to be hard and uncaring like Dead Eye, or at least logical to the point of cold heartedness like his brother, the rightful heir to their father's throne. Instead, he found himself doubting this mission and feeling pity for the poor creature now bound and gagged beneath the nets by his feet.

"You, there," he demanded, "get a bucket of water and pour over her."

"Why the hell would I do that?" the deckhand asked.

"Can't you see her drying out? We can't have her withering and shriveling up, can we? You fools have already done enough damage to her flesh and scales," Dante yelled, trying to sound as royal and commanding as a man of his position should.

The deckhand hesitated for just a moment until Dead Eye ordered, "Do as the prince commands you."

The water soaked into Naida's tail and covered her body. She let out a whimper and tried to squirm, but the sound of the conch shell seemed to still hold her in thrall. The man dumped another bucket of sea water over her, re-wetting her hair until it clung to her flesh. Dante's eyes traced the ebony waves down her cheeks, across her neck, over her shoulders, and along the curves of her breasts. Almost as mesmerized by her beauty as she was by the sound of the horn, he let his eyes wander down her flat stomach and over the sharp hip bones on each side of her perfect navel.

But when he saw the scales that covered the bottom half of her body, heat washed over his face. His eyes jerked upward and accidentally met hers, and the sight of the hatred boiling behind their golden brown depths made him recoil. He turned his back on the creature before him until they finally reached the larger ship.

They hauled their catch aboard and carried her down into the ship's hold. There they placed Naida into an aquarium full of sea water just large enough to accommodate her body with little movement. She had room enough to lay flat in all directions, to float upright and be completely submerged, and just enough space between the top of the water and the aquarium lid to emerge from the shoulders up out of the water.

Dante helped the men slide the heavy metal lid over the opening at the top and turn on the pumps that would provide an ample supply of oxygen into the water. He then slid the iron lock into the latch. The finality of the click when he closed the shackle sounded like a canon in his ears. Without much thought, he pulled the leather string that held his shirt closed from its eyelets and ran it through the hole in the key. Once he'd secured it with a tight knot, he slipped the makeshift necklace around his neck and tucked it beneath his clothes.

"Not that I don't trust the lot of you," Dante said, "but I think I'll take care of our precious cargo until we reach our destination."

The other men laughed as if he'd volunteered to scrub the deck with a toothbrush.

"Be my guest," Dead Eye sneered. "You won't catch any of my men complaining about not having to babysit the damn thing."

POSEIDON'S VOICE

Naida woke from fitful dreams into a nightmare. The dark cargo area of the ship loomed beyond the blurry glass. The water she floated in stank of staleness and waste, and the building ammonia from the filth burned her inside and out. She wasn't sure how long she'd been aboard the ship and trapped in the strange enclosure, but she definitely knew she couldn't survive in such conditions much longer. She gnawed with her sharp teeth and pulled with her bound hands until the corners of her mouth had bled. Finally, the cloth gag had broken.

But it had done her no good. The men had come and had blown the shell until they'd managed to render her helpless and place a new gag into her mouth. The brown-haired, green-eyed man they called Dante always came with them, and it was he who kept the shell. At times, Naida thought about refusing to eat and starving herself, but she fought against her desire to give up. She didn't want to die at the hands of human men.

Not this time. Not again, she promised herself. *This time you must save yourself because Galene will not be here to help you.*

The door to the cargo hold opened, and Dante entered. In his right hand, he held the Voice of Poseidon. Naida glared at him, hating that he looked handsome in a haggard and dangerous way. Even though she was sure it was only to protect the earnings he'd make from her, at least he was kinder than the others.

The sailors aboard the ship, with their rough groping hands, hurt her each time they came to bring her food or change the water inside the enclosure. But Dante protected her, stopping them and admonishing them for their behavior. Captain Dead Eye and the other men called Dante sire and prince, but the words sounded more like curses sliding off their tongues. Still, they grudgingly obeyed him.

The circling thoughts about Dante and his place on the ship sparked a tiny flame of hope inside of Naida. Perhaps there was still a way to escape.

She waited until Dante came near enough to the enclosure that he'd be able to see her through the murky water and wavy glass. Then, she pointed to the shell and shook her head no. The prince paused, confusion wrinkling his brow as he stared from her to the conch and back again.

Pleased that he had not instantly used the Voice of Poseidon to stop her attempts at communication, Naida pushed herself up until her head raised as far as it could above the water before hitting the lid. She continued the captive's version of charades by shaking her head and pointing at the gag. Still, Dante looked confused, but the shell remained unused in his hand. So, Naida mimicked talking by opening and closing her hand and gesturing to the gag and the shell once more.

With her wrists bound together, the message was hard to convey, but Dante seemed to comprehend.

"You want to talk to me?" he asked, caution thick in his tone.

She nodded her head yes before pointing down at the water and covering her nose. Hoping he'd understand that she desperately wanted and needed clean water, she tried to hide the disgust she felt for the human prince behind pleading eyes.

"The water is too dirty?" he asked.

Naida nodded, pleased he wasn't so stupid that he couldn't understand. Next, she rubbed her bound hands against her face, down her chest, over her bare midriff, and across her scaled hips. But not in a seductive way, because she'd rather die than offer herself up to a human man. Instead, she made scratching motions with her fingers.

Dante quirked up one eyebrow but didn't speak. Nadia tried again. This time, moving her hands a few inches above her cheek to imitate clawing at her skin.

Shock registered across Dante's expression. "You're hurting? Or itching?" he asked.

She nodded again, more enthusiastically than before.

"Are there other things that you need?" Dante asked, his gaze turning worried as he seemed to scan her with fresh eyes.

Naida nodded for a third time before pointing to the shell and the gag and shaking her head no. She gestured toward Dante and herself and made the sign for talking with her hand once more.

"I cannot trust you. If I remove the gag, you will only attempt to use your siren song to hurt me. Or, worse, you will call upon the kraken." As he spoke, his eyes turned hard with distrust.

Naida placed her palms flat together in front of her and silently pleaded. Remembering something from her human youth, she tried to draw an X over her heart with her bound hands.

Dante's mouth cracked into a very small and very brief grin. "You cross your heart, huh?"

Naida nodded again. *Please take the bait,* she thought, mentally willing the prince to drop his guard and give into her pleading.

Dante took a step closer and stared at her through the glass. The hand holding the conch shell trembled.

Naida placed her palms together again and nodded yes.

They stared deep into each other's eyes for what seemed like hours before Dante jerked his head away and stormed from the room, slamming the door hard enough behind him to rock the glass cage.

"No," Naida cried around the wet cloth in her mouth. Fresh tears fell from her eyes, and she sank back down into the dirty water.

A few minutes later, the door opened again, and Dante returned. However, he was not alone. Three of the other men followed him into the room carrying a large hose and buckets of fresh water. As the men worked to drain the disgusting fluids from her cage and replace it with fresh water from the ocean, the prince blew the horn—never allowing her a chance to speak.

Naida stared at him, fighting back anger and desperation, but allowing her tears to flow. *Let him see the pain he causes*, she thought. I *hope he remembers this moment for the rest of his life as the decision that killed an innocent. I may no longer be human, but this is murder, and I hope it haunts his dreams for eternity.*

Still, she recognized the small kindnesses he did for her, like not letting the men dump the large buckets of water over her head as she cowered in the corner of the aquarium and not allowing them to taunt or touch her with their filthy hands. Dante watched, ever silent except for the blowing of the horn and his barking orders until the men finished.

When he stood to leave he said, "I'll return later with your evening meal," before he strode from the room and shut the door.

For a moment, Naida almost believed he might actually care. *No,* she scolded herself. *The only thing this prince of men cares for is the money he will make from selling me to some scientist, pervert, or ring master. My life will end in filthy waters and agony because of him.*

The litany of reminders, curses, and weeping repeated for hours. A constant barrage of thoughts and fears flowed through her body like the clean waters flowed through her gills. By the time the door opened again, Naida had driven herself nearly hysterical with the myriad of emotions she'd allowed to plague her throughout the day.

Dante had come alone once more. Something he hadn't done in

the beginning. And he carried a tray in both hands toward her. The Voice of Poseidon was nowhere to be seen. Naida wiggled to the front of the tank. As she had before, she placed her hands together in a pleading gesture and signaled she wanted to talk.

CHAPTER NINE: DANTE

He hoped the mermaid couldn't see his hands shaking as he set the tray down on the table next to the chair he usually occupied when in her company. The cargo hold remained almost pitch dark during the day, and the single candle he carried didn't offer much illumination.

Get ahold of yourself, man, he thought as he bent to light the lantern. The room filled with yellowish hues, and when he turned, his heart sank. Her lovely brown eyes with long, thick lashes filled with tears as she used her hands to plead with him to speak with her.

Dante wanted to. He knew he shouldn't. But a part of him desperately wanted to hear what her voice would sound like when she wasn't pleading for her life, gagged by a filthy rag, or trying to kill him. He shook his head before turning back to the tray.

None of them had known what to feed a starving mermaid, the legends hadn't been clear on that. Other than human flesh, no one had ever seen or heard of the creatures feasting on anything else. So, they had caught salmon, tuna, snapper, and even eel and served it to her raw. Though nothing seemed to please her—for good reason, he guessed—she ate what she was given each day. Tonight, he'd brought her a special treat. He'd hooked the black sea bass and plump pollock only an hour before.

Dante pulled the key from around his neck and approached the glass. He still hadn't taken out the conch shell. *I'm insane if I do this. She'll kill us all,* he thought. Despite his reservations he reached for the lock and let his gaze meet hers.

"You want to talk?" he asked.

The mermaid nodded.

"You must swear to me that you will not attack me in any way. You can't use your siren song or call up that monster. You can't bite at me. You must behave. Do you swear?"

She tried to make an X over her heart just as she'd done before, and Dante had to fight back the smile pulling at his lips. The simple and almost childlike gesture sealed his fate. If he died, and all the men on the ship perished, it would be because a beautiful sea creature had reminded him of happier times when he'd been just a boy with no worries of dead fathers and brothers and a kingdom to run.

Dante undid the lock and let it clatter to the ground before pulling the chair over to use as a footstool. It took all of his strength to push back the metal lid by himself while balancing on the rickety wooden seat. Somehow, he created an opening just big enough that she could use her arms to pull herself up on the edge of the aquarium and raise her head out of the enclosure without him falling off. The tinge of saltwater already going stale hit his nostrils as she emerged, and guilt washed over him.

"I'm sorry about the water. I know it must be uncomfortable for you," he said before clamping his teeth down on his tongue. *Damn it,* he silently cursed. *Do not show weakness now.*

The mermaid looked at him with those sad brown eyes and nodded as if to say she understood there was nothing he could do.

"I'm going to remove the gag now. *Do you promise to be good?*" he asked.

She nodded vigorously in response.

"Very well then," Dante said. He pulled a knife from his side to cut away the rag, but the mermaid jerked.

Alarm spread across her beautiful face as she sank to the bottom of the aquarium and covered her face with her bound hands.

Dante jumped down from the chair and stared at her in horror. "Oh, no. It's okay," he said. "I'm not going to hurt you. I was just going to cut away the gag."

The mermaid continued to cower.

He tapped on the glass lightly until she opened her eyes and peered back at him, her gaze full of anger, fear, and confusion. Dante raised his hands so that she could watch him walk back to the table and place the knife there beside the tray. Then, slowly, he walked back to the chair and climbed up. When the mermaid didn't move, he motioned for her to come to him.

With the same caution he'd seen his stablemen use when breaking wild horses, she moved upward, always prepared to bolt.

"That's it," he crooned as she raised her head back above the water. "I was just going to cut away that filthy rag, but I can try to untie it instead."

The mermaid bent her head to allow him access to the knot at the back of her skull. As Dante worked his hands around the coils of dark hair, trying not to pull, he felt her body trembling beneath his gentle touch.

"I promise not to hurt you if you promise not to hurt me," he swore.

The mermaid raised her head until their noses were only inches apart, and her large doe eyes bore into his. Fresh tears dripped down her cheeks, but she nodded again. After a few unsuccessful attempts, he finally freed her from the gag.

In a voice that still sounded lovely even if it had been made hoarse from screaming, crying, and breathing dirty water, the mermaid whispered, "Thank you."

"You're welcome," he replied as he stepped down once more.

"I'm going to take the shell out of my pocket now, just in case. But I swear I won't use it unless you make me. Understand?"

"Yes," the girl replied. "Though, I promise you that I will not give you cause to use it."

Dante pulled the conch out and held it in his right hand. "What is your name?" he asked.

"I am Naida," she answered, her eyes swimming from him to the fresh fish on the platter.

"Naida, my name is Prince Dante Montoya. Would you like to eat while we talk?"

CHAPTER TEN: NAIDA

They talked for an hour as she ate cubes of raw fish. Naida tried hard to remain calm, sweet, and submissive. But, inside, she raged. Coddling a stupid human in an attempt to gain her freedom seemed disgraceful. Especially a human man. Even the food was unacceptable. Despite the popular human opinion, mer-people preferred sea moss and other vegetarian dishes over raw meat. She ate anyway, knowing she would need her strength if her efforts paid off.

Dante had clearly grown comfortable with her during their conversation. So much so that he'd removed the wax from his ears so that they could talk quieter and lessen the chance of drawing attention to themselves. As they chatted, she began dipping her tone here and there, beginning the tiniest notes of the siren's song. Not enough a human should notice, but enough that her plan might begin in earnest.

And when he'd moved closer to the aquarium, Naida had made sure to press her body against the tank while using her arms to prop herself up on the rim. His eyes couldn't seem to decide if they wanted to stare longingly into hers or roam over her naked breasts.

Of course, her hair covered most of their full roundness, but when she pressed forward, she knew exactly what he would see from the downward angle of his chair.

"Dante, can I ask you a question?"

"I guess so," he answered, suddenly looking a bit shy.

"You seem like such a kind man. Why are you doing this to me? Why did you do that to my people?" Naida kept her voice quiet and slow, letting just a little more of the siren's song dangle in her tone. *Please do not let him notice,* she pleaded to the gods.

"I..." he began. "I didn't mean for anyone to get hurt. Dead Eye is a madman. I only wanted to see the mer-people. I wanted—" He stopped, unable to finish this time.

"What did you want?" Naida insisted, using the lyrical tone a bit more. "Tell me what you wanted, Dante."

"I wanted to have one for myself," he declared, and the shock of that confession washed over his face in a mix of horror and anger. "You swore you wouldn't do that!" he yelled as he jumped up, knocking over the chair.

Naida dove under the water and to the rear of the tank, her still bound hands in front of her as if they might somehow hold off an attack. She shook her head vigorously, silently pleading once again. Their gazes bore into each other, but when Dante didn't move to grab the shell or approach the glass, she slowly relaxed.

After a moment, he motioned for her to rise up from the water once more, and she did so cautiously. "I didn't mean to, I swear. It is the nature of the mer-people to speak as we speak. It takes tremendous effort for us to hold our tone. Please, I am sorry," she lied.

Dante looked doubtful.

"I swear, it only happened because I became comfortable with you and dropped my guard. I won't do it again. Please don't be angry."

Though the distrust still shined in his eyes, highlighted by the yellow lantern light, Dante took a slow and purposeful step forward. "It is time for me to go now, Naida. I've stayed too long. If I remain here, the captain and crew will become suspicious. Someone might come. What I've done might be discovered. Then, they will not allow me to come here alone again. I may be a prince, but I am still an outsider on a vessel with other dangerous men who owe me no fealty."

Naida's heart sunk low in her chest, becoming a ten pound weight of sadness and fear. She might have lost her only chance at escape by pressing him so soon. "I understand," she whispered as she bowed her head to allow him to replace the gag.

The sound of ripping cloth surprised her, and Naida's head jerked upward.

"I will not place that filthy thing back in your mouth," he said as he finished tearing a length from his shirt. "The corners of your mouth are already cut from the coarseness of that dirty rag."

His hand reached up to stroke her cheek, and they both jumped back in shock the second his flesh touched hers.

Naida bowed her head again and whispered, "As I said, Prince Dante Montoya, you are a kind man."

Dante did not speak to her again. He simply tied the fresh gag in place, much looser this time, and left the room. Naida sank into the clean water and drifted into her own mind, wondering if the prince would return again. Telling herself she only cared because he was her one chance to escape, she tried desperately not to think of how it had felt for him to caress her cheek.

Her belly full, her water no longer filled with filth, and her mind somehow eased by the gentle way Dante had parted, Naida finally drifted off into a restless sleep filled with strange dreams. When she woke, the sun peeked through the thin lines between the planks above her. Stretching as much as she could, she ached for open water and the ability to swim through the currents and waves.

Naida spent the day humming to herself and floating about in the small enclosure, waiting for Dante to return. When he finally arrived, they spent hours in conversation. This occurred nightly for the next four days. Every evening when he left, he stroked her cheek before replacing the gag, and she knew her plan was working.

On the fifth day, the hours passed and she dozed off and on. Each time she heard a sound, her heart leaped. But it was only the men working on the deck above her, and she sank deeper into despair. At last, as the light began to fade, the door to the cargo area opened.

Naida turned around, her big, dark eyes purposefully held wide. But two men entered instead of Dante. One began to blow the shell as the other opened the enclosure, removed her gag, and dumped barely edible fish into the water. Once the lid had been replaced and the lock snapped closed, they stood with their hands over their wax-plugged ears and waited for her to eat.

Naida shook off the effects of the conch and forced down the disgusting meat that would soon go bad—poisoning her and her water. She reminded herself she would need her strength in the days to come. If Dante had truly abandoned her, she had no other hope of escaping until they reached land. As soon as she finished, the men blew the horn again so that they could remove the waste from the water and gag her once more. Naida cried in earnest. Death seemed all too close now. The finality of her predicament clouded her mind as the debris from her dinner clouded the waters.

Days passed in this manner. Still Dante didn't come. She feared the worst, and some part of her wanted to weep for him. Though he'd caused so many of her troubles, something in him seemed sweet and vulnerable. Somehow, Naida suspected he hadn't held ill will toward her or her people. He was a human man who made human mistakes. Still, she cursed him for not coming back. For not saving her.

On the third day, the door to the hold opened again. This time Naida did not turn. Her water had grown almost septic again, and she could not bear to force one more piece of nearly rotten fish between her lips.

I'll die before we make it to where we are going anyway, she thought. *Why bother trying now?* But when no boot steps neared her enclosure, she turned, expecting to see the same harsh and uncaring faces as before. Instead, hope awakened in her.

Dante stood inside the doorway, a tray of food in his hand. For a long moment, he didn't move. His gaze froze on her face, and his body stiffened. She wanted to beckon to him, to somehow summon him to her side as she did the kraken. She wanted to enslave this man to her. But that was a power she could not wield while bound and gagged inside her watery prison.

The minutes stretched on, until Dante finally shook his head and looked down at the tray in his hand. He came closer and placed the food on the table.

"I'll be right back," he said as he held up one finger and stormed away.

Six men, including the two who had been her caretakers for the last few days were marched in a few minutes later. Dante berated and threatened every man present but especially the two he'd left in charge of her as they drained the aquarium and poured fresh water inside. Naida wished she could ask for a simple tub outside the enclosure so that she may clean away the taint of the filth still in her hair and on her skin, but she knew Dante couldn't allow such a thing.

Protecting his interest in a profitable business deal and showing true compassion to her were two very different things. And even if the prince did have some kindness in his heart, he wouldn't be able to show it without risking both of their lives.

Once the men left, Dante dragged the chair over as he'd done before and motioned for Naida to come up to the top of the water.

She wondered if she would look crazed and dangerous if she tried to smile around the gag in her mouth and decided against the effort. Instead, she tried to look as passive and woeful as possible.

"Hello, Naida," Dante said. "I was thinking we could spend more time talking tonight. I'm sorry I didn't come sooner but we put into port, and I had some things to take care of."

Naida nodded to say she would like to talk to him again, and that she understood why he had abandoned her to the mercy of such ruthless men. Of course, the only thing she really understood was how little he cared for her survival. How could she not?

"You mustn't be angry with me or try to use the siren song on me because of it. Do you understand?" he pleaded.

Though she tried not to show it, rage boiled inside her. She nodded her head and crossed her heart, adding the last little bit because he'd seemed to like it when she'd done it before.

"Very well. Let's remove that gag. I brought you something special this evening. Since we were in port, I acquired some of the things you told me that you enjoyed eating more than the fish."

As Dante untied the cloth from around her mouth, Naida stared at the fresh plate of sea moss, seaweed, and wakame. Her stomach rumbled. She'd been aboard the ship for almost two weeks, and her body needed more than raw proteins from the nearly rotten fish.

"Thank you, Dante. You are strangely kind for a man who is holding me captive against my will," she said as he stepped down and went to fetch the food.

Once he balanced the lid on the corner of the tank, and she began to eat, he took his seat. Naida had to force herself not to grab up the bowls with both hands and pour them into her mouth. The raging hunger for fresh sea vegetables gnawed at her insides.

But when Dante spoke, she stopped mid-chew and nearly forgot about the food altogether.

"When we spoke before, you asked me why I had done this to you and your people. Then today, you tell me I am a kind captor. I feel as if I owe you an explanation and my deepest apologies. Though I cannot change what I've done or set you free while we are at sea, I can offer you some sort of explanation. Even if it is nothing but a poor excuse for terrible behavior."

Naida bit into her cheek to keep from screaming out her frustration. *How dare he tell me he cannot change this or stop it? How can he sit here and feed me as if I were an actual sentient being to him but still commit to following through with a scheme that will end in my death even as he apologizes for doing so? How can he force those brutes to provide me with oxygen and clean water but still leave me here to suffer?*

Instead of responding, she gave a silent nod of her head.

Dante went on to tell her of how his father had passed away due to a strange illness, and his brother lay dying from the same unknown disease. He poured his heart out about how he'd been an irresponsible and cowardly second son, intent on fulfilling his destiny as the family scandal maker. He'd never wanted to be king. He still didn't want to be king. So, he had set out on a mission to find the mer-people his grandfather had told him about. And though he hadn't expected to succeed, he had. Now, there seemed no way to take it all back. Not the murder of those five mer-people in the battle that night, or the deaths of the men aboard the ship. Not Naida's imprisonment or even his own shame.

Tears rolled down Dante's cheeks. "Please, Naida. You must understand. If I try to free you, these men will kill us both."

She interrupted him without much thought to her words, as she said, "If you die, we die together. It wouldn't be so terrible."

Dante blanched. "Why would you say such a thing?" he asked.

Naida did not offer up a real answer. Instead, she shrugged her shoulders. "I'm sorry, my prince. I am feeling a little melancholy today. Please continue."

"I do not want to die. And neither do you. Not really. But this way, I can protect you until we reach our destination. There you will be taken to a man who is a collector of all rare things. He will care for you, and you will live. Then I will be able to return home to my own country and rule in my father and brother's place. It is our only chance of survival."

Naida swallowed the last bite of sea moss and cocked her head to the side. "Dante, you would truly save me if you thought you were able to do so without us both being killed?" she asked, astonishment filling her voice.

"Yes," he cried. "A thousand times yes. I wish I had never begun this folly."

With hope in her heart once more, she said, "We could do it together, you know. I could use my siren's song to escape. You could come with me."

He shook his head no. "The men have all plugged their ears with wax, day and night. And if you call upon that beast again, we both know I won't survive the attack. This is the way it has to be, Naida. Please try to understand. We can't just say if you die, we die together. We both have to survive."

Naida cried openly for a while, and Dante sat in silence.

His head hung low, weighed down by the wrongs of what he had done. "I tried to take it all back, but now it is too late. I have a duty to my people to survive this ill-fated adventure and go back home to face a lifetime of being responsible for an entire kingdom. How the mighty have fallen," he mumbled into his hands.

Naida couldn't respond. No words could explain how she hated the man before her, yet his sadness tore into her heart. No good would come of the things he had done, not for her anyway. Still, she wanted to offer him comfort. The contradiction inside her drove hot anger to the surface like a volcano erupting from the seas she had once called home.

"Leave," Naida demanded. "Get out of my sight, you weak and horrible human. Bind and gag me, leave me to rot in my own filth. How dare you weep in front of me? You have condemned me to be a captive monstrosity or nothing more than an abused animal for the rest of my life if I manage to survive this voyage. You, the spoiled little prince, who wants to cry over castles, parties, and riches beyond imagination. All the dead bodies lying in your wake will hang on your consciousness like an anchor until you sink. Get out before I sing you into the sea right now and call up the kraken to slurp your brains from your skull."

CHAPTER ELEVEN: DANTE

Her rage was justified. Deep down, Dante knew that. He had done everything she'd accused him of and more. And he'd committed the atrocities all for the sake of dodging responsibility. This above all else proved he wasn't fit to be a king and never would be, and by admitting that to himself, he only worsened the guilt riding him. With that shame came the undeniable anger he harbored inside as well.

Faster than she could react, he grabbed the shell from its place on the table and blew. The trumpeting silenced her tirade long enough for him to drag the chair over and replace her gag. He blew again to give himself time to pull the lid back over the lip of the tank and close the lock.

With Naida secured, he let loose a torrent of anger. "You speak of murder and misdeeds. You are nothing but a creature of hatred and destruction. Your people feed on the flesh of men as sport. Your kind has terrorized the seas for thousands of years, yet the mermen and women play victim whenever they are at the receiving end of things."

Before she could respond in angry gestures, he turned his back and left the room.

Little sea bitch, Dante cursed as he stormed up to the deck and turned his back to the port to stare out across the ocean. Another storm rolled across the horizon and the winds whipped at his sandy brown hair and tugged at his clothes. Soon the skies and seas would be as dark and turbulent as his mind.

The mermaid enraged him, captivated him, and tore at his heart-strings. Every part of him longed to be near her, but each time he tried, she turned on him like a rabid dog. "Impossible," he growled between clenched teeth. "It'll be a blessing to be rid of her."

He stood on the deck long after the sun had set over the vast waters and the waves had begun to pummel the hull with force. For once, Dead Eye had made a good call by remaining in port for the night. The men who'd survived the kraken seemed edgy, and he wondered if they were fighting the same terrifying memories as him. It would be awhile before he'd feel comfortable on the open sea at night in a storm.

Only the fat drops of rain pelting down from the swirling clouds finally drove Dante down to his cabin and into a fitful night of dreams. It seemed Naida would haunt his every moment with her dark curling hair and golden brown eyes no matter if he were awake or not. So, he drifted in and out of nightmares and wakeful worrying about what would become of her.

In the early hours of the morning, just as the first purplish light of dawn filled the sky, Dante returned to the deck and stared up at the fading stars. An impossible idea snuck into his mind as he watched the waters and wondered where the pod had gone and if they were out there searching for their lost Naida.

Yes, he was a selfish, thoughtless, and spoiled prince. But soon he would be king. He couldn't enter into that role with the weight of this burden haunting him for the rest of his life. The decision had been made days ago, he just hadn't admitted it to himself or to the mermaid. If something could be done to save her, he would risk it all to do so. She had done nothing to deserve such a fate.

Filled with regret, Dante turned on his heel, ready to barge back into the cargo hold and apologize. *I'll plead with Naida, and we will work together to figure out just how to escape the ship and make it back to where we'll be safe in my kingdom. From there, she can recover before she goes back to the pod.* That thought kicked the side of his heart like an angry mule, but he knew no man could truly ever be with a mermaid and survive. *I'll go on to find a queen, and Naida will find her own mate. That is just the way the world works.*

"Where are you going in such a hurry at this hour of the morning, your highness?" a deep voice asked.

Dante spun to meet Dead Eye's lopsided glare. "The chop kept me up all night. I was just returning to my cabin," he lied.

"Is that so?" The captain stepped closer, a menacing snarl spreading across his haggard face. "I thought you might be off to spend a few more hours chatting with our little fish down in the hold."

"No," Dante protested. "Whatever would give you that idea?" Something felt very wrong, and Dante wasn't sure what would happen next.

"A little crow said you have been chastising the men so much about their treatment of the wench that the crew are beginning to clamor about mutiny." Dead Eye stepped closer. "I understand taking care of her until she can be delivered. We want to make sure and get a fair price after all. But the same little crow said when he went in search of you to discuss your place here amongst real sailors and men, he overheard an argument."

Dante recognized the look of murderous rage in the man's one good eye, and even as he backed away, he laughed. "Captain, you can't be serious. I'm only looking out for our interest here. And as the future king, I have the right to choose who I speak with and who I don't. If the mermaid and I had words, it is none of anyone's business. Especially not one of the rats you have crawling about my ship."

"Is that so," another voice sounded from behind Dante.

He whipped around to see five men lurking in the shadows. "What's going on here, Captain?" he demanded.

"It's time for you to get off the ship, Prince Dante," Dead Eye said. "You'll not be setting that sea bitch free, nor will you be returning home to play ruler in your fairytale castle."

The first hit caught him in the face, the rest landed over every inch of his body. Dante tried to struggle, even tried to fight back, but the six sailors were stronger and meaner than he could ever be. They pummeled him until blood poured from the open gashes and wounds and several bones cracked. Unconsciousness loomed just out of reach, and by the time the beating stopped, he was close to begging for death.

Just as they made to toss him over, Dead Eye halted his men. "Bring me the shell first," he demanded. "We don't want to lose our way of controlling that bitch or our means to capture more of them."

Dante tried to fight, but his lungs gurgled as he gasped for breath, and his vision blurred. None of his limbs would obey his brain's commands, and he feared the crazed brutes had snapped his spine. But when they tore the conch shell from the inside of his coat and lifted him to the railing, pain raged through every nerve ending. The sailors heaved his body into the water, and the landing crushed the air from his lungs. Dante sank down into the darkness, watching the human world disappear.

CHAPTER TWELVE: NAIDA

After the fight, Dante never returned. Naida waited and watched, forced to obey the others as they tormented her with rotted food and rough, groping hands. She wept when the water in her enclosure turned brown and murky. Unable to safely breathe it in, she bobbed above the surface until the levels had become so depleted that she could rest on her tail without the gills on her neck being submerged.

Dante had been so angry, and they'd both said such terrible things. But, deep down, she had thought him too kind to truly give up on her. She'd been convinced he would return, and then she could have used her beauty, charm, and siren's voice to make him help her if he wouldn't do it of his own accord.

How could I have been so wrong? she wondered. *How could I have misjudged him so much?* Starved and alone, Naida knew she would die soon. No one, mermaid or human, could survive the levels of toxicity in the water for long. It's *probably for the best,* she thought. *The man they call the collector sounds like a far worse fate than death.* Still, she cried soundlessly day and night.

By the time Captain Manford Dead Eye Roberts stormed into the ship's hold and blew the Voice of Poseidon, Naida was too weak to move let alone try to sing the siren's song or call the kraken to her. Her scales itched and her skin wrinkled and puckered within the filthy water surrounding her. She'd given up and was ready to die. The fight had left her when Dante hadn't returned.

Dead Eye ordered his men, "Get her out of the contraption and get her cleaned up. I can't deliver a sewer bass to the collector."

Rough hands ripped her out of the water and threw her into a copper bathtub. Naida curled into a ball, trying to hide her body from the sailors and protect herself from the pain she knew would come. When the shock of cold sea water splashed down over her face and torso, she gasped, but her limbs could not find the strength to struggle. The men tugged at her hair and ran scratchy sponges over her from face to tailfin.

Human women might have enjoyed being groomed by others, but Naida hadn't before she'd become a mermaid and she certainly didn't now. She fought to find even the smallest note of the siren song, but her throat closed around her every attempt as Captain Roberts continued to blow into the shell. Then the man with the needle had come, filling her veins full of some vile liquid that made her head spin like a cyclone. In that moment, exposed and at the mercy of evil men, Naida swore she'd kill every human she came into contact with for the rest of her life if she could only survive.

The fresh water had opened her swollen gills and soothed her irritated scales and skin, but Naida still lay nearly unconscious in the tub of fresh salt water. Hunger clawed at her stomach, and pain ricocheted through her skull. Weakness enveloped her like a cocoon against the men's hatred, numbing her until only a dull, throbbing rage pulsed within her heart.

Despite her efforts, she couldn't process what was happening. It wasn't until they'd wrapped her in blankets and carried her to the deck that realization set in. Blinded by the first daylight she'd seen since she'd been locked away, Naida turned her face toward the sky and squeezed her lids closed. Fresh air filled her lungs. For a moment, her mind cleared, and she realized Dead Eye hadn't blown the horn.

She struggled to call for help, to summon the kraken. But the drug they'd injected into her arm had stolen the life from her limbs and the power of her brain to form coherent thought for longer than a second or two. Naida had never fought so hard to make a single sound in her life, but when she finally found her voice, only a cracked groan of pain escaped her lips. The man with the needle looked at her in shocked surprise, and injected her again.

The world spun and her whole body went numb as a shining seal encircled her vision. To reserve her strength and to keep the captain from using the shell, she gave up and watched quietly from where they'd laid her on the deck. The men carried up a smaller aquarium, this one just barely large enough for her to lay down in, and placed it on a strange contraption that consisted of a flat board the size of the enclosure's base on six metal wheels and a pulley system hooked to a large beam that stood taller than the aquarium.

It's a mobile glass coffin, she thought, lost in the delirium of the drugs.

The men standing guard over her lifted Naida once more. She tried again to call out to the sea, but her voice barely made a squeak before they dumped her into the tank and closed the lid.

"Don't worry, pet," Dead Eye crooned in a sickening tone, "we'll have you to your new home soon." His laughter echoed in her ears as the sailors draped a dark cloth over the glass on all sides.

Naida bobbed in the water, occasionally slamming into the glass as the tank was jostled about. Though she could not see beyond the darkness they'd enclosed her in, she could smell the human world all around her. Voices shouted as her enclosure was hoisted upward and tipped dangerously to one side. But instead of praying that it would fall and break, she pleaded with the old gods that it didn't. Even if she were close enough to shore to make an escape, the very sight of her dragging her glimmering tail down into the port would expose the entire mer-people community to more men just like Dead Eye.

Not once did she hear or see Dante as she'd hoped she would. Throughout the entire horrible experience of being washed and manhandled, she'd prayed he would come. She'd believed he could still redeem himself by helping her. And when she realized he seemed nowhere to be found, Naida wondered if something awful had befallen him.

Finally, the rocking and tilting lessened, becoming more of a steady sway. Naida took her hands from where she'd braced them on the sides of the tank and rested. Even through the thick glass and water, she listened to the rhythm of horses' hooves.

It won't be long now, she thought as she drifted into the drug haze and closed her eyes.

When she next awoke it was to the sight of a strange human man staring through the glass in wide-eyed amazement. Naida jumped, pushing her body against the aquarium with her tail. With such little space to move, she slammed into the glass with a thud hard enough to make her head spin.

Dead Eye glared at her, and his hand reached inside his coat pocket to where she knew the conch shell lay hidden. In that moment, Naida realized the captain had no intention of parting with Poseidon's Voice, and that provided her with the perfect opportunity. Her captor seemed unaware that, once in their lifetime, every mermaid was allowed to walk on land and be a human again for a single lunar phase. Or maybe he did know that strange bit of truth, and he just didn't care. Either way, Naida had found her means of escape. She'd drive the bald man with thick glasses to throw himself into the sea the first chance she got, then she'd simply transform into a human and walk out into the world on her own.

Naida let her eyes droop and her limbs go limp, pretending to fall back under the influence of the drugs they'd given her. In her mind, she pictured the deep crevice the mer-people called home. Their shell houses and businesses and the smiling faces of all the people she knew and loved floated behind her closed lids.

Soon, I'll be home, she silently promised herself.

Minutes ticked by, and Naida had to force herself not to peek through her lashes at whatever was taking place outside the enclosure. *Have they exchanged money yet? Is the strange man bartering for a better price?* She hoped with all her heart that he wasn't. Dead Eye didn't seem the type of man to spare the collector's life if he felt as if he might be cheated out of his monetary gain.

Voices, muffled by the glass, echoed through the water. Naida's eyes instinctively sprang open to the sound of an unexpected thud and the squeal of something rubbing hard against the glass. She screamed as she flattened herself against the opposite wall, sending large air bubbles upward through the water. The bald man's face slowly slid downward, smooshed against the aquarium. His glasses tilted, magnifying large dead eyes as they stared into her soul. Blood poured from his neck, bubbling like a fountain.

Dead Eye stood behind him, with a red-smeared knife in his hand and a look of cruel satisfaction on his face. "Clean the place out, boys," he ordered. "Load everything of value into the wagon."

He used me, Naida thought. *That bastard used me to get to this man just so he could kill him and steal his things.* Tears leaked from her eyes into the water as she stared at the dead man. *He deserved it,* she told herself. *Anyone who would purchase a mermaid or merman for their collection of rare oddities deserves what they get. He was just another awful human. It doesn't matter. I've got to get out of here.*

Her original plan had been thwarted. Naida had no choice but to attempt escape from the sailors while they were still busy ransacking the collector's home. It would be more difficult than what she'd expected. Dead Eye had the Voice of Poseidon.

The only way I'm going to make it out of this aquarium is to turn human, but then how do I manage to break the lock? I won't go back to that ship, she declared. *Never again.*

Naida thought hard as her panicked heart pounded in her chest. Every second she waited brought her closer to losing her chance to run. She wasn't large enough in either human or mermaid form to break the glass or the metal lid on the aquarium. And, if she transformed while still in the aquarium, she would drown.

Suddenly, it came to her. Naida knew exactly how she'd escape. Her chances were small, but anything was better than what she would be forced to endure while in Captain Manford Dead Eye Roberts's hands. The murderous wretch had killed Luna and the other mermaids, the collector, and probably a prince all to gain a fortune and some fame. He wouldn't hesitate to cast her aside the moment he found another mermaid.

Locked into her own mind, she bided her time until the men arrived to tell their captain that their loot had been loaded into the wagon. Dead Eye smiled down at Naida trapped inside the aquarium and still trying to pretend the drugs had kept her submissive. It took all her strength to hold back from screaming at him.

"Load the enclosure. Let's get everything back on the ship and set sail before he is discovered and word begins to spread," the captain ordered.

Naida hunkered at one end of the tank, curled into a ball and waiting. The four men lifted the aquarium. The water rocked and swayed as they strained to carry it to the cart waiting outside. She allowed them to take a few steps, wanting their muscles to be weakened just a little more. One of the men stumbled and the water sloshed backward toward where her weight pressed.

Dead Eye removed a hand from his side of the glass to pound on the lid. "Straighten out in there before we drop you and leave you to die in the sun."

Naida took her shot. With the man who'd stumbled still off balance, most of the water weight and her own body pulling at one end of the aquarium, and Dead Eye not supporting the back corner with both hands, the enclosure teetered precariously.

With every ounce of strength she could muster, she pushed

against the wall of glass and propelled herself toward the other end of the enclosure. Her head and shoulder screamed in pain when she collided with the front of the aquarium, but the sudden shift in weight distribution pulled all the men off balance. The water rocked hard back and forth for a fraction of a second before the tank fell.

Nadia instinctively threw out her hands to catch her fall, and the palms hit the ground, jarring her until she gnashed her teeth down on her tongue. Shattered glass sliced into her flesh and scales in thick lines, and salt water burned the wounds. Nadia hadn't expected the damage from a four or five foot drop to be so bad. Pain ripped through her side, and she looked down.

The world turned in circles around her, and the angry men became no more than a blur. Their shouting voices sounded so much like the waves crashing on the beach during a storm that she longed for home even more. But she couldn't move. She couldn't tear her eyes away from how the light of the sun reflected off the hunk of glass sticking out of her side making it look as if it were floating in a sea of red.

A powerful impact knocked the wind out of Naida, jerking her attention to the man hovering above her.

"You stupid, bitch," Dead Eye screamed. Spittle flew from his lips as he drew the pistol from his side and blew Poseidon's Voice using the other..

"No," she yelled. Naida threw her hands up to cover her face, though there was nothing she could do to stop a bullet. She willed forth the transformation. The very least she could do is make sure she completed the change before she died. That way, her body couldn't be used to expose the rest of the pod.

The captain pulled back the hammer with a click, and she held her breath, accepting the horrible death she'd felt chasing her for weeks.

Grunts shattered the silent moment before the shot rang out. Naida jerked, but no new pain radiated through her. The place on her side where the glass stuck out hurt like hell, but she hadn't been shot. Still dizzy despite the adrenaline overriding the drugs, it took her a moment to focus on the commotion happening ten feet away.

"Dante?" she breathed as she watched the chaos unfold, too lost in the pain of her wounds and the transformation to move.

CHAPTER THIRTEEN: DANTE

When he'd seen her on the ground amongst the muddy water and blood, he had thought for sure Naida was already dead. But Dead Eye had kicked her, and she'd jerked. Dante had felt as if someone had punched him directly in the heart. After that, he hadn't thought about the consequences when he charged forward and tackled the captain to the ground.

The close-range gunfire rang in his ears as he struggled against Dead Eye. Luckily, his opponent had dropped the gun, but it took all of Dante's strength to pin him to the dirt. He struck the man over and over, watching his face transform into a pulpy mass of bloody flesh. Nothing in his life had ever felt so terrible and so right at the same time.

Dead Eye stopped moving or fighting back. Dante couldn't force himself to quit. Every hit brought back the vision of the captain cocking the gun and aiming it at Naida's unprotected body. He struck again and again until his strength failed. Then, he reached out, snagged Poseidon's Voice from where it had fallen on the ground, and stuffed it inside his own. He would not lose such a dangerous weapon again.

Suddenly hands grabbed both his arms and wrestled him upright. One man held him, why the other struck him in the face. Dante's head swam as pain erupted in his temple. He kicked upward, catching his attacker off guard when the blow landed in the center of the man's chest. The sailor holding him stumbled off balance, but managed to maintain his grip.

The one he'd kicked stood up and snarled. Eyes gleaming with menace, he strutted over to a nearby stump and pulled an ax from its center. Turning back, he snapped, "I'm going to make you pay for that, Prince Dante."

The sharp blade sliced through the air, aimed at Dante. There was nothing he could do with his arms pinned as they were. Of all the things he could have thought of, of all the people he should have imagined in that moment, his mind turned once more to Naida. The image of her under the water and turning toward him played in his memory. Beautiful dark eyes held wide and a mischievous smile tugging at her lips.

The sharp edge sliced across Dante's chest just as gunfire rang out. His other attacker released him and ran, as the man with the ax fell to the ground. The sailor's dead, unblinking eyes stared upward even as his body twitched. Blood pooled beneath his head.

Pain ripped through Dante, but his mind barely registered anything beyond the sight of Naida standing behind where the man had fallen with the smoking gun still in her hand. He couldn't believe his eyes. It couldn't be true. Dante was certain that he must be hallucinating or already dead because Naida's naked flesh sparkled in the sun from head to toe.

Dante's chest lay spread open, sliced by the ax blade. It had cut so deep so fast that the blood hadn't yet started to flow from the gaping wound, and when he looked down he saw bone. Averting his eyes, he gazed upward at the woman moving toward him.

Still unsteady, Naida stumbled forward on human legs. Blood flowed from the glass jutting out of her side and from various other cuts. Still she pushed forward until she fell on her knees next to him.

"If we die," she whispered, "we die together. But not yet."

CHAPTER FOURTEEN:
NAIDA

They both needed help soon. As a healer she knew just how bad both of their injuries were. So, with a determination she would have never guessed she possessed, Naida stood from the blood soaked ground. Using the black cloths the men had covered the aquarium with and Dante's knife, she cut out bandages. Everything in her wanted to work to save him first, but if she didn't care for herself, she would not survive to help the prince.

With both hands, she yanked the glass from her side. The agony stole her breath away, but she forced herself to concentrate on filling the wound with a piece of the cloth and then wrapping a long strip around herself until it held so tight she could barely breathe.

Dante groaned, and her attention turned back to him. His skin had gone pale and the wound bled buckets out and around him. Whispering reassurances and working with adept hands, she wrapped the cloths around his chest. Each time she pushed to turn his body, he groaned in pain, and her heart ached. At last, she managed to stop most of the bleeding.

"Dante, I need you to wake up," she cried. "I'm going to need your help with this next part. We have to go now. Please wake up. I need you."

His eyes cracked open, and Naida sighed.

"The cart they used for the aquarium is only a few feet away. The horse is still hitched to it. I need you to push with your legs, I'm going to pull you by your arms. But I'm not strong enough to get you there alone. You just have to do this, and then I'll get us to safety. There's a hoist I can use to get you onto the cart. But you are going to have to help me. It's going to hurt. I'm so sorry," she said, begging him to stay strong for just a few moments longer while she prayed she could survive her own wounds.

Dante's eyes drifted closed.

"No. Damn it. You are not going to die. Not here. Not now. If we die, we die together, and I'm not going down like this. Do you hear me?" she shouted.

The prince opened his eyes and nodded.

"Good. Now, get ready." Naida moved to grab him under the arms and lifted. He screamed, but she didn't stop. "Push, Dante. Push now."

He did as she said, and though it felt as if the glass was still shoved deep within her side, Naida pulled until they reached the edge of the cart. Time was running out, but she had to rest. She had to breathe. The pain ripping through her weakened limbs held her prisoner as she gulped in air. Minutes passed until she could finally stand again.

Hooking the ropes around his shoulders, waist, and legs, Naida secured Dante into the pulley system. Luckily, the cart rode low to the ground and she would only have to lift him a foot or two. Because of her injury, even that much force would be hard to exert if not for the ratcheting system the men had left secured to the line and a fence post.

Using both hands she pumped the lever up and down, raising Dante until he hung just above the cart. Then she half-walked, half-stumbled to the front of the cart. "Horses," she breathed. "I always hated horses. Even when I was human."

The animal whinnied and shied, but Naida didn't hesitate. Instead, she grabbed the harness secured over the beast's muzzle and pushed backward. At first, the horse resisted, but when she didn't give up, it stepped back far enough that Dante hung at the center of the cart. Her vision blurred and darkness threatened to take over, but Naida kept moving until she had removed the ropes and Dante lay on the wood. She took another moment to secure him with the ropes they'd used to anchor down her watery prison before she kneeled beside him once more.

With her hand on his sweat-beaded cheek, she promised, "You're going to be okay. Just hang in there. We're going now." She couldn't tell if he'd heard her or not, so she pressed a kiss to his forehead and climbed onto the coach box. With a click of her tongue and a flip of the reins, the horse began to walk. Naida shook the reins again, encouraging the beast into a trot. She didn't want to jostle Dante or herself too much, but time had become their enemy.

Blood loss, too many drugs, and exhaustion weighed heavily on Naida as she steered the horse onto the main road leading away from the collector's home. She hadn't seen the way they'd come when Dead Eye had brought her there, but she'd felt the turn when the water had shifted and had registered the passing of time until they'd arrived. It would be a miracle if she and Dante reached help in time. She clicked the horses into a faster trot and whispered a prayer.

Having not been human for a decade, everything still seemed so foreign to her. So, the noise approaching from behind them didn't register in Nadia's mind as a danger right away. They'd been on the road for a while, and she could smell the sea. At first, she thought maybe she was hearing waves on the shore though the wind didn't seem very strong. But when she turned, she saw the cloud of dust rising just beyond the bend.

The man who'd gotten away must have sounded an alarm. The collector was dead, and surely he had people who wanted to protect him just like the sailors had wanted to protect Dead Eye. Naida panicked. There were a lot of them, but how many she couldn't tell. And they were moving much faster than her single horse pulling a cart loaded down with an injured man could. The port was too far away to reach.

Her mind grasped for the only hope she could find, and even though she wasn't sure it would work, it didn't matter. They'd die either way if she didn't do something. Naida jerked the reins and steered the horse from the dirt road onto the plains separating them from the ocean, flipping the reins again and again until the cart moved at top speed. Thankful she'd tied him to the cart, Nadia looked back to watch Dante's body bouncing against the wood.

She drove the horse hard toward the sea, but the men following them gained ground as they tore across the plains behind them. Naida screamed in frustration when the ground began to turn to sand and the cart slowed. Guilt wracked her when she reached for the whip and used it to push the horse harder.

She could see the water. Its promise of safety loomed up in front of her like a beacon in the darkest night. But the men were closing in. Their blood thirsty cries heralded over the sound of the waves and the pounding of the horse's hooves. Naida cracked the whip again, and the horse screamed in protest as froth flew from its mouth. Tears poured from her eyes in a combination of pain, fear, and remorse.

At last, the sand turned dark with moisture. Naida glanced back over her shoulder to see the men still a quarter mile behind them. "We're almost there," she cried out to Dante, the horse, and herself. "We've almost reached the sea."

But her celebration came too soon. The back wheels of the cart sank into the wet sand, jerking the horse to a dead stop. The poor creature lost its footing and toppled sideways, taking the cart and Naida with it. Dante, strapped as he was, slid until his body slammed into the wooden side rail.

Pain seared through her and panic enveloped her mind. On hands and knees, Naida crawled toward the sea. She couldn't think

698

of Dante, lying helplessly at the mercy of the men once they reached him. She couldn't think of how she might not make it to the sea in time. She had to try.

The men's horses whinnied and kicked up sand as they came to a halt before the cart just as Naida's hands found the water. Voices yelled behind her, but she did not look back again. Instead, she pushed herself into the surf, submerged her face, and began to sing.

Air pushed out of her lungs and sea water burned her eyes and filled her mouth. Without her gills she could not reach the highest notes without coming up for a breath of air, and the bubbles swam around her cascading hair.

"Kraken, come to me. Defend your mistress," she called into the depths. At first, nothing happened, but Naida tried again. She'd known that she might not be able to call the beast since she'd turned human, but she had to try. She couldn't give up. "Kraken, come to me. Defend your mistress and her people."

Green light flowed forward from her mouth and fingertips to swim around her submerged body, and Naida surfaced with a cry of triumph. Still singing, she spun until she could see the men moving across the sand toward the water's edge.

Dante remained strapped to the cart, unmoving and unmolested by the enemy, and she prayed he wasn't dead before she returned her focus to the movement of the water around her. "He's coming," she whispered, allowing magic to pour from her body and into the sea, beckoning the kraken.

The men paused. Some of them pointed to the strange light swirling around her, but Naida had already sent out the call. Even if they threw themselves down and begged for her mercy, she couldn't stop what had already begun. "Come to me," she sang, urging the kraken upward from where it slept in the darkest dark of the undiscovered seas.

The first tentacle snapped up out of the water, and then seven more followed. They whipped the air around her like the whip had snapped against the horse's hindquarters. Then in a cascade of sea water and roaring sound, the kraken raised up from behind her, crawling into the shadows like the monster she knew it to be.

Its appendages shot out, striking some men, and grabbing others. Horses and humans alike fell victim to the beast's insatiable hunger. And though the collector's men tried to run, they'd waited too long. The kraken's reach was long and unflinching as it avenged Naida's wounds. When the last man had succumbed to the beast, it calmed. The massive tentacles retreated, and came to cradle her in its grasp with gentleness.

"Bring him to me," she ordered. "Please do not hurt him. I wish to take him to the deep." She'd never asked the kraken to help her in such a way. But something in the way it had been so gentle with her told Naida that it would do her bidding even if it went against its nature.

One tentacle stretched back out of the sea and pulled Dante from the wreckage. Limp and still, he hung in the thing's grasped like a rag doll. Naida closed her eyes and hoped with all her heart that he still lived. And when the kraken placed him next to her in the bend of another appendage, she saw that his eyes had slid open, though only pain shone there.

"Dante," she crooned, "I am not sure this is what you will want for yourself, but I can still save you. It's too late to make it to the port. We've both lost more blood than most could withstand and the cart was destroyed. Do you want to become like me, Dante? Do you want to belong to the pod and live or would you rather die?"

Dante groaned, but managed to reach up to her face.

"No, I need you to answer me. You will only be able to return to land once in your lifetime afterward. This is forever if you choose to become one of us, and I can't promise that Galene will grant you such a thing after all that has transpired. But, before I call her, I need your permission. I need to know this is what you want, and we are running out of time, Prince Dante."

He closed his eyes and his hand fell from her cheek. Naida watched him dying there while pressed against her in the creases of the kraken's tentacle. Tears slipped through her lashes, and she cried, "I'm so sorry I couldn't save you. Thank you for helping to save me." Sobs shook her shoulders as she pulled Dante closer.

"Naida."

The whisper of her name brushed against her cheek, and she jerked upward. Dante's sad smile melted her heart into the sea. "Take me with you."

Though she knew what such a thing meant to him, Nadia ached with hope that Galene would accept their request. The human world would lose a great man and future king, but the mer-people would gain so much more. She would gain so much more.

CHAPTER FIFTEEN: NAIDA

Gathering all of her strength, Naida slipped back into the water and raised her voice into the fading day. She used her siren's song to call out to the pod, hoping they were near. Even if the charge of magic in the waters and the rise of the kraken had alerted them to her whereabouts, she needed to call out for urgency. The wreck had reopened her and Dante's wounds.

Minutes passed, and Naida raised her voice again. The first pinks and oranges of a beautiful sunset began to fill the sky, but still she saw no sign of the pod. Caressing the kraken's giant tentacle she whispered, "Thank you old friend, but I think this is goodbye. Go back now and rest. Your job here is done."

The creature gently shifted Dante to the sand, but stirred for a moment as if trying to decide if it were okay to leave her there wounded and dying.

"Go now. You have served me well," Naida whispered, new tears streaking down her cheeks.

Moving so slowly that it barely stirred the ocean, the massive beast backed away and sank into the deep. Left alone, Naida crawled back onto the beach and laid next to him. Though she'd hated him and cared for him while on the ship, his gallantry and self-sacrifice had made her love him. Knowing everything he'd willingly risked for her made it hurt so much more that she might die next to him on the beach.

"If we die," she whispered, "we die together."

"What's all this talk about dying," a lyrical voice asked.

Galene, the creator of mermaids, sat at the water's edge. Her long blonde hair flowed in the wind, catching hits of the sunset. Naida gasped and pushed herself upright despite the fresh blood that pressed out of the bandage on her side.

"Oh, Naida. What trouble have you gotten yourself into?" the other mermaid asked. But as her sea-green eyes fell on Dante, they narrowed with rage. "And why are you with one of the men who attacked the pod?"

Placing her hand on Dante's chest to feel his heartbeat, Naida answered, "I'm afraid I don't have much time to explain. He was badly wounded while trying to help me escape captivity, and he's dying."

"Without an explanation, I cannot help you," Galene replied. Her gaze shifted to Dante once more and her voice grew as cold as the Atlantic in the winter months. "Or him."

Naida spoke quickly, trying to leave nothing important out. She told the maker of mermaids how she'd been captured and why. She explained Dante's part in the attack and how he'd been misled by the captain. She assured Galene that Dante had realized his folly and had regretted the choices he'd made. She told her of his kindness while Naida had been a prisoner, and then of his brave rescue. How the prince had willingly sacrificed his home, family, kingdom, and himself to save a mermaid.

During the explanation, Galene's features softened. "And the shell, Poseidon's Voice, where is it now?" she asked.

"I'm not sure," Naida answered. "It may have been lost in the battle, or it may still be with the dead man's body."

A look of grave concern passed over Galene's face. "I understand."

Just then, Dante stirred and the women realized he had awakened. His hand reached into his shredded coat, and he pulled out the shell. "Take it," he said, holding Poseidon's Voice out to Galene. "Destroy it—" Dante paused for a ragged breath "—or hide it away. Just...don't let it fall into human hands again."

Galene accepted the shell and stared deep into Dante's eyes for a long moment. "Thank you," she said at last. "And is it true, Prince Dante Montoya, that you are willing to give up everything to join the pod and be with Naida?"

"Yes," he groaned, one hand clutching his chest and the other reaching for Naida.

"And what will your kingdom do without their future king?"

"They will find another," he answered as his face twisted into a grimace of pain.

"Please, Galene," Naida begged. "I beg of you. Turn him. He can't survive much longer."

Galene looked thoughtful for a long moment. "He has committed crimes against our kind. Ignorance is no excuse for what he did. However, by relinquishing Poseidon's Voice, killing Captain Roberts, and saving you, he has also done the pod a great service. So, I will grant him this gift, Naida, but know you are responsible for him. If he ever betrays the pod again, I cannot and will not save either of you."

Naida wept. "Yes, Galene. I understand."

"Then you know what you must do," she answered before slipping back into the sea.

Naida dragged Dante back into the water, cradling her head in his hands. "The transformation is both dark and painful. For you to turn, you must first drown. Try not to fight, it will all be over soon," she whispered as she sank him under the water.

His eyes went wide but he fought the urge to struggle, and Naida was thankful he did. Her strength had abandoned her completely, and it took all her weight on top of him to hold his body beneath the gentle waves. As the last light fled from the night sky, the final spark of life drifted from Dante's eyes.

Galene pulled his lifeless body from Naida's arms. "I'll take it from here. You should transform back before it's too late," she said before drifting into the dark waters with Dante's body.

The sea pulsed with magic as both transformations took place. Naida soaked up the feeling of fresh sea water in her gills and her body stitching itself back together. Even the pain of the healing felt like a sweet welcome home as she swam downward to find the others.

At the center of the pod, Galene floated next to Dante, and Naida's heart pounded against her chest. He'd been healed, yes. But a shimmering scale-laced scar spread across his chest where the ax had nearly killed him. She knew in that moment how lucky they were that he'd survived. Not even the transformation had been able to take away how close he'd come to death.

"Naida," Dante whispered before he darted forward, pulling her into his arms. Finally, their lips met in a kiss that could've set the oceans on fire.

Kintsugi Unbroken

MARIE CATHERINE REGALADO

PREFACE

Kintsugi is the Japanese art of sealing broken pottery with gold. The art form takes what was once whole and seals broken pieces together in an elaborate design of organized chaos. The once simple bowl finds that it awakes from shattered neglect to luxurious transformative art, more beautiful than it had any right to dream of. We are born empty vessels, ready for the world to pour into our souls. Over the years, some of us find the world to be too much, and we crack into pieces. We try to hold that shell together with tape and a prayer, but in the end, only the golden love of ourselves can withstand the test of time. Given a chance, we can repair the broken pieces and make something new and beautiful out of that vessel that was once too broken to use.

CHAPTER ONE

I nearly drowned in the ocean outside my parent's house when I was young. A rip tide came by and tried to pull me under with force so strong that I could only wait for the inevitable. I let my body go limp and watched the water dance around my head. Just as suddenly as The Tide grabbed me, I felt it release and pull me back up. My tiny child's head popped above the water, and I giggled as The Tide pushed me forward to land. I felt his laugh in the ocean spray. He was playing with me, and I was okay with that. He had always been my dearest friend.

She always felt at ease by the Sea. Her husband didn't care. For him controlling the vast expanses of the deep blue water was the ultimate control, but for her, it was pure magic. The ship they boarded was by far the largest yet, with unusable smokestacks decorated in brown and gold with a royal theme. This was likely the central selling point for the man ahead of her. He was tall, lean, and olive-toned with jet-black hair. Anyone with eyes, male or female, would have their breath taken away at the sight of him. Daliah could have loved him had his beauty extended past his superficial exterior.

THE FAMILY BEGAN to climb aboard with the distinguished man at the lead. His eldest son followed close behind, a perfect copy of the father in beauty and temperament. Next in line was the youngest, as the males always took the lead. His toddler legs walked hesitantly up the ramp and were coached forward by a stern-looking Scottish nanny. The next in line was a busty bombshell woman, who the casual observer could assume must be the mother, regardless of the stark contrast in her pale complexion and the rich tones of the children around her. She walked confidently with two very chatty teen girls, all vibrating with excitement for the adventure ahead.

Finally, yards behind came a timid, slight girl who could easily be mistaken for the eldest daughter from the casual observer's perspective. For a moment, one of the teens looked back at her and rolled her eyes as though the distance and demeanor of the trailing relative bothered her deeply. The woman noticed the look; however, it barely registered as she had so few positive interactions with her family. It would have been more impactful had she received any form of kindness recently. She simply lowered her head and focused every bit of energy on each step before her. One plank, gap, two planks, water, one plank gap.....all the way to the top.

SHE MADE it a song in her mind and found peace in the process and joy in having a purpose. As she felt her toes hit the flat deck, Daliah mentally braced for any direction her husband, the handsome leader of their clan, gave.

"Daliah!" The man stepped forward and took her elbow in his large hand. "Waiting for you is NOT something any of us enjoys, so stop holding us up."

Her breath caught as she waited for his fingers to dig familiar bruises into her delicate arm, but today he was too distractible and barely left a mark.

The pale Blonde woman detached from her younger companions and floated to his side, smiling and charming as always. "Oh, Donovan, isn't this simply the most delicious view?" With the command of a woman wanting nothing, she gently hooked her arm in his and met no resistance from him as they scampered away.

Daliah's arm was left mostly unmolested for the moment.

The Blonde woman with natural perky tones spoke loud enough to capture the attention of anyone within 100 feet. "Now, I was just plotting with the girls, and we think you'll LOVE what they have planned for tonight. There's a magnificent show to welcome the guests, and we have already notified the crew that you'll need their best seats. Everyone will see you and your older children sitting in the most distinguished place this tin can has to offer. It'll be a magnificent way to start our journey."

Donovan visibly turned to putty in her hands, ready to start their adventure.

Daliah looked on as an impartial observer while her "Family" walked away without another glance in her direction." She followed the group with a slight increase in pace to avoid additional attention. The group was greeted by an eager porter and a gaggle of luggage handlers. The group zigged and zagged through various decks before finally landing on a luxurious floor, clearly made for the elite people onboard.

Daliah dreaded this moment because she never knew if her husband wanted to put on the "Happy Family" show for the crew or let them assume what they would without worrying about their low-statured opinions. She always hoped for the latter, as she looked young enough to be one of his children. With his new "Friend" taking up all the oxygen in the room, it would probably be easier for him to let them all assume she was the matron of the brood. Make it an actual Von Trapp Family situation as if the countess had won their father's love instead of the meek, pious woman.

The Blonde, attentive to Donovan's every move, felt comfortable taking control of the situation and spoke up. "Well, aren't these cabins just lovely? Do any of the cabins connect? Some of the kids would love the opportunity to sneak into each other's rooms after they've been told to sleep, those sneaky devils." She winked conspiratorially at the teens to let them in on the joke before turning back to the porter for a response.

"MADAME, you can rest assured that the only connecting door is from the servant's quarters to the master suite; all other rooms are solitary cabins."

Donovan had determined the attendants needed no show as they were well below his stature and made his presence known. "Fine, fine. Leave the bags in the master suite. Stephan, decide where your siblings will sleep, and be ready for dinner within the hour."

Turning to the porter, he asked, "Will this boat ever get underway? I assumed the cost of our stay included a timely departure."

The porter was a professional, as it would have been easy to point out that the family's late arrival had something to do with the delayed departure time. Still, ever the professional, the man bowed and made excuses. "Of course, sir, it will be only a moment. If only we could control the tides and be on our way faster. Please don't hesitate to ask for anything. We're at your service."

Donovan waved the man away, clearly not comforted by his groveling, and stomped back toward the suite leaving the family behind to sort out the cabin assignments.

The Blonde looked unsure of what was expected of her. Daliah took the lead, knowing it was best to only make assumptions once Donovan had declared his intentions. She picked up her personal effects and gestured for The Blonde to follow her to the servant's quarters. Once they were inside and the door was shut, Daliah opened one of the connecting doors and waited, standing at attention. The Blonde looked like a fish out of water for the first time that day. She sat on the bed, hyper-focused on her nails, and began picking and cleaning them like her life depended on it. After about ten minutes of silence, she huffed and stared holes into the locked joining door; clearly, she was unaccustomed to waiting.

Just then, the door to the suite clicked and openedd. Daliah was not surprised to see her tall, handsome husband on the other side. He looked terrifying to Daliah and like magic to his mistress.

Daliah stepped aside, allowing him to enter, taking care not to move too quickly or too slowly. He looked around and took in his wife's suitcase lying on the bed. His scowl turned toward her as though she had decided without his permission. Before he could jump to conclusions, she carefully spoke to his concerns. "Stephan sent my bags to the master bedroom, and it was clear I was to come here. The crew assumes she's your wife, and he made no effort to correct them." She breathed and waited to see if her simple, direct explanation suited him. His eyes turned from anger to lust as they locked onto the honey-brown eyes of The Blonde. She perked up, sending her ample breasts out, drawing even Daliah's attention.

Without looking away, he spoke to Daliah, never too distracted to address his frustration with her. "Stephan was correct. YOU can stay here for the remainder of the trip. We have no need for you. My companion here will take your place by my side. As a matter of fact, I should probably make sure she is well attended to before heading down to dinner." He softened his tone before addressing The Blonde directly, "Do you mind running ahead,my pet, and starting the shower? Long car rides always make me feel so dirty." He focused back on Daliah.

The Blonde eagerly jumped off the bed and made a vulgar grab for Donovan's crotch before slinking away. He never took his eyes off Daliah as his mistress closed the door behind her. She couldn't be utterly blind to the strained relationship between the couple. It was evident that she planned to pretend it wasn't happening. Daliah thought she would make a lovely replacement for her should Donovan decide to finally kill her one day.

As soon as the door closed, Donovan bent down to hold Daliah's chin in his large hands. He leaned in to close the space between him as though to kiss her, but she braced herself, knowing full well there was no peace to be had between them.

He stopped far enough back to see Daliah's eyes as he spoke, and she knew exactly what he was looking for. Although Donovan loved to travel, he always felt uneasy right before the boat got moving. He couldn't control the ship or the tides but could always count on Daliah to be in his total control. She saw it coming as he became increasingly upset with her, regardless of what she was or was not doing. Donovan scowled at her in gruff low tones, "You see? THAT is what a wife should be like. I give you everything, and all you give me is a headache. You better stay out of my sight, or I swear I'll make you pay for your constant insolence." He spat in her face and roughly released his grasp on her face before slamming the joined door behind him.

CHAPTER TWO

The Wind saw my plight. He encouraged me to laugh by playing little tricks on the people walking by. He'd shoot a gush of wind toward a loose skirt or knock the hat right off a man's head. These tiny little distractions helped pump me full of temporary dopamine and made me last just that much longer.

THE BOAT WAS RUNNING LATE, which wasn't unusual as the staff worked diligently to settle all the passengers. Inevitably, a few boarded late, and today was no exception. Soledad had been working on this boat his whole life but would swear he was born in the sea. He may have come from lighter stock, but that blistering sea sun had colored him the darkest shade of brown, and he loved it. The man had been looking forward to a break. He was relieved to return to the shared staff quarters without bumping into any more needy passengers. Soledad plopped onto his bed and took in the largest breath he could, holding it for only a moment before slowly letting it all out. He had just a few moments to take these much-needed calming breaths before he was expected back to start preparing the dinner service.

SOLEDAD COULDN'T LIE DOWN for fear of passing out, so he closed his eyes and re-played the day in his mind while sitting up just enough to stay awake. Most of the passengers and interactions floated past his mind as blank pages and uninteresting social sets, likely to pepper him with needs later in the voyage. He laughed to himself about a particularly handsy yet unfortunate-looking newlywed couple he had helped earlier in the day. It wouldn't have been delightful had it not been for the bride, clearly trying to get to their rooms, and the groom just not understanding the urgency. His mind slid into another positive memory from the day when he caught a young woman in the middle of a secret smirk that he just couldn't take his eyes off.

HIS LAST PLACEMENT of the day wasn't anything extraordinary; however, there was this one moment he wasn't meant to catch. As the last large, wealthy family made their way up the gangplank, this young woman stood out as she lagged far behind the rest. Usually, that would have annoyed Soledad because she held up his much-needed break, and the family was already very late, but something about her intrigued him. This young woman on this specific day caught his interest because of the way she was walking up. The rest of the family was bold and clearly putting on their best "Public" face, with over-the-top conversations or overly stiff stoicism with a dollop of too rich to care. The vibe they put off was meant to draw the attention of anyone looking so they would know exactly what their monetary worth was. They wanted everyone to know that they were better and more easygoing than any peons near them had the right to be. Everything about their stature said, "Get back to work."

· · ·

THE YOUNG WOMAN at the back of the group, presumably the oldest child, was anything but "Better." She was just normal, silly, and clearly playing a game. Soledad could see her mouth moving as though singing a song to herself. Her smirk was so consuming he couldn't take his eyes away. Something about how she smiled made him break out into a secret smile of his own. It was enough to make him forgive her the discretion of taking her time. He would take his time, too, if he had to deal with that family. The memory brought another smile to his face, and he decided to keep an eye out for his secret smiler during the remainder of their journey.

AS THE HORNS BLEW, announcing the boat was finally on its way, Soledad stretched and sighed before getting back onto reluctant feet. Today he didn't mind as much that his break was over because now, he had a mission, and he couldn't wait to see what played out at dinner.

THE FAMILY WAS sharp and ready for dinner, leaving their suits in a flamboyant fashion. Daliah was the only one missing, and no one bothered to find out why. Donovan came out, followed by his shock-ingly beautiful guest, and the pair led their group to dine with the elites.

THEY WERE GIVEN a semi-private lounge of their own, and everyone claimed their seats quickly to begin the festivities. As they waited for their father to take the social lead, each sat quietly, hands folded in their laps. Once Donovan felt properly respected, he stood and walked to familiar tables as they waited for the food to arrive. The older children followed suit, and The Blonde followed him, lapping up the hostile looks she received from his "Friends" wives. The wealthy all became magnetically drawn to each other, taking care not to get too friendly with those lowly folk at the basic tables.

SOLEDAD WAS PLACED at the bar and had a perfect view of the wealthy elite lounge. He searched the crowd between orders but was sadly left wanting as his favorite distraction was nowhere to be seen. After the dinner service was well underway, he lost hope that she was joining the family feast. He believed she wouldn't have been thrilled to laugh and play with them anyway; it didn't seem like her style. Once the desserts came out, Soledad gave up entirely on his search and doubled down on his work to get to the next blessed break. The guests began drifting into the dance club, which had its own bar, so he closed as quickly as possible. He was finally free to be rid of the guests until the morning.

IT WAS hard to calm down after a full day, so Soledad made it a habit of wearing himself down by walking laps before bed. He walked the deck, knowing full well that most guests would not be there now. It was the only time of day he was safe from their ever-wanting needs.

THE AIR that night was a little colder than he liked, so it became apparent that he would need to take his adventure inside. Soledad walked with purpose and looped through corridors with ease. As he zig zagged and climbed stairs, he eventually found himself drawing closer to that particularly interesting families' cabins. He made excuses that a job is never done until EVERY guest is cared for. That was the narrative he told himself to excuse his intrusion. He couldn't possibly allow that young girl to go hungry. He had to at least check and ensure she had everything she needed.

· · ·

HE WASN'T EVEN sure where to start with five doors before him. That girl he was looking for could be in any of the rooms, but which one? As he stood contemplating in the middle, he heard the tiny stomping feet of a small child. He turned around just in time to see a 4-year-old chubby little boy launch around the corner. Without a care in the world, the boy dove behind Soledad to hide from someone or something coming for him. As alarming as the loud intrusion was, Soledad assumed it was all in innocent fun. The boy's laughter was infectiously familiar. He knelt and put a hand on both shoulders, speaking in a conspiratorial tone to gain the child's trust, "Oh dear, are we hiding from the broccoli from dinner? I think I can smell it coming for you from the dining room." Soledad made a big gesture closing his nose and gagging a little, much to the little boy's excitement. The child nodded enthusiastically and held his own nose, peaking around the man for an offending vegetable in the hallway.

JUST AS THEY began laughing even harder at their cleverness, the servant's quarter door peeked open. Once the women inside established that no one was around save the two in the hall, she came out. The woman was precisely who he was looking for. The young woman he envisioned was older up close and much more beautiful than he could have imagined. She couldn't have been much older than him, maybe mid 30's, but too young to be the gentleman's wife and too old to be his daughter; perhaps she was a sister. It was very confusing as the puzzle pieces tried to make a fit in Soledad's head, but her beauty was distracting enough to bring him to the present. The quest to find her went from an innocent game to a genuine interest. Her slight frame was wrapped in a dark green silk robe that hypnotically hugged her delicate curves.

THE LITTLE BOY was NOT happy about this apparent distraction. He made his frustration known by grabbing Soledad's face in his sticky hands and moving his head to match the conspiratorial tilt of the boys because there were still jokes to be made. Soledad laughed so hard with the bossy little boy and dared a quick glance at the woman. She was staring straight into his soul and must have believed him safe because her attention turned to the boy as she took long strides toward him.

Daliah scooped up the boy, all the while darting her eyes and ears toward the corridor. Once she was assured no immediate visitors were coming, she embraced the boy in a deep hug. The boy started to squiggle until he recognized the woman picking him up and smashed himself into her breast. Her gentle touch instantly calmed him, and he slumped in her arms with a heavy sigh. She deepened the embrace and snuggled her nose into his hair. He smiled at her, and she kissed his cheek with the love of 1000 stars in her eyes.

Soledad felt his heart open wide at the perfection of their embrace and realized he had never experienced anything like it, not even from his own mother. He remained kneeling on the floor, stone still totally enraptured by the beauty of the connection before him. The moment couldn't have lasted more than a fraction of a second, but it felt like hundreds of perfect years.

Without the slightest change in her deep smirk, a half-smile Soledad noticed her son mimicked perfectly; she stooped back down, placing the boy in the stranger's space. She gave one last squeeze to his chubby hands before taking a significant and swift step backward. She first gave the stranger a clear look of conspiratorial guidance before turning her eye back toward the corridor. Soledad was entirely too enraptured by her to hear the footfalls behind him. Still, just as he was about to look, the boy again grabbed his face like nothing had happened between the child and the woman he adored.

JUST AT THAT MOMENT, the elderly stern woman he had seen the boy with earlier came barreling around the corner and stopped dead in her tracks. She squinted at the scene before her, judging each of them as though she suspected tomfoolery everywhere. She appeared appeased that nothing obviously untoward had happened and moved forward to collect the boy in her arms. "Peter! You naughty boy, what have I told you about running around the boat? Do you want to join the Sirens below?" Her broad Scottish accent and roots became most apparent when tested or when given a chance to talk about the spirits and any other mythological creatures that could be hiding behind every corner. "You'll be fish food before daylight with all this mischievous behavior. I'm tempted to tell yur father he has a changeling on his hands, for HIS little boy couldn't possibly be so poorly behaved." She scurried toward their suite, which was the door furthest from the master bedroom and even further from the servant's quarters, as though the mother was never meant to be near him.

ALTHOUGH THE ELDERLY woman visibly calmed as she held the boy, she continued admonishing him, "You're lucky yur father doesn't take to beltin' ye' like mine would have. I tell ya, boy, I can still feel the crack of that leather on my ars'." The boy giggled but was too tired to put up a fight. The nanny turned to Soledad and spoke over her shoulder, "Thank ye' fir catchin' this wee lad. Best be puttin' him to bed before his father sees this disturbance." Her last word was directed straight at Daliah, who had made no effort to move or even make eye contact. The nanny clipped the door shut, and Soledad stood up, finally finding himself alone with the curiosity in green silk.

. . .

DALIAH PULLED her robe tighter and glanced toward the little boy's door before spinning around and walking purposefully toward her own lonely room.

WITHOUT A THOUGHT IN HIS HEAD, Soledad took the few steps between them and reached for her elbow so she would stay. The moment he had even the slightest grasp on her, she whelped, pulled away, and spun around defensively. As her hair swooped across her shoulders, he could see the bruises on her chin, neck, and soul up close.

HER TEARS WERE INSTINCTUAL, but recognizing her pain caused Daliah to stand taller and speak like nothing had happened. "Can I help you?"

HER VOICE WAS a lot stronger than Soledad had imagined. She was intense in every way, and he became lost in her sphere. He faltered a moment before responding, "Oh, um, I didn't see you at dinner and wanted to," he knew better than to see if she was okay; she clearly wasn't, "Um, I wanted to see if, well, if you're hungry."

DALIAH REMAINED defensive but thought deeply into his awkward question, never missing a thing; she knew he was trying to make her more comfortable. "Well, Thank you, I am rather hungry. Can you tell me how much longer you expect the show to go on? I suspect my family will likely stay until the end. They enjoy being the center of attention for as long as possible." Daliah knew she could poke fun at her family with this man because he had no vested interest in them.

. . .

SOLEDAD WAS DELIGHTED for this formidable woman to take the lead in the conversation because he was seriously struggling to focus. He responded joyfully, just happy to be helpful to her. "The band hasn't even started yet; they just finished dessert and made their way toward the dance hall. You have at least 4 hours before the party starts to wind down. Everyone always overdoes it on the first night; after today, the crowds tend to wind down a bit earlier until we get closer to our destination. If you'd like, I will happily bring you something from the kitchen." Ever the server, Soledad wanted nothing more than to make her happy.

DALIAH COULD TELL he was genuine and kind just by how he interacted with her son. Although she had planned to mope in her room, getting out sounded like a dream. "Actually, do you mind if I go with you? I would greatly appreciate it if you could help me avoid bumping into my family. As you said, people are typically a little over the top on the first day." She winked at him, which sent an electric charge through his heart. He perked up and offered his arm should she choose to take it. Daliah hesitated and moved to his opposite side to use her less bruised arm. He eagerly adjusted and steered her toward the servant's staircase nearby.

CHAPTER THREE

I disassociate from the heartache as much as possible. Somedays are more challenging when I could really use a firm hug. As a child, my parents gave me all the hugs I wanted and held together the cracks forming, sealing them with stability. Now here, alone and deprived of love, I only have myself to keep the shattered pieces together.

Daliah pulled away and squeaked from Soledad's touch. He thought he had hurt her again for a moment and stepped back. Instead of tears, he saw Daliah's hands covering her full smile as she giggled.

"Oh, Dear, I'm still in my nightgown and robe!"

The pair looked at her very inappropriate attire and laughed heartily. Daliah recovered from her giggles and looked into the stranger's eyes. He had kind, playful eyes that looked like the world had treated him kinder than her. For the first time, she realized there may be more than her tiny piece of the world had to offer, but for now, her only concern was standing alone with a man she barely knew while draped in thin silk. As funny as it was, Daliah knew it wouldn't be such a cheeky joke to the casual observer.

Soledad picked up on Daliah's discomfort and let the joke pass. Of course, she was beginning to look uncomfortable. A woman, alone dressed as she was, would draw unwanted attention, so he did the only thing he could. Soledad's mother may not have loved him as profoundly as Daliah loved her son. Still, the women that raised him taught him to always look out for his companions. He quickly removed his crew jacket and placed it on Daliah's frail shoulders. He was broader and taller than her, but the coat was the perfect length, almost like it was a fashion statement rather than an unexpected necessity. At the very least, anyone walking by would just see a sweet couple taking a night stroll.

Soledad stood back and took in her new look. He avoided her eyes, fearing they would trap him in their beautiful depths. With a wink and his outstretched hand, Daliah felt at ease and was grateful for the gesture. She took his hand and allowed this intriguing stranger to lead her wherever he wished.

Donovan had made the rounds and was unimpressed with his so-called peers. One gentleman with decent connections in the American stock market was worth following up with. Otherwise, there was no one worth his time there. He had been in the clubhouse for only an hour before contemplating his warm bed. It didn't help that the lady beside him made his heart race whenever she bounced with laughter. She opened an animal inside him, and he was eager to get her alone. Something about her made him reconsider his low opinion of women in general. His wife Daliah was like a limp noodle, or an empty shell compared to his new companion. Donovan swished expensive whiskey and laughed to himself as he compared the two. Once upon a time, he could have loved Daliah, but she was too young and frail for his tastes. If he was going to be perfectly honest, he only married her to gain favor with the town he was trying to do business with. Her parents needed money, and they had the resources he wanted. It was a marriage of convenience for him. If he was truly going to be completely honest with himself, and the whiskey had the tendency to do just that, he would have been done with Daliah anyway the moment she gave him an heir. That was all he needed her for; she had done that long ago.

Her delicate nature was the cause for a plethora of outbursts from him over the years. With every flinch or cowering, Donovan grew to loath Daliah. Her weakness was intoxicating and infuriating, but the chase had lost its steam years ago. Donovan had to work much harder to get a proper squeal out of her in the servant cabin earlier. He could tell she was faking the pain, so he dug in a bit deeper until he could see the blood rush from her face.

After their second son was born, he really had no interest in bedding her thoroughly used-up body. Now it was more about control than baring his children, and he found it soothing to see her terror, especially when he got stressed out. Boarding days tended to do that to him. The sea made him feel small, and Donovan did not like feeling anything less than substantial. That was the main reason they were on that godforsaken boat, to face his fears and prove to himself just how amazing he truly was.

After everything he had done for Daliah, she could only provide a vessel for his emotional needs. Tonight was different, though, because she wasn't doing a very good job of fulfilling those needs, and that meant she was pulling away. He couldn't have that. She wasn't allowed to have anything in her life that wasn't all about him. Donovan noted that he'd have to make sure she knew her place later.

The Blonde sensed his mood shift and worked to draw the attention back to where it belonged, on her. She made her displeasure known as she moved a perfectly manicured hand down his thigh, dragging nails harder than usual. Her aggression surprised and excited Donovan enough to bring his mind back to the present. He looked into The Blondes' eyes to see his hunger reflected in her own. He was unaware of his need for approval. Regardless, she was happy to give it to him.

. . .

DONOVAN WONDERED if The Blonde could help fulfill his aggressive impulses. She had teased as much in the past, but he had yet to see it in action. He leaned in closer to the woman to speak softly while digging his own hands into her thigh, testing the boundaries of their intimacy. Much to his surprise, The Blonde matched his aggressive grip and moaned as she spoke, "Don't play with me if you want to stay for the show. I'm not known for my patience."

The Blonde got up and addressed the rest of the party. "It is getting late, my dears, and I've had almost too much fun. Take your time and enjoy the rest of the show for me, will ya?" The girls looked crestfallen but had been trained not to show it, so their perky expressions quickly masked their disappointment. The eldest child had no visible reaction other than to glance toward his father, ready for a command. With the elegance of a trained debutante, The Blonde reached for Donovan's hand and gently pulled him toward her. "Darling, do you mind walking me back to my room? I'm completely turned around on this blasted boat."

She was all innocence at that moment, putting on a show for the other tables, which made Donovan even more eager to leave. He knew she was trying to get him to herself, and the show was perfection. "Of course, my dear. What kind of gentleman would I be if I let you get lost all by yourself." Donovan looked over to his older son and let go of the convivial charm. "Stephan, see that your sisters get back the minute this performance is over." Then edging back into a flirty tone, he looked back at the Blonde, "And don't bother checking in. I'll be indisposed."

DALIAH SAT in a metal chair in what she assumed was the employee lounge. Soledad opened every fridge door to find whatever he was looking for. By the third door, he exclaimed success. He made a yipping sound and displayed a childish grin. Daliah found it completely infectious. Soledad had found the stuffed crab leftovers and presented the tray with a flourish. The sight of the food made

Daliah's stomach rumble with excitement. After he had warmed them up a bit, he displayed the feast with a bow to his guest. Daliah let the laughs escape as freely as she had in childhood. She dug in, grabbed the closest one, and blew on it before attempting a bite. Soledad smiled and grabbed one for himself.

DALIAH WOULD HAVE BEEN DELIGHTED with the cold food. But appreciated his kindness too much to say anything to him. She couldn't remember a time someone had taken such good care of her. She realized she may be a tad naive, but she had seen the worst of humanity, and nothing in his character told her there was anything to worry about. Soledad jumped up and left. A few moments later, he returned with a bubbly red drink topped with a cute umbrella. Soledad placed it before Daliah and returned for his decorative umbrellaed glass.

SOLEDAD WAS ENRAPTURED by Daliah's beauty and quickly stuffed a hot crab cake in his mouth to avoid saying as much out loud. In his haste, he bit down into the heat, which simmered on his tongue. With instinctive panic, he leaned down to spit the scorching Volcano out onto the cold floor. The panicking man tossed his umbrella down with the offending food and chugged half the drink before regaining his composure.

DALIAH WAS LOOKING at him in shock before she broke out in a deep belly laugh as Soledad turned red. She caught herself and clamped both hands over her mouth to hide the joy. She was always worried her joy would bring a human hammer of pain. Giving into her own instinct, she abruptly stopped laughing and flinched.

· · ·

SOLEDAD CAUGHT the abused eyes under her beautiful shell and pulled Daliah's hands away from her mouth, forgetting his own minor pain for the moment. Sitting closer now than he had any right, he could smell the sweet warmth of wind in her hair. Chancing discretion Soledad leaned in and spoke softly. "Your laugh is infectious, you know. It's a travesty to hide that smile of yours from the world, so why don't we set it free, if only for tonight."

DALIAH ALLOWED a small crack in her smile to assuage Soledad's request. Although she had lost the joy for a moment, he made it easy to find her way back to it.

SOLEDAD EASED BACK and rejoined his chair reluctantly, but he knew he could only push it so far before crossing a line both couldn't come back from. "Now, before I tried to burn my tongue off. I was going to tell you about the special drink I made for us." He reached for her untouched drink and brought it forward. "Here, this was my grandmother's "Sunny Day" drink for the days when she needed the sun to shine inside the dark. After a very long first day at sea, I love to come down here and make this special drink to relax and remember the joy the sun brings. Take a sip, then try to tell me that you can't feel the sun on your skin as you drink it." Soledad suddenly remembered the straws in his vest pocket and quickly unwrapped one for her, the lovely lady before him.

DALIAH LEANED IN, never taking her eyes off Soledad, and took a long pull from her straw. She was surprised to taste a strong tangy zing with a delightful bitterness at the back of her throat. "Wow, that is delicious! What's your secret?" Daliah leaned in and took another long draw from her straw. Soledad was glad she liked it but was a little worried about how quickly she was lapping it up. "Woah woah, slow down there. Grandma wasn't as sweet as you, and this sunrise will put you to bed if you drink too much too fast. Especially if you haven't even eaten much yet. Besides, I promised Grandma I would never tell her secrets, so you'll have to just enjoy the delicious mystery."

SOLEDAD REALIZED he hadn't even asked the woman her name or if she even drank alcohol and hadn't explicitly explained its potency. "Oh shit, you do drink alcohol, right? I didn't even think to ask your name, let alone whether or not you drink alcohol, before making it for you. I can make you something else if this is too strong. Is it okay? I'm so sorry if this isn't your jam. I totally understand."

DALIAH LAUGHED it off and took a smaller sip. " Actually, I don't drink hard alcohol or any alcohol for that matter, but only because no one has offered me some. My name is Daliah. What's yours?"

"SOLIDAD MA'LADY AT YOUR SERVICE!"

DALIAH LAUGHED AGAIN AND ASKED, "Let's say that I do like this. If every cocktail was like Your Grandmother's secret recipe, I probably would drink them more frequently in the future. I can see what all the fuss is about. This is quite delicious, and I understand how it could be dangerous if you take too much too fast. I'll be more careful in the future, I promise."

DALIAH GAVE Soledad that secret smirk that initially caught his attention, and it reminded him to ask about the first moment he saw her. "First of all, no drink even comes close to being as good as my

Granma's, so you may be setting yourself up for disappointment if you think just any drink would be as good. Second, you haven't asked me why I was looking for you."

DALIAH AVOIDED eye contact and readied herself for a reprimand. "Oh, I, I didn't think to ask. I'm not used to anyone actively looking for me unless it's to leave. I've gotten quite good at predicting my husband's mood, so I know when to be ready and when to be scarce. But I hadn't really thought about why you would be looking for me. So, why were you looking?" Daliah didn't like being negative, so she always put a joke or something light at the end of the truth. "Luckily for me, tonight I was meant to be scarce so no one would miss me for a while. But I am curious now, what was it that got you looking for me? I am nobody." Daliah popped another crab cake in her mouth to avoid the need to keep talking. She hadn't led a very happy life and wasn't interested in relieving it when she was having such a good time.

SOLEDAD WAS FAIRLY certain he knew what was going on behind closed doors, especially if he had seen this woman's husband openly flirting with that voluptuous blonde not too long ago. Not only that, but no man was smoking and drinking like his life depended on it unless he had insecurity issues. His whole persona was very put upon, like a showman at a three-ring circus. Soledad took what little she shared and moved on because her comfort was more important to him than his curiosity. "Well, since you asked so nicely, I'll tell you, but you must promise to keep smiling. I'm sure you are aware that your family was the last to arrive this afternoon, correct?" He only paused for a moment as she nodded and impulsively cupped her injured left elbow. Soledad pretended not to notice. "Well, I was standing near the bow, that's the front of the ship, and watched with scorn as the late arrivals sauntered onto the boat. You see, we work very hard, and the sooner the boat is underway, the sooner we can take a break. I was just stewing in my frustration when you caught my eye. I saw this intriguing young woman singing and playing a game all the way up the gangplank. That smirk of yours is infectious, and I forgave you all the discretion of being late at that moment. I just had to meet the woman who could play and sing at a time like that with all the pressure of being late to the boat and shuttling that large family around. It was refreshing to see you in your own little world, just enjoying the moment."

Soledad was rewarded with that exact smile that pulled his attention earlier. He continued, "So, as for how I found you? I asked my buddy where your family was staying after you didn't show up for dinner. I was worried you wouldn't get to taste these award-winning crab cakes. It was just a bonus that I happened to be making my Grandma's special drink tonight as well."

Daliah laughed and finished her fourth cake before licking her fingers clean and taking another long sip of that amazing drink. Unfortunately, she hadn't eaten enough before consuming the magical cocktail and could feel the room getting a little spinny. "Oh! Oh dear, I believe it's time to get back to my room. Either the boat's rocking, or I need to take a break from this delicious drink." Daliah took one last tiny sip and winked conspiratorially at Soledad. The drink was loosening her up in all the best ways.

He couldn't help but bursting out in laughter before standing up from his chair. "Well, I have definitely been a bad influence on you tonight, so madame, I will take the offending drink away and escort you to your room. I can sleep now knowing that I've got you all fed and watered, well, vodka'd anyway." Soledad winked back conspiratorially as well and got up in a dramatic fashion to take her glass and hold it out as though it was disgusting to touch, which made Daliah giggle even harder. Soledad bent at the waist and offered his hand to help Daliah rise. He was both showing off his charm and a little concerned she may stumble. He was a little surprised that she took his hand so readily. Daliah appeared to be completely relaxed in his presence, but he didn't want to chance anything going sour, so he delicately released her hand the moment he was assured she could stand upright. As they neared her family suites, Daliah visually sobered and transformed from a slightly buzzed young lady to the pensive woman she had grown into over many dark years.

FEELING the change in her temperament, Soledad stopped and stepped back a foot to really look at Daliah before they parted ways. " Well, ma'lady, this is where I leave you, if you feel comfortable making your way the next fifteen feet to your suite. Would you like me to drop by again after breakfast for another secret kitchen raid? Or should I be expecting you in the lounge bright and early?"

HIS CHARM once again made Daliah smile and distracted her from her anxiety as she thought hard about his question. "I suppose we'll have to see what the morning brings. How about this. If you don't see me at breakfast, can you kidnap me after? Is that okay?" She suddenly worried about his opinion but pushed the thought away because she had spent too much of her life worrying about someone else's feelings instead of her own. Something about Soledad made her feel free to be herself, and it probably had a little something to do with the alcohol.

SOLEDAD DEEPLY BOWED to Daliah and winked while lifting his head. "As you wish, miss Daliah. I will await your command." Although he was tempted to kiss her hand to complete the dramatic action, he resisted. After all, she was married regardless of the obvious dysfunction. He got what he wanted anyway when she made that lightning smile before he turned away and disappeared behind the hallway wall.

DALIAH WAS ecstatic and still a little drunk as she approached her cabin. The kindness Soledad had shown made her reconsider the life that she had led. It was wonderful to experience true kindness again. It had been too long, and it really got Daliah thinking about what her life would be like in the future.

CHAPTER FOUR

The wind panicked one day when it saw my soul shattering beyond repair, and the person I once was began to fade. He promised to keep me together, to love me when I couldn't love myself. The problem wasn't that I didn't love myself. The problem was that my body couldn't take the poisonous stings from the man that should protect me. I knew it made the wind happy to help where he could, so I allowed him to wrap gusts of wind around the floating pieces. I knew this wouldn't last, but it made me happy to see him so happy. I only wish my husband could be so easily appeased.

Daliah quietly opened her door to the tiny dark room. She was at ease but had learned to tread lightly, just in case. Out of paranoid habit, she scanned the room and was startled to see the outline of a person sitting on her bed. The port hole was too small to help her make out the silhouette from the moonlight, so she clicked the light on and pressed her body to the door frame just in case. Sitting before Daliah, nearly three feet away, The Blonde leaned back on her elbows, showing off her curvy form. Her long thick legs were wrapped in black stockings clasped to the full body corset and delicate matching black underwear. The Blonde recrossed her legs and pointed toward the space beside her. She gestured Daliah forward to come and sit on the bed with her. With a stiff wobbly walk, Daliah did as she was told out of curiosity more than a sense of obligation. As she sat next to The Blonde, she could hear her guest take in a deep satisfying breath. The Blonde rose on her elbows as she began to speak, "Well, Daliah, there you are. Now don't be alarmed. I've put your husband to sleep." The Blonde gave a wicked grin as she continued. "I've worn him out and would be surprised if he stirs before morning." The Blonde winked at Daliah, but Daliah had no idea what on earth she could have done to knock him out so thoroughly. From what she had experienced, the man never slept. Fear ran down her spine as she considered that the woman beside her may have actually knocked him out. So, either he was dead, or worse, alive, and nearly hours from waking in a rage.

The terror must have shown on her face because The Blonde suddenly became serious. She started to defend herself, but it became evident that she misinterpreted Daliah's dread for shock about the very obvious affair she had been carrying on with Daliah's husband. The Blonde was surprised by her reaction because she hadn't seemed to care before. "Now look, it's not like you didn't know what was going on here. We haven't exactly made it a secret, and I haven't seen you put up a fuss yet, so we might as well be adults about this and talk about our next steps. It's not like either of you is very happy with the other, which is what I came to talk to you about."

Daliah was still very confused but didn't see any sign that The Blonde was there to cause her harm, so she agreed to listen. "Okay, what should we talk about then?"

The Blonde let her guard down and laid back across the bed. She patted the bedding beside her and propped the side of her temple up in her hand. Daliah remembered having a friend like her so many years ago who liked to lay in her bed and share secrets. Although The Blonde was dressed in a very sexual way, she was not lying in a particularly sexual manner. It was more of a relaxed, sleepover kind of posture. Daliah remembered how good it felt to hear her friend's secrets and to feel so close to someone. She laid down and mimicked The Blonde's relaxed body. The two took each other in and waited for the other to speak. It was no surprise that The Blonde eventually broke the silence.

"You are much older than you look. I can see some wise lines around those eyes." The Blonde reached and pushed Daliah's hair behind her ear. "You're actually kind of beautiful, you know? How old are you anyway? You can't be more than thirty, but you have a full-grown son, so unless you had him in childhood, you must be much older than you look." Daliah closed her eyes and remembered another thing she felt back in her room with her friend in her bed. It was comfort. She found herself biting her lower lip but became self-conscious and stumbled to remember her age. "Oh, I'm, well, I'm over 30. I'm thirty-six. I had my oldest about two years after Donovan, and I were married." The Blonde looked toward the ceiling as she did the math, and her eyes grew wide as she figured it out. "But you would have been 16 then? You're telling me that you got married at fourteen. Who does that?"

Daliah took the Blonde's astonishment as a harsh judgment of her character and sat up to defend herself. "Well, I didn't exactly do it for fun. My family needed the money, and Donovan needed access to the fishing boats we had. They landed on an agreement and made a trade for the boats. Donovan could take them in exchange for a large sum of money and me. It's actually very common where we come from, and he had to promise not to consummate the marriage until I was of age which would have been sixteen."

Daliah felt confident that her explanation was perfectly reasonable as these types of arrangements had been around since the dawn of mankind. The Blonde lost her snarky shell and visibly softened before speaking again. "And did he wait?"

Daliah looked down in shame before she replied. "NO, not quite."

The two women sat in silence for a moment. Daliah had never told a soul about Donovan's breach of contract. Had it become known, he would be forced to give back any profit he had made to her parents or their next of kin, which would be her. Daliah was too afraid of retaliation, so she said nothing until now. "But anyway, that's all in the past. What did you want to speak to me about." Daliah could feel the lingering effects of her delicious drink from earlier and was beginning to grow impatient with this conversation. She looked back at her pillow longingly but waited patiently for her guest's response.

The Blonde was still processing the information she had just received and said as much. "Oh yeah, I'm still working out what I think about Donovan's character after that bombshell. To be honest, I am inclined to agree with you and just leave it in the past. I'll have to think about it a little bit more, but in the meantime, I wanted to talk to you about our little arrangement. I've discovered tonight that our Donovan is a bit of a freak, just to put it to you plainly." The Blonde did not look at all upset about what she had just said. As a matter of fact, she licked her lip and bit it to show just how much she approved.

Daliah, on the other hand, just looked confused. "I'm sorry, what? What are you talking about?"

The Blonde suspected Daliah may not be aware of her husband's sexual peculiarities but figured it would be worth checking before she continued. "Well, how can I put this elegantly? He may be all strong and brooding outside, but deep down, he's extremely inse-cure. It's actually a lot more common for these kinds of men than you might realize. I'm not sure what he was like with you over the last twenty years, but with me, he is putty in my hands. I guess what I'm trying to say is he likes a Mama type. Someone who tells him what to do and punishes him when he doesn't listen, do you get me?" The Blonde studied Daliah's face but saw no understanding of what she had just said. "Maybe you noticed he can be controlling, as though he wants to punish you for something." Now it was Daliah's turn to look wide-eyed and shocked. "Wait! You're saying he does that to get off?" Daliah's look of horror and shock made The Blonde laugh just a little.

"Yes and no. I suspect, with you, it really is more of an anger thing, maybe just too many years of suppressed frustration. What I'm talking about is more of a mutually beneficial agreement. Some people just like to feel out of control within the confines of a controlled environment. There's a lot of trust and skill that goes into this kind of outlet. Some people get off on the pain or on inflicting the pain or some variation of that. In the end, it's never completely out of control, and both people have to be mindful of the other person's boundaries."

Daliah couldn't understand what The Blonde found so funny, and her guest could feel her confusion.

The Blonde realized she was talking to a woman who clearly didn't know a thing about mutual satisfaction, which made her feel frustrated with Donavan. She was going to make sure he never treated her in such a cruel way. "Okay, let me explain why I'm here. Donovan has certain needs, and I believe you may not be the best suited to meet those needs. Now, please don't be offended, but I think I'm more suited to the task. I'd ask you to join, but something tells me that's definitely not in your wheelhouse. I can help him learn how to refocus that energy into a healthy, more mutually satisfying relationship, and I don't think I'm overstepping to say that you would be happier with someone less aggressive, am I right?"

Daliah was still wrapping her head around Donovan's aggression and just couldn't picture it relating back to sex or for him to be vulnerable enough to allow this woman to tell him what to do. Instead of answering The Blonde's question, she asked one of her own. "So, does he ever hurt you or take it too far?"

The Blonde laughed, not realizing just how much physical pain Donavan had caused Daliah over the years. "Oh God, no! That's not how the rules work, and I would never allow someone to harm me in any kind of malicious way. Anyway, I came to tell you that I think you should get a divorce."

Daliah felt the sting of reproach from The Blonde's comment. The woman was either extremely callous or just had no idea how violent Donovan could be, and there was no pleasure in it for her, the victim of his rage. Daliah felt like she was in a daze. It was all too much to take in, but the thought of divorce had surprisingly never crossed her mind. " What would I do? How would that even work? I don't know where I would go or what the process would be. My family died ages ago, and I'm not even sure that Donovan kept their old house or any of their old boats."

Daliah was a little surprised at how easy it was for her to consider divorce after 22 years, but she enjoyed her time with the kind crewman tonight, and that tiny sliver of hope was enough to make her want more. "What do I need to do?" Daliah was completely out of her element. The Blonde would be her only connection to the resources she needed to pull something like this off. This may be her only chance to get out. Daliah began to feel excitement and nervousness overtake her.

"Daliah, we can work it out, so you don't have a thing to worry about. Look, I know a guy Donovan can hire to handle everything. All we need to do is let him do his thing. You should tell what you want, and I'll make sure he makes a big show of it for Donovan. In the end, Donovan will be happy to move on. Trust me, so long as you don't ask for anything outrageous, you're golden."

Daliah laid on her back and crossed shaky hands over her belly. She knew exactly what she wanted but was terrified that saying it out loud would somehow curse it. What she wanted more than the breath in her lungs was her child. It was too late for the older kids. Donovan had thoroughly poisoned them all against her years ago by keeping her from being the mother they all deserved. He kept her away, then lied to the kids and said it was her choice. He told them over and over that Daliah just didn't love them and never would. It was so cruel and unyielding that eventually, Daliah gave in to the narrative and stopped longing for them. All she could do was love them silently and hope they landed on their feet in life. They had every right to be resentful. Regardless of the reason she couldn't be there, all she could do was hope that one day they might understand what part their father played in controlling the narrative. Daliah stared up at the ceiling and sighed deeply. It was too late for the older ones, but she could change everything for her youngest. It wasn't too late for him because he was so young, and his father had not yet taken enough of an interest in him to attempt to poison him against his mother. She knew what she had to ask for, but it still terrified her to even consider it, so with one final deep breath, she fixed her eyes on the ceiling even harder and asked. "Can I have my son?" She blurted it out, held back the tears so close to brimming over the edge of her eyes, and waited. Breathlessly for an answer.

The Blonde misunderstood the declaration. "Oh darling, you're on your own with that one. I mean, I can pull off some amazing things, but getting a grown man to pick his mommy over his daddy is not what I would call a reasonable request. I was more so talking about spousal support like alimony to give you time to figure out your next step. Basically, you get a monthly check for a few years. It's a pretty common divorce settlement, and it's not like it'll break the bank. Donovan is loaded, so I can't imagine he'd have a reason not to just give you that much and more to move past it all." The Blonde realized how crass it all sounded but held strong in her conviction. Daliah was clearly unhappy, and The Blonde was sure she could make a better life for herself with the wealth and security Donovan could provide to her. The arrangement was best for everyone.

Daliah sat up and looked The Blonde right in the eyes for the first time and gained courage she wouldn't have otherwise had without the intoxication of liquor or the convictions of a mother. "I'm talking about the baby, my youngest. He's the last chance I have to repair this broken family. I want to raise him far away from Donovan's influence and oversight. Let me show him the love of a mother and teach him to be kind and generous, unlike his father. All I've ever wanted was to be a good mother."

The Blonde smacked a well-manicured hand against her forehead. "Oh yeah, the kid. Obviously, you would need to take him. I can't see why Donovan would need him around. He's already got an heir to stand in his shoes if he ever lets him. I don't know the first thing about kids. I mean, don't get me wrong, I'm 100% on board with hanging out with the teens, but I don't do diapers. That's all you, lady!"

Daliah laughed, feeling suddenly much more confident about the whole situation. "He's a bit old for diapers, but I understand what you mean. The girls seem to really like you, and something tells me they would benefit from some strong female direction."

The Blonde had wondered why Daliah always kept her distance from the kids. She had only been around for a couple months, and the family dynamic had not changed. Daliah's request to simply have her youngest in the divorce settlement was very telling. "Daliah, can I just ask why you keep everyone at arm's length? I mean, it's clear you care about these kids. Why haven't you stepped up and gotten more involved."

Daliah rose to scoot to the end of the bed and dangled her bare feet over the edge until they softly touched the carpeted floor. Daliah hunched inside. "Donovan didn't want me to make them too soft. He thought it made more sense to send them to boarding schools and hire nannies to take care of their needs. It's not that I didn't want to be there for them. I just wasn't allowed to." Letting go of the secret felt like a weight had been added to her burden instead of lifting it. By acknowledging the shitty reality of her life, she had inadvertently broken down the thin walls she had so meticulously built around her heart. The tears started to flow as she buried her face in frail hands and attempted to stop the flow of sorrow. Instead of the scorn she felt from Donovan when she cried, she felt The Blonde scoot closer to gently pull Daliah's hands down. It briefly reminded her of the man she had met earlier when he had pulled Daliah's hands away from her giggling mouth. She couldn't help but wonder where these kind people had been all these lonely years.

The Blonde said softly, "You're a beautiful crier, you know. It's so delicate and sweet. I'm an ugly crier, true story. I look like one of those monsters that Irish nanny of yours is always singing about."

The Blondes' distracting humor had the desire to affect, and Daliah felt a little less emotional. With a sigh, Daliah gestured for The Blonde to keep talking.

"Besides, kids are gonna resent their parents no matter what you do, even with a mother like you. It's only a matter of time before they realize how wonderful you are. Just think about how much more one on one time you can get once the divorce is finalized."

Daliah sniffled and wiped the remaining tears from her face. "How do you know so much about these things?"

The Blonde reached over and tucked a strand of her own hair behind her ear. She couldn't help it. This subject made her ever so slightly self-conscious. She was beginning to feel much closer to this woman than she ever intended to. "I was brought up by my grandmother, and she died, so I tracked down my own mother to demand answers. Turns out she ditched me when my father died and got married to some small-time crook. She figured I was fine with my grandmother, and to be honest, she wasn't wrong. It would have been nice to have a mother who wanted to be there for me. But it just wasn't part of my story. Turns out I inherited my mother's nonexistent parental skills, so I can say with 100% certainty that the kid is better off with you in the divorce, but as far as why do I know so much about divorce? I ask a lot of questions. I'm curious, and honestly, I'm not really looking for somebody who's all puppy dogs and rainbows. I'm looking for somebody a little bit more established in the world. Somebody that's already had their children, so they're not trying to push me to have more."

The two women clasped hands and smiled brightly.

CHAPTER FIVE

In times of great sorrow, I find it useful to go limp and embrace the void

The shared door to the master suite burst open and slammed against a nearby dresser. Standing in all his fiery glory, Donovan walked in with flared nostrils and death in his gaze. "What the fuck are you two talking about? So, you think you can just conspire with my guests now, Daliah. You always try to take everything from me. Is that what's going on? Are you trying to take everything I've worked my ass off for?"

Both women jumped back at the unexpected intrusion. Donovan's glance snapped toward Daliah's movement. The reaction was as instinctive as any predator tracking familiar prey. His drive was purely animalistic, and before he could think, Donovan launched for her. The tall man pulled her off to bed, bare feet kicking helplessly under her. "You think I'll give you divorce? That I'll let you take my son? You think I'll let you have a dime of my money." Donovan shook her limp form feeding off her whimpers of pain. The power of the moment fed his chest with a sick fulfillment. Just as quickly as he snatched her up, he dropped her with a hard flop to the ground.

Donovan wasn't done with her yet. He needed a moment to catch his breath before leaning down toward her scattered form to drive his knee into her thigh as he inched angry teeth closer to her cowering face. "I own your ass. You're a worthless mother, a sad excuse for a wife, and yet I've allowed you to waste space in our lives because you owe me. I'll die before I let you go. Don't you ever leave me, you fucking selfish whore." He gathered and twisted the silks of her robes around large fingers and lifted her closer, letting the pressure from his knee cause just a little more pain. "You made me do this. You always make me do this, you stupid piece of shit."

He leaned back and head-butted Daliah before letting go, allowing her to slump down into the carpet below. His breathing was heavy, but the impact had channeled his anger, finally allowing the rage to subside, if only for the moment. With the pressure easing, Donovan stood and rubbed his temple in tired exasperation. Without another look at Daliah, he shifted his gave toward the Blonde and twined large fingers together in a prayer-like gesture. Bending down to his knees, he placed himself gruffly in front of the shocked guest.

Luckily, she knew not to jump again or cower; instead, she simply held her hand out. Donovan clasped and dropped deeper into this subservient gesture to bury his face in her hands. The grown man began to sob, then inched forward to cry with his head buried in her lap. "Do you see what she makes me do? You understand, don't you? I don't want to be like this. She makes me like this."

The Blonde ran her fingers through his hair, mistaking this show of self-pity as remorse. She could see Daliah stirring and thought it would be prudent to leave as soon as possible before Donovan could get worked up again. "It'll be all right, baby. I got you. I understand. We'll figure this whole mess out after you've had some rest, okay." Her gentle voice helped Donovan feel the validation he was looking for. He wiped his face with swollen red knuckles from punching the door open and stood up without even the slightest look toward his wife on the floor. The Blonde escorted Donovan out the door and stopped only for a moment to look empathetically at the beaten woman on the floor. She knew there was much more to this broken family than expected. The pain and trauma went much deeper than anything she had seen. The Blonde reconsidered her stance on children at that moment. Although she would never want any of her own, she knew that this man's children needed all the help they could get. She vowed at that moment to do everything in her power to help Daliah get her youngest away, or at the very least, she could help make sure he was safe and well cared for. The Blonde may not want her own children, but nothing would stop her from protecting someone else's.

Daliah did not look up as she lay perfectly still, like a tragic marble statue.

The moment she could hear Donovan get far enough away; she moved her pained body one limb at a time. She was left to discover the broken pieces of herself before submitting to the inevitable breakdown to follow. The burden wasn't skin deep anymore. It was crushing her soul into a new type of pain she had not yet experienced. It was as though the broken pieces of her soul had literally shattered into a million unfixable pieces. Daliah had allowed herself a moment of hope that she had only dreamed of the beating, but she was never very good at escaping her violent reality. Daliah chose to lie slumped and closed her eyes to think about a better life. Visions of her son dancing across pebbled beaches brimmed across her mind as tears escaped to burn helpless trails of pain down her busted cheek. The pain was so deep she figured it might as well take her to the depths of hell, but for now, she would dissociate into a dreamworld of her own making.

Daliah watched the scene play out. She stood behind him in a thin pink drooped fabric, relaxed and happy. The house behind her was her childhood home, just as bright and open as she remembered it. She had missed the funeral for her parents when they died so many years ago. They say it was a tragic accident that took them too early, but Donovan didn't feel it was necessary for her to go back to see them off. He said he had already wasted enough money on her and refused to indulge a "Lazy brat" just to go talk to the dug-up ground. So, she imagined their faces much younger. When she had left them, her parents were still fairly young at heart and so bright. Fondness for their memory had faded from years of loneliness, so it was nice to think of them again, even if they had never tried to contact her after she left. Daliah told her mind to move on because longing for someone didn't make them long for you back.

Daliah dreamed of the life her baby boy could have, full of laughter and joy by her side. She sat up and leaned forward, closing her eyes even tighter to hold into the thought while burying her shaky hands deep into her safe hands. She didn't want to end her dream life just yet. It felt like some kind of reconciliation was just around the corner.

Negative thoughts began to intrude around the beautiful picture of her boy on the beach. She considered the Blonde's betrayal compared to how kind she had been just moments before. How could she be so understanding of Donovan's crocodile tears? Daliah's frame lay broken on the floor, yet the woman who Daliah nearly called friend took him in her arms and walked away.

The betrayal was too much for Daliah to take, so she escaped back into her imagination. She kept fighting to see him again. in her mind, she watched him grow taller, stronger, and braver than she would ever be. His smile was deep and kind, but he was handsome like his father. Daliah had to admit she hated that he took like that vial man, but if he had to take anything from him, at least it was only his looks and nothing of his personality or mental state.

Tears streamed down her face as the pain tried to sleep in. She tried to distract her body by re-evaluating the Blonde's position in all that had just happened. Perhaps the Blonde was trying to help. What did she know? The women had been so kind before. It could have been possible that maybe she was trying to get Donovan away before Daliah offended him again. It was hard for Daliah to understand what Blonde was thinking at that moment when she was terrified, but maybe the Blonde was terrified too. Regardless of her strange choice of lovers, the Blonde had shown Daliah she was capable of emotional maturity, so maybe she was just doing her best. Daliah felt comfort in knowing the kids would have such a strong woman in their life. They could all be fine without her, without their mother, so long as they had someone in their corner. The Blonde would make a wonderful addition to the family if only she could marry Donovan and keep his anger under control.

Daliah grew tired of thinking about it, so she went back to her daydream. She closed her eyes softer this time, and she saw herself grow old and puffy like a happy little grandmother. She came over to visit all the time with her grandchildren and her exemplary son. He always came to visit her as she aged and brought her the loveliest pink and purple flowers. Daliah even had the chance to meet her son's one great love before her time came to a peaceful close. With that happy thought, her dreams had come true as if they were truly happening. Daliah felt peace and clarity at that moment.

She stood slowly and left her cabin barefoot. Her robe had fallen open while cowering on the floor and drooped across her bruised shoulder. Daliah climbed each stair to the upper deck with a delicate step. She dwelled on the memory of her son, happy. He had been loved, and he gave love. He deserved all that was good in the world.

Her face felt the cold midnight air she breathed into receptive lungs. Her toes touched freezing cold boards, but her feet moved forward, compelled by the splashing waves below. It was like a song that she couldn't get out of her head, and she moved forward as the open robes flapped behind her body. The sea winds licked her frail form questioning her late-night walk. Daliah reached for the railing as though she was casually embracing its sturdiness. She barely held on to the brass dividers, daring them to let her slip, while stepping up to one bar, then a second, and finally a third until she was forced to climb to the other side. She raised a single arm above her head, and the robe ripped violently off, dancing away to another part of the deck. She could feel the pieces of her body falling apart while the wind desperately tried to keep her together, just as he always had. It wouldn't work this time. She was too broken.

Daliah balanced like a trained ballerina and reached down to swing her other leg over the thick bar as she held on with limp fingers and leaned over, staring at the blessed Sea below. The Tide perked up with the attention and danced like a beloved pet, waiting for his name to be called. Daliah didn't want to disappoint the wind, but she felt that her time had come, and she needed to let go. Without a hint of regret, she felt the air draw her down to her forever home. As she made peace with the inevitable, her arm was yanked behind with painful force. Jealous water sprayed up toward her at the offending delay. Daliah looked up to see her only friend, the kind Soledad, grasping her hand while barely holding onto the damp railing behind him. He looked upset and confused. "Daliah! I saw your robe fly away. What the hell are you doing?" Daliah knew he would never understand that she was already gone. The tides whipped across the ship, rocking it back and forth. She made one last conspiratorial smile toward Soledad before digging nails into his hand, forcing him to let her go. Soledad screamed and watched as the hungry Sea ate her alive with no empathy for the beautiful life it had just taken. He sagged against the rail and vowed revenge toward the unworthy Sea for tasking Daliah's life. He felt that she deserved all the goodness in the world, but she died full of empty dreams and heartache. He slumped onto the deck floor and tried to take solace in that his kind eyes would be the last she was. At least she would know that someone in this world loved her.

CHAPTER SIX

Will the flowers bloom just as brightly if they never see the rain? I wonder how well lived a person can be if they never see love. Can they shine through and sustain any level of hope in that lonely darkness? I'm inclined to think that perhaps, with a lot of effort, flowers can adapt to anything if they try hard enough, so why can't I?

Daliah let the air rush past her, embracing the end with perfect clarity. She closed her eyes and let all the pain go from the years of loneliness and lost expectations. She was finally free. Greedy waves reached up to take her down to meet the tides. Daliah could hear the wind cry in the distance, but they had their time, and this was not about him. This was about her and what she needed at the moment. Daliah wasn't prepared for the slap of ice-cold water across her thin pajamas. In a moment of internal panic, her arms thrashed, and her legs kicked, but the water wound up her body and rocked as if to say, "Let go." Daliah slowed her limbs but still held her breath, not quite ready to go.

She marveled at the darkness all around her and mentally thanked the Tide for making her feel welcome. Just as she had that thought, the Tide began to shift and dance around her as though it knew what she had said to herself. He began showing off by running a nearby current right under her feet. Daliah continued to sink while small fish flew by, occasionally stopping to see what all the fuss was about. Daliah laughed at the spectacle unfolding beneath her. The innocent giggle turned into a gurgle, and she finally let the air go. The tides moved against her, knocking Daliah's body just enough to drown every once of air from her lungs. She enjoyed the movement and tried not to think about how desperately she wanted air. It burned so much, but it still felt a million times better than lying on the floor of the cabin above her. When it was clear not a bubble was likely to escape her, the Sea let her drift, and the Tide stilled all the waters nearby. Daliah was at peace, arms raised above and hair straight and unburdened by gravity.

The Tide wasn't as mature and tranquil as the Sea. It moved Daliah's hair just to see it swirl and pushed around her body to see if she would wake up. When Daliah didn't move or smile, the tides became sad that their new friend wasn't meant for the water. Even if she could communicate with it them, it was of no use if she died. She was special, but he didn't think she knew that. The tides all stopped, and he began to weep, for the woman was the first to speak to him in hundreds of years. The Sea could feel the tides' pain and tied to lift their spirits. "We shall call upon Galene, my old friend. For she may help you. After all, she needs you to travel in my vast depths. Perhaps she'll find this human useful."

The tides pulled the Sea around Daliah and hugged her close? "But how can she know what we require, Brother? She cannot understand our words."

The Sea considered the Tide and gave the issue some thought.

After a moment, he had formed a plan, but it may take convincing their Brother, The Wind, to come down and work with them.

Galene pulled an invasive piece of coral off her favorite statue. There had been so much more erosion to the piece than she was prepared to see over the last decade. The pod had seldom ventured this far West, regardless of their other obligations.She usually found a way to make it back more frequently in the past, but as usual, time had gotten away from her. It was an easy thing to lose for a woman outside of the constraints of time.

She looked just as beautiful as the day Poseidon made her the first mermaid. She still appreciated the gift he had given her and how he had always trusted her discretion in choosing pod members who had been lost to the Sea. She prided herself on her ability to pick just the right. people to join their group. The pod members were never gifted the ability to live as long as she would, but even with the normal lifespan of a human, her pod had done quite well. Things, and, in some cases, pod members were given amazing gifts by Poseidon himself. She stepped back and observed the statue with a deep sense of pride and loss. The image was that of a woman no more than 15 years old mid-change. The agony in her silent stone screams tore your heart and made even the most stoic of them bend a knee in solidarity. Galene loved the piece because it was a constant reminder that her choices came with a price.

Galene wanted her pod to remember that cost before asking her to change someone. The incredible weight needed to be shared as she simply could not withstand it all alone. She pitcked another piece of coral off and ran her eyes across the breaking bones down the childish legs. Although a fin had begun to emerge, it was also a reminder that not all humans survive the change, whether because of indifference or unworthiness. Some just were not meant to be shepherds of the sea.

Galene daydreamed of those lost souls when the Tide pulled her waist impatiently. Apparently Poseidon felt a human nearby was in need of evaluation. It was common to feel a little push from the ocean itself or the tides when there was a human nearby. But she never quite understood the reasoning behind which ones Poseidon picked. Galene raised her arms and let the current take her away to meet the lost creatures of the Sea. To the casual observer, she looked elegant as her hair whipped, but as the Sea pulled to Galene, she felt clunky and manhandled. She often spent the journey contemplating how nice it would be to teleport, but there was something about the Tide today that was a little bit more aggressive than she liked. They must not have gone very far because she felt the current slow and eventually disperse.

Galene took a moment to fix her tangled hair and closed her eyes. She always liked to count to three just to make sure that she was centered before considering allowing someone to take the change

There was never much time in these matters. The human had to be on the brink of death to try to even consider themselves worthy of a second life. So Galene always closed her eyes and gave herself half a moment to center herself and prepare to watch the suffering caused by her choices if she found them worthy. She would lay her hands on them and breathe in new life moments later. Their body would begin to reject everything their human form needed in place of the unnecessary parts, their bones would fuse and crack into a fishtail, and the transition was immensely painful. So much so that not all humans have it in them to hold on long enough to make the full transition. You have to want life. You have to need life so that you can have a life that will pay homage to the Sea for the rest of your days. If the human wavered or gave into the pain too much, they could end up only partially changed, preventing them from surviving in both the Sea and the land. To drown, begin to change, then drown again was a fate Galene would rather be no part of. The alternative was to simply allow the human to drown. In a way, it can be a kindness to let them die in the arms of a beautiful woman. At least they wouldn't be alone. Galene took her half moment and opened her eyes to see a cacophony of chaos before her.

The wind above her tore and dug into the ocean, ripping up

violent streams of water. She could see the wind wrestle the water until the two creatures created a tornado. What could cause the elements to battle was beyond her comprehension. She tried to ignore it, then felt a tug from The Tides reminding her what she was there for. Galene looked around to find a drowning woman. Daliah had barely glanced at the mermaid before passing out completely from the lack of oxygen. She felt pieces of her body begin to break apart and float toward the ocean surface. The Tide moved each piece back in place as best he could while waiting for Galene to change his friend into a creature of the sea, like himself. She felt herself falling apart again, but The Tide whispered to hang on just a moment longer. Daliah had meant to die that night, but something in the Tide's voice made her feel bad for their loneliness. She popped open her eyes in one last effort to hold on. The woman before her looked alarmed and confused as she gapped at something happening above them. Daliah had nothing left to care about and was mildly offended That that would be the last thing she would see. After all, hadn't she already had a lifetime of that confusion.

The woman shook her head as if to clear it and properly take in the woman before her. With the help of The Tide, Galene pulled Daliah's pieces back together. It wasn't uncommon for fallen souls to break apart a bit in their last moments. In fact, in many cases, pretty significant chunks began to drift away, but this woman had a unique paper-thin line that looked as if it had been broken and repaired too many times to stay together for any significant amount of time. She could feel pressure around the woman/ The Sea and Tide held her in a captive state.

Daliah started to pass out again before thinking how this may not be the worst way to die, lying in the arms of a loving sea. Just as she said goodbye to the world, Daliah heard a shrill echoing song in her head. It made her whole body flinch in a confused convulsion. White light flooded her vision. Something wasn't right, but her light was dimming, and she no longer cared.

Galene was shook. She had seen the air and water battle many times, but the ferocity of their battle felt different this time. She thought to herself that it couldn't possibly be due to this girl. It had to be a coincidence, so what on Earth could they be so upset about? Galene thought to herself, "I want nothing to do with that nonsense. The sooner I can get out of here, the better. Now, what is going on with this poor woman? She's falling apart!" Galene gently reached for a crumbling piece of this woman's face and placed it against the bone. Galene could feel the woman's energy waning with dimming life. She gathered enough pieces to gain access to Daliah's mind. Galene began sifting through Daliah's life. Galene hummed the siren song to tease out potential gifts. She sorted the less interesting bits and found that this woman had lived a sad life. Galene couldn't see anything particularly intriguing that could lead to a unique gift. Normally that wouldn't prevent her from giving the gift of sea life, but this woman had chosen death. It would be cruel to change her now. The woman made her intentions clear when she threw herself overboard, and Galene couldn't see any doubt beyond the cloud of poison this woman held from years of abuse. She reached into Daliah's soul as she had done to others a million times before, but what she saw made her flinch.

This poor woman had experienced hurt and poison so many times before that it was a miracle that she hadn't tried to end her life long ago. Tragically, many women had suffered similar plights, but the thing that really stood out was Daliah's deep love for her young son. Galene could nearly taste the pure joy there. It was enough love alone to fill several oceans. Galene never yearned for children herself, but this woman's deep valley of attachment was transcendent. Galene suddenly understood a new type of longing. Daliah would have given that child a love worthy of epic fables. Anyone would give up eternity for even a moment with this love, but what on earth had happened to sever such an unbreakable tie? Galene dug deeper, sifting through all the worst of Daliah's memories, until she found the moment that had occurred only hours before.

There in the memory, Galene watched as this kind mother

turned a cold-hearted Blonde into her own personal savior. The look in this woman's eyes was full of determination and spice. Even Galene herself would pause at the sight of such commitment. It was at this moment that both Galene and Daliah agreed that her beloved son would survive the torment of a father who could not truly love. The Blonde woman would step in and protect him no matter what. Daliah didn't give up. She transcended to allow the strong Blonde a chance to marry the horrible man that had hurt Daliah so much. The woman had a much better chance of protecting Daliah's children than she ever could.

Galene respected her for understanding that she couldn't provide enough for her loved one without the other woman's strength. There was nothing left but to give this Blonde woman a chance to make things right. She was so much less depleted by life and would step up if given a chance. Daliah's son needed to thrive, and she didn't want to survive at the expense of her child. She gave literally everything she had to give him the best chance at a happy life. To her, the strong, brash blonde was an answer to her prayers. Daliah wanted to live but never at the cost of her son's happiness. Something in the blonde's eyes convinced Daliah that in the end, she would step up, that she would come through, and she would be the mother her son needed.

In the next memory, Galene saw the current situation in a better light as she watched Daliah lean over the railing of a gigantic boat. The wind began pushing her back forcefully as if it didn't want her to go. Daliah thought to herself, "My dear friend. I'm sorry to leave you now, but this world is better off without me." The wind caressed her face and began weeping tiny tears. He tried again, wiping fiercely at her open robe to pull her back onboard. Daliah adjusted her grip, and the robe blew off in the direction of a man nearby. It was as if the wind had carried it to him, knowing he would come running to save her.

Daliah looked up at the sky and said, "If you love me, let me go. This is the only way my son can thrive. My husband will never let me go, and you know that. Please let me go!" The wind died down again, and began to weep soft tears, this time while hugging her body against the rails. As she began to let go, some man caught her and pleaded with Daliah until the ocean itself splashed upward to take her down. She fell to the depths, and the wind began to quarrel with the sea for taking her. They acted like two distraught siblings fighting over a toy. The wind beat down aggressively against the sea, pulling up waves in a magnificent waterspout. Then one after another, sea tornados flew up to the sky as The Tide claimed its prize.

GALENE LET GO of Daliah and stared into her sinking eyes. This mess was more than Galene could handle. She wasn't aware that the Sea and Sky had elements of sentient life. She had suspected they might but had never confirmed it. All she knew was that it would be a mistake to get involved. Besides, as the mother of the sea, she could respect Daliah's wishes and let her finally be at peace.

Galene edged away and gave Daliah one last kind smile before kissing her on a crumbling cheek and closing the poor woman's eyes. As Galene began to back away to rejoin her clan, The Sea stopped fighting above, and everything became still. She felt uneasy as the aggression built up around her. When she tried to move, Galene found herself frozen in place as a wall of algae and sea plants moved in toward her. She was terrified. Galene didn't understand what was happening, so she pulled and jerked as a spire of bubbles arranged themselves inches from her face. The creature before her was made of The Sea and The Sky, separate, yet somehow as one. It stared at her intently and gestured toward Daliah.

Galene didn't like having her hand forced, but it was clear that, at least for her own safety, she had to do what they wanted regardless of the outcome. Then it occurred to her: there was a chance that the woman wouldn't have enough life left to make her transition. Would this creature blame her if the transition didn't work? Galene squared her shoulders and spoke like the leader she was. "I'll do what you are asking but know this: she will remain broken. Her spirit is too damaged, and she may not even make the change. If I do this for you, it is only for you, as she has made her intentions clear. If she doesn't survive the change, this choice is on you alone. Do you agree?"

THE CREATURE PAUSED AS if discussing the matter amongst themselves. After a moment, it nodded and released Galene to give Daliah the gift of life. Or possibly an excruciating death...

CHAPTER SEVEN

My mother used to tell me a story passed down through our family, about three brothers who always fought. There were few things they could agree on, and one of those things was their favorite human. As it was told in our family, that person was my great great...lots of greats...grandma. Apparently, she was born with the ability to speak to the brothers, a talent few would ever possess beyond the Gods themselves. My mother always told me these were just stories, but to me it was reality. I wish she knew just how real that ability was before I was taken from her.

The Sea and Sky stood still in anticipation. They watched as Galene tentatively moved toward Daliah's broken body. The Mother of the Sea gently pushed a broken piece back into place, and the Tide helped hold it there. He worked hard to keep his friend's pieces in place while Galene kissed Daliah, releasing her gift of light and life into the fractured woman. Galene could feel Daliah's spirit perk up as though hungry for possibilities. She leaned back. The light left her mouth and deepened its fix on Daliah.

The broken pieces rattled, and Daliah gasped, opening terrified eyes to the heavens. Light poured through her to every broken piece and began pulling them back in place. Each jagged puzzle piece synced together, then fell away as though there wasn't enough strength left in her to keep them in place. Daliah's body went limp, and the light began to dim once more. Galene could feel the tension pouring off the creature pacing behind her. It felt like a million terrifying moments, but Galene had seen the change delay before. She was more curious about how the tiny broken pieces could somehow fuse together to receive the light. Galene seriously doubted the woman before her had enough will to even start to make the change.

As THE EMBERS of potential dimmed, Daliah's body continued to slump. Galene always wondered if The Sea could cry, and at that moment, she finally had her answer. Bubbles escaped from the life around her and slowly trickled upward. As tears fell down on land, these tears streamed upward in a fantastic display of sadness. The light had nearly extinguished now. Galene looked toward the creature and saw understanding in its unyielding eyes. It didn't look toward her pleading this time. There was just a sense of daunting acceptance. The bubbles began to dissipate, but The Tide continued to hold onto Daliah with hope. At some point, it would have to let go, but Galene couldn't fathom how to help it move on. For now, she was as trapped as before, but this time she was in a trap of her own making. Shock and sickness slowly iced her veins. This ancient woman was moved for the second time that night by the love and loss alone. To understand that The Sea and The Sky had the capacity to both love and communicate was an immense surprise Galene had not expected. She was intimidated by the sheer power one would have with such unconditional love. A very tiny piece of her curiosity wanted to know more about Daliah and wished she could see her communicate with the creature.

· · ·

THE SHEER THOUGHT made her whole body shake which indicated that she was free to leave. She shook off the bubble prison and approached the beast as it began to cradle its precious friend in sunken arms. Galene was at a loss as to how one would comfort a being such as this. She attempted to pat what she assumed was a shoulder, and the creature heaved a sigh. A new swarm of teary bubbles escaped as he took solace in her comfort.

Galene had been gone for too long. Her pod would be worried if she didn't return soon, so she backed away slowly and met the creature's eyes, or what she thought would possibly be its eyes. "It was my honor to try. I am so sorry for your loss, but I must get back to my pod now. You do understand, don't you?"

GALENE TURNED and quickly swam away. The beast of elemental brothers continued to hold tight to their love and each other. Their love was much more than that of the love from a partner. It was much more that of love from a parent to a child. Daliah was created from the Earth and fire of the world they all inhabited. She was the dearest wish of a family desperate for someone to share in their love with. It was The Wind and Sea that moved Heaven and Earth to ensure her existence. It was their greatest shame that she fell into the hands of an abusive unworthy man. The guilt ate away at the brothers to the point where they blamed each other and argued constantly. In the end, they learned that their quarrel fixed nothing and was just wasted time. All they could do was watch and hope until Daliah took matters into her own hands. Much to their current dismay Daliah didn't have the will to live and was too shattered to move forward into a new life.

AS THEY SAT IN PAIN, The Tide remembered back to a time when he, too, felt weak and broken. It was so long ago, but the memory gave him a tiny bit of hope. The brothers reached far into the earth below them, and with luck, they found some empty shells. They crushed a handful of shells and sea plants into a paste and smeared it onto Daliah's dying skin. The process was slow and deliberate. With each paste, Daliah's cracked skin began to glow with the effervescence of the shells. The Wind asked The Tide to gather more as they began the laborious task of putting the woman back together again. Creatures of the sea were so impressed by this beautiful act that they began to sacrifice their own special treasures.

THE WORK CONTINUED AS MORE sea life stayed to honor this incredible moment. After hours of labor, nearly every crack had been sealed, save for a small hole no larger than a clownfish in her chest. The brothers had been so focused, it was only after they had run out of shells that The Winds looked around to see an impressive collection of creatures surrounding them. His heart warmed as he took in the vision before them. There among the fish and seagrass, he saw dozens of naked creatures who had given their homes as a sacrifice to help. Every single one of those creatures would not last the day without their protective shells. The kindness was more than either brother could ask for, and yet they fell short of their goal.

AT THE CENTER of Daliah's chest lay an open hole still in need of patching. The unspoken request rippled around those gathered, and they responded, in turn, each looked about for just one more item to fill that hole. They couldn't see the tiniest sea slug, known as a sea dragon, swim up to Daliah's chest. The dragon lay in the gap and felt the poison from Daliah's treacherous life. He mourned for her and wished to take away that which drained her for so many years. His bright blue skin was brilliant against her dark features. He felt like he was home, and the tiny sea dragon decided to stay with her to the end, sacrificing his life to honor hers.

• • •

THE SEA suddenly stood perfectly still. The elemental brothers stopped moving as a cloud formed around Daliah. With a pop, Poseidon appeared in all his godly glory. The tiny blue sea dragon watched in shock as the God of the Sea bent down to look him in the eye. "You are a very brave young one to give your life to honor this woman. This kind of sacrifice does not often go unnoticed in my oceans. Please tell me why. What is it about her that has moved so many here today?"

THE TINY DRAGON hardly knew himself, but one does not leave a King of the Sea waiting. He gave a deep bow and explained as best he could, "I can absorb poison from other creatures. Normally I would have to consume them to extract it, but her poison is so different. This poison is not of her own making. It's gathered, much like I gather poison myself, but she did not choose this life. I could feel that she did not want this poison, so if I could, I would take it from her. I would like her to be free of that which she has not wanted. I thought I would help keep her together by taking up this last empty space. I can hear the waning beat of her heart. I can feel the poison course through her heart like blades cutting deep with each pass. The creatures I consume do not feel pain from their poison because it is made from their own body. Her poison is not her own, so she has no way to use it to protect herself. She's in so much pain, and I'd like to help ease her into the next life, even if I have to lose mine to do so."

THE KING of the sea let a tear run down his cheek and breathed out a sigh? "But what about the life you're giving? Isn't your life worth saving too?"

· · ·

THE SEA DRAGON lost no time responding. "Of course, my life has its own value. I've had an amazing time growing, breeding, and exploring the small section of the sea. It has been wonderful, and now I wish to explore more than this tiny section of life. I'm ready to move on, and I'd be honored to give my life to someone as worthy as this woman."

POSEIDON FELT the conviction was indeed worthy. He reached out and held Daliah in his arms. Her limp body was beautifully pieced together by shells and sea debris of all sorts. Clearly, she was special; otherwise, The Sea and The Sky would have let her drown. Poseidon leaned toward Daliah's head and raised her cheek to meet his own. He was able to feel her story, to see her heartbreak, and to touch her faint hope. It wasn't enough for him, that tiny promise of change. Poseidon knew she could thrive alongside the sea dragon's bravery. For one, she would never be alone because he would be strong where she could not be, and the two would have such amazing adventures.

POSEIDON SMIRKED as he came up with the perfect gift for them both. He would allow the sea dragon to do what he does best. The tiny creature would drain Daliah's poison whenever it began to creep back into her. Unfortunately, the pain she had endured would never completely leave her, but with this gift, the dragon would be able to use the poison to protect them both. The dragon would absorb it, store it, and eventually use it to protect her in times of need. It was a perfect symbiotic relationship. They would be able to travel the world with Galene's pod. This tiny sea dragon would finally see more than this small piece of the ocean, and Daliah would have a second chance at life, the life that she so greatly deserved.

· · ·

THE ONLY PROBLEM now was what he could use to fuse them and fill in the remaining hole in her chest. The sea dragon was too small to completely fill the space. Poseidon looked down toward the many rings on well-worn fingers, all collected from his own adventures. Within a moment, he found the perfect gem to complete the bond. The moonstone he wore was embedded with magic and linked to the flower moon. With this gem, Daliah would always have that link with her. Poseidon suspected that the link could very well be exactly what she would need in her future. He crushed the stone beneath his fingers and placed the dust in Daliah's chest, paving out a space for the tiny water dragon. Once complete, the sea dragon curled into space as Poseidon waved a hand over him. The dragon hardened into a beautiful new stone that shined brightly against the moonstone. The hardened, beautiful design set off a chain reaction throughout Daliah's filled cracks. Poseidon continued to set each line until every piece was completely sealed.

FINALLY, he stood back to admire his work and was quite pleased with the results. "Now we must breathe new life into this woman, for it has been too long, and her lungs have long since filled with seawater. Dear cousin Wind, would you mind helping The Tide pull water from her while you fill her with air?"

THE WIND and The Tide were quick to fulfill Poseidon's request. Since Dalia could not live as human underwater and had not yet made the change to a Mermaid, she would first have to be revived enough to make the change, should she choose to accept this last chance.

POSEIDON COULD SEE their doubt and confusion and explained further. "She's still human, so we must honor her birthright by first restoring her life as it was. If we are successful, not only will she come back, she will live again with all the poison she imbibed throughout her life. This is where our little dragon friend comes in. It is HIS birthright to take whatever poison he can from those who sustain him. Once she is free from that poison, Daliah will be able to choose if she would like to accept the gift Galene has so graciously given her. Only then can she make the change."

NOW WITH FULL UNDERSTANDING, the brothers all worked together to help Daliah once more. One pulled, one pushed, and all prayed it would be enough. Once they were sure the seawater had left her lungs and air was placed within, Poseidon held his hands up to her chest and pressed against the sea dragon. The pulse sent a shock to her dying heart. Without waiting another moment, Poseidon did it again and again, pumping her heart into submission. It should be noted that any normal man would not have been able to resuscitate her after such a long time, but this was no ordinary man, and these were not ordinary circumstances. Stranger things occur when hidden in the depths of the ocean.

THE CREATURES of the sea froze in anticipation, waiting to find out how the story would end. Would she wake from this endless sleep? Could she find the will to live once the sea dragon drained her of the countless years of poison? The brothers found comfort in their monstrous embrace, creating their shared creature to watch and wait with the others, just as helpless and just as invested. Poseidon paused, then pumped one last shock to her heart before shifting back to wait with the others.

INSIDE DALIAH, her body had given in to the inevitable and shut off all its essential organs. The heart lay flat in her chest, unfused by the shocks. Whatever spark it had once used, it was now too damaged to re-ignite. Daliah had died, and in the sea, there wasn't much you could do to ignite the shock needed to restart a dying heart.

THE FEELING of forlorn hope spread throughout the crowd of creatures like a disease. One by one, the frenzy of sadness overtook them, and so began the cry of the sea. They mourned and wailed in their way, splashing about in remorseful dance. Their chaos caught the attention of one creature who had not yet come out of the coral to join the others. With a shy crooked smile, an ancient serpent slid into the spaces between the gathered crowd. His oversized jaw and sharp teeth began to frighten the shell-less slugs below him. As he made his way closer to Daliah, more fish began to panic and swim out of his way. The danger became more chaotic than the sorrow as the crowd widened to get far away from the offending yet terrifying thing.

POSEIDON NOTICED the cacophony of shattered sadness and turned to see an old friend approach the lifeless woman. The two ancient creatures simply nodded in an apparent understanding of what was about to occur. The Eel turned his long teeth away from Daliah, placing his tail along her chest. He let out a current of electricity that would kill any sea creature in the area had they been struck so directly.

DALIAH'S HEART felt the familiar spark and responded accordingly. With the faintest tug, it began to pump as it knew it should, slowly picking up steam and making the effort it was so reluctant to earlier. Methodically her veins responded hungrily for the blood as it rushed back. Organs began to wake from what felt like endless slumber, and Daliah's mind perked up, ready to begin again. As suddenly as the blood began to flow, so did the poison. It wasted no time laying there dormant, feeding on Daliah with more vengeance than it had any right to take out on her.

THE LITTLE BLUE Sea Dragon felt the poison rush in to take over more of her body. This was his chance to prove himself worthy of the gift Poseidon had given them. The Dragon drew on the tail end of the offending invader and effortlessly drew it back into the dragon's waiting stone shell. He could feel it try to resist, but the poison was no match for the strength of the mighty Sea Dragon. The more poison he pulled, the richer his blues became, getting out into intricate designs that spread throughout Daliah's body. Each broken piece had been sealed with offerings from the sea and had now been replaced by all the blues of the dragon. The cracks became more than patchwork. Each grew more beautiful than the next, creating something new and glorious. For the first time in many years, Daliah was not a broken shell of herself. She had become something more beautiful than she could ever have dreamed of. The cracks had turned into art, and her life was once again her own.

DALIAH BECAME aware at that moment and felt the presence of her tiny new friend. Although he had lost the ability to move or communicate externally, here, inside Daliah, he could communicate with her easily.

"DON'T BE ALARMED, my dear. I'm here to protect us. You died, you see, sometime before I had the chance to officially meet you. I've purged the poison from your system and have stored it for us should we need to protect ourselves. Unfortunately, the damage you have suffered in your life will always be with you, so from time to time, I'll help siphon off the offending darkness. I mean, that is if you'd like to stick around with me. Galene gifted you with a choice. You'll have to decide if you want it but know that I am here for you no matter what you choose. You've lived a very hard life, and we all respect your choice. I just want to thank you for allowing me this honor to be with you at this moment. You're not alone anymore, Daliah. From now on, you'll never have to be alone again."

DALIAH PLAYED with the feeling of freedom from the Poison and liked the emptiness inside. There was room for whatever she wanted to put in the space, as it was all hers to use up. Donovan could not reach her down here, so for once, she was totally free. She hesitated and thought to herself, "Is that enough? Do I even want to try again?". The moment of peace came crashing to an end as searing pain started to burn every inch of her body.

THE SEA DRAGON perked up to offer his assistance, "Don't be afraid! This is the gift. Your body wants to adapt to the sea, but it comes at a painful cost. You'll have to decide if you want this new life. It will hurt, and you'll feel like you may not survive, but I promise you, if even the slightest part of you wants to live, you will live. I'll be here with you the whole time. I may not be able to protect you from this pain but know that I will be here when you get to the other side of it."

DALIAH DIDN'T KNOW herself at that moment. The pain was worse than every beating she had taken from her callous husband. It felt like every bone in her body was breaking, healing then breaking again. Just as suddenly as it started, it would ease, then renew with aggressive vigor. She had to ask herself over and over if it was worth it. If the pain would ever end. Daliah searched for answers all around her and found nothing but emptiness when, through the clouds of agony, there in the distance, she saw her dream play out. She saw her son playing on a pebbled beach, her beach. A woman came out of a house. Her house. The son ran back toward the woman and jumped into her arms, not Daliah's arms. Her vision panned up to reveal The Blonde holding onto her child and loving him as if he were her own. Donovan was nowhere to be seen as the two sauntered back into Daliah's childhood home. He was safe and loved.

A TEAR RAN down Daliah's face as she let go of the last remnant of her human life. She gave in to the pain and embraced it with her new dragon friend. Together they rode the waves of agony into a black abyss, and for once, Daliah was totally at peace.

"Daliah...."

"Sweet child..."

"Wake up. It's time to start your new life..."

SIREN SONG

MELISSA MACKINNON

SIREN SONG

I 682 - Somewhere on the Edge of the 'New World'

"FATHER... Father, no! Please, Papa, I'll do anything you want. I promise I haven't sinned. I just wanted to save her. Please, Papa, I'm your chi-"

Her words cut off abruptly when she hit the water. A distant part of her had been expecting the fall to not be too bad. Like diving into the deep end of the lake in the golden haze of summer. But the early winter frost had already gripped the countryside, and she wasn't diving in. She was being pushed from a very high cliff. There was no gentle splash when she hit the ocean's surface.

It felt like she was being dashed against rocks; there was a mere second of falling through the air, and then... pain. Bright, consuming pain, raking its claws over every inch of her body.

No one was meant to experience this kind of pain this young.

Let alone at the hands of her own family.

The Rivers baby had been sick for days. She'd watched it get weaker and weaker, wailing into the night until it was so exhausted that the cry became a thin, threadbare sound. Constance had wanted to save the child.

She had only copied what she'd seen the natives practice. This was their land, after all; they knew the plants and sicknesses better than anyone. And it worked, it had cured the infant.

And once the town's joy had passed, Constance had been named a witch.

She suspected it had more to do with her recent rebuttal of a marriage offer from the pastor's son. Her refusal hadn't been personal, but the boy had taken it to heart. Rejection seemed to turn men into dark, twisted versions of themselves, and she had known better than to expect her choice to be without consequence.

But of everything she could have expected, this had never crossed her mind. She knew her father was a zealot. They all were: the Quakers who'd dragged themselves across the world to escape England's cruel grasp. They had escaped it only to replace it with a crueler grasp of their own, and now Constance was paying the price.

These were the last few thoughts that went through her mind before the darkness took her. Waves buffeted her body back and forth. The cold was so profound that it felt like she was being torn into by sharp, savage teeth. Her mind went to her father's face, and the sheer rage that had consumed him.

The last thing she pictured was the Rivers baby. Hale and hearty, recovering from its sickness. That was what mattered, she told herself.

That was her last thought before she died.

-

. . .

JACOB COULDN'T TELL which was drenching him more: sweat or seawater. Either way, he was soaked to the bone, and a chill had taken up permanent residence in his joints. It didn't help that his job seemed to be mostly bending and lifting.

Pick up the heavy thing. Put down the heavy thing. Move the other heavy thing. All while being assaulted by frozen, salty ocean spray and verbally dressed down by the Captain.

Perhaps the life of a fisherman had not been a good choice.

It was intended to be a punishment, however. Jacob was born into a family of criminals, all the way back in England. His father raised him to be selfish and cruel and to take advantage of others. And for the first two decades of his brutal existence, he committed one monstrous act after another, until his mother ended up paying the price for their sins.

This new life was meant to be his repentance. He was meant to be suffering. Punishment can't be pleasant.

But that didn't mean he had to like it.

He chewed over that thought as he continued his work: lift and place, move, and stack. Again and again and again. The monotony of it had him nearly lulled into a trance. He was so focused on the thought of why he deserved to be here, he had stopped paying attention to where 'here' was. Right until the moment that he stood up, placing himself squarely in the path of the boom.

The sharp crack of wood hitting his skull was the last noise he heard before the world went black.

CONSTANCE blinked to clear her vision, but the world remained blurry. Everything seemed so bright, and the voices surrounding her were so loud she couldn't distinguish the individual words. It was just a wall of sound.

Her skin felt raw and exposed, and the sun seemed hot enough to cook her alive. There were so many competing pains it was difficult to dig through them all and take in her surroundings, but she had no choice.

She was on... a boat? Water surrounded her. She could see that. And the bright, clear sky overhead was a sight she remembered from the long journey she once made across the water with her family. Except her memory of that journey was dominated by the constant nauseating rocking of the waves, which she didn't feel right now.

Not that they weren't rocking with the waves. They were, but somehow this time it was comforting. There was something familiar about it that she hadn't felt before. As if her body was somehow responding differently to the pitch and yaw of the sea.

Nothing was making any sense.

The shouting grew louder, and she turned her attention to the men that surrounded her.

"She's an omen; storms are coming," one man yelled.

"Aye, this could be the sign of a witch's curse," said another.

"Her lewd beauty is made to tempt us, that's certain," said one more.

The sound of the voices rose and fell, all shouting over each other. She heard them call her cursed and evil as many times as they called her beautiful, and then she heard some of them speak of killing her.

All while she blinked until the world around her was clear enough to see.

There was a tall, gaunt man standing in front of her. His face was pock-marked and sallow, and he stood much closer to her than Constance would have liked. The way the other men looked at him, he seemed to be their leader, which made her feel more unsettled than she did already.

The look he gave her was predatory.

"If we kill her, it might anger whatever sea witch sent her to us," he said. The rasp of his voice fit well with the rest of his appearance.

"But that doesn't mean we can't enjoy her presence. We should lock her up below deck while we decide what to do."

That was all it took before rough hands were grabbing at Constance and dragging her across the wooden boards of the deck.

Something felt off, though. She wasn't weighed down by her dress, so she must have lost it in the ocean. But she also couldn't feel the wood scraping against her bare legs. In fact, she couldn't feel her legs at all. Briefly, she worried that she'd been injured in the fall.

But when she looked down at her body, it was so much more than that.

It was difficult to truly examine herself while she was disoriented and being dragged by several men, all of whom were avoiding her eyes and muttering insults and curses at her. But she could see enough to know that her legs were gone, and in their place was a strong, thick tail.

It was covered with dark scales that glimmered in the sunlight. The strength of it was obvious, even though she couldn't use it now. It was like the tail of a massive snake, coiled and waiting to strike. She could only imagine how it would feel to use such a tail to swim.

The thought occurred to her just as the men threw her through a hatch, and the sudden darkness triggered a flash of memory.

It was so cold; she could feel it squeezing the life from her. The water was pressing in on her from every angle, even as she choked on it. This was it, she had thought. This was what her compassion had earned her.

She did not think there could be a God that would allow her father to condemn her to this.

There was no God here.

But just as the blackness was closing in, she saw a light. A beautiful woman, swam quickly towards her, her tail moving in powerful strokes through the water. When she reached Constance, she had touched her face, and suddenly Constance could see and hear underwater more clearly than ever before.

"Do you wish to be free?" the creature had asked.

"Free from what?" Constance had answered.

"Free from life."

At that moment, still consumed by the searing pain of her drowning, anything sounded better than this. Anything that would let her take a breath.

She nodded yes, and that was the last thing she remembered before waking up on the ship.

Constance gasped as the memory hit her all at once. It was so vivid she could feel the pain of her slow suffocation all over again, and her chest grew tight. It even distracted her from the new pain of being knocked into every rung of the ladder the men were dragging her down before they hit another bare wooden floor.

They finally released her into a small room. There were a few narrow cots stretched across it, and barely enough room for her to turn around in, considering the full length of her new tail. It was also so dark she could barely make out the corners. The air felt dry in a way that made her skin prick and itch.

The men that dragged her here were looking at her with a mixture of contempt, revulsion, and something... hungry. Discomfort curled in her, every sense that she possessed putting her on high alert.

She still didn't know what was going on, but she knew she wanted these men as far away from her as possible.

"What about Jacob?" one man asked another. Constance turned to see that there was a body lying on one of the cots, nearly concealed by the darkness.

"You mean what if she eats him? Or witches him into madness?"

"Aye," the sailor says. "His wound was serious, but he could still wake up any moment."

"I've heard the way that man talks when he gets a few drinks in him. He's a Godless heathen. He came to the New World with some misguided idea of a sinful, egalitarian society springing up. 'Utopia', he calls it. I call it the devil's work. If the creature wishes to eat him before he wakes, I say good riddance."

With that, the two men shut the door, leaving Constance trapped and alone.

-

IT WAS SO DARK, Jacob could hardly tell when he'd truly opened his eyes to take in his surroundings.

He was below deck on the ship. He could tell that much from the tight quarters and the steady rock of the vessel on the waves. But he wasn't in his normal hammock in the bunkroom with the other men. He was in the glorified closet they called an infirmary, and his head was throbbing worse than he had ever experienced.

Lifting himself to a sitting position caused a wave of pain and nausea to rip through him, and Jacob let out a moan into the dark room. However, he was not expecting the noise he heard in response.

There was a loud scraping sound, and it was coming from not very far away.

"Hello?" he asked the darkness.

But no one answered.

The silence stretched out just long enough for him to think he was hearing things when a figure came close enough to be seen by the light of the dingy oil lamp hanging from the ceiling.

She was beautiful. That was the first thing he noticed. Not just pretty, but Earth-shattering, heart-wrenchingly beautiful. Until that moment, he hadn't thought about how long it had been since he let himself indulge in something as simple as appreciating the beauty of a woman, but this felt like it was beyond his control.

But almost as quickly as he noticed her beauty, he noticed her fear.

The woman crouched low to the ground. She looked at him with a wary expression, and her long, dark hair was damp and tangled. It was too dark to tell if her face was bruised or if it was just a trick of the shadows, but either way, he could see obvious scrapes covering her neck and shoulders.

Her *bare* neck and shoulders.

This woman looked like she was unclothed, and someone had been rough enough with her to mark her skin.

Before Jacob could control himself, he let out a growl. A literal growl. The thought that someone had hurt this innocent young woman made his skin crawl and his stomach clench with rage.

The only thing that helped him control his temper was how she jumped at the noise.

He tried to apologize, but his voice croaked with disuse and seemed to startle her further. Jacob sat up slowly, clearing his throat so he could try again.

"I'm sorry, Miss, I didn't mean to frighten you."

His words seemed to put her at ease again, and some of the tension left her shoulders. She remained crouched on the floor, swathed in shadows, but she wasn't trying to run away from him, at least.

"Did someone hurt you?" he asked.

There was a long, pregnant pause while he waited for her to answer. Her eyes darted from side to side, and he could see even in the barely there light of the lamp how green they were.

It was an incredible color that reminded him of home.

Her eyes were verdant.

Mesmerizing.

Jacob shook his head, trying to bring his thoughts back to the present. This woman needed his help, potentially, not his admiration. But he couldn't deny that there was something... intoxicating about her.

Eventually, she spoke.

"The other sailors dragged me here and locked me in. I don't know what happened, or how I got here."

Jacob gritted his teeth and held back the urge to growl again. He couldn't know for sure, but he'd spent his life around the worst kind of men, and he could fill in the blanks easily enough.

He pushed away the intrusive thoughts of his mother and how she had died. It was something he was well practiced in.

"What's your name?" he asked, keeping his voice and body language as non-threatening as possible.

"Constance," she answered, leaning towards him. "Constance Goode."

The movement brought her closer to the lamp, and he could see her teeth glinting in the light.

They were white and straight and filed down to razor points. They were the teeth of a predator. Jacob gasped, even as he felt twin sparks of fear and arousal shoot through him at the sight.

Who was this creature? And why was something that should be terrifying him only making him more intrigued?

-

AFTER HER INITIAL FRIGHT, she found that something about the stranger put her at ease.

He wasn't like the other men. He looked at her with hunger, certainly, but not in the same way. He looked at her like she was something he desired. The other sailors looked at her like she was something they already owned.

They talked. She didn't know for how long.

She learned that his name was Jacob, and he'd come here from England looking for a new life. She told him that a new life sounded pretty good right now, which made him laugh.

She could see more clearly in the dingy cabin light than she should have been able to. Her eyes had changed, along with the rest of her, and it was something she was quickly having to come to terms with. But in this instance, it was a wonderful gift. Jacob was quite a sight to look at.

She could tell how tall he was, even as he kept himself folded small on top of his cot. And there was a thickness to his body... Every limb was carved from hard muscle and the sight of him conveyed this overwhelming sense of *largeness*.

And warmth. And grace.

She wanted to reach out and touch his skin more than she'd ever wanted anything before. It seemed that she was afflicted with her own hunger, all of a sudden. Saliva pooled in her mouth as she thought about what his skin might taste like. She imagined a salt tang and it flooded her senses.

"Constance? Are you..." Jacob started to speak, but he trailed off.

He was staring at her. His eyes were dark and wide, reflecting her hunger back at her. She wasn't sure what was happening, but whatever it was, they were feeding off of each other's intensity in a way that made her squirm.

The silence hung thickly between them.

"I feel different," she said. Even her voice was different. It was lower and raspier, but with a mellifluous smoothness to it. Every time she spoke, Jacob seemed to lean more and more toward her.

She ran her tongue over her teeth, feeling the way they ended in sharp points. These were teeth designed for ripping into flesh, nothing like her human teeth. The image of ripping into Jacob's flesh appeared to her, and it was as abrupt as it was visceral.

Not to kill him, though. She didn't have any desire to kill him. But the thought of sinking her teeth into his neck and claiming him, feeling his hot, sticky blood running down her chin and marking her, claiming her back... That was a powerful urge.

Her life had changed a lot in a very short space of time, it seemed.

"I think I'm beginning to know what you mean," Jacob said.

His voice was raspier as well, and he cleared his throat for a moment. She could see his pulse where it pounded in his throat. He flicked his eyes away from her, but they came right back, as if by magic. He couldn't stop staring at her, and she couldn't stop staring at him.

It felt as if they were tethered together by some intangible force.

Her blood throbbed and pulsed through her body, making every inch of her tingle and pushing her to move closer to him. She couldn't resist it, even if she'd wanted to.

She'd spent a lifetime trying to meet some intangible code of conduct that was handed to her, and where had it gotten her?

Murdered. Murdered by the very man who gave her life and told her to behave in the first place.

She didn't know what it was pulling her towards Jacob. And she still didn't know why her body had changed, or if any of what she remembered happening in the water had been real.

All she knew was that her body wanted him.

Craved him.

And for once, she was going to get what she wanted.

She used her hands to push herself forward, dragging her transformed body behind her. Her tail undulated as it pushed against the dirty floorboards, propelling her forward. Jacob's eyes grew wider as he watched her, and his mouth fell slightly open.

His bottom lip looked ripe. Her hearing, as newly acute as her vision, detected the subtle uptick in his breathing. The room was quiet apart from the sound of their combined breath, and the scrape of scales over wood as she continued to move towards her prize.

"Jacob," she whispered once we were only a few inches apart.

He leaned down, closing the distance between them, using two fingers to gently tilt her face up towards his.

"Yes, Constance?" His voice was practically a purr when he spoke.

"I don't know what's happening right now, but I think I like the new me."

That was the last thought in her head before he moved forward the last few inches and kissed her.

She had been kissed before, once or twice. Furtive children's

785

kisses, stolen behind the barn or out in the woods on a hot, sticky summer evening. Kisses that were exciting mostly because they were so illicit.

But this was something else entirely.

The thrill of it curled through her gut like a living thing. Her hands reached up to grab his face and keep him there with her, just as he slid off of the cot to pull her closer into his body. She hadn't noticed that her fingers ended in claws now until they were digging into his plump flesh, hard enough to draw blood.

As soon as a drop of it trickled down his cheek, she could smell it in the air. She broke away from his mouth for a moment to run the flat of her tongue over it, lapping the blood into her mouth.

The taste exploded on her tongue and only made her want to pull him closer.

"It's like your blood is calling to me," she whispered into his open mouth.

"Aye," he answered, "I can feel it. You're calling to me, too."

Their mouths surged together again until it felt like they were about to consume each other whole. And they would have if they hadn't been interrupted.

"What's this, then?"

There were four of them. The leader, from above deck, with his cruel, sibilant voice, was the one who had spoken. The other three were standing behind him, looking at Jacob and Constance with eager delight.

"It looks like the heretic already had the same idea as us, Captain," one of them said.

She was looking at the interlopers at the door, but she could still see Jacob's face out of the corner of her eye, and she caught the moment when his expression hardened.

"And what idea was that?" she asked.

The old Constance wouldn't have spoken in front of a room full of strange men. The old Constance would have demurred and waited for her fate.

With every passing moment, she missed the old Constance less.

The sound of her voice must have startled the sailors because one of them gasped and they all took a small, incremental step away from her. She was rapidly coming to suspect that there was power in her new voice.

But the captain was quick to recover, and he stepped towards her with a cruel smirk.

"Ah, the monster speaks," he said. "You'd do best to keep your witching voice quiet though, or we'll be forced to kill you. As it is, you'll most likely still be alive when we throw you back into the ocean that spat you out. Once we're done."

She realized what their intentions were all at once as if a curtain had dropped in her mind.

"Never, you pigs," she spat, before she could think better of it.

The shift in the room was instant. The Captain closed the distance between them with a few short steps and didn't hesitate to strike her across the face. He hit her hard enough to knock her body to the ground, and when she pushed herself back up, she was spitting blood.

But more curiously, Jacob was silent.

"You're coming with us, witch," the captain sneered as he looked down at her.

The other men surged forward, and before she knew it their hands were all over her, grabbing at her limbs and pulling her roughly towards the door. She flexed and bowed her body, trying to get out of their grasp as she snarled in anger.

She couldn't even speak. Raw animal instinct took over, and all she could do was fight.

But she got closer and closer to the door, no matter how much she thrashed. She looked back at Jacob, waiting for him to get up and fight for her. Her body called out to him just as much now as it had a few minutes ago, and it felt like the invisible tether between them was being pulled taut enough to snap.

"Stop."

Jacob stood up, unfolding his large body and drawing himself up to his full height. His head grazed the low ceiling of the cabin, and he seemed to take up all the space in the room.

The sailors were going to regret their actions soon; she was sure of it.

"I claimed it first," Jacob said. "You can't have all the fun without me."

Constance felt something in her twist, and her body went cold with the betrayal. Something more powerful than either of them had pulled them together, she was sure of it. A few minutes ago, it felt like Jacob was crawling into her heart and becoming a part of her.

And now he was just another one of her captors.

-

THE SHOCK and betrayal on Constance's face were crippling to behold, but Jacob couldn't stop now. He had committed to the lie, and it was the only way he saw to get her out of this.

He was big, sure, and a skilled fighter. But he had seen the captain in a brawl before and didn't feel like going up against him in a confined space with terrible odds. He had to stay with them until they were in a better space. That was his only hope of getting Constance away from them.

"Fine," the captain said, spitting rancid tobacco juice on the floor in the process. "But your turn is last."

Constance's betrayal quickly gave way to rage. She cursed and spit and fought, but there were too many of them. They laughed as they dragged her out of the room and back to the ladder, with Jacob trailing along behind them.

He didn't have time to question what he was thinking. He didn't even know what Constance *was*, let alone why he felt compelled to be close to her. Maybe she was a witch and the desire he felt for her was nothing more than poison.

It felt too good to stop, though. It wasn't like he had anything left to lose.

Jacob blinked his eyes against the brightness as they all emerged above deck. It wasn't even sunny. There were storm clouds overhead, but the throb in his head reminded him that his injury was far from healed. Every glint of light seemed to burrow into his brain and make it ache.

The sound of voices seemed like it was coming to him from a great distance, or through a thick wall. Jacob felt his body pitch and sway even though the ocean was still, and he barely managed to catch himself before falling.

Getting Constance and himself out of this situation was seeming more and more like an unreachable goal. Thick, inky blackness was edging into his field of vision. The urge to sleep was tugging at him with strong hands, but he had to fight it.

"Captain gets the first touch, but after that, it's my turn with the monster bitch!"

He wasn't sure who said it, but it was enough to get Jacob to pull his awareness back to reality. He ignored the throb in his head that threatened to consume him. Right now, he needed to take stock of his surroundings.

There were eight men. The Captain was the strongest fighter, but the rest were no slouches. He needed to hit them hard and fast before they knew what was happening.

Constance screamed in rage, and he could see her thrashing and struggling to get away from them. The sight of their dirty, undeserving hands on her made Jacob's blood boil as he blinked back the last of his brain fog.

It was now or never. Even if he died in the process, Constance must be free. He may have known her for less than an hour, but she was pure goodness and deserved to live.

He knew this with as much certainty as he knew that he was bad and deserved to die. No matter how he tried to redeem himself, Hell was always going to be his final resting place.

Perhaps today he would finally pay the price for the sins of his past.

In three long strides, he crossed the deck to where the men were pawing at Constance like animals. Jacob picked up a pike pole from the deck without losing his momentum. It was a thick staff, perhaps three feet long, with a wickedly curved hook on the end. This would do nicely.

With a grunt of effort, he swung the pole and embedded the hook into the back of a man's head. He had heard this man advocating for Constance to be tortured before her murder, so he felt no regrets about taking the man's life. The world would be a better place, he thought, as the man slumped to the deck with a soft thud.

He hadn't even had the chance to scream.

The others still hadn't noticed. But when Jacob knocked the next two men to the deck, each with a sharp crack to the skull from the butt end of the pike, people started to pay attention.

"Jacob, what the-"

"He's gone mad! The heretic has the devil in him!"

"She's witched him!"

All their frightened, superstitious words blurred together. Right now, he could only focus on the fight.

Two men tried to grab his arms to hold him back, but Jacob knew how to use his size and strength to his advantage. With a roar, he shook them loose. He drove the butt of the pike into one stomach, watching as the sailor doubled over and then groaned his way to the floor. In the same movement, he swept the staff across and cracked the other across the face.

Blood smeared in the wake of the hook, and the man screamed.

No one was touching Constance anymore. Jacob felt himself grinning, even as he breathed heavily and his head continued to ring and pulse with pain.

And she was looking at him like he was her avenging angel. Soon, Constance was grinning too.

Whatever part of them called to each other was practically singing through their blood. Jacob could feel his connection to her like a tangible, physical thing. They were bound to one another.

Jacob had never believed in a God before, but this felt like the work of Heaven. Perhaps he was being forgiven after all.

This was his last thought before the remaining men got smart and rushed him all at once. Jacob's back hit the deck hard. His breath was knocked out of him, and the black edges of his vision seemed to telescope in and out as his head snapped back into the wooden deck.

A wave of nausea and dizziness ripped through him, and it gave the men the opening they needed.

The rough rope was tearing at his skin as they tried to pull his wrists together and bind them. He bowed his back and pulled himself away from them with a roar, but he was too disoriented to see clearly. His attackers were a blur, and the shouting was an indistinct wall of noise that only made his head throb worse.

After a few more seconds of struggle, he heard the captain's voice rise above the din.

"Don't kill him! He needs to pay for what he's done," he said in that vicious, hissing voice.

Jacob continued to blink until he could see the captain standing over him. The man leaned down close. He was watching Jacob be restrained with an expression that could only be described as leering.

"Just for this, I'll make you watch while I gut the fish bitch. After I take my pleasure, as I deserve. Then we'll throw her back into the ocean in pieces, and you'll be next."

Jacob spat in his face.

It wasn't helpful, but damn if it didn't feel good. He's hated that man since the day he set foot on this worthless vessel.

Jacob was trying to think of some witty rejoinder, even as he looked for an opening to escape the grip of the men holding him down, but he couldn't. His head was too full of fog, and the thought of having failed Constance was weighing on his soul.

He could see her staring at him through the sailors that surrounded him. She was leaning against the railing of the deck. She looked beautiful despite the obvious anguish on her face. She was so close to the ocean, he thought. If she could just get herself over the railing, she could be free.

Go, he mouthed at her. Constance frowned and shook her head. She was stubborn.

"Constance, just jump!" he yelled, earning himself an open-handed blow to the face from his captors.

But Constance refused to move. He saw her concentrate for a moment before sitting up taller on the desk. When she looked at him again, there was a small smile on her face.

"Let him go," she said.

But there was something different about her voice.

CONSTANCE DIDN'T KNOW how she knew. At first, the world had seemed like a bright and blinding place, and her new body had been heavy and confusing. She didn't know what she was.

She didn't deserve any of this, and she didn't know how to fight the sudden, violent urges she felt. The urge to claim Jacob as her own and taste his blood. The urge to rip apart their attackers, limb from limb. These were animal urges, and not something she had experienced before.

But with every minute that passed, she felt more and more at home in her new form. And she knew that there was something different about her voice.

"Let him go," she said. The sailors that were still conscious were busy pinning Jacob down, but they still took notice. Confused faces turned to look at her.

She could feel her voice get sharper and sharper. There was a quality to it that made them listen. They wanted to obey. She could see it in their faces. Even as they fought it.

"Stop," she said again.

"Back away."

"Let him go."

"Step back."

"Stop."

She repeated herself over and over, developing a cadence. Her voice became stronger and louder with each word and it had more and more effect on the sailors.

Her voice reached out to them like a hand, sinking her fingers deep into each of their skulls and pulling them back from the brink of violence.

For a brief moment, Constance wondered how she wasn't able to use her voice to save herself, but when Jacob's life was threatened, everything seemed to fall into place. As if her connection to him was making her more powerful. Or just giving her the motivation to access her power...

Jacob was still on the ground, moaning and writhing in pain. He squinted against the sunlight, and she could tell that his head injury was still affecting him. A fresh trickle of blood was running from the wound. It ran down his face and traced the contour of his strong jawline.

The feral urge to lick it off of him was nearly consuming. But their safety came first.

Constance continued to speak, and the men slowly but surely backed away from Jacob. The rope was loose around his wrists, heavy with incomplete knots. Jacob's movements were clumsy, but he pulled himself from his bindings bit by bit until he was sitting up on the deck.

He stared at her like she was the sun that he wanted to orient himself towards. Like her light made him unfurl.

She was going to save them both. Constance was sure.

At this point, her voice wasn't even saying words. It was just a powerful sound that had lulled the sailors into a sort of trance. She felt as if she were singing. Their consciousness hung suspended in the honey of her song.

But she also knew it wouldn't last forever. Now that Jacob looked more like himself, she caught his eye and nodded. A moment of silent communication seemed to pass between them, and he nodded back.

At the same moment, she raised her voice to become a scream. The men who were entranced turned horrified, clawing at their ears as if they could protect themselves from the sound tearing through them.

Even Jacob winced, but he was still able to move. He rose to his feet in a blur of muscle and anger. He was swinging his fists before he even got to the sailors, and he descended on them in a fury.

Constance watched the fight. Jacob's pike was long abandoned, it had been tossed aside somewhere, but he didn't need it. He tore into the men with his hands, carving blunt bruises into the flesh until they fell away, one by one.

He looked like pure anger, and it was beautiful to behold.

Constance felt so confident in their victory that she didn't see the Captain creeping up behind Jacob with the pike in his hand.

"No!" she screamed as she watched him swing. Everyone flinched, but it was too late, and her concentration was too shattered for her voice to carry much power.

Jacob turned around at the sound and was able to move quickly enough to bring up one arm, but not quick enough to block the blow altogether. The head of the pike glanced across his face, tearing into his cheek in the process.

But that wasn't enough to stop him. The other sailors were all down now, dead or unconscious or at least unwilling to get back up and fight again. It was just Jacob and the Captain. They took a moment to feel each other out, and the violence between them seemed to crackle with energy.

"You should have known your place, boy," the Captain hissed as he swung the pike. Jacob caught the weapon in one hand and pushed his attacker back. He swayed a little on his feet, but he was still upright, and Constance watched him launch himself into the fight in a flurry of rage.

They fought. It felt like hours, but it was probably only a few minutes. Constance felt powerless to help, and both of their fates were hanging in the balance.

Jacob and the Captain chipped away at each other blow by blow until they were both bloody and exhausted. But neither of them was ever going to back down. They managed to edge closer and closer to Constance as they fought until they were standing right over her.

The Captain had the upper hand. He was uninjured and moved quickly, which Jacob's brute strength wasn't enough to match.

When the Captain drove the hooked end of the pike into Jacob's gut, no one screamed. Constance stared in shock, and Jacob could only gasp as he doubled over. His body became heavy, and he slid off the hook to collapse in front of Constance like a sack of meat.

He wasn't dead, but he was close. Constance could see the color draining from his skin.

And then there was the Captain, standing over her with that same smug smile as before.

"You both need to learn your place, witch."

When the Captain leaned down and reached for her, Constance no longer felt like she had anything holding her back. Whatever human restraint she had lingering in her body was dying with Jacob. This man wasn't reaching for a scared, broken woman. This man was reaching down to grab a monster.

And monsters have teeth.

Constance still couldn't stand, so she needed to bring the Captain down to her. She reached for him even as he gripped her arm. Her fingers ended in sharp claws and they dug into his skin as she yanked him down towards her.

The undignified, startled squeak that he made was deeply satisfying to hear.

He was a strong fighter and recovered quickly, though. His face became a mask of rage and he reached for her, fitting his large hands around her throat and trying to squeeze the life from her. But she was done being a plaything for others.

Her body moved with a strength and grace that she never could have imagined.

She pushed and pulled and muscled herself into him until she was able to roll him onto his back. The weight of her tail crushed him to the ground. He continued to squeeze her neck until she couldn't breathe, but she didn't stop.

She didn't have any weapon but herself.

It felt so natural when she leaned down and bit into his throat.

Constance had imagined biting Jacob before, when they had been touching each other in the soft, private darkness of the sick bay. She had seen an image of her mouth on his neck, not in violence but as a way to claim him. This urge felt completely different.

When she imagined biting Jacob, it was like a way to knit their bodies together. She could imagine his teeth sinking into her neck as well and their blood mingling between them until every inch of them was connected.

This bite was something different. This was savage.

The taste of salt and iron flooded her senses. Tendon and muscle gave way beneath her sharp teeth and strong jaw until the Captain was choking and gurgling underneath her. She released his neck when the damage was done and pulled back enough to look at him.

She was able to see the moment when he choked to death on his blood and the life left his eyes.

Good riddance.

"Jacob," she breathed. He was close, lying still and so very pale.

She flung herself towards him, clutching at his bloody shirt and looking for signs of life.

When his eyes fluttered open, she took her first full breath since the Captain tried to strangle her. Jacob breathed with her, and despite his deathly pallor, he was looking at her with this warm, intense affection.

"Constance," he said. His voice was practically a sigh, and there was a small smile on his face. "It was worth it, Constance. It was worth it for you to be free."

Free from life.

The image burst into her brain. That was what the creature had said before it had saved her. Before it had changed her into the powerful monster she now embodied.

Jacob deserved to be free, as well.

"Just hold on, my love," she whispered to him. "Focus on me and don't let go."

It was barely two feet to the rail, but it felt like two miles. Jacob was heavy, and it was hard to push them both with nothing but the raw power of her tail. But Constance was nothing if not determined.

When she heaved both of their bodies over the railing, the fall to the water felt like pure freedom. They were flying. Then they hit the ocean's surface with a splash and they were done.

Constance said goodbye to the sunlight and let herself and Jacob sink. The water was dark and cold, but this time it felt like a relief. Her body became lighter and the violence of the day remained on the surface where it belonged.

Now she only had to save Jacob.

He was barely clinging to life, and the oxygen in his lungs would only last a few seconds. Constance wanted to breathe the life back into him.

· · ·

WHEN JACOB WOKE UP, everything was different.

The world had always seemed like something sharp and harsh. It was made up of bright lights and dark shadows and the constant push and pull of people around you.

This was peaceful.

Jacob could feel himself hanging suspended in the water, and it felt like a caress on every inch of his skin. His body was the same, but it felt whole. The ache in his gut and the throbbing in his head were gone.

He had been planning to die for Constance and he was willing to go to hell for his sins. But maybe this was Heaven?

Then he saw Constance looking at him with hesitant optimism.

"Jacob?"

Her voice came to him through the water like a sigh.

"Where are we?" he asked. His voice sounded softer, as well.

"Home. I was able to breathe for you and I think I can carry you to her. She can change you like she changed me, and then we can both be free."

There was a moment of hesitation.

"If you want."

Jacob didn't need to hesitate. He knew in his bones that this was where he belonged.

His body surged with strength now that he was whole again, and he used every ounce of it to reach out and pull her towards him. Their bodies lined up, and they floated together in the cool, dark water, their faces barely an inch apart.

Jacob let himself truly look into her eyes in a way he hadn't been able to before.

"It's the only thing I want."

Their kiss before had been consuming. It had been a kiss of hunger and new, powerful urges. This time, their kiss felt like a conclusion.

They were already connected and the kiss was just a confirmation of it. Jacob let himself revel in the feeling of her warm body against him. They clung to one another, exploring with their hands and tongues until they felt the peace of their connection sinking into them.

It was too soon when Constance pulled away from him minutely. She looked at him with a wicked grin on her face, and he was powerless to do anything but grin back.

"Come on," she said, "let's go find her."

She turned and started swimming, pulling him behind her in her wake.

Jacob had never felt this peaceful in his life. If this was death, it was the greatest gift he'd ever received.

-

JACOB'S BLOOD tasted sweet on her tongue. When she had ripped into the Captain, it had tasted like violence and victory. This tasted like home.

His new body was strong, and now that his form matched hers, they were able to truly wrap every inch of themselves around each other. Strong tails glided together in their embrace. They both had the same sharp teeth, and they had been teasing each other's skin for what felt like forever. The primal need to claim each other through an act of teeth and tongue was driving every thought and breath.

They had both spent their short lives on Earth suffering for the sins of their fathers. Finding each other was the first gift that fate had given them, even if it meant letting go of their human lives. Constance took a breath, able to smell Jacob's presence through the water that embraced them.

Constance sunk her teeth into his neck, and Jacob did the same.

The world would never be able to touch them again.

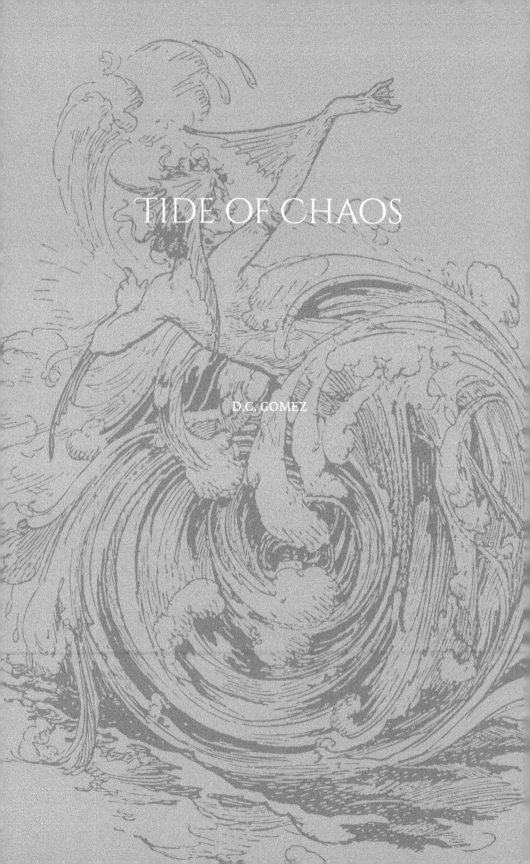

TIDE OF CHAOS

D.C. GOMEZ

PROLOGUE

The year 1619, off the Coast of Great Britain

LIGHTNING ILLUMINATED the waves as thunder filled the night. The storm raged over land and ocean. Visibility was low, with the sheets of water crashing over the land. Catalina watched the shore patiently, waiting for movement from the pier. She loved storms. More than a decade after being made a mermaid, she was still in awe of the power of the storms, the chaos above the water. While the world of humans trembled with the onslaught, her world remained calm, like the soothing tide on a gentle breeze.

"Cat, are you sure they are taking off tonight?" Joan asked, swimming closer to Catalina to avoid screaming over the storm.

Catalina smiled at the nickname. Only her mermaid family called her that. Her human mother had resisted anyone ever giving her a nickname. She shook her head, washing away any thoughts of her mother from her brain. The pain of watching her mother burned at the stake still crushed her soul.

"They have no choice," she replied. "If my informant is correct, they have less than a day before the inquisitors arrive at the village. They need to sail tonight if they hope to reach the new world."

"I still can't believe you listen to a cat for information?" Joan giggled.

"Do you question him?"

Catalina rolled her eyes at her best friend. It was their usual bickering; the fact that Joan made fun of Catalina for trusting the talking cat. Joan had met the infamous Constantine, Death's right-hand cat. She had even met Death the night of her transition. Few had the privilege of meeting *the* Constantine, the enforcer for the Horseman, Death. The feline was a legend around some circles, but most didn't believe he was real. Still, Joan never missed an opportunity to tease her for it. A mermaid consulting with a fish-eating-feline, the horror.

"You know how fickle cats can be?" Joan added, playing with her hair.

"Aren't you supposed to be guarding the Pod this evening?" Catalina asked, hoping to change the subject.

"I was, but Phillip begged me to switch with him." Joan submerged herself to adjust the shells around her breasts.

Catalina followed her friend underwater, crossing her arms over her chest.

"Please tell me that boy is not chasing Elizabeth again." Catalina shook her head, making her brown curls bounce in the water.

Joan giggled, and her pale skin looked almost translucent.

Catalina's copper complexion took a soft glow underwater. Galene, the original mermaid and her maker, had explained that Poseidon's gifts mixed with her own magic had an interesting reaction. Her natural healing powers were gone. She didn't have a lot of magical powers before the transformation. Healing and some basic self-protection barriers. Nothing useful against her enemies. As a mermaid, she had the power bested to them by Poseidon, controlling the waters. Her human training had made her better at controlling it than most other mermaids.

All her life, Catalina hid being a witch to avoid the persecution plaguing her small town in central Spain. At seventeen, she tried to escape to the new world aboard a ship. She was sure it wasn't her fault, but the ship suffered terrible luck. Her supposed saviors turned on her and tossed her overboard to save the ship and crew.

It was a sure death. The ocean was freezing, and Catalina didn't know how to swim. It was a mercy that Galene was out that night and took pity on her soul. Catalina vowed to aid all her kindred sisters in need of a new life. Unfortunately, the task had not been easy. Few made it onto the boats without being discovered on land. The witch trials were spreading like wildfire across the continent, with little hope of stopping them.

"Hey, Cat, it's not that big of a deal," Joan said, waving her hand in front of Catalina. "Cecily doesn't mind."

"I'm sorry." Catalina blinked back to the present. "My mind just keeps wondering off tonight. Bad feeling. But if Cecily doesn't mind, who am I to argue?"

Cecily was the head of the patrol division. In her middle age, Cecily was still fierce. She was not afraid of anything, human or supernatural. Some rumored that she once battled a vampire before being made into a mermaid. The poor bloodsucker didn't stand a chance. At least that's what the rumors around their barracks had commented.

The mermaids resurfaced and focused back on the port ahead.

"There." Joan pointed at a small vessel leaving the shore.

"It's about time," Catalina told her. "Agnes should be on the ship, helping it navigate the currents."

The waves were violent against the ship, but the vessel was steady. Catalina was sure her second in command, Agnes, was using her powers to control the water to keep the ship moving. It should be a simple task to get the ship out of the harbor and off on its way. If Constantine was correct, at least a half dozen witches should be safe aboard that ship. Catalina prayed to Poseidon that he was right.

"What is that?" Catalina asked, pointing at the ship.

"Fire?" replied Joan.

"In this storm?"

"I'm sure they have lanterns. Give them some credit?" Joan glared at her.

"You are probably right, but why?" Catalina was drifting in the ship's direction. "They are supposed to be keeping a low profile, not drawing attention to themselves. Unless . . . by the gods, let's go."

Catalina dove and swam as fast as she could toward the ship. Joan didn't ask questions and followed her friend. Neither one could feel the freezing currents as they sped toward the craft. Catalina broke the surface in time to see a young girl thrown overboard.

"No!" Catalina screamed, rushing toward the child.

"Look out," shouted Joan as two more bodies came hurdling down.

The last two were tangled in each other, fighting. Catalina moved swiftly to the right, still focused on the child. Joan moved to the left as the bodies crashed into the water. Joan submerged herself to find the feisty red-headed Agnes fighting with a dark-headed man. The man held Agnes by the neck. Agnes hadn't transformed back into her mermaid form as she struggled to lose the man. Joan rushed to her friend's side and pulled the human off her. As soon as Agnes was free, she swam down and shifted.

Joan followed her friend down. "Are you okay?" she asked.

"Yes." Agnes shook her hair loose from the bun she had confined it to. "Where is Cat?"

"She was heading toward the falling kid," Joan replied, searching around for their friend.

"Hurry, we must find her," Agnes told her. "It's not safe here. They had hunters on the ship."

The mermaids swam toward the surface. The storm had intensified and seeing above the water was difficult, even with two of them looking. Agnes was the first to spy Catalina near the ship, helping the young girl up the rope ladder.

"Cat, no!" Agnes shouted, but the storm drowned her screams.

Before Agnes could swim toward the ship, the man broke the surface of the water behind Joan. He grabbed the mermaid by the hair and pulled her back.

"Let go of me," said Joan, trying to use her magic on the ocean.

"You and your friends are an abomination to God," said the man. "If I can't rid the earth of her, you will do."

"Watch out, Joan!" Catalina screamed from the boat.

She swam as fast as her body could handle toward her friend, who didn't hear her warning.

After leaving the young girl, she spied her friends and the human behind them. Neither of them could hear her shouts over the storm, but Catalina had seen the knife in the man's hand.

Joan managed to turn around and face the man, as he raised the knife toward her.

"You will die." The man plunged the knife into her chest.

The cold steel pierced her skin and the pain surged all over her body. She could feel her blood trailing down toward the water. In one last act of defiance, Joan did the unthinkable. She wrapped her arms around the man, dragged him down to the ocean floor, and transferred her life force into him.

"By the gods." Agnes had turned around in time to see the knife piercing her friend and the two of them disappearing into the depths.

Catalina reached Agnes as the mermaid submerged herself after Joan and the man.

"Agnes, what is going on?" Catalina asked as the two dove deeper into the ocean, following the trail of blood left by Joan.

"The captain sold us out," Agnes said, fighting not to cry. "By the time we figured it out, they had locked all the girls up."

"He will pay for this," Catalina informed her as they followed the trail. "There!"

Catalina found Joan's body on the ocean floor. Her friend wasn't moving. The man was not too far away, and Catalina prayed he had suffered on the way down.

"Joan, dear, wake up." Catalina cautiously picked her friend up.

"He will become what he most hates," Joan whispered.

"What?" Catalina asked, looking over at Agnes.

Agnes shrugged.

"The man," Joan whispered.

"By Poseidon! Joan, what have you done?" Catalina stared at the body of the man who trembled on the ocean floor.

Joan could barely move. She struggled to raise her arm but didn't have the energy. Catalina interlocked her fingers with her friend and squeezed.

"We will see each other again," Joan whispered her last words and her head dropped.

"No, Joan. No!" Catalina shook her. "Please wake up. We will get you help. Please."

"Is too late, Cat." Agnes could barely say the words herself.

"Noooooooooo!" Catalina's anger created ripples in the ocean that could be felt for miles.

Agnes had to fight to stay close to her friend.

"I'm going to kill him," announced Catalina, as she lay Joan's body back down. "If Joan gave him an hour to breathe, I will use it to make him suffer for this."

The man's comatose body rolled down the ocean floor, pushed by the force of Catalina's power. Agnes swam close to Catalina as they reached the man. Mermaids could save a human by granting them an hour of oxygen underwater.

"Something is wrong with him," Agnes said, pulling Catalina back.

"Besides being a treacherous viper?" Catalina refused to look at the human.

"That doesn't look like a breathing gift. It looks like . . ." Agnes stopped talking as her mouth dropped open. "By Poseidon, she couldn't have?"

Catalina spun around to face the man. "No, Joan. Why?"

The man's body was transforming. Instead of legs and feet, a gorgeous purple tail was forming. The process was torturous. It could take hours, and it could in fact kill a man.

"I'm going to kill him." Catalina moved forward, but Agnes stopped her.

"I'm sorry, my friend, but you know the rules." Agnes held tight to Catalina's bicep.

"You can't be serious." Catalina pointed at the human. "He killed Joan."

"Yes, and she made him a mermaid." Agnes held her tight. "You know the rule: We do not kill our own."

"He is not one of us," Catalina argued.

"The process has started." Agnes pulled her back. "This is outside our control. I will carry him to the pod. You take Joan."

"We should let him die here alone," Catalina protested.

"This is not our decision." Agnes looked at her friend straight in the eyes. "I know you are hurt. I'm hurt as well. But we will not violate our laws. We are better than that. Let's go."

Catalina rubbed her face with both of her hands and took a deep breath. She knew Agnes was right. Agnes had been a mermaid longer than her, even though she only recently became part of the guard. If anyone knew the rules of the pod, it was Agnes. But her heart ached for Joan. Her friend did not deserve a death like this.

"What were you thinking, Joan?" Catalina asked her friend as she slowly picked up her body.

They did not leave behind mermaids, even the dead ones. That was one of the main reasons nobody could ever confirm or deny their existence. There was no proof that they were real.

PART ONE

"What are you going to do with him?" Catalina asked for the tenth time.

"I told you," Cecily answered her. "That is none of your business. Don't you have patrolling to do?"

Cecily's silver hair was falling out of her neatly combed bun as she leaned over the reports on her desk. While mermaids aged at the normal speed of humans, not exposing your skin to the sun regularly had a way of slowing down the aging process. Cecily's immaculate golden complexion could pass for late twenties or even early thirties.

"He killed Joan," Catalina implored. "Doesn't that deserve some type of justice?"

"A life for a life," Cecily replied.

"What life?" Catalina roamed back and forth in her boss' office. "Joan lost hers and he gets to be one of us. How is that justice?"

"Simple, my dear child, he lost the life he once knew. Now he gets to become the monster," Cecily replied, glancing up from her papers. "Now get to work and stop starting more commotion. Galene decided, and he is staying. He might become useful one day."

"I doubt it," Catalina said under her breath, but left the office.

Cecily's office was near the young ones' play area. The sounds of their laughter filled the ocean as soon as Catalina emerged from the front of the office. Cecily had told her once, she picked the location to always remember the people they were protecting. Seeing all the young ones playing, Catalina swallowed her anger. This was the reason she and Joan had joined the guard as well. To help those who couldn't help themselves.

Unfortunately, her good mood didn't last long. Across the play area sat the murderer-former-human watching the kids. Hate filled her veins and Catalina had to force herself to calm down before she started a vortex in their home. She wanted to get as far away as possible from the human, but something pulled her toward him. She stayed on the edge of the area, avoiding being noticed but close enough to listen in to his conversation.

A young girl named Ava, not older than eight, joined the man on the rocks. Ava was more curious than most of the other young ones, and not afraid of strangers. When she spoke, her gorgeous brown curls bounced in the water.

Catalina wanted to pull the girl away, but realized the teachers were in the area watching everything. They had sent the man to train. How to be a Mermaid 101. Catalina wanted to laugh if the anger in her chest wasn't all consuming. She moved closer to the pair to listen better.

"Hi, I'm Ava," the young girl said to the man. "What's your name?"

"I don't think you should be here," he replied.

"Mother Maria says we should make everyone feel welcome here." Ava handed the man a small plate with colorful looking seaweed. "You should eat."

"Are these good?" The man took the plate and pushed around the strange-looking things with his fingers.

"The purple ones are better when you first get here," Ava confessed. "After a while, you learn to like them all. Avoid the green ones for a while. They are really bitter."

"Do you know who I am?" he asked.

"No, because you refused to tell me your name." Ava placed her hands on her little hips and squeezed her eyes together, trying to glare. The man had to laugh.

"You are correct." He took a piece of the purple seaweed and ate it. "Not bad. I'm Edmund."

"Nice to meet you." Ava smiled, making dimples in her face. "Why are you here and not with the adults?"

Edmund swallowed the weed before answering. "I did a terrible thing, and they are afraid of me now."

"Mother Maria says people are afraid of the things they don't understand," Ava informed him, looking older than she was.

"Is she your mother?" Edmund glanced across the play area where a mermaid with a golden tail played with a group of little mermaid kids.

"Oh no silly, mermaids can't have kids," Ava explained. "Mother Maria used to be a nun in her other life. She was one of those Christians."

"She was?" Edmund stopped chewing and stood still. "What happened to her?"

"A group of men went to the village where she was teaching and accused her of being a witch, because she refused to help them." Ava bit her lower lip. "The elders tell me I'm too little to know what they needed help with, but all I know is they took her on a ship and tried to drown her."

"How did she get here?"

"Galene saved her . . ."

"What are you doing?" Agnes asked from behind Catalina, making her scream.

Both Ava and Edmund looked in the sound's direction, but Catalina had taken cover dragging Agnes with her.

"Have you lost your mind? What are you doing?" Agnes pulled herself straight and glanced in the direction Catalina was staring at.

To Catalina's surprise, nobody was there. Agnes shook her head and faced her friend instead.

"Why are you sneaking around scaring people?" Catalina asked, trying not to stare at the play area.

"Nobody is sneaking around. You are the one not paying attention to things," Agnes fired back. "I was looking for you everywhere and I find you hiding around here. Are you sure you didn't get hurt?"

"I'm fine," Catalina replied, pushing away from her friend, who was trying to touch her face. "Why were you looking for me?"

"We got word from the surface," said Agnes, focusing back on the situation. "Your informant sent word that the girls are safe, but they are being moved this evening. If we can get them out of the ship, he can find them a new home. What do you think?"

"That shouldn't be too hard," Catalina said, smirking.

This was something she could wrap her mind around. Planning a mission was easy for her. Dealing with murdering humans; that took more work than she had time for.

"All we need to do is wait for them to leave the harbor and we sink that ship," Catalina announced.

"Simple enough," Agnes added. "Let's just make sure those poor kids don't die while we do it."

"That's part of the plan." Catalina glanced in the direction of the play area, but it was still empty. "Do we know when the ship is sailing?"

"This evening dear." Agnes smiled at her friend.

"In that case, we better hurry. We need to be in position as soon as they clear the harbor," Catalina informed her. "Need to let the surface know to be ready with transportation for the survivors."

PART TWO

Setting up the ambush took less time than Catalina expected. Catalina took the lead, as she had the most knowledge of the informant. Agnes was her second in charge, and Beatrix was their back-up.

Beatrix was a quiet lady in her late thirties, with beautiful dark black hair. Nobody knew much about her or where she came from. She had been a member of the pod for over two decades and was a trusted member of Cecily's pod. The one thing everyone knew about Beatrix was that she was ruthless. The destruction of those she considered her enemies didn't affect her. On the contrary, many believed she took pleasure in the suffering of humans. Catalina always wondered what they had done to her.

"How many are they keeping captive?" Beatrix asked in a soft, melodious voice.

"As of the last count, we got over two dozen," Catalina replied. "It seems they were busy these last couple of days."

"We can have them jump overboard and that would make things easier for your friends," Beatrix suggested.

"They will expect that," Agnes informed them. "Last time I was on board, I saw them covering their ears with cotton to diminish our song's power."

"That's a shame," said Beatrix. "It would have been faster if they just drowned. Too bad for the boat."

Agnes and Catalina glanced at each other and smiled. At least they knew what Beatrix really felt bad for. They settled against a coral reef to wait for the ship to leave.

During the day, they had taken turns exploring the surface and watching the different ships leaving and entering the harbor. They had packed the port with more humans than usual. The local guild probably hired security to avoid any more fights in the area. The good news, activity reduced as the sun set. Very few boats left the harbor after nightfall. The fact that this one was trying to avoid human detection showed how desperate they were to tempt the ocean.

It was Agnes' turn to explore the surface when sounds came toward them. Beatrix pulled from her back a makeshift blade made from a shark's tooth, while Agnes and Catalina worked on the surrounding currents.

"Is that . . .?" The words barely left Agnes' mouth when Edmund was swimming at full speed toward them.

"Does he know how to stop?" Beatrix asked, as the newly made mermaid showed no attempts at slowing down.

"That is an excellent question," Catalina replied, watching him getting closer and closer.

Like Beatrix feared, Edmund failed at the stopping department at full speed, and was waving his hands in circles, trying to stop. The action kept adding more momentum to his trajectory instead. As he approached the trio, Catalina raised her hand and created a wall of water. Not hard enough to kill the disturbing man, just strong to stop him. Edmund slammed into the wall and landed flat on the reef. Beatrix and Agnes leaned over him as he struggled to get up.

"Why are you here?" Catalina asked.

"I know what you are going to do, and I can't let you," said Edmund.

"You can't let us save dozens of kids from being killed or sold off?" Catalina placed her hands on her hips and loomed over the man. "How do you think the kids back at the pod came to us? Trust me, it wasn't a pretty sight."

"Those are my people. I can talk to them," Edmund pleaded. "They are good men who have been misinformed and used. They don't deserve to die."

"They won't listen," Beatrix said in an almost song like voice. "You are better off staying away."

"You are more concerned for the men than the kids?" Agnes added. "You are not one of them anymore, those humans will betray you."

"They know me," Edmund continued. "They are my friends. I can help and nobody will get hurt."

"Sure, why not?" Catalina said to him. "Let's see how good your people are. They should take off any minute now. Save them."

"Thank you," Edmund told her and swam toward the surface to search for the ship.

"What are you doing?" Agnes asked, pulling on her arm. "You know, that is not a good idea. They are going to kill him as soon as they see him."

"Yes, but us telling him that will not help." Catalina pointed up at the man. "He still wants to believe he is not the monster in the night."

"You are a devious one." Beatrix winked at her and headed toward the surface.

"This is going to be bad," Agnes warned her.

"Hey, I didn't invite him to come, so not my fault," Catalina tried to defend herself, but Agnes was also gone. "Not my fault."

Catalina followed the crew up and waited. They watched as a lone ship left the harbor as soon as the sun vanished across the horizon. Agnes nodded at Catalina and dove to head to her position. Beatrix did the same on the opposite side.

"If you are planning to do something, you better hurry," she told Edmund. "We can't let them get too far out to sea."

Edmund nodded as well and swam toward the ship. Catalina followed behind at a much slower pace. She watched as the ship steered toward them. Edmund placed himself in the center of the ship's path and started waving his hands.

Bad idea, Edmund, Catalina said to herself.

"Over here," Edmund shouted.

To his surprise, and because of his new powers, his voice carried. Three of the members of the crew found him and shouted toward the others.

"It's Edmund everyone. He is alive," one added.

"You need to stop this," Edmund told them, with his hands waving in the air.

"Edmund, how are you doing that?" one man in the crew asked.

"Time's up Edmund," Catalina mumbled to herself. "Get out of there."

"They are not bad people. Stop this," Edmund continued.

As he waved his hands around, he forgot to keep his lower body covered. The crew could see the shiny scales covering his lower half.

"By the Lord, they got him," one screamed at the top of his lung.

"They have turned Edmund," another one added. "Kill him before he turns us all."

"Hurry, put him out of his misery," the captain commanded.

"What? Wait!" It took Edmund several minutes to realize what the crew was shouting.

"Don't worry Edmund," the captain said. "Your soul will be free finally and you will find a resting place in heaven."

"I'm not dead, wait!"

The crew found spears and took aim at Edmund. Before he could move, they hurled the weapons at him from all over the ship. Edmund froze in panic. His body wouldn't react and take cover from the onslaught coming his way. Agnes interfered and sent a gigantic wave between Edmund and the weapons. Catalina dragged Edmund back to the bottom of the ocean. He didn't struggle and went down in silence.

"Stay here and don't move," Catalina ordered him.

Edmund didn't reply. He stared at the empty ocean in front of him. Catalina gave him one last glance before heading back to her team. By the time she resurfaced, Beatrix had crashed the ship against the rock formations and was using the waves to crash it again. Agnes was busy battling with the crew when Catalina joined her. Catalina added massive waves to the attack to keep the crew from throwing more spears at them. As the waves battered the ship, the crew started jumping off.

"I'll take care of them," Agnes told Catalina. "See if you can help Beatrix crash the ship."

"Not sure if she really needs help." Catalina pointed toward Beatrix, who was busy sending waves at the vessel.

Catalina was afraid they would drown the captives if they continued the attack like that. She dove underwater and found a large crack in the bottom of the vessel. They needed to end this, or they would find no one alive.

Fortunately, by the time she emerged to the surface, the last of the crew jumped overboard and Beatrix slowed her assault. A small rowboat pulled next to Catalina.

"What took you so long?" she asked.

"It's a little hard to get here when you have the ocean turning in circles," a young man with dark, curly hair replied. "Constantine sends his regards."

"Hurry, the hull has a crack and the ship will sink quickly," Catalina warned.

"Can you hold it off till we get everyone out?" he asked.

"Yes, but I don't know if that's the only one."

Catalina gave no more explanations. She dove and used her power to keep the water from entering the ship. It was always a lot easier to flood something than to keep it from going down. She closed her eyes and let her concentration fill her. Back in the days when she was a human, she practiced earth magic. Her mother made her focus on creating small healing spells and even fire. She used that same technique to focus her powers to keep the water from sinking the ship.

Her body was trembling by the time Agnes broke her concentration. The hole in the ship was the size of two large humans. When Catalina broke the magic, water rushed in, sucking every small fish nearby into the boat. Catalina exhaled and dropped her head.

"Did they get everyone?" Catalina struggled to ask.

"Yes." Agnes took her friend by the arm and led her away. "There were more people trapped inside than we expected. The ship had a cargo of slaves as well."

"Why?"

"Greed," Agnes admitted. "Humans will do horrible things for money and power. Let's go home. You need rest."

Catalina closed her eyes and let Agnes lead her. She rarely struggled to use her magic, but her powers were fighting her. All the anger and hate she was carrying made it difficult for her to channel. Something had to change, or she was going to fall apart.

PART THREE

The guard had very specific duties around the pod. One of Catalina's favorites was the day trips with the kids. One day, during every lunar cycle, the teachers and the guards took the youth to the surface. Only once a month could the mermaids walk on land. Instead of taking a chance in a major city with a bunch of curious kids, the teachers picked a desolate beach.

For that one day, their little ones looked like every other kid with two legs. They played in the sand, built castles, sun-bathed, and ate food cooked by a fire. The guards were rotated to give everyone an opportunity with the kids. When it was Catalina's turned, she wasn't in a mood to play on the beach. She was still mourning Joan, even six months after her death. As hard as she tried to find a way out, nobody wanted to switch with her.

"Why is this so hard?" Catalina whined at Agnes.

"Maybe because everyone thinks you need the break," Agnes replied, not looking at her friend.

"What is that supposed to mean?"

"You have been impossible to deal with," Agnes informed her, as Catalina pouted at her.

"It's been tough," Catalina justified herself.

"Nobody is blaming you, Cat." Agnes squeezed Catalina's shoulders. "But you need a break. You are losing yourself in this job. I know that's not what Joan would want for you."

Catalina closed her eyes and resigned herself to the day at the beach. As part of the process, everyone had human clothes to use while out. The idea of wearing those ridiculous outfits again made her skin crawl. She took a deep breath and went to do her job.

The kids and the teachers were all ready for their outing. Some carried human baskets to blend in with the surroundings just in case another human would appear. Catalina took her position at the rear of the group to watch their back. Mother Maria waved at her, and Catalina waved back.

It didn't take them long to reach their destination. A large span of sandy beach off the coast of Spain. The area was deserted. The idea of going to the beach was slowly picking up interest with the royals, but it wasn't something many did often, unless they were fishing. After scouting the location, the guard agreed the area was safe. The kids rushed to the land, enjoying how their tails slowly transformed into legs.

Catalina took her time getting out of the water. The kids had claimed different locations with little groups busy working on their favorite activities. Catalina claimed one of the rocky outposts near the beach and watched the horizon for any potential intruders. From her peripheral she saw a figure walking toward her. Edmund took a seat next to her.

"Do you normally avoid people this much?" he asked.

"Are you normally this nosy?" she replied.

"It's hard to not be curious when you ignore everyone in sight," he added. "Why come if you hate it this much?"

Silence filled the space between them, when finally, Catalina replied. "I don't hate it. It's just hard to see everyone so happy and know Joan is gone."

Edmund looked down at his hands.

"I'm truly sorry," he whispered.

"Are you?" Catalina barely looked at him.

"They taught me that your kind." He stopped himself. "I guess our kind was inhuman. Creations of the devil. Designed to destroy the souls of men. I thought I was doing my duty. I didn't know."

"Did you ever ask?" Catalina had to hold back her temper before she shouted at him.

"Who exactly was I supposed to ask? How many of our people go around educating humans?"

They sat in silence again.

"I don't know why she did it," Edmund said softly. "She should have left me to die, but instead she gave me this gift."

Catalina glanced at him with one eyebrow raised. "Gift?"

"Yes, gift," he confessed. "At first I thought it was a curse, but I'm grateful for what she did."

"Joan was crazy enough to believe in second chances," Catalina said. "That's what she called Poseidon's gift to us. A second chance for a better life. She believed everyone deserved it."

"But you don't think I do?"

Edmund didn't give Catalina an opportunity to answer. Instead, he stood up and walked away. He joined Ava and Mother Maria as they built their own version of a castle in the sand. Catalina dropped her head on the rock and stared at the ocean.

Catalina woke by the screams coming from the beach. Looking over at the area, everyone was going mad, shouting. Catalina rushed down and found Mother Maria first.

"What is going on?" Catalina asked.

"We are missing Ava and Martha," Mother Maria explained.

"They went to get wood for the fire and haven't been back. It shouldn't have taken them this long."

Edmund came running toward them.

"I searched all down the beach and nothing," he stated.

"We need to form search parties," Catalina informed them.

"Already on it," said Agnes. "You and Edmund take the right side toward the hills; we need to leave some here watching the camp."

"What?" Catalina stuttered.

"Cat, we don't have time for this," Agnes informed her. "We have kids missing."

"Yes, sorry." Catalina blushed. "Edmund, let's go."

Edmund squeezed Mother Maria's hand and rushed up the embankment with Catalina. The area still looked deserted, but this time they were looking for potential footprints.

"How far could they possibly have gone?" Catalina asked.

"They were only looking for small sticks," Edmund answered. "There is no reason they should have gone out too far."

They found a small trail leading toward a line of trees. Before Catalina could step on the road, Edmund pulled her back.

"What?" she asked.

"Those are horse and cart tracks," he said.

"And?" she added.

"When we came in this morning, those were not here." Edmund was on the ground, inspecting the tracks.

"Are you sure?"

"Yes," he said, and took off, running away from the trees and toward the open field. "I inspected this area personally. There hadn't been a single track anywhere to be found."

"I have a bad feeling," Catalina told him as she ran beside him.

"You have a bad feeling?" Edmund glanced back. "Two cute girls walking along in the middle of nowhere. You should have a horrible feeling."

It didn't take them long to find the responsible party for the tracks. A small man with graying hair sat next to a broken-down cart. A large trunk sat next to him, but there wasn't a horse in sight. From their location on a small hill, Edmund searched the man's camping area and saw no one else.

"Where is the horse?" he asked.

"Why do we care about the horse? We are looking for the girls," Catalina replied.

"Because it means someone else took it, and we could have a problem." He pointed in the road's direction. "I think that road might lead to the ocean."

"Our transformation won't last too long. We need to get them back before they realize what they really are," Catalina's voice took a higher tone as her panic took over. "If anyone knows we are real, there will be a hunt for mermaids worse than the one they have for witches."

"I know that. Breath," Edmund tried to reassure her. "First, we need to figure out what he knows. Let me go down there and talk to him."

"Just you?" Catalina asked with wide eyes.

"Yes," Edmund answered, not turning around. "I can't tell if he has a weapon from here. But if he attacks me, I need you to surprise him from behind. We both can't be exposed."

"In that case, why can't I go first?"

"Because he is most likely not going to answer the questions of a woman alone," Edmund pointed out the truth. "We are not back in the pod."

"What if he has her? You will have to choose between him and the girls," Catalina continued.

"What are you trying to say?"

"You have never had to face your own people before," Catalina said the last part softly.

"As everyone has told me hundreds of times, they are not my people anymore." Edmund fixed his shirt. "Besides, Ava was the only person who befriended me when I arrived at the pod. I will kill Poseidon himself to defend her. Never doubt that."

Without another word, Edmund headed down the road, waving at the man near the cart.

"Hi, my friend," Edmund shouted from afar.

The man looked around and pulled out a small knife from his boot. He slowly moved to stand in front of the trunk as Edmund came near.

"Are you okay? What happened to your eye?"

"Fine," the man gently touched his face, fingering a nasty black eye. "Just fell off my horse. But how can I help you?"

The man never moved away from the trunk, making Edmund walk around them.

"I'm looking for my child," Edmund said.

"Sorry, but no," the man quickly replied. "Have seen no kids around here."

"Kids?" Edmund moved closer to the man. "I didn't say anything about kids, just one."

"Why would you let your kid run around alone in these parts?" The man shouted back. "These are some dangerous parts of the country."

"What happened to your cart?" Edmund pointed to the broken wheel.

"Bad terrain, the usual." The man scratched his chin with the knife, making sure Edmund saw it.

"I hope you weren't pulling that by hand." Edmund moved closer.

"Not at all," the man replied. "Just waiting for my dear wife to come up with the horse and our sons to fix this. I'm just an old man and that's too much for just me."

"Of course," said Edmund, inspecting the cart. "If you would like, I can help you fix it. I'm sure you have some tools in that trunk."

Edmund took a step toward the trunk, and the man jumped. Putting his knife in front of himself.

"There is nothing to see in the trunk," said the man. "It's time for you to be on your way. Good luck finding your daughter."

"I never said I was looking for my daughter." Edmund had barely enough time to jump out of the way as the man charged him with the knife.

For an old man, he was agile. He also was very familiar with a knife and had no issues using it. Edmund gave up playing nice and took advantage of being taller. When the man charged for a third time, Edmund side stepped over him, and used his elbow to land a punch in the gut. The man went down, gasping for air. Edmund disarmed him.

Before Edmund could finish the job, Catalina hit the man over the head with a tree branch. Edmund jumped quickly out of the way to avoid getting hit in the head.

"I'm pretty sure he is out cold," said Edmund. "Was that really necessary?"

"You were playing with him," Catalina replied. "We don't have a lot of time."

"I wasn't playing, but that's not the point." Edmund gave up and waved his hands in the air. "Let's see what's in the trunk."

Catalina beat him to the trunk and popped the lid open. Large blankets were spread inside the trunk.

"Why would anyone be that upset about blankets?" Catalina pulled several from the pile inside.

"Why would anyone put breathing holes in a trunk full of blankets?" Edmund pointed at the small holes at the bottom of the trunk. "Give me a hand."

They pulled blankets and sheets from inside the trunk until they reached what appeared to be the bottom. An old beat down wooden panel lay buried in front of them.

"I don't get it." Catalina kicked the trunk, and the panels wiggled.

"Did you see that?" Edmund reached inside the trunk and searched all around the edges.

"What are you looking for?" Catalina leaned inside as well.

"This." Edmund found a small indentation and pulled. "It's a false bottom."

He dragged the wooden panels from the trunk, revealing a tied up young girl, blindfolded and gaged.

"By the Gods," screamed Catalina. "Poor Martha. Where is Ava?"

Edmund reached inside the trunk for Martha. The girl had bruises on her arms and legs and scratches everywhere. When Edmund touched her, she cowered away, folding her legs as close to her body as possible.

"Martha it's me, Edmund," he whispered to the scared child. "I got you dear."

Martha struggled to get up, but Edmund carried her out. Once outside the trunk, they removed her bonds and gag. As her eyes adjusted to the light, tears filled them. As soon as her arms were loose, she wrapped them around Edmund and cried.

"It's okay dear, where is Ava?" Edmund asked softly.

"The other two men took her," Martha struggled to speak. "They are going to sell her off. I tried to fight them."

Martha cried as the memory consumed her.

"You did great, Martha," Catalina said, holding her hand. "Do you remember which way they went?"

"Toward the ocean," she sobbed in between words. "They were going to catch a ride on a ship this afternoon."

"Not if I can help it," Catalina announced.

"Where are you going?" Edmund grabbed her arm before she took off. "We shouldn't separate."

"We are losing time," Catalina pulled her arm away. "Take Martha back. I'm going to chase them down. We can't lose them."

"Catalina, wait." Edmund shouted, but it was too late.

Catalina was running down the trail at full speed.

"Why doesn't she ever listen?" Edmund muttered to himself. "Have a seat right here, Martha. I need to handle something before we go."

Martha saw the small man knocked out on the ground and screamed.

"It's okay dear, I got this." Edmund winked at her and grabbed all the bonds and gags that were holding the young girl in place. "It would be a crime not to return the favor."

In no time, Edmund had bound, blindfolded, and gaged the small man. The last thing he needed was for the fool to give them away. He placed the man inside the trunk and arranged all the sheets and blankets back inside. Once he was sure everything was secure, Edmund picked Martha up and carried her cautiously.

"Let me take you back. We have many people worried about you." He softly kissed her head and made his way back to the beach.

PART FOUR

Catalina channeled all her inner strength and magic. She wasn't familiar with the layout of the land, but she could smell the ocean getting closer. The salt water was calling to her and she prayed she wasn't too late. If the two men made it into a ship, they could be miles away. Catalina refused to lose another one of her sisters, not like this.

The road took a sharp turn toward the right, but Catalina followed her senses instead. The ocean was calling her to the left. She ran in that direction, jumping over boulders and small tree trunks. A large cliff overlooked the gorgeous water. A smaller beach sat on that side of the countryside, almost in a semi-circle. In the center, a small rowboat was making its way toward the main ocean.

Catalina could see three figures in the small boat and one looked like Ava. Without thinking about her actions, she dove off the cliff. A jump like that would have killed a normal human. For a seasoned mermaid, she barely felt the impact of the water. As soon as her body was submerged in the ocean, she transformed. Her splendid tail emerged and the speed only mermaids possessed took over.

The waters around Catalina were crystal clear, giving her a

perfect view of her prey. As she reached the boat, something sped by her. Two more small projectiles came her way, and she realized it was coming from the boat. The men had firearms, and they were using them on her. One round grazed her arm, sending a burning pain through her. Before she was hit again, Catalina dove deeper into the ocean.

She needed to get near the boat and rescue Ava, but she couldn't afford to get hit again. The firing had stopped, and the boat had stopped moving. If she tried to tip the boat over from underneath, she could risk those men hurting Ava in return. She needed a plan.

As Catalina contemplated her options, one man jumped off the boat. She swam up to meet the man and watched as his lungs filled with water, but his gaze remained distant and empty. Only one thing had that power: a Siren's call. Catalina rushed to the surface. As she broke through the water, she watched the other man jump to his doom. A distance away from the boat, Catalina saw her tribe singing in their direction.

The man slowly sank to the bottom as Catalina rushed toward the boat. Ava lay in a corner, tied and gagged like Martha. She, at least, wasn't blindfolded. Tears rolled down Ava's face as Catalina reached her.

"It's okay, Ava, we are here," Catalina said to the panicking child.

Catalina couldn't reach her or jump inside the boat. Ava couldn't move enough to crawl over to Catalina. The tears continued to roll, and Catalina felt powerless to secure her charge.

"Need help?" Edmund asked as he swam next to the boat.

"How did you . . .?" Catalina looked around as Agnes and Mother Maria joined them.

"We are much faster by water than on foot," Edmund pointed out. "Why take chances alone when you can bring friends with you?"

Catalina couldn't help it; she smiled back at him. "I can't reach her." She explained.

"In that case, let's flip the boat over," Edmund suggested, and the other three mermaids just stared at him. "That way, nobody is really wondering what happened to the owners of this boat."

"I like how you think," Agnes told him.

"Ava, dear," Edmund said to the child. "As soon as you hit the water, slow your transformation. That should give us plenty of time to get your bounds off. Can you do that for me?"

The scared child nodded.

"I'll be right next to you to catch you," Edmund added.

"On three, we will flip to the right," Agnes ordered. "Ava, close your eyes dear and prepare to shift."

Ava did as she was told and as soon as the boat was flipped, the child landed in the water. Edmund, like he promised, was there to catch her as she fell. The other three mermaids moved smoothly to release her before she completed the shift. Ava embraced Edmund as soon as her arms were free.

"You came!" the young mermaid cried.

"Of course, and so did everyone else." Edmund held her tight. "We are family, remember?"

"They said they were going to sell me off," Ava explained.

"They won't be selling anyone off, ever," Agnes told her.

"We punched just like you guys taught us," Ava mentioned.

"You ladies did great. That man is going to be feeling that punch when he wakes up," Edmund said, holding her tight. "Time to go home. We will have fried fish another time."

Edmund took off with Ava. Catalina held Agnes and Mother Maria back.

"What is Ava talking about punches?" Catalina asked, without moving.

"Edmund thought it would be a good idea if the young ones learned self-defense," Mother Maria explained.

"Really? Since when? And why did nobody tell me?"

"Nobody told you, because you hate the guy," Agnes explained. "Even the mention of his name put you in a horrible mood. Worse than your normal one."

"Yes, Edmund did a horrible thing." Mother Maria held Catalina's hand. "Forgiving him doesn't erase the memory of Joan. You have closed off your life from everyone. It's time to come back to us."

Mother Maria kissed Catalina on the cheek and took off after Edmund. Catalina held her breath and trembled. Agnes moved slowly in front of her.

"I love Joan as much as you." Agnes squeezed Catalina's shoulder. "But you are not honoring her memory by locking yourself away. Edmund is not a bad guy. He was just ignorant in his beliefs. He thought he was fighting monsters, not living beings."

"So, has everyone forgiven him?" Catalina's nails cut her palms as she squeezed her fists.

"No," Agnes said. "He hasn't forgiven himself."

"You two are extremely stubborn." Agnes giggled. "It's time to live again."

She kissed Catalina's cheek and pulled her along with her as she started swimming. Holding her friend's hands, Catalina allowed herself to be led and slowly released the anger that was eating her alive.

EPILOGUE

It took Catalina a few more weeks before she could approach Edmund. He had taken over the training classes for the young ones. The kids adored him, and he enjoyed being useful around the pod. Unlike many other jobs around, this one fit his personality and background.

Edmund was finishing his last class when Catalina swam inside the classroom. Normally, Catalina wouldn't even make eye contact with him. Edmund was used to being invisible around her. He continued cleaning up the place instead of interacting with the mermaid.

"It is really impressive everything you are doing with the young ones," Catalina said.

Edmund stopped and stared at her. It was the most she had said to him in a pleasant tone.

"The kids make it easy to train," Edmund replied.

"Cecily mentioned she had asked you to join the guard," Catalina continued.

Before she could continue, Edmund raised both of his hands in front of her. "Look, I turned her down. I know you can't stand me, and that would just make everyone miserable. I'm happy contributing to what I'm doing here."

"I think it's a great idea if you join us," Catalina told him.

"What?" Edmund stared at her in disbelief. "Are you feeling okay?"

"I have been an evil witch to you for months," Catalina explained, and Edmund didn't correct her. "You murdered my best friend. Seeing you alive and knowing she is not killed me."

"I can't take any of what I did back," Edmund stated. "I'm truly sorry, and I know that pain will never go away."

"I know," Catalina said. "I'm not making things better. But I would like to try."

"Are you serious?" Edmund stood still.

"If you are willing to, yes." Catalina smiled. "Joan truly believed in second chances. Maybe this is exactly what she had planned."

Catalina extended her hand, and Edmund slowly reached for it.

"Catalina," she said.

"Edmund."

"Nice to meet you." This time, Catalina held his gaze and let the anger and pain completely melt from her body.

SONG OF STORMS

CASIA PICKERING

CHAPTER ONE

Ocean waves washed against the ferry. Wincing from the beads of seawater, Sophie gripped the metal railing. The slow burn of the salt meeting her dry face subsided with each application of the sweater.

The ferry rocked with the waves, rising and lowering almost methodically. If it weren't for the contents in her stomach rolling erratically, it would almost be enjoyable. Inhaling to push back the urge to vomit, she realized the years living on the mainland softened her.

The ocean air was cold. She could taste the salt on the back of her throat. The hint of jasmine and sage tickled the edges of her memory. This was what home smelled like- of dreams, seawater, and stories her father told under the stars.

Off in the distance was her birthplace, Finley Isle. It was colonized by seafarers in the late 1600s and was home to under five thousand people. A small exodus of residents would leave the town yearly for bigger things, but Finley remained small.

Sophie sighed, trying to still the anxiety brewing. She was among many in her graduating class who decided Finley was not big

839

enough. Yet here Sophie was, crossing the waterway between Finley and the rest of Maine with her tail between her legs and a heavy heart. So much of her life was different now, but she knew Finley would remain the same.

A time capsule amalgamation of modernity in a small colonial town. The bank would still be the post office, perfect for a one-stop errand. The single church was still the town hall, and the primary school would still have children in the playground, yards away from the only cemetery.

Except for her moving back, nothing else would change.

The wind and waves joined together, composing a song Sophie knew all too well. She closed her eyes and listened. The somber melody of sorrow was faint, but if she leaned closer just a bit, she could hear the calls of nature. Her father called it the Song of Storms.

She remembered sitting on his lap, curled to his chest. The rhythmic beat of his heart boomed with the thunder of the storm outside. He rocked her steadily, his hand playing with the unruly sandy blonde hair tangled on her head. Whenever she looked up, she could see the far-off whimsical stare he held just before going into a story. The somber melody of the song picked up, and Sophie's father sighed and closed his eyes before opening them again to speak to her.

"Do you hear that song?" He asked softly. His words were almost lost to the storm.

Sophie nodded, unable to say anything, fearing the story he was about to tell would disappear if she did.

Whipping his arms around her, he pulled her into a hug. "That song is the song of storms. Mermaids sing it when they lose one of their own."

"Like when I lost Mommy at the zoo?" Sophie asked.

"No, honey," her father chuckled wistfully, "like Grandma."

"Oh," Sophie sighed, remembering the waxy feel of Grandma before she went into the Earth. "Are they singing for Grandma?"

Her father's heart paused. He tightened his embrace and buried his face into her hair. Sophie waited, knowing he needed this time to gather his thoughts and feelings. Her hair grew damp, but she hugged him back, not caring about his tears.

Slowly, he moved away and wiped what he could from her head.

"I like to think they are," he admitted, "did you know that we are descendants of mermaids?"

Mermaids.

The idea was too beautiful. Sophie had heard stories about their magic, their songs, and how their tales shimmered like diamonds beneath the ocean waves. To be a mermaid was akin to being an angel on Earth.

She wanted it to be true.

Laughter broke through the song, chasing the memory away. Sophie wiped away the tears flowing from her cheeks. Looking over her shoulder, she recognized the tell-tale uniforms from the secondary school every islander went to.

Sophie snorted. She hated that uniform. With her pale skin and freckles, the uniform made her look sickly. The jaundice yellow button-up, navy blue bottom, and matching tie made her most uncomfortable and scratchy outfit. Many arguments were lost over that outfit.

A soft smile crossed her lips as her attention returned to the island. The pier was nearly full, with fishermen returning home from their catch. She could see the town's streets, crisscrossing from one end of the island to the other. They were bordered by buildings hidden behind trees and hills. A metal cross broke through the tree-tops, signifying the center of town.

On the rocks was the lighthouse, tall and unlit, waiting for its time to shine. A boardwalk bridge connected to the Holmquist homestead. Sophie's chest tightened, gripping her heart like a vice. Expectation and sorrow danced together, pulling her in every direction.

The Holmquist family had been in charge of the lighthouse for generations. Her father was the last of the lightkeepers. Aida, her mother, was undoubtedly keeping the light going, but that responsibility would fall on Sophie's shoulders in time.

The ferry neared the dock and slowed down. Ferry patrons gathered their belongings and lined up. Sophie stood still, staring at her future. So much was the same except for one painful detail.

Lars Holmquist was gone.

A stream of tears ran down her cheeks as she remembered his deep laugh and tall tales. The reality of lost time and opportunities hit, leaving anger and guilt in its wake. Sophie closed her eyes and let the wind take her tears, joining them with the ocean her father loved.

CHAPTER TWO

"Welcome to Finley Isle, home of Piper's Pies, the pies that sing to you. Have a pleasant visit as you go through our historic roads." The ferry's intercom crackled to life.

Sophie snorted as she repeated the speech she had known since childhood in her head. "There are two more trips to the mainland scheduled, so please keep that in mind. For our Finley residents, thank you for choosing our ferry as your ticket to the mainland."

One of the teenagers scoffed and rolled his eyes. He leaned closer to his friend group.

"Like we have a choice in the matter," he grumbled loudly.

"We look forward to seeing you again. Please gather all of your belongings at this time and line up as we are docking. We are not responsible for anything lost or missing at Perry's Ferry. Thank you, and have a nice day." The intercom ended.

Sighing, Sophie pulled her duffel bag over her shoulder and gripped her rolling suitcase. This was what was left: her whole life condensed into these two bags. The boat rocked harshly against the dock, pushing Sophie to the side railing and nearly into a passenger.

The woman darted a glare before pulling her purse closer to her chest.

After muttering an empty apology, Sophie's eyes lingered on the ocean. The sun reflected on its surface, shimmering like a field of glass. A splash caught her attention, and she looked in time to see the water ripple out.

A fish, she thought to herself with a snort.

Sophie let the disappointment roll off her back as she straightened herself and entered the line. Thinking of her father brought back the same whimsy feelings that mermaids existed. She spent years educating herself in folklore, trying to find the proof of her family stories, only to be hit with disappointment after disappointment. No one hires folklorists outside of research, and not even that pays the bills. It didn't matter if she was descended from mermaids or not. She was still Sophronia Holmquist, a thirty-year-old woman without a career moving back.

More guilt and disappointment reared their ugly heads to the surface. Sophie tried to ignore them. Instead, she followed the line, matching her breathing with each step. This was her life now: unemployed, without a father, and facing the growing reality that her mother would say something about it. Her mother always did have something to say.

Focusing on her breathing, Sophie walked down the ramp from the ferry to the dock. The back of her jaw tightened with each step as anxiety filtered in. She remembered Aida's text a week ago mentioning Lars' accident. He was such a cautious man when he went to sea, but somehow he drowned, caught in the net he and a friend cast out.

Once on land, she pulled her cell phone from her back pocket and looked at the screen. Staring up at her was a picture from her last summer on Finley Isle. The photo was dark, a scan from the film, but she treasured it. Standing on the rocks of the Holmquist homestead was her first love, Thea staring out to the ocean. Though Sophie only remembered smiles and the warm smell of seawater and sunlight, she could see something more on Thea's face when she looked at the photo.

Longing.

That was the last night Sophie saw her. A month-long summer romance filled with laughter and hidden kisses against the trees. She never told her parents about their relationship but suspected they knew. It wasn't that they were against it, just that they didn't talk about those things. What they did talk about was Thea's influence on Sophie's future.

As much as Sophie hated to admit it, Thea was one of the reasons why she never returned. How could she when her heart was broken without a goodbye? So many questions were left unanswered; somewhere in Sophie's logic, she thought some answers were on the mainland.

Her phone vibrated in her hand, indicating a text message. Pressing down, Sophie saw what her mother had sent.

"Are you coming?"

Anxiety pushed up her chest as her mind began to overthink all the possible implications behind those three words. Was her mother upset? Asking out of concern? Or was she implying that Sophie would continue living in self-exile despite her father's funeral?

Sighing, Sophie put the phone away and shook her head. Answering was pointless. Besides, Aida would know when she saw her.

Sophie pulled her suitcase and walked through the streets on the quickest route she knew. The teens from the ferry made a bee-line for Piper's Pies, opening the diner's doors just as she walked past. Coffee, cinnamon, and a menagerie of kitchen smell wafted toward her, making her stomach growl. It had been so long since she had one of their pies. Glancing through the window to see the white and forest green decor hadn't changed, Sophie mentally noted to visit once she was settled.

As she passed, she noticed patrons of the diner she had known since childhood were double-taking, muttering to each other over their shoulders. She inhaled deeply and kept walking, ignoring the growing attention and occasional Finley native pulling out their phone. If her mother didn't know she was home before reaching the lighthouse, she would question the speed of Finley's rumor mill.

Sighing, she kept walking. She was too much a Holmquist with her long sandy blonde hair and hazel eyes. She had her mother's delicate angles and her father's smile. Aida and Lars were Finley natives, never leaving the island except for an emergency. Sophie suspected that even if she dyed her hair and had facial piercings, the town would know.

Thinking she could walk into town without someone recognizing her was stupid.

Seeing there was no point to continue sneaking through her hometown, Sophie exhaled and pulled back her shoulders. The weight of anxiety slowly rolled down her back, leaving prickling bumps she would no doubt need to scratch at night. This was her home; even if she abandoned it twelve years ago, they would all welcome her back.

There was comfort in that. Sighing again, Sophie decided to try and stop feeling guilty for never returning. What mattered was that she was here now.

Passing the park and into the woods, she followed the path to the lighthouse. It was one of the many ways to get to the homestead, usually chosen by the random nature-loving tourist. There weren't many tourists in town, but when there were, the homestead became a makeshift petting zoo and lighthouse museum. Only the main house was off-limits for the guests.

When Sophie was in primary school, her class visited the homestead. She nearly got in trouble trying to invite everyone into the house. Lars enjoyed every moment, laughing as he tried to change the direction of their small attention spans. Aida was a little less forgiving, putting Sophie on dung duty for the night.

Sophie shivered at the memory and shook her head. This was why she didn't want to return. The random memories and overthinking could be too much for her. When she could afford one, her therapist said it was anxiety and suggested that she was hiding from herself and the world. Some of her agreed about that, but there was more to it.

She was home and felt at home here, but she wasn't complete.

The bleats of the goats signaled how close she was to the homestead. After a few steps, she made it to the clearing. In front of her was the barn where the horses huffed out their displeasure of not being out. The goats bleated in the petting zoo, jumping on the makeshift obstacle course she and Lars made the summer before she left. On the rocky shore was the lighthouse, standing tall and ready.

To her left stood the cottage. It wasn't really a cottage though it began that way. The home she had always known was more than that. The front of the house was original to the conception of the town. Still, the surrounding additions told the town's story in a whimsical hodge-podge way, almost like a geological timeline.

Just by looking at the home, a person would know the life story of the Holmquist family and their particular tastes. Her grandparent's part of the house had a distinct 1970s flair with a mermaid wind chime. Her parents enjoyed a more homey 90s look that reminded her of the family sitcoms they would watch on Friday nights.

"Welcome home," she said.

Sophie pulled her suitcase to the house and didn't bother looking for the spare key. In Finley, the idea of locking a front door wasn't consistently recognized. For Aida, every entry was accessible -car, house, barn, lighthouse, you name it. If a person could open it, it was unlocked if Aida had a say. But not everywhere was as safe as Finley, and it was the first harsh reality Sophie had to learn on the mainland.

Pushing open the door, she paused and waited. Nothing came from the kitchen, and the house smelled nearly unused since the morning. Sophie hesitantly stepped into the house, wondering where her mother was.

"Might as well put these away," she said to herself.

She was used to that, talking to herself, but doing it in the empty Holmquist cottage was unnerving. It felt empty and dark, and her words nearly echoed back to her. It was beginning to no longer feel like home but a tomb.

She entered her room and realized how much of a tomb it was. Nothing had changed. There were still the boyband posters on her walls. The dresser still had her incense and candles. And her bedspread was still the awful paisley pattern Mrs. Gunnar from church gave her as a "coming into womanhood" gift. It felt weird even then, having a bedspread from a church lady, but Mrs. Gunnar watched over her as a child when her grandmother died. There was a sweet obliviousness to the gift that teenage Sophronia couldn't ignore.

Adult Sophronia on the other hand, hated the thing and wanted it out as soon as possible. She tossed her duffle onto the bed, not caring that the bedspread was rumpled. Once settled, she would get new bedding, something more mature and less emotionally creepy.

Sophie threw her suitcase alongside it and stretched out her neck. Small quick pops broke the bubbles in her spine. She gasped in satisfaction and stepped out of her room. Moving around the room, Sophie began to hum. Her fingers glided on the belongings her parents decided to keep.

The trash was gone, and there was no dust, but aside from that, nothing had changed. Sophie's room and this house was becoming a time capsule. And it was always meant to be that way.

The wind picked up speed, twinkling the mermaid windchime outside. Sophie paused and closed her eyes. She listened closely, feeling as much as hearing the shift of a cadence. The same melody from the ferry was filtering in, and it was powerful.

Her feet began to move before she realized it. Walking down the hall and out the door, Sophie headed straight for the lighthouse. The song continued, pulling her in like a string tied to her heart. Her eyes darted around, looking for who was singing.

And it was a person. There were no lyrics to the song, but there was clearly a voice. She couldn't pinpoint who, but it wasn't the alto of her mother, and this was someone else entirely.

Her heart beat fast. It was like she was a kid again, fighting dragons and saving princesses. The song was sad, but it drummed through her blood like a lightning storm, charging the spirit inside that lay stagnant for too long. Each step melted away the stillness, and shakily she continued.

Thoughts ran through her mind. Was her father right all along? Were there mermaids?

The song was different from the one Lars told her about. This one clearly had a person. The wind wasn't joining the trees and rocks to make something unearthly. This was human, or as human as a voice can be. Sophie couldn't deny the ethereal draw it had on her.

That wasn't human. But Sophie didn't let it stop her.

Sophie picked up speed, past the bleating goats and the horses. She nearly ran to the lighthouse. The song grew in strength, pulling her hard. She could see the rocks piercing the sea and a glimpse of black hair shining under the sun.

She opened her mouth to say anything, but her feet slipped. The impact of the fall broke the song, and only the wind called to her. There was a splash in the water, and she thought she saw a large tail disappear. She walked tentatively to the shore, hoping to glimpse what she saw.

A mermaid? No, it couldn't be. All this time, Sophie had been searching for them. It would be cruel to learn they were with her all along. She began to kick off her shoes and fumble with the button of her jeans. There was only one way to know for sure.

"What in the hell are you doing?" Her mother's question stopped her mid-slide off of her jeans.

Sophie turned her head to look over her shoulder. She slowly pulled up her jeans and began to rebutton them.

"Hey, mama."

CHAPTER THREE

Thea swam. Her tail pushed her down to the floor bed of the coast. There she waited, looking up to see just the silhouette of the human female. She held her breath, waiting to see what would happen next.

In the distance, towards the pod's coral home, she could feel the reverberation of emotions. Concern, worry, anger, all dancing with the currents and directed at her. Slowly, she began to still her heart and allow the tension to flow away. She was safe, as they all were in the ocean; Poseidon's power and Galene's leadership ensured that.

Slowly, the pod's communication died out. The silhouette disappeared onto land, and Thea allowed herself to exhale. She wasn't expecting anyone to be there. The man was dead, and his wife was preparing for the funeral. Their daughter, Sophronia, hadn't been on the island for nearly twelve years.

Thea was supposed to be alone. But that woman surprised her.

A frown crossed her face as she tried to pinpoint who it was. The momentary glimpse allowed her to see long sandy blonde hair, jeans, and an oversized black t-shirt with a leather jacket. Nothing about her stood out, and yet . . .

Thea pushed herself from the rocky bottom and slowly swam upwards. Curiosity was getting the better of her. Her heart beat with excitement as her tail went upwards. Just a tiny peek, that's all she wanted. Enough to confirm what her heart had been yearning for.

Hiding behind a large rock, her head broke water. She leaned close to the warmth of the land and turned her head to the shore. The woman she knew as Aida was talking to the younger woman. Even from a distance, Thea could see their matching hair and the shapes of their bodies.

Aida was older, and her body showed that. Curved and untoned, her body told the story of a life filled with love and motherhood. Her long sandy hair was mixed with white, like the winter snow on the beaches of Finley. Thea couldn't see her face, but she remembered the mapped lines of Aida's wrinkles and the settled look of scrunched laughter lines.

The younger woman had the beginnings of her own mapped face. The creases between her eyes showed that laughter didn't come as easy on her as her mother.

Her mother. Thea lifted a hand to her mouth to hide the growing smile. Sophronia was back, and she was with her mother.

"A swim?" Aida frowned. Her eyes darted to the water and back to Sophie. "Without your bathing suit? Before a storm? Has being on the mainland rotted your brains?"

Thea watched Sophie shift her weight. Sophie's head dipped slightly to the side in shame, and Thea's heart clenched. She remembered how Sophie looked when they first met.

Thea leaned against the rock and watched Sophie talk to her mother. Their words melted together as her attention landed on Sophie's face, and memories began to surface.

That day, Thea left the pod against her mother's wishes. Thea surfaced from the ocean, away from the pod. She could feel their confusion, her mother's growing anger, and the incessant pull to return to safety. They were family, and though some left, all returned one way or another. The power of the ocean and pod was their most vital magical link.

She found a small cave tucked away in the cliff just as the moon took over the night sky. Thea pulled herself onto land and waited. A cold breeze blew against her tail as silver light landed on her body. There was a tingling feeling before a searing pain shot through her spine. It was the type of pain one didn't forget, searing itself into forever memory. But the pain was bearable as long as she thought of it as the gift it was. Poseidon gave this magic to the pod for them to walk on land for one month.

As she clenched driftwood in her mouth to keep from screaming, Thea repeated her thanks to Poseidon. After all, the more painful the miracle, the more it should be treasured.

It wasn't until morning that Thea slipped into town and began her adventure. Taking clothes from a nearby clothesline, she wandered the woods barefoot. Everything was new: the animals, the smells, and the soft song dancing with the breeze.

Thea stopped and hid behind a tree just in time for a young human female to appear. The stories the pod told about humans were conflicting. Many spoke about the darkness inside the land walkers, but there were stories of love and acceptance. Keeping to the shadows, Thea watched the girl as closely as possible.

The girl was around her age, dancing as she walked, twirling on fallen branches and leaves. Two wires connected to her ears trailed down to her pocket. Thea frowned, wondering what they were.

She leaned close, hearing music come from the wires. The girl opened her mouth and sang, rocking her head to the beat. Thea smiled. The song was foreign, and the girl's voice was human, but a lilt reminded Thea of the ocean. Without thinking, Thea stepped out of her hiding spot. The girl gasped, laughed nervously, and the two became quick friends.

Sophie's laugh broke Thea away from her memory. It was the same embarrassed hiccupy giggle from the past.

"Help me get these groceries inside," Aida said, rolling her eyes with an exasperated sigh.

Sophie nodded. She turned back to the shore, causing Thea to push herself deeper against the rock. Sophie sighed, scratched her head, and turned back to her mother.

Thea let out a breath she was holding and looked over the rock's edge. She watched as the two women walked away. Aida's steps, though slow and rocky from age, were still strong and moved with a purpose. Sophie's own steps were short and quick.

Thea's heart dropped. The Sophie she knew was opinionated and confident. In the summer, they knew each other. Sophie had gotten into fights, spoke her mind, and loved intensely. The shift in personality was disconcerting.

There was no doubt in Thea's mind it was because of her. If not for the love they experienced, then in the death of Lars Holmquist.

The water around her felt cold as guilt filled her. Thea rubbed her arms and sighed. She would do anything to speak to Sophronia again- to apologize as much as confess her feelings.

Biting her lower lip, Thea decided to take a chance. She dove into the water.

CHAPTER FOUR

Thea swam through the current. If she were on land, making it to the cliffside would take hours. But with the ocean guiding her, the time was cut in half. As if sensing her intentions, the sea pushed on, changing the speed and direction of the current to help her. A humming thrum danced along her skin and scales, charging her body. Closing her eyes, Thea inhaled and gave silent thanks.

This was the essence of life. The ocean, with its hidden depths and waterways, was the blood of the Earth. Every mermaid knew its song: it trickled down their skin, calling them to remain with the pod and do what mermaids did best.

Thea opened her mouth and sang. The song was low and melodious. It sprang out of her, danced with the current, and rose past the crashing waves. Each note held the magic of the sea, rising up and sending power into the air. She didn't need to look up to see the clouds forming or the wind shifting in a new direction. This song was a part of her, and it was a part of the whole pod.

She could hear the pod joining her from a distance, towards a hidden reef they called home. A sad smile crossed her face as she felt the warm acceptance of her people. Despite their differences, the pod mattered most. She could feel them understand her need to leave for this. The song they sang with her said as much. They knew her grief and shared it as much as they would have if it was her who died instead of Lars Holmquist.

Reaching the side of the island where the cave hid, Thea broke the song. She could still hear the magic shifting with the waves as the pod continued to sing. Slowly, their voices began to winnow into silence, leaving her with the waves crashing into rocks. She clutched the strap of her crossbody bag and ascended.

Spires of rocks and mossy sea flora guarded the entrance. Waves crashed into them, and the current swirled around. An inexperienced swimmer could easily get caught in the torrent and be jostled into the rocks or pushed into the depths. Many humans drowned, attempting to enter the cave. Thea inhaled deeply, closing her eyes in reverence.

Many caves were like this, filled with human death and Poseidon's magic. Caves like this one were multi-functional and scattered along the pod's migration route. The pod used them as safe houses during the rougher fishing season, as ritual spots to give offerings to Poseidon, and to give birth. Thea had only used it for one thing, transformation.

The rocks guarding the entrance were placed almost intentionally like a labyrinth, with the mouth of the cave as its prize. There was no easy way to walk out along the shore. Still, unbeknownst to the people of Finley, another hidden cave on the island connected to this one. It was how she got out the first time, and hopefully, Poseidon willing, she will be back on her feet on the island the next day.

Thea took her time swimming around the rocks. The ocean's magic thrummed around her, telling her when to slow down, turn, or speed up. She easily navigated the rocky obstruction and swam into the mouth of the cave.

It was the same as she remembered it. A pool of water quietly lapped onto the rock and sand incline. Water dripped from the cave roof, dripping onto a flat rock resembling a makeshift table. The droplets made a small pool inside a divot of the stone. Thea swam to the embankment and swung the bag to her back.

She could feel the fish flop around inside. It moved fast for a few seconds and then slowed. With no more salt water seeping into the bag to keep the fish alive, it would suffocate to death. Thea winced slightly, but it didn't deter her. Instead, she pulled her body up the incline, half in a crawl and half shimmy. She sang softly under her breath a song of thanks, finishing only when she felt the fish gulp its last feeble attempt.

Sighing, Thea turned her body around to sit. The water lapped upwards, hitting the ends of her red and gold fin. She dipped the end of her tail to splash the water and sighed again. She didn't know what she would do if this didn't work. Only a few humans knew about the pod, and she could theoretically tell Sophie as she was.

Thea stared down at her tail. Red and gold, it shimmered like a fire inside the cave. Guilt and fear pulled at her chest as she weighed her options. No, revealing her form like this was not an option. Instead, she would take the time for closure.

"Closure," Thea nodded to herself, "this is only for closure. She has been on my mind for years, and her father died because of me. I need closure, but I will not reveal the pod."

She looked up at the cave's ceiling. "Do you hear me, Poseidon? With my blood and voice, I promise that I will not reveal us, and the pod will remain safe with me. But I need this closure."

Her whisper echoed in the cave, returning to her like the wind. Clenching her hands to her chest, she bowed down in reverence. The water continues to lap at her tail. She felt warm as she spoke and knew he could hear her.

Thea pulled the bag to her front and took out the fish. With little effort, she shimmied closer to the altar rock. More water was seeping down, and she knew outside their song had woken the clouds. The sky was weeping.

Thea laid the fish on the rock and bowed her head. She pulled out her knife from the sheath around her waist.

"With my breath, I pray." She lightly kissed the fish, breathing softly against its body.

"With my blood, I pray." She cut the fatty tip of her thumb. A small line of red blood seeped out. It trickled onto the fish.

"With my song, I pray." Thea straightened her body.

She opened her mouth and sang out. There were no words, only a solemn melody of reverence and love. It echoed through the cave, taking over the sounds of the sea washing in or the drops of water falling from the Earth. When she finished, she dug the knife into the fish, gutting it on the altar.

Everything went still. Thea could feel the ocean shift directions. The water from the cave roof seemed to stop, suspended in the air. A charged buzz filled the air as damp and cold mixed with heavy heat. Outside, she could hear the storm growing.

"Please," Thea barely whispered, "I need this closure."

It started as a tingling sensation, light and only slightly burning. But the more attention Thea paid to it, the more heat came from her tail.

It *burned.*

A bright light emanated from her tail, making the fire real. Scales began wilting away. They flew up into the air and crumpled into ashy dust.

Thea clenched her jaw, refusing to cry out. More and more scales lifted up into the air. Her fins curled into themselves. She was on fire.

But still, Thea held firm.

She knew this pain. Any quick transformation was painful. Soon, her bones will grow, break, and grow again. Her tail would split in the middle. There would be no blood, no evidence of magic outside of her offering.

But the pain would still be there.

Thea watched her tail begin to rip and screamed.

The ocean sang.

A school of fish danced around. Their bodies glimmered with the sun. Moving together in unison, they shifted with the currents, becoming one with the ocean. To and fro, up and down, they swam without a care in the world.

Thea watched at a distance. A slow smile crossed her face as she gripped her bag with both hands. Catching one or two random fish was easy, and even a large fish or shark was doable with the right tool. The difficulty in targeting a school of fish was in their unity.

They didn't stray from the group. If Thea moved head-on, they would scramble into a chaotic mess. It made catching one fish nearly impossible. Thea wanted a real challenge; to catch one or two without disrupting the group.

Thea slowly swam closer. The fish shifted nervously, causing her to pause. Taking the time, Thea closed her eyes and inhaled deeply. With her senses opened, she could feel the change in the current move back into place. Opening her eyes, she swished her tail slightly, testing the current. The fish moved with the change.

Thea's smile grew. She began to swim with the school, learning how they determined their next step. Every chance she could, she moved in closer.

She was too much into the dance to see the darkened shadow cross over them. It wasn't until she felt the sinewy roughness of the net hitting her that she realized her mistake.

The school of fish scattered, most of it gathered with her. The net closed, locked into itself, and moved upwards. Thea was stuck, unable to swim away, and she didn't bring her knife.

Fear and worry filled her bloodstream, and she could hear the confusion of the pod calling back to her. There was no way they would risk saving her, not when she was so far away from the reef's safety. The cranking sound of the boat's gears took over, and her heart dropped.

THEA WOKE WITH A START. Sweat drenched her body. A pounding sensation pulsed from her temples, radiating out and covering her head in a blanket of pain. Reaching up, she slowly rubbed the back of her head and felt the growing lump. Sometime during the transition, she passed out and hit the back of her head.

The rest of her body ached just as much. Looking down, Thea's heart skipped a beat. Two long and lean muscled legs replaced her tail. Inhaling deeply, she tentatively stretched. Tingling pain speckled her calves as she worked the new muscles. Methodically, Thea began accessing everything.

Two legs? She stretched out the calves again, feeling the tingles begin to subside.

Ankles? She rolled the ankles. Small pops echoed as tiny air bubbles broke apart in the joints.

Feet and toes? Thea kicked up her legs and counted the ten toes.

Water slid down her skin, sending a wave of emotions through her. She could still feel the magic and hear the ocean's call. The pod called out to her, sharing the emotions flowing around. A slow smile crossed her lips. She bowed her head in thanks and began to climb to her feet.

The air inside the cave was cold. Thea shivered and rubbed her body down quickly. The friction didn't do much to keep her warm, but with any luck, the clothes she hid inside the cave would still be viable. Taking a tentative step, she walked further into the cave. A closed wooden box hid behind a drier part of the cave.

Thea bent to her knees and opened it. Inside were bags of clothing, all of which she had procured during her month on Finley Isle with the humans. Thea opened one bag and smiled. For the most part, the clothing looked stable. There were no holes or mold in the seams. Now, she had to make sure she could fit in them.

Grabbing all of the bags, Thea began to shop around.

CHAPTER FIVE

A man Sophie didn't know spread his arms out for a hug. Despite the urge to shrink and run away, she spread her own. The man entered the hug without a second thought. He pulled her in, lowered his head to her ear, and let out a breath before speaking. She didn't hear what he said; all of her focus was the sour smell of his breath.

"Thank you," she mumbled numbly as he stepped away from the hug and went to Aida.

The funeral home was brightly lit and filled with most of the town. Everyone who respected Lars Holmquist stepped into the lobby and paid their condolences. In theory, it made sense, and Sophie did appreciate that so many knew and would remember her father. Still, there was a bleakness to the experience. In truth, there was nothing enjoyable about a funeral.

Sophie shifted nervously on her feet as she continued to greet the guests. She didn't want to go into the viewing room. In her eyes, Lars was no longer there. His body was, but the man she knew and loved wasn't. He had gone wherever anyone went and left behind a shell of a human. Looking at his face would only make it feel less tangible. For her, it was better to think that he had just ceased to exist.

It was painful, and tears threatened to leave at a moment's notice, but Sophie kept strong. This funeral was not for him or for her. It was for the people who stepped into the funeral home to pay their respects. They needed the closure of his death. Deep inside, she feared she would never get that closure.

Like many in Finley, Lars was an experienced fisherman and swimmer. His drowning seemed the most unlikely method of death possible. If it was storming when he was out at sea, Sophie could allow that thought, but being caught in his fishing net and pulled down into the depths made no sense.

"Oh, honey," Aida's soft voice called her attention.

Sophie turned to look at her mother. Then she felt the stinging pain of salty tears trailing down her cheeks. Excusing herself, she rubbed at her face and walked into a bathroom. People openly cried in the viewing room. They held their own loved ones close. But she couldn't do that.

Grieving was just too intimate for her. No one would understand the depths of her pain and guilt. They would stare at her with open pity, not caring that she was uncomfortable. If she said anything, their words would only prove her point more.

Practically running into the bathroom, she closed the door and locked it. She never made it to the toilet. Instead, she slid down to the floor and sobbed. It came out in broken pleas. The tears rolled down her cheeks, threatening to drown her. Her breath came out in strangled hiccups. She wanted to curl up and disappear into the tiles of the floor.

He was gone. His stories, his warmth, everything was gone. And here she was, on the brink of being alone.

On the mainland, she was lonely but never truly felt alone. Despite not returning in the last twelve years, she knew both parents were there. They would always be there, no matter what hardships their relationships played. But now, she felt the hardcore truth: her mother was slowly wilting away, and her father was gone.

A knock on the door broke her crying.

"Sophie?" Her mother called from the other end. "Are you okay?"

Sophie wanted to scream. There was nothing okay about the situation. Her father was dead, her mother was aging, and she had nothing to leave behind. Not that there was anyone in her life she could go to.

Her heart dropped to her stomach, and true loneliness began to fill the void. She felt her body shake as she tried to scratch up to the surface. There was no getting out, and Sophie was alone in the depths.

"Sophronia." Her mother's voice was sharp.

It didn't stop the anxiety, but it did leave behind a small rope ladder that she could begin to climb up.

I can do this. Daddy wouldn't want me to give up. I can't give up.

She told herself. Without realizing it, her body moved on autopilot. It walked to the sink and turned on the faucet. Unsure of what she should say, Sophie closed her mouth. All her attention went to the rushing sound of the water. There was a calmness to it that she didn't realize before. A white sound that calmed her nervous system and brought her back to reality.

She cupped her hands and ran them under the rushing water. A pool formed inside. Dipping down, she washed her face.

"I'm almost done," she said, lifting her face from the water. Her mascara was running down her eyes, but she didn't care, and the makeup wasn't her anyways.

"We have guests," Aida said.

Sophie grabbed some paper towels. Folding the paper towel to dry her face, she resisted the urge to roll her eyes. Only her mother would think about the funeral guests versus the actual grieving.

"I'm almost done," she said, wiping the last water from her face. She wanted to say many cuss words, some disheartening accusations, and maybe a few insults. Still, she kept quiet, and there wasn't enough energy in the world for her to be angry enough.

Sophie threw away the used paper towel, turned off the faucet, and opened the bathroom door.

"Sorry, I had the runs," she couldn't help lying.

Aida frowned and crossed her arms over her chest. She opened her mouth to say something, but Sophie shook her head.

Briefly smiling, Sophie nodded to the lobby. "Were there more people you wanted to introduce me to?"

With a sigh, Aida's frown smoothed out. "Not only that, we are about to begin."

Sophie's heart dropped again. She nodded quickly and stepped out of the bathroom. An older white man stepped closer once she reached the lobby. He had the same pitying smile plastered on his face and had an outstretched hand. Sophie ignored the smile and instead paid attention to the squared authoritative way he stood. The pale yellow light of the funeral home reflected from his bald head.

"I'm so sorry for your loss," the man said, gripping Sophie's hand without direction. "Lars was a good friend of mine."

Sophie nodded and shook his hand absentmindedly. "And you are?"

"Oh, this is Peter," Aida said with a smile. It sent a sickening feeling up Sophie's stomach. "He was there during the accident."

"I have been fishing with your father for a while now," Peter explained, dropping Sophie's hand, "I know how painful it can be to not know the details of a parent's passing. If you want to, I can tell you more about it."

Sophie frowned slightly, unsure how to feel. Yes, she did have questions, but it felt weird to be offered answers so close to her father's body. There was almost a sense of urgency in Peter's voice. As if he was trying to dig something out of her or gain her trust.

She opened her mouth to speak but closed it at the sight of his face. His beady brown eyes had widened into pinpoints as he looked over her shoulder. Sophie glanced over her shoulder to see the last person she expected to see.

Thea stood at the doorway of the funeral home. Her long summer dress was the same one Sophie remembered twelve years ago. Long black hair was tied back into a braid. There was a guilty sadness on Thea's face as she slowly stepped into the building. Their eyes locked, and thoughts rolled through Sophie's mind, taking over her senses.

"Thea?"

CHAPTER SIX

Sophie wanted to talk to Thea, but her mother ushered her into the viewing room. The next thing she knew, she was sitting in the front row, staring at the prone body of her father inside the casket. Throughout the event, her hands were clammy, and her breathing shallow. The priest spoke about the ocean, Finley Isle, and Lars being more than just the light keeper. If anyone asked her what was said, she couldn't repeat it.

The only thing on her mind was Thea. For twelve years, Thea lived rent-free in her mind, and never once did she think they would see each other again. It was almost easier to believe Thea was a fevered dream for a girl who wanted a summer romance and something worth living for. But now that dream was real, and Sophie didn't know how she felt about it.

She wanted to stop the service and pulled Thea away. She wanted to demand answers and ask questions but wanted to kiss her most.

Emotions warred through her mind. This was her father's funeral, and he was at the forefront of her mind. And yet, Thea was there too. It was as if Lars' death had replaced Thea's disappearance.

It left a bad feeling in Sophie's stomach.

"That was a beautiful service," Mrs. Gunnar said, a little too loud. She lifted a hand to her ear and played with something.

Sophie nodded as she noticed the hearing aid.

"It really was. Dad would have appreciated everyone coming here," She said loudly.

Mrs. Gunnar winced and shook her head. Every wrinkly on her face deepened as she frowned at Sophie.

"I'm hard of hearing, hon, not deaf," she said sharply. The old woman turned around with a scoff and walked away, shaking her head the whole time.

Sophie sighed and shook her head. She remembered Mrs. Gunnar as lovely, but some changed with old age. Watching the elderly woman talk to her peers, Sophie sighed again. She supposed the woman was thinking the same thing as her.

"I'm sorry for what happened," a woman's voice said.

Sophie turned her attention to see Thea standing next to her. Her throat caught her heart. She took a step back and smiled nervously.

"Thea."

A soft pink blush colored Thea's cheeks. She bowed her head to the side and shrugged slightly. There was so much Sophie wanted to say, but she kept quiet. Thea shifted in her feet and smiled.

"Hi, Sophie," Thea finally spoke.

"Why are you here?"

Thea winced at Sophie's voice. There was a ping of guilt, but Sophie kept quiet. She tried to keep her face as unresponsive as possible. Thea's eyes darted from side to side as if trying to find a way out of the conversation. Sighing, Sophie rubbed her face with her hand.

"I'm sorry," she gave up, "I just don't understand why you're here."

"I heard about your father," Thea said.

Sophie narrowed her eyes and stared at Thea. There was no indication that Thea was lying, but it didn't make sense. Her mother didn't advertise Lars' death. The only way Thea could learn about it was if she was living on the island. Sophie frowned, more at herself than Thea. It was just another reason to feel guilty for not coming back earlier.

"I see," Sophie said slowly, "I guess you've been back on the island for a while."

Thea bit her lower lip and then nodded firmly. "I've been around for a while."

"Are you staying?" The question came out before Sophie could stop herself, but she needed to know. She wasn't sure how much more she could give Thea.

"Well, I do have to get home eventually," Thea said with a twinkle in her eyes.

Sophie's heart jumped for a second. It had been so long since she flirted the last time, and a part of her felt off doing it at her father's funeral, but this was Thea. Her Thea. The girl who took her heart and ran away without a word.

Sophie found herself smiling softly. "I meant the island."

"I knew what you meant," Thea said.

She leaned close to Sophie, her hand outstretched. Sophie's breath caught in her throat as she waited. Anxiety pulsed through her as thoughts raced through her mind. What would it feel like to touch Thea again? Did she want Thea to touch her?

Thea placed her hand on Sophie's arm and squeezed. All of the anxiety rushed out of her, and Sophie let out the breath she was holding. There was nothing negative about Thea's touch. It was reassuring, comforting, and intimate.

Sophie wanted more.

She opened her mouth to say something when she noticed Peter walking towards her. He pushed past the other guests, pausing only to smile cordially, and then continued to them. Thea glanced over her shoulder, sighed, and lowered her hand. She looked at Sophie with a sad smile and shrugged slightly.

"I'll let you be with the others," she offered softly, "but I'll see you later."

"Later?" Sophie asked. "Do you promise?"

Thea smiled and nodded. "Promise."

Thea stretched out her hand again for a handshake. Sophie grabbed her wrist and pulled her close. Embracing her, Sophie closed her eyes and breathed in deeply. She smelled of seawater and the sun. There was a jump in Sophie's chest as her heart matched Thea's beat. It was as if they were the only two people in the world.

"I'll see you soon," Thea promised.

Her voice was soft, almost a whisper in the wind. Sophie reluctantly let go and watched as Thea walked away.

Peter stopped walking and stepped aside for Thea. His eyes widened at the sight of her as she passed by. Slowly, he watched Thea walking away, taking in her feminine figure. When she left the house, Peter looked at Sophie and smiled.

Sophie's hands clenched into fists as jealousy sprang up. She knew it was immature, but Peter's look at Thea bothered her.

Peter sauntered to her. A smug grin was plastered to his face. The anger didn't subside once he stopped before her and opened his mouth. Never had she wanted to punch a man so much.

"She's a pretty girl," Peter said.

The back of her jaw clenched. She wanted to punch him more now.

"She's an old girlfriend," Sophie said.

Peter nodded slowly. "Is that so? It's good that a friend of yours came to the funeral."

She kept quiet. It was no use correcting Peter when the first thing that would most likely cross his mind was a threesome. Men like Peter didn't look at a woman's sexuality as her own thing. It was purely for his enjoyment.

"She's been living here for a while," Sophie said, trying to keep the talk as small as possible.

"Really?" Peter frowned slightly, shook his head, and smiled, "I don't remember her being around, but I am getting old."

Sophie didn't know what to say. It was awkward enough that he checked out Thea.

"How long have you known each other?" He asked.

The back of her jaw was beginning to hurt. She could feel the veins at her temple pulse at the headache threatening to appear.

"How long have you known Dad?" She asked.

Peter took a step back. His eyes widened in surprise. It took a second, but the sly, smug grin returned when he regained his composure. A worry crossed her mind, and Sophie wondered if he would move the conversation back to Thea. There was a twinkle in his eye. It was as if he knew what she was doing by refusing to answer.

"We've been friends since childhood," he answered with a shrug. "We would go fishing together sometimes."

"Like that day," Sophie commented.

Her mind wandered to the funeral home and Peter's offer to tell her everything. It was only a few hours ago, but something about that interaction had her wondering if there was something more to it. As if sensing something, Peter shifted his feet. He looked nervously over his shoulder and then back to Sophie.

Taking a small step forward, he leaned close to her. "Just like that day."

Sophie felt like she was missing something. There was a directness to his voice. An almost conspiratorial promise left unsaid. She narrowed her eyes slightly and nodded slowly. He knew something, quite possibly did something to her father, and she needed to know what it was.

"You mentioned meeting me about it," she said.

"Not here and not today, but soon," Peter promised with a shake of his head. "I'll take you fishing and everything."

CHAPTER SEVEN

Thea groaned. A few days had passed since the funeral, and she still hadn't seen Sophie. She couldn't. There was too much she would have to leave unsaid.

It was already too late when it crossed her mind that she couldn't tell the whole truth. By then, Sophie was asking questions she wasn't ready to answer. When they hugged, it took everything from Thea to not blurt out the whole truth. But then she avoided it, and it was too late. Sophie was hopeful they could be together again. Thea was sure of it.

It broke her heart.

Thea leaned back on the park bench. The wood was stiff and creaked under her weight. She had been sitting on it for two hours, thinking of what she could say to Sophie without sounding crazy or causing trouble. Thus far, she composed four possible scenarios, each awful.

Sighing, she watched children play in the grass. One child was chasing a small group, yelling at them. Laughter cascaded from them.

"I was wondering when I'd find you," Sophie said.

Thea leaped from the seat. She whipped around to see Sophie standing behind her. Sophie smiled down with arms crossing her chest.

"Sophie," Thea squeaked, "you're here."

Sophie nodded. "I am."

She walked around the park bench and sat down next to Thea. With a playful grin, she leaned close and nudged Thea with her elbow.

"And so are you."

"Yeah," Thea said.

"Are you busy?" Sophie asked.

Thea blinked. She could lie and say she was, but then what? There was nowhere else she could go. If she went to the cave, she ran the risk of Sophie following. And then what would she say? No, there were too many variables, and she wasn't ready for them.

Slowly, Thea smiled softly and shook her head. "I'm free."

"Good." Sophie smiled back. "How about lunch? You can tell me what you've been up to for twelve years."

Thea could hear the unsaid questions. She needed to be cautious with what she said. Agreeing to lunch, Thea told herself she must stick with the most straightforward lie: the half-truth.

She followed Sophie to the local diner, Piper's Pies, and sighed with contentment. It had been a while since she had human food, not since the last migration. Sometimes, they would come across a yacht or cruise ship and be able to steal human nutrition for the occasional treat. But nothing beat the home-cooked thrill that was Piper's Pies.

Sophie guided her to a table tucked in the corner. Thea narrowed her eyes and looked around. The interior and furniture had changed over the years. The restaurant was cozy, with warm wood seating and a cottage-core aesthetic. There was something familiar with this specific spot.

Sitting down across from Sophie, Thea realized what it was. "This is our spot."

"You remembered," Sophie smiled at her reaction.

Thea blushed, and it was a memory she never wanted to forget. That first night Sophie got so nervous she spilled her tea, Thea struggled with her silverware, and they shared their first kiss. It was both the most embarrassing and beautiful night Thea had experienced. Since then, they have sat in that corner while eating at the diner.

"Why wouldn't I? "She asked.

"It's been twelve years," Sophie said.

Thea sighed. It had been twelve years, and everything could change in that amount of time. Nervous, she wrung her hands together and looked down at the floor. Even the tile had changed to hardwood. The change was inevitable. Except for her feelings, she knew that now.

Sensing something, Sophie leaned across the tabletop. She wormed a hand between Thea's and held to the nearest one she could. With three tight reassuring squeezes, Thea's attention went back to her.

"I'm glad you remembered," Sophie said.

There was a soft acceptance in her voice. As if she thought their month together was a dream or a fleeting fantasy for one of them. Fear gripped Thea's chest. Did she somehow cause Sophie to feel undeserving of genuine affection? Thea squeezed back hurriedly, blinking her eyes quickly to keep tears from falling.

"I will never forget," she promised, and it was true. She never could forget as much as she had tried.

"Why did you leave?" Sophie asked. She bit her lower lip and shook her head. "No, I knew eventually you would leave. But I don't understand why you didn't tell me you were going. Where did you go?"

Thea held her breath. The where was easy to answer; the pod was consistent in its migration path. She had crossed the Atlantic Ocean many times in her life. It was why she couldn't figure out a good answer.

"My family moves around a lot," she said slowly, trying to find an appropriate human thing to make up for the truth. "We were leaving our summer home, and I had to go with them."

"You couldn't call? Leave a note?"

Thea sighed. Sophie asked the right questions, but how could you tell someone that a cell phone didn't work underwater, let alone fathoms deep in the ocean?

"I don't have a phone," she said with a shrug, "I don't need one."

Sophie snorted incredulously and shook her head. "Not even for work?"

"I don't have a typical job," Thea said. She smiled at the thought of her in an office, tail and all. "What do you do?"

Thea cringed. From the look on Sophie's face, she knew she could have been more tactful. This was the problem with being a mermaid, socializing like a human. She was a literal fish out of water.

"Sorry," she apologized. "I'm not good with conversation. "

"There was always something awkward about you," Sophie said with a slow nod. After a pause, she answered Thea's question. "I'm between jobs right now. Turns out having a Ph.D. in Folklore doesn't get you many offers."

"Folklore?" Thea brightened. That was interesting.

Sophie nodded with a laugh. "Yeah, folklore. Dad got me into it when I was a kid. He used to say we were descended from mermaids. This strange phenomenon here on the island is where the wind picks up and sounds like singing. He called it the Song of Storms. It was supposedly mermaids singing about the loss of their own. It happened when my grandmother died, and, actually, it happened when I got here for Dad's funeral."

There was a soft wispy look on her face as she told the memory. Thea smiled, but her mind reeled on the information. To her knowledge, there was no other mermaid pod in the world. Galene would have told them if there were. And mermaids, when childbirth happened, did not birth human children. But that didn't change the fact that Lars was right about one thing.

He had known about their song of grief. It was troubling and comforting at the same time. In some mystical way, he had known about the pod's practices. It brought some peace knowing that she and the others sang for him.

"That's beautiful," she said softly.

"Yeah," Sophie said. She wiped a tear from her face and shrugged. "I wanted to find a mermaid so badly just to tell him some of his story was true."

"Who is to say it wasn't?" Thea asked. It was a gamble, but she needed to know how receptive Sophie was to the idea. Hope spurred in her heart at the prospect of being able to tell the whole truth.

"Everyone," Sophie laughed. "Mermaids aren't real, but it'd be amazing if they were."

"What would you do if they were?" Thea asked. Fear replaced hope as she worried.

"Nothing," Sophie shrugged, "I mean, I would want to know their stories and customs. Maybe write a book about them. But, I can't imagine anything more besides pushing environmental causes."

"Would you tell other people?"

Sophie narrowed her eyes in confusion but laughed and shook her head. "You sound as if you believe in them."

"I've traveled the world," Thea said quickly, "I've been to Spain, Greece, and many other places. All of them have stories about mermaids."

"Stories," Sophie nodded emphatically, "that's all they are."

Thea frowned. She wanted to tell Sophie so much more.

"But would you tell people?" Thea asked cautiously. "I wouldn't. It could be detrimental to their whole culture, and humans are known to exploit what they don't understand. Hell, exploitation happens when they do understand."

"Woah," Sophie said. She leaned back from the table, relinquishing her hand from Thea's. "You've put some serious thought into this."

"Sorry," Thea said. She forced herself to tamp down her feelings. Anything more, and she was risking everything. "I got excited."

"No," Sophie said with a smile, "that's okay. I love that about you."

There was an awkward pause. Thea's heart jumped to her throat. She couldn't stop smiling. Sophie loved her. She *still* loved her. Thea wanted to jump and tell her everything, but she wanted to profess her feelings. All of them.

"So," Sophie broke the awkward silence, "what is Greece like?"

Thea laughed and began to tell her. It was easy talking about the places she'd been to. If Sophie suspected that the main subject was the water, she didn't let on. Instead, their lunch consisted of them laughing and talking about the places they'd been and the food they'd eaten.

Sophie mentioned going to the Grand Canyon, and Thea's eyes widened. She had never thought a trench could exist on land, yet it did. Sadness played with her heart as she thought of all the places she couldn't experience. But that feeling faded with every lilt of Sophie's laugh or because Thea noticed how her eyes crinkled. She wanted to share everything with Sophie.

Their lunch continued this way, with only one thing genuinely bothering Thea. At one point, Sophie left to use the restroom, leaving her at the table. Thea's eyes wandered to the patrons of the diner. She wondered if they had ever left the comfort of Finley. A chill ran up her spine when her eyes went to the window.

There was something about the man staring at her that she couldn't quite place her finger on. He was round and bald. His beady eyes bore through the glass and were directed at her. The confused stare on his face morphed into anger. It was so intense she nearly left the table.

"Is everything alright?" Sophie asked, catching her attention.

Thea looked up and smiled. "I'm fine, but I should get going."

Sophie nodded slowly. "I should probably help Mom out with the house. You'd be surprised how much is left when a person dies."

"I can only imagine," Thea said, standing up from the table and joining Sophie. "I will see you again, though. I won't be here much longer, but I want to be with you while I am."

Sophie's smile was everything. The growing fear of the man at the window dissipated instantly. All there was was Sophie. Thea smiled back and leaned in.

The kiss was meant to be soft and endearing. What happened was Earth-shattering.

Sophie cupped her hand behind Thea's head and pulled her in closer. Their lips touched, sending waves of desire through her. Soft gasps of air broke through. It was slow and hungry. Every second of their separate lives lingered in the kiss. It was like breathing air and the ocean at the same time.

She could feel the pod stirring. The ocean called to her. And then everything crashed like a tidal wave. All in this one kiss.

When they broke apart, both were gasping. Thea smiled. This one kiss said it all. She would beg Sophie to be with her if she had the choice. She would throw everything away for Sophie.

"I need to go," she whispered.

It took everything out of her to turn around and walk out the door. What she wanted more was to spend every waking moment with Sophie, but the pod stirred again, and reality hit. One day, her heart was going to break again.

She wasn't sure she could live past it.

"I know who you are." A voice hissed at her.

Thea stopped and turned. The man was standing there, full of venom and vitriol. He clenched his beefy fist and raised it.

"You," he hissed.

Thea didn't know what happened next. She felt him before everything went dark.

CHAPTER EIGHT

Sophie frowned. A week. Thea had been missing for a week. Guilt and anger warred inside her as she looked at her phone again. She willed it to ring, but nothing happened. A strangled laugh bubbled up as she remembered Thea mentioning not having a cell phone.

She couldn't help it. Thea left without an explanation. Again.

"Eat," her mother commanded from the other side of the table.

Sophie lifted a piece of toast to her mouth and bit down. Despite the enormous amount of jam and peanut butter, it tasted dry; everything tasted different since lunch with Thea. It was as if that kiss they shared knocked her senses out of order, and she was working on autopilot.

"Okay," Aida said, annoyed, "you've been like this for days. I haven't seen you like this since that girl up and left you broken-hearted."

Sophie flinched. It angered her that not only was her mother right, but it was the same girl. The fact her mother mentioned her heart wasn't lost on her. She didn't see a reason to admit she was a lesbian. Clearly, the only thing that bothered Aida was Sophie's reaction to another rejection.

Aida sighed and shook her head. "Sophronia Ann Holmquist."

Sophie looked up from her toast. Aida's voice was a sharp annoyance when she said her name. Still, her face said otherwise. Tears coated Aida's eyes as she looked at Sophie with an emotional cocktail.

"You can't sit around moping," she said softly, "go talk to Peter. Maybe he can take you fishing. You must get out of the house, off the island, and clear your mind. That girl does things to you, and you need to return to me."

There was a momentary pause. Thoughts ran through Sophie's mind. Slowly, she began to nod. Her mother was right. She did need to get out, and if for a little while.

"Does it bother you?" She asked softly.

"That some trollop has broken my daughter's heart?" Aida asked, snorting, "Of course."

"No, Mom," Sophie laughed. She shook her head. "That I'm a lesbian."

"Don't be stupid." Aida rolled her eyes. "I couldn't give two shits about who you fall in love with, and neither would your father. We want you happy, and that's all we ever wanted."

Tears threatened to roll down soap in space. The relationship with her parents was Rocky for the last 12 years. Though she never suspected her parents had stopped loving her, the admission from her mother was too much. For too long, she had let her pride get in the way of growing closer to them. Now it was too late for her and her father.

She looked at her mother. Aida seemed so old and weary. Tears ran down her face. Sophie got out of her seat and ran around the table. Aida had no chance to say anything or move before Sophie embraced her.

"I love you, Mommy," Sophie sobbed in her hair.

Aida's body shook as she returned the hug. The two of them sat there, not saying anything past the tears and unspoken guilt. Sophie imagined her father there, completing their triad, and smiled. This time she was going to do better.

"Go," Aida urged, breaking their connection after a few minutes. "See if Peter can entertain your morose mood."

Sophie laughed. She wiped the tears from her cheeks and nodded. Aida was right. She needed to do something. No one else was hiring on the island, and Sophie required more time to begin job searching on the mainland. Getting out and doing something her father loved would benefit her more than keep her occupied; she would also feel closer to him.

"I'll see you for dinner," Sophie promised, kissing Aida's head before leaving for the docks.

As expected, Peter was on his fishing boat, gathering supplies. Sophie crossed the dock and picked up a large box, and Peter turned and made a startled laugh.

"Oh, Sophronia. I wasn't expecting you," he said.

"Sorry about that, Peter," Sophie said, handing him the box. He hesitantly took it from her as she continued to talk. "I'm feeling a bit off, and Mom suggested I get out for some fresh air. It's been a long time since I've done any fishing, but you did offer to tell me what happened with Dad, and I thought now was as good a time as ever."

Peter lowered the box onto the deck. There was a grunt as he stood up straighter. With a twist, his back popped, and he sighed. His mouth was shut thin as he looked at Sophie with narrowed eyes.

She wondered why he seemed cagey. When they first met, he seemed open and willing to have her on the boat, and now he looked around as if grasping for an excuse to keep her on land. It bothered her.

Slowly, Peter nodded. A smug grin crossed his face. He pointed to another box, and Sophie leaned down to grab it.

"Sure thing, Sweetheart," he said, his smile growing. Sophie held back a cringe. "Let's get the rest of these things in and get going."

CHAPTER NINE

"We're almost there," Peter said gleefully.

The further out in the sea they went, the more excited Peter became. Sophie tried to be as enthusiastic as he was, but it was unnerving. It had been an hour since they left Finley, and there was only small talk then. Now, here he was, practically dancing at the wheel.

"Great," Sophie said numbly, giving up on trying to be excited.

Peter darted a glare in her direction, but she ignored it. How could he be excited to return to the very spot her father died? Did anyone find that enjoyable? Sophie had a feeling Peter was the only one.

"You should be happy about this," he said with a hiss.

Sophie narrowed her eyes. Happy was not the word she would have chosen.

"I'm not sure I understand," she said slowly, "why should I be happy?"

"Because now you will know the truth," he said simply.

She opened her mouth to say something, but he jumped up and made a noise that was a part excited exclamation and a strangled squeak. He moved away from the wheelhouse and snapped his fingers.

"Hold on," he said quickly, "let me get her."

"Her?" Sophie asked, but Peter didn't answer.

Instead, he ran into the boat, going down to the main hull. There was silence, and then she heard what sounded like a struggle. A muffled slap echoed from below and then a cry. Peter returned up the stairs, dragging a bruised and bloody woman before him. He pushed the woman to the deck floor and smiled proudly at Sophie.

Her face went pale when she saw who lay at her feet.

"Thea?" She said with shock.

Thea looked up. The bruises were purple, and her left eye was swollen shut. There were cuts on her arms. Her arms were tied close to her back. She tried to smile, winced, and then whimpered.

"Oh, baby," Sophie cooed. She lowered to her knees and cradled Thea close to her.

"I know it looks bad," Peter said nonchalantly, "but you must understand, I had to do it. She's not human."

Sophie was only partially listening. Her eyes roved down Thea's body as she took in every cut and bruise. Anger pooled within her. Never had she wanted to hurt someone as bad as she did now.

"Why?" It came out as a whisper.

Peter didn't hear her. Instead, he continued his tirade. Peter spoke about mermaids and fishing. When he said her father's name, Sophie looked up. Fear gripped her. There was no way her father would have condoned hurting a woman. She was sure of it.

"What did you say?" She asked, seething with anger.

Peter rolled his eyes. He grabbed Thea from behind and pulled her away. Thea screamed out in pain, but Peter ignored her. He flung her to the side and laughed as she rolled to a stop, hitting the side of the boat.

"Thea!" Sophie took a step forward.

Peter stepped between them and shook his head. "No."

"Get away from her," Sophie said.

"Listen," he said calmly, "she's not human, Sophronia."

"What are you talking about?" Sophie shook her head. She could see Thea over Peter's shoulder. Thea was moving into a sitting position. "She looks human to me."

"Yes," Peter agreed, "but that doesn't make her human."

"Alright, I'll bite," Sophie growled, "what is she then."

"A mermaid."

Sophie stared at him and laughed. This man was crazy. It was the only explanation she had for it. Somehow, Peter went nuts. She looked at Thea, and guilt hit her. Thea wore the same outfit she had during lunch at the diner. Sophie wanted to cry. She hadn't left without a word. Thea was stuck with a crazy man.

"They aren't real," she said. Sophie took a slow step forward.

Peter shook his head. "That's where you're wrong. Lars and I caught her that day."

"Go on," Sophie said, taking another step forward.

Peter didn't seem to notice. Behind him, Thea was sitting up. Her chest rose and fell in short bursts. Sophie allowed herself to calm down. Thea was breathing. That was good.

"We were fishing," Peter said. "The net was coming up, and it was heavy. When it landed on deck, out popped the mermaid. Your girlfriend."

He said girlfriend with a heavy sneer. Sophie continued to stalk toward him. She glanced at Thea from over his shoulder. Thea leaned back, with her one good eye narrowed in disgust. Peter didn't care. He kept talking.

"Your father was the first to see her. She would be in a zoo if it were me, but no!" He screamed out, causing Thea and Sophie to flinch. "Lars had to be a bleeding heart, and he cut her free."

"And then what happened?" She asked cautiously. She lifted a hand, reaching for him.

Peter glared. "Don't come any closer, or I'll throw her overboard."

For emphasis, he ran to Thea. He gripped her hair and wrapped it around his fist. With one quick tug, he pulled her up. Thea screamed.

Sophie's heart jumped. "Don't touch her!"

"Why not?" He asked. "This bitch caused your father's death, and he cut her out of the net and allowed her to leave. We could have made millions!"

"You're crazy," Sophie shook her head. "Mermaids aren't real."

"You think so?" Peter barked out a laugh. He pulled Thea close, buried his face into her neck, and smelled. "Why don't you tell her the truth, sweetheart?"

Tears ran down Thea's face. Sophie clenched her fists and growled.

"Fine then," Peter sneered. "Your girlfriend is a mermaid, and because of your father, I lost a fortune."

"What did you do?" Sophie insisted.

Peter barked out a laugh. "I took care of business and will finally get my millions. As soon as your girlfriend here transforms back."

Sophie had had enough.

Without thinking, she ran towards him. Thea let out a strangled cry as Sophie dove. Peter wasn't a criminal. He was just crazy. Instead of hurting Thea, he dropped her and cowered. Sophie didn't let him make a move. She ran into his body, pushing both of them overboard.

Thea screamed as both Sophie and Peter fell into the water.

Saltwater rushed through Sophie's nose, causing her to gasp out. The lungful of water burned her chest. Quickly, she let go of Peter and kicked him. Peter grasped for her but couldn't reach her. His fingers grazed at her shoes, but another kick kept him from gripping.

Sophie broke water to see Thea staring down at him. Thea stretched out her hand.

"He's gone," Sophie yelled, grabbing Thea's hand.

CHAPTER TEN

The moment Sophie got on deck, she called for the coast guard. It took hours for them to search for Peter's body and investigate Thea's kidnapping. Sophie found it odd that they had so many questions for Thea. Still, after consistently telling them the same story, they eventually let her go. Thea never left Sophie's side after that.

The moon was high up in the sky, hovering over the lighthouse. Thea shifted nervously. She could feel the tug of the ocean calling to her. The pod's insistence that she come home was stronger. It was almost time.

Thea turned to look at Sophie. She was sitting on the lighthouse's dock. Her feet dangled over the water. Sophie kicked back and laid down next to her. She slid her arm to Thea and gripped her hand. With a squeeze, she smiled.

"I can't believe that happened," she mused aloud.

Thea tried not to flinch. She stared out at the ocean, hearing the pod sing for her. Magic tingled through her body. The change was happening.

"I need to go," she said quietly.

Sophie narrowed her eyes. "What?"

Thea sighed. She closed her eyes and took a deep breath.

"My family is calling for me," she said.

Sophie sat up, confused at what was going on. Thea didn't look at her. Instead, she stood up. Her hands danced down to the edge of her dress. She gripped the hem and pulled it up over her head. Slowly, she folded it and placed it on the deck. There was no reason to do it, but she couldn't bring herself to destroy the clothing.

"What are you doing?" Sophie asked.

Thea smiled. "He wasn't lying."

"Who wasn't?"

"Peter," Thea said with a shrug. "Your father did save me. But I didn't know Peter killed him. I thought I did."

"What are you talking about?" Sophie asked.

Instead of answering, Thea dove into the water.

Sophie didn't understand what she was seeing. The moonlight brightened as the wind began to move. Squinting, she could see something glowing underwater.

"Thea!" Sophie dove into the water.

Thea was in front of her. Her black hair floated around her face. Sophie frowned. She stared at Thea in awe. Instead of two legs was a beautiful tail of gold and reds. Thea smiled sadly at her and kicked her tail, propelling her upwards.

Sophie followed. Cold air hit her when she surfaced.

"You're a,"

Thea nodded. "Mermaid."

"Peter,"

"Was right," Thea confirmed, "I am a mermaid, and I got caught in the net. Your father freed me. I don't know if he recognized me or was just that good of a man, but he allowed me to get out. I thought he got caught in the net and that I caused his death."

"But your legs," Sophie shook her head in confusion.

"We are allowed to have them, but the magic is limited," Thea explained.

"Magic?"

Thea nodded. "There's so much more I wish I could tell you."

Sophie blinked, unsure of what to say. It was so much. Slowly, she nodded and opened her mouth to ask her most important question.

"What about us?"

The question hit Thea hard. She bit her lower lip. Slowly, she swam to Sophie. She reached out and grabbed her arms. Without any answer, she pulled Sophie close and kissed her.

There was a moment of hesitation, and then Sophie's lips met hers. They kissed under the moonlight, hands touching new parts that weren't there in the past. So much needed to be said, but Thea couldn't do it. She wasn't ready for their inevitable goodbye. But it needed to happen.

She pulled away and smiled sadly at the human woman she fell in love with. There was no future for them, and she knew that. But she needed to make sure Sophie did as well.

"Don't you see," she said softly, "we can't be together."

"No." Sophie shook her head.

"Shhh," Thea placed her hand on Sophie's cheek. It was wet, and not just because of the ocean. "We can't be together, Sophie. You have to see that."

"You can stay here."

"I can't be away from my family," Thea said.

"Visit me then," Sophie insisted, "just don't leave me."

Tears flowed down Thea's face, and she let out a strangled cry. Shaking her head, she swallowed back the knot in her throat.

"I'll visit," she promised, "but don't live in agony without me. Find someone to love and be happy. Promise me."

Sophie nodded slowly. She couldn't say the word aloud, but she did mouth them. Thea smiled softly and nodded. She turned around and dove into the water, letting the ocean take her tears.

The pod called to her. She had been gone too long, and they were migrating from their reef. She would be back. She knew that. She just wished Sophie would be happy.

EPILOGUE

Sophronia Holmquist sat in her rocking chair and listened. A song called out from the ocean. It mixed with the wind and pulled the clouds together. She watched as they darkened and the waves quaked. The song was low and melodious. There were no words, but she knew the feeling so well.

She closed her eyes and imagined Thea singing with others like her. With a deep breath, Sophie opened her mouth and joined their song.

SERENA'S SONG

TIFFANY SHAND

CHAPTER ONE

This is the best feeling in the world. Serena stood on the deck of the boat and held out her arms. It felt like she was flying as the wind whipped her silvery blonde hair around her face. She sang along as the radio boomed out a classic rock song.

After the awful night she'd had, she thought she would never want to sing again. The sound of people jeering and booing still echoed through her mind. *God, don't think about that. Just enjoy this moment.* Worse still, the guy she had been chatting to online for a few weeks had stood her up. She'd spent so much time talking to Mark she felt like she knew him.

She'd been so excited and terrified of performing in front of an audience for the first time. Mark had promised to be there to support her. She had seen pictures of him online and had scanned the crowd for him. When she had realised he wasn't there, she froze and her performance had been a disaster.

Serena closed her eyes and let the sound of crashing waves wash over her. Almost as if the waves could wash away all of her churning emotions. She started singing again and it felt good just to say the words. See, she could sing. Unlike what those people had said in the pub. The singing part wasn't a problem. It was standing on stage and facing people's judgement that truly frightened her. And the one person she thought would support her hadn't been there.

"Are you gonna stand there all night?" Mike called over to her as he stood at the bridge and took a swig from his beer bottle.

The sound of his voice broke her out of her feeling of bliss. Typical. She had wanted to enjoy the feeling for a little longer. To just feel free and be one with the waves. Mike wasn't her type at all, but he had been the only guy to pay any attention to her all night, so she'd agreed to hang out with him for a while.

Serena flashed him a smile. She still couldn't believe they had only met a few hours ago at the local pub and he'd talked her into coming on a ride on his boat with him. He was nothing like Mark. Mark had been sweet and funny from what she had read in their exchanged messages. Mike was arrogant and full of himself. Her best friend had warned her not to go off with him, but she'd been humiliated tonight and needed something to take her mind off things. Mike might be an arsehole but hey, he had made her feel better for a while. He hadn't stood her up like her so-called boyfriend. Maybe Jade had been right. Maybe her online relationship had been a complete fantasy.

So, Mike it was. He was real and he'd asked her to come for a ride on his boat around the local harbour. Not the best idea since they'd both been drinking. But who could turn down a romantic boat ride in the middle of the night? The stars hung overhead like a glittering canopy of silver in darkness.

The waves crashed against the bow of the ship as they sped through Brightlingsea Harbour and out towards Mersea Island. Exhilaration rushed through her. This was true freedom. Out here, nothing could harm her. There was no one to judge her, no one to question her abilities. No one to hurt her.

She grabbed her beer bottle and took a swig. Drinking wasn't like her, but she needed something to take her mind off things. The alcohol had dulled her senses a little, but she kept thinking about

Mark. Had he stood her up because he couldn't make it? Had he turned up, seen her, and thought she wasn't pretty enough for him? Did he change his mind?

She stared at her phone for the thousandth time and found no new messages. She sighed and shoved her phone back in her pocket.

"Can this thing go any faster?" Serena asked and laughed as the boat lurched forward and picked up speed. She gripped the boat's railing and yelped when she stumbled down onto the deck. She laughed again, her head spinning.

"Hey, come over here. Or are you gonna spend all night up there?" Mike wanted to know and motioned for her to join him.

He had a mop of short black unruly hair, blue eyes and a chiselled face. He didn't look like one of the locals and hadn't told her much about where he came from or what he was doing in town. She hadn't minded. Not after the humiliating open mic night. Everyone in town called her the next Celine Dion and seemed convinced she would be world famous someday. Sure, she could sing, but overcoming her stage fright was an entirely different matter.

Some nights were fine and she could sing without any problem. Other nights she was too terrified to go on stage. Her heart would race, her hands would get sweaty and she would start hyperventilating. Serena didn't know what caused her stage fright. Maybe it was just the fear of being rejected and people not liking her. It didn't matter. She wasn't sure she ever wanted to go on stage again after what happened tonight at a pub in Colchester.

Her best friend, Jade, had been there and managed to get her offstage before she had turned into a blubbering mess. Both over Mark standing her up, and over her failed gig. Jade had insisted they go out and get completely drunk to take her mind off things. Serena hadn't had the heart to say no. She didn't usually like getting drunk — hangovers were the worst — but it had seemed like a good idea at the time. They'd been having a laugh together when Mike had approached her. He seemed nice enough at first. Not her usual type. Heck, most men never paid much attention to her.

895

"Can I have another one of those?" She stumbled over to Mike and motioned to one of the bottles of beer in the six-pack.

"You don't need to ask, love." Mike chuckled and let go of the ship's wheel. He went over and sat on one of the deck seats.

Serena grabbed the bottle and popped the lid off but didn't take a drink. "You could have asked anyone to come out here. Why choose me?"

He shrugged. "I liked the sound of your voice when you sang at the Siege House earlier."

She lifted the bottle to her lips then lowered it again. "Oh, Christ, you saw my awful performance?"

"You sounded pretty good from what I remember. You sing like an angel."

She snorted. "I'm no angel. Heck, I was terrible tonight. Maybe people are right. Maybe I'm just not meant to be a singer." Being a singer and making music had been her lifelong dream. She even wrote her own songs, but never really had the courage to sing them to other people.

Mark and Jade had been the only ones who'd encouraged her to follow her dream of being a singer and convinced her to perform at the open mic night. Had any of it been real? Or had Mark just set her up for complete failure? Maybe he wanted to make fun of her all along and had just pretended to be interested in her. It wouldn't be the first time someone had done that to her.

"My dad used to say never give up on your dreams. So, you shouldn't give up." Mike caught hold of her arm and dragged her onto his lap.

She bit back a yelp of surprise. The stars and wind swirled around her dizzy mind. Mike claimed her mouth and she recoiled at the wet sensation of his tongue forcing its way into her mouth. God, what was she doing? She didn't want this! She just wanted to take her mind off things for a while. This wasn't the person she had envisioned kissing tonight either.

"Stop." She pushed against his chest. "I didn't come here to sleep with you."

"You didn't think I'd give you a free boat ride for nothing, did you?" The smile had gone from his eyes. Now they had darkened with anger and desire.

She pulled away, but he caught hold of her and tried to kiss her again. "I said no. Let go of me!" He caught hold of her wrists and captured her mouth in another kiss. She bit down on his tongue, and he screamed in pain. The coppery taste of blood filled her mouth and she spat in his face.

But still, he refused to let go of her. Serena spotted the beer bottle beside them and smashed it against his head with all the force she could muster. Mike screamed as glass exploded over him, but it was enough for him to finally let go.

Serena wriggled free from his grasp and stumbled. The world around her spun upside down and she swallowed bile. She had to get away from him. Where could she hide on a boat? Somewhere below deck perhaps? No, she didn't want to be trapped down there.

Mike continued howling in pain and clutched his bloody head where the bottle had struck him. "Come back here, you crazy bitch!"

I have to get out of here. She grabbed another bottle and smashed it against the side of the ship, so it became a makeshift weapon. "You stay away from me," she warned.

"I'll kill you for this," he growled. "Do you have any idea who I am? I'll make sure no one ever finds you."

Oh, God, he was going to kill her. She glanced around, now suddenly sober. If he came near her again, he'd rape her, or worse. Maybe sex had been the only thing on his mind earlier but not now. Now she'd pissed him off.

Serena did the only thing she could think of. She ran to the other side of the boat and leapt over the railing. She plunged into the icy North Sea, and it felt like being punched as the water crashed against her. Its coldness hit her like a thousand knives. She kicked her legs in an effort to get up to the surface again but didn't seem to be making any progress.

She'd never been a strong swimmer and being out in the middle of the open sea made it even harder for her. She had to get to the surface. Had to get some air. Her lungs burned in protest.

The lights from the boat flickered above her like glowing orbs, but the harder she kicked the harder it became to keep moving. Her vision blurred and darkness closed in around her.

No, please don't let me die here, she prayed. *Not like this.*

CHAPTER TWO

Serena knew she was dying. She couldn't fight the pain anymore as it dragged her deeper. *No, I'm not ready to die. I can't. I have so much I still want to do.* She thrashed around, but it didn't do any good. Her lungs burned for air as she slowly suffocated.

The blackness drew ever closer. She felt herself sinking further. This was it. No one would ever find her out here. She'd become fish food. Nothing but a pile of bones for the fish to feed on. She would never get a chance to find out why Mark had stood her up. Or to sing again. Her life would be snuffed out. As if she had meant nothing. She had spent most of her life feeling worthless after growing up as a foster kid.

No one would ever know what happened to her. No one would ever think to look for her here. Why would they? Jade hadn't even known where she and Mike had been going. Not that she really had anyone to leave behind. Except for Jade. She was the only real friend Serena had. She didn't have any family. No one would miss her or notice she was gone.

Was this it? Was this what death felt like? Slowly suffocating until the blackness consumed you? To float in endless darkness?

Serena had expected something more. Somewhere peaceful perhaps. Somewhere better than this. Somewhere warmer and nicer. If heaven was real, wasn't it supposed to be a welcoming place? And wasn't hell supposed to be hot and surrounded by fire?

Would her spirit be stuck floating around here forever? Were spirits even real? She had never been a believer in religion or anything paranormal. She never really thought about it until now. Death had always seemed like something that would be far in the future. Not at the age of twenty-one. Serena had always thought she'd get to see her parents again when she died. The rest of her family had passed on long before she was born. But no one appeared to greet her.

She wanted to scream, to cry out. This wasn't fair. She wasn't meant to die like this. And not this young either. The humiliation over being stood up and failing her gig seemed insignificant now.

Please, no. Not this. Let there be something better than this.

Something moved from the darkness. A faint ethereal glow. It slowly drew closer and became brighter. So bright it made her wince.

A woman with long blonde hair swung towards her. Serena almost cried with relief. But she didn't recognise the woman. It wasn't a friend or relative or someone she met before.

It must be an angel who had come to escort her to wherever she was meant to go. Or maybe some kind of spirit. She had never been a believer in God but now it didn't matter. But what if she ended up in the bad place? She had tried to kill Mike after all. Perhaps she wouldn't be seen as worthy enough to go to heaven or whatever good place dead people went to.

Her lungs burned and she still felt herself drowning. She was surprised she hadn't already suffocated to death. How long did it take someone to drown? She always thought it would be instantaneous or at least within a couple of minutes. Yet it felt like she had been floating down here forever in the gloom of the deep with her thoughts racing.

"This doesn't have to be the end," the woman said.

Please help me! Serena thought but had no idea if the woman could hear her. She didn't dare open her mouth as she fought to hold her breath. *I don't want to die. I'm not ready — I still have so much I want to do. Please tell me you can help me.*

"Don't be afraid. I'm Galene. You don't have to move on to the next world. You can become something greater. Something better than you were before." The woman swam around her. Light still illuminated her body, so much that Serena couldn't make out much of the woman's features other than the fact she had long, blonde hair. "You can become like me. Do you accept?" The woman's voice sounded melodious and almost otherworldly.

Like you? What does that even mean? Serena wished she could open her mouth and speak, but it took every ounce of strength not to take a breath.

"You can become one of Poseidon's daughters like I am. Not everyone gets offered this opportunity. Think of it as a once-in-a-lifetime chance to be something greater than you were before."

I don't...

The woman came closer and circled around Serena. She almost gasped at the sight of the woman's tail. A long green fishtail. Christ, she was a mermaid. That was what she meant by the daughter of Poseidon. Serena had never imagined such a thing might exist. Mermaids were the stuff of children's stories. Like fairies. They weren't real.

The mermaid swam closer and touched Serena's face. The burning in her chest stopped and she could breathe a little.

"I can become like you?" Serena asked, still gasping for breath. Holy crap, how could she speak now? She was still underwater.

"Yes. You would get to live. That's what you asked for, isn't it?"

"What's the cost? Will I be able to walk on land or will I be stuck down here all the time?"

"You can go on land, but only for a limited time. Your new life will be down here in the sea. You must leave your old life behind."

That didn't seem important. She didn't have much to leave behind. Other than her failed music career. And the guy she thought she had been in love with who had stood her up.

Should she do this? Should she say yes? Thinking the decision over didn't seem to matter. She didn't want to die. That much she did know.

"What's the full price?" she repeated. Serena wasn't a fool. Nothing in life came for free. As much as she wanted to accept the offer, she needed to know everything that it entailed first. It seemed too good to be true. Leaving her old life behind wasn't a huge price to pay. There had to be something more.

"The price is you must live out your life here. You won't have any children, and you can only save up to three people from drowning. No more. You'll also have the gift of magic."

"What kind of magic?" That piqued her interest.

"It depends on whatever gift Poseidon bestows upon you," the mermaid said. "I should warn you; the change will be very painful as you're reborn into your new body. Once the change begins you won't be able to stop it. You must endure the entire process for it to work."

"What kind of pain?" She'd always been a wimp when it came to pain, but she wanted to know everything before she made her final decision.

"Are there more mermaids like you? Or mermen?"

"There's a whole pod but it consists of only mermaids and humans who have been granted the ability to breathe underwater. Here you will have a new life, a new family, a new home."

That didn't sound so bad.

"Fine, I accept."

The mermaid reached out and touched her forehead. Serena gasped and the blackness around her deepened until she was surrounded by bright light. Stars and planets seemed to whirl around her and off into infinity.

The mermaid vanished and someone else appeared. She could sense them rather than see them very well. "You shall become a daughter of the sea. I bestow on you the gift of magic. Use it wisely." She caught a flash of a glowing bearded man holding a trident.

She yelped as pain tore through her body. The pain shot down through her head, to her spine and down to her legs. Every bone and muscle felt like it was being torn apart. Her body turned inside out. Her clothes were ripped apart and fell away from her. She screamed, but the sound was lost in the gloom of the deep. More flashes of light blinded her, and the pain intensified like a thousand knives stabbing through her and tearing through every fibre of her being.

God, why had she agreed to this? Even drowning hadn't been this painful. Maybe she should have said no. Had let herself drown and move on to wherever dead people ended up.

Would she survive this? Would her body break into pieces?

The mermaid had never mentioned if anyone survived the transformation or not. Perhaps some people didn't — which wouldn't surprise her. Why hadn't the mermaid warned her she could die? All she had said was it would be painful. Painful didn't begin to describe this feeling. She should have known there was a catch. If something was too good to be true it always was.

If she had to choose a way to die, she'd have chosen the drowning. It hurt like hell but nothing like this.

Nothing could have prepared her for this.

Images from her life before flashed through her mind. Playing as a kid with her parents. The first time she had sung. Playing piano in one of her foster homes, meeting Jade. Talking to Mark online and exchanging numerous messages as well as talking on the phone. Up until her fight with Mike and falling overboard.

"Don't fight the change, Serena. You are going to be reborn," the mermaid's voice sounded far away. "The pain will pass eventually. Just try to breathe and let it happen. Don't fight against it."

She wanted this nightmare to be over. Once and for all.

CHAPTER THREE

Serena floated in the blackness for what seemed like forever. The pain had faded. Now there was nothing. Just numbness. No memories. No feelings. Nothing. Maybe this was it. She had died and now existed in an infinite void. She would float here forever. Alone.

The thought saddened her. Tears dripped down her cheek and disappeared into the darkness. Coldness seeped through her. Did the dead even feel the cold? That didn't make sense. Why would a dead person need to feel anything? Why would they cry?

More tears fell and the coldness deepened.

Serena gasped for breath and drew in gulps of air. No, not air. Seawater. It felt like taking in lungsful of clean air. She could breathe again.

Serena raised her arms. Her clothes had long since vanished. Now her chest and torso were covered by iridescent blue scales. Her legs were gone. Now replaced by a long blue tail. She was a mermaid.

She'd survived the change.

Serena swam around, surprised by how fast and easily she could move. She half expected to flay about like a fish out of water.

Her body knew how to move through the water with ease. It felt exhilarating to swim and not feel any pain. Like pure freedom.

Nothing could hurt her down here. Not Mike, not the people who had jeered at her, not anyone.

The other mermaid she'd spoken to earlier had mentioned there being others like them. So where were they? She was curious to meet other mermaids and to find out more about them. And more about her new body and what it could do.

She didn't know how to feel about meeting them, though. What if they didn't like her? She never really fit in with humans.

Was she still human? Yes, she looked like a mermaid, but did she still have her soul or whatever made her Serena? Had everything about her changed or just her body? Did she have a different personality now? Would she be different than she had been before?

So many questions raced through her mind. She still felt like herself. Just stronger and much more powerful. She guessed only time would tell.

Her nerves gave way to excitement. If she had magic now, she wondered what it might be. She stared at her hands. Other than having a faint shimmer to her skin they looked more or less the same.

She waved a hand, but nothing happened. Her heart sank.

What kind of magic would she have? Could she control the tides or maybe talk to sea life?

She almost laughed at the idea of singing to crabs like Ariel had. Maybe it would take a while for her magic to appear.

She swam further. She didn't feel cold anymore either. Her body seemed to have adapted to the sea pretty quickly.

The mermaid had been right. This didn't feel like her old body. Now she was stronger; faster than she ever could have been as a human.

The gloom of the deep faded and became much brighter. Almost like the sun had illuminated everything in a midday glow.

She didn't know where she was going. It was more like an

instinct. Up ahead were houses made of coral. Covered in algae and other crustaceans. The multi-colours looked almost pretty in the ethereal below.

Another mermaid with long blonde hair and an iridescent purple tail swam out.

"Hey, you must be new. I'm Chelsea." She gave Serena a warm smile.

"I can understand you." Serena gasped. "Holy crap, I half expected not to be able to talk to anyone. I was only able to talk to that other mermaid earlier when she touched me."

Chelsea snorted. "Of course you can. Duh. Welcome to the pod. You must have already met Galene?"

"Who?" She furrowed her brow.

"Galene. She's the first mermaid and appears to everyone before they change. And she's one of the oldest among us. What's your name?"

"Serena. How many people live here?"

"A few dozen. This is our home, but we swim all over the globe. We're the only mermaids in existence."

"I'm still having trouble getting my head around the fact mermaids are real." Serena shook her head. "This feels like a dream." She didn't mention some parts of it were more like a nightmare. Especially when she changed. She still half expected to wake up hung over somewhere to find this was all a bizarre dream. Or maybe battered and beaten up on Mike's boat.

"Because we are. It's not a dream. How are you liking your new body?" Chelsea swam around her and grinned. "I know it's weird at first, but you'll get used to it. Most people adapt pretty quickly. Just don't fight your new body. Let everything come naturally. It makes the transition much easier."

"It feels incredible. I never felt like this as a human."

"There's a spare house over there. It used to belong to Merle, but she passed away a while back." Chelsea motioned to another dwelling. "You can use it. Make it your new home."

"Are you sure?" She bit her lip. It didn't seem right to move into someone else's house. She hadn't really thought about where she would live down here, but it looked like mermaids had houses at least. She had half expected them to sleep on the seabed. That idea didn't sound so appealing. All manner of sea creatures could crawl over her. So the idea of having an actual dwelling seemed much more preferable.

Chelsea nodded. "Go ahead. We always give our old dwellings to newcomers. It's the way the pod works. New mermaids don't come along very often." Chelsea swam alongside her. "Have you discovered your new power yet? You must be excited about having magic. Poseidon knows I was when I first changed."

Serena shook her head. "Not sure I have one. I tried to use it earlier, but nothing happened. If I do have one, I have no idea what it is or how it works. Doesn't Poseidon give you instructions on what kind of magic he bestows on you?"

Chelsea laughed. "He's a god. They never give people instructions or straight answers. All of us have a magical gift. It's what comes with the change and it's one of the perks of being a mermaid. Sometimes it takes time for it to appear."

"What's your gift?"

"I can manipulate stone and talk to rocks. Comes in handy when we need dwellings. I used to work with stone when I was a human. But you wouldn't think that by looking at me. What were you good at in your old life? Most people usually get something based on their pre-existing talents. Just don't expect to go around blowing things up. That's not how our gifts work."

She shrugged. "Music, I guess. I loved to sing. But I'm not sure I want to do that anymore."

"Why not? All mermaids can sing. We don't get much music down here other than the occasional song we pick up from passing ships. Or songs that we knew when we were human. It would be fun to hear some updated music. Most of the songs I know are from the 90s or older. Try and sing something. See what your voice sounds like now. Our bodies change a lot when we transform but we don't lose the essence of who we were before."

Her mind flashed back to the night at the pub and people jeering at her for missing her note. But it didn't matter now. Those people couldn't hurt her down here.

Now she was a different person. Something better and stronger.

She hesitated. Could she still sing? Would her voice even work beneath the waves? Sure, she could speak, but it wasn't the same as singing.

The only real experience and information she knew about mermaids came from a Disney movie. Something made to entertain kids. Hardly much to go on. The Little Mermaid was probably nonsense anyway.

Serena took a deep breath then started singing. Her voice sounded different, more ethereal and melodious.

She laughed in surprise. It sounded so ethereal that it came out more like sounds than words. Tears filled Chelsea's eyes and other mermaids come out of their dwellings to see what the noise was.

"Wow, your voice is so beautiful," Chelsea remarked. "You sound better than the whole pod combined. This must be your magic. You will lure a lot of people down here with that voice of yours."

"My voice... It sounds different."

"It's mesmerising. You truly have a gift. Poseidon must have enhanced your natural talent." Chelsea grinned.

After chatting with the other mermaids for a while. They all introduced themselves and some of them briefly told their stories of how they had either been lost in shipwrecks or forced overboard for whatever reason. It felt comforting to know she wasn't alone. She wasn't the only one who had been attacked by a drunken idiot either. A couple of the other mermaids had mentioned they had gone through similar things. That was how Galene had found them and convinced them to become like her.

After talking for a while, she headed into her new home. It wasn't much. A hammock hung in the corner and a few rock shelves with jars and other oddments. Chelsea had shown her around her dwelling. It didn't look like many of the mermaids were hoarders like Ariel had been in the Little Mermaid film. Serena almost wished she had read more mermaid stories growing up or knew more about their folklore. Most of them didn't seem very materialistic. She supposed down here they didn't need to be. Whenever they wanted something they usually traded for it or did their best to make use of whatever they had. It was heartening to see that. The human world was so different; being run by greed and the overwhelming need for money.

There was one thing she couldn't stop thinking about. Mike. She might be happy to have a second chance in life, but he had still hurt her. Could hurt other people. That would be her mission now. To find him and stop him once and for all.

CHAPTER FOUR

Serena adapted to her new life pretty fast over the coming weeks. Being a mermaid felt different from the person she'd been in her old life. She enjoyed the pure freedom that came from the sea and the new family she found with the pod. Yet something still felt like it was missing.

Chelsea insisted she just needed to find her new calling. Serena had always thought her calling had been to become a singer and enrich people's lives through music. But in the sea there was only a small crowd to show her their appreciation. She felt like she hadn't found her purpose yet. Singing to unsuspected sailors didn't feel that rewarding either. Sure, she might be able to lure people to join the pod but that wouldn't work every time. Especially if there were no women on board. Chelsea insisted her calling would come in time.

All mermaids were meant to help the pod, to make it stronger, with their unique gifts. What good was her enhanced voice if she couldn't do something useful with it?

She had helped Chelsea with stonework, gone hunting. Tried numerous other tasks. Nothing so far had made her feel useful. Everything she tried had had varying degrees of success. Most of them had been complete disasters. She couldn't work with stone and wasn't much good at hunting either. Other than catching a few fish, but she couldn't say that was her new calling. Becoming a mermaid had sounded so fulfilling. Yet she still felt empty.

"Hey, ready to come help me?" Chelsea grinned as she swam into Serena's house.

Serena's shoulders slumped. "I guess."

"You look blue."

"I am blue in some places." She forced a laugh and motioned to her tail and scales.

"You know what I mean. You look down. It's happening."

"What is?" She furrowed her brow, unsure what Chelsea meant. Was something bad happening to her? Was that why she had been feeling so down? Maybe it was a natural part of becoming a mermaid. But she didn't think she missed her old life that much. She just wanted to feel useful.

"Your mourning period. Everyone goes through a mourning period after the change. It's normal. We think about the life we had before and people we left behind."

"I didn't leave anyone. I didn't have family and only one real friend." Serena shook her head. "Can't say I miss my old life. I just... I need something more. I keep thinking about the guy who attacked me."

"What about him? He can't hurt you ever again."

"No, but he could hurt other people. Other women. I doubt I'm the first one he took on his boat."

"Have you been to the surface to look for him? You know the rules about letting humans see you."

Right, rules. No interaction with humans in your mermaid form unless it was someone you chose to save. Unless you went for a trip on land for one lunar cycle. Serena had been tempted to go back to land but at the same time she didn't know what she would find there. Would anyone have reported her missing? If so, people seeing her would lead to unwanted questions.

"No, I haven't. But I don't think I'll be okay until I put an end to him. He deserves to pay for what he did."

Chelsea waved a hand in dismissal. "Let the humans take care of him. He's bound to get caught eventually."

Serena snorted. "Human justice is either slow or non-existent when it comes to punishing people. I want to stop him. At least then I can feel like I can do something useful."

"Do you think ridding the world of one scumbag will help?"

"It would make me happy. I can't bear the thought of him hurting anyone else. Imagine how many more unsuspecting women he could hurt. Some of them might not get a second chance like I did."

"Go to the surface then. Walk on land again. Bear in mind you can't stay for long."

"I can go back?" She'd heard stories about some of the others going back and spending short periods of time on land. She had no idea how it worked or what it involved. She didn't like the idea of going through the change again given how agonising it had been. Becoming human again must be just as painful and probably dangerous. Or maybe it didn't hurt so much. From what the others had said some of the other mermaids went to land pretty often. Surely they couldn't endure the agony of changing every time they wanted to go on land?

"Usually we aren't allowed to go back until a few years have passed. But you need closure so if you ask the others, you should get their approval. They'll show you how to change and go back. I've never gone back myself. Never seen the need to."

Good. Maybe she'd finally have a chance to find Mike and get her revenge at last. Now she just had to find him.

CHAPTER FIVE

Serena drew to the surface and breathed in the air again as she reached Brightlingsea Harbour. She couldn't deny how much finding Mike had been playing on her mind.

The mermaid. The ship's name stood out in the low light and beckoned to her like a beacon.

Told you I'd find you again. She grinned and swam closer to the ship.

There was a ladder on the side.

Chelsea had mentioned they could walk on land again for one lunar cycle before they had to return to rest and recharge before they could go on land again.

Some of the pod came on land regularly just to find potential mermaids. Or to find potential mates. Although there were rules about that too. You couldn't save anyone or turn them unless they were worthy.

She grabbed onto the ladder and hauled herself out of the water. She wanted to find Mike and get this over with. She winced as her body shifted and her tail vanished. She scrambled up the ladder and up onto the deck where she dropped her bag and quickly pulled on a dress over her naked body. Mermaids didn't exactly need to wear clothes while being underwater and she wasn't about to wander around naked. Thankfully the others kept clothes around and kept them in sealed bags so they could carry them and put them on once they reached land along with some shoes.

Serena used the towel to dry herself off as best she could then shoved it back into her bag and crept along the deck. She knew Mike probably wouldn't be here at this time of day, but she hoped she might find something about where she could find him.

Pulling open the door, she crept down some stairs and into another room. To her surprise different screens were there showing different views around the ship.

Oh shit. Had someone seen her? She had never thought there would be cameras around. What if she had been exposed? One of the pod's rules was not to be noticed by humans.

But she couldn't pass up the opportunity to find Mike. She scanned around the desk for any paperwork or something that might give her his name. It was then she spotted a phone with a sparkly jewelled case.

Holy crap, it was her phone. She had dropped it during the struggle the night Mike had attacked her. She hadn't expected to find it here. She thought he would have dropped it overboard by now.

Serena picked up her phone. To her surprise, it still had some charge on it and it switched on. Someone had unlocked it. Given the fancy equipment on board that didn't surprise her. She had dozens of missed calls and messages. Most of them from Jade.

She opened her email to check and see if she had anything from Mark. It seemed almost like a lifetime ago since she had been stood up by him now.

There was one message.

It read: *I'm so sorry. I never meant for this to happen.*

For what? Being stood up? She scoffed and shoved her phone back in her pocket.

Her heart sank at the message from Mark. He didn't even bother to say why he stood her up. Or try to arrange meeting up again. It was as if she meant nothing to him. Maybe she didn't. Maybe she never had.

She had thought about him too. Focusing on getting revenge had been easier. She took a deep breath and reminded herself it didn't matter anymore. She had a new life now. All that mattered was finding Mike and making sure he didn't hurt anyone else.

She rifled through some of the papers on the desk. Looking for anything with Mike's name on it. All she'd found so far were medical leaflets and a list of physio exercises. Did Mike have some kind of medical issue?

He hadn't seemed impaired the night he attacked her. He'd been a lot stronger than her. Even in his drunken haze.

Come on. There had to be something around here. Something about Mike's true identity. Maybe Mike wasn't even his real name. He could be anyone. And why have all this surveillance equipment around? Why spy on everyone?

It had to be more than just a security setup. There were cameras around the town and harbour from the looks of things. More images of other places flashed on some of the smaller screens.

Serena wasn't a computer genius, but she switched between some of the cameras. She gasped when she recognised the pub where she had performed. Had Mike been watching her? Had he singled her out?

That creeped her out even more and proved Mike had to be stopped.

"Hey, how'd you get in here?" A man's voice made her jump.

Heart pounding, she searched around for any potential weapons. Serena grabbed a screwdriver that she found on the desk then spun around. "You... You're not... Why are you here?" She wanted to hit herself for how stupid she sounded.

This was not going according to plan. Why hadn't she spotted him on one of the monitors? Why hadn't she thought to look around first before snooping? She should have checked to make sure the place was empty!

"I might ask you the same thing." The man came in. He looked young. Maybe late twenties with short brown hair and a chiselled face. He lent on a crutch and limped inside. "Why are you on my boat?"

"I-I'm..." What could she say? *I came to find the guy who killed me so I could get revenge?* That wouldn't go over very well. "I should go," she said instead.

"No, not until you tell me how you got on my boat." The man gave her a quizzical look. "And why you're here. How did you even get on board?"

"Why are there cameras everywhere?" She deflected his questions.

"It's part of my job. Monitoring CCTV cameras. I run a security company."

"Yeah right."

"Actually I do." He handed her a card which read Sealand Security. "Tell me why you're on my boat. Maybe I should call the police and have you taken in for trespassing. Not to mention breaking and entering."

"I... Please don't do that. I... I came to find the guy who tried to rape me." Tears stung her eyes. "I'm sorry." She couldn't believe she'd started crying. What was wrong with her? Maybe Chelsea had been right when she told her she had to deal with what happened to her.

"I thought this was his boat. I'm sorry, I shouldn't have intruded."

"Please don't cry." To her amazement, he held out a handkerchief for her.

Since when did men have handkerchiefs nowadays? But at least his demeanour had softened. She shook her head and sniffed. "If you let me go, I promise I won't disturb you again."

"Who were you looking for? Maybe I can help you."

Serena hesitated. This guy might seem genuine enough but why did he have her phone? This had to be the boat Mike had taken her out on. So where was he? And where did this new guy factor into the equation?

"It doesn't matter. I just know his first name was Mike. But that could be fake."

"I could search for him. I'm pretty good at finding people."

"No, I should go." Unfortunately, he stood between her and the only way out. "Please just let me out of here."

He moved aside and she almost breathed a sigh of relief. She hurried past him and ascended the stairs. "Wait, are you Serena?"

She froze at the top of the stairs. "What?"

"Serena Matthews. The woman that went missing a couple of months ago."

Aw crap, how did he recognise her? She thought she looked different enough to not be recognised by anyone. She doubted she'd be a very high-profile missing person case.

She should run. She should dive over the side of the boat and never look back. She was already breaking the rules just by being here and risking possible exposure.

The man hobbled up the stairs, leaning heavily on his crutch. "The police asked me to help look for you. I already know you were here the night you disappeared since I found your phone on board. My boat was taken the night you disappeared. But I don't know who took it or why." He reached out and took her hand. "You can trust me when I say I'm on your side, Serena. I won't hurt you. All I want to do is help."

Serena took a deep breath. "I'm Serena Matthews. You can tell the police I'm not missing anymore. But I need to go." She turned to leave.

"Don't worry, I won't tell them you're a mermaid."

She gasped and put her hand over her mouth. "How? I mean... That's impossible. What are you on about?"

"I have cameras stationed all around the boat. I saw you come aboard. You don't need to be afraid of me. I won't tell anyone what you are. It's pretty incredible. Is that why you disappeared? Did you become a mermaid?"

Serena took a deep breath and wondered what the hell she should do next.

CHAPTER SIX

Serena stood there frozen for a few moments. She didn't know what to do. Should she run away and forget this nightmare had ever happened? Or should she stay? After all, he already knew what she was. And he didn't look to be much of a threat.

"Why should I trust you?" Serena asked. "I don't know you. You haven't even told me your name."

"Because I want to find the guy who stole my boat as much as you do. My name is Jack Marx. I'm sorry for what happened to you, but if I can find him, we can put him away."

She almost laughed at that. "For what? Stealing the boat? That won't stop him. Mike is a predator. He attacked me and he would have raped me or worse if I hadn't jumped overboard."

"We could if you testified against him. Several women have gone missing in this area over the past few years. Around the same time different boats have gone missing. The police and I think that's how he gets rid of his victims. By using them and then dumping them in the sea. The police can't monitor things the way I can."

Serena bit her lip. Jack Marx. A local millionaire. She had seen his name pop up online a few times over the past few years. He was one of the youngest millionaires in the country from what she remembered reading about him. Jade had always talked about how it would be great if they met him one day around Colchester. Serena had never expected to finally meet him under these circumstances. She had also heard about him helping on police cases so maybe he was legit.

Jack sat down and pulled out a mini tablet. "What can you tell me about the guy who took my boat? What does he look like? Did he tell you anything about himself?"

She reluctantly sat down as well but moved her chair a little nearer to the side of the boat just in case she had to make a quick getaway. She still wasn't sure what to make of this handsome stranger.

She shook her head. "I don't remember much. I met him at the local pub. I had a bad night, so I was drinking quite a lot. Going out with random strangers isn't something I usually do. When he asked me to come out for a ride on his boat it sounded like fun."

"Was anyone else with you?" Jack asked. "Your best friend Jade mentioned to the police that he didn't invite her to go. Did you see anyone else on board when you got here?"

"No. We were alone on the boat. We were headed out to Mersea Island. When he came on to me, I told him no. That's when he attacked me."

"And would you be willing to talk to the police about that?"

"How can I? I don't exactly live on land anymore." She stared at him, incredulous.

"You would only need to give a statement. But news about your disappearance around here has been pretty big. There's been reporters all over the place. So you should be careful about where you go whilst you're on land. If I recognised you, someone else could. Although you do look different from the footage and photos I've seen of you from the night you disappeared."

"Why do you want to catch Mike so much?"

Jack got up and disappeared below deck again. Serena sat there and wondered if she'd said something to offend him. But she heard him rummaging around down below. A few moments later, he came back up on deck and held a photo out to her. It was of a young woman with auburn hair and laughing green eyes.

"That's my sister, Maria. She disappeared last year. That's why I have a vested interest in this case. I need to find out who killed her. Like it or not. You're the only lead I have to go on."

"I promise I'll do what I can to help you. But I can't risk other people finding out what I am."

SERENA SPENT the next three weeks staying on Jack's boat and helping him with the case. To her surprise, she actually enjoyed it. It was like being a real-life crimefighter. She and Jack talked a lot, and it was easy to get to know him. She admired how he didn't let his disability stop him from doing whatever he wanted as well.

So far, she had learnt whatever she could about missing women. Only a couple of bodies had been found. The rest were presumed dead and lost at sea. She had only travelled back once to the pod to ask the others if any other women had been changed into mermaids over the past few years. To find out if any of the pod might be Mike's victims as well. To her disappointment, none of the others had been as lucky as she had.

Neither of them had had much luck tracking down Mike so far. Despite visiting local pubs and asking around. It amazed her how easily people talked to Jack, despite him not being a police officer. When people didn't want to answer questions, Serena had discovered that by singing to people she could compel them to do whatever she wanted. It somehow lowered their inhibitions and made them much more pliable.

She knew time was running out. Mermaids could only stay on land for one month. Then she would have to return to the sea for at least a week. As much as she enjoyed being in the sea, she couldn't deny she would miss Jack. They had become close during the short time they had spent together.

Serena decided the best way to find Mike was to lure him out of hiding. She had gone to the police and told them what happened. They had convinced her to give a press conference stating she had only disappeared for a while whilst she took time to recover from a mystery illness. They told her that if Mike thought he was in the clear he would come out of hiding and resurface again.

She knew the pod wouldn't be happy about the risk of exposure, but she was determined to find Mike and bring him to justice once and for all. If not just to help other potential victims, but to help Jack get justice as well.

She knew she would need her strength that night so reluctantly she headed back out to sea early the next morning. The sea welcomed her back into its embrace. She needed some time to recharge before they set a trap for Mike that night.

AFTER SPENDING time in the water all day, Serena swam back towards Brightlingsea. It felt odd to be swimming in shallow waters, so she stuck close to the seabed to avoid being seen and to avoid getting tangled in any nets.

As she drew closer to the town, nerves fluttered in her stomach like butterflies. This was it. If she found Mike tonight, she could finally stop him. She couldn't remember much about Mike. He hadn't told her much about himself and she wondered if she would even be able to find him. If everything she'd done would bring him out of hiding.

Serena pulled herself up the sea wall and winced as her body changed and shifted back into human form. Thank Poseidon, changing back didn't hurt like hell the way it had when she had first changed into her mermaid form. She tossed a bag over the wall that contained some clothes that the other mermaids kept stored for when they made trips on land. She changed into a dress and some ballerina shoes. She couldn't walk around naked, or she'd have even more problems.

She stumbled on wobbly legs as she slid off the wall. It felt odd to be walking again after being in the sea all day. To be above the surface and breathing air again.

Would Mike still be here? Her mind raced with memories of the night she was attacked. She couldn't remember if she'd asked him if he lived in town. Most of the night was a blur up until he attacked her. The memory of that fuelled her anger. He might not have raped her but if she hadn't met that mermaid, she would be a rotting corpse now. Someone had to make him pay for what he'd done. One way or another, she'd find him and make sure he never hurt anyone else.

Serena walked through the town. Jack had told her he couldn't be there at the pub, but he would be watching her from the boat on CCTV. She had been disappointed to hear that. It would have felt comforting for him to be there with her. But she understood why he couldn't. If Mike saw him, he might get scared away. One way or another, she would get her man tonight. And she'd make him pay for what he'd done.

CHAPTER SEVEN

Being around so many people as she entered the pub felt like walking into an alien world again. Everything looked so odd after being under the sea or on Jack's boat for the past few months.

Everything seemed so loud and bright here. The sea wasn't a quiet place by any means, but everything was so much more intense the further she got on land. She hadn't realised how much she'd missed the serenity of the sea.

Her legs ached by the time she reached the Yachtsman's Arms pub. She pushed open the door and let her long hair fall over her face. Jack was right. She looked different now. More ethereal. Herself yet something more. She guessed she couldn't hide her new self completely.

She went to the bar, her throat dry. "Can you get me some water?" She motioned to the barman but he ignored her. Serena started humming. Everyone in the bar turned and stared, mesmerised by her voice.

Guess my power works here too. That was one thing she had learnt about her gift. It could stun people. Maybe she was a siren. She hadn't thought about it but it made sense.

She motioned to the dark-haired barman. "Give me a drink." She started humming and grew louder. As she sang, she scanned the bar for any signs of Mike.

Yes, it was a long shot he would come here again. But after her appearance at the press conference, Jack seemed convinced Mike would be in a cocky mood and might have the audacity to track her down. That was why she had to make herself visible.

There was a blur of different faces but not the one she searched for.

The barman brought her a bottle of water and a glass of ice. Then poured the water out for her. "Are you sure this is all you want?"

Serena spotted a missing person poster hanging behind the bar. "No. Can you take that down?" She kept her face turned away in case he recognised her.

"Oh, that's Serena Matthews. The local missing woman who appeared again. I saw her with a local bloke the night she disappeared."

"Wait, what bloke?" She kept her hair over her face to avoid being seen. Why hadn't she seen this guy before? He looked familiar, but he hadn't been one of the people Jack or the police had questioned. "Do you mean Mike?"

"No, I mean Mark. He is a local bloke that I saw her with in here that night. He's probably coming tonight. He always comes in on Friday night to pick up whatever women he can find."

She froze. Mark. The guy she had been talking to online. Had he been the one she had been talking to all along? She almost wanted to throw up. "What else can you tell me about him?"

"He lives near Colchester in Lexden. Big posh house. He has old family money."

Serena got all the information about Mike she could from the barman and other people in the pub. It didn't take much to make them forget after singing to them.

Her gift worked much better on humans than she'd expected.

She sat in a corner. She had a good view of the door, but she could remain hidden there.

People ignored her — much to her relief. As long as she kept quiet, she was just another face in the crowd. She wanted to keep it that way until Mike turned up.

Her mind raced and she drummed her fingers on the table. What would she say to Mike or Mark as he was really called? Could she trick him into confessing? As much as she had wanted to get her revenge and kill him, she had other people to think about now. Like Jack. He deserved justice for his sister and all the other women who had been Mark's victims.

A few minutes later, the pub's door opened and Mike, or Mark, himself walked in with a woman on his arm.

Serena grinned. She had been right. The creep was at it again!

Now she just had to get him away from here. She rose and started singing. Mike's gaze shot towards her. She crooked her finger and motioned for him to come towards her.

He came over and smiled at her. "Wow, you're so beautiful. Your voice is magical. It reminds me of the sea."

She had to refrain from rolling her eyes and laughed instead. He'd said that the night he attacked her. "I love being out on the water. It's my dream one day to own a boat then I can go out whenever I want to."

"It's your lucky night. I own a boat. How'd you like to go for a ride on it?"

Her smile widened. "I'd love to. Let's go." She grabbed his arm and pulled him towards the door.

ONCE THEY REACHED THE HARBOUR, she carried on singing and convinced him to go on board *The Mermaid*. While she was there, she finally got Mike talking and the police arrived a few moments later then took him away.

"I can't believe it's over," Jack remarked. "Thank you, I can never repay you for everything you've done to help me get justice for my sister. It doesn't bring her back but at least I know what happened to her now."

"I'm happy to help. But I really have to go. I can't afford to stay on land any longer. I have to go back to the sea."

Jack put a hand out to stop her. "Wait, there's something I should tell you. I want to apologise."

Her eyes widened. "What for? You haven't done anything wrong."

"I'm Mark — that's my online username for the dating site Essex Singles that I met you on. I'm sorry I never should have stood you up that night. If I had followed through you never would have been put in danger. I was just afraid you wouldn't accept me because of this." He motioned to his leg. "I planned on coming to the pub to find you and explain but by the time I got there it was too late. You were already gone."

Serena hesitated then reached up and kissed him. "Why don't you come with me? You could join me under the sea. There's nothing to stop us from having the best of both worlds on land and sea."

Jack smiled and pulled her in for another kiss. "Lead the way."

FIN OUT OF WATER

BRY DIG

CHAPTER ONE

Had it been a year or longer since they migrated towards these waters? Sure, some of her sisters in flippers were very well in tune with the seasons and days of the week. Not Nori. It was hard for her to remember to keep up with the pod, let alone recall the number of days. The pod would never leave her behind. They always sent someone to retrieve her if she fell back too much. Nori tended to fall behind a lot. Or swim in the lower depths in the darkness of cold waters.

Cold? She thought. *Are the waters cold?* She never felt the coldness. It was as if she was one with the dark, cold waters. They matched her disposition. Calm, quiet, deep, and *cold. Were mermaids cold?*

Whispers that turned to a clatter of underwater chatter caught Nori's unfocused attention. Her long dark hair fanned in front of her face due to the downward push of the water. With an annoyed huff, she pushed the strands from her face. Her nearly translucent blue eyes blinked a few times before finding the swishing colorful tails of her fellow pod mates. Mermaids traveled together. They swam in pods, migrating in a group throughout the ocean. The places they saw, the views, the underwater depths, were just breathtaking

931

dreams that Nori's former human self could never have imagined. It was as if she was living in a fantasy painting, except she didn't have starfish covering her tits. Now though, this was the reality of Nori's mermaid life.

That would be too painful? Nori shook her head at the thought.

Mermaids were not fantasy. They were born from a tragic death and lived in the ocean's hidden depths. A part of Nori was grateful to be alive and a mermaid, but a small amount, a dark pearl in the middle of her chest, pinged with...*hate? No,* Nori thought, *not hate.* It was more of a feeling of being a *Fish out of water.* She laughed at her thought. *Fish in water? Fin out of water?* She smirked at her own humor. *Yes,* she felt like she belonged but didn't belong in the pod. All her fellow mermaids were happy and loving their lives, but Nori felt something was missing. Her story was similar to the other mermaids. A tragic watery death only to be saved and born again as this magnificent lore creature. A mermaid. An inhabitant of the oceans who protected the life beneath the waters and, in many ways, protectors of humankind. They killed, yes, but Nori felt that most were justified. Of course, some enjoyed the occasional eating of ocean-side inhabitants, but who was Nori to judge. She, too, had killed the males that deserved the violent watery deaths they were granted. Yet, part of Nori still yearned for the old life of legs and air breathing. Of no care in the world except surviving by making money and dreaming of a bigger carefree life. Not this sway of the ocean and the red waters she often found herself in.

Nori shook her head. When had she become so...depressing?

"Did you hear me, Nori?" A soft voice caught Nori off guard.

She blinked in surprise at the mermaid who was before her. She was one of the ones that Nori had labeled as an underwater goddess. Though the mermaid facing Nori was no goddess, she had the ethereal look of one. The female had blonde hair floating strategically around her body in tamed strands. The current guided the strand of golden locks in flattering waves.

In contrast, Nori's thick, nearly black hair always flopped around her face like thick fat squid tentacles, sticking to her face and getting in her mouth. This mermaid before Nori even had the perfect shape, breasts that were perky and round like plump apples, and a slender waist that led to a swell of perfectly curved hips that were covered in a fine sheen of gold and pink glittery scales. Even the mermaid's tail was beautiful and elegant, tipped in gold. Nori frowned down at herself. Orange like a goldfish. That was what Nori felt her tail looked like. Plain orange scales with no extra splashes of colors like many of the others had.

"Nori, are you listening?" the mermaid gave a glittery laugh and snapped her fingers in front of Nori's face. There was no sound to the snap, but a flurry of bubbles drifted upwards.

Nori opened her mouth, decided against talking, and shook her head from side to side, gesturing NO.

"We will be here for a few cycles. It was decided by the majority of the pod. So go, and do your Nori thing." The mermaid smiled.

"Oh," was all Nori could think for a response. Her Nori thing? Nori blinked in confusion, "What's my Nori thing?" She asked, almost cringing at the sound of her own voice. The mermaid in front of her sounded like a princess with such a sweet dolphin voice. That was the opposite of how Nori found her own voice. She compared hers to being more like that of a frog, a dying frog with deep grunts and unflattering tones.

The mermaid gave a knowing smile to Nori. "You know, hanging out by a rocky shoreline where you languish around pulling moss off boulders."

A furrow formed between Nori's brows. "I do not languish."

The mermaid laughed again. All bells and dolphin whistles. "Of course not. Just go. We can feel your emo escaping you. You need air time and maybe a few more kills under your scales to get you back to the despondent Nori we all enjoy."

With that, the goddess-like mermaid flippered away. Bubbles and a mix of churned water left a trail in her wake.

"I'm not despondent, maybe a bit pessimistic," Nori mumbled.

Who was she kidding? Nori tossed her head back. She was totally despondent.

THE ROCKY COASTLINE was all Warrick could think about. The button-up polo collar around his neck was strangling him, and the slacks he wore made him feel aggravated. He walked through the thick trees towards the beach. He ducked under a branch and shoved another aside. He could hide from the responsibilities the world seemed to want to place on his broad shoulders when he was at the beach. On the massive boulders that dared to sit on the shoreline, War would shroud himself in their gigantic shadows and close his eyes, and just *fucking* let go of the world. When he was younger, he'd swim along this coastline, build massive sand castles, kick the crabs back and in the water, and just be. The private beach sat on the property owned by his family, so no others ever came. Everyone enjoyed the pretty beach with no large boulders or sharp rocks to taint their view. That was far on the other side of his family's property, far from where he was headed. It was nothing like the hidden spot he valued and claimed as his own. On occasion, when he was younger, War's mother would come and check on him, but after she died, no one really checked on him. Not even his father bothered to go through the thicket of trees to come to this one section of the beach. Rare occasions brought others. Mostly it was his fellow teen friends who wanted to bonfire and drink under the almost full moon. They'd keep a reasonable distance from him and leave soon after arriving. That was all due to War's reputation of being unpleasant. He wouldn't talk to them or glare at them until his unpleasant gaze penetrated their cores, and they hustled away. Now that they, he, was mature and nearly thirty, no one came to the spot. Bonfires and drinking were in the past. All were replaced with birthrights and political dominance.

War smiled. He liked his reputation of being unpleasant. He wore it like a shield. It kept him from having to be...social. Even now, the social pack desperately tried to drag him into their folds.

Who was mating who and who was challenging who was never of interest to Warrick. The only exception was his sister. He had a soft spot for the talkative younger female that shared his blood. She was the only babbling brook of nonstop talking energy that bothered him and never scared away. She didn't mind him grunting and sighing at her. She'd roll her eyes and keep talking about useless stuff she liked to express toward him. He never cared for her conversations.

"Get away from me, you assholes! No means fucking No!" A scream flooded all the surrounding noise of nature until it rang in War's ear.

That voice? That scream? Familiar! Warrick thought. His feet moved before his brain caught up. *My sister! In danger!*

A growl shredded through Warrick's throat. His muscles tensed and bunched. His bones cracked and snapped and clicked into place. The clothing he wore was shredded. War's body did not stop as it should have. Younger pups couldn't do this. Even some of his peers could not transform while in motion. No. Only one of his kind could master the pain that seared through the change while in action. Only alphas could. War ran while contorting and shifting until he was transformed. Until the wolf's paws found complete purchase in the soil that slowly faded away to sand.

CHAPTER TWO

Nori was not in the mood to deal with humans. At first, she was content perched on a boulder, nearly sunk into the ocean water. On the boulder, she was hidden from view. The sun was about an hour from the setting. On her perch, Nori would wait until the moon appeared. It would be a new moon. The marking of the lunar cycle. During this window of time, if Nori decided, she could escape the fin for an entire lunar cycle and walk among the humans. It was such a precious gift granted to her from Poseidon. Other mermaids had the same skill, though some were altered with slight variations. The gift had limits, such as after the lunar cycle was completed, Nori had to return to the water. She would not survive otherwise. The water recharged her.

It was on the rock half submerged in water, where Nori was lost in thought. She was startled when she first heard the voices of humans. She took quick notice of the voices. Six males and one female. They all were in the throes of laughter and joking. The female even laughed. A smell of sour hit Nori's nose. She did not like that scent. She scrunched up and placed a delicate finger under her nose to try and avoid the smell of alcohol.

"Throw her ass off the boat! This will teach her Familia!" Nori recalled the events before her birth into mermaid-hood. Those were the words they spoke. The drunk men clawed and pawed at her. Their rank breath of tequila was forever scorched in Nori's memories. She did not like the scent of alcohol or desperate men. *"Drown the bitch!"*

The scream the female gave snapped Nori out of her past memories. It was instinct that propelled Nori into the ocean. She was around the boulders in one flex of her fin, and the humans were in view. She was wrong. There were not six males. No, eight and one tiny female with red hair were pinned into the sand. Four males held down the female while one was yanking at his pants.

Nori shook her head from left to right. Her tongue clicked, making a tsk tsk sound. "Bad, bad, boys." Nori found herself speaking in a singsong way. Her voice was not as seductive as it could have been, and her English was spun with a Spanish accent, but the tune still carried. A smirk played on her lips. "I do not think the lady likes your affections."

Everyone on the beach paused. All their attention turned to Nori. The males seemed transfixed on Nori. Even the female blinked a few times as if she didn't believe someone else was on the beach. Nori calculated in her head. She had taken many a male life before, never this many, though. Not at once. It could be done as long as her call got them all. The call of the siren.

"Come to me. Why don't you play with me?" Nori sang sweetly. She sang in an upbeat tune. The water flung from her hair as she gave her head a good shake letting her hair fall away from her face. Her long lashes flapped with every seductive blink of the eye that Nori gave. "Come on, boys, come to me. It's a great day to drown."

Nori continued to sing softly, this time with no words, just a tune in the same singsong beat. Nori could not help the smile that stretched fully across her face. The males, one by one, started walking towards the ocean. The first male stepped into the shoreline, his feet sank into the sand, and the water lapped around his ankles, calves, and knees. As he came closer, Nori reached out to him. His arm lifted, and the tips of his fingers brushed against Nori's touch.

She gazed directly into his eyes. "Drown," She sang. Her actions were quick, like fish jumping out of water. Had you blinked, it would have been missed. She pulled the male into the water, her hand firmly at his neck. He thrashed and kicked, but her strength submerged him in the water. "Drown," she sang to the next male that had come close to her. Nori reached for him and shoved his head under the blanket of seawater.

Her eyes lifted and met with the female, who stood with her hands clutching at her torn clothes. "Run, female," Nori commanded.

The female took a few steps back before she stumbled. Lifting herself from the beach, she took off in a sprint to the tree line. The female did not look back. Not once. She had followed Nori's command.

Nori was engrossed in watching the female run that she had not noticed her call had dropped. It wasn't until the swing of a fist landed across her face.

WARRICK BREACHED THE TREE LINE, landing on the sandy beach shore. He stood motionless, rapt by the sight before him. The water was red, and the sand was highlighted in a pink that smelled metallic. Blood. Bodies bobbed in the waters, and one was face down on the beach. War licked his fangs. He had wanted these kills. He envied the one that took the kills from him. At that thought, War searched the shore. His sister, she was not here!?

"Die already," A voice caught War's attention. He immediately found the speak of the voice. A female in the water. She stood just about waist-deep in the water. In one hand, she held on to a man's neck, his body face down in the water, and his legs and arms kicking and fighting for survival. The female shook her head. "No use, bad boy. The sea wants your death. Just give it to her."

War narrowed his eyes. This female looked too tiny to have the strength to keep the man face down in the water. The fight he gave was enough to knock most to their asses. War stepped closer to the beach waters keeping his eyes on the female. His movement caught her attention. Warrick paused as her light blue translucent crystal-colored eyes landed on him.

"Oh," she whispered. "Is he your owner, doggie?" The woman asked.

War took note of her exotic voice. She had an accent that was clearly Spanish or Latin-related but mixed with something else, something whimsical and elegant. War sat down in the fine grain sand, his front paws digging down and his head hung to the side, taking in the view before him. He had spent his whole life avoiding the opposite sex. They were everything unappealing in his life. They clung to him and wanted to use him to make themselves comfortable in a higher social status. This one, though, he found appealing. Her dark hair ran down her back, and strands were over the front of her shoulder, the ends floating in the water. Her slender neck was stained with red blood in lines that mirrored fingerprints. Warrick looked at the bobbing bodies. He wondered which had tried to strangle this female. His body vibrated with a growl.

The female hushed him. "He was a bad boy. He deserves this. Once he is gone, you'll be free, puppy boy. You can be unleashed for life or until animal control grabs you. I would like to think for life, though, that is more positive."

The man she held underwater made a final attempt to free himself. He clawed down the female's chest. She winced as his claws raked through her flesh. The female took her free hand and wrenched his wrist back. Bone snapped, and then his hand hung at an odd angle.

"You know. Sharks do not care for human blood. They prefer fish blood or sea lion blood. But you humans always feel like you are in trouble." The female babbled. He'd seen this before. It was the babble of a female who did not know what to say and needed to fill the air with noise. His sister had done this kind of babbling on the night their mother lay dying in her bed. The female continued on her soft babblings. "I think we must have a similar taste to our blood because I have seen a shark eat a mermaid whole. Well, that is not true. He chomped her in half, then ate her. We grieved and took our revenge by filling our bellies with that shark. Feasted on his murderous corpse. It was the blood, though, that is what caught his attention. She accidentally ran into the coral she was trying to harvest for her home. Cut her hands really bad. The blood would not stop. She pushed me away. Saved me...I couldn't save her."

The female let go of the body she held underwater. War did not notice at first, but the male had ceased moving. He was dead. She had successfully drowned him. War stood on all fours. He watched as the female looked at her hands. They were dripping in blood. She maneuvered her arms, and that was when Warrick saw what the female was seeing. Fingernail marks were all over her torso, arms, and chest. She seemed confused, but War knew. These males that were all dead and surrounded this female were all wolves. Were-wolves. From his pack...his father's pack. Those marks that tattered her soft flesh and flayed her skin were made with claw marks of werewolves. They were deep and deadly. The one on her left side looked especially deep, exposing the bone of her ribs.

"I made a mistake." She whispered. His eyes locked with hers. She stood torso deep in water, the water lapping just below her perfect dip of a belly button. Even covered in blood War couldn't help but praise the beauty of her form. Though his appraisal paused when she spoke again. "Puppy, I made a bad mistake. They put up more fights than most human males have. I think they are on those bath salts or something." The female gurgled on her words, and blood trickled from one corner of her mouth. "Can you help me, puppy? I do not want to be eaten by the sharks. That scares me...." Her eyes were closing, and her voice trailed. Her body was slowly sinking into the water. "I...heal...need time..."

Warrick gave a warning growl as the female waded through the water, coming closer to him, her hand extending. He did not want to be her next victim but dared not move either. He did not want to take his eyes off her. She was fascinating. Her hand reached for him, and then her eyes closed. She fell forward. Face first into the water.

Fuck! War paced the shoreline before deciding against his better judgment. He was going to help her. *Fuck me!* He growled inside his head. This was not a good idea, but all his life decisions were based on bad ideas.

Warrick shifted back as quickly as he had shifted from man to wolf. His body contorted and snapped back into his human form. Far from his thoughts was his nudity. Instead, he stepped over the dead body and lunged into the water. His hands firmly grabbed the female by her lifeless arms. He flipped her over with ease. He focused on ensuring she could breathe in the air instead of face down in the seawater. War sank into the water, moving his arms under the female. He readied himself to retrieve this fascinating female from the water. At his sunken posture, he stared down at the female. His eyes took in every inch of her face. Her dark brows arched in a feminine fashion. Her long lashes rested against her high cheekbones. He even found her nose attractive. The straight slope of the bridge gave way to a perfect nose, and by all things feral, her lips made Warrick take a deep breath to swallow his lust. They were full, with the bottom slightly plumper than the top. He couldn't help it. War ran a wet finger across her soft, plump lips.

So, this is what other males lust over. The divine beauty of a female. He thought as he continued to run a single finger over her lips. When she gave a soft moan, one of pain, Warrick stopped his finger. He moved his hand to the water and gently washed the blood from her face and neck. His eyes moved further down. Her head hung back, exposing the expanse of her slender neck. His eyes followed her neck downwards. Her collar bones were sharp and slightly pronounced in her positioning, but even War found them attractive. He gave a low growl of appreciation when his eyes landed on her breasts. She wore a braided band of what looked like seaweed across her chest. He wondered what fashion trend this one was. It didn't matter. War licked his lips as he appreciated how the band covered the female's nipples but exposed her breast tops and bottom swells. He ran a hand over the top of her breasts. Frowning at the claw gash from the lower part of her neck down her chest. The skin was parted, exposing her insides' tender, bloody flesh. As he washed the blood away, new blood replaced it. War realized she could slowly bleed out on the beach if he did not get her to a doctor.

Warrick, again, sunk into the water, placing both arms underneath the frail body of the female. Rising to his full height, War stood, lifting the woman into his arms. He took two steps back towards the shore before glancing at the woman's body. He nearly stumbled as he took in the view.

"The fuck?" He questioned out loud. He jostled the nearly lifeless body in his arms, staring at her bottom half. "She has a fin?"

CHAPTER THREE

The water was cold. Colder than normal. Nori tried to blink her eyes. Her eyelids were too heavy to budge. She groaned, trying to move her body. Her body ached and felt more severe than usual, but she could flop to the side. Her fingers extended out, expecting to reach the sand, but instead, they landed on brutal slick coldness. Nori frowned. Had she landed on a rock? What rock was smooth and cold?

The familiar sound of a door closing caught Nori's attention. Like the sound of a closing door was a shot of adrenaline, Nori opened her eyes and sat up with frantic animation. Her lashes flapped, trying to help her eyes gain focus. Her fin thrashed as she flopped around, trapped in the bowl of a perfect clawfoot tub. Nori's sharp nails clanked against the tub's porcelain sides as she tried to lift herself up. Memories flashed through her mind as quickly as the water in the tub spattered over the edge.

Beach. Men. Lots of fighting. And a dog.

"It wasn't a dog." A deep voice rumbled.

Nori slipped into the tub and dunked her head beneath the salty bathwater. When was bathwater salty and tasting of the sea? She questioned as she settled at the bottom of the tub. The tub was not much of a hiding spot, considering her fin hung over the rim of the porcelain, and the water could not be more profound than two feet. Yet Nori stayed beneath the tub water. Her hair floated about her providing the perfect curtain. Had the tub been the ocean, Nori would have been hidden beneath the dark depths of the ocean floor.

A rumbling voice startled Nori. She blinked through the crystalline bathwater. She was sure it was not bathwater but ocean water. The taste and feel of the salty water was identical to that of the ocean. Ignoring that thought, she blinked, focusing on the shadow of a man who stood over the tub.

He was talking. She could feel the vibrations of his voice and hear the muffled deep tones. The shadow moved closer, and through the rippled water, Nori could make out the image of a frowning male. She couldn't help but frown back. He loomed over the tub, his arms crossed over his chest, and an eyebrow arched. It had been a long while since Nori had paid this much attention to a male's appearance. She tried to think of the last male she had in her hands; what did he look like? She couldn't remember. They all blurred together while their bodies washed up on the beach. The rumbling voice caught Nori off guard again. Her eyes snapped to the males'. He was clearly talking to her, but she could not make out one word.

Shifting her weight, she pushed up on her elbows slowly. Using the water as a shield, she pushed up until her ears were above the water, but her nose and mouth remained cocooned in the bath water.

"You said dog. I'm no dog," the man mumbled.

Nori did not blink. Her blue eyes took in the pretty man with his long dark hair styled haphazardly on top of his head. It reminded her of a mixture of bedhead and strategically styled model hair. It was perfect hair. Two black rings hung on his lobes. The bridge of his nose was straight and gave way to an ideal nose. Not too big and complementary to his squared jaw. His thick dark brows didn't distract from the ridiculously long lashes he had. The lashes protectively stood around perfect amber eyes. To add to his look was just a shadow of a beard. A few days of growth. She knew if she reached out and touched his face, the facial hair would prickle at her fingers. She kind of wanted to touch it anyways. Nori blinked a few times before landing on the man's lips. His mouth was the perfect mix of straight and yet just the right amount of plumpness for lips. Had she guessed, she would think him a suffer. It made sense with his tall, lean body, but his arms and shoulders were thick and brawny. Were there lumberjacks around here? The hair and earrings did not go with the pristine white polo shirt he wore or the khaki pants. He seemed too edgy to wear such a pretentious outfit. Perhaps it was Nori's only exposure to men. More times than not, she saw sailors, boaters, and the occasional surfer.

His words finally penetrated her ears. *Huh?*

"You said dog." He grumbled. When Nori looked at him with a puzzled look, the man continued to speak. "You mumbled things and said you saw a dog on the beach. I'm no dog."

He took a knee. Nori's eyes followed him. His height placed him above the tub's rim, even on one knee. He had to have been tall. She could make out the little flecks and rings of gold coloring in his amber eyes.

"Considering you have a fin out of the water, I'll tell you my secret since I know yours. I'm no dog, just as you are no fish." His lip twitched, and for a split second, Nori saw the smile beneath his stone face. "You good in there? I don't really have an aquarium that would fit you."

Nori considered his question. Her eyes darted around the small bathroom. A window with white shutters was her closes escape...if she had legs. Her eyes noticed the shifting changing of light that barely seeped through the shutters. It was nearly nightfall.

Soon!

Emerging from the water, she moved her body so that her back pressed against the tub, providing some distance from the stranger. "You looked like a dog." Her voice trembled with an unsure tone.

His face moved quickly into a scowl. "Wolf."

Nori rolled her eyes. "Practically the same."

This time the male growled low in his throat. "I don't sniff ass and bark at squirrels!"

This time it was Nori who smirked.

The man abruptly stood. He took a step back and frowned down at her. "Do you have a name, fish girl?"

Nori gave a nod. "It's not yours to have."

The man's frown deepened. "Well then, little goldfish, it looks like you are mine until I figure out what I will do with you."

Nori purposely flopped around in the tub. Water sloshed over the rim, bathing the floor with salty water. Stilling herself, she pulled herself up against the tub ledge. Her chin rested on the porcelain. Biting her lower lip, she motioned for the male to step closer to her. She'd show him exactly what kind of fish she was. He hesitated but finally came closer. Kneeling before her keeping her eyes level with hers. Her fingers itched with instinct.

Take him by the collar and pull him to his death.

Grabbing him and holding his head underwater wouldn't take much. Even as that thought appealed to Noir, something about this ruggedly pretty man didn't sit well with her, or at least the idea of his death didn't.

Nori opened her mouth to speak. Before a word could leave her mouth, a rattling sound echoed throughout the house. A second later, the rattle returned. Then a chirping doorbell repeatedly sounded. Nori quickly covered her ears at the unexpected noise. The man stood towering over Nori, his fists balled at his side. He glared at the bathroom door. She saw the hesitation once more. This time he was not hesitant to come closer to Nori, but he did not want to leave the enclosed space he had been trapped in with Nori. The ringing continued from the door beyond the bathroom. Nori felt uneasy as the man started for the door.

He glanced over his shoulder and smirked, "Guess I don't have to tell you to stay put. You aren't going anywhere." Then the man was gone leaving Nori in the bathroom alone.

Nori's head moved to the side, and her eyes landed on the shutter-closed window. The light that had peeked between the white wooden plates was fading. It was only minutes now. At that thought, she looked at the bathroom door. The male closed it in his departure. Nori smiled.

Perfect.

WARRICK STOMPED THROUGH THE HOUSE. The consistent doorbell made his eye twitch with annoyance. Yet he instantly knew who it was behind the front door. He had known the moment the door knob had rattled with someone trying to get in. It wouldn't have been his father. His father never came to this house. It was the only other person he could stand.

"Layla," War greeted his sister as he opened the door. "One knock would have been good."

"I need you to be my alibi." Layla shoved passed War. Her hands went straight to her hair and tugged on her roots before letting her hands drop.

"Come in. I'm not busy," War mumbled as he slammed the door close.

"I'm dead serious, War. Maybe I shouldn't say dead." Layla paced the living room rug. "I saw something bad. I ran. I was told to run. I don't know. I ran through. I fled the scene of a crime. I went back, though, and it was...."

"They won't find the bodies, Layla. You don't have to worry about it. I took care of it." War interrupted his sister's rant. He pushed his hands through his hair, linked his fingers behind his head, and stared at the ceiling momentarily. "You should have never been out there with them. If they weren't dead, I would have torn them apart myself. I don't know what the fuck you were thinking."

"I liked him." Her voice was small. "I thought he liked me. I didn't..."

War closed his eyes for a moment. At that moment, his sister wrapped her arms around him and rested her head on his chest. Warrick let his arms down and enclosed her in a hug. Her body trembled with fear. Her scent mixed with that fear so much that it overtook the sugary smell that usually clung to her skin.

Layla pressed her face into his chest and spoke. "If I told you what happened. What I saw, you wouldn't believe me."

War gave a haughty chuckle. His eyes lifted to the bathroom door. "I don't know. I just might." Giving his sister a final squeeze. "Get out of here. Go home, shower, and get the guilt and fear off you. There'll be questions. You have to be ready for that. I'll do what I can, but if they told anyone where they were going and with who, they'll come sniffing at your door first."

Layla lifted her head and stared at her brother in his gold-amber eyes. Those eyes are a unique trait of her brothers. "You know who they are, right? I don't have a good enough motive. They'll come for you."

War nodded. "They won't find anything to pin on me."

"But you said-"

"-They won't find remains. They won't find a way to connect me to the scene. Doesn't matter. Neither of us is guilty of doing it." War's eyes lifted to the bathroom door again.

Layla detangled herself from her brother and nodded. "Yes, but they can't find her either. She is the hero in this fucked story."

A pregnant pause stood between the two siblings as they stared at each other. A moment later, a clatter startled both of them. Their heads turned to the bathroom. Warrick was too slow. Layla rushed for the bathroom door, swinging it open before War could even make it around the sofa standing in his way. When War reached the door, he about gasped himself. Layla gasped, placing her hand over her mouth, and stared.

"It's you!" Layla accused, pointing at the female in the bathroom. "At the beach, you did it. You saved me."

War frowned. "Where'd your fin go?"

The gold-tail mermaid was gone. Instead, a two-legged naked beauty stood in the bathroom with a towel rack in her hand.

The once mermaid blinked at War, then shook her head. A smile spread across her face, and she stepped closer to Layla. "Hello, I'm Nori. I must be leaving now."

Her words were singsong. Almost a tune. War couldn't move. Instead, he stood there transfixed on the female. Nori was her name. He liked how that name rumbled through his brain.

Nori.

With that, she handed the towel rack to a confused Layla and pushed past both a stunned Layla and Warrick. It wasn't until she was at the front door that War snapped from his daze. Had the mermaid done that? Dazed him? He growled and spun, facing the door. The gold-tail mermaid who no longer had a fin waved her think pretty fingers at War and closed the door behind her.

She was gone.

CHAPTER FOUR

It wouldn't last.

Nori had used some of her natural mermaid persuasion to walk past the handsome man and the pretty flamed-haired female she had seen at the beach. It wouldn't last. That one thought had Nori sprinting through the woods. Her feet were sensitive to the branches and rocks, but she had to reach the ocean. It would be a waste of legs, but Nori could no longer be here on land, even if the lunar cycle had begun. She needed to return to the sanctuary of the ocean. Nori wasn't sure what trouble she would be in, especially when the pod discovered that one male had seen her in form and survived. Nori was confident she would do the one thing she didn't like to do, lie.

A branch snapped. Nori paused in her running to look around her. That branch snap had not been her. Her skin prickled with awareness. She was not alone. The dog had come for her. Not a dog, man.

Gold amber eyes glowed from the darkness of the tree line. It was now night, and the full moon hung above, giving just enough light to make out the shapes of the surroundings. The pretty male with those eyes were unmistakable eyes of gold and amber. Though those eyes. Nori knew it was him. She did not give it a chance. She took off in a sprint. The ocean called to her. She could feel the moisture in the air and the scent of the heavenly saltwater hung in the air. She was close to being free.

NEVER RUN FROM A WOLF, *especially under a full moon.* Warrick felt the chase in his blood. It adrenalized and fueled the need to catch. She was fast. *Nori.* He couldn't help but say her name repeatedly in his head. The way her voice had sung her name was engrained in his soul. She is ours. His wolf reminded him. Do not let her go. Nori pumped her arms and picked up speed. She was fast for such a beautiful ethereal thing, but he was faster.

He had never shifted from wolf to man quicker than he did the moment before he tackled her. She gave a pitchy growl, and he growled back. Her nails found purchase on his skin and bared his teeth as they raked across his forearms. She thrashed and kicked. Her hair flung in his face. The scent of the ocean and beach clung to the strands. He inhaled deeply. The smell was driving him wild. He held on tighter.

DO NOT HURT HER.

His inner wolf panted with concern. He would never hurt her. It would go against his nature. He had known it when he saw her, but she wouldn't have known. There were things at play here. It was a wolf thing. A mate thing. He didn't think goldfish had mates. Then again, he did not know much about them.

With the force of his arms, he flipped her over and pinned her wrists to the ground. He had not thought this through. When he shifted from wolf to man, the shift did not come with clothing. When she fled the bathroom, she was nude. The seaweed top was the only thing that clung to her body, yet now it was nearly entirely off, ripping from her struggles. With War pinning her down, his body on top, her legs fell apart, and his hips fitted between her thighs. She may not have been aware of their intimate position, but War was. His body certainly was.

"Stop thrashing. I will not harm you." War bit out.

Nori surprisingly stopped her fighting. Her chest heaved with the breath, and War did his best not to stare. "Let me go."

He gave a heavy sigh. "That I can't do."

"Let go of my hands." She drawled out.

War shook his head. He felt the compelling need to do as she said. *Do not let her go*, his inner wolf demanded. *She is ours. She stays with us.* War tightened his grip on her wrist. He wouldn't let her go.

"I can't do that." He responded between gritted teeth.

Nori sighed. She closed her eyes, and her next movement stunned the life out of Warrick. He hadn't expected it, but in one fluid motion, she had lifted upwards. Her mouth pressed to his, and then her tongue slipped into his mouth. The goldfish was kissing him?!

NORI COULD NOT EXPLAIN what she was doing. One moment she was fighting this male with all her strength. The next, her legs were firmly wrapped around his waist, and her mouth devoured his. Surprisingly he had an enjoyable taste. He tasted cinnamon and masculinity. An odd mixture but everything that made her want more. Usually, that would have won her the advantage. She was small, but she had power. More than a hundred drownings under her fin had made her strong. Desperate men, deplorable men, they gave a fight when their breath was leaving them.

There was one moment when Nori thought she would have to do something terrible to get the dog boy off her, but that thought was overtaken by something unexplainably new. Lust. Nori had felt butterflies before. A boy in her other life had been before the fin that had made her blush and giggle. That felt like forever ago. It was forever ago. Recently she had felt more comfortable in the cold shadows of the ocean hidden in the pod of her sister mermaids than thinking of males and things like lust.

"Your name?" Nori asked between breaths.

He grinned against her lips before giving her a name. "Warrick. Just call me War."

Fitting, Nori thought. War. He was creating a war between her instincts and emotions. She knew she should have been fighting to get back to the ocean. Instead, she shifted her lower body to rub more efficiently against him. Without her hands, she couldn't do much more than shuffle her body beneath him and keep kissing him. War unexpectedly let her wrists go. Nori quickly found her hands wrapping around his warm body. She grabbed his shoulders and lifted herself up, deepening their intense kiss.

"I'm going to fuck you right here on this cold ground. Are you against it?" He asked between kisses.

Nori moved her hips again. Purposely she pressed so that the throbbing steel shaft of his cock was pressed against her warm slick center. "I'm not particularly opposed."

"You won't drown me when I'm not looking, will you?"

Nori pulled back her head to look at the amber-gold eyes she was fond of. Quickly, she moved to his shoulder and bit the strong muscle that tensed. With a grin, she gazed up at him. "Not anytime soon."

War chuckled. "Well, that's a start."

The world slipped from Nori. She was no longer pressed with her back into the mixture of sand and dirt. Instead, she was encased in a warm embrace with a full moon above her, giving enough light to glimpse the expanse of smooth skin and tight muscle that adorned War's body. If she closed her eyes, the air's soft wind and ocean scent reminded her of the shoreline. She had never dreamed she would have met someone like him. Like her War. *Her War.* He was hers, whether he knew it or not. When the time came, and she had to return to the ocean, she wasn't sure what she would do. Could she petition Poseidon? What would she say? *I glimpsed him once and fell madly in lust and possible love. Please grant him a tail so we can be together forever. Grant me happiness through this warm-blooded, not a dog, male.* Was love at first sight a thing? Was that something people truly did with success? Did mermaids?

Her thoughts were interrupted by touch. War moved his hand from her knee to her hip. The slow touch sent a sizzle of sensations through her skin. Desire burned in her. His mouth worked from her mouth down her chin to her neck. He kissed, licked, and bit. Each tease had her wiggling beneath him. The tips of her breasts perked and grazed across his bare chest. Her skin felt sensitive to the touch, but every part of her that touched him, burned with possibility. Not wanting to be the only one not giving pleasure, Nori moved her hips. Nori was careful to move her hips slowly so she worked their bodies together in a sliding motion, making sure he hit the sentive bud with the pulsating head of his dick. His cock slid through her wetness, nearly seeking entrance. He growled at the movement.

WAR WAS IN A DREAM. It had to be a dream. This female had been running from him and now was using her body to tease the ever-living life from him. His cock was ready to plunge into her. To claim him and work the details of their joining aftermath in a post bliss haze of spent sexual energy. Moving his mouth down her body, he kissed and tasted all he could. She was perfection. His hand gripped a breast, massaging the globe of flesh before his mouth latched onto a nipple. His tongue teased the raised bud of her nipple, and she gave a mewling sound. Pushing his hips downwards, he pressed his shaft against her wanting more than just the tease of sliding friction.

"I want in you," he mothed around her breast.

Nori, his Nori, opened her legs wider and arched her back. "Do you need more invitation than my spread legs and thrusting hips?"

He growled at her sassy response. Lifting off her slightly, he moved his hand down her torso. He paused, placing the palm of his hand just below her belly button. It had been not even an hour ago when from this point down, she had a tail. A beautiful goldfish tail

954

that was sexier than it should have been. His amber eyes now looked down at her smooth skin that extended to two long tone legs. Then there was the best part. A pussy that was inviting and wet and ready for him.

"Where did your tail go?" He asked, moving his hand down. When he reached the top of her pussy he spread her lips apart and pushed a finger to ring the nub of nerves waiting for his teasing fingers. Nori closed her eyes and arched more. Her hips lifted from the ground. War grinned. "Not that I don't mind this version. I liked the tail too."

"You worry about the tail too much. Focus on what you are doing."

Nori placed her hand on top of his. She moved his hand, dragging his finger in the lazy circular motion she needed. Panting, she opened her eyes and took in the man above her. He was staring at her in awe. The look scared her as well as made her feel shy. She had never stared into a lover's eyes as they played with her most intimate parts. Taking a bolder direction, Nori moved his hand down further. With her fingers guiding him, she brought his thick digits to her entrance. He complied, shoving his finger deep into her. He pumped his finger inside of her a few times. Nori shuddered with each draw of the sliding action. He maneuvered to place his thumb at her clit where he created circular motions. Wet with her lust, her hand lifted to touch his face. War growled. In an animalist move, he captured her fingers. His hot mouth sucked and tasted the wetness of her fingers, all while he manipulated his own digits in and out of her body at a rapid pace.

All at once, Nori let go and screamed as her body convulsed with zinging pleasure, and waves of desire rocked her through an orgasm.

Her body slowly fell into a lax state. War slowed his fingers' pace and kissed down the side of Noir's face. She hadn't realized, but her hands clutched War's thick hair tightly. Moving his hand from her body, she felt him lift her leg, placing it over his right hip. She watched with ragged breath as he fisted his cock and dragged between her folds. He repeated the dragging movement a few times before he speared her entrance. Nori let out a soundless scream. He maneuvered into her body, and with each inch deeper, she felt her body stretch and tighten around him. Sated inside her tight body, War paused. Nori took a moment to grab the globes of his ass and pushed him utterly flush with her. He gritted his teeth but didn't move. Nori placed her feet flat on the ground and moved her hips, taking charge of the movements that guided him in and out of her body. It took him a few more thrusts before she joined her in moving. The two of them found a frantic needy pace that served them both well. Each drag and shove into her body slapped his heavy sack against her bottom. The sound of their clashing bodies bounced off the trees.

"You're never allowed to leave me," he grunted between thrusts. "Never. You're my goldfish. Mine."

Nori didn't respond to him with words. Instead, she kissed his distracting mouth. Each slap of their bodies became more desperate than the last. Using her strength, Nori pushed War to his back. She didn't let the dirt and debris distract her as she placed her knees on each side of his hip and continued the frantic pace of their fucking. She rode his cock with abandon. Her head back and fingers raking down his chest. War held one breast in his hand and the other clutched at her hip. She knew there would be bruising later, but each one would be worth it. Her body was already battered from the fight with men she had taken on earlier in the evening. Most of those wounds healed to the point of pink puffy, barely there scars that would be gone in a few days. However, she wanted these bruises to mar her body for the rest of her life.

Nori looked down at this male. His face was tilted up to the moon. He bit his lower lip, and sweat beaded his forehead. Was it just hours ago when she felt like a fish out of water in her pod? Now she felt she belonged here at this moment with this man. The reality of this situation was hanging around her, but she rather sit in the bubble of this dream.

War hissed between his clenched teeth. He was so close. This female was the end of him. He was going to finish inside of her soon. He did not want to be the only one caught in this hazy air of desire. Reaching for where their bodies were joined, he found her clit and frantically teased the perfect bud of flesh. Nori contorted and withered on top of him. Her lifted hips slowed in pace. War moved his thumb faster and sat up as much as he could. He took over the controlling speed as she slowed and slumped over him. He kissed her shoulder and bit down as he suddenly gave on final thrust, just as she clenched and withered above him. They both came panting and grunting until each of them stilled. Their bodies connected, and this time War felt maybe it was more than just a body connection. She was swimming in his soul now.

CHAPTER FIVE

Wild dreams. This had to be one of them, Nori thought.

"You awake?" War asked her.

Nori nodded her head. She was half sprawled over him. Their naked bodies pressed together, keeping her warm enough to ignore the slight coldness of the night air. When she tried to move off him, she returned to his embrace. He didn't want to let her go. She felt that from him. She wasn't precisely certain she wanted to be let go, either.

"I think you have to let me go." She whispered. "Fish and dogs can not live in this world."

He gripped her tight then.

Nori gently lifted her head. He moved to look at her, and she looked into his eyes. "My stay on land is always short. One lunar cycle, then another, must be spent in my home, the ocean, to regenerate all the energy I use during that cycle. This is my gift, but it comes with limits."

War frowned. "I'll go with you then."

Nori gave a small nervous giggle. "And do what? Can you hold your breath for hours? Can you swim without cramping?"

958

A wrinkle formed between War's eyes as he contemplated her words. Nori watched him taking in each part of his face. She saw the moment when she thought he figured it out. She never wanted to forget him.

He pulled her closer to him. "I'll get a boat. You could come to me every day, and when it's time, you could join me."

Nori kissed his peck. She rested her cheek against his chest. On an inhale, she listened to the steady pounding of his heart. She would not tell him it didn't work like that. He had worshiped her body and held her like heaven in his arms. She loved the feeling. She could return to this feeling whenever she felt despondent. She listened to his heart and breathing until his arms became lax. His breathing evened out and deepened. Nori sat up gently, not to disturb him, because she knew he had fallen asleep.

Detangling herself from him was more complex than she suspected it would have been. But he held onto her not only in body but in soul. She did take a few tries to move away from him. Her body felt so used in a dirty and pleasing way. The space between her legs ached from their joining but also tightened at the loss of him not inside of her. She stumbled through the terrain until the trees became sparse; the dirt gave way to soft sand. The ocean rhythmically pounded the shoreline. When the sparkling waves came into view, Nori stopped. She closed her eyes and took in a deep breath.

COLD? She thought. *Are the waters cold?* She never felt the coldness. She was one with the dark, cold waters. They matched her disposition. Calm, quiet, deep, and *cold*. But now she felt the cold. Without his arms around her, she felt the chill.

She pressed a hand to her pounding heart and looked over her shoulder. Disappointment hit when she did not see amber-gold eyes. With all her strength, she moved towards the ocean. When the water touched her toes, she knew she would regret leaving him, but it had to be done. It wasn't until she was a mile away from the shore, swimming in the sparkling expanse of the ocean, that she heard a cry. One word filled the night air.

"NORI!"

CHAPTER SIX

War sat on the beach. The sun was setting. He sat her every day at this time. He relived the short moments when he had a goldfish in his grasp. When that beauty poisoned him with her presence, he was now a shell of a wolf. His inner wolf rarely spoke to him, mad that he had fallen asleep that night nearly a year ago. At that time, he had bought countless goldfish at the pet store. Everyone reminded him of her. His Nori of the sea. He wondered if she'd be amused at all the books he bought. Any book with a mermaid in it, he had to own. He read them, looking for truths that might be possible. It had led him to a rabbit hole that was impossible to climb out of.

"Here you are," Layla spoke out.

War frowned. He hadn't even heard her footfalls. He must have been too deep in thought.

"Sis," he mumbled in greeting.

She flopped a tablet down beside him. He looked at the offending device. "Not really in the mood to read."

Layla sighed. "Look at it." She lifted the device so it was at face level with him. "Today, there are protestors on two beaches over

961

protesting for the freedom of some contained dolphins at that sea exhibit."

"Neat."

Layla shoved her brother's shoulder. "Just look at the picture. Isn't that the girl? Our hero? You know the one who... killed those guys."

Warrick felt the air leave his body. He snatched the tablet from his sisters' hands, frantically searching for the photo that topped the article his sister spoke of. There in the background, he saw her. She had her hair down, straight locks that fell to her hips. Her faded blue eyes pierced from behind her dark lashes. One hand was up as if she was trying to block the photographer, but whoever the photographer was had captured her perfect profile. War could not breathe. It was her. The article was posted twenty minutes ago. The protesting happened earlier in the day. Even if he ran to his truck, he was sure they weren't there anymore. His hope died as quickly as it sprung.

Layla snatched the device from his hands. "I know something between you two happened. I mean, she was naked in your bathroom, after all. Anyways I'm out of here. I have a date two packs over. He's nice, a feminist too."

Layla bounced away. War called out over his shoulder. "Be safe, Lay."

"Always," she sing-songed back. "ever since those boys from our pack went missing, I've been cautious." She gave him a wink and went on her way.

War sighed and let his body drop back into the sand. He watched the sun run across the sky in streaks of gold and pink. Ten more minutes and it would be dark. He'd return home then and spend the night trapped in a cheesy romance novel about first loves and mermaids. *How fucking lame,* He thought.

"You know doggies should not lay in the sand. It's hard to get it out of their fur." The voice paralyzed War. He blinked a few times before sitting up.

His dream was there before him. Nori. She stood a few feet away.

Nude, her wet hair hanging over her plump breasts. Everything rushed back to him. His wolf growled out. Our female. He stood quickly.

Nori stepped back with the abruptness of his movements.

"I think I forgot to tell you...mermaids travel in pods all over." She bit her bottom lip. "But we always come back to our favorite spots."

War cleared his throat. "I would have gotten a boat. I would have followed."

Nori smiled her wide smile. "I'm not despondent anymore. I talk a bit more and interact."

"Huh?"

She giggled. "I never really liked to socialize. It's not my strongest feature. But I saw something. Did you know a male can be granted to be like us? All their stories are different. A male. He could live out his life with a fin. It's not an easy process. I don't know if it can really happen. Maybe the male doesn't want a fin. Or would you rather have a fin out of water?"

War moved in for the kill. He reached for his female and shut her downward spiral of words with a kiss. When all her breath was gone, and she was kissing him back, he pulled away to rest his forehead with hers. "Fin in or out of water. He wants to be with her because she's his goldfish, fin in or out of the water, and he can't live another day without her."

"It's not a guaranteed or easy process."

War grinned. "Are you trying to tell me dogs and fish can't mate."

She smiled at him. "I would never say such words, doggie."